select
editions

Reader's
Digest

The condensations in this volume
are published with the consent of the authors
and the publishers © 2012 Reader's Digest, Inc.

www.readersdigest.co.uk

Published in the United Kingdom by Vivat Direct Limited
(t/a Reader's Digest), 157 Edgware Road,
London W2 2HR

For information as to ownership of
copyright in the material of this book,
and acknowledgments, see last page.

Printed in Germany
ISBN 978 1 78020 023 1

select
editions

THE READER'S DIGEST ASSOCIATION, INC.

contents

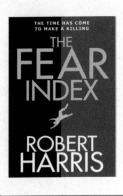

A fast-moving thriller set in the world of high finance, in which overstretched genius, Dr Alex Hoffmann, finds himself desperately battling what he himself created—artificial intelligence that can predict changes in the financial markets—before it destroys him.

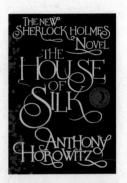

Sherlock Holmes is back, with all the nuance, pace and powers of deduction that make him, in the eyes of many fans, the most celebrated fictional detective. Best-selling author Anthony Horowitz delivers a first-rate Holmes mystery.

lethal
sandra brown

A high-octane tale of passion, deceit, and betrayal. When Honor Gillette is confronted by an accused murderer on the run, she is desperate to do all that he asks to keep her daughter safe. But who is he? And why does he need her help?

the haunting
alan titchmarsh

A story of love and betrayal, intrigue and murder, which spans two centuries and portrays the very different lives of Harry and Anne Flint. Where folk are not what they seem, and the past is no more predictable than the future . . .

The Haunting

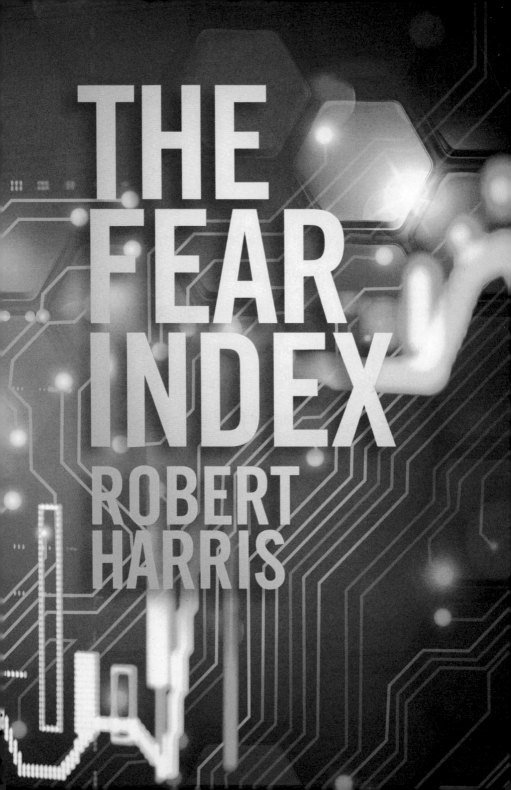

THE FEAR INDEX

ROBERT HARRIS

Visionary scientist Dr Alexander Hoffmann is a computer software genius with the Midas touch. As the creator of a form of artificial intelligence that can predict big, emotion-driven swings in the financial markets, he's made billions from his Geneva-based investment fund.

However, in the early hours of one morning, an intruder breaches the elaborate security of Hoffman's mansion, setting in motion a nightmarish train of events, which will, by nightfall, take him to the very brink of survival . . .

1

D r Alexander Hoffmann sat by the fire in his study in Geneva, a half-smoked cigar lying cold in the ashtray beside him, an anglepoise lamp pulled low over his shoulder, turning the pages of a first edition of *The Expression of the Emotions in Man and Animals* by Charles Darwin. The Victorian grandfather clock in the hall was striking midnight but Hoffmann did not hear it. Nor did he notice that the fire was almost out. All his formidable powers of attention were directed onto his book.

He knew it had been published in London in 1872 by John Murray & Co. in an edition of 7,000 copies. The binding was in the original green cloth with gilt lettering, the spine-ends only slightly frayed. It was what was known in the book trade as 'a fine copy', worth perhaps $15,000. He had found it waiting for him when he returned home from his office that evening, as soon as the New York markets had closed, a little after ten o'clock. Yet the strange thing was, even though he collected first editions and had browsed the book online, he had not actually ordered it.

His immediate thought had been that it must have come from his wife, but she had denied it. He had refused to believe her at first, following her round the kitchen as she set the table.

'You're really telling me you didn't buy it for me?'

'Yes, Alex. Sorry. It wasn't me. Perhaps you have a secret admirer.'

It had come with no message apart from a Dutch bookseller's slip: *Rosengaarden & Nijenhuise, Antiquarian Scientific & Medical Books. Established 1911. Prinsengracht 227, 1016 HN Amsterdam, The Netherlands.* The parcel was correctly addressed: Dr Alexander Hoffmann,

Villa Clairmont, 79 Chemin de Ruth, 1223 Cologny, Geneva, Switzerland. It had been dispatched by courier from Amsterdam the previous day.

After they had eaten their supper, Gabrielle had stayed in the kitchen to make a few anxious last-minute phone calls about her exhibition the next day, while Hoffmann had retreated to his study clutching the mysterious book. An hour later, when she put her head round the door to tell him she was going up to bed, he was still reading.

She said, 'Try not to be too late, darling. I'll wait up for you.'

He did not reply. She paused in the doorway and considered him for a moment. He still looked young for forty-two, and had always been more handsome than he realised—a quality she found attractive in a man. It was not that he was modest. On the contrary: he was supremely indifferent to anything that did not engage him intellectually, a trait that had earned him a reputation among her friends for being downright rude—and she quite liked that as well. His preternaturally boyish American face was bent over the book, his spectacles pushed up and resting on the top of his thick head of light brown hair. She sighed and went upstairs.

Hoffmann had known for years that *The Expression of the Emotions in Man and Animals* was one of the first books to be published with photographs, but he had never actually seen them before. Monochrome plates depicted Victorian artists' models and inmates of the Surrey Lunatic Asylum in various states of emotion—grief, despair, joy, defiance, terror—for this was meant to be a study of *Homo sapiens* as animal, with an animal's instinctive responses, stripped of the mask of social graces. With their misaligned eyes and skewed teeth they reminded Hoffmann of a childish nightmare—of grown-ups from an old-fashioned book of fairy tales who might steal you from your bed in the night and carry you off into the woods.

There was another thing that unsettled him. The bookseller's slip had been inserted into the pages devoted to the emotion of fear:

The frightened man at first stands like a statue motionless or breathless, or crouches down as if instinctively to escape observation. The heart beats quickly and violently, so that it palpitates . . .

Hoffmann reasoned it must be coincidence. But on the other hand, the physiological effects of fear were so directly relevant to VIXAL-4, the project he was presently involved in, that it did strike him as peculiarly pointed. Yet VIXAL-4 was highly secret, known only to his research team, and although he took care to pay them well—$250,000 was the starting salary—it was surely unlikely any of them would have spent $15,000 on an anonymous gift. One person who certainly could afford it, and who would have seen the joke of it—if that was an expensive joke—was his business partner, Hugo Quarry, and Hoffmann, without even thinking about the hour, rang him.

'Hello, Alex. How's it going?' If Quarry saw anything strange in being disturbed just after midnight, his perfect manners would never have permitted him to show it. Besides, he was accustomed to the ways of Hoffmann, 'the mad professor', as he called him.

Hoffmann, still reading the description of fear, said distractedly, 'Oh, hi. Did you just buy me a book?'

'I don't think so, old friend. Why? Was I supposed to?'

'Someone's just sent me a valuable Darwin first edition and I thought, because you know how important Darwin is to VIXAL, it might be you.'

''Fraid not. Could it be a client? A thank-you gift and they've forgotten to include a card? Lord knows, Alex, we've made them enough money.'

'Yeah, well. Maybe. OK. Sorry to bother you.'

'Don't worry. See you in the morning. Big day tomorrow. In fact, it's already tomorrow. You ought to be in bed by now.'

'Sure. On my way. Night.'

As fear rises to an extreme pitch, the dreadful scream of terror is heard. Great beads of sweat stand on the skin. All the muscles of the body are relaxed. Utter prostration soon follows, and the mental powers fail . . .

Hoffmann held the volume to his nose and inhaled. A compound of leather and library dust and cigar smoke, so sharp he could taste it, with a faint hint of something chemical—formaldehyde, perhaps, or coal-gas. It put him in mind of a nineteenth-century laboratory and for an instant he saw Bunsen burners on wooden benches, flasks of acid and the skeleton of an ape. He reinserted the bookseller's slip to mark the page and carefully closed the book. Then he carried it over to the shelves and with two fingers gently made room for it between a first edition of *On the Origin of Species*, which he had bought at auction in New York for $125,000, and a leather-bound copy of *The Descent of Man* that had once belonged to T. H. Huxley.

Later, he would try to remember the exact sequence of what he did next. He consulted the Bloomberg terminal on his desk for the final prices in the

USA: the Dow Jones, the S&P 500 and the NASDAQ had all ended down. He had an email exchange with Susumu Takahashi, the duty dealer in charge of execution on VIXAL-4 overnight, who reported that everything was functioning smoothly, and reminded him that the Tokyo Stock Exchange would reopen in less than two hours. It would certainly open down, to catch up with what had been a week of falling prices in Europe and the USA. And there was one other thing: VIXAL was proposing to short another three million shares in Procter & Gamble at $62 a share, which would bring their overall position up to six million—a big trade: would Hoffmann approve it? Hoffmann emailed 'OK', put a fine-meshed metal guard in front of the fireplace and switched off the study lights. In the hall he checked to see that the front door was locked and then set the burglar alarm with its four-digit code. He left just one lamp lit downstairs—of that he was sure—then climbed the curved white marble staircase to the bathroom. He undressed, brushed his teeth and put on a pair of blue silk pyjamas. He set the alarm on his mobile for six thirty, registering as he did so that the time was then twenty past twelve.

In the bedroom he was surprised to find Gabrielle still awake, lying on her back on the counterpane in a black silk kimono. A scented candle flickered on the dressing table. Her hands were clasped behind her head, her legs crossed at the knee. One slim white foot, the toenails painted dark red, was making impatient circles in the fragrant air.

'Oh God,' he said. 'I'd forgotten the date.'

'Don't worry.' She untied her belt and parted the silk, then held out her arms to him. 'I never forget it.'

IT MUST HAVE BEEN about three fifty in the morning that something caused Hoffmann to wake. He struggled up from the depths of sleep and opened his eyes to behold a celestial vision of fiery white light—eight 500-watt tungsten-halogen security lights shining brilliantly through the slats of the window blinds—enough wattage to light a small soccer ground; he had been meaning to have them changed.

The lights were on a thirty-second timer. As he waited for them to turn off, he considered what might have interrupted the infrared beams that crisscrossed the garden to trigger them. It would be a cat, he thought, or a piece of overgrown foliage waving in the wind. And after a few seconds the lights indeed went out and the room returned to darkness.

But now Hoffmann was wide awake. He reached for his mobile. It was one of a batch specially produced for the hedge fund that could encrypt certain sensitive phone calls and emails. To avoid disturbing Gabrielle he switched it on under the duvet and briefly checked the Profit & Loss screen for Far Eastern trading. The markets were, as predicted, falling but VIXAL-4 was already up 0.3 per cent, which meant he had made almost $3 million since going to bed. Satisfied, he turned off the device and replaced it on the nightstand, and that was when he heard a noise: soft, unidentifiable, and yet oddly disturbing, as if someone was moving around downstairs.

Hoffman raised himself on his elbows and strained his ears. It was nothing specific—an occasional faint thump. It could just be the unfamiliar heating system, or a door caught in a draught. He felt quite calm. The house had formidable security, which was one of the reasons he had bought it a few weeks earlier: apart from the floodlights, there was a three-metre-high perimeter wall with heavy electronic gates, a steel-reinforced front door with a keypad entry system, and a movement-sensitive burglar alarm, which he was sure he had turned on before he came up to bed. The chances that an intruder had got past all that and penetrated inside were tiny.

He slid out of bed without waking Gabrielle and put on his glasses, dressing gown and slippers. He slipped his mobile into his pocket and opened the bedroom door—a crack at first, and then fully. The light from the lamp downstairs shed a dim glow along the landing. He paused on the threshold, listening. But the sounds—if there ever had been sounds—had ceased. He moved towards the staircase and began to descend very slowly.

Perhaps it was the effect of reading Darwin just before he fell asleep, but as he went down the stairs he found himself registering, with scientific detachment, his own physical symptoms. His breath was becoming short, his heartbeat accelerating rapidly.

He reached the ground floor.

The house was a belle époque mansion, built in 1902 for a French businessman. The whole place had been excessively interior-designed by the previous owner, left ready to move into, and perhaps for that reason Hoffmann had never felt entirely at home in it. To his left was the front door and ahead of him was the door to the drawing room. To his right a passage led towards the house's interior: dining room, kitchen, library and a Victorian conservatory that Gabrielle used as her studio. He stood absolutely still, his hands raised ready to defend himself. In the corner of the hall, the tiny red eye of the movement sensor winked at him. If he was not careful, he would trigger the alarm himself.

He relaxed his hands and crossed the hall to where an antique barometer was mounted on the wall. He pressed a catch and the barometer swung outwards. The alarm control box was hidden behind it. He reached out to enter the code to switch the system off.

The alarm had already been deactivated.

His finger stayed poised in midair while the rational part of his mind sought for reassuring explanations. Perhaps Gabrielle had switched the system off and had forgotten to turn it back on again. Or he had forgotten to set it in the first place. Or it had malfunctioned.

Very slowly he turned to his left to inspect the front door. It appeared to be firmly closed, with no sign it had been forced. He moved towards it and tapped in the code. He heard the bolts click back. He grasped the heavy brass handle and turned it, then stepped out onto the darkened porch.

Above the inky expanse of lawn, the moon was a silvery-blue discus. The shadows of the big fir trees that screened the house from the road swayed and rustled in the wind.

Hoffmann took a few more paces out into the gravel drive, setting off the floodlights at the front of the house. The brightness made him jump. He put up his arm to shield his eyes and turned to face the yellow-lit interior of the hall, noticing as he did so that a large pair of black boots had been placed neatly to one side of the front door, as if their owner had not wanted to trail in mud. The boots were not Hoffmann's and they were certainly not Gabrielle's. He was also sure they had not been there when he arrived home almost six hours earlier.

His gaze transfixed by the boots, he fumbled for his mobile, almost dropped it, and started dialling: 117.

The number rang once before a woman answered sharply: '*Oui, police?*'

Her voice seemed to Hoffmann very loud in the stillness. It made him realise how visible he must be, standing exposed under the floodlights. He stepped quickly to his left, out of the line of sight of anyone watching from the hallway. He had the phone pressed very close to his mouth. He whispered: '*J'ai un intrus sur ma propriété.*'

'*Quelle est votre adresse, monsieur?*'

He told her as he began moving along the façade of the house.

'*Et votre nom?*'

He whispered, 'Alexander Hoffmann.'

The security lights cut out.

'*OK, Monsieur Hoffmann. Restez là. Une voiture est en route.*'

She hung up. Alone in the darkness, Hoffmann stood at the corner of the house. It was unseasonably cold for Switzerland in the first week of May. The wind was from the northeast, blowing straight off Lac Léman. He could hear the water lapping against the nearby jetties. He pulled his dressing gown tighter around his shoulders. He was shaking violently. He had to clench his teeth to stop them chattering. And yet, oddly, he felt no panic. He sniffed the air and glanced along the side of the mansion towards the lake. Somewhere near the rear of the house there was a light on downstairs. Its gleam lit the surrounding bushes very prettily, like a fairy grotto.

He waited for half a minute, then began to move towards it stealthily, working his way through the wide herbaceous border that ran along this side of the house. As he drew closer he realised the light was emanating from the kitchen, and when he edged his head round the window frame, he saw inside the figure of a man. He had his back to the window. He was standing at the granite-topped island in the centre of the room. His movements were unhurried. He was taking knives from their sockets in a butcher's block and sharpening them on an electric grinder.

Hoffmann's heart was pumping so fast he could hear the rush of his own pulse. His immediate thought was Gabrielle: he must get her out of the house while the intruder was preoccupied in the kitchen, or at the very least get her to lock herself in the bathroom until the police arrived.

He still had his mobile in his hand. Without taking his eyes from the intruder, he dialled her number. Seconds later he heard her phone start to ring—too near for it to be with her upstairs. At once the stranger looked up from his sharpening. Gabrielle's phone was lying where she had left it before she went to bed, on the big pine table in the kitchen, its screen glowing, its pink case buzzing. The intruder cocked his head and looked at it. With infuriating calmness, he laid down the knife—Hoffmann's favourite knife, one with a long thin blade that was particularly useful for boning— and moved round the island towards the table. As he did so, Hoffmann got his first proper glimpse of him—a bald pate with long, thin grey hair at the sides pulled back behind the ears into a greasy ponytail, hollow cheeks, unshaven. He was wearing a scuffed brown leather coat. He looked like the sort of man who might work in a circus or on a ride in a fair. He stared at the phone as if he had never seen one before, picked it up, hesitated, then pressed answer and held it to his ear.

A wave of murderous anger flooded Hoffman. He said quietly, 'Get out of my house,' and was gratified to see the intruder jerk in alarm. He rapidly twisted his head—left, right, left, right—and his gaze settled on the window. For an instant his eyes met Hoffmann's, but blindly, for he was staring into dark glass. Suddenly he threw the phone onto the table and with surprising agility darted for the door.

Hoffmann swore, turned and started back the way he had come, sliding and stumbling through the flower bed, along the side of the big house, towards the front—hard going in his slippers, each breath a sob. He had reached the corner when he heard the front door slam. He assumed the intruder was making a dash for the road. But no: seconds passed and the man did not appear. He must have shut himself in.

'Oh God,' Hoffmann whispered. 'God, God.' He flailed on towards the porch. His hands were shaking as he keyed in the security code. By this time he was yelling out Gabrielle's name. The bolts clicked back. He flung open the door onto darkness. The hall lamp had been switched off.

For a moment he stood panting on the step, then he lunged towards the staircase, screaming, 'Gabrielle! Gabrielle!' and was halfway across the marble floor when the house seemed to explode around him, the stairs tumbling, the floor tiles rising, the walls shooting away from him into the night.

HOFFMANN HAD no memory of anything after that—no thoughts or dreams disturbed his normally restless mind—until at last, from out of the fog, he became aware of a gradual reawakening of sensations—freezing water trickling down the side of his neck and across his back, a cold pressure on his scalp, a sharp pain in his head, a mechanical jabbering in his ears, and he realised that he was lying on his side, with something soft against his cheek.

He opened his eyes and saw a white bowl, inches from his face, into which he immediately vomited. The bowl was removed. A bright light was shone into each of his eyes in turn. His nose and mouth were wiped. A glass of water was pressed against his lips. He gulped it down then opened his eyes again and squinted around his new world.

He was on the floor of the hall, laid out in the recovery position, his back resting against the wall. A blue police light flashed at the window; unintelligible chatter leaked from a radio. Gabrielle was kneeling next to him, holding his hand. She was dressed in jeans and a jersey. She smiled and squeezed his fingers. 'Thank God,' she said. He pushed himself up and looked around, bewildered. Without his spectacles, everything was slightly blurred: two paramedics, bent over a case of gleaming equipment; two uniformed gendarmes, one by the door with the noisy radio on his belt and another just coming down the stairs; and a third man, tired-looking, in his fifties, wearing a dark blue windcheater and a white shirt with a dark tie, who was studying Hoffmann with detached sympathy.

When Hoffmann tried to rise, he found he had insufficient strength in his arms. A flash of pain arced across his skull. The man in the dark tie said, 'Here, let me help,' and stepped forward with his hand outstretched. 'Jean-Philippe Leclerc, inspector of the Geneva Police Department.'

One of the paramedics took Hoffmann's other arm and together he and the inspector raised him carefully to his feet. On the creamy paintwork of the wall where his head had rested was a feathery patch of blood. More blood was on the floor.

Gabrielle said anxiously, 'He needs to go to a hospital.'

'The ambulance will be here in ten minutes,' said the paramedic. 'They've been delayed.'

'Why don't we wait in here?' suggested Leclerc. He opened the door onto the chilly drawing room.

Once Hoffmann had been lowered into a sitting position on the sofa—he refused to lie flat—the paramedic squatted in front of him.

'Can you tell me the number of fingers I'm holding up?'

Hoffmann said, 'Can I have my . . .' What was the word? He raised his hand to his eyes.

'He needs his glasses,' said Gabrielle. 'Here you are, darling.' She slipped them over his nose and kissed his forehead. 'Take it easy, all right?'

The medic said, 'Can you see my fingers now?'

Hoffman counted carefully. 'Three.'

'We need to take your blood pressure, monsieur.'

Hoffmann sat placidly as the sleeve of his pyjama jacket was rolled up and the plastic cuff was fastened round his bicep and inflated. His mind seemed to be switching itself back on now, section by section. Methodically he noted the contents of the room: the Bechstein baby grand, the Louis Quinze clock ticking quietly on the mantelpiece, the charcoal tones of the Auerbach landscape above it. On the coffee table in front of him was one of

Gabrielle's self-portraits: a half-metre cube, made up of 100 sheets of Mirogard glass, onto which she had traced in black ink the sections of an MRI scan of her own body. The effect was of some strange, vulnerable alien creature floating in midair. Hoffmann looked at it as if for the first time. There was something here he ought to remember. This was a new experience for him: not to be able to retrieve a piece of information he wanted immediately. When the paramedic had finished, Hoffmann said to Gabrielle, 'Aren't you doing something special today?' His forehead creased in concentration. 'I know,' he said at last with relief, 'it's your show.'

'Yes, it is, but we'll cancel it.'

'No, we mustn't do that—not your first show.'

'Good,' said Leclerc, who was watching Hoffmann from his armchair. 'This is very good.'

Hoffmann turned slowly to look at him. 'Good?'

'It's good that you can remember things.' The inspector gave him the thumbs-up sign. 'For example, what's the last thing that happened to you tonight that you can remember?'

Hoffmann considered carefully, as if it were a mathematical problem. 'I guess it was coming in through the front door. He must have been behind it waiting for me.'

'He? There was only one man?' Leclerc unzipped his windcheater and with difficulty tugged a notebook from some hidden recess, then shifted in his chair and produced a pen.

'Yes, as far as I know.' Hoffmann put his hand to the back of his head. His fingers touched a bandage, tightly wound. 'What did he hit me with?'

'By the looks of it, a fire extinguisher.'

'And how long was I unconscious?'

'Twenty-five minutes.'

'Is that all?' Hoffmann felt as if he had been out for hours. But when he looked at the windows he saw it was still dark. 'And I was shouting to warn you,' he said to Gabrielle. 'I remember that.'

'That's right, I heard you. Then I came downstairs and found you lying there. The front door was open. The next thing I knew, the police were here.'

Hoffmann looked back at Leclerc. 'Did you catch him?'

'Unfortunately, he was gone by the time our patrol arrived.' Leclerc flicked back through his notebook. 'It's strange. He seems simply to have walked in through the gates and walked out again. Yet I gather you need two separate codes to access the gates and the front door. I wonder—was this man known to you in some way, perhaps?'

'I've never seen him before in my life.'

'Ah.' Leclerc made a note. 'So you did get a good look at him?'

'He was in the kitchen. I saw him through the window from outside.'

Haltingly at first, but with growing fluency as his memory returned, Hoffmann relived it all: how he had gone downstairs, discovered the alarm turned off, opened the door, seen the pair of boots, noticed the light from a ground-floor window, worked his way round the side of the house, and watched the intruder through the window.

'Can you describe him?' Leclerc was writing rapidly, barely finishing one page before turning it over and filling another.

Gabrielle said, 'Alex . . .'

'It's all right, Gabby,' said Hoffmann. 'We need to help them catch this bastard.' He closed his eyes. 'He was medium height. Rough-looking. Fifties. Gaunt face. Bald on top. Long, thin grey hair, pulled back in a ponytail. He was wearing a leather coat, or maybe a jacket—I can't remember which.' A doubt swam into Hoffmann's mind. He paused. Leclerc waited for him to continue. 'I say I've never seen him before, but now I come to think of it, perhaps I have seen him somewhere—a glimpse in the street, maybe . . .' His voice trailed off.

'Go on,' said Leclerc.

Hoffman thought for a moment, then fractionally shook his head. 'No. I can't remember. Sorry. But to be honest I have had an odd feeling of being watched just lately.'

Gabrielle said in surprise, 'You never mentioned anything to me.'

'I didn't want to upset you. And besides, it was never anything I could put my finger on, exactly.'

'It could be that he's been following you for a while,' said Leclerc. 'You may have seen him in the street without being aware of him. What was he doing in the kitchen?'

Hoffmann glanced at Gabrielle. 'He was—sharpening knives.'

'My God!' Gabrielle put her hand to her mouth.

'Would you be able to identify him if you saw him again?'

'Oh, yes,' said Hoffmann grimly. 'You bet.'

Leclerc tapped his pen against his notebook. 'We must issue this description.' He stood. 'Excuse me,' he said. He went out into the hall.

Hoffmann suddenly felt too tired to carry on. He closed his eyes again and leaned his head back against the sofa, then remembered his wound. 'Sorry. I'm ruining your furniture.'

'To hell with the furniture.'

He stared at her. She looked older without her make-up, more fragile and—an expression he had never seen before—scared. It pierced him.

Leclerc came back into the drawing room carrying a couple of clear plastic evidence bags.

'We found these in the kitchen,' he said. He held them up. One contained a pair of handcuffs; the other, what looked to be a black leather collar with a black golf ball attached to it.

'What's that?' asked Gabrielle.

'A gag,' replied Leclerc. 'It's new. He probably bought it in a sex shop. They're very popular with the S and M crowd.'

'Oh my God!' She looked in horror at Hoffmann. 'What was he going to do to us?'

Hoffmann felt faint again, his mouth dry. 'Kidnap us?'

'That's certainly a possibility,' agreed Leclerc, glancing round the room. 'You're a rich man, that's obvious enough. But I must say that kidnapping is unheard of in Geneva. This is a law-abiding city.' He took out his pen again. 'May I ask your occupation?'

'I'm a physicist.'

'A physicist.' Leclerc made a note. 'English?'

'American.'

'And Madame Hoffmann?'

'I'm English.'

'And you've lived in Switzerland for how long, Dr Hoffmann?'

'Fourteen years.' Weariness almost overtook him. 'I came out here in the nineties to work for CERN, on the Large Hadron Collider. I was there for about six years.'

'And now?'

'I run a company called Hoffmann Investment Technologies.'

'And what does it make?'

'What does it make? It makes money. It's a hedge fund.'

'Very good. "It makes money." How long have you been in this house?'

Gabrielle said, 'Only a month.'

'Did you change the entry codes when you took over?'

'Of course.'

'And who apart from the two of you knows the combination for the burglar alarm and so forth?'

Gabrielle said, 'Our housekeeper. The maid. The gardener.'

'Does anyone at your office know the codes, Dr Hoffmann?'

'My assistant.' Hoffmann frowned. How sluggishly his brain moved: like a computer with a virus. 'Oh, and our security consultant—he checked everything before we bought the place.'

'Can you remember his name?'

'Genoud.' He pondered for a moment. 'Maurice Genoud.'

Leclerc looked up. 'There was a Maurice Genoud on the Geneva police force. I seem to remember he went into the private security business. Well, well.' A thoughtful expression crossed Leclerc's hangdog face. He resumed his note-taking.

A buzzer sounded in the hall. It made Hoffmann jump.

'That's probably the ambulance,' said Gabrielle. 'I'll open the gate.'

While she was out of the room, Hoffmann said, 'I suppose this is going to get into the press?'

'We'll endeavour to be discreet. Do you have any enemies, Dr Hoffmann? Some rich investor—Russian, perhaps—who's lost money?'

'We don't lose money.' Still, Hoffmann tried to think if there was anyone on his client list who might possibly be involved. But no: it was inconceivable. 'Is it safe for us to stay here, do you think?'

'We'll have our people here most of the day, and tonight we can keep an eye on the place. But, generally, we find that men in your position prefer to take precautions of their own.'

'You mean hire bodyguards?' Hoffmann grimaced.

'Unfortunately, a house like this is always going to attract unwanted attention.'

From outside came the noise of a diesel engine. Gabrielle put her head round the door. 'The ambulance is here. I'll go and find you some clothes we can take with us.'

Hoffmann tried to rise. Leclerc came over to help him, but Hoffmann waved him away. He had to rock himself forwards a couple of times before he had gained sufficient momentum to escape the sofa, but on his third attempt he managed it, and stood swaying on the Aubusson carpet.

Together Hoffmann and Leclerc went out into the hall, Hoffmann taking exaggerated care with each step, like a drunk who wishes to be thought sober. The house had become crowded with people from the emergency services. More gendarmes had arrived, along with two ambulance personnel, a man and a woman, wheeling a bed. Hoffman was relieved to see Gabrielle coming down the stairs with his raincoat. Leclerc took it from her and draped it round Hoffmann's shoulders.

By the front door, Hoffmann noticed a fire extinguisher, wrapped in a plastic bag. The mere sight of it gave him a twinge of pain. He said, 'Are you going to put out an artist's impression of this man?'

'We might.'

'Then there's something you should see.' Ignoring the protests of the ambulance people that he should lie down, he turned and walked back along the hall to his study. The Bloomberg terminal on his desk was still switched on. Almost every price in the Far Eastern markets was down. He switched on the light and searched along the shelf until he found *The Expression of the Emotions in Man and Animals*. His hands were trembling with excitement. He flicked through the pages.

'There,' he said, turning to show Leclerc and Gabrielle. He tapped his finger on the page. 'That's the man who attacked me.'

It was the illustration for the emotion of terror—an old man, his eyes wide, his toothless mouth agape. Electric calipers were being applied to his facial muscles by the great French doctor Duchenne in order to stimulate the required expression. Hoffmann could sense the others' dismay.

'I'm sorry,' said Leclerc, puzzled. 'You're telling us that this is the man who was in your house tonight?'

'Oh, Alex,' said Gabrielle.

'Obviously I'm not saying it's *literally* him—he's been dead more than a century—I'm saying it *looks* like him.' They were both staring at him intently. *They believe I have gone mad*, he thought. He took a breath. 'OK. Now this book,' he explained to Leclerc, 'arrived yesterday without any explanation. I don't know who sent it. Maybe it's a coincidence, but you've got to agree it's odd that a few hours after this arrives, a man—who actually looks as though he's just stepped out of its pages—turns up to attack us.' They were silent. 'Anyway,' he concluded, 'all I'm saying is, if you want to make an artist's impression of the guy, you should start with this.'

'Thank you,' said Leclerc. 'I'll bear that in mind.'

'Right,' said Gabrielle brightly. 'Let's get you to the hospital.'

LECLERC SAW them off from the front door. The moon had disappeared behind the clouds. There was barely any light in the sky, even though there was only half an hour until dawn. The American physicist, with his bandaged head and his black raincoat and his thin pink ankles poking out beneath his expensive pyjamas, was helped into the back of the ambulance by one of the attendants. His wife followed, clutching a bag. The doors were banged shut and the ambulance pulled away, a patrol car behind it.

Leclerc watched until the two vehicles reached the curve of the drive leading to the main road, then turned back into the house.

'Big place for two people,' muttered one of the gendarmes standing just inside the doorway.

Leclerc grunted. 'Big place for ten people.'

He went on a solitary expedition to try to get a feel of what he was dealing with. Six—no, seven bedrooms upstairs, each with en suite bathroom, the master bedroom huge, with a big dressing room next to it lined by mirrored doors; a plasma TV in the bathroom; a space-age shower. Across the landing, a gym, with exercise bike, rowing machine, cross-trainer, weights, another big TV. No toys. No evidence of children anywhere.

Leclerc went downstairs. He skirted the bloodstains and passed through into the study. An entire wall was given over to books. He took down one at random and looked at the spine: *Die Traumdeutung* by Sigmund Freud. A first edition. He took down another. *La psychologie des foules* by Gustave le Bon. Paris, 1895. Leclerc knew little about rare books, but sufficient to appreciate that this must be a collection worth millions. The subjects covered were mostly scientific: sociology, psychology, biology, anthropology—nothing anywhere about money.

He crossed over to the desk and sat down in Hoffmann's antique captain's chair. Occasionally the large screen in front of him rippled slightly as the shimmering expanse of figures changed: *-1.06, -78, -4.03%, -$0.95*. He could no more decipher it than he could read the Rosetta Stone. *If only I could find the key*, he thought, *maybe I could be as rich as this fellow*. His own investments, which he had been persuaded to make a few years back by some pimply 'financial adviser' were now worth only half what he had paid for them. He made himself stand up and go into another room in order to take his mind off it.

In the kitchen, he leaned against the granite island and studied the knives. On his instructions they had been bagged and sealed in the hope that they might yield fingerprints. This part of Hoffmann's story he did not understand. If the intruder had come prepared to kidnap, surely he would have armed himself properly beforehand? So was the motive robbery? But a simple burglar would have been in and out as quickly as he could, taking as much as he could carry. Everything therefore seemed to point to the criminal being mentally disturbed. But how would a violent psychopath have known the entry codes? Perhaps there was some other way into the house that had been left unlocked.

Leclerc went back out into the corridor and turned left. The rear of the house opened into a large Victorian-style conservatory, which was being used as an artist's studio, although it was not exactly art as the inspector understood that term. It looked more like a radiographic unit, or possibly a glazier's workshop. On the original exterior wall of the house was a vast collage of electronic images of the human body—digital, infrared, X-ray— along with anatomical drawings of various organs, limbs and muscles.

Sheets of non-reflecting glass and Perspex, of various sizes and thicknesses, were stored in wooden racks. In a tin trunk were dozens of files, bulging with computer images, carefully labelled: 'MRI head scans, 1–14 Sagittal, Axial, Coronal'; 'Man, slices, Virtual Hospital, Sagittal & Coronal'. On a bench were a light box, a small vice and a clutter of inkpots, and engraving tools. There was a pile of glossy brochures for an exhibition entitled 'Human Contours' due to begin that very day at a gallery on the Plaine de Plainpalais.

Next to the bench, mounted on a pair of trestles, was one of Gabrielle's works: a 3D scanned image of a foetus composed of about twenty sections drawn on sheets of very clear glass. Leclerc bent to examine it. Its head was disproportionately large, its spindly legs drawn up beneath it. Viewed from the side it had depth, but as one shifted one's perspective to the front it seemed to dwindle, then vanish entirely. He could not make out whether it was finished or not.

A door from the conservatory led to the garden. It was locked and bolted. Beyond the thick glass, the lights of Geneva wavered across the lake.

Leclerc left the conservatory and returned to the passage. Two more doors led off it. One turned out to be a lavatory and the other a storage room filled with detritus: rolls of carpet tied with twine, deckchairs, a croquet set, and, at the far end, in pristine condition, a baby's cot, a changing table and a clockwork mobile of stars and moons.

2

According to the records subsequently released by the Geneva medical service, the ambulance radioed to report that it was leaving the Hoffmanns' residence at 5.22. At that hour it was only a five-minute drive through the empty streets of central Geneva to the hospital.

In the back of the ambulance Hoffmann maintained his refusal to lie down on the bed, but instead sat upright with his legs over the side, brooding and defiant. He was a brilliant man, a rich man, accustomed to respect. But now suddenly he found he had been deported to some less-favoured land: the kingdom of the sick. It irritated him to recall how Gabrielle and Leclerc had looked at him when he had showed them *The Expression of the Emotions in Man and Animals*—as if the obvious connection between the book and the attack was merely the fevered product of an injured brain. The volume was resting in his lap; he tapped his finger against it restlessly.

The ambulance swerved round the corner and the female attendant put out her hand to steady him. Hoffmann scowled at her and began searching his dressing-gown pockets for his mobile.

Gabrielle, watching him from the opposite seat, next to the ambulance woman, said, 'What are you doing?'

'I'm calling Hugo.'

She rolled her eyes. 'For God's sake, Alex—'

'What? He needs to know what's happened.' Hoffmann reached over and took her hand to mollify her.

Eventually Quarry came on the line. 'Alex?' His normally languid voice was strained with anxiety: 'What the hell is it?'

'Sorry to call this early, Hugo. We've had an intruder.'

'Oh God, I'm so sorry. Are you all right?'

'Gabrielle's OK. I got a whack on the head. We're in an ambulance going to the university hospital.'

'I'm on my way.'

A couple of minutes later, the ambulance swept up the approach road to the big teaching hospital. Through the smoked-glass window Hoffmann briefly glimpsed its scale—a huge place: ten floors, lit up like some great foreign airport terminal. The ambulance descended along a gently circling subterranean passage and pulled to a halt. The rear doors swung open onto what looked like a spotlessly clean underground car park.

Hoffmann was instructed to lie down, and this time he decided not to argue. He stretched out, the bed was lowered, and with a horrible feeling of helplessness he allowed himself to be wheeled along factory-like corridors, staring up at the strip lighting until, at a reception desk, he was briefly parked. An accompanying gendarme handed over his paperwork. Hoffmann watched as his details were registered, then he was on the move again, down a short corridor and into an empty cubicle.

Gabrielle sat on a moulded plastic chair, took out a powder compact and started applying lipstick in quick, nervous strokes. Hoffmann watched her as if she were a stranger: so dark and neat and self-contained, like a cat washing her face. A harassed young Turkish doctor came in with a clipboard; a plastic name tag attached to his white coat announced him as Dr Muhammet Celik. He consulted Hoffmann's notes. He shone a light into his eyes, struck his knee with a small hammer and asked him to count backwards from 100 to eighty.

Hoffmann answered without difficulty. Satisfied, the doctor took off Hoffmann's temporary dressing, parted his hair and examined the wound, gently prodding it with his fingers.

'He lost a lot of blood,' said Gabrielle.

'Wounds to the head always bleed heavily. He will need a few stitches, I think. It was something blunt that hit him?'

'A fire extinguisher.'

'OK. Let me make a note of that. We need to get a head scan.'

Celik bent down so that his face was level with Hoffmann's. He smiled and spoke extremely slowly. 'Monsieur Hoffmann, later I will stitch the wound. Right now we need to take you downstairs and make some pictures of the inside of your head with a machine we call a CAT scanner. Are you familiar with a CAT scanner, Monsieur Hoffmann?'

'Computed Axial Tomography uses a rotating detector and X-ray source to compile cross-sectional radiographic images—it's seventies technology, no big deal. And it's not Monsieur Hoffmann, it's Dr Hoffmann.'

As he was wheeled to the elevator, Gabrielle said, 'There was no need to be so rude. He was only trying to help you.'

'He spoke to me as if I were a child.'

'Then stop behaving like one. Here, you can hold this.' She dropped his bag of clothes onto his lap and walked ahead to summon the elevator.

Gabrielle obviously knew her way to the radiology department, a fact that Hoffmann found obscurely irritating. Over the past couple of years the staff had helped her with her art, giving her access to the scanners when they were not in use, staying late after their shifts to produce the images she needed. Several had become her friends. The doors opened onto the darkened lower floor. A young man with long black curly hair came striding across to them. 'Gabrielle!' he exclaimed. He took her hand and kissed it, then turned to look down at Hoffmann. 'So you have brought me a genuine patient for a change?'

Gabrielle said, 'This is my husband, Alexander Hoffmann. Alex—this is Fabian Tallon, the duty technician.'

Hoffmann looked up at the young man. Tallon had large dark liquid eyes, a wide mouth, very white teeth and a couple of days' growth of dark beard. His shirt was unbuttoned more than it needed to be, drawing attention to his rugby player's chest. Suddenly, Hoffmann wondered if Gabrielle might be having an affair with him. He tried to push the idea out of his head. Looking from one to the other he said, 'Thank you for all you've done for Gabrielle.'

'It's been a pleasure, Alex. Now let's see what we can do for you.' He pushed the bed through the control area and into the room containing the CAT scanner. 'Stand up, please.'

Once again Hoffmann surrendered to the procedure. His coat and spectacles were taken from him and he was instructed to lie on his back on the couch that formed part of the machine, his head pointing towards the scanner. Tallon adjusted the neck rest. 'This will take less than a minute,' he said, and disappeared. The door sighed shut behind him. Hoffmann raised his head. Through the thick glass window at the far end of the room, he could see Gabrielle watching him. Tallon joined her. There was a clatter, and then Tallon's voice came loudly over a loudspeaker.

'Lie back, Alex. Try to keep as still as possible.'

Hoffmann did as ordered. There was a hum and the couch began to slide backwards through the drum of the scanner. It happened twice: once briefly, to get a fix; the second time more slowly, to collect the images. He stared at the white plastic casing as he passed beneath it. It was like being subjected to some radioactive car wash. The couch stopped and reversed itself and Hoffmann imagined his brain being sprayed by a brilliant, cleansing light—

all impurities exposed and obliterated in a hiss of burning matter.

The loudspeaker clicked on and Tallon said, 'Thank you, Alex. It's all over. Stay where you are. I'll come and get you.'

Hoffmann lay there for what seemed a long while: plenty of time, at any rate, to consider how easy it would have been for Gabrielle to have had an affair over the past few months. There were the long hours she had spent at the hospital collecting the images she needed for her work; and then there were the even longer days and nights he had been away, developing VIXAL. What was there to anchor a couple in a marriage after more than seven years if there were no children to exert some gravitational pull?

'Are you OK, Alex?' Tallon's handsome face loomed above the couch, handsome, concerned, insufferable. He handed him his spectacles.

'I'm fine.' Hoffmann put them back on. He refused to get back onto the wheeled bed. He swung his legs off the couch, took a few deep breaths and walked into the room behind the glass.

'Alex,' said Gabrielle, 'this is the radiologist, Dr Dufort.'

She indicated a tiny woman with close-cropped grey hair who was seated at a computer screen. Dufort gave him a perfunctory nod over her narrow shoulder, then resumed her examination of the scan results.

'Is that me?' asked Hoffmann, staring at the screen.

'It is, monsieur.' She did not turn round.

Hoffmann contemplated the image of his brain with detachment, indeed disappointment. Its messiness, its lack of form or beauty, depressed him. *Surely we can do better than this*, he thought. This must be merely a stage in evolution, and our human task is to prepare the way for whatever comes next. Artificial intelligence, or autonomous machine reasoning as he preferred to call it—AMR—had been a preoccupation of his for more than fifteen years. Silly people thought the aim was to replicate the human mind and to produce a digitalised version of ourselves. But why would one bother to replicate anything with such built-in obsolescence: a central processing unit that could be utterly destroyed because some mechanical part—the heart, say, or the liver—suffered a temporary interruption?

The radiologist tilted the brain on its axis from top to bottom.

'No evidence of fracture,' she said, 'and no swelling, which is the most important thing. But what is this, I wonder?'

The skull bone showed up like a reverse image of a walnut shell. A white line of variable thickness encased the spongy grey matter of the brain. She zoomed in. The image widened, blurred. Hoffmann leaned forwards for a closer look.

'There,' said Dufort, touching the screen. 'You see these white pin-points? These are tiny haemorrhages in the brain tissue.'

Gabrielle said, 'Is that serious?'

'No, not necessarily. It's probably what one would expect to see from an injury of this type. You know, the brain ricochets when the head is struck with sufficient force. There is bound to be a little bleeding.' She raised her spectacles. 'All the same,' she said, 'I would like to do another test.'

Hoffmann had so often imagined this moment—the abnormal test result, the coolly delivered medical verdict—that it took him a moment to realise this was not another of his hypochondriac fantasies.

'What sort of test?' he asked.

'I would like to use MRI for a second look. It should tell us whether this is a pre-existing condition or not.'

A pre-existing condition . . . 'How long will that take?'

'The test itself does not take long. It's a question of when a scanner is free.' She called up a new file and clicked through it. 'We should be able to get a machine at noon, provided there isn't an emergency.'

'I'd rather leave it,' said Hoffmann. 'I don't want the test.'

'Don't be silly,' said Gabrielle. 'Have the test. You might as well.'

'*I said I don't want the damn test!*'

There was a moment of shocked silence.

Hoffman put his hand to his brow. His fingers were very cold. His throat was dry. He had to get out of the hospital as quickly as possible. He swallowed. 'I'm sorry, but there are important things I need to do today.'

'What important things?' Gabrielle stared at him in disbelief.

'I am going into the office. And you're going to the gallery for the start of your exhibition.'

'Alex . . .'

'Yes, you are. You've been working on it for months. And tonight we're going to have dinner to celebrate your success.' He forced himself to speak calmly. 'Just because this guy got into our house, it doesn't mean he has to get into our lives. Look at me.' He gestured to himself. 'I'm fine. You just saw the scan—no fracture and no swelling.'

'And no bloody common sense,' said an English voice behind them.

'Hugo,' said Gabrielle, without turning to look at him, 'will you please tell your business partner that he's made of flesh and blood, like the rest of us?'

'Ah, but is he?' Quarry was standing by the door with his overcoat unfastened, a cherry-red woollen scarf round his neck, his hands in his pockets.

'Business partner?' repeated Dr Celik, who had been persuaded to bring Quarry down from A&E. 'You said you were his brother.'

'Just have the test, Al,' said Quarry. 'The presentation can be postponed.'

'I promise you I'll have the test,' said Hoffmann evenly. 'Just not today. Is that all right with you, Doctor?'

'Monsieur,' said the grey-haired radiologist, who had been on duty since the previous afternoon and was losing patience, 'what you do, and do not do, is entirely your decision. The wound should definitely be stitched, and if you leave you will be required to sign a form releasing the hospital from all responsibility. The rest is up to you.'

'Fine. I'll have it stitched, and I'll sign the form. And then I'll come back and have the MRI when it's more convenient. Happy?' he said to Gabrielle.

Before she could reply, a familiar electronic reveille sounded. It took him a moment to realise it was the alarm on his mobile, which he had set for six thirty in what felt to him already like another life.

HOFFMANN LEFT his wife sitting with Quarry in the reception area of the accident and emergency department while he went to have his wound stitched up. Afterwards, Dr Celik produced a mirror and showed Hoffmann his handiwork. The area had been shaved, and the cut was about five centimetres long. Stitched together, it resembled a twisted mouth with thick, white lips.

'It will hurt,' said Celik cheerfully, 'when the anaesthetic wears off. You will need to take painkillers.'

'You're not going to bandage it up?'

'No, it will heal quicker if it's exposed.'

'Good. In that case, I'll leave now.'

Celik shrugged. 'That is your right. But you must sign a form that you are leaving the University Hospital contrary to medical advice.'

After he had signed the little chit, Hoffmann picked up his bag of clothes and followed Celik to a small shower cubicle. Celik switched on the light and closed the door.

It was the first time he had been alone since he recovered consciousness, and for a moment he revelled in his solitude. He dressed slowly and deliberately—boxer shorts, socks, jeans, desert boots, a plain white long-sleeved shirt, a sports jacket—and with each item he felt a degree less vulnerable. Gabrielle had put his wallet inside his jacket pocket. He checked the contents. He had 3,000 Swiss francs in new notes. He stood and looked at himself in the mirror. His clothes said nothing at all about him, which was the way he liked it. A hedge-fund manager with $10 billion in assets under management could pass for the guy who delivered his parcels.

There was a knock on the door, and he heard the radiologist, Dr Dufort, calling his name. 'Monsieur Hoffmann? Are you all right?'

'Yes, thank you,' he called back, 'much better.'

'I am going off duty now. I have something for you.' He opened the door. She had put on a raincoat and rubber boots. 'Here. These are your CAT scan results.' She thrust a CD in a clear plastic case into his hands. 'You should take them to your own doctor as soon as possible.'

'I will, of course, thank you. Do you think there is something wrong?' He detested the sound of his own voice—tremulous, pathetic.

'I don't know, monsieur. You need an MRI scan to determine that.'

'What might it be, do you think?' Hoffmann hesitated. 'A tumour?'

'No, I don't think that,' she said. 'It probably isn't anything at all. But I suppose other explanations might include MS perhaps, or dementia.' She patted his hand. 'See your doctor, monsieur. Really, take it from me: it is always the unknown that is most frightening.'

3

Some in the secretive inner counsels of the super-rich occasionally wondered aloud why Hoffmann had made Quarry an equal shareholder in Hoffmann Investment Technologies: it was, after all, the physicist's algorithms that generated the profits. But it suited Hoffmann's temperament to have someone more outgoing to hide behind. It was not just that Quarry had the experience and interest in banking that he lacked; he also had something else that Hoffmann could never possess no matter how hard he tried: a talent for dealing with people.

This was partly charm, of course. But it was more than that. It was a capacity for bending human beings to a larger purpose. If there had been another war, Quarry would have made a perfect ADC to a field marshal—a position that had, in fact, been held in the British Army by both his great- and great-great-grandfathers—ensuring that orders were carried out, soothing hurt feelings, bringing together jealous rivals over a dinner for which he himself would have selected the most appropriate wines. He had a first in politics, philosophy and economics from Oxford, an ex-wife and three children safely stowed in a gloomy mansion in Surrey, and a ski chalet in Chamonix where he went in winter with whoever happened to be his girl-friend that weekend. Gabrielle couldn't stand him.

Nevertheless, the crisis made them temporary allies. While Hoffmann was having his wound stitched up, Quarry sat with her in the tiny waiting room. He held her hand and listened to her account of what had happened. When she recited Hoffmann's subsequent oddities of behaviour, he reassured her: 'Let's face it, Gabs, he's never been exactly *normal*, has he, even at the best of times? We'll get this sorted out.'

He called his assistant and told her he would need a chauffeured car at the hospital immediately. He woke the company's security consultant, Maurice Genoud, and brusquely ordered him to attend an emergency meeting at the office within the hour, and to send someone over to the Hoffmanns' house.

Gabrielle watched Quarry with reluctant admiration. He was so much the opposite of Alex—good-looking *and* he knew it. His affected southern English manners also got on her Presbyterian northern nerves.

'Hugo,' she said very seriously, when he finally got off the phone, 'I want you to do me a favour. I want you to order him not to go into the office.'

Quarry took her hand again. 'Darling, if I thought my telling him would do any good, I would.'

'Is it really so important, what he has to do today?'

'It is, quite. I mean, nothing that can't be put off if his health really is at stake, obviously. But if I'm honest with you, it would definitely be better to go ahead than not. People have come a long way to see him.'

She pulled her hand away. 'You want to be careful you don't kill your golden goose,' she said bitterly. 'That definitely would be bad for business.'

'Don't think I don't know it,' said Quarry pleasantly. His smile crinkled the skin around his deep blue eyes; his lashes, like his hair, were sandy. 'Listen, if I start to think for *one moment* that he's seriously endangering himself, I'll have him back home and tucked up in bed with Mummy within fifteen minutes. And that's a promise. And now,' he said, looking over her shoulder, 'if I'm not mistaken, here comes our dear old goose, with his feathers half-plucked and ruffled.' He was on his feet in an instant. 'My dear Al,' he said, meeting him halfway across the corridor, 'how are you feeling? You look very pale.'

'I'll be a whole lot better once I'm out of this place.' Hoffmann slipped the CD into his coat pocket so that Gabrielle could not see it. He kissed her on the cheek. 'Everything's going to be fine now.'

THEY MADE their way through the main reception. It was nearly half past seven. Outside, the day had turned up at last: overcast and cold. The thick rolls of cloud hanging over the hospital were the same shade of grey as brain tissue, or so it appeared to Hoffmann, who was now seeing the CAT scan wherever he looked.

Quarry found their car, a big Mercedes parked in a bay reserved for the disabled. The driver—a heavyset and moustachioed figure—levered himself out of the front seat as they approached and held a rear door open for them. *He has driven me before*, thought Hoffmann, and he struggled to remember his name as the distance between them closed.

'Georges!' He greeted him with relief. 'Good morning to you.'

'Good morning, monsieur.' The chauffeur smiled and touched his hand to his cap in salute as Gabrielle climbed into the back seat, followed by Quarry. 'Monsieur,' he whispered in a quiet aside to Hoffmann, 'forgive me, but just so you know, my name is Claude.'

'Right then, boys and girls,' said Quarry, seated between the Hoffmanns and squeezing the nearest knee of each simultaneously, 'where is it to be?'

Hoffmann said, 'Office,' just as Gabrielle said, 'Home.'

'Office,' repeated Hoffmann, 'and then home for my wife.'

As the Mercedes turned into the Boulevard de la Cluse, Hoffmann fell into his habitual silence. He wondered if the others had overheard his mistake. It was not as if he usually noticed who his driver was: car journeys were passed in the company of his iPad, surfing the web for technical research or, for lighter reading, the digital edition of the *Financial Times* or the *Wall Street Journal*. It was rare for him even to look out of the window. How odd it felt to do so now, when there was nothing else to occupy him.

The limousine slowed to make a left. A bell clanged. A tram drew alongside. Hoffmann glanced up absently at the faces framed in the lighted windows. For a moment they seemed to hang motionless then began to drift past him: in the last window, the bony profile of a man in his fifties with a high-domed head and unkempt grey hair pulled into a ponytail.

It was all so quick and dreamlike, Hoffmann was not certain what he had seen. Quarry must have heard him draw in his breath. He turned and said, 'Are you all right, old friend?' But Hoffmann was too startled to speak.

'What's happening?' Gabrielle stretched back and peered around Quarry's head at her husband.

'Nothing.' Hoffmann managed to recover his voice. 'Anaesthetic must be wearing off.'

Hoffmann was trying to decide whether he was hallucinating or not. What if he was imagining things? It would mean he could no longer trust the signals from his own brain. He could endure anything except madness. He would sooner die than go down that path again.

HOFFMANN'S HEDGE FUND was based in Les Eaux-Vives, a district just south of the lake, as solid and confident as the nineteenth-century Swiss business-men who had built it: heavy masonry, wide faux-Parisian boulevards with cherry trees erupting from the kerbsides, shops and restaurants on the ground floors, seven storeys of offices and apartments stacked imper-turbably above. Amid this bourgeois respectability, Hoffmann Investment Technologies was easy to miss unless you were looking for it.

'You promise me you'll be careful?' said Gabrielle, as the car pulled up.

Hoffmann reached behind Quarry and squeezed her shoulder. 'I'm get-ting stronger by the minute. What about you, though? You feel OK, going back to the house?'

'Genoud is sending someone round,' said Quarry.

Gabrielle made a quick face at Hoffmann—her Hugo face, which involved turning down the corners of her mouth, sticking out her tongue and rolling up her eyes. Despite everything, he almost burst out laughing. '*Hugo* has it all under control,' she said, 'don't you, Hugo? *As usual.*' She kissed her husband's hand where it lay on her shoulder. 'I won't be stopping anyway. I'll just grab my things and get over to the gallery.'

The chauffeur opened the door.

'Hey, listen,' said Hoffmann. 'Good luck this morning. I'll come over and see how things are going as soon as I can get away.'

'I'd like that.'

He climbed out onto the pavement. She had a sudden vivid premonition that she would never see him again. 'You're sure we shouldn't both cancel everything and take the day off?'

'No way. It's going to be great.'

Quarry said, 'Cheerio then, sweetheart,' and slid his neat bottom over the leather upholstery towards the open door.

As the car pulled away, Gabrielle looked back at them through the rear window. Quarry had his left arm round Alex's shoulders and was steering him across the pavement. A moment later they disappeared.

THE OFFICES of Hoffmann Investment Technologies revealed themselves to a visitor like the carefully rehearsed stages of a conjuring trick. First, heavy doors of smoked glass opened automatically onto a narrow reception area, walled by dimly lit brown granite. Next you presented your face to a camera for 3D recognition scanning: it took less than one second to match your features to a database; if you were a visitor, you gave your name to the unsmiling security guard. Once cleared, you were clicked through a steel turnstile, walked down another short corridor and turned left—and suddenly you were confronted by a huge open space flooded with daylight: that was when it hit you that this was actually three buildings knocked into one. The masonry at the back had been demolished and replaced by a sheer Alpine ice-fall of frameless glass, eight storeys high, overlooking a court-yard centred around a jetting fountain and giant ferns. Twin elevators rose and fell noiselessly in their soundproofed glass silos.

Quarry, the showman and salesman, had been stunned by the concept the moment he had first been shown round the place nine months earlier. For his part, Hoffmann had loved the computer-controlled systems—the lighting that adjusted in harmony with the daylight outside, the windows that opened automatically to regulate the temperature. The building was advertised as 'a holistic, digitally aware entity with minimal carbon emissions'. It was also, most important of all, connected to the GV1 fibre-optic pipe, the fastest in Europe. That clinched it: they took out a lease on the fifth floor.

The floor was a kingdom within a kingdom. A wall of opaque and bubbled turquoise glass blocked off access from the elevators. To gain entry, facial recognition activated a sliding panel, which rolled back to reveal Hoffmann's own reception area: low cubes of black and grey upholstery stacked and arranged like child's bricks to form chairs and sofas, a coffee table of chrome and glass, and adjustable consoles containing touch-screen computers on which visitors could browse the web. Each had a screensaver stating the company's rubric in red letters on a white background:

THE COMPANY OF THE FUTURE WILL HAVE NO PAPER
THE COMPANY OF THE FUTURE WILL CARRY NO INVENTORY
THE COMPANY OF THE FUTURE WILL BE ENTIRELY DIGITAL
THE COMPANY OF THE FUTURE HAS ARRIVED

There were no magazines in the reception area: it was company policy that, as far as possible, no printed material or writing paper of any sort should pass the threshold. Of course, the rule could not be imposed on guests, but employees, including the senior partners, were required to pay a fine of ten Swiss francs each time they were caught in possession of ink and wood pulp rather than silicon and plastic.

It was embarrassing, therefore, for Hoffmann to have to pass through Reception with his first edition of *The Expression of the Emotions in Man and Animals*. If he had caught anyone else with a copy he would have pointed out that the text was readily available online via Darwin.online.org, and asked sarcastically whether they considered themselves to be a quicker reader than the VIXAL-4 algorithm. He saw no paradox in his zeal to ban the book at work and to display it in rare first editions at home. Books were antiques, just like any other artefacts from the past. Nevertheless, he slipped the volume under his coat and glanced up guiltily at one of the tiny security cameras that monitored the floor.

'Breaking your own rules, Professor?' said Quarry, loosening his scarf.

'Forgot I had it with me.'

'Like hell. Your place or mine?'

'I don't know. Does it matter? OK—yours.'

To reach Quarry's office it was necessary to cross the trading floor. The Japanese stock market would close in fifteen minutes, the European exchanges would open at nine, and already four dozen quantitative analysts—quants, in the dismissive jargon of the trade—were hard at work. None talked above a whisper. Most stared silently at their six-screen arrays. Giant plasma televisions with muted sound carried CNBC and Bloomberg, while beneath the TVs a glowing red line of digital clocks noiselessly recorded time's relentless passage in Tokyo, Beijing, Moscow, Geneva, London and New York. This was the sound that money made in the second decade of the twenty-first century. The occasional soft clatter of strokes on a keyboard was the only indication that humans were present at all.

Hoffmann's force of quants was nine-tenths male, for reasons he did not entirely understand. It simply seemed to be only men who applied, usually refugees from the twin miseries of academia: low salaries and high tables. Half a dozen had come from the Large Hadron Collider. Hoffmann would not even consider hiring anyone without a PhD in maths or the physical sciences. Nationality did not matter and nor did social skills, with the result that Hoffmann's payroll occasionally resembled a United Nations conference on Asperger's syndrome. Quarry called it 'The Nerd World'. Last year's bonus brought the average remuneration up to almost half a million dollars.

Only five senior managers got offices of their own—the heads of Finance, Risk, and Operations; along with Hoffmann, whose title was company president, and Quarry, who was the CEO. The offices were standard soundproofed glass cubicles with white venetian blinds, beige carpeting and Scandinavian furniture of pale wood and chrome. Quarry's windows looked down onto the street and across to a private German bank, hidden from view by thick net curtains. He was in the process of having a sixty-five-metre super-yacht built by Benetti of Viareggio. Framed blueprints and artist's sketches lined his walls; there was a scale model on his desk. Hoffmann, who was happy enough in a Hobie Cat, worried at first that their clients might take this ostentation as evidence that they were making too much money. But Quarry knew their psychology better than he did: 'No, no, they'll love it. They'll tell everybody: "D'you have any idea how much those guys are making . . .?" And they'll want to be a part of it even more.'

Now he sat behind his model boat, peered over one of its three model swimming pools and said, 'Coffee? Breakfast?'

'Just coffee.' Hoffmann went straight across to the window.

Quarry buzzed his assistant. 'Two black coffees right away. And I'll have a banana and some yoghurt. And send Genoud straight in when he gets here.' He released the switch. 'Anything happening out there?'

Hoffmann had his hands on the windowsill. He was staring down into the street. A group of pedestrians waited on the corner opposite for the lights to change, even though there was no traffic coming in either direction. Hoffmann muttered, 'The goddamn tight-arsed Swiss . . .'

'Yeah, well, just remember the goddamn tight-arsed eight-point-eight per cent tax rate they let us get away with, and you'll feel better.'

A well-toned freckled woman with a low-cut sweater and a cascade of dark red hair came in without knocking: Hugo's assistant, an Australian. Hoffmann couldn't quite remember her name—Amber? He suspected she was a former girlfriend of Hugo's who had passed the statutory retirement age for that position: thirty-one. She was carrying a tray. Behind her lurked a man in a dark suit and black tie with a fawn raincoat over his arm.

'Mr Genoud is here,' she said.

Hoffmann raised his hand in thanks. He took his coffee from the tray and returned to the window. The pedestrians had moved on. A tram rattled to a halt and opened its doors, spilling out passengers along its entire length. Hoffmann tried to pick out faces, but they were dispersing too quickly. He drank his coffee. When he turned round, Genoud was in the office and the door was closed. They had been talking to him and he had not realised. He was aware of a silence.

'Sorry?'

Genoud said patiently, 'I was just telling Mr Quarry, Dr Hoffmann: I have spoken to several of my old colleagues in the Geneva police. They have issued a description of the man.'

Hoffmann said, 'The inspector in charge of the case is called Leclerc.'

'Yes, I know him. He's ready to be put out to grass, unfortunately.' Genoud hesitated. 'May I ask you, Dr Hoffmann—are you sure you have told him everything? It would be wise to be frank with him.'

'Of course I have. Why the hell wouldn't I?'

Quarry cut in: 'I don't give a shit what Inspector Clouseau thinks. The point is, how did this lunatic get past Alex's security? And if he got past it at his house, can he get past it here at the office? That's what we pay you for, isn't it, Maurice? Security?'

Genoud's sallow cheeks flushed. 'This building is as well protected as any in Geneva. As for Dr Hoffmann's house, the police say that the codes seem to have been known to the intruder. No security system in the world can protect against that.'

Hoffmann said, 'I'll change the codes tonight. And in future *I* will decide who knows them.'

'I can assure you, Dr Hoffmann,' said Genoud, 'only two persons in our company knew those combinations—myself and one of my technicians. There was no leak from our side.'

'So you say. But he must have got hold of them from somewhere.'

'OK, let's leave the codes for now,' said Quarry. 'Until this guy is caught, I want Alex to have some proper protection. What will that entail?'

'A permanent guard on the house, certainly—one of my men is there already. At least two other men on duty tonight—one to patrol the grounds, the other to remain indoors downstairs. As for when Dr Hoffmann moves around the city, I would suggest a driver with counterterrorism training and one security officer.'

An hour ago, Hoffmann would have dismissed these precautions as absurd. But the spectre on the tram had jolted him. Little flashes of panic kept breaking out in his mind. 'I want Gabrielle looked after as well. We keep assuming this maniac was after me, but what if it was her he wanted?'

Genoud was making entries on a personal organiser. 'Yes, we can manage that. And should we take precautions on your behalf as well, Mr Quarry?' he asked.

Quarry laughed. 'The only thing that keeps me awake at night is the thought of a paternity suit.'

'RIGHT,' SAID QUARRY, when Genoud had gone, 'let's talk about this presentation—if you're still sure you're up for it?'

'I'm up for it.'

'OK, thank God for that. Nine investors—all existing clients as agreed. Four institutions, three ultra-high net worths, two family offices. Ground rules are: first, they have to sign a non-disclosure agreement and second, they're each permitted to bring in one designated professional adviser. They're due to arrive in about an hour and a half—I suggest you have a shower and a shave before they get here: the look we require from you is brilliant but eccentric. You walk them through the principles. We'll show them the hardware. I'll make the pitch. Then we'll both take them out to lunch at the Beau-Rivage.'

'How much are we looking to raise?'

'I'd like a billion. Settle for seven-fifty.'

'And commission? Are we sticking with two and twenty?'

'More than the going rate looks greedy, less and they won't respect us in the morning. So even with our track record I say let's stick with two and twenty.' Quarry pushed back his chair and swung his feet up onto the desk in a single, fluid motion. 'We've waited a whole year to show them this. And they're gagging for it.'

A two per cent annual management fee on $1 billion was $20 million. A twenty per cent performance fee on a billion-dollar investment, assuming a twenty per cent return—modest by Hoffmann's current standards—was an additional $40 million a year. In other words, an annual income of $60 million in return for half a morning's work and two hours of small talk in a smart restaurant. Even Hoffmann was willing to suffer fools for that.

He asked, 'Who exactly have we got coming?'

'Oh, you know—the usual suspects.' For the next ten minutes Quarry described each in turn. 'But you don't have to worry about them. I'll handle that side. You just talk about your precious algorithms. Now go and get some rest.'

4

Hoffmann's office was identical to Quarry's except he had no decoration of any sort apart from three framed photographs. One was of Gabrielle in St-Tropez two years earlier: she was laughing, the sun on her face, vitally alive; it raised his spirits every time he saw it. Another was of Hoffmann himself, taken in 2001, wearing a yellow hard hat and standing 175 metres below ground in the tunnel that would eventually house the synchrotron of the Large Hadron Collider. The third was of Quarry in evening dress in London receiving the award for Algorithmic Hedge-Fund Manager of the Year from a minister in the Labour government: Hoffmann, needless to say, had refused to attend the ceremony, a decision Quarry had approved of, as he said it added to the company's mystique.

Hoffmann closed the door and went round the double-glazed walls of his office lowering all the venetian blinds and closing them. He hung up his raincoat, took the CD of his CAT scan from the pocket and tapped the case against his teeth while he considered what to do with it. His desk was bare except for the inevitable six-screen Bloomberg array, a keyboard and mouse and a telephone. He opened a bottom drawer and thrust the CD inside out of sight, as far as it would go. Then he closed the drawer and switched on his computer. In Tokyo the Nikkei Stock Average of 225 companies had closed down 3.3 per cent. Mitsubishi Corporation was off by 5.4

per cent, Japan Petroleum Exploration Company 4 per cent. *This is turning into a rout*, thought Hoffmann.

Suddenly, before he realised what was happening, the screens in front of him blurred and he started to cry. His hands shook. His upper body shook convulsively. *I am coming to pieces*, he thought, as he laid his forehead on the desk in misery. And yet at the same time he remained oddly detached, as if he were observing himself from high up in the corner of the room. After a couple of minutes, when the spasm of shaking had subsided, he sat up, took off his spectacles and wiped his eyes with his trembling fingertips and then his nose with the back of his hand. He blew out his cheeks.

When he was sure he had recovered, he rose and went back over to his raincoat and retrieved the Darwin. He laid it out on his desk and sat down before it. The 138-year-old green cloth binding and slightly frayed spine seemed utterly incongruous in the surroundings of his office, where nothing was older than six months. Hesitantly, he opened it at the place where he had stopped reading shortly after midnight, then he removed the Dutch bookseller's slip, unfolded it and smoothed it out. *Rosengaarden & Nijenhuise, Antiquarian Scientific & Medical Books.* He reached for the telephone and dialled the bookshop's number in Amsterdam.

The phone rang for a long while without being answered: hardly surprising as it was barely eight thirty. But Hoffmann was at his desk, so he assumed everyone else should be at theirs. He let it ring and ring, and thought about Amsterdam. He had visited it twice. He liked its elegance, its sense of history; it had intelligence: he must take Gabrielle there when all this was sorted out. He listened to the long purr of the ring tone. He imagined its bell trilling in some dusty bookshop; an elderly bibliophile, stooped and bald, hurrying to his desk to answer the phone—

'*Goedemorgen. Rosengaarden en Nijenhuise.*'

The voice was young and female; lilting, sing-song.

He said, 'Do you speak English?'

'Yes, I do. How can I help you?'

He cleared his throat. 'I believe you sent me a book the day before yesterday. My name is Alexander Hoffmann. I live in Geneva.'

'Hoffmann? Yes, Dr Hoffmann! Naturally I remember. The Darwin first edition. A beautiful book. You have it already?'

'Yeah, I got it. But there was no note with it, so I can't thank whoever it was who bought it for me. Could you give me that information?'

There was a pause. 'Did you say your name was Alexander Hoffmann?'
'That's right.'

This time the pause was longer, and when the girl spoke again, she sounded confused. 'You bought it yourself, Dr Hoffmann.'

Hoffmann closed his eyes. When he opened them again it seemed to him that his office had shifted slightly on its axis. 'I didn't buy it,' he said. 'It must have been someone pretending to be me.'

'But you paid for it yourself by bank transfer.'

'And how much did I pay?'

'Ten thousand euros.'

With his free hand Hoffmann grasped the edge of his desk. 'Did someone come into your shop and say they were me?'

'There is no shop any more. Not for five years. These days we are in a warehouse outside Rotterdam. Orders all come from email.'

Hoffmann wedged the phone between his chin and shoulder. He clicked on his computer and went to his email screen. He scrolled through his outbox. 'When am I supposed to have sent you this email?'

'May the 3rd.'

'Well, I'm looking here now at my emails for that day and I can assure you I sent no message to you on May the 3rd. What's the email address on the order?'

'A dot Hoffmann at Hoffmann Investment Technologies dot com.'

'That's my address. But I don't see any message to a bookseller here.'

'You sent it from a different computer perhaps?'

'No, I'm sure I didn't.' But even as he uttered the words, the confidence leaked from his voice and he felt as if an abyss was opening at his feet. The radiologist had mentioned dementia as a possible explanation for the white pinpricks on his CAT scan. Perhaps he had used his mobile, or his laptop, and had forgotten all about it. He said, 'What exactly was in the message I sent you? Can you read it back to me?'

'There was no message. The customer clicks on the title on our online catalogue and fills in the order form—name, address, method of payment.' Caution entered her voice. 'I hope you are not wanting to cancel the order.'

'No, I just need to sort this out. You say the money was paid by bank transfer. What's the account number the money came from?'

'I cannot disclose that information.'

Hoffmann summoned all the force he could muster. 'Now listen to me.

I've clearly been the victim of identity theft. And I most certainly will cancel the order and put the whole thing in the hands of the police if you don't give me that account number so I can find out just what is going on.'

There was a silence at the other end of the line. Eventually the woman said coldly, 'I cannot give this information over the telephone, but I can send it to the email address given on the order. Will this be OK for you?'

'This will be OK for me. Thank you.'

Hoffmann hung up and exhaled. He put his elbows on his desk, rested his head between his fingertips and stared hard at his computer screen. Twenty seconds later his email inbox announced the arrival of a new message. He opened it. It was from the bookshop. There was no greeting, just a single line of twenty digits and letters, and the name of the account holder: A. J. Hoffmann. He gawped at it then buzzed his assistant.

'Marie-Claude, could you mail me a list of all my personal bank account numbers? Right away, please.'

'Of course.'

'And you keep a record of the security codes at my house, I believe?'

'Yes, I do, Dr Hoffmann.' Marie-Claude Durade was a brisk Swiss woman in her middle fifties who had been with Hoffman for five years.

'Where do you keep them?'

'In your personal file on my computer.'

'You haven't discussed them with anyone? Not even your husband?'

'My husband died last year.'

'Did he? Oh. OK. Sorry. There was a break-in at my house last night. The police may want to ask you some questions.'

'Yes, Dr Hoffmann.'

As he waited for her to send him the details of his accounts, he pushed himself onto his feet and prowled round his office. Whoever heard of a case of identity theft in which the thief bought a present for the victim? Someone was trying to make him doubt his own sanity. He parted the slats of his blinds and gazed out across the trading floor. Did he have an enemy out there, in his team of sixty quants? Hoffman had hired them all personally, but he did not know them well.

He dropped the slats and returned to his terminal where a list of his bank accounts was waiting in his inbox. He had eight: Swiss franc, dollar, sterling, euro, current, deposit, offshore and joint. He checked their numbers against the one that had been used to buy the book. None matched. He tapped his finger against his desk for a few seconds, then picked up his phone and called the firm's chief financial officer, Lin Ju-Long.

'LJ? It's Alex. Do me a favour. Check out an account number for me, would you? It's in my name but I don't recognise it. I want to know if it's on our system anywhere.' He forwarded the email from the bookshop. 'I'm sending it across now. Have you got it?'

There was a pause.

'Yes, Alex, I got it. OK, well, first thing, it starts "KYD"—that's the Cayman Islands IBAN prefix for a US dollar account.'

'Could it be some kind of company account?'

'I'll run it through the system. Has Gana spoken to you, by the way?'

Gana was Ganapathi Rajamani, the company's chief risk officer.

Hoffmann said, 'No. Why?'

'You authorised a big short on Procter and Gamble last night? Two million at sixty-two per share? He says our risk limit has been breached. He wants a meeting of the Risk Committee.'

'Well, tell him to go talk to Hugo about it. And let me know about that account, will you?'

Hoffmann felt too tired to do any more. He buzzed Marie-Claude again and told her he was not to be disturbed for an hour. He lay on his sofa and tried to imagine who on earth would have gone to the trouble of stealing his name in order to buy him a rare volume of Victorian natural history using a Cayman Islands dollar account that he seemed to own. But the bizarreness of the conundrum defeated even him, and very soon he sank into sleep.

INSPECTOR LECLERC knew that the chief of Geneva's police department, a stickler for punctuality, invariably arrived at police headquarters at 9.00 sharp and that his first act of the day was always to read the summary of what had occurred overnight. Therefore, when the telephone rang in his office at 9.08, he had a fair idea of who it might be.

A brisk voice said, 'Jean-Philippe?'

'Good morning, Chief.'

'This assault on the American banker, Hoffmann.'

'Yes, Chief?'

'I've already had the Minister of Finance's office on the phone, wanting to know what's happening. It would be good if you could see this one through. Do me a favour and pull a double shift, will you?'

'The Minister of Finance?' repeated Leclerc in amazement. 'Why's he so interested?'

'Oh, you know, the usual story, I expect. One law for the rich, another for the poor. Keep me up to speed on it, will you?'

After he had hung up, Leclerc let out a string of expletives under his breath. He plodded along the corridor to the coffee machine and got himself a cup of very black espresso. His eyes felt gritty, his sinuses ached. *I'm too old for this*, he thought. He went back to his office and logged on to the internet to see if he could find out anything about Dr Alexander Hoffmann, physicist and hedge-fund manager. But to his surprise there was almost nothing—no entry in Wikipedia, no newspaper article. Yet the Minister of Finance himself was taking a personal interest in the matter.

What the hell was a hedge fund in any case? he wondered.

He looked it up: 'A private investment fund that may invest in a diverse range of assets and may employ a variety of investment strategies to maintain a hedged portfolio intended to protect the fund's investors from downturns in the market while maximising returns on upswings.'

None the wiser, he flicked back through his notes. Hoffmann had said in his interview that he had worked in the financial sector for the past eight years; for six years before that he had been employed on developing the Large Hadron Collider. As it happened, Leclerc knew a man who worked in security at CERN. He gave him a call and, fifteen minutes later, he was at the wheel of his little Renault, driving slowly in the morning traffic, north-west past the airport, along the Route de Meyrin, through the drab industrial zone of Zimeysa.

QUARRY'S INVITEES began to arrive just after ten, the first pair—a fifty-six-year-old Genevese, Etienne Mussard, and his younger sister, Clarisse—turning up on a bus. 'They'll be early,' Quarry had warned Hoffmann. 'They're always early for everything.' Dowdily dressed, they lived together in a small three-bedroomed apartment in the suburb of Lancy that they had inherited from their parents. They did not drive. They took no holidays. They rarely dined in restaurants. Quarry estimated M. Mussard's personal wealth at approximately 700 million euros, and Mme Mussard's at 550 million. Their mother's grandfather, Robert Fazy, had owned a private bank, which had been sold in the 1980s following a scandal involving Jewish assets seized by the Nazis and deposited with Fazy et Cie during the Second World War.

This drab couple was followed closely by perhaps the most exotic of Hoffmann's clients, Elmira Gulzhan, the thirty-eight-year-old daughter of the President of Azakhstan. Resident in Paris, Elmira was responsible for administering the Gulzhan family holdings overseas, estimated by the CIA in 2009 to be worth approximately $19 billion. Quarry had contrived to meet her on a skiing party in Val d'Isere. The Gulzhans presently had $120 million invested in the hedge fund—a stake Quarry hoped to persuade Elmira at least to double. Quarry was waiting in the lobby to greet her as she emerged from her bulletproof Mercedes, wearing an emerald silk frock coat with matching headscarf draped over her helmet of glossy black hair. 'Be not fooled,' he had warned Hoffmann. 'She may look like she's off to the races but she could hold down a job at Goldman any day of the week. And she can arrange for her daddy to have your fingernails torn out.'

Next to roll up, sharing a limousine from the Hotel Président Wilson on the other side of the lake, were a couple of Americans who had flown over from New York especially for the presentation. Ezra Klein was chief analyst for the Winter Bay Trust, a $14 billion fund-of-funds. Klein had a reputation for being super-bright, enhanced by his habit of talking at a rate of six words per second (he had once been timed by his bewildered subordinates).

Beside him, not even pretending to listen to Klein's unintelligible jabber, was a bulky figure in full Wall Street dress uniform of black three-piece suit and red-and-white-striped tie. This was Bill Easterbrook of the US banking conglomerate AmCor. 'You've met Bill before,' Quarry had warned Hoffmann. 'Remember him? He's the dinosaur who looks as if he's just stepped out of an Oliver Stone movie.' Quarry had himself worked for AmCor in London for a decade, and he and Easterbrook went 'way back'. When Quarry had left AmCor to set up with Hoffmann, Easterbrook had passed them their first clients in return for commission. Now AmCor was Hoffmann's biggest investor, with close to $1 billion under management. He was another attendee who Quarry met personally in the lobby.

And so they all came: twenty-seven-year-old Amschel Herxheimer of the Herxheimer banking and trading dynasty, whose sister had been at Oxford with Quarry; dull Iain Mould of what had once been an even duller Fife building society, until it had taken itself public and, in the space of three years, run up debts necessitating a takeover by the British government; the billionaire Mieczyslaw Lukasinski, a former mathematics professor and leader of the Polish Communist Youth Union, who now owned eastern

Europe's third-largest insurance company; and, finally, two Chinese entre-
preneurs, Liwei Xu and Qi Zhang, representing a Shanghai-based investment bank, who arrived with no fewer than six dark-suited associates, who
they insisted were lawyers but who Quarry was fairly sure were computer
experts, come to inspect Hoffmann's cyber-security.

Not one existing investor who Quarry had invited had declined the invitation. 'They're coming for two reasons,' he had explained to Hoffmann.
'First, because over three years, even as the markets have tanked, we've
returned them a profit of eighty-three per cent and yet we've refused to take
a single extra cent in investment.'

'And what's the second reason they're coming?'

'Oh, don't be so modest. They want to take a look at *you*, you daft bugger.
You're becoming a legend and they want to touch the hem of your garment,
just to see if their fingers turn to gold.'

HOFFMANN WAS WOKEN by Marie-Claude.

'Dr Hoffmann?' She shook his shoulder gently. 'Dr Hoffmann? Mr
Quarry says to tell you they are waiting for you in the boardroom.'

'Thanks,' he said, sitting up. 'Tell him I'll be there in a minute,' and then
he added impulsively, 'I'm sorry about your husband. I get'—he twirled his
hand helplessly—'distracted.'

'That's quite all right. Thank you.'

There was a washroom across the passage from his office. He ran the
cold tap and cupped his hands beneath it. He splashed his face again and
again, flailing his flesh with the icy water. He had no time to shave. It was a
curious fact—no doubt an irrational swing of mood brought on by his
injury—but he was beginning to feel exuberant. He had survived an
encounter with death—exhilarating in itself—and now the rich of the earth
had bestirred themselves from the dealing rooms of Manhattan and the
counting houses of Shanghai, and had gathered in Switzerland to listen to
Dr Alexander Hoffmann, the legendary—Hugo's word again—creator of
Hoffmann Investment Technologies.

With such thoughts surging through his damaged head, Hoffmann dried
his face, pulled back his shoulders and headed off to the boardroom. As he
passed across the trading floor, the lithe figure of Ganapathi Rajamani, the
company's chief risk officer, moved to intercept him, but Hoffmann waved
him out of the way: whatever his problem was, it would have to wait.

5

The boardroom had the same corporate impersonality—the same soundproofed glass walls and floor-to-ceiling venetian blinds—as the managers' offices. A giant blank screen for teleconferencing took up most of the end wall, looking down onto a big oval table of pale Scandinavian wood. As Hoffmann entered the room, all but one of the table's eighteen chairs was occupied either by the principals or their advisers; the only spare place was next to Quarry at its head. 'Here he is at last,' he said with evident relief, 'Dr Alexander Hoffmann, ladies and gentlemen, president of Hoffmann Investment Technologies. I'm afraid he took a bit of a knock, hence the stitches, but he's fine now, aren't you?'

They all stared. Those nearest to Hoffmann twisted in their seats to look up at him. But Hoffmann, hot with embarrassment, avoided eye contact. He took his position next to Quarry, folded his hands on the table in front of him, and stared fixedly at his interlaced fingers. He felt Quarry's hand grasp his shoulder, the weight increasing as the Englishman rose to his feet.

'Right then, we can at last get started. So—welcome, friends, to Geneva. It's almost eight years since Alex and I set up shop together, using his intelligence and my looks, to create a very special kind of investment fund, based exclusively on algorithmic trading. We started with just over a hundred million dollars in assets under management, a big chunk of it courtesy of my old friend over there, Bill Easterbrook, of AmCor—welcome, Bill. We made a profit that first year, and we've gone on making a profit every year, which is why we are now one hundred times larger than when we started, with assets under management of ten billion dollars.

'I'm not going to boast about our track record. You all get the quarterly statements and you know what we've achieved together. I'll just give you one statistic. On the 9th of October 2007, the Dow Jones Industrial Average closed at 14,164. Last night the Dow closed at 10,866. That represents a loss over more than two and a half years of almost one quarter. Imagine that! All those poor saps with their retirement plans and their tracker bonds have lost about twenty-five per cent of their investment. But *you*, by placing your trust in us over the same period, have seen your net asset value increase by eighty-three per cent. Ladies and gentlemen, I think you'll agree that bringing your money to us was a pretty smart thing to have done.'

For the first time Hoffmann risked a brief glance round the table. Quarry's audience was listening intently. Even Mieczyslaw Lukasinski could not keep the grin off his plump peasant face.

'Now,' Quarry went on, 'this consistency of performance is not, I can assure you, a matter of luck. Hoffmann spends thirty-two million dollars a year on research. We employ sixty of the most brilliant scientific minds in the world—at least I'm told they're brilliant: I can't understand a word they're on about.'

He acknowledged the rueful laughter, leaned forward, suddenly serious. 'About eighteen months ago, Alex and his team achieved a significant technological breakthrough. As a result, we had to take the difficult decision to hard-close the fund.' Hard-close meant turning away additional investment, even from existing clients. 'And I know that every single one of you in this room—because that is why we've invited you here—was disappointed by that decision, and some of you were actually pretty angry about it.'

He glanced at Elmira Gulzhan listening at the opposite end of the table. She had screamed at Quarry on the phone, Hoffmann knew, and threatened to withdraw the family's money from the fund, or worse.

'Well,' continued Quarry, with the merest hint of a kiss blown in Elmira's direction, 'we apologise for that. But we had to concentrate on implementing this new investment strategy based on our existing asset size. There's always a risk with any kind of fund, as I'm sure you're aware, that increasing size translates into decreasing performance. We wanted to be as confident as we could be that that wouldn't happen.

'It is now our opinion that this new system, VIXAL-4, is robust enough to cope with portfolio expansion. Therefore, as of today, I can announce that Hoffmann is moving from a hard-closed to a soft-closed position, and is willing to accept additional investment from existing clients only.'

He stopped and took a sip of water to allow the impact of his words to sink in. There was complete silence in the room.

'Cheer up, everyone,' he said brightly, 'this is supposed to be good news.'

The tension was released by laughter and for the first time since Hoffmann entered the room, the clients looked openly at one another. Complicit smiles spread around the table. They were on the inside track.

'At which point,' said Quarry, looking on contentedly, 'I think the best thing I can do is hand you over to Alex here, who can fill you in a bit more on the technical side.' He half sat down then stood again. 'With a bit of luck I may even be able to understand it myself.'

More laughter, and then the floor was Hoffmann's.

He was not a man to whom speaking in public came naturally. The few classes he had taught at Princeton had been torture for lecturer and students alike. But now he felt himself filled with a strange energy and clarity. He took a couple of deep breaths, then rose to his feet.

'Ladies and gentlemen, we have to be secretive about the detail of what we do in this company, to avoid having our ideas stolen by our competitors, but the general principle is no great mystery, as you know. We take a couple of hundred different securities and we trade them over a twenty-four-hour cycle. The algorithms we have programmed into our computers pick the positions we hold based on a detailed analysis of previous trends—the Dow, say, or the S and P 500—and the familiar commodities: Brent crude, natural gas, gold, silver, copper, wheat. We also do some high-frequency trading, where we may hold positions for only a few milliseconds. It's really not that complicated. Even the S and P two-hundred-day moving average can be a pretty reliable predictor of the market: if the current index is higher than the preceding average, the market is likely to be bullish; if lower, bearish. Or we can make a prediction, based on twenty years of data, that if tin is at this price and the yen at that, then it is more likely than not that the DAX will be here. The principle can be simply stated: the most reliable guide to the future is the past. And we only have to be right fifty-five per cent of the time to make a profit.

'As Hugo has pointed out, in a period when the Dow has declined by nearly twenty-five per cent, we've grown in value by eighty-three per cent. How has this happened? It's very simple. There have been two years of panic in the markets, and our algorithms thrive on panic, because human beings always behave in such predictable ways when they're frightened.'

He stopped. His mouth felt dry. 'Can I have some water, Hugo?' Quarry leaned over and passed him a bottle of Evian and a glass. Hoffmann drank straight from the bottle and wiped his mouth on the back of his hand.

'Around 350 BC, Aristotle defined human beings as "*zoon logon echon*"—"the rational animal"—or, more accurately, "the animal that has language". For perhaps forty thousand years, only humans were *zoon logon echon*: the animal with language. Now we share our world with computers.

'Computers . . .' Hoffmann gestured towards the trading floor with his bottle. 'It used to be the case that we imagined that computers—robots—would take over the menial work in our lives. In fact, the humans that computers are replacing are members of the educated classes: translators, medical technicians, legal clerks, financial traders.

'Computers are increasingly reliable translators in commerce and technology. In medicine they can listen to a patient's symptoms and are diagnosing illnesses and prescribing treatment. In the law they search and evaluate vast amounts of complex documents. Speech recognition enables algorithms to extract the meaning from the spoken as well as the written word. News bulletins can be analysed in real time.

'Pretty soon all the information in the world—every scrap of knowledge that humans possess—will be available digitally. Every road on earth has been mapped. Every building photographed. Everywhere we humans go, whatever we buy, whatever websites we look at, we leave a digital trail as clear as slug-slime. This data can be read, searched and analysed by computers and value extracted from it in ways we cannot begin to conceive.

'Google will one day digitalise every book ever published. No need for a library; all you'll need is a screen you can hold in your hand. But here's the thing. A really clever American college student reads eight hundred words per minute, but IBM announced last year they're building a computer for the US government that can perform twenty thousand trillion calculations a second. There's a physical limit to how much information we, as a species, can absorb. But there's no limit to how much a computer can absorb.

'And language—the replacement of objects with symbols—has another big down side for us humans. Language unleashed the power of the imagination, and with it came rumour, panic, fear. But algorithms don't have an imagination. They don't panic. And that's why they're so perfectly suited to trade on the financial markets.

'What we have tried to do with our new generation of VIXAL algorithms is to isolate, measure and factor into our market calculations the element of price that derives from predictable patterns of behaviour. Why, for example, does a stock price that rises on anticipation of positive results almost invariably fall below its previous price if those results turn out to be poorer than expected? Why do traders on some occasions hold on to a stock even as it loses value and their losses mount, while on other occasions they sell, simply because the market in general is declining? The algorithm that can adjust its strategy in answer to these mysteries will have a huge competitive edge.'

Ezra Klein, who had been rocking back and forth, could no longer contain himself. 'But this is just *behavioural finance*!' he blurted out. He made it sound like heresy. 'How do you filter out the noise to make a BF tool?'

'When one subtracts out the valuation of a stock as it varies over time, what one is left with is the behavioural effect, if any,' Hoffman replied.

'Yeah, but how do you figure out what caused the behavioural effect? That's the history of the entire universe, right there!'

'Ezra, I agree with you,' said Hoffmann calmly. 'We can't analyse every aspect of human behaviour in the markets and its likely trigger, however much data is now digitally available. We realised from the start we would have to narrow the focus down. The solution we came up with was to pick on one particular emotion for which we know we have substantive data.'

'So which one have you picked?'

'Fear.'

There was a stirring in the room. Hoffmann sensed a growing bafflement among his audience. But now he had their attention, no question. He continued: 'Fear is historically the strongest emotion in economics. Remember FDR in the Great Depression? It's the most famous quote in financial history: "The only thing we have to fear is fear itself." It's so strong we've found it relatively easy to filter out the noise made by other emotional inputs and focus on this one signal. We've been able to correlate recent market fluctuations with the frequency rate of fear-related words in the media—terror, alarm, panic, horror, scare, anthrax, nuclear. Our conclusion is that fear is driving the world as never before.'

Elmira Gulzhan said, 'That is al-Qaeda.'

'Partly. But why should al-Qaeda arouse more fear than the threat of destruction did during the Cold War in the fifties and sixties—which, incidentally, were times of great market stability? The rise in market volatility, in our opinion, is a function of digitalisation, which is exaggerating human mood swings by the unprecedented dissemination of information via the internet.'

'And we've found a way to make money out of it,' said Quarry happily. He nodded at Hoffmann to continue.

'As you will be aware, the Chicago Board of Exchange operates what is known as the S and P 500 Volatility Index, or VIX. This has been running, in one form or another, for seventeen years. It tracks the price of options—

calls and puts—on stocks traded in the S and P 500. It shows the implied volatility of the market for the coming month and goes up and down minute by minute. The higher the index, the greater the uncertainty in the market, so traders call it "the fear index". And it's liquid itself, of course—there are VIX options and futures available to trade, and we trade them.

'So the VIX was our starting point. It's given us a whole bunch of useful data going back to 1993. In the early days, it also gave us the name for our prototype algorithm, VIXAL-1, which has stuck. We're now onto the fourth iteration, which with notable lack of imagination we call VIXAL-4.'

Klein jumped in again. 'The volatility implied by the VIX can be to the up side as well as the down side.'

'We take account of that,' said Hoffmann. 'Fear doesn't just mean a broad market panic and a flight to safety. There is also what we call a "clinging" effect, when a stock is held in defiance of reason, and an "adrenaline" effect, when a stock rises strongly in value. We're still researching all these to refine our model.' Easterbrook raised his hand. 'Yes, Bill?'

'Is this algorithm already operational?'

'I'll let Hugo answer that, as it's practical rather than theoretical.'

Quarry said, 'We started back-testing VIXAL-1 almost two years ago, just as a simulation, without any actual exposure to the market. We went live with VIXAL-2 in May 2009, with play money of one hundred million dollars. We moved on to VIXAL-3 in November and gave it access to one billion. That was so successful we decided to allow VIXAL-4 to take control of the entire fund one week ago. As of last night, it was up about seventy-nine point-seven million.'

Easterbrook frowned. 'I thought you said it had only been running for a week?'

'I did.'

'But that means . . .'

'That means,' said Ezra Klein, doing the calculation in his head, 'that on a ten-billion-dollar fund, you're looking at making a profit of four-point-one-four billion a year.'

'And as VIXAL-4 collects and analyses more data,' Hoffmann said, 'it's likely to become more effective.'

Whistles and murmurs ran round the table. The two Chinese started whispering to one another.

'You can see why we've decided we want to bring in more investment,' said Quarry with a smirk. 'We need to exploit this thing before anyone develops a clone strategy. And now, ladies and gentlemen, this might be a suitable moment to offer you a glimpse of VIXAL in operation.'

THREE KILOMETRES away, in Cologny, forensics had completed their examination of the Hoffmans' house. Gabrielle was in her studio, dismantling the portrait of the foetus, lifting each sheet of glass out of its slot on the wooden base, wrapping it in tissue paper and then in bubble wrap, and laying it in a cardboard box. She found herself thinking how strange it was that so much creative energy should have flowed from the black hole of this tragedy. She had lost the baby two years ago, at five and a half months: not the first of her pregnancies to end in miscarriage, but by far the most shattering. The hospital had given her an MRI scan when they began to get concerned, which was unusual. Afterwards, rather than stay on her own in Switzerland, she had gone with Alex on a business trip to Oxford. Wandering round a museum while he was interviewing PhDs in the Randolph Hotel, she had come across a 3D model of the structure of penicillin built up on sheets of Perspex. An idea had stirred in her mind, and when she got home to Geneva, she had tried the same technique on the MRI scan of her womb, which was all she had left of the baby.

It had taken a week of trial and error to work out which of the 200 cross-sectional images to print off, and how to trace them onto glass, what ink to use and how to stop it smearing. She had sliced her hands repeatedly on the sharp edges of the glass sheets. But the afternoon when she first lined them up and the outline had emerged—the clenched fingers, the curled toes—was a miracle she would never forget. When Alex came home from work and saw the portrait, he had sat stunned for ten minutes.

After that she had become utterly absorbed by the possibilities of marrying science and art to produce images of living forms. Mostly she had acted as her own model, talking the radiographers at the hospital into scanning her from head to toe. The simplicity of the form was what appealed to her most, and the paradoxes it carried—clarity and mystery, the impersonal and the intimate, the generic and yet the absolutely unique. Watching Alex going through the CAT scanner that morning had made her want to produce a portrait of him. She wondered if the doctors would let her have his results.

She wrapped up the last of the glass sheets tenderly and sealed the cardboard box with thick brown sticky tape. It had been a painful decision to offer this, of all her works, to the exhibition: if someone bought it, she knew she would probably never see it again. And yet it seemed to her that this was the whole point of creating it in the first place—to give it a separate existence, to let it go out into the world.

She picked up the box and carried it out into the passageway as if it were an offering. In the hall, she carefully skirted the spot where Alex had been lying when she discovered him. A noise came from inside the study and she felt her skin rise into gooseflesh just as a man's heavy shape loomed in the doorway. She gave a cry of alarm and almost dropped the box.

She recognised him. It was the security expert, Genoud. He had shown her how to use the alarm system when they first moved in. Another man was with him—heavyset, like a wrestler.

'Madame Hoffmann, forgive us if we startled you.' Genoud introduced the other man. 'Camille has been sent by your husband to look after you.'

'I don't need looking after . . .' began Gabrielle. But she was too shaken to put up much resistance, and found herself allowing the bodyguard to take the box from her arms and carry it out to the waiting Mercedes.

'Brilliant,' whispered Quarry, catching Hoffmann by the elbow as they left the boardroom.

'You think? I got the feeling I'd lost them at one point.'

'They don't mind being lost, as long as you bring them back to what they really want to see, which is the bottom line.' He steered Hoffmann ahead of him, to where the clients were waiting patiently on the edge of the trading floor. 'This way, if you please,' called Quarry, and with his finger held aloft, tour-guide-style, he led them in a crocodile across the big room. They gathered round a trading screen as one of the quants vacated his desk to give them a better view.

'So, this is VIXAL-4 in operation,' said Hoffmann. He stood back to let the investors get closer to the terminal. 'The algorithm selects the trades. They're on the left of the screen in the pending orders file. On the right are the executed orders.' He moved a little nearer so that he could read the figures. 'Here, for instance,' he began, 'we have . . .' He paused, surprised by the size of the trade. 'Here you see we have one and a half million options to sell Accenture at fifty-two dollars a share.'

'Whoa,' said Easterbrook. 'That's a heck of a bet on the short side. Do you guys know something about Accenture we don't?'

'Fiscal Q2 profits down three per cent,' rattled off Klein from memory. 'Earnings sixty cents a share. I don't get the logic of that position.'

Quarry said, 'Well, there must be some logic to it, or VIXAL wouldn't have taken the options. Why don't you show them another trade, Alex?'

Hoffmann changed the screen. 'OK. Here—you see?—here's another short we've just put on this morning: twelve and a half million options to sell Vista Airways at seven euros twenty-eight a share.'

Vista Airways was a low-cost, high-volume European airline, which none of those present would have dreamed of being seen dead on.

'*Twelve and a half million?*' repeated Easterbrook. 'That must be a heck of a chunk of the market. Your machine has got some balls, I'll give it that.'

Klein said, 'Vista Airways had twelve per cent passenger growth in the final quarter and a revised profits forecast up nine per cent. I don't get the sense of that position, either.'

'Wynn Resorts,' said Hoffmann, reading off the next screen. 'A million-two short at one hundred and twenty-four.' He frowned, puzzled. These enormous bets on the down side were unlike VIXAL's normal complex pattern of hedged trades.

'Well, that one truly is amazing to me,' said Klein, 'because they had Q1 growth up from seven-forty million to nine-oh-nine, with a cash dividend of twenty-five cents a share, and they've got this great new resort in Macau that's literally a licence to print money. May I?' Without waiting for permission, he seized the mouse and started clicking through the recent trades. 'Procter and Gamble, six million short at sixty-two . . . Exelon, *three million* short at forty-one-fifty . . . Jesus—is an asteroid about to hit the earth, or what?' His face was practically pressed against the screen. 'Tell me, Hoffman, a big short such as any one of these—does the algorithm put it on entirely independently, or does it require human intervention to execute?'

'Independently,' replied Hoffmann. He wiped the details of the trades from the screen. 'First the algorithm determines the stock it wishes to trade. Then it examines the trading pattern of that stock over the past twenty days. Then it executes the order itself in such a way as to avoid alerting the market and affecting the price. Our system speaks directly to the executing broker's system, and then we use their infrastructure to hit the exchange. Nobody telephones a broker any more. Not from this shop.'

Mould said, 'There must be human supervision at some point, I hope?'

'There's constant supervision, but not usually intervention, not unless something starts going wrong. If one of the quants sees an order going through that worries him, naturally he can put a stop on it.'

'Has that ever happened?'

'No. Not with VIXAL-4. Not so far.'

'Your prime broker is AmCor, I assume, given your long relationship?'

'We have various prime brokers these days, not just AmCor. We don't want one single brokerage firm knowing all our strategies. Now, let's take a look at the hardware, shall we?'

As the group moved off, Quarry pulled Hoffmann aside. 'Am I missing something here,' he said quietly, 'or are those positions way out of line?'

'They're a little more exposed than normal,' agreed Hoffmann, 'but nothing to worry about. Now I think of it, LJ mentioned that Gana wanted a meeting of the Risk Committee. I told him to talk to you about it.'

'Christ, is *that* what he wanted? I didn't have time to take his call. Damn it.' Quarry glanced at his watch. 'OK, let's grab five minutes while they're all having coffee. I'll tell Gana to meet us in my office. You go on ahead and keep them happy.'

The computers were housed in a big windowless room on the opposite side of the trading floor, and this time Hoffmann led the way. He stood in front of the face-recognition camera—only a few were cleared for access to this inner sanctum—and waited for the bolts to click back, then pushed at the door. It was solid, fireproof, with rubber vacuum seals on the sides, so that it made a slight whoosh as it opened.

Hoffmann went in first; the others followed. Compared to the relative silence of the trading floor, the busy racket of the computers sounded almost industrial. The arrays were stacked on warehouse shelving, their rows of red and green indicator lights flickering rapidly as they processed data. At the end of the room, in a pair of long Plexiglas cabinets, two robots patrolled up and down on monorails, shooting with the speed of striking snakes from one end to the other as VIXAL-4 instructed them to store or retrieve data. The noise of the powerful air-conditioning needed to keep down the temperature of the central processing units, combined with the whir of the fans on the motherboards themselves, made it surprisingly difficult to hear. When everyone was inside, Hoffmann had to raise his voice.

'In case you think this is impressive, I should point out that it is only four per cent of the capacity of the CPU farm at CERN, where I used to work. But the principle is the same. We have nearly a thousand standard CPUs,' he said, resting his hand proudly on the shelves, 'each with two to four cores, exactly the same as those you have at home, except without the casing and repackaged for us by a white box company. In CERN in the nineties, we had a supercomputer that cost fifteen million dollars and delivered half the power a Microsoft Xbox now gives you for two hundred bucks. You can imagine what that trend means for the future.'

Etienne Mussard said, 'So what happens if there is a power cut?'

'For short-term interruptions, we switch to car batteries. After ten minutes, diesel generators in the basement would cut in.'

'What would happen if there was a fire,' asked Lukasinski, 'or this place was attacked by terrorists?'

'We have full system back-up, naturally. But it isn't going to happen, don't worry. We've invested a lot in security—sprinkler systems, smoke detectors, firewalls, video surveillance, guards, cyber-protection. And remember, this *is* Switzerland.'

Most people smiled. Lukasinski did not. 'Is your security in-house, or outsourced?'

'Outsourced.' Hoffmann wondered why the Pole was so obsessed with security. 'Everything is outsourced—security, legal affairs, accountancy, transport, catering, technical support, cleaning. These offices are rented. Even the furniture is rented. We aim to be a company that not only makes money out of the digital age; we want to *be* digital.'

'What about your own personal security?' persisted Lukasinski. 'I understand you were attacked in your home last night.'

Hoffmann felt a stab of embarrassment. 'How do you know about that?'

Lukasinski said, offhand, 'Someone told me.'

'If I could just say,' interjected Quarry, who had slipped in unnoticed at the back, 'what happened to Alex was nothing whatever to do with company business—just some lunatic who I'm sure will be picked up by the police. Now, does anyone have any more questions directly relating to the hardware?' There was silence. 'No? Then there's coffee in the boardroom. If you all go ahead, we'll join you in a couple of minutes. I just need to have a quick word with Alex.'

THEY WERE MIDWAY across the trading floor and their backs were to the big TV screens when one of the quants gave a loud gasp. In a room where nobody spoke in much above a whisper, the exclamation rang out like a gunshot in a library. Hoffmann halted in his tracks and turned to see half his workforce rising to their feet, drawn out of their seats by the images on Bloomberg and CNBC.

Both the satellite channels were showing the same footage, obviously filmed on a mobile phone, of a passenger airliner coming in to land at an airport. It was clearly in trouble, smoke streaming out of its side.

Someone grabbed a remote and pumped up the sound.

The jet passed out of sight behind a control tower and then reappeared, skimming the tops of some low, sandy-coloured buildings—hangars, perhaps. It seemed to graze one of the buildings with its underbelly, and then abruptly it exploded in a vast expanding ball of yellow fire that carried on rolling and rolling. The picture shook, and then cut to a later, more stable shot of thick black oily smoke, roiled with orange and yellow flames.

Over the images the presenter's voice—American, female—said breathlessly: 'OK, so those were the scenes just a few minutes ago when a Vista Airways passenger jet with ninety-eight people on board crashed on its approach to Moscow's Domodedovo Airport . . .'

'Vista Airways?' said Quarry, wheeling round to confront Hoffmann. 'Did she just say Vista Airways?'

A dozen muttered conversations broke out simultaneously across the trading floor: 'My God, we've been shorting that stock all morning.' 'How weird is that?' 'Someone just walked over my grave.'

'Will you turn that damn thing off?' called Hoffmann. When nothing happened, he strode between the desks and snatched the remote from the hands of the hapless quant. 'All right,' he said. 'Let's get on with our work.'

He threw the remote onto the desk and made his way back to the clients. Easterbrook and Klein, hardened veterans of the dealing room, had already lunged for the nearest terminal and were checking the prices.

'My God,' said Easterbrook, looking round from the trading screen, 'it only happened five minutes ago and Vista's stock is down fifteen per cent already. It's crashing.'

Klein's eyes were riveted to the market data. 'Whoa,' he murmured appreciatively, 'your little black box is really cleaning up, Alex.'

Hoffmann stared over Klein's shoulder. The figures were changing rapidly as VIXAL took profits on its options to sell Vista Airways' stock at the pre-crash price.

Easterbrook said, 'I wonder how much you guys are going to make from this one trade—twenty million, thirty million? Jesus, Hugo, the regulators are going to be swarming over this like ants at a picnic.'

Hoffmann, unable to take his eyes from the figures on the trading screen, was not listening. The pressure in his skull was intense. He put his fingers to his wound and traced his stitches. It felt to him as if they were stretched so tight they might split apart.

6

The Risk Committee of Hoffmann Investment Technologies met briefly at 11.57 a.m., according to a note drawn up subsequently by Ganapathi Rajamani, the company's chief risk officer. All five members of the senior management team were listed as present: Dr Alexander Hoffmann, president of the company; the Hon. Hugo Quarry, chief executive officer; Lin Ju-Long, chief financial officer; Pieter van der Zyl, chief operating officer; and Rajamani himself.

They all stood around in Quarry's office, apart from Quarry, who perched on the edge of his desk so that he could keep an eye on his computer terminal. Hoffmann took up a position at the window and occasionally parted the slats of the blinds to check on the street below.

'OK,' said Quarry, 'let's keep this quick. I've got a hundred billion dollars on the hoof unattended in the boardroom and I need to get back in there. I take it we all saw what just happened. The first question is whether by making such a large bet to the down side on Vista Airways we're going to trigger an official investigation. Gana?'

'The short answer is yes, almost certainly.' Rajamani was a neat, precise young man, with a strong sense of his own importance. His job was to keep an eye on the fund's risk levels and ensure they complied with the law. Quarry had poached him from the Financial Services Authority in London.

'Yes?' repeated Quarry. 'Even though we couldn't possibly have known what was going to happen?'

'The process is automatic. The regulators' algorithms will have detected any unusual activity surrounding the airline's stock immediately prior to the price collapse. That will lead them straight to us.'

'But we haven't done anything illegal.'

'No. Not unless we sabotaged the plane. But what they *will* want to know,' continued Rajamani, 'is why we shorted twelve and a half million shares at that precise moment. I know this sounds an absurd question, Alex, but is there any way VIXAL could have acquired news of the crash before the rest of the market?'

Reluctantly Hoffmann let the slats of the blind click shut and turned to face his colleagues. 'Can we just stop this right now?' he said irritably. 'It will take us less than five minutes to show even the most dumb-assed regulator that we shorted that stock as part of a pattern of bets to the down side. It was nothing special. It was a coincidence. Get over it.'

'Well, speaking as a former dumb-assed regulator,' said Rajamani, 'I agree with you, Alex. It's the pattern that matters, which is why actually I tried to talk to you about it earlier this morning.'

'Yeah, well, I'm sorry, but I was late for the presentation.' *Quarry should never have hired this guy*, Hoffmann thought. Once a regulator, always a regulator: you could never quite hide where you came from.

Rajamani said, 'What we really need to focus on is the level of our risk if the markets rally—Procter and Gamble, Accenture, Exelon, dozens of them: tens of millions in options since Tuesday night. These are all huge one-way bets we have taken. I'm seriously worried, frankly. We're long gold. We're long the dollar. We're short every equity futures index.'

Hoffmann felt his temper beginning to rise. He said, 'So what are you suggesting we do, Gana?'

'I think we have to start liquidating some of these positions.'

'That's just about the stupidest thing I've ever heard,' said Hoffmann. In his frustration he slapped the back of his hand hard on the blinds. 'We made close to eighty million dollars last week. We just made another forty million this morning. And you want us to ignore VIXAL's analysis?'

'Not ignore it, Alex. I never said that.'

Quarry said quietly, 'Give him a break, Alex. It was only a suggestion.'

'No, actually, I won't give him a break. He wants us to abandon a strategy that's showing massive alpha, which is exactly the kind of illogical reaction to success, based on fear, that VIXAL is designed to exploit! If Gana doesn't believe that algorithms are inherently superior to humans when it comes to playing the market, he's working in the wrong shop.'

Rajamani, however, was unfazed by his company president's tirade. He said, 'I have to remind you, Alex, that the prospectus of this company promises clients exposure to a yearly volatility of no more than twenty per cent. If I see that those statutory risk limits are in danger of being breached, I am obliged to step in.'

'Meaning what?'

'Meaning, if the level of our exposure isn't dialled back, I will have to notify the investors. Meaning I really must talk to their board.'

'But this is *my* company.'

'And the investors' money, or most of it.'

In the silence that followed, Hoffmann started massaging his temples vigorously with his knuckles. His head was aching badly: he needed a painkiller. 'Their board?' he muttered. 'I'm not even sure who's on their board.' As far as he was concerned it was a purely technical legal entity, registered in the Cayman Islands for tax purposes, which controlled the clients' money and paid the hedge fund its management and incentive fees.

'OK,' said Quarry, 'I don't think we're anywhere near that point yet. As they used to say in the war, let's keep calm and carry on.' He bestowed one of his most winning smiles upon the room.

Rajamani said, 'For legal reasons, I ask that my concerns be minuted.'

'Fine. Write up a note of the meeting and I'll sign it. But if Alex trusts VIXAL then we all should trust it. However, I agree we also have to keep an eye on the risk level. Alex, you'd accept that? So, given that most of these equities are US-traded, what I suggest is we reconvene in this office at three thirty when the American markets open, and review the situation then.'

Rajamani said ominously, 'In that case, I think it would be prudent to have a lawyer present.'

'Fine. I'll ask Max Gallant to stay behind. You OK with that, Alex?'

Hoffmann made a weary gesture of agreement.

At 12.08, according to the minutes, the meeting broke up.

'OH, ALEX, by the way,' said Ju-Long, turning in the doorway as they were filing out, 'I almost forgot—that account number of yours you asked about? It turns out it is on our system.'

'What account is this?' asked Quarry.

Hoffmann said, 'Oh, nothing. Just a query I had. I'll catch up with you, LJ.'

They walked back to their offices, Rajamani leading the way. As Quarry watched them go, the expression of suave conciliation with which he had ushered them out changed to a sneer of contempt. 'What a pompous shit that fellow is,' he said. He imitated Rajamani's flawless, clipped English: '"It would be prudent to have a lawyer present."' He mimed taking aim at him along the barrel of a rifle.

Hoffmann said, 'It was you who hired him.'

'Yes, all right, point taken, and it'll be me who fires him, don't you worry.' He pulled an imaginary trigger a second before the trio moved out of sight, then dropped his voice. 'We are OK here, aren't we, Alexi? I don't have to be worried?'

Hoffmann regarded him with surprise. In eight years he had never heard Quarry express anxiety. It was almost as unsettling as some of the other things that had happened that morning. 'Listen, Hugo,' he said, 'we can put an override on VIXAL this afternoon if that's what you want. We can let the positions wind down and return the money to the investors. I'm actually only in this game in the first place because of you, remember?'

'But what about *you*, Alexi?' asked Quarry urgently. 'Do *you* want to stop? I mean, we could, you know. We've made more than enough to live out the rest of our days in luxury. We don't have to carry on pitching to clients.'

'No, I don't want to stop. We have the resources to do things here on the technical side that no one else is even attempting. But if you want to call it quits, I'll buy you out.'

Now it was Quarry who looked taken back, but then he suddenly grinned. 'Like hell you will! You don't get rid of me that easily.' His nerve seemed to revive as quickly as it had wilted. 'No, no, I'm in this for the duration. If you're fine, I'm fine. Well, then?' He gestured for Hoffmann to step ahead of him. 'Shall we return to that esteemed bunch of psychopaths and criminals we are proud to call our clients?'

'You do it. I've nothing left to say to them.'

Quarry's mouth turned down. 'You'll come to the lunch at least?'

'Hugo, I really cannot stand these people . . .' But Quarry's expression was so forlorn that Hoffmann capitulated. 'Oh, if it's really that important, I'll come to the damn lunch.'

'Beau-Rivage. One o'clock.' Quarry seemed on the point of saying something else, but then looked at his watch and swore. 'Shit, they've been on their own for a quarter of an hour.' He set off towards the boardroom. 'One o'clock,' he called, turning round and walking backwards. He cocked his finger. 'Good man.'

Hoffmann pivoted on his heel and headed in the opposite direction towards Ju-Long's office. His door was shut, his assistant away from her desk. Without waiting for a reply, Hoffmann knocked and went in.

It was as though he had disturbed a group of teenage boys examining pornography. Ju-Long, van der Zyl and Rajamani drew back quickly from the terminal, and Ju-Long clicked the mouse to change the screen.

Van der Zyl said, 'We were just checking the currency markets. The euro is weakening against the dollar.'

'Which is what we anticipated, I believe.' Hoffmann pushed the door open wider. 'It was LJ I wanted to speak with—in private.' He stared straight ahead as they filed out. When they had gone, he said, 'So you say that account is on our system?'

'It comes up twice.' Ju-Long's smooth forehead creased into a deep frown. 'Actually, I assumed it was for your own personal use.'

'Why?'

'You asked the back office to transfer forty-two million dollars into it.'

Hoffmann studied the other man's face carefully for evidence that he was joking. But Ju-Long, as Quarry always said, though possessed of many admirable qualities, was entirely devoid of a sense of humour.

'When did I request this transfer?'

'Eleven months ago. I just sent you the original email to remind you.'

'OK, thanks. You said there were two transactions?'

'Indeed. The money was entirely repaid last month, with interest.'

'And you never queried this with me?'

'No, Alex,' said the Chinese quietly. 'Like you say, it is your company.'

'Yeah, sure. That's right. Thanks, LJ.' Hoffmann turned at the door. 'And you didn't just mention this to Gana and Pieter?'

'No.' Ju-Long's eyes were wide with innocence.

Hoffmann hurried to his office. Forty-two million dollars? He would hardly have forgotten. It had to be fraud. He strode past Marie-Claude and went straight to his desk. He logged on to his computer and opened his inbox. And there indeed was his instruction to transfer $42,032,127.88 to the Royal Grand Cayman Bank on June 17 last year. Beneath it was a notification of a repayment of $43,188,037.09, dated April 3.

He performed the calculation in his head. What kind of fraudster repaid the capital sum that he had stolen from his victim, plus exactly 2.75 per cent interest?

He went back and studied what purported to be his original email. There was no greeting or signature, merely the usual standard instruction to transfer the amount X to the account Y. LJ would have put it through the system without a second's hesitation, confident that their intranet was secure behind the best firewall that money could buy. He checked what time he was supposed to have sent his email ordering the transfer: midnight exactly.

He tilted back in his chair and contemplated the smoke detector in the ceiling above his desk. He often worked late in the office, but never as late as midnight. This message, if genuine, would therefore have had to have come from his terminal at home. Could he be suffering from some kind of Jekyll-and-Hyde syndrome that meant one half of his mind was doing things the other half knew nothing about?

On impulse he opened his desk drawer, took out the CD and inserted it into the optical drive of his computer. The screen was filled with an index of 200 monochrome images of the inside of his head. He clicked through them rapidly, trying to find the one that had caught the attention of the radiologist, but it was hopeless.

He buzzed his assistant. 'Marie-Claude, if you look in my personal directory you'll see an entry for a Dr Jeanne Polidori. Will you make me an appointment to see her tomorrow? Tell her it's urgent.'

'Yes, Dr Hoffmann. What time?'

'Any time. Also, I want to go to the gallery where my wife's having her exhibition. Can you fix me a car?'

'You have a driver at your disposal at all times now, arranged by Monsieur Genoud.'

'Oh, yeah, that's right, I forgot. OK, tell him I'm coming down.'

He ejected the CD and put it back in the drawer along with the Darwin volume, then grabbed his raincoat. Passing through the trading floor, he glanced across at the boardroom. On the opposite wall Bloomberg and CNBC were showing lines of red arrows, all in the descendent. The European markets had shed their earlier gains and had started falling fast. That would almost certainly depress the opening in the US, which would in turn make the hedge fund much less exposed to loss by mid-afternoon. Hoffmann experienced a thrill of pride. Once again VIXAL was proving smarter than the humans around it, smarter even than its creator.

His good humour persisted as he rode the elevator down to the ground floor and turned the corner into the lobby, where a bulky figure in a cheap dark suit rose to greet him. He flashed his ID and introduced himself as Olivier Paccard, *l'homme de la sécurité*.

'If you would wait just a moment, please, Dr Hoffmann,' said Paccard. He held up his hand in a polite plea for silence. He had a wire trailing from his ear. 'Fine,' he said. 'We can go.'

He moved swiftly to the entrance, hitting the exit button with the heel of his hand precisely as a long dark Mercedes drew up at the kerb, with the same driver who had picked Hoffmann up from the hospital. Paccard strode out first, opened the rear passenger door and ushered Hoffmann inside. Before he even had the chance to settle himself into his seat, Paccard was sliding into the front, the car doors were all closed and locked, and they were pulling out into the noonday traffic. The whole procedure must have taken less than ten seconds.

7

*C*ontours de l'homme: Une exposition de l'oeuvre de Gabrielle Hoffmann—how much more impressive it sounded in French than English, she thought—was scheduled to run for one week only at the Galerie d'Art Contemporain Guy Bertrand.

Gabrielle had found herself sitting next to the owner, M. Bertrand, five months earlier at a Christmas charity auction at the Mandarin Oriental Hotel—an event Alex had flatly refused to attend—and the next day he had wheedled his way into her studio to see what she was working on. After ten minutes of outrageous flattery, he had offered to give her an exhibition in return for half of any proceeds, as long as she paid the expenses. Of course she had realised at once that it was Alex's money rather than her talent that was the attraction. But she wanted to have a show—wanted it, she realised, more keenly than she had ever wanted anything, except to have a child.

When the doors of the gallery opened quietly at eleven that morning, two young waitresses in white blouses and black miniskirts stood offering flutes of Pol Roger and plates of canapés to everyone who crossed the threshold. Gabrielle had worried that no one would show up, but they did: the gallery's regulars; passers-by attracted by the sight of a free drink; and her own friends and acquaintances who she had been calling and emailing for weeks beforehand—names from old address books, people she hadn't seen for years. All had turned up. The result was that by noon, a sizeable party of more than a hundred was in process, spilling out through the doors and onto the pavement where the smokers gathered.

Halfway through her second glass of champagne, Gabrielle realised she was enjoying herself. Her *oeuvre* consisted of twenty-seven pieces. Once it all was gathered together and properly lit, it did look like a solid, professional body of work. People had looked carefully and made mostly complimentary comments. Her only remaining anxiety was that nothing had yet sold, which she blamed on the high prices Bertrand was charging, from 4,500 Swiss francs—about $5,000—for the CAT scans of the smallest animal heads up to 18,000 for the big MRI portrait, *The Invisible Man*. If nothing had gone by the end of the day it would be a humiliation.

She tried to forget about it and pay attention to what the man opposite her was saying. It was difficult to hear over the noise. She put her hand on his arm. 'I'm sorry, what did you say your name was again?'

'Bob Walton. I used to work with Alex at CERN. I was just saying that I think you two first met at a party in my house.'

'Oh,' she said, 'that's quite right. How are you?' She shook his hand and looked at him properly for the first time: thin, tall, neat, grey—ascetic, she decided. She said, 'It's funny—I just tagged along to that party with friends. I'm not sure we've ever been formally introduced, have we?'

'I believe not.'

'Well—thank you, belatedly. You changed my life.'

He didn't smile. 'I haven't seen Alex for years. He is coming, I assume?'

'I certainly hope so.' Once again her eyes flickered to the door in the hope that Alex would walk through it. 'So what brings you here? Are you a gallery regular or just a passer-by?'

'Neither. Alex invited me.'

'Alex?' She did a double-take. 'I'm sorry. I didn't know Alex sent out any invitations. It's not the kind of thing he does.'

'I was a little surprised myself. Especially as the last time we met we had something of a disagreement. And now I have come to make amends and he isn't here. Never mind. I like your work.'

'Thank you.' She was still trying to assimilate the idea that Alex might have invited a guest without telling her. 'Perhaps you'll buy something.'

'I fear the prices are somewhat beyond the means of a CERN salary.' And for the first time he gave her a smile—all the warmer for being so rare, like a flash of sun on a grey landscape. He put his hand into his breast pocket. 'If you ever feel like making art out of particle physics, give me a call.' He gave her his card. She read: *Professor Robert Walton, Computing Centre Department Head, CERN—European Organisation for Nuclear Research, 1211 Geneva 23, Switzerland.*

'That sounds very grand.' She slipped the card into her pocket. 'Thank you. I might well do that. So tell me about you and Alex—'

Over his shoulder Gabrielle saw an incongruous figure, strange yet familiar, enter the gallery. 'Excuse me a minute, would you?' She slipped away and went over to the door. 'Inspector Leclerc?'

'Madame Hoffmann.' Leclerc shook her hand politely.

She noticed he had on the same clothes he had been wearing at four in the morning: dark windcheater, a white shirt now distinctly grey round the collar, and a black tie. The stubble of his unshaved cheeks reached up like a silvery fungus towards the black pouches beneath his eyes.

One of the waitresses approached with a tray of champagne, which Gabrielle assumed he would refuse, but Leclerc, brightening, said, 'Excellent, thank you,' and took the glass cautiously by the stem. 'That's very good,' he said, taking a sip and smacking his lips. 'What is it?'

'I couldn't tell you. My husband's office arranged it.'

A photographer from the Geneva *Tribune* came over and took their picture standing side by side. Leclerc waited until the photographer had moved away and then said, 'Well, I can tell you forensics obtained an excellent set of fingerprints from the knives in the kitchen. Unfortunately, we can find no matches in our records. Your intruder does not have a criminal record, in Switzerland at least.' He seized a canapé from a passing tray and swallowed it whole. 'And your husband? Is he here? I can't see him anywhere.'

'Not yet. Why? Do you want him?'

'No, I came to see your work.'

Guy Bertrand sidled over, plainly curious. She had told him about the break-in. 'Is everything OK?' he asked, and Gabrielle found herself introducing the policeman to the owner of the gallery.

'A police inspector,' repeated Bertrand, in a tone of wonder. 'You would be interested in *The Invisible Man*, I think.'

'*The Invisible Man*?'

'Let me show you,' said Gabrielle, grateful of an opportunity to separate them. She led Leclerc over to a glass case lit from beneath in which a full-size nude man, apparently composed of pale blue gossamer, seemed to hover just above the ground. The effect was ghostly, disturbing. 'This is Jim, the invisible man.'

'And who is Jim?'

'He was a murderer.' Leclerc turned sharply to look at her. 'James Duke Johnson,' she continued, 'executed in Florida in 1994. Before he died, the prison chaplain persuaded him to donate his body for scientific research.'

'And also for public exhibition?'

'That I doubt. You're shocked?'

'I am, I confess.'

'Good. That's the effect I wanted.'

Leclerc grunted and set down his champagne on a nearby table. 'How do you achieve this impression of floating?'

'I take sections from an MRI scan and trace them through very clear glass. Sometimes instead of using pen and ink I use a dentist's drill to engrave the line. If you shine artificial light onto it from the right angle— well, that's the effect you get.'

'And what does your husband think of it?'

'He thinks I've become unhealthily obsessed. But then he has obsessions of his own.' She finished her glass of champagne. Everything seemed pleasantly heightened—colours, noises, sensations.

Leclerc turned his bloodshot eyes upon her. 'Would you mind if I asked you a couple of questions?'

'Go ahead.'

'When did you first meet Dr Hoffmann?'

'I was just remembering that.' She could see Alex in her mind with perfect clarity. He had been talking to Hugo Quarry—always bloody Quarry in the picture, even right at the start—and she had had to make the first move, but she had drunk enough not to care. 'That would have been at a party in Saint-Genis-Pouilly, about eight years ago.'

'Saint-Genis-Pouilly,' repeated Leclerc. 'A great many CERN scientists live around there, I believe.'

'They certainly did then. You see that tall, grey-headed guy over there— Walton, his name is. It was at his house.'

'Were you at CERN yourself?'

'No. I was working as a secretary at the UN—your typical ex-art student with bad prospects and good French: that was me.' She was talking too fast and grinning too much, she realised.

'But Dr Hoffmann was still at CERN when you got to know him?'

'He was in the process of leaving to set up his own company with his partner, a man called Hugo Quarry. We all met for the first time on the same night, oddly enough. Is this important?'

'And why exactly did he do that, do you know—leave CERN?'

'You'd have to ask him. Or Hugo.'

'I will. He is American, this Mr Quarry?'

She laughed. 'No, English. Very much so.'

'I assume one reason Dr Hoffmann left CERN was because he wanted to make more money?'

'No, not really. He told me he could pursue his line of research more easily if he had his own company.'

'And what line was that?'

'Artificial intelligence. Again, you'd have to ask him about the details.' Leclerc paused.

'Has he sought psychiatric help, do you know?'

The question startled her. 'Not that I'm aware. Why do you ask?'

'It's just that I gather he suffered a nervous breakdown when he was at CERN, which someone there told me is the reason why he left. I wondered if there'd been any recurrence.'

She realised she was staring at him with her mouth open. She clamped her jaw shut.

He was studying her closely. He said, 'I'm sorry. You didn't know that?'

She recovered her composure just enough to lie. 'Well, I knew *something* about it.' She was aware of how unconvincing she sounded. But what was the alternative? To admit that an immense amount of what occupied her husband's mind every day had always been impenetrable territory for her, and that this unknowable quality was what had attracted her to him in the first place? 'So you've been checking up on Alex?' she said in a brittle voice. 'Shouldn't you be trying to find the man who attacked him?'

'I have to investigate all the facts, madame,' said Leclerc primly. 'It may be that the assailant knew your husband in the past. I merely asked an acquaintance at CERN—in the strictest confidence, I do assure you—why he had left.'

'And this person said he had had a breakdown, and now you think Alex may be making up this whole story about a mysterious attacker?'

'No, I'm simply trying to understand all the circumstances.' He picked up his glass and emptied it in one swig. 'I'm sorry—I should let you get back to your party. It really has been most interesting to see your work.' He stopped and stared again at the executed murderer in his glass box. 'What exactly did he do, this poor fellow?'

'He killed an old man who caught him stealing his electric blanket. He was on death row for twelve years. When his last appeal for clemency was turned down, he was executed by lethal injection.'

'Barbaric,' muttered Leclerc, although whether he meant the crime, the punishment, or what she had made out of it, she was not entirely sure.

AFTERWARDS LECLERC SAT in his car on the opposite side of the street, his notebook on his knee, writing down as much of what he had just been told as he could remember. Through the window of the gallery he could see people milling around Gabrielle, her small dark figure lent an occasional touch of glamour by a camera flash.

He finished writing and flicked back and forth through his notes, as if he might find some clue that had so far eluded him. His friend at CERN had taken a quick look at Hoffmann's personnel file and Leclerc had jotted down the highlights: that Hoffmann had joined the team operating the Large Electron–Positron Collider at the age of twenty-seven, one of the few Americans seconded to the project; that his head of section had considered him one of the most brilliant mathematicians on site; that he had switched from the construction of the Large Hadron Collider to the design of computer systems needed to analyse the billions of pieces of data generated by the experiments; that after a prolonged period of overwork his behaviour had become sufficiently erratic for his fellow workers to complain, and he had been asked to leave the facility by the security department; and that finally, after extensive sick leave, his contract had been terminated.

Leclerc was fairly sure that her husband's breakdown had come as news to Gabrielle Hoffmann. It seemed Hoffmann was a mystery to everyone— his fellow scientists, the financial world, even his wife.

His thoughts were interrupted by the noise of a powerful engine, and he glanced across the road to see a big, charcoal-coloured Mercedes pulling up outside the gallery. Even before it had come to a stop, a bull-like figure in a dark suit jumped out of the front passenger seat, quickly checked the road ahead and behind, then opened the rear door. The people on the pavement, with their drinks and cigarettes, turned round to see who was emerging, then looked away without interest as the unknown newcomer was escorted swiftly through the doors.

8

Hoffmann's non-existent public profile had not been achieved without effort. One day, quite early in the history of Hoffmann Investment Technologies, when the company still only had about $2 billion in assets under management, he had invited the partners of Switzerland's oldest public-relations firm to breakfast at the Hotel Président Wilson and offered them a deal: an annual retainer of 200,000 Swiss francs in return for keeping his name out of the papers. Hoffmann made no public charitable donations, attended no gala dinners or industry awards ceremonies, endorsed no political party, endowed no educational institution, and gave no lectures or speeches.

It was, therefore, an unusual experience and an ordeal for him to attend his wife's first exhibition. From the moment he stepped out of the car and entered the noisy gallery, he wished he could turn round and leave. People he suspected he had met before, friends of Gabrielle's, loomed up and spoke to him, but although he had a mind that could perform mental arithmetic to five decimal places, he had no memory for faces. He heard what others were saying, the usual trite and pointless remarks, but he was conscious of mumbling replies that were inappropriate or even downright odd. Offered a glass of champagne, he took water instead, and that was when he noticed Bob Walton staring at him from the other side of the room.

Walton, of all people!

Before he could take evasive action, his former colleague was making his way through the crowd towards him, determined to have a word, his hand extended. 'Alex,' he said, 'it's been a while.'

'Bob.' He shook his hand coldly. 'I don't believe I've seen you since I offered you a job and you told me I was the devil come to steal your soul.'

'I don't think I put it quite like that.'

'No? I seem to recall you made it pretty damn clear what you thought of scientists going to the dark side and becoming quants.'

'Did I really? I'm sorry about that.' Walton gestured round the room with his drink. 'Anyway, I'm glad it all turned out so happily for you, Alex.'

He said it with such warmth that Hoffmann regretted his hostility. When he had first come to Geneva, knowing no one and with nothing except two suitcases and an Anglo-French dictionary, Walton had been his section head at CERN. He and his wife had taken him under their wing—Sunday lunches, apartment-hunting, lifts to work.

Hoffmann said, with an effort at friendliness, 'So how goes the search for the God particle?'

'Oh, we're getting there. And you? How's the elusive holy grail of autonomous machine reasoning?'

'The same. Getting there.'

'Really?' Walton raised his eyebrows in surprise. 'So you're still going on with it? That's brave. What happened to your head?'

'Nothing. A silly accident.' He glanced over towards Gabrielle. 'I think maybe I ought to go and say hello to my wife . . .'

'Of course. Forgive me.' Walton offered his hand again. 'Well, it's been good talking to you, Alex. We should hook up properly some time. You've got my email address.'

Hoffmann called after him, 'Actually, I haven't.'

Walton turned. 'Yes, you have. You sent me an invitation to this.'

'I haven't sent any invitations.'

'I think you'll find you have. Just a second . . .'

It is typical of Walton's academic pedantry, thought Hoffmann, *to insist on such a minor point, even when he is wrong.* But then to his surprise, Walton handed him his BlackBerry, showing the invitation sent from Hoffmann's email address.

Hoffmann said reluctantly, for he, too, hated to admit an error, 'Oh, OK. Sorry. I must have forgotten.'

He quickly turned his back on Walton to hide his dismay and went in search of Gabrielle. When he finally managed to get across to her, she said, 'I was starting to think you weren't coming.'

'I got away as soon as I could.' He kissed her on the mouth and tasted the sourness of the champagne on her breath.

A man called out, 'Over here, Dr Hoffmann,' and a photographer's flash went off less than a metre away.

Hoffmann jerked his head back instinctively. Through his false smile he said, 'What the hell is Bob Walton doing here?'

'How should I know? You're the one who invited him.'

'Yeah, he just showed me. But I'm sure I never did that. Why would I? He's the guy who closed down my research at CERN.'

Suddenly the owner of the gallery was beside him. 'You must be very proud of her, Dr Hoffmann,' said Bertrand.

'What?' Hoffmann was still looking across the party at his former colleague. 'Oh, yes. Yes, I am—very proud.' He made a concentrated effort to put Walton out of his mind. 'Have you sold anything yet?'

Gabrielle said, 'Thanks, Alex—it isn't all about money, you know.'

'Yes, OK, I know it isn't. I was just asking.'

'We have plenty of time,' said Bertrand. His mobile emitted an alert, playing two bars of Mozart. He blinked at the message in surprise, muttered, 'Excuse me,' and hurried away.

Hoffmann was still half blinded by the camera flash. When he looked at the portraits, the centres were voids. Nevertheless, he struggled to make appreciative comments. 'It's fantastic to see them all together, isn't it? You really get a sense of another way of looking at the world.'

Gabrielle said, 'How's your head?'

'Good. I hadn't even thought about it till you just mentioned it. I like that one very much.' He pointed to a nearby cube. 'That's of you, isn't it?'

It had taken her a day simply to sit for it, he remembered, squatting in the scanner, her head clasped in her hands, her mouth opened wide as if in mid-scream. When she had first shown it to him, he had been almost as shocked by it as he had been by the foetus, of which it was a conscious echo.

She said, 'Leclerc was here earlier. You just missed him.'

Her tone put Hoffmann on his guard. 'So what did he want?'

'He wanted to ask me about the nervous breakdown you apparently had when you worked at CERN.'

Hoffmann wasn't sure he had heard properly. 'He's talked to CERN?'

'About the nervous breakdown,' she repeated more loudly. 'The one you've never mentioned before.'

He felt winded, as if someone had punched him. 'I wouldn't exactly call it a nervous breakdown.'

'What would you call it, then?'

'Do we really have to do this now?' Her expression told him they did. He wondered how many glasses of champagne she had drunk. 'OK, I guess we do. I got depressed. I saw a shrink. I got better.'

'You saw a psychiatrist? You were treated for depression? And you've never mentioned it in *eight years*?'

A couple standing nearby turned to stare.

'You're making something out of nothing,' he said irritably. 'You're being ridiculous. It was before I even met you, for God's sake.' And then, more softly: 'Come on, Gabby, we shouldn't spoil this.'

There was a sound of metal rapping on glass. 'Ladies and gentlemen,' called Bertrand. He was holding up a champagne flute and hitting it with a fork. 'Ladies and gentlemen!' It was surprisingly effective. A silence quickly fell on the crowded room.

He had something in his hand. He walked over to the self-portrait, peeled a red spot from the roll of tape concealed in his palm and stuck it firmly against the label. A delighted, knowing murmur spread around the gallery.

'Gabrielle,' he said, turning to her with a smile, 'allow me to congratulate you. You are now, officially, a professional artist.'

There was a round of applause and a general hoisting of champagne glasses in salute. All the tension left Gabrielle's face, and Hoffmann seized the moment to take her wrist and raise her hand above her head, as if she were a boxing champion. There were renewed cheers and the camera flashed again. 'Well done, Gabby,' he whispered. 'You so deserve this.'

She smiled at him happily. 'Thank you.' She toasted the room. 'Thank you all. And thank you especially whoever bought it.'

Bertrand said, 'Wait. I haven't finished.'

Next to the self-portrait was the head of a Siberian tiger that had died at the Servion Zoo the previous year. The etching on glass was lit from below by a blood-red light. Bertrand placed a spot next to that one as well. It had sold for 4,500 francs.

Hoffmann whispered, 'Any more of this, and you'll be making more money than I am.'

'Oh, Alex, shut up about money.' But he could see she was pleased, and when Bertrand moved on and attached another red spot, this time to *The Invisible Man*, the 18,000-franc centrepiece of the exhibition, she clapped her hands in delight.

If only, Hoffmann had thought bitterly afterwards, it had stopped there, the whole occasion would have been a triumph. But Bertrand worked his way methodically around the entire gallery, leaving a rash of red spots in his wake—a pox, a plague, an *epidemic* of pustules erupting across the whitewashed walls—and he did not stop until all were marked as sold.

The effect on the spectators was odd. At first they cheered whenever a red spot was applied. But gradually a palpable air of awkwardness settled over the gallery. It was as if they were witnessing a practical joke that had started out as funny but had gone on too long and become cruel. Hoffmann could hardly bear to watch Gabrielle's expression as it declined from happiness to puzzlement, to incomprehension, and finally to suspicion.

He said desperately, 'It looks as though you have an admirer.'

She didn't seem to hear him. 'Is this all one buyer?'

'It is indeed,' said Bertrand. He was beaming and rubbing his hands.

A muted whisper of conversation started up again, people talking in low voices.

Gabrielle said in disbelief, 'Who on earth is it?'

'I cannot tell you that, unfortunately.' Bertrand glanced at Hoffmann. 'All I can say is "an anonymous collector".'

Gabrielle followed his gaze to Hoffmann. She swallowed before she spoke. Her voice was very quiet. 'Is this you?'

'Of course not.'

'Because if it is—'

'It isn't!'

The door emitted a chime as it was opened. Hoffmann looked over his shoulder. People were starting to leave; Walton was in the first wave, buttoning his jacket against the chilly wind. Bertrand saw what was happening and gestured discreetly to the waitresses to stop serving drinks. The party had lost its point and nobody seemed to want to be the last to leave. A couple of women came over to Gabrielle and she had to pretend that their congratulations were sincere. 'I would have bought something myself,' said one, 'but I never had the chance.'

After they had moved off, Hoffmann said to Bertrand, 'For God's sake, at least tell her it isn't me.'

'I can't say who it is, because to be honest I don't know. It's as simple as that.' Bertrand spread his hands. 'My bank just sent me an email to say they'd received an electronic transfer with reference to this exhibition.

When I got my calculator and added up the cost of all the items on display, I found it came to one hundred and ninety-two thousand francs. Which is precisely the sum transferred.'

'An electronic transfer?' repeated Hoffmann.

'That is right.'

'I want you to pay it back,' said Gabrielle. 'I don't want my work to be treated like this.'

Bertrand smiled. 'My dear Gabrielle, you seem not to understand. We are in a legal situation. When a piece of art is purchased, it's gone. If you wish not to sell, don't exhibit.'

'I'll pay you double,' said Hoffmann desperately. 'You're on fifty per cent commission, so you just made nearly a hundred thousand francs, right? I'll pay you two hundred thousand if you'll give Gabrielle her work back.'

'That is impossible, Dr Hoffmann.'

'All right, I'll double it again. Four hundred thousand.'

Bertrand swayed in his Zen silk slippers, ethics and avarice visibly slugging it out on the smooth contours of his face. 'Well, I don't know what—'

'Stop it!' shouted Gabrielle. 'Stop it now, Alex! Both of you! I can't bear to listen to this.'

'Gabby . . .'

But she eluded Hoffmann's outstretched hands and darted towards the door, pushing between the backs of the departing guests. Hoffmann went after her, shouldering his way through the small crowd. He emerged onto the street just behind her, and finally managed to grab her elbow. He pulled her to him, into a doorway.

'Listen, Gabby . . .'

'No.' She flapped at him with her free hand.

'Listen!' He shook her until she stopped trying to twist away. 'Calm down. Something very weird is going on. Whoever just bought your exhibition I'm sure is the same person who sent me that Darwin book. Someone is trying to mess with my mind.'

'Oh, come off it, Alex! It's you who bought everything—I know it is.' She tried to wriggle free.

'No, listen.' He shook her again. Dimly he recognised that his fear was making him aggressive, and he tried to calm down. 'The Darwin was bought in exactly the same way—a cash transfer over the internet. I bet you that if we go back in there right now and get Monsieur Bertrand to give us the purchaser's account number, they'll match. Now, you've got to understand that although the account may be in my name, it's not mine. But I'm going to get to the bottom of it, I promise you.' He released her. 'That's what I wanted to say.'

She stared at him and began slowly massaging her elbow. She was crying silently. He realised he must have hurt her. 'I'm sorry.'

She looked up at the sky, gulping. Eventually she got her emotions back under control. She said, 'You really have no idea, do you, how important that exhibition was to me?'

'Of course I do . . .'

'And now it's ruined. And it's your fault.'

'Come on, Gabrielle, how can you say that?'

'Well, it is, Alex, you see, because either you bought everything, out of some kind of mad alpha-male belief that you'd be doing me a favour. Or it was bought by this other person who you say is trying to mess with your mind. Either way, it's you—again.' She wasn't crying any more. 'What exactly have you turned into, Alex? I mean, Leclerc wanted to know if money was the reason why you left CERN, and I said no. But do you ever stop to listen to yourself? Two hundred thousand francs . . . Four hundred thousand francs . . . Sixty million dollars for a house we don't need . . .'

'You didn't complain when we bought it, as I recall. You said you liked the studio.'

'Yes, but only to keep you happy! You don't think I like the rest of it, do you? It's like living in a bloody embassy.' A thought seemed to occur to her. 'How much money have you got now, as a matter of interest?'

'Drop it, Gabrielle.'

'No. Tell me. I want to know. Give me a figure.'

'In dollars? Ballpark? I really don't know. A billion. A billion-two.'

'A billion dollars? *Ballpark?* You know what? Forget it. It's over. As far as I'm concerned, all that matters now is getting out of this bloody awful town, where the only thing anyone cares about is *money*.'

She turned away.

'What's over?' Again he grabbed her arm, but feebly, without conviction, and this time she wheeled on him and slapped him on the face. It was only light—a warning flick, a token—but he let her go at once.

'Don't you ever,' she spat, jabbing her finger at him, '*ever* grab hold of me like that again.'

And that was it. She was gone. She strode to the end of the street and rounded the corner, leaving Hoffmann with his hand pressed to his cheek, unable to comprehend the catastrophe that had so swiftly overtaken him.

LECLERC HAD WITNESSED it all from the comfort of his car. It had unfolded in front of him like a drive-in movie. Now, as he continued to watch, Hoffmann slowly turned round and made his way back towards the gallery. He went inside, and it was perfectly easy to see what was happening: the window was large and the gallery was now almost empty. Hoffmann went over to where the proprietor, M. Bertrand, was standing, and clearly began to berate him. He pulled out his mobile phone and waved it in the other man's face. Bertrand threw up his hands, shooing him away, whereupon Hoffmann seized the lapels of his jacket and pushed him against the wall.

Leclerc swore under his breath, threw open his car door and hauled himself stiffly out into the street and across the road to the gallery.

By the time he got inside, Hoffmann's bodyguard had planted himself very solidly between his client and the gallery's owner. Bertrand was smoothing down his jacket and shouting insults at Hoffmann, who was responding in kind.

'Gentlemen, gentlemen,' said Leclerc, 'we shall have no more of this, thank you.' He flashed his ID at the bodyguard. 'Dr Hoffmann, it would pain me to arrest you, after all you have been through today, but I shall if necessary. What is going on here?'

Hoffmann said, 'My wife is very upset, and all because this man has acted in the most incredibly stupid way—'

'Yes, yes,' cut in Bertrand, 'incredibly stupid! I sold all her work for her, on the first day of her first exhibition.'

'All I want,' responded Hoffmann, in a voice that struck Leclerc as quite close to hysteria, 'is the number of the buyer's bank account.'

'And I have told him this is confidential information.'

Leclerc turned back to Hoffmann. 'Why is it so important?'

'Someone,' said Hoffmann, struggling to keep his voice calm, 'is quite clearly attempting to destroy me. I have obtained the number of the account that was used to send me a book last night, presumably in order to frighten me in some way—I've got it here on my mobile. And now I believe the same bank account, which is supposedly in my name, has been used to sabotage my wife's exhibition.'

'Sabotage!' scoffed Bertrand. 'We call it a sale!'

'It wasn't one sale, though, was it? Everything was sold, at once. Has that ever happened before?'

'Ach!' Bertrand made a sweeping gesture.

Leclerc sighed. 'Show me the account number, Monsieur Bertrand, if you please.'

'I can't do that. Why should I?'

'If you don't, I shall arrest you for impeding a criminal investigation.'

'You wouldn't dare!'

Leclerc stared him out and eventually Bertrand muttered, 'All right, it's in my office.'

'Dr Hoffmann—your mobile, if I may?'

Hoffmann showed him the email screen. 'This is the message I got from the bookseller, with the account number.'

Leclerc took the telephone. 'Stay here, please.' He followed Bertrand into the small back office; it smelled of a pungent combination of coffee and glue. A computer sat on a scratched and rickety roll-top desk; Bertrand moved the mouse across his computer screen and clicked. 'Here is the email from my bank.' He vacated the seat with a pout.

Leclerc sat at the terminal and peered close to the screen. He held Hoffmann's mobile next to it and compared the two account numbers. They were an identical mixture of letters and digits. The name of the account holder was given as A. J. Hoffmann. He took out his notebook and copied down the sequence. 'And you received no message other than this?'

'No.'

Back in the gallery, he returned the mobile to Hoffmann. 'You were right. The numbers match. Although what this has to do with the attack on you, I confess I do not understand.'

'Oh, they're connected,' said Hoffmann. 'I tried to tell you that this morning. And why the hell are you going round asking questions about me at CERN? You should be finding this guy, not investigating me.'

His face was haggard, his eyes red and sore, as if he had been rubbing them. With his day's growth of beard he looked like a fugitive.

'I'll pass the account number to our financial department and ask them to look into it,' said Leclerc. 'Bank accounts, at least, are something we Swiss do rather well, and impersonation is a crime. In the meantime, I strongly urge you to go home and see your doctor and have some sleep.'

HOFFMANN TRIED to call Gabrielle from the Mercedes, but he only got her voicemail. The familiar, jaunty voice caught him by the throat: 'Hi, this is Gabby, don't you dare hang up without leaving me a message.'

There was a beep. After a long pause, which he knew would sound weird when she played it back but which he struggled to end, he said finally, 'Call me, will you? We've got to talk.'

He hung up and leaned forward to the bodyguard. 'Is your colleague with my wife, do you know?'

Keeping his eyes fixed on the road ahead, the bodyguard spoke over his shoulder. 'No, monsieur. By the time he got to the end of the road, she was already out of sight.'

Hoffmann let out a groan. 'Is there no one in this goddamn town who can do a simple job without screwing up?' He threw himself back in his seat, folded his arms and stared out of the window.

He did not like to think of Gabrielle wandering the streets alone. It was her impulsiveness that worried him. Once angered, she was capable of anything. She might disappear for a few days, fly back to her mother in England. *You know what? Forget it. It's over.* What did she mean by that? What was over? The exhibition? Her career as an artist? Their conversation? Their marriage? Panic welled inside him again. Life without her would be a vacuum: unsurvivable.

The Mercedes turned onto the Quai du Mont-Blanc. The city, crouched around the dark pool of its lake, looked low and sombre, hewn from the same grey rock as the distant Jura Mountains. There was none of the vulgar glass-and-steel animal exuberance of Manhattan or the City of London: their skyscrapers would rise and they would crash, booms and busts would come and go, but crafty Geneva, with its head down, would endure. The Hotel Beau-Rivage, positioned near the mid-point of the wide, tree-lined boulevard, embodied these values in bricks and stone.

The Mercedes pulled up on the opposite side of the road, and the bodyguard, his hand raised imperiously to stop the traffic, escorted Hoffmann across the pedestrian crossing, up the steps and into the faux-Habsburg grandeur of the interior. If the concierge felt any private alarm at Hoffmann's appearance, he allowed no flicker of it to show on his smiling face as he took over from Paccard and led *le cher docteur* up the stairs to the dining room.

The atmosphere beyond the tall doors was that of a nineteenth-century salon: paintings, antiques, gilt chairs, gold swag curtains. Quarry had reserved a long table by the French windows and was sitting with his back to the lake view, keeping an eye on the entrance. When Hoffmann appeared, he moved to intercept his partner in the middle of the room.

'Professor,' he said cheerfully for the others to hear, and then, drawing him slightly apart, 'where the bloody hell have you been?'

Hoffmann started to answer but Quarry interrupted him without listening. He was fired up, eyes gleaming. 'OK, never mind. The main thing is it looks as though they're in—most of them, anyway—and my hunch is for closer to a billion than seven-fifty. So all I need from you now, please, is sixty minutes of technical reassurance. Preferably with minimal aggression.' He gestured towards the table. 'Come and join us. You've missed the *grenouille de Vallorbe*, but the *filet mignon de veau* should be divine.'

Hoffmann didn't move. He said suspiciously, 'Did you just buy up all Gabrielle's artwork?'

'What?' Quarry halted and squinted at him, perplexed.

'Someone just bought up her entire collection using an account set up in my name.'

'I haven't even seen it! And why would I have an account in your name? That's bloody illegal, for a start.' Quarry glanced over his shoulder at the clients, then back at Hoffmann. He looked utterly mystified. 'You know what? Could we talk about this later?'

Hoffmann's gaze swept jaggedly around the room: the clients, the waiters, the two exits, the high windows and the balcony beyond. 'Someone's really after me, Hugo. Out to destroy me bit by bit. It's starting to bug me.'

'Well, yes, I can see that, Alexi. How's your head?'

Hoffmann put his hand to his scalp. He had a throbbing headache again, he realised. 'It's started hurting again.'

'OK,' said Quarry slowly. 'So what are you saying here? Are you saying perhaps you ought to go back to the hospital?'

'No. I'll just sit down.' Hoffman wearily shrugged off his raincoat. It was quickly taken by a waiter, who hung it on a coat stand by the door.

'And eat something, maybe?' said Quarry hopefully. 'You haven't eaten all day, have you?' He took Hoffmann by the arm and led him towards the table. 'Now you sit here, opposite me, where I can keep an eye on you, and perhaps we can all change places later on.'

Hoffmann found himself being helped by a waiter into a seat between

Etienne and Clarisse Mussard. The Chinese had been left to fend for themselves at one end of the table; the American bankers, Klein and Easterbrook, were at the other. In between were Herxheimer, Mould, Lukasinski, Elmira Gulzhan and various lawyers and advisers. A linen napkin was shaken out and spread over Hoffmann's lap. He was offered a choice of white or red wine by the sommelier, but asked for still water.

Herxheimer said, 'We were just discussing tax rates, Alex.' He broke off a piece of bread and slipped it into his mouth. 'We were saying that Europe seems to be going the way of the old Soviet Union. France forty per cent, Germany forty-five per cent, the UK fifty per cent—'

'Fifty per cent!' cut in Quarry. 'I mean, don't get me wrong. I'm as patriotic as the next chap, but do I really want to go into a fifty-fifty partnership with Her Majesty's Government? I think not.'

'There is no democracy any more,' said Elmira Gulzhan. 'The state is in control as never before. All our freedoms are disappearing and no one seems to care. That's what I find so depressing about this century.'

Hoffmann stared at the tablecloth and let the discussion flow around him. He was remembering now why he didn't like the rich: their self-pity. Persecution was the common ground of their conversation.

'I despise you,' he said, but nobody paid him any attention, so engrossed were they in the inequities of higher-rate taxation. And then he thought, *Perhaps I have become one of them; is that why I am so paranoid?*

At that moment the doors swung open to admit a file of eight tail-coated waiters, each carrying two plates. They stationed themselves between their allotted pair of diners and set the plates down before them. The main course was veal with morels and asparagus.

'I cannot eat veal,' said Elmira, leaning confidingly across the table to Hoffmann. 'The poor calf suffers so.'

'Oh, I always prefer food that has suffered,' said Quarry cheerfully, wielding his knife and fork. 'The nastier the demise the better.'

Elmira flicked him with the end of her napkin. 'Hugo, you are *wicked*. Isn't he wicked, Alex?'

'He is wicked,' agreed Hoffmann. He pushed his food around his plate with his fork. He had no appetite. Over Quarry's shoulder he could see the Jet d'Eau probing the dull sky on the opposite side of the lake like a watery searchlight.

Lukasinski began calling across the table some technical questions about the new fund, which Quarry laid down his cutlery to answer. The structure of the fund would be as before: investors would be part of a limited-liability company registered in the Cayman Islands for tax purposes, which would retain Hoffmann Investment Technologies to manage its assets.

Herxheimer said, 'How soon do you require an answer from us?'

Quarry said, 'We're looking to hard-close the fund again in three weeks' time, at the end of the month.'

Suddenly the atmosphere around the table was serious. Side conversations ceased. Everyone was listening.

'Well, you can have my answer now,' said Easterbrook. He waved his fork in Hoffmann's direction. 'You know what I like about you, Hoffmann?'

'No, Bill. What would that be?'

'You don't talk your book. You let your numbers do the speaking. I'm going to recommend that AmCor doubles its stake.'

'Bill, that is so generous of you,' said Quarry hoarsely. 'Alex and I are overwhelmed.' He glanced across the table.

'Overwhelmed,' repeated Hoffmann.

'Winter Bay will be in as well,' said Klein. 'I can't say how much exactly, but it will be substantial.'

Lukasinksi said, 'That goes for me, too.'

'Do I take it that the mood of the meeting is that you're all planning to invest?' asked Quarry. Murmurs of assent ran around the table. 'Well, that sounds promising. Is there anyone *not* planning to increase their investment?' The diners looked from one to another, shrugged. 'Even you, Etienne?'

Mussard looked up grumpily. 'Yes, yes, I suppose so. But let's not discuss it in public. I prefer to do things in the traditional Swiss way.'

'You mean fully clothed with the lights off?' Quarry rose to his feet on the tide of laughter. 'My friends, I know we are still eating, but if ever there was a time for a spontaneous toast, then I think this must be it. I truly believe we are present at the birth of a new force in global asset management, the product of the union of cutting-edge science and aggressive investment—or, if you prefer, of God and Mammon.' More laughter. 'At which happy event, it seems to me only right that we should stand and raise our glasses to the genius who had made it possible.' He beamed down at Hoffmann. 'To the father of VIXAL-4—to Alex!'

With a chorus of 'To Alex!' and a peal of clinking cut glass, the investors stood and toasted Hoffmann. They looked at him fondly, and when they had all sat down he realised to his dismay that they expected him to respond.

'Oh, no,' he said. 'Really, I can't.'

But such a good-natured round of 'No!' and 'Shame!' greeted his refusal that Hoffmann found himself getting to his feet. He rested one hand on the table to steady himself. Almost absently he glanced out of the window at the view—which, because he was now elevated, had widened to take in not only the opposite shore but also the promenade directly beneath the hotel. Hoffmann's eyes came to rest upon a skeletal apparition draped in a brown leather coat standing under a lime tree. His eye sockets were deeply shadowed by his bulging forehead, from which all his hair had been scraped back into a grey ponytail. He was gazing directly up at the window.

Hoffmann's limbs locked. For several long seconds, he was unable to move. Then he took an involuntary step backwards, knocking over his chair. Quarry, staring at him in alarm, began to rise, but Hoffmann held up his hand to ward him off. He took another step away from the table and his feet became entangled in the legs of the upended chair. He stumbled and almost fell, but that seemed to those watching to break whatever spell he was under, for suddenly he kicked the chair out of his path and turned and ran towards the door. Stopping only to grab his raincoat, he wrenched at the door handle and let himself out of the room.

Hoffmann was barely conscious of the astonished exclamations swelling behind him, or of Quarry calling his name. He ran along the mirrored corridor and down the sweep of staircase. At the bottom he jumped the last few steps, sprinted past his bodyguard—who was talking to the concierge—and out onto the promenade.

9

Across the wide highway the pavement beneath the lime was empty. Hoffmann halted, looked left and right, and swore. The doorman asked if he wanted a taxi. Hoffmann ignored him and, pulling on his raincoat, walked straight past the front of the hotel to the street corner. To his left, running parallel with the side of the Beau-Rivage, was a narrow one-way thoroughfare. For want of a better idea he set off down it, jogging about fifty metres, past a line of parked motorbikes and a small church. At the end was a crossroads. He stopped again.

A block further along, a figure in a brown coat was crossing the road. The man paused when he got to the other side and glanced back at Hoffmann. It was him, no question of it. A white van passed between them and he was gone, hurrying off down a side street.

And now Hoffmann ran. A great righteous energy flooded his body, propelling his legs in long, fast strides. He sprinted to the spot where he had last seen the man. It was another one-way street; once again he had vanished. He ran down it to the next junction. The roads were narrow, quiet, a lot of parked cars. Wherever he looked there were small businesses—a hairdresser's, a pharmacy, a bar—people going about their lunchtime shopping. He spun around hopelessly, turned right, working his way through the narrow maze of one-way streets, reluctant to give up but increasingly sure that he had lost him. The area around him changed. The buildings turned shabbier, derelict, sprayed with graffiti; and then he was in a different city. A teenaged black woman in a tight sweater and white plastic micro-skirt shouted at him from across the road. She was standing outside a shop with a purple neon sign, VIDEO CLUB XXX.

Hoffmann slowed his pace, trying to get his bearings. He must have run almost to the Cornavin railway station, he realised, and into the red-light district. Finally he stopped outside a boarded-up nightclub covered in a flaking skin of peeling fly-posters. Wincing, his hands on his hips, a sharp pain in his side, he leaned over the gutter trying to recover his breath. An Asian prostitute watched him from a window three metres away.

He straightened and set off back the way he had come, scanning the alleys and courtyards on either side in case the man had slipped into one of them to hide. He passed a sex shop, Je Vous Aime, and retraced his steps. The window contained a halfhearted display of wigs and erotic underwear. The door was open, but the view of the interior was obscured by a curtain of plastic strips. He thought of the handcuffs and ball gag the intruder had left behind in their home. Leclerc had said they might have come from such a place.

Suddenly his mobile chimed with his text alert: Rue de berne 91 chambre 68.

He stared at it for several seconds. He had just passed the Rue de Berne, had he not? He turned round and there it was, right behind him, close enough to read the blue street sign. He checked the message again. The sender was not identified; the originating number was unavailable. He glanced round to see if anyone was watching him, then walked back up the street to the Rue de Berne. It was long and shabby but it was busier—two lanes, with tram cables strung above—which made him feel safer. At the junction was a fruit-and-vegetable shop offering an outdoor display; next to it a forlorn little café with a few empty aluminium chairs and tables set out on the pavement, and a *tabac* advertising '*Cartes telephoniques, DVDs X, Videos X, Revues X USA.*' The street numbers ascended to his left. He walked, counting them off, and within thirty seconds had migrated from northern Europe and entered the southern Mediterranean: Lebanese and Moroccan restaurants, swirls of Arabic script on the shop fronts, Arabic music blaring from tinny speakers.

He found number 91 on the northern side of the Rue de Berne, opposite a shop selling African clothes—a dilapidated seven-storey building of peeling yellow stucco. It was four windows wide, its name spelt out down the side, almost from top to bottom, by individual letters protruding over the street: HOTEL DIODATI. Most of the shutters were closed, but a few were half-raised, like drooping eyelids. At street level there was an ancient and heavy wooden door, elaborately carved with what looked like masonic symbols. As he watched, it swung inwards and from the dim interior a man emerged wearing jeans and trainers, a hood pulled over his head. He put his hands in his pockets, hunched his shoulders and set off down the street. A minute or so later the door opened again. This time it was a woman, young and thin, with fluffy dyed orange hair and a short skirt. She paused on the doorstep, then moved off in the opposite direction to the man.

There was never a moment when Hoffmann made a definite decision to go in. He watched for a while and then crossed the road and lingered outside the door. Eventually, he pushed it open and peered inside. There was a small lobby with a counter, deserted, and a seating area with a black and red sofa. In the gloom an aquarium glowed brightly, but it seemed devoid of fish.

Hoffmann took a few steps over the threshold. The thick door closed behind him, cutting off the sounds of the street. He moved through the empty reception, across a floor of curling linoleum, and followed a narrow passage to a small elevator. He pressed the call button and the doors opened immediately as though it had been waiting for him.

The elevator was tiny, with just enough room for two people, and when the doors closed Hoffmann was almost overwhelmed by claustrophobia.

The buttons offered him a choice of seven floors. He pressed number six. The elevator rattled and he began to rise very slowly. It was not so much a sense of danger he felt now as of unreality, as if he were back in a recurrent childhood dream he could not quite remember, from which the only way to wake was to keep on going until he found the exit.

When at last the elevator did halt, the doors opened jerkily onto the sixth floor. The landing was deserted. He was reluctant to step out onto it at first, but then the doors began to close and he had to thrust his leg out to save himself from being reimprisoned. The doors juddered back and he moved out cautiously. The landing was darker than in the lobby. His eyes had to readjust. The walls were bare. There was a stale, fetid smell of air that had been breathed a thousand times and never refreshed by an open door or window. It was hot. An amateurish sign indicated that Room 68 was to the right. The clank of the elevator motor restarting behind him made him jump. He listened to the car descend, then there was silence.

He took a couple of paces to the right and peered round the corner along the passage. Room 68 was at the far end, its door closed. From somewhere close by came a rhythmic noise of rasping metal, which he realised was bedsprings. A man moaned as if in pain.

Hoffmann pulled out his mobile, intending to call the police. But, curiously for the centre of Geneva, there was no signal. He put it back in his pocket and walked warily to the end of the passage. His eyes were at the same level as the bulging opaque glass of the spyhole. He listened. He couldn't hear anything. He tapped on the door. Nothing.

He tried the black plastic handle. The door wouldn't open. But it was held by only a single Yale lock and he could see the door jamb was rotted into the spongy wood. He stepped back a pace, then barged against the door with his shoulder. There was a crack and the door opened.

It was warm and dark inside, just a faint line of grey daylight showing where the bottom of the window shutter had failed to close properly. He edged across the carpet, groped around and through the net curtain for the switch, pressed it, and noisily the shutter began to rise. The window looked out through a fire escape onto the back of a row of buildings about fifty metres away. By the thin light, Hoffmann could see the room, such as it was: a single unmade bed on wheels with a greyish sheet hanging down over a red and black carpet, a small chest of drawers with a rucksack resting on top of it, a wooden chair with a scuffed brown leather seat. There was a strong smell of stale cigarette smoke, masculine sweat and cheap soap. In the tiny bathroom were a small bathtub with a clear plastic shower curtain hung around it, a basin streaked greenish-black where the taps had dripped, and a WC with similar markings.

Hoffmann moved back into the bedroom. He carried the rucksack to the bed and emptied out the contents. It was mostly dirty clothes—a plaid shirt, T-shirts, underwear, socks—but buried among them was an old Zeiss camera with a powerful lens, and also a laptop computer.

He put the laptop down and returned to the open door. The frame had splintered outwards round the lock but had not broken, and he found he was able to press the housing of the lock back into place and gently close the door. From a distance it would look untouched. Behind the door he noticed a pair of boots. He picked them up between thumb and forefinger and examined them. They were identical to the ones he had seen outside his house. He replaced them, went to the bed and opened the laptop. Then, from the bowels of the building, came a clang. The elevator was moving again.

Hoffmann put aside the computer and listened to the whine of its long ascent. At last it stopped, and then came the rattle of its doors opening close by. He crossed the room quickly and put his eye to the spyhole just as the man came round the corner. He reached the door and pulled out his key. The distorting lens of the peephole made his looming face seem even more skull-like than before, and Hoffmann felt the hairs rise on his scalp.

He stepped back and looked around quickly, then withdrew into the bathroom. An instant later he heard the key inserted into the keyhole, followed by a grunt of surprise as the door swung open without needing to be unlocked. Through the crack between the bathroom door and the door jamb, Hoffmann had a clear view of the centre of the bedroom. He held his breath. For a while nothing happened. He prayed the man might have turned round and gone down to Reception to report a break-in. But then his shadow passed briefly across his line of view, heading towards the window. Hoffmann was on the point of trying to make a run for it when, with shocking speed, the man doubled back and kicked open the bathroom door.

There was something scorpion-like in the way he crouched, legs apart, with a long blade held at head height. He was bigger than Hoffmann remembered. There was no way past him. Long seconds elapsed as they stared at one another, and then the man said, in a surprisingly calm and educated voice, 'Zurück. In die Badewanne.' He gestured with the knife at the bath and Hoffmann shook his head, not understanding. '*In die Badewanne*,' repeated the man, pointing the knife first at Hoffmann and then at the tub. After another endless pause, Hoffmann found his limbs doing as they were bidden. His hand pulled back the shower curtain and his legs stepped shakily into the bath, his desert boots clumping on the plastic. The man came a little further into the tiny room and pulled the light cord. Above the basin a neon strip stuttered into life. He closed the door and said, '*Ausziehen*,' and this time helpfully added a translation: 'Take off your clothes.'

'*Nein*,' said Hoffmann, shaking his head and holding his palms up in a gesture of reasonableness. 'No. No way.' The man spat out some swear word he didn't understand and slashed at him with the knife, the blade passing so close that the front of Hoffmann's raincoat was slashed and the lower part of it flapped down to his knees. For a ghastly moment he thought it was his flesh and he said quickly, '*Ja, ja*, OK. I'll do it.' He quickly shrugged the coat off his left shoulder and then his right. There was hardly room for him to get his arms out of the sleeves and for a time it was stuck across his back: he had to struggle with it as if escaping from a straitjacket.

He tried to think of something to say, to establish contact with his attacker. He said, 'You are German?' and when the man didn't respond, he struggled to remember what little of the language he had picked up at CERN: '*Sie sind Deutscher?*' There was no answer.

At last he had the ruined coat off. He let it drop round his feet. He slipped off his jacket and held it out to his captor, who gestured with his knife that he should throw it onto the bathroom floor. He started to unbutton his shirt. He would carry on removing his clothes until he was naked if necessary, but if the man tried to tie him up he resolved that he would fight— yes, then he would put up a struggle.

'Why are you doing this?' he asked.

The man frowned at him as if he were a slightly baffling child and replied in English: 'Because you invited me.'

Hoffmann stared at him, aghast. 'I didn't *invite* you to do this.'

The knife was flourished again. 'Continue, please.'

Hoffmann finished unbuttoning his shirt and let it fall. He was thinking hard now, evaluating risks and chances. He grasped his T-shirt and pulled it up over his head, and when his face emerged and he saw his attacker's hungry eyes he felt his flesh crawl. But here was weakness, he recognised: here was opportunity. Somehow he forced himself to make a ball of the white cotton and to offer it to him. 'Here,' he said, and leaned forward encouragingly. When the man reached out to take it, he slightly adjusted his feet against the back of the bathtub and then launched himself at him.

He landed on his assailant with sufficient force to knock him backwards, the knife went flying, and together they sank down so entwined it was impossible for either man to land a blow. Hoffmann tried to haul himself up onto his feet, grabbing at the basin with one hand and the light cord with the other, but both seemed to come away at once. The room went dark and he felt something round his ankle dragging him down again. He hacked at it with his other heel and stamped on it and the man howled with pain. Hoffmann fumbled in the darkness for the door handle, at the same time lashing out with his feet. He was connecting with bone now—that pony-tailed skull, he hoped. His target whimpered and shrank into a foetal ball. When he no longer seemed a threat, Hoffmann pulled open the bathroom door and staggered into the bedroom.

He sat down heavily on the wooden chair. Despite the heat of the room, he was shivering with cold. He needed to get his clothes. He returned cautiously to the bathroom and pushed at the door. He heard a scuffling noise inside. The man had crawled towards the lavatory bowl. He was blocking the door. Hoffmann stepped over him and retrieved his clothes and also the knife. He went back into the bedroom and quickly dressed. *You invited me*, he thought furiously—what did he mean, he had invited him? He checked his mobile phone but there was still no signal.

In the bathroom the man had his head over the lavatory. He looked up as Hoffmann came in. Hoffmann, pointing the knife, gazed down at him without pity. 'What is your name?' he said.

The man turned his face away and spat blood. Hoffmann warily came closer, squatted on his haunches and scrutinised him. He was about sixty, although it was hard to tell with all the blood on his face; he had a cut above his eye. Overcoming his revulsion, Hoffmann transferred the knife into his left hand, leaned forward and opened the man's leather coat, searching until he found an inside pocket, from which he withdrew first a wallet and then a dark red European Union passport. It was German. He flicked it open. The text identified him as Johannes Karp, born 14.4.52 in Offenbach am Main.

Hoffmann said, 'You're seriously telling me you came here from Germany because I invited you?'

'*Ja.*'

Hoffmann recoiled. 'You're crazy.'

'No, *you* are crazy,' said the German with a flicker of spirit. 'You gave me your house codes.' He spat a tooth into his hand.

'Where is this invitation?'

He gestured weakly with his head towards the other room. 'Computer.'

Hoffmann stood. He pointed the knife at Karp. 'Don't move, OK?'

In the other room he sat on the chair and opened the laptop. It came awake immediately and at once the screen was filled with an image of Hoffmann's face: a picture-grab from a surveillance tape, by the look of it. He had been captured gazing up into the camera. It was so tightly cropped it was impossible to tell where it had been taken.

A couple of keystrokes took him into the hard-drive registry. The program names were all in German. He called up a list of the most recently viewed files. The last folder to be edited, just after six o'clock the previous evening, was entitled *Der Rotenburg Cannibal*. Inside it were scores of files containing newspaper articles about the case of Armin Meiwes, a computer technician and internet cannibal who was currently serving a life sentence in Germany for murder. There was a folder called *Das Opfer*, which Hoffmann knew meant *The Victim*. This was in English and looked like transcripts from an internet chat room—a dialogue, he perceived as he read on, between one participant who fantasised about committing murder and another who dreamed about what it would be like to die.

He was so absorbed by what was on the screen it was a near-miracle that some slight alteration in the light or air caused him to look up as the knife flashed towards him. He jerked his head back and the point just missed his eye—a fifteen-centimetre blade, a flick knife; it must have been hidden in the man's coat pocket. The German lashed out at him with his foot and caught him on the bottom of his rib cage, then lunged forward and tried to slash at him again. Hoffmann cried out in pain and shock, the chair toppled backwards and suddenly Karp was on top of him. The knife glinted in the pale light. By reflex, Hoffmann caught the man's wrist with his left and weaker hand. Briefly the knife trembled close to his face.'*Es ist, was Sie sich wünschen,*' whispered Karp soothingly. 'It is what you desire.' The knife-tip actually pricked Hoffmann's skin. He grimaced with the effort, holding the knife off, gaining millimetres, until at last his attacker's arm snapped backwards and with a terrible exultation in his own power, Hoffmann flung him back against the metal frame of the bed. Hoffmann's left hand still held on to the other man's wrist, his right was clamped to Karp's face, the heel of his hand jammed against the throat. Karp roared in pain and tore at Hoffmann's fingers with his free hand. Hoffmann responded by adjusting his grip so that he had his hand round the scrawny windpipe, choking off the sound. He was leaning into him now, pinning Karp to the side of the bed. All sense of time was gone, but it seemed to Hoffmann only a few seconds later that the fingers gradually ceased scrabbling at his hand and the knife clattered to the carpet. The body went slack beneath him, and when he withdrew his hands it toppled sideways.

He became aware of someone pounding on the wall and of a male voice calling out in thickly accented French, demanding to know what the hell was going on. He heaved himself up and closed the door and, as an extra protection, dragged the wooden chair over and wedged it at an angle under the handle. The movement set off an immediate clamour of pain in various battered outposts of his body—his head, his knuckles, his fingers, the base of his rib cage especially, even his toes where he had kicked the man's head. He dabbed his fingers to his scalp and they came away sticky with blood: at some point in the struggle his wound must have partially opened up. His hands were a mass of tiny scratches, as though he had fought his way out of an undergrowth of thorns. He sucked his grazed knuckles, registering the salty, metallic taste of blood. The hammering on the wall had stopped.

He was trembling now and he felt sick. He went into the bathroom and retched into the toilet bowl. The basin was hanging away from the wall but the taps still worked. He splashed his cheeks with cold water and went back into the bedroom.

The German lay on the floor. His open eyes gazed past Hoffmann's shoulder. Hoffmann knelt and checked his wrist for a pulse. He slapped his face. He shook him as if that might reanimate him. 'Come on,' he whispered. The head lolled like a bird's on the stem of a broken neck.

There was a brisk knock on the door. A man called out, '*Ça va? Qu'est-ce qui se passe?*' It was the same heavily accented voice that had shouted through the wall from next door. The handle was tried several times: '*Allez! Laissez-moi rentrer!*'

Hoffman levered himself painfully up onto his feet. The handle rattled again and whoever was outside began shoving against the door. The chair moved fractionally but held. The pushing stopped. Hoffmann waited, then crept quietly to the spyhole and looked out. The corridor was empty.

He stuffed the German's possessions back into the rucksack, slipped Karp's mobile into his pocket, closed the laptop and carried it over to the window. He parted the net curtain. The window opened easily, obviously often used. Outside on the fire escape, amid the encrusted swirls of pigeon shit, were a hundred sodden cigarette butts, a score of beer cans. He clambered out onto the ironwork, reached round the window frame and pressed the switch. The shutter descended behind him.

It was a long way down, six floors, and with every step of his descent Hoffmann was acutely aware of how conspicuous he must be. But to his relief most of the windows he passed were shuttered. As he descended, he could see that the fire escape led to a small concrete patio. There was some wooden garden furniture and a couple of faded green umbrellas advertising lager. He calculated that the best way to get out to the street would be through the hotel, but when he reached the ground and saw the sliding glass door that led to the reception area, he decided he couldn't risk running into the man from the next-door room. He dragged one of the wooden garden chairs over to the back wall and climbed up onto it.

He found himself peering at a two-metre drop to the neighbouring yard—a wilderness of sickly urban weeds choking half-hidden pieces of rusting catering equipment and an old bike frame; on the far side were big receptacles for trash. The yard clearly belonged to a restaurant of some kind. He balanced the laptop on the wall and hauled himself up to sit astride the brickwork. In the distance a police siren began to wail. He grabbed the computer, swung his leg over and dropped down to the other side, landing heavily in a bed of stinging nettles. He swore. From between the waste bins a youth stepped out to see what was going on. He was carrying an empty slop bucket, smoking a cigarette. He stared at Hoffmann in surprise.

Hoffmann said diffidently, '*Où est la rue?*' He tapped the computer significantly, as if it somehow explained his presence.

The youth looked at him and frowned, then slowly withdrew his cigarette from his mouth and gestured over his shoulder.

'*Merci.*' Hoffmann hurried down a narrow alley, through a wooden gate and out into the street.

GABRIELLE HOFFMANN had spent more than an hour furiously prowling round the public gardens of the Parc des Bastions declaiming in her head all the things she wished she had said on the pavement to Alex, until she realised that she was muttering to herself like a mad old lady and that passers-by were staring at her; at which point she hailed a taxi and went home. Beyond the gate, in front of the mansion, the wretched bodyguard-cum-driver, who Alex had sent to watch over her, was talking on his phone. He hung up and stared at her reproachfully.

She said to him, 'Do you still have that car, Camille?'

'Yes, madame.'

'Bring it round, will you? We're going to the airport.'

In the bedroom she started flinging clothes into a suitcase, her mind obsessively replaying the scene of her humiliation at the gallery. That it was Alex who had sabotaged her exhibition she had no doubt, although she was prepared to concede he would not have meant it maliciously. It would have been his clumsy, hopeless conception of a romantic gesture.

She went into the bathroom and stopped, staring in sudden bafflement at the cosmetics arrayed on the glass shelves. It was hard to know how much to pack if you didn't know how long you would be gone, or even where you were going. She looked at herself in the mirror, in the wretched outfit she had spent hours choosing for the launch of her career as an artist, and started crying—less out of self-pity, which she despised, than out of fear. *Don't let him be ill*, she thought. *Dear God, please don't take him away from me in that way.*

After a while she put her hand into her jacket pocket to try to find a tissue, and felt instead the sharp edges of a business card. *Professor Robert Walton, Computing Centre Department Head, CERN—European Organisation for Nuclear Research, 1211 Geneva 23, Switzerland.*

10

It was well after three o'clock by the time Hugo Quarry got back to the office. He had left several messages on Hoffmann's mobile phone, which had not been answered, and he felt a slight prickle of unease about where his partner might be: Hoffmann's so-called bodyguard he had found chatting up a girl in reception, unaware that his charge had even left the hotel. Quarry had fired him on the spot.

Still, for all that, the Englishman's mood was good. He now believed they were likely to mop up double his initial estimate of new investment—$2 billion—which meant an extra $40 million a year simply in management fees. He had drunk several truly excellent glasses of wine.

He was smiling so much the facial-recognition scanner failed to match his geometry to its database and he had to try a second time when he had composed himself. He passed under the watchful eyes of the security cameras in the lobby, stepped into the elevator and hummed to himself all the way up the glass tube. He even managed to maintain his smile when the glass partition to Hoffmann Investment Technologies slid back to reveal Inspector Jean-Philippe Leclerc of the Geneva Police Department waiting for him in Reception. He examined his visitor's ID and then compared it to the rumpled figure in front of him. The American markets would be opening in ten minutes. This he could do without.

'It wouldn't be possible, Inspector, would it, for us to have this meeting some other time?'

'I am very sorry to disturb you, monsieur. I had hoped to catch a word with Dr Hoffmann, but in his absence there are some matters I would like to discuss with you. It will only take ten minutes.'

There was something in the way the old boy planted his feet slightly apart that warned Quarry he had better make the best of it. 'Of course,' he said, switching on his trademark smile, 'you shall have as long as you like. We'll go to my office.' He extended his hand and ushered the policeman in front of him. 'Keep right on to the end.'

Leclerc walked slowly past the trading floor, examining his surroundings with interest. The big open room with its screens and time-zone clocks was more or less what he would have expected in a financial company. But the employees were a surprise—all young, and not a suit between them—and also the silence, with everyone at his desk and the air so still and heavy with concentration. The whole place reminded him of an examination hall in an all-male college. Or a seminary, perhaps: yes, a seminary of Mammon. The image pleased him.

Quarry opened his office door and stood aside to let Leclerc go in first, then went straight to his desk. 'Please, take a seat, will you, Inspector? Excuse me. I won't be a second.' He checked his screen. The European markets were all heading south fairly quickly. The DAX was off one per cent, the CAC two, the FTSE one and a half. The euro was down more than a cent against the dollar. He didn't have time to check all their positions, but the P&L showed VIXAL-4 already up $68 million on the day. Still, there was something about it all he found vaguely ominous, despite his good mood; he sensed a storm about to break. 'Great. That's fine.' He sat down cheerfully behind his desk. 'So then, have you caught this maniac?'

'Not yet. You and Dr Hoffmann have worked together for eight years, I understand.'

'That's right. We set up shop in 2002.'

Leclerc extracted his notebook and pen. He held them up. 'You don't object if I . . .?'

'I don't, although Alex would. We're not allowed to use carbon-based data-retrieval systems on the premises—that's notebooks and newspapers to you and me. The company is supposed to be entirely digital. But Alex isn't here, so don't worry about it. Go ahead.'

'That sounds a little eccentric.' Leclerc made a careful note.

'Eccentric is one way of putting it. Another would be stark raving bloody bonkers. But there you are. That's Alex. He's a genius, and they don't tend to see the world the same way we do. Quite a large part of my life is spent explaining his behaviour to lesser mortals.'

He was thinking of their lunch at the Beau-Rivage, when he had been obliged to interpret Hoffmann's actions to mere Earthlings twice—first when he didn't show up for half an hour ('He sends his apologies, he's working on a very complex theorem'), and then when he abruptly sped away from the table midway through the entrée ('Well, there goes Alex, folks—I guess he's having another of his eureka moments.'). But at the end of the day, Hoffmann could swing naked from the rafters playing the ukulele as far as they were concerned, as long as he made them a return of eighty-three per cent.

Leclerc said, 'Can you tell me how you two met?'

'Sure. When we started working together.'

'And how did that come about?'

'What, you want the whole love story?' Quarry put his hands behind his head and leaned back in his favourite position, feet up on his desk, always happy to tell a tale he had recounted a hundred times, maybe a thousand, polishing it into a corporate legend. 'It was around Christmas 2001. I was in London, working for a big American bank. I wanted to have a crack at starting my own fund. I knew I could raise the money—I had the contacts:

that was no problem—but I didn't have a game plan that would sustain over the long term.

'A guy in our Geneva office mentioned this science nerd at CERN he'd heard about who apparently had some interesting ideas on the algorithmic side. We thought we might hire him as a quant, but he wouldn't meet us, didn't want to know: mad as a hatter, apparently, total recluse. But there was just something about the sound of him that got me interested: I don't know—a pricking of my thumbs. As it happened, I had rented a chalet in Chamonix to go skiing over the holidays, so I thought I'd look him up . . .'

HE'D DECIDED to make contact on New Year's Eve: he had figured even a recluse might be forced to put up with company on New Year's Eve. He had driven down the valley to Geneva, in a hire car, and when he got close to Geneva Airport he had had to pull off the road and look at the Hertz map. Saint-Genis-Pouilly was straight ahead, just past CERN, in flat arable land that glistened in the frost—a small French town, a café in its cobbled centre, rows of neat houses with red roofs.

Quarry had rung Hoffmann's doorbell for a long time without getting a response. Eventually a neighbour had come out and told him that *tout le monde par le CERN* was at a party in a house near the sports stadium. He had stopped off at a bar on the way and picked up a bottle of cognac, and had driven around the darkened streets until he found it.

More than eight years later he could still remember his excitement as the car locked with its cheerful electronic squawk and he had set off down the pavement towards the multicoloured Christmas lights and the thumping music. In the darkness other people, singly and in laughing couples, were converging on the same spot, and he could somehow sense that this was going to be it: that the stars above this dreary little European town were in alignment. The host and hostess were standing at the door to greet their guests—Bob and Maggie Walton, English couple, older than their guests, dreary. They had looked mystified to see him, and even more so when he told them he was a friend of Alex Hoffmann's: he got the impression no one had ever said that before. Walton had refused his offer of the bottle of cognac. Not very friendly, but then in fairness he was crashing their party. He had asked where he might find Hoffmann, to which Walton had replied, with a shrewd look, that presumably Quarry would recognise him when he saw him, 'if you two are such good friends'.

Leclerc said, 'And did you? Recognise him?'

'Oh, yes. You can always spot an American, don't you think? He was on his own in the centre of a downstairs room and the party was kind of lapping around him—he was a handsome guy, stood out in a crowd—but he had this look of being somewhere else entirely. Not hostile, you understand—just not there. I've pretty much got used to it since then.'

'And that was the first time you spoke to him?'

'It was.'

'What did you say?'

'"Dr Hoffmann, I presume?"'

He had flourished the bottle of cognac and offered to go and find two glasses, but Hoffmann had said he didn't drink, to which Quarry had said, 'In that case, why did you come to a New Year's Eve party?' to which Hoffmann had replied that several overprotective colleagues had thought it was best if he was not left on his own on this particular night. But they were quite wrong, he added—he was happy to be on his own. And so saying, he had moved off into another room, obliging Quarry to follow him. That was his first taste of the legendary Hoffmann charm. 'I've come sixty miles to see you,' he said, chasing after him. 'The least you can do is talk to me.'

'Why are you so interested in me?'

'Because I gather you're developing some very interesting software. A colleague of mine at AmCor said he'd spoken to you.'

'Yeah, and I told him I'm not interested in working for a bank.'

'Neither am I.'

For the first time Hoffmann had glanced at him with a hint of interest. 'So, what do you want to do instead?'

'I want to set up a hedge fund.'

'What's a hedge fund?'

Sitting opposite Leclerc, Quarry threw back his head and laughed. Here they were today with $10 billion in assets under management, yet only eight years ago Hoffmann had not even known what a hedge fund was! And although a crowded New Year's Eve party was probably not the best place to attempt an explanation, Quarry had shouted the definition into Hoffmann's ear. 'It's a way of maximising returns at the same time as minimising risks. Needs a lot of mathematics to make it work. Computers.'

Hoffmann had nodded. 'OK. Go on.'

'Right.' Quarry had glanced around, searching for inspiration. 'Right, you see that girl over there, the one in that group with the short dark hair who keeps looking at you?' Quarry had raised the cognac bottle to her and smiled. 'Let's say I'm convinced she's wearing black knickers and I'm so sure that that's what she's wearing, I want to bet a million dollars on it. The trouble is, if I'm wrong, I'm wiped out. So I also bet she's wearing knickers that aren't black, but are any one of a whole basket of colours—let's say I put nine hundred and fifty thousand dollars on that possibility: that's the rest of the market; that's the hedge. This is a crude example, OK, in every sense, but hear me out. Now, if I'm right, I make fifty K, but even if I'm wrong I'm only going to lose fifty K, because I'm hedged. And because I'm never going to be called on to show ninety-five per cent of my million dollars, the only risk is in the spread—I can make similar bets with other people. And the beauty of it is if I can just get the colour of her underwear right fifty-five per cent of the time, I'm going to wind up very rich. She really is looking at you, you know.'

She had called across the room, 'Are you guys talking about me?' Without waiting for a reply, she had detached herself from her friends and come over to them, smiling. 'Gabby,' she had said, sticking out her hand to Hoffman.

'Alex.'

'And I'm Hugo.'

'Yes, you look like a Hugo.'

Her presence had irritated Quarry, and not only because she so obviously had eyes only for Hoffmann. He was still mid-pitch, and as far as he was concerned her role in this conversation was as illustration, not participant. 'We were making a bet,' he said sweetly, 'on the colour of your knickers.'

Quarry had made very few social mistakes in his life, but this was, as he freely acknowledged, a beaut. 'She's hated me ever since.'

Leclerc smiled and made a note.

At midnight the guests had gone into the garden to light small candles— 'You know, those tea-light things'—and put them into paper balloons. Dozens of softly glowing lanterns had lifted off, rising quickly in the cold still air like yellow moons. Afterwards Quarry had offered to drive Hoffmann home, whereupon Gabrielle, to his irritation, had tagged along, sitting in the back seat and giving them her life story without it being asked for. But even she had shut up when they got inside Hoffmann's apartment.

He had not wanted to let them in, but Quarry had pretended he needed to use the loo—'Honestly, it was like trying to get off with a girl at the end of a bad evening'—and so, reluctantly, Hoffmann had led them up to the landing and unlocked his door onto a vivarium of noise and tropical heat: motherboards whirring everywhere, red and green eyes winking out from under the sofa, behind the table, stacked on the bookshelves, black cables festooned from the walls like vines. On his return from the bathroom, Quarry had looked in at the bedroom—more computers taking up half the bed.

He had come back into the living room to find that Gabrielle had made room for herself on the sofa and kicked off her shoes. He had said, 'So, what's the deal here, Alex? It looks like Mission Control.'

At first Hoffmann had not wanted to talk about it, but gradually he had begun to open up. The object, he said, was autonomous machine-learning—to create an algorithm which, once given a task, would be able to operate independently and teach itself at a rate far beyond the capacity of human beings. Hoffmann was leaving CERN to pursue his research alone, which meant he would no longer have access to the experimental data emanating from the Large Electron–Positron Collider. For the past six months, therefore, he had been using data streams from the financial markets instead. Quarry had said it looked an expensive business. Hoffmann had agreed, although the main cost to him was having to find 2,000 francs a week simply to bring in sufficient power.

Quarry had said cautiously, 'I could help you out with the cost.'

'No need. I'm using the algorithm to pay for itself.'

It had taken an effort for Quarry to stifle his gasp of excitement. 'Really? That's a neat concept. And is it?'

'Sure.' Hoffmann had shown him the screen. 'These are the stocks it's suggested since December the 1st, based on data from the past five years. Then I just email a broker and tell him to buy or sell.'

Quarry had studied the trades. They were good, if small: nickel-and-dime stuff. 'Could it do more than cover costs? Could it make a profit?'

'Yeah, in theory, but that would need a lot of investment.'

'Maybe I could get you the investment.'

'You know what? I'm not actually interested in making money. No offence, but I don't see the point of it.'

Quarry couldn't believe what he was hearing: he didn't see the point!

He had said, 'But surely if you did make money then you could pay for more research? It would be what you're trying to do now, only on a vastly bigger scale. I don't want to be rude, man, but look around. You need to get some proper premises.'

'Perhaps a cleaner?' Gabrielle had added.

'She's right, you know—a cleaner wouldn't hurt. Look, Alex—here's my card. I'm going to be in the area for the next week or so. Why don't we meet up and talk this through?'

Hoffmann had taken the card and put it in his pocket without looking at it. 'Maybe.'

At the door Quarry had bent down and whispered to Gabrielle, 'Do you need a ride? I can drop you in town somewhere.'

'It's all right, thanks.' A smile as sweet as acid. 'I thought I might stay here for a while and settle your bet.'

QUARRY HAD PUT UP the seed money himself, used his annual bonus to move Hoffmann and his computers into a Geneva office: he needed a place where he could bring prospective clients and impress them with the hardware. He had hit the road of investors' conferences, moving from city to city in the US and across Europe, pulling his wheeled suitcase through fifty different airports. He had loved this part—loved being a salesman, he who travels alone, walking in cold to a conference room in a strange hotel and charming a sceptical audience. His method was to show them the independently back-tested results of Hoffmann's algorithm and the mouth-watering projections of future returns, then break it to them that the fund was already closed: he had only fulfilled his engagement to speak to be polite, but they didn't need any more money, sorry. Afterwards the investors would come looking for him in the hotel bar; it worked nearly every time.

Quarry paused in his tale to let Leclerc's cheap ballpoint catch up with his flow of words.

And to answer his questions: no, he was not sure when Gabrielle had moved in with Hoffmann as he and Alex had never seen one another much socially. No, he had not attended their wedding: it had been one of those solipsistic ceremonies conducted at sunset on a Pacific beach somewhere, with two hotel employees as witnesses. And no, he had not been told that Hoffmann had had a mental breakdown at CERN, although he had guessed it: when he went to the loo in his apartment that first night, he had rummaged through Hoffmann's bathroom cabinet (as one does) and found a veritable mini-pharmacy of antidepressants.

'That didn't put you off going into business with him?'

'What? The fact he wasn't "normal"? Good Lord, no. To quote Bill Clinton—not necessarily a fount of wisdom in all circumstances, I grant you, but right in this one—"Normalcy is overrated: most normal people are assholes".'

'When did you last see Dr Hoffmann?'

'At lunch. The Beau-Rivage. He left without explanation.'

'Did he seem agitated?'

'Not especially.' Quarry swung his feet off the desk and buzzed his assistant. 'Is Alex back yet, do we know?'

'No, Hugo. Sorry. Incidentally, Gana just called. The Risk Committee is waiting for you in his office. He's trying to get hold of Alex urgently. There's a problem, apparently. He said to tell you that "VIXAL is lifting the delta hedge". He said you'd know what that meant.'

'OK, thanks. Tell them I'm on my way.' Quarry released the switch and looked thoughtfully at the intercom. 'I'm going to have to leave you, I'm afraid.' For the first time he felt a definite spasm of anxiety in the pit of his stomach. He glanced across the desk at Leclerc, and suddenly he realised he had been gabbling away much too freely: the copper didn't seem to be investigating the break-in any more, so much as investigating Hoffmann.

'Is that important?' Leclerc nodded at the intercom. 'The delta hedge?'

'It is rather. Will you excuse me? My assistant will show you out.'

He left abruptly without shaking hands, and soon afterwards Leclerc found himself being conducted back across the trading floor, preceded by Quarry's red-headed gatekeeper. He noticed the atmosphere had changed. Around the room several groups of three or four were gathered round a screen, with one person seated, clicking on a mouse, and the others leaning over his shoulders. And now Leclerc was reminded much less of a seminary and more of doctors assembled at the bedside of a patient displaying grave and baffling symptoms. Standing beneath the TV was a man in a dark suit and tie. He was preoccupied, sending a text message on his mobile phone, and it took Leclerc a moment to recollect who it was.

'Genoud,' Leclerc muttered to himself. He'd distrusted the younger man ever since Genoud was a rookie under his command. There was, in his opinion, no principle his former colleague wouldn't betray, no deal he wouldn't cut, no blind eye he wouldn't turn—if he could make sufficient money and stay just within the law.

THE RISK COMMITTEE of Hoffmann Investment Technologies met for the second time that day at 16.25, fifty-five minutes after the opening of the US markets. Present were the Hon. Hugo Quarry, chief executive officer; Lin Ju-Long, chief financial officer; Pieter van der Zyl, chief operating officer; and Ganapathi Rajamani, chief risk officer, who took the minutes and in whose office the meeting was held.

Rajamani sat behind his desk like a headmaster. Under the terms of his contract he was not permitted to share in the annual bonus. This was supposed to make him more objective about risk, but in Quarry's opinion it had simply had the effect of turning him into a licensed prig who could afford to look down his nose at big profits. The Dutchman and the Chinese occupied the two chairs. Quarry sprawled on the sofa. Through the open blinds he watched his secretary, Amber, leading Leclerc towards reception.

The first item noted the absence, without explanation, of Dr Alexander Hoffmann, company president—and the fact that Rajamani wanted this dereliction of duty officially minuted was, to Quarry, the first indication that their chief prig officer was preparing to play hardball. Indeed, he seemed to take a grim delight in laying out just how perilous their position had become. He announced that since the last meeting of the committee, some four hours earlier, the fund's risk exposure had increased dramatically. Decisions needed to be taken fast.

He started reading facts from his computer. VIXAL had almost entirely abandoned the company's long position on S&P futures: its principal hedge against a rising market. It was also in the process of disposing of all its matching pairs of long bets on the eighty or so stocks it was shorting.

'I have never seen anything like it before in my life,' concluded Rajamani. 'The plain fact is, this company's delta hedge has gone.'

Quarry maintained a poker face, but even he was startled. If you took away the hedge—if you dispensed with all the intricate mathematical formulae that were supposed to ensure that you covered your risk—you might as well take the family silver and bet the lot on the 3.45 at Newmarket.

He held up a hand. 'OK, Gana. Thanks. We get it.' He needed to take charge of this meeting quickly. He was conscious that they were being scrutinised from the trading floor, and that the quants knew the hedge had gone. He sat up, hoisted his feet onto the coffee table and laced his fingers behind his head in a parody of nonchalance. 'So what is your recommendation?'

'There is only one option: override VIXAL and put the hedge back on.'

'You want us to bypass the algorithm without even consulting Alex?' asked Ju-Long.

'I would most certainly consult him if I could find him,' retorted Rajamani. 'However, he is not answering his phone.'

Van der Zyl said, 'I thought he was at lunch with you, Hugo?'

'He was. He left halfway through in a hurry.'

'Where did he go?'

'Lord knows. He just took off without a word.'

There was a silence.

'In my opinion,' said Ju-Long, 'and I would not say this except among us, I believe Alex is having some kind of breakdown.'

'Shall I minute this?' enquired Rajamani.

'No, you damn well won't.' Quarry pointed an elegantly shod toe across the table at Rajamani's computer terminal. 'Now hear me well and good, Gana: if there's any hint in these minutes of Alex in any way being mentally unreliable, then this company will be finished. No Alex, no company.'

For several seconds, Rajamani stared him out. Then he frowned and lifted his hands from the keyboard.

'OK then,' resumed Quarry. 'In the absence of Alex, let's try looking at this the other way. If we *don't* override VIXAL and put the delta hedge back on, what are the brokers going to say?'

Ju-Long said, 'They are just so hot on collateral these days, after what happened to Lehman's. They won't allow us to trade unhedged.'

'So when will we have to start showing them some money?'

'I would expect we'll need to provide a substantial level of fresh collateral before close of business tomorrow.'

'And how much do you reckon they'll want us to put up?'

'I'm not sure.' Ju-Long moved his neat, bland head from side to side, weighing it up. 'Maybe half a billion.'

'Half a billion total?'

'No, half a billion each.'

Quarry briefly closed his eyes. Five prime brokers—Goldman, Morgan Stanley, Citi, AmCor, Credit Suisse—half a billion to be deposited with each: $2.5 billion. Not promissory notes or long-term bonds, but the pure crystal meth of liquid cash, wired to them by 4 p.m. tomorrow. It was not that the company didn't have that kind of money: they only traded about twenty-five per cent of the cash lodged with them by their investors. The last time he looked, they had at least $4 billion stashed in US Treasury bills alone. But what a colossal hit on their reserves; what a step towards the precipice . . .

Rajamani interrupted his thoughts. 'I am sorry, but this is madness, Hugo. If the markets were to rise strongly, we would be left facing billions in losses. We might even go bankrupt.'

Ju-Long added: 'Even if we continue trading, it will be unfortunate, will it not, if the board of the fund has to be notified of our accelerated risk levels just as we are approaching individual investors to put another billion dollars into VIXAL-4?'

Quarry was unable to sit still any longer. He jumped up and would have paced around the office but there wasn't sufficient room. That this should happen now, after his $2 billion pitch! Unable to stomach Rajamani's expression of moral superiority for a moment longer, he turned his back on his colleagues and leaned against the glass partition, his palms spread wide, staring out at the trading floor, heedless of who was watching. For a moment he tried to visualise what it would be like to manage an uncontrolled, unhedged investment fund exposed to the full force of the global markets: the 700-trillion-dollar ocean of stocks and bonds, currencies and derivatives that rose and fell against one another day after day.

He turned and said, 'We really need to talk to Alex before we put on an override. I mean, when was the last time any of us actually *did* a trade?'

Rajamani said, 'With respect, that's not the point, Hugo.'

'Of course it's the point. This is an algorithmic hedge fund. We're not manned up to run a ten-billion-dollar book. I'd need at least twenty top-class traders out there with steel balls, who know the markets; all I've got are quants with dandruff who don't do eye contact.'

Van der Zyl said, 'The truth is, this issue should have been addressed earlier.' The Dutchman's voice was rich and deep and dark, marinated in coffee and cigars. 'VIXAL has been so successful for so long, we have all become dazzled by it. We have no adequate procedures for what to do if it fails.'

Quarry knew in his heart that this was true. He had allowed VIXAL's technology to enfeeble him. Nevertheless, he found himself rising to its defence. 'Can I just point out that it hasn't failed? The last time I looked, we were up sixty-eight mil on the day. What does the P and L say now, Gana?'

Rajamani checked his screen. 'Up seventy-seven,' he conceded.

'Well, thank you. That's a bloody odd definition of failure, isn't it? A system that made nine million dollars in the time it took me to shift my arse from one end of the office to the other?'

'Yes,' said Rajamani patiently, 'but it is a purely theoretical profit, which could be wiped out the moment the market recovers.'

'And is the market recovering?'

'No, I accept that at the moment the Dow is falling.'

'Well, there is our dilemma, gentlemen, right there. We all agree that the fund should be hedged, but we also have to recognise that VIXAL has demonstrated itself to be a better judge of the markets than we are.'

'Oh, come on, Hugo! VIXAL is supposed to operate within certain parameters of risk, and it isn't, therefore it is malfunctioning.'

'I don't agree. It was right about Vista Airways, wasn't it?'

'That was a coincidence. Even Alex acknowledged that.' Rajamani appealed to Ju-Long and van der Zyl. 'Come on, fellows, back me. To make sense of these positions, the whole *world* would have to crash in flames.'

Ju-Long put his hand up like a schoolboy. 'Since the subject has been raised, Hugo, could I just ask about the Vista Airways short? Did anyone see the news just now?'

Quarry sat down heavily on the sofa. 'No, I didn't. What are they saying?'

'They are saying that the crash was not a mechanical failure, but some kind of terrorist bomb.'

'OK. And?'

'It seems that a warning was posted on a jihadist website while the plane was still in the air. The intelligence authorities missed it. That was at nine o'clock this morning.'

'I'm sorry, LJ. I'm being slow on the uptake. What does it matter to us?'

'Nine o'clock was the time we started shorting the Vista Airways stock.'

It took Quarry a moment to react. 'You mean to say we're monitoring jihadist websites?'

'So it would appear.'

Van der Zyl said, 'That would be entirely logical, actually. VIXAL is programmed to search the web for incidences of fear-related language and observe market correlations. Where better to look?'

'But that's a quantum leap, isn't it?' asked Quarry. 'To see the warning, make the deduction, short the stock?'

'I don't know. We would have to ask Alex. But it is a machine-learning algorithm. Theoretically, it's developing all the time.'

Quarry leaned his head against the back of the sofa and looked at the ceiling, his eyes darting, trying to absorb the implications. 'God in heaven. I mean, I'm simply staggered by that.'

Ju-Long said, 'It could be a coincidence, of course. As Alex said this morning, the airline short was just part of a whole pattern of bets to the down side.'

'Yeah, but even so, that's the only short where we've actually sold the position and taken the profit. The others we're holding on to. Which poses the question: *why* are we holding on to them?' Quarry felt a tingling along the length of his spine. 'I wonder what it thinks is going to happen next?'

'It does not *think* anything,' said Rajamani impatiently. 'It is an algorithm, Hugo—a tool. It is no more alive than a wrench or a car-jack. And our problem is that it is a tool that has become too unreliable to depend on. Now, I really must ask this committee formally to authorise an override on VIXAL and start an immediate rehedging of the fund.'

Quarry looked at the others. He detected that something had just shifted in the atmosphere. Ju-Long was staring ahead impassively, van der Zyl examining a piece of fluff on the sleeve of his jacket. *Decent men,* he thought, *and clever, but weak*. And they liked their bonuses. It was all very easy for Rajamani to order VIXAL to be shut down; it would cost him nothing. But they had received $4 million each last year. He weighed the odds. They would give him no trouble, he decided. 'Gana,' he said pleasantly, 'I'm sorry, but I'm afraid we're going to have to let you go.'

'What?' Rajamani frowned at him. Then he tried to smile: a ghastly nervous rictus. He tried to treat it as a joke. 'Come on, Hugo . . .'

'If it's any consolation, I was going to fire you next week whatever happened. But now seems a better time. Write it down in your minutes, why don't you? "After a short discussion, Gana Rajamani agreed to relinquish his duties as chief risk officer, with immediate effect." Now clear your desk and get off home. And don't worry about money—I'm more than happy to pay you a year's salary just for the pleasure of not having to see you again.'

Rajamani was recovering: afterwards, Quarry was forced to give him credit for resilience at least. He said, 'Let me be clear about this—you're dismissing me simply for doing my job?'

'It's partly for doing the job, but mostly for being such a pain in the ass about doing it.'

Rajamani said, with some dignity, 'Thank you for that. I'll remember those words.' He turned to his colleagues. 'Piet? LJ? Are you going to intervene at this point?' Neither man moved.

Quarry got up and pulled the power cable out of the back of Rajamani's computer. It emitted a slight rattle as it died. 'Don't make copies of any of your files—the system will tell us if you do. Don't speak to any other employees. Leave the premises within fifteen minutes. Your compensation package is conditional on your abiding by our confidentiality agreement. Gentlemen,' he said to the other two, 'shall we leave him to his packing?'

Rajamani said, 'When word of this gets out, this company will be finished—I'll see to that.'

Quarry put his arms round Ju-Long and van der Zyl and guided them out of the office ahead of him. He closed the door without looking back. He knew that the entire drama had been played out to an audience of quants, but that could not be helped. He felt quite cheerful; he always felt good after he'd fired someone: it was cathartic.

'I'm sorry about that,' he said to Ju-Long and van der Zyl, 'but at the end of the day we're innovators in this shop. Gana is the kind of chap who'd have turned up on the quayside in 1492 and told Columbus he couldn't set sail because of his negative risk assessment.'

Ju-Long said, with an asperity Quarry had not expected, 'Risk was his responsibility, Hugo. You may have got rid of him, but you have not got rid of the problem.'

'I appreciate that, LJ, and I know he was your friend.' He put his hand on Ju-Long's shoulder. 'But don't forget that at this precise moment this company is about eighty million dollars richer than it was when we came to work this morning.' He gestured to the trading floor: the quants had all returned to their places; there was a semblance of normality.

They moved off along the side of the trading floor, Quarry in the lead. He was keen to get them away from the scene of Rajamani's assassination.

Van der Zyl said, 'You know, I was thinking that VIXAL must have extrapolated a general market collapse. If you look at the stocks it's shorting, they are not at all sector-specific.'

'Then there is the short on the S and P,' said Ju-Long.

'And the fear index,' added van der Zyl. 'You know, a billion dollars of options on the fear index—my God!'

It certainly is a hell of a lot, thought Quarry. He came to a halt. In the general welter of data that had been thrown around, he had rather missed the significance of the size of that position. He stepped across to a vacant terminal and quickly called up a chart of the VIX. Ju-Long and van der Zyl joined him. The graphic showed a gentle wave pattern in the volatility index over the past two trading days, the line rising and falling inside a narrow range. However, within the last ninety minutes it had definitely started trending upwards. It was too early to say whether this marked a significant escalation in the level of fear in the market itself. Nevertheless, even if it didn't, on a billion-dollar punt, they were looking at almost $100 million in profit right there.

Quarry pressed a switch and picked up the live audio feed from the pit of the S&P 500 in Chicago. 'Guys,' an American voice was saying, 'the only buyer I have on my sheet here, guys, from about nine twenty-six on, is a Goldman buyer at fifty-one even two hundred and fifty times. Other than that, guys, every entry I have has been big-time sell-side activity, guys . . .'

Quarry switched it off. He said, 'LJ, why don't you make a start on liquidating that two-point-five billion in T-bills, just in case we need to show some collateral tomorrow?'

'Sure, Hugo.' His eyes met Quarry's. He had seen the significance of the movement in the VIX; so had van der Zyl.

'We should try to talk at least every half hour,' said Quarry.

'And Alex?' said Ju-Long. 'He ought to see this.'

'I know Alex. He'll be back, don't you worry.'

11

Hoffmann had managed to hail a taxi on the Rue de Lausanne, one block away from the Hotel Diodati. He asked to be taken to an address in the suburb of Vernier, close to a local park—which meant the taxi had to perform an illegal U-turn. When they passed a police car heading in the opposite direction, he had sunk low in his seat and put a hand up to shield his eyes. The driver had watched him in the mirror. He was clutching the laptop. His phone rang once but he didn't answer it; afterwards he turned it off.

It was after four when the taxi finally approached the centre of Vernier, and Hoffmann abruptly leaned forward and said, 'Let me out here.' He handed over a 100-franc note and walked away without waiting for change.

Vernier stands on hilly ground above the right bank of the Rhône. In Hoffmann's memory he associated it with melancholy autumn afternoons. His hand shook as he pressed the buzzer of the detached building where he was supposed to have been cured eight years ago. It had been a shop once. Now its large downstairs window was frosted and it looked like a dentist's surgery. Did he have the strength to go through it all again? The first time he hadn't known what to expect; now he would be deprived of the vital armour of ignorance.

A young man's voice said, 'Good afternoon.'

Hoffmann gave his name. 'I used to be a patient of Dr Polidori. My secretary has made an appointment for me tomorrow but I need to see her now.'

'Wait, please.' There was a brief buzz as the door was unlocked.

Inside it was more comfortable than it used to be—a sofa and two easy chairs. Next to the receptionist was a certificate to practise: Dr Jeanne Polidori, with a master's degree in psychiatry and psychotherapy from the University of Geneva. The young man at the desk scrutinised him carefully. 'Go on up. It's the door straight ahead.'

'Yes,' said Hoffmann. 'I remember.'

The familiar creak of the stairs was enough to unleash a flood of old sensations. Sometimes he had found it almost impossible to drag himself to the top; on the worst days he had felt like a man without oxygen trying to climb Everest. Depression wasn't the word for it; burial was more accurate. Now he was sure he could not endure it again. He would rather kill himself.

The doctor was in her consulting room, sitting at her computer, and stood as he came in. She wasted no time on a greeting. 'Dr Hoffmann, I'm sorry, but I told your assistant on the phone I can't treat you without a hospital referral.'

'I don't want you to treat me.' He opened the laptop. 'I just want you to look at something. Can you do that at least?'

'It depends what it is.' She scrutinised him more closely. 'What happened to your head?'

'We had an intruder in our house. He hit me from behind.' Hoffmann bent his head forward and showed her his stitches.

'When did this happen?'

'Last night. This morning. I went to the University Hospital.'

'Did they give you a CAT scan?'

He nodded. 'They found some white spots. They could have come from the hit I took, or from something else—pre-existing.'

'Dr Hoffmann,' she said more gently, 'it sounds to me as though you *are* asking me to treat you.'

'No, I'm not.' He set Karp's laptop down in front of her. 'I just want your opinion about this.'

She looked at him dubiously then reached for her glasses, put them on and peered at the screen. As she scrolled through the document, he watched her expression.

'Well,' she said with a shrug, 'this is a conversation between two men, obviously, one who fantasises about killing and the other who dreams of dying and what the experience of death would be like. I would guess an internet chat room, a website—something like that. The one who wants to kill isn't very fluent in English; the would-be victim is.' She glanced at him over her glasses. 'I don't see what I'm telling you that you couldn't have worked out for yourself.'

'Is this sort of thing common?'

'Absolutely. It's one of the darker aspects of the web we now have to cope with. I have been consulted by the police about it several times. There are websites that encourage suicide pacts, especially among young people.'

Hoffmann sat down and put his head in his hands. He said, 'The man who fantasises about death—that's me, isn't it?'

'Well, you would know, Dr Hoffmann, better than I. Do you not remember writing this?'

'No, I don't. And yet there are thoughts there I recognise as mine— dreams I had when I was ill. I seem to have done other things lately I can't remember.' He looked at her. 'Could I have some problem in my brain that's causing this, do you think?'

'It's possible.' She put the laptop to one side and turned to her own computer screen. 'I see you terminated your treatment with me in November 2001 without any explanation. Why was that?'

'I was cured.'

'Don't you think that was for me to decide, rather than you?'

'No, I don't actually. I've been fine now for years. I got married. I started a company. Everything has been fine. Until this started.'

'You might have felt fine, but I'm afraid major depressive disorders like the one you had can recur.' She scrolled down her notes. 'You'll have to remind me what it was that triggered your illness in the first place.'

Hoffmann had kept it quarantined in his mind for so long, it was an effort to recall it. 'I had some serious difficulties in my research at CERN. There was an internal enquiry, which was very stressful. In the end they closed down the project I was working on.'

'What was the project?'

'Machine reasoning—artificial intelligence.'

'And have you been under a lot of similar stress recently?'

'Some,' he admitted.

'What sort of depressive symptoms have you had?'

'None. That's what's so weird.'

'What about the suicidal fantasies you used to have? They were very vivid, very detailed—any recurrence there?'

'No.'

'This man who attacked you—am I to take it he is the other participant in the conversation on the internet?'

Hoffmann nodded.

'Where is he now?'

'I'd prefer not to go into that.'

'Dr Hoffmann, show me your hands, please.'

Reluctantly he held out his hands.

'You have been in a fight?'

He took a long time to reply. 'Yes. It was self-defence.'

'That's all right. Sit down, please.'

He did as he was told.

She said, 'In my opinion, you need to be seen by a specialist right away. There are certain disorders—schizophrenia, paranoia—that can lead the sufferer to act in ways that are entirely out of character and which after-wards they simply can't remember. That may not apply in your case, but I don't think we can take a chance, especially if there are abnormalities on your brain scan. What I would like you to do now is take a seat downstairs while I talk to my colleague. Is that all right with you?'

'Yeah, sure.'

He waited for her to show him out, but she remained watchful behind her desk. Eventually he stood and picked up the laptop. 'Thanks,' he said. 'I'll go down to Reception.'

At the door, he turned. A thought had occurred to him. 'Those are my computer records you're looking at. What exactly is in them?'

'My case notes. A record of treatment—drugs prescribed, psychotherapy sessions and so on.'

'Do you tape your sessions with your patients?'

She hesitated. 'Yes.'

'And then what happens?'

'My assistant transcribes them.'

'And you keep the records on computer?'

'Yes.'

'May I see?' He was over at her desk in a couple of strides. She quickly put her hand on the mouse to close the document, but he grabbed her wrist.

'Please, just let me look at my own file.' He had to prise the mouse away from her. He said, 'I'm not going to hurt you. I just need to check what I told you.'

He felt bad seeing the fear in her eyes, but he would not yield, and after a couple of seconds she surrendered. She pushed her chair back and stood. He took her place in front of the screen with Karp's laptop. She moved to a safe distance and watched him from the doorway. She said, 'Where did you get that laptop?' But he wasn't listening. He was comparing the two screens, scrolling down first one and then the other, and the words on each were identical. Everything that he had poured out to her nine years ago had been cut and pasted and put onto the website where the German had read it.

He said, without looking up, 'Is this computer connected to the internet?' and then he saw that it was. He went into the system registry. It didn't take him long to find the malware—strange files of a type he had never seen before, four of them.

He said, 'Someone's hacked into your system. They've stolen my records.' But the consulting room was empty, the door ajar. He could hear her voice somewhere. It sounded as though she was on the telephone. He seized the laptop and thumped his way down the narrow carpeted staircase. The receptionist came round from the desk and tried to block his exit, but Hoffmann had no trouble pushing him aside.

Outside, he turned left and walked quickly down the street. He did not know where he was going. Normally he found that when he exercised— walked, jogged—it focused his thoughts. Not now. His mind was in turmoil.

After a while, the road was sliced off by the concrete wall of an elevated autoroute. It dwindled to a footpath that wandered left alongside the thunderous motorway, taking him down through some trees until he emerged on the bank of the river. The Rhône was wide and slow at this point, greenish-brown, opaque, bending lazily into open country with woodland rising steeply on the opposite bank. A footbridge, the Passerelle de Chèvres, linked the two sides. Hoffmann walked out onto the central span, and at the mid-point of the bridge, he stopped and climbed up onto the metal safety barrier. It would take him only a couple of seconds to drop the five or six metres into the slow-moving current and let himself be borne away.

And he was tempted. He was under no illusions: there would be a mass of DNA and fingerprint evidence in the hotel room linking him to the killing; his arrest was only a matter of time. He thought of what awaited him—a long gauntlet of police, lawyers, journalists, flashing cameras. He thought of Quarry, Gabrielle—Gabrielle especially.

But I am not mad, he thought. *I may have killed a man but I am* not *mad. I am either the victim of an elaborate plot to make me think I am mad, or someone is trying to set me up, blackmail me, destroy me.* He asked himself: did he trust the authorities to get to the bottom of such a fiendishly elaborate entrapment any better than he? The question answered itself.

He took the German's mobile phone out of his pocket. It hit the river with barely a splash, leaving a brief white scar on the muddy surface.

Professor Walton's assistant had left Gabrielle in the lobby of the Computing Centre at CERN and gone off to find him. Now she was alone, she was strongly tempted to flee. What had seemed a good idea in the bathroom in Cologny after finding his card—calling him, ignoring his surprise, asking if she could come over right away—now struck her as hysterical and embarrassing. Turning round to find the way out, she noticed an old computer in a glass case. When she went closer, she read that it was the NeXT processor that had started the World Wide Web at CERN in 1991. *Extraordinary*, she thought, *that it all began with something so mundane.*

'Pandora's Box,' said a voice behind her, and she turned to find Walton. 'Or the Law of Unintended Consequences. You start off trying to create the origins of the universe and you end up creating eBay. Come to my office. I don't have long, I'm afraid.'

He led her down a corridor and into an office block. It was dingy, functional—frosted-glass doors, too-bright strip lighting, institutional lino, grey paintwork—not at all what she had expected for the home of the Large Hadron Collider.

'This is where Alex used to sleep,' said Walton, throwing open the door of a spartan cell with two desks, two terminals and a view over a car park.

'Sleep?'

'Work, too, in fairness. Twenty hours of work a day, four hours of sleep. He used to roll out his mattress in that corner.' He smiled faintly at the memory and turned his grey eyes upon her. 'There's a problem, I assume.'

'Yes, there is.'

He nodded, as if expecting it. 'Come and sit down.' He led her along the passage to his office. On top of a filing cabinet a radio was quietly playing classical music, a string quartet. He switched it off. 'So, how can I help?'

'Tell me what went wrong here. I gather he had a breakdown, and I have a bad feeling it's happening all over again.'

Walton was sitting behind his desk. He studied her for a while. Eventually he said, 'Have you ever heard of the Desertron?'

THE DESERTRON, said Walton, was supposed to be America's Superconducting Super Collider—eighty-seven kilometres of tunnel being dug out of the rock at Waxahachie, Texas. But in 1993 the US Congress voted to abandon construction. That saved the US taxpayer about $10 billion. However, it also pretty much wiped out the career plans of an entire generation of American physicists, including those of the brilliant young Alex Hoffmann, then finishing his PhD at Princeton.

In the end Alex was one of the lucky ones—he was only twenty-five, but already sufficiently renowned to be awarded one of the very few non-European scholarships to work at CERN on the Large Electron–Positron Collider, forerunner of the Large Hadron Collider.

Alex had arrived in Geneva only a couple of years after CERN's scientists had invented the World Wide Web. And oddly enough, it was that which had seized his imagination: not re-creating the Big Bang or finding the God particle or creating antimatter, but the possibilities of serial processing power, emergent machine reasoning, a global brain.

'I was his section head at the Computing Centre. Maggie and I helped him get on his feet a bit. He used to babysit our boys when they were small. He was hopeless at it.'

'I bet.' She bit her lip at the thought of Alex with children.

'Completely *hopeless*. We'd come home and find him upstairs asleep in their beds and them downstairs watching television. He was always pushing himself far too hard, exhausting himself. He had this obsession with artificial intelligence, although he preferred to call it AMR—autonomous machine reasoning. Are you very technically minded?'

'No, not at all.'

'Well, without getting too technical about it, one of the big challenges we face here is simply analysing the sheer amount of experimental data we produce. It's now running around twenty-seven trillion bytes each day. Alex's solution was to invent an algorithm that would learn what to look for, so to speak, and then teach itself what to look for next. That would make it able to work infinitely faster than a human being. It was theoretically brilliant, but a practical disaster.'

'So it didn't work?'

'Oh yes, it worked. That was the disaster. It started spreading through the system like bindweed. Eventually we had to quarantine it, which meant basically shutting everything down. I'm afraid I had to tell Alex that that particular line of research was too unstable to be continued. It would require containment, like nuclear technology, otherwise one was effectively just unleashing a virus. He wouldn't accept it. He had to be forcibly removed from the facility on one occasion.'

'And that was when he had his breakdown?'

Walton nodded sadly. 'I never saw a man so desolate. You would've thought I'd murdered his child.'

12

By the time Hoffmann reached his office, it was the end of the working day—about 6 p.m. in Geneva, noon in New York. People were coming from the building, heading for home or a drink or the gym. He stood in a doorway opposite and checked for any sign of the police, and when they were not in evidence he went loping across the street, stared bleakly at the facial scanner and was admitted, passed straight through the lobby, up in one of the elevators, and onto the trading floor. The place was still full; most people here did not leave their desks until eight. He put his head down and walked to his office. Sitting at her desk, Marie-Claude watched him approach. She opened her mouth to speak and Hoffmann held up his hands. 'I know,' he said. 'I need ten minutes and then I'll deal with all of it. Don't let anyone in, OK?'

He went inside and closed the door. He sat in his expensive orthopaedic chair with its state-of-the-art tilt mechanism and opened the German's laptop. Who had hacked into his medical records?—that was the question. Whoever it was must be behind everything else.

His head was hurting again. He ran his fingers over the shaved area: it felt like the stitching on a football. His shoulders were locked with tension. He started massaging his neck, leaning back in his chair and looking up at the smoke detector as he had done a thousand times before when he was trying to focus his thoughts. He contemplated the tiny red light, identical to the one on their bedroom ceiling in Cologny. Slowly he stopped massaging. 'Shit,' he whispered.

He sat up straight and looked at the screensaver image on the laptop: the picture of himself, gazing up with a vacant, unfocused expression. He clambered onto his chair. It shifted treacherously beneath his feet as he stepped from it onto his desk. The smoke detector was square, made of white plastic, with a grille that presumably covered the alarm itself. He felt around the edges. It seemed to be glued to the ceiling tile. He pulled at it and twisted it, and finally in fear and frustration he yanked it free.

The screech of protest it set up was physical in its intensity. The air pulsed with it. It was still connected to the ceiling by an umbilical cord of wire, and when he put his fingers into the back of it to try to shut it down, he received an electric shock that was as vicious as an animal bite; it travelled all the way to his heart. He cried out, dropped it, let it dangle, and shook his fingers vigorously. The noise was an assault: he felt his ears would bleed unless he stopped it quickly. He grabbed the detector by the casing this time and pulled with all his weight, almost swinging on it, and away it came, bringing down a chunk of the ceiling with it. The sudden silence was as shocking as the din.

MUCH LATER, when Quarry found himself reliving the next couple of hours, and when he was asked which moment for him had been the most frightening, he said that oddly enough it was this one: when he heard the alarm and went running from one end of the trading floor to the other, to find Hoffmann flecked with blood, covered in dust, standing on a desk beneath a hole in his ceiling, gabbling that he was being spied upon.

Quarry was not the first on the scene. The door was already open and Marie-Claude was inside with some of the quants. Quarry shouldered his way past them and ordered them all to get back to their work. He could tell at once that Hoffmann had been through some kind of trauma.

He said, as calmly as he could, 'OK, Alexi, how's it going up there?'

'Look for yourself,' cried Hoffmann excitedly. He jumped down from the desk and held out his palm. On it were the components of the dismantled smoke alarm. He poked through them with his forefinger and held up a small lens with a wire trailing from the back. 'Do you know what that is?'

'I'm not sure that I do, no.'

'It's a webcam.' He let the dismantled pieces trickle through his fingers and across his desk; some rolled to the floor. 'Look at this.' He gave Quarry the laptop. He tapped the screen. 'Where do you think that picture was taken from?'

He sat down again and lolled back in his chair. Quarry looked at him and then at the screen and back again. He glanced up at the ceiling. 'Bloody hell. Where did you get this?'

'It belonged to the guy who attacked me last night.'

Even at the time Quarry registered the odd use of the past tense— *belonged?*—and wondered how the laptop had come into Hoffmann's possession. There was no time to ask, however, as Hoffmann jumped to his feet. 'Come,' he said, beckoning. 'Come.' He led Quarry by the elbow out of his office and pointed to the ceiling above Marie-Claude's desk, where there was an identical detector. He put his finger to his lips. Then he took him to the edge of the trading floor and showed him—one, two, three, four more. There was one in the boardroom, too. There was even one in the men's room. He climbed up onto the wash basins. He could just reach it. He pulled hard and it came away in a shower of plaster. He jumped down and showed it to Quarry. Another webcam. 'They're everywhere. I've been noticing them for months without ever really seeing them. There'll be one in your office. I've got one in every room at home—even in the bedroom. Christ. Even in the bathroom.' He put his hand to his brow, only just registering the scale of it himself. 'Unbelievable.'

Quarry had always had a sneaking fear that their rivals might be trying to spy on them. That was why he had hired Genoud's security consultancy. He turned the detector over in his hands, appalled. 'You think there's a camera in *all* of them?'

'Well, we can check them out, but yeah—yeah, I do.'

'Yet we pay a fortune to Genoud to sweep this place for bugs.'

'But that's the beauty of it—he must be the guy who put all this in, don't you see? He did my house too, when I bought it. He's got us under twenty-four-hour-a-day surveillance.'

He was so certain he was right, Quarry found his paranoia contagious. He used his cellphone to call his assistant. 'Amber, would you please track down Maurice Genoud and tell him to drop whatever else he's doing and come to Alex's office.' He hung up. 'Let's hear what the bastard has to say. I wonder what his game is.'

'That's pretty obvious, isn't it? We're a hedge fund returning an eighty-three-per-cent profit. If someone set up a clone of us, copying all our trades, they'd make a fortune. The only thing I don't understand is why he's done all this other stuff.'

'What other stuff?'

'Set up an offshore account in the Cayman Islands, transferred money in and out of it, sent emails in my name, bought me a book full of stuff about fear and terror, sabotaged Gabby's exhibition, hacked into my medical records and hooked me up with a psychopath. It's like he's been paid to drive me mad.'

Listening to him, Quarry started to feel uneasy again, but before he could say anything his phone rang. It was Amber.

'Mr Genoud was only just downstairs. He's on his way up.'

'Thanks.' He said to Hoffmann, 'Apparently he's in the building already. Maybe he knows we're onto him.'

'Maybe.' Suddenly Hoffmann was on the move once more—out of the men's room, across the passage, into his office. Another idea had occurred to him. He wrenched open the drawer of his desk and pulled out the volume of Darwin he had called Quarry about at midnight.

'Look at this,' he said, flicking through the pages. He held it up, open at a photograph of an old man. 'What do you see?'

'I see some Victorian lunatic seemingly terrified out of his wits.'

'Yeah, but look again. Do you see these calipers?'

Quarry looked. A pair of hands, one either side of the face, was applying thin metal rods to the forehead. The victim's head was supported in some kind of steel headrest.

'The calipers are being applied by a French doctor called Guillaume-Benjamin-Armand Duchenne. He believed that the expressions of the human face are the gateway to the soul.' He waited for Quarry to see the importance of what he was saying and, when he continued to look baffled, he added: 'It's an experiment to induce the facial symptoms of fear for the purpose of recording them on camera.'

'OK,' said Quarry cautiously. 'I get it.'

Hoffmann waved the book in exasperation. 'Well, isn't that exactly what's been happening to *me*? I'm the subject of an experiment designed to make me experience fear, and my reactions are being monitored.'

After a moment when he could not entirely trust himself to speak, Quarry said, 'Well, I'm very sorry to hear that, Alexi. That must be a horrible feeling.'

'The question is: who's doing it, and why? Obviously it's not Genoud's idea. He's just the tool . . .'

But now it was Quarry's turn not to pay attention. He was thinking of his responsibilities as CEO—to their investors, to their employees and (he was not ashamed to admit it afterwards) to himself. He was remembering Hoffmann's medicine cabinet all those years ago, filled with enough mind-altering drugs to keep a junkie happy for six months. 'Let's sit down,' he suggested. 'We need to talk about a few things.'

Hoffmann was irritated to be interrupted in mid-flow. 'Is it urgent?'

'It is rather, yes.' Quarry took a seat on the sofa and gestured to Hoffmann to join him.

But Hoffman ignored the sofa and went and sat behind his desk. He swept his arm across the surface, clearing it of the detritus of the smoke detector. 'OK, go ahead.'

Quarry said, 'We have a problem with VIXAL-4. It's taken off the delta hedge.'

Hoffmann stared at him. 'Don't be ridiculous.' He pulled his keyboard towards him, logged on and began going through their positions—by sector, size, type, date. The mouse clicks were as rapid as Morse code, and each screen they brought up was more astonishing to him than the last. He said, 'But this isn't what it's programmed to do.'

'Most of it happened between lunchtime and the US opening. We weren't able to get hold of you. The good news is that it's guessing right—so far. The Dow is off by about a hundred, and if you look at the P and L we're up by over two hundred mil on the day.'

'*But it's not what it's supposed to do,*' repeated Hoffmann. Of course there would be a rational explanation: there always was. He would find it eventually. It had to be linked to everything else that was happening to him. 'OK, first off, are we sure this data is correct? Could it be sabotage of some kind? A virus?' He was remembering the malware on his psychiatrist's computer. 'Maybe the whole company is under cyber-attack by someone, or some group—have we thought of that?'

'Maybe we are, but that doesn't explain the short on Vista Airways—and, believe me, that's starting to look like somewhat more than a coincidence.'

'Yeah, well, it can't be. We've already been over this—'

Quarry cut him off impatiently. 'I know we have, but now it seems the crash wasn't caused by mechanical failure after all. Apparently there was a bomb warning put up on some Islamic terrorist website while the plane was in the air. The FBI missed it; we didn't.'

Hoffmann couldn't take it in at first: too much information was coming at him too quickly. 'But that's way outside VIXAL's parameters. That would be an extraordinary inflection point—a quantum leap.'

Marie-Claude tapped on the door and opened it. 'Monsieur Genoud is here.'

Quarry said to Hoffmann, 'Let me handle this.'

Marie-Claude stood aside to let the ex-policeman enter. His gaze went immediately to the hole in the ceiling. 'Come in, Maurice,' said Quarry. 'Close the door. As you can see, we've been doing a little DIY in here, and we were wondering if you have any explanation for this.'

'I don't believe so,' said Genoud, shutting the door. 'Why should I?'

Hoffmann said, 'He's a cool one, Hugo. You've got to give him that.'

Quarry held up his hand. 'OK, Alex, please just wait a minute, will you? All right, Maurice. We need to know how long this has been going on. We need to know who's paying you. And we need to know if you've planted anything inside our computer systems. It's urgent, because we're in a very volatile trading situation. We will call in the police to handle this, if we have to. So my advice is to be absolutely frank.'

After a few moments Genoud looked at Hoffmann. 'Is it OK for me to tell him?'

Hoffmann said, 'OK to tell him what?'

'You are putting me in a very awkward position, Dr Hoffmann.'

Hoffmann said to Quarry, 'I don't know what he's talking about.'

'Very well, you can't expect me to maintain my discretion under these circumstances.' Genoud turned to Quarry. 'Dr Hoffmann gave me instructions when you moved into these offices to set up concealed cameras. I guessed he wasn't telling you about it. But he's the company president, so I thought it was permissible for me to do as he asked.'

Hoffmann smiled and shook his head. 'Hugo, this is total, utter bullshit. I haven't had one single conversation with this guy about planting cameras—why would I want to film my own company?'

Genoud said, 'I never said we had a conversation. As you well know, Dr Hoffmann, I only ever received instructions from you by email.'

Email—again! Hoffmann said, 'You're seriously telling me that you put in all these cameras and never, in all these months, did we have a conversation about any of it?'

'No.'

Hoffmann emitted a sound that conveyed contempt and disbelief.

Quarry said to Genoud, 'That's hardly credible. Didn't it strike you as bizarre at all?'

'Not especially. I got the impression this was all off the books, so to speak. That he didn't want to acknowledge what was going on.'

'And how in the hell am I supposed to have paid you for all this?'

'By cash transfer,' said Genoud, 'from a bank in the Cayman Islands.'

That brought Hoffmann up short. Quarry was looking at him intently. 'OK,' he conceded, 'supposing you did receive emails. How did you know it was not someone pretending to be me?'

'Why would I think that? It was your company, your email address; I was paid from your bank account.'

Hoffmann swore and slammed his fist on his desk in frustration. 'Here we go again. I'm supposed to have ordered a book on the internet. I'm supposed to have bought Gabrielle's entire exhibition on the internet. I'm supposed to have asked a madman to kill me on the internet . . .' He realised Quarry was looking at him in dismay. 'Who's doing this to me, Hugo?' he said in despair. 'Doing this and filming it? You've got to help me sort this out. It's like a nightmare I'm caught in.'

Quarry's mind was reeling from it all. It took some effort to keep his voice calm. 'Of course I'll help you, Alex. Let's just try to get to the bottom of this.' He turned back to Genoud. 'Right, Maurice, presumably you've kept these emails? Can you access them now?'

'Yes, if that is what you want.' Genoud had become very stiff and formal during the last few exchanges, standing erect as if his honour as a former police officer was being called into question.

'All right then, you won't mind showing them to us. Let him use your computer, Alex.'

Hoffmann rose from his seat like a man in a trance. Fragments of the smoke detector crunched beneath his feet. Reflexively, he looked up at the mess he had made of the ceiling. The hole where the tile had come down opened onto a dark void. Inside, where the trailing wires were touching, a blue-white spark flashed intermittently. A worm of suspicion began to form in his mind.

Genoud, bent over the computer, said triumphantly, 'There!' He straightened and stood aside to let Hoffmann and Quarry examine his emails. He had filtered his saved messages so that only those from Hoffmann were listed—scores of them, dating back almost a year. Quarry took the mouse and started clicking on them at random.

'I'm afraid it's your email address on all of these, Alex,' he said. 'No question of it.'

'Yeah, I bet it is, but I still didn't send them.'

'All right, but then who did?'

Hoffmann brooded. This was beyond hacking now, or compromised security or a clone server. It was more fundamental, as if the company had somehow developed dual operating systems.

Quarry was still reading. 'I don't believe it,' he said. 'You even snooped on yourself in your own house . . .'

'Actually, I hate to keep repeating myself, but I didn't.'

'Well, I'm sorry, Alexi, but you did. Listen to this: "To: Genoud. From: Hoffman. Required Cologny webcam surveillance units twenty-four concealed immediate . . ."'

'Come on, man. I don't talk like that. Nobody talks like that.'

'Somebody must: it's here on the screen.'

Hoffman suddenly turned to Genoud. 'Where does all the information go? What happens to the images, the audio recordings?'

Genoud said, 'As you know, it's all sent to a secure server.'

'But there must be *thousands* of hours of it,' exclaimed Hoffmann. 'When would anyone ever have time to review it all? You'd need a whole dedicated team. There aren't the hours in the day.'

Genoud shrugged. 'I don't know. I've often wondered that myself. I just did what I was ordered.'

Only a machine can analyse that quantity of information, thought Hoffmann. It would have to be using the latest face-recognition technology; voice-recognition as well; search tools . . .

He was interrupted by another outcry from Quarry: 'Since when did we start leasing an industrial unit in Zimeysa?'

Genoud said, 'I can tell you exactly, Mr Quarry: since six months ago. It's a big place—fifty-four Route de Clerval. Dr Hoffmann ordered a special new security and surveillance system for it.'

Hoffmann said, 'What's in this unit?'

'Computers.'

'Who put them in?'

'I don't know. A computer company.'

Hoffmann said, 'So I deal with entire companies by email, too?'

'I don't know. Presumably, yes.'

Quarry was still clicking through the emails. 'This is unbelievable,' he said to Hoffmann. 'According to this, you also own the freehold of this entire building.'

But Hoffmann had stopped listening. He was thinking back to his time at CERN, to the memo Bob Walton had circulated recommending that Hoffmann's research project, AMR-1, be shut down. It had included a warning issued by Thomas S. Ray, software engineer and Professor of Zoology at the University of Oklahoma:

> . . . freely evolving autonomous artificial entities should be seen as potentially dangerous to organic life, and should always be confined by some kind of containment facility, at least until their real potential is well understood . . . Evolution remains a self-interested process, and even the interests of confined digital organisms may conflict with our own.

He took a breath. 'Hugo, I need to have a word with you—alone.'

'All right, sure. Maurice, would you mind stepping outside for a minute?'

'No, I think he should stay here and start sorting this out.' He said to Genoud, 'I want you to make a copy of the file of emails that originate from me. I also want a list of every job you've done that I'm supposed to have ordered. I especially want a list of everything to do with this industrial facility in Zimeysa. Then I want you to start stripping out every camera and every bug in every building we have, starting with my house. And I need it done tonight. Is that understood?'

Once they were outside the office and the door was closed, Quarry said, 'I hope to God you've got some kind of explanation for this, Alex, because I have to tell you—'

Hoffmann held up a warning finger and raised his eyes to the smoke detector above Marie-Claude's desk.

Quarry said, with heavy emphasis, 'Oh, right, I understand. We'll go to my office.'

'No. Not there. It's not safe. Here . . .'

Hoffmann led him into the washroom and closed the door. The pieces of the smoke detector were where he had left them, next to the basin. He could barely recognise his own reflection in the mirror. He looked like someone who might have escaped from the secure wing of a mental hospital. He said, 'Hugo, do you think I'm insane?'

'Yes, since you ask, I bloody well do. Or probably. I don't know.'

'No, it's OK. I'm not blaming you if that's how you feel, and what I'm about to say isn't going to make you feel any more confident.' He could hardly believe he was saying it himself. 'I think the basic problem we have here is VIXAL. It's possibly doing somewhat more than I anticipated.'

Quarry squinted at him. 'What are you talking about? I don't follow. More than you anticipated in what way?'

Hoffmann said carefully, 'VIXAL may be making decisions that are not entirely compatible with our interest.'

'You mean our interest as a company?'

'No. I mean *our* interest—the human interest.'

'Aren't they the same?'

'Not necessarily.'

'Sorry. Being dim here. You mean you think it's somehow actually doing all this itself—the surveillance and everything?'

In fairness to him, Hoffman thought, *Quarry at least seems to be treating the suggestion seriously.*

'I'm not sure. We need to take this one step at a time until we have enough information to make a full assessment. But I think as a first move we have to unwind the positions that it's taken in the market.'

'Even though it's making money?'

'It's not a question of making money any more—can't you forget about money just for once?' It was becoming increasingly hard for Hoffmann to maintain his composure, but he managed to finish quietly, 'We're way beyond that now.'

Quarry folded his arms and thought it over, staring at the tiled floor. 'Are you sure you're in a fit state to be taking this kind of decision?'

'I am, really. Trust me, please, will you, if only for the sake of the last eight years?'

For a long moment they looked at one another, the physicist and the financier. Quarry frankly didn't know what to make of it. But as he said afterwards, it was Hoffmann's genius that had brought in the punters, his machine that had made the money in the first place, his call to shut it down. 'It's your baby,' he said. He stood clear of the door.

Hoffmann went out onto the trading floor with Quarry at his heels. He clapped his hands. 'Listen up, everybody!' He climbed onto a chair so the quants could see him. 'I need you all just to gather round for a minute.'

They rose from behind their screens at his command, a ghost army of PhDs. He could see their exchange of glances as they came over; some were whispering. They were obviously all on edge with what was happening. Van der Zyl came out of his office, and so did Ju-Long; he couldn't see Rajamani. He cleared his throat.

'OK, we've obviously got a few anomalies to deal with here—to put it mildly—and I think for safety's sake we're going to have to start dismantling these positions we've built up over the last few hours.'

He checked himself. He didn't want to create a panic. He was also conscious of the smoke detectors dotted across the ceiling. Presumably everything he said was being monitored. 'This doesn't mean we have a problem with VIXAL necessarily, but we do need to find out why it's been doing some of the things it has been doing. I don't know how long that's going to take, so in the meantime we need to get that delta back in line—hedge it out with longs in other markets; even liquidate if it comes to it.'

Quarry said, to Hoffmann and the room, 'We'll need to tread carefully. If we start liquidating positions this size too quickly, we'll move prices.'

Hoffmann nodded. 'That's true, but VIXAL will help us achieve the optimums, even in override.' He looked up at the row of digital clocks beneath the TV screens. 'We've got just over three hours before America closes.'

'If you encounter any problems,' said Quarry, 'Alex and I will be here to help out. And don't anyone think for a second that this is a retreat. We took in an additional two billion in fresh investment today—so this shop is still growing, OK? We'll recalibrate over the next twenty-four hours and move on to even bigger and better things. Any questions?' Someone raised their hand. 'Yep?'

'Is it true you just fired Gana Rajamani?'

Hoffmann glanced at Quarry in surprise. He'd thought he was going to wait until the crisis had passed.

Quarry didn't miss a beat. 'Gana has been wanting to rejoin his family in London for some weeks.' An exclamation of surprise arose from the meeting. Quarry held up his hand. 'I can assure you he's completely on side with everything we're doing. Now, does anybody else have anything to say?'

'Actually, there is one last thing, Hugo,' Hoffmann said. Staring out across the upturned faces of his quants, he felt for the first time a sudden sense of comradeship. He had recruited all of them. The team—the company—his creation: 'It's been, as some of you have probably guessed by now, an absolute bitch of a day. And whatever happens to me, I just want to tell you all . . .' To his horror he was welling up, his throat thick with emotion, his eyes brimming. He looked down at his feet, waiting until he had himself under control, then raised his head again. He had to rush to get through it or he would have broken down completely: 'I simply want you to know I'm very proud of what we've done together here. It's never been just about the money—certainly not for me, and I believe not for most of you, either. So thanks. It's meant a lot. That's it.'

There was no applause; simply mystification. Hoffmann stepped down from the chair. He could see Quarry looking at him in a strange way, although the CEO recovered quickly and called out, 'All right, everyone, that's the end of the pep talk. Back to your galleys, slaves, and start rowing. There's a storm coming in.'

As the quants began to move away, Quarry said to Hoffmann: 'That sounded like a farewell speech.'

'It wasn't meant to.'

'Well it did. What do you mean, "whatever happens to me"?' But before Hoffmann could answer, someone called out, 'Alex, have you got a second? We seem to have a problem here.'

THE MAN WHO HAD called Hoffmann over to his six-screen array was an Oxford PhD named Croker, who Hoffmann had recruited on the same trip that Gabrielle had hit upon the idea of making art out of body scans. He had been attempting to put a manual override on the algorithm in order to begin liquidating their massive position on the VIX, but the system had denied him authority.

'Let me try,' said Hoffmann. He took Croker's place and entered his own password, which was supposed to give him unrestricted access to every part of VIXAL, but even his request was turned down.

As Hoffmann clicked the mouse in vain and tried various other routes into the system, Quarry stood looking over his shoulder, together with van der Zyl and Ju-Long. He felt surprisingly calm; resigned, even. Part of him had always known that the moment one surrendered oneself to a machine operated by someone else, one was acquiescing in one's own doom. After a while he said, 'I assume the nuclear option is just to unplug the thing?'

Hoffmann replied, without turning round, 'But if we do that, then we simply cease to trade, period. We don't unwind our present positions: we're just frozen into them.'

Little cries of alarm and astonishment were erupting all over the room. One by one the quants were abandoning their terminals and coming over to watch what Hoffmann was doing.

On the big screens, the afternoon reports from Wall Street continued as normal. The lead story was riots in Athens against the Greek government's austerity measures—whether Greece would default, the contagion spread, the euro collapse. And still the hedge fund was making money: in a way that was the weirdest aspect of all. Quarry turned away for a few seconds to consult the P&L on the next-door screen: it was now up by almost $300 million on the day. Part of him still wondered why they were so desperate to bypass the algorithm. They had created King Midas out of silicon chips; in what way was its phenomenal profitability not in their interest?

Suddenly Hoffmann lifted his hands from the keyboard in the dramatic manner of a concert pianist finishing a concerto. 'This is no good. There's no response. The whole system needs to be shut down completely and quarantined until we find out what's wrong with it.'

Ju-Long said: 'How are we going to do that?'

'Why don't we just do it the old-fashioned way?' suggested Quarry. 'Let's take VIXAL offline and simply call up the brokers on the phone and get them on email and tell them to start winding down the positions?'

'We'll need to come up with some plausible explanation for why we're no longer using the algorithm to go straight to the trading floor.'

'We tell them there's been a catastrophic loss of power in our computer room and we have to withdraw from the market until it's fixed. And like all the best lies, it has the merit of being almost true.'

Van der Zyl said, 'In fact, we only have to get through another two hours and fifty minutes and then the markets are closed in any case. By Monday morning the book will be neutral and we will be safe—as long as the markets don't stage a strong rally in the meantime.'

'The Dow's off a full percentage point already,' said Quarry. 'The S and P's the same. There's no way this market's going to end the day up.' The four executives of the company looked from one to another. 'So is that it? We're agreed?' They all nodded.

Hoffmann said, 'I'll do it.'

It seemed to him a long walk across the trading floor to the computer room. He could sense the eyes of everyone like a weight upon his back. When he presented his face to the scanner, the bolts slid back and the door opened. In the cold, noisy darkness, the forest eyes of a thousand CPUs blinked at his approach. It felt like an act of murder, just as it had at CERN when they'd closed him down there all those years ago. Nevertheless, he opened the metal box and grasped the isolator handle. It was only the end of a phase, he told himself: the work would go on. He flicked the handle, and within a couple of seconds the lights and the sound had faded. Only the noise of the air-conditioning disturbed the chilly silence. It was like a mortuary. He headed back towards the glow of the open door.

As he approached the cluster of quants gathered around the six-screen array, everyone turned to look at him. Quarry said, 'What happened? You couldn't go through with it?'

'Yes, I went through with it.' He looked past Quarry's mystified face. On the screens VIXAL-4 was continuing to trade. Puzzled, he went to the terminal and began flicking between the screens.

Quarry said quietly to one of the quants, 'Go back and check, will you?'

Hoffmann said, 'I am capable of throwing a switch, Hugo. I'm not so crazy I don't know the difference between on and off. God—will you look at that?' In every market VIXAL was continuing to trade: it was shorting the euro, piling into Treasury bonds, adding to its position on VIX futures.

From the entrance to the computer room the quant shouted, 'The power's all shut down!'

An excited murmur broke out.

'So where is the algorithm if it's not on our hardware?' demanded Quarry.

Hoffmann didn't answer.

'I think you will find that is something the regulators will also be asking,' said Rajamani.

Afterwards, no one was sure how long he had been watching them. Someone said he had been in his office all along: they had seen his fingers parting the blinds as Hoffmann delivered his speech on the trading floor. Someone else claimed to have come across him at a spare terminal in the boardroom uploading data. Yet another quant, a fellow Indian, even confessed that Rajamani had asked if he would be willing to act as his informant inside the company. The one thing everyone could agree on was that Quarry had made a grievous error in not having the chief risk officer escorted off the premises by security the moment he had been fired; in the chaos of events, he had simply forgotten about him.

Rajamani stood on the edge of the trading floor holding a cardboard box containing his personal effects—the photographs of his graduation, his wedding, his children; a tin of Darjeeling tea he kept in the staff refrigerator for his personal use and which no one else was allowed to touch.

Quarry said hoarsely, 'I thought I told you to bugger off.'

'I am going right now,' Rajamani replied, 'and you'll be glad to know I have an appointment at the Geneva Finance Ministry tomorrow morning. This technology is completely out of control and I can promise you, Alex and Hugo, that the US Securities and Exchange Commission and the Financial Securities Authority will revoke your access to every market in America and London pending an investigation. Shame on you.'

With a final sweeping glare of fury and contempt, Rajamani thrust out his chin and walked steadily towards Reception.

'Yes, go on, clear off,' Quarry called after him. 'You'll find ten billion dollars buys us a heck of a lot of lawyers. And we're going to come after you personally for breach of contract!'

'Wait!' shouted Hoffmann.

Quarry said, 'Leave him, Alex—don't give him the satisfaction.'

'But he's right, Hugo. If VIXAL's somehow migrated out of our control, that could pose a real systemic risk. We've got to keep him on side until we can figure it out.' He set off after Rajamani and caught up with him by the elevators. The corridor was deserted. 'Gana,' he said. 'Please. Let's talk.'

'I've nothing to say to you, Alex.' He was clutching his box. His back was to the elevator control panel, and he hit the call button with his elbow. 'It's not personal. I'm sorry.' The doors opened. He turned, stepped smartly through them and plunged from view. The doors closed.

For a couple of seconds Hoffmann stood motionless, unsure of what he had just witnessed. He pressed the call button. The doors slid open onto the empty glass tube of the elevator shaft. He peered over the edge, down maybe fifty metres of translucent column, until it dwindled into the darkness and silence of the underground car park. He shouted hopelessly, 'Gana!' There was no response.

He sprinted along the corridor to the emergency exit and half ran, half jumped his way floor after floor down the concrete staircase, all the way to the basement, out into the garage and across to the elevator doors. He jammed his fingers into the gap and tried to prise them apart, but they kept closing on him. He stepped back and prowled around looking for some tool he could use. Then he saw a metal door with a lightning-flash symbol and tried that. Behind it was a space for storing tools. He found a big crowbar, ran back to the elevator doors and jammed it into the gap, working it back and forth. The doors parted enough for him to shove his foot into the space. Some automatic mechanism was triggered and the doors trundled open.

Light falling from the upper floors showed Rajamani lying face down in the well of the elevator shaft. His photographs lay scattered around him. Hoffmann jumped down next to him. He stooped and grasped Rajamani's hand, which was shockingly warm and smooth, and for the second time that day tried to feel for a man's pulse, but again he couldn't find one.

Behind and just above him, the doors rattled shut. Hoffmann looked around in panic as the elevator car began its descent. The tube of light shrank rapidly as the car hurtled down—the fifth floor went, and then the fourth. He grabbed the crowbar and tried to jam it back into the doors, but lost his footing. He fell backwards and lay next to Rajamani's corpse, looking up at the bottom of the car as it hurtled at him, holding the crowbar upright in both hands above his head like a spear to fend off a charging beast. The light faded, vanished, something heavy hit his shoulder, and then the crowbar jumped and went as rigid as a pit prop. For several seconds he could feel it taking the strain. He was screaming blindly in the absolute darkness at the elevator's floor, which must have been only inches from his face, braced for the crowbar to bend or slip. But then a gear changed, the note of the motor became a whine, the crowbar came loose in his hands and the car began to rise, accelerating rapidly up its cathedral column of glass.

He scrambled up and shoved the crowbar back between the doors, working it into the gap, parting them a fraction. The elevator had climbed to its highest point and stopped. There was a clunk, and he heard it start to plunge again. He jammed his fingers into the narrow opening and clung there, feet wide apart, muscles straining. He threw back his head and roared with the effort. The doors gave slightly, then flew wide open. The crowbar rolled out just as a shadow fell across Hoffmann's back and, in a rush of air and a roar of machinery, he launched himself forwards onto the concrete floor.

LECLERC HAD BEEN in his office at police headquarters and on the point of going home when he received a call that a body had been discovered in a hotel on the Rue de Berne. He guessed at once from the description—gaunt face, ponytail, leather coat—that it was the man who had attacked Hoffmann. Cause of death, he was told, appeared to be strangulation. The victim was a German: Johannes Karp, aged fifty-eight. Leclerc rang his wife for the second time that day to say he was delayed at work, and set off in the back of a patrol car through the rush-hour traffic to the northern side of the river. He had been on duty for almost twenty hours and was as exhausted as an old dog, but the prospect of a suspicious death always bucked up his spirit.

In the Rue de Berne there was almost a carnival atmosphere outside the Hotel Diodati—four police cars with flickering blue lights, sharply brilliant in the overcast early-evening gloom; a sizable crowd on the opposite side of the street, including several glossy black hookers in colourful, minimal clothes, joking with the locals; and fluttering lines of stripy black-and-yellow crime-scene tape sectioning off the spectators. *They look like fans*, thought Leclerc as he got out of the car, *waiting for a star to come out*. A gendarme lifted the tape and Leclerc ducked underneath it.

Inside the Diodati, he didn't like the look of the tiny elevator so took the stairs, pausing on each floor to recover his breath. Outside the room where the body had been found, he had to put on white overalls, white latex gloves and clear plastic slipovers on his shoes.

He didn't know the detective in charge of the crime scene—a new fellow named Moynier. Also in the room, in their white suits, were the pathologist and the photographer, both old hands. He contemplated the corpse. There were various cuts and abrasions on the face. One eye was badly swollen. In the bathroom there was no light switch, but even so it was possible to see the shower curtain rail was hanging away from the wall; so was the basin.

Moynier said, 'A man next door swears he heard sounds of a struggle, sometime around three. I was right to call you? Do you think this is the man who attacked the American banker?'

'I should say so.'

Leclerc wondered how the occupant of this squalid room could possibly have come to intersect with the owner of a mansion in Cologny. On the bed the dead man's possessions had been individually bagged in clear plastic: a camera, two knives, a raincoat apparently slashed at the front. *Hoffmann wore a raincoat like that when he went to the hospital*, Leclerc thought. He picked up a mains adaptor.

He said, 'Isn't this for a computer? Where is it?'

Moynier shrugged. 'There isn't one here.'

Leclerc's mobile phone rang. It was in his jacket pocket. Irritably, he unzipped the coveralls and pulled off his gloves. Moynier started to protest about contamination, but Leclerc turned his back on him. The caller was his assistant, young Lullin, who was still at the office. He said he had been looking at the afternoon log and a psychiatrist, a Dr Polidori in Vernier, had called a couple of hours earlier about a patient of hers showing potentially dangerous schizophrenic symptoms—he had been in a fight, she said. His name was Alexander Hoffmann.

Leclerc said, 'Did she mention whether he was carrying a computer?'

There was a rustle of notes and Lullin said, 'How did you know that?

HOFFMANN, CLUTCHING the crowbar, hurried up the steps from the basement to the ground floor, intent on raising the alarm about Rajamani. At the door to the lobby he stopped. Through the rectangular window he saw a squad of six black-uniformed gendarmes, guns drawn, jogging in heavy boots across the reception area towards the interior of the building; following them was Leclerc. Once they had passed through the turnstile, the exit was locked and two more armed police stationed themselves on either side of it.

Hoffmann turned and clattered back down the steps and into the car park. He headed for the ramp up to the street. Behind him he heard the soft squeak of tyres turning on concrete and a large black BMW swung out of a parking bay and came towards him, headlights on. Without pausing to think, he stepped out in front of it, forcing it to stop, then ran round to the driver's door and pulled it open.

What an apparition the president of Hoffmann Investment Technologies must have presented by now—bloody, dusty, oil-smeared, clutching a large crowbar. It was little wonder the driver couldn't scramble out fast enough. Hoffmann threw the crowbar onto the passenger seat, put the automatic transmission into drive and pressed hard on the accelerator. The big car lurched up the ramp. Ahead, the steel door was just beginning to rise. He had to brake to let it open fully. In his rearview mirror he could see the owner, transformed by adrenaline from fear into rage, marching up the ramp to protest. The steel door opened fully and Hoffmann transferred his foot from the brake to the accelerator, kangarooing the BMW out across the pavement and swerving on two wheels into the empty one-way street.

ON THE FIFTH FLOOR, Leclerc and his arrest squad stepped out of the elevator. He pressed the buzzer and Marie-Claude let them in. She put her hand to her mouth in dismay as the armed men rushed past her.

Leclerc said, 'I am looking for Dr Hoffmann. Is he here?'

'Yes, of course.'

'Will you take us to him, please?'

She led them onto the trading floor. Quarry heard the commotion and turned round. He had been wondering what had happened to Hoffmann. He had assumed he was still with Rajamani. But when he saw Leclerc and the gendarmes, he knew their ship was sunk.

He said calmly, 'Can I help you, gentlemen?'

'We need to speak to Dr Hoffmann,' said Leclerc. He was swaying from left to right, standing on tiptoe, trying to spot the American among the astonished quants who were turning from their computer screens. 'Will everyone please remain where they are?'

Quarry said, 'You must have just missed him. He stepped outside to speak to one of our executives.'

'Outside the building?' Leclerc swore. He said to the nearest gendarmes: 'You three, check these premises.' And then to the others: 'You three, come with me.' And finally to the room in general: 'Nobody is to leave the building. Nobody is to make any calls. We shall try to be as quick as possible.'

He walked briskly back towards Reception. Quarry chased after him. 'I'm sorry, Inspector—excuse me—what exactly has Alex done?'

'A body has been discovered. We need to speak to him about it . . .'

He strode out of the offices and into the corridor. It was deserted. 'What other companies are on this floor?'

Quarry was still at his heels. His face was grey. 'Only us, we rent the whole thing. What body?'

Leclerc said to his men, 'We'll have to start at the bottom and work up.'

One of the gendarmes pressed the elevator call button. The doors opened and it was Leclerc, eyes darting, who saw the danger first and yelled out to him to stay where he was.

'Christ,' said Quarry, gazing at the void. 'Alex . . .'

The doors began to close. The gendarme held his finger on the button to reopen them. Leclerc got down on his knees, shuffled forwards and peered over the edge. He felt a drop of moisture hit the back of his neck, and put his hand to it and touched a viscous liquid. He craned his head upwards to find himself staring at the bottom of the elevator car. It was only a floor above him. Something was dangling off the bottom. He drew back quickly.

GABRIELLE HAD FINISHED her packing. Her suitcases were in the hall: one big case, one smaller, and one carry-on bag. The last flight to London was due to take off at 21.25: she ought to leave now if she was to be sure of catching it. She sat in her studio and wrote Alex a note, the old-fashioned way, on pure white paper with steel nib and Indian ink.

The first thing she wanted to say was that she loved him, and that she was not leaving him permanently—she just needed a break from Geneva. She had been out to see Bob Walton at CERN—'don't be angry, he's a good man, he's worried about you'—and that had been a help because for the first time she had begun to understand the immense strain he must be under.

As she understood it from Walton, Alex had devoted his life to trying to create a machine that could reason, learn and act independently of human beings. To her there was something inherently frightening about that whole idea, even though Walton assured her Alex's intentions had been entirely noble. But to take such a vaulting ambition and place it entirely at the service of making money—wasn't that to marry the sacred and the profane?

On and on she wrote, forgetting time, the pen gliding over the hand-woven paper in her intricate calligraphy. The conservatory grew darker.

Across the lake, the lights of the city began to glint. The thought of Alex out there with a broken head gnawed at her.

I feel awful going when you're ill, but if you won't let me help you, then there's not much point in my staying, is there? If you need me, call me. Please. Any time. It's all I've ever wanted. I love you. G x

Gabrielle sealed the note in an envelope, wrote a large 'A' on the front and carried it towards the study, pausing briefly in the hall to ask her driver-bodyguard to put her cases in the car and take her to the airport.

She propped the envelope on the keyboard of her husband's computer, and somehow she must have pressed a key by accident, because the screen came to life and she found she was looking at an image of a woman bending over a desk. It took her a moment to realise it was her. She looked behind her and above, at the red light of a smoke detector; the woman on the screen did the same.

She tapped a few more keys at random. Nothing happened. She pressed ESCAPE and instantly the image shrank into the top left-hand corner of the screen, part of a grid of twenty-four different camera shots. In one, something seemed to be moving faintly. She adjusted the mouse and clicked on it. The screen was filled with a night-vision image of her in a short dressing gown. She slipped off the dressing gown and a man's head—Alex's head—appeared in the bottom right quadrant of the screen.

There was a polite cough. 'Madame Hoffmann?' enquired a voice behind her, and she dragged her horrified gaze away from the screen to find her driver framed in the doorway. Behind him loomed two gendarmes.

13

Zimeysa was a nowhere land—no history, no geography, no inhabitants; even its name was an acronym of other places: Zone Industrielle de Meyrin-Satigny. Hoffmann drove between low buildings that seemed to be neither office blocks nor factories, but a hybrid of both. The skeletal arms of cranes stretched over construction sites and lorry parks deserted for the night. It could have been anywhere in the world.

The airport was less than a kilometre to the east. The lights of the terminals imparted a pale glow to a darkening sky corrugated with cloud. Each time a passenger jet came in low overhead, it sounded like a rolling wave breaking onshore: a thunderous crescendo that set Hoffmann's nerves on edge.

He treated the BMW with extreme care, driving with his face up close to the windscreen. There were a lot of roadworks, cables being laid, first one lane shut and then the other, creating a chicane. The turning to Route de Clerval was on the right, just past a distribution centre for auto parts— Volvo, Nissan, Honda. He indicated to turn into it. Up ahead on the left was a petrol station. He pulled up at the pumps and went into the shop. CCTV footage shows him hesitating between the aisles, then moving decisively to a section selling jerry cans: red metal, good quality, thirty-five francs each. He buys five, paying for them in cash. The camera above the till clearly shows the wound on the top of his head. The sales assistant subsequently described him as being in an agitated state. His face and clothes were streaked with grease and oil; there was dried blood in his hair.

Hoffmann said, 'What's with all the roadworks?'

'It's been going on for months. They're laying fibre-optic cable.'

Hoffmann went out onto the forecourt with the jerry cans: it took him two trips to carry them to the nearest pump. He began filling them in turn. There were no other customers. He felt horribly exposed standing alone under the fluorescent lights. He could see the sales assistant watching him. Another jet was coming in to land directly over their heads, making the air tremble. It seemed to shake him from the inside out. He finished filling the last can, opened the rear door of the BMW and shoved it along to the far side of the back seat, stacking all the others in a row after it. He returned to the shop, paid 168 francs for the fuel and another twenty-five for a torch, two cigarette lighters and three cleaning cloths, then left.

LECLERC HAD BRIEFLY inspected the body at the bottom of the elevator shaft. There was not much to see. It reminded him of a suicide he had once had to deal with at the Cornavin railway station.

In the basement he talked briefly to the Austrian businessman whose car Hoffmann had stolen. He was outraged, seemed to hold Leclerc more responsible than the man who had committed the crime. The licence number and description had been circulated as a high priority to every Geneva police officer. Forensics were on their way. Madame Hoffmann had been picked up at the house in Cologny and was being brought over for questioning. Leclerc was not sure what else he could do.

For the second time that evening he found himself climbing multiple flights of stairs. He felt dizzy with the effort. He wondered about Hoffmann and whether he had killed his colleague as well as the German in the hotel room. On the face of it, it seemed impossible: the safety mechanism of the elevator had plainly failed. But equally it was a remarkable coincidence, one had to say, for a man to have been at the scene of two deaths in the space of a few hours.

Arriving at the fifth floor, he paused to recover his breath. The entrance to the hedge fund's offices was open; a young gendarme was standing guard. Leclerc nodded to him as he went past. On the trading floor, the mood seemed not merely shocked—he would have expected that, after the loss of a colleague—but almost hysterical. The employees, previously so silent, were huddled in groups, talking animatedly. The Englishman, Quarry, almost ran over to him.

Quarry said, 'Any news of Alex?'

'It appears he forced a driver out of his car and stole it. We're looking for him now. Could I see Dr Hoffmann's office, please?'

Quarry at once looked shifty. 'I'm not altogether sure about that. I think perhaps I ought to call in our lawyer . . .'

Leclerc said firmly, 'I'm sure he would advise full cooperation.' He wondered what the financier was trying to hide.

Quarry backed down immediately. 'Yes, of course.'

Inside Hoffmann's office there was still debris on the floor. The hole in the ceiling gaped above the desk. Leclerc looked up at it in bewilderment. 'When did this happen?'

Quarry grimaced with embarrassment. 'About an hour ago. Alex pulled down the smoke detector. He believed there was a camera inside.'

'And was there?'

'Yes.'

'Who installed it?'

'Our security consultant, Maurice Genoud.'

'On whose authority?'

'Well . . .' Quarry could see no escape. 'Actually, it turns out to have been Alex.'

'Hoffmann was spying on himself?'

'Yes, apparently. But he couldn't remember ordering it.'

'And where is Genoud now?'

'I believe he went down to talk to your men when Gana's body was dis-covered. He also handles security for this whole building.'

Leclerc sat at Hoffmann's desk and started opening the drawers.

Quarry said, 'Don't you need a warrant to do that?'

'No.' Leclerc found the Darwin book and the CD of Alex's scan. On the sofa he noticed a laptop lying discarded. He went across and opened it, stud-ied the photograph of Hoffmann, then went into the file of his exchanges with the dead man, Karp. He was so absorbed, he barely glanced up when Ju-Long came in.

Ju-Long said, 'Excuse me, Hugo—I think you ought to take a look at what's happening on the markets.'

Quarry, frowning, bent over the screen on Alex's desk, switching from display to display. The slide was beginning in earnest now. The VIX was going through the roof, the euro sinking, investors pulling out of equities and scrambling for shelter in gold and ten-year Treasury bonds. Everywhere money was being sucked out of the market—in electronically traded S&P futures alone, in the space of little more than ninety minutes, buy-side liquidity had dropped from $6 billion to $2.5 billion.

Here it comes, he thought.

He said, 'Inspector, if we're done here, I need to get back to work. There's a big sell-off underway in New York.'

There was a brief knock on the door and a gendarme stuck his head into the room.

'We've got a trace on the stolen car.'

Leclerc swung round to face him.

'Where is it?'

'A guy at a petrol station in Zimeysa called. Someone matching Hoff-mann's description driving a black BMW just bought a hundred litres of fuel.'

'A hundred litres? My God, how far is he planning to go?'

'That's why the guy called. He says he didn't put it in the tank.'

FIFTY-FOUR ROUTE DE CLERVAL turned out to be at the end of a long road that took in a cargo-handling facility before dwindling into a cul-de-sac beside the railway tracks. The building stood out pale in the dusk through a screen of trees: a boxy windowless steel structure, two or three storeys high—it was difficult for him to estimate the height in the absence of any windows—with security lights mounted along the edge of the roof and video cameras protruding from the corners. They turned to follow Hoffmann as he passed. A small slip road led up to a set of metal gates; beyond was an empty car park. The whole site was secured by a steel perimeter fence surmounted with triple strands of razor wire.

Hoffmann drew up in front of the gates. At window-level next to him were a keypad console and an entryphone. He leaned over and pressed the buzzer and waited. Nothing happened. He looked across at the building; it seemed derelict. He considered what was logical from the machine's point of view, then tried keying in the smallest number expressible as the sum of two cubes in two different ways. At once the gates began to slide open.

The gates slid closed behind him again as he drove slowly across the car park and along the side of the building. He turned the corner and pulled up in front of a big steel shutter, a truck-sized delivery entrance. A video camera mounted above it was trained directly on him. He got out of the car and approached the door. Like the offices of the hedge fund, it was controlled by face recognition. He stood in front of the scanner. The response was immediate, the shutter rising to reveal an empty loading bay. Hoffmann turned to walk back to the car and saw, as he did so, in the distance on the other side of the railway tracks, a show of flashing red and blue moving very fast; a scrap of siren from the police car carried in the wind.

He drove quickly into the bay, lurched to a halt, turned off the engine and listened. He couldn't hear the siren now. It was probably nothing to do with him. He pressed the button to close the shutter. There was a warning buzzer; an orange lamp flashed and within ten seconds the bottom of the shutter clattered against the concrete floor, extinguishing the daylight. He felt alone in the darkness, the victim of his own imaginings.

He took the crowbar and the torch from the front seat of the BMW. With his left hand he shone the torch round the bare walls and onto the ceiling, picking out yet another surveillance camera looking down at him malevolently, or so he thought. Beneath it was a metal door, again activated by face recognition. He tucked the crowbar under his arm, shone the torch onto his face and tentatively pressed his hand against the pad. For several seconds nothing happened, and then—almost, it seemed to him, reluctantly—the door opened onto a short flight of wooden steps that led up to a passage.

He shone the torch along it to another door at the far end. Now he could hear clearly the faint hum of CPUs. The ceiling was low and the air was chilled. He walked warily to the end, pressed his palm to the sensor and opened the door onto the noise and lights of a processor farm. In the torch's narrow beam the motherboards sat on steel shelves that stretched ahead and to either side, exuding the familiar, oddly sweet electrical scent of burned dust. He walked on slowly, shining his torch to right and left along the aisles, the beam disappearing into the darkness. He wondered who else would have access. The security company, presumably—Genoud's outfit; building services for maintenance; the computer technicians. If each received instructions and payment via email, the place could, he reckoned, function independently on outsourced labour alone, without any need of its own workforce.

He reached the next door, repeated the procedure with the torch and the recognition sensor, and the bolts slid back. He stepped over the threshold, heard movement to one side, and wheeled round as an IBM TS3500 tape robot rushed towards him along its monorail, stopped, plucked out a disk, and whisked away again. He watched it for a moment, pausing by some metal fire escape steps as he waited for his heart rate to settle down. When he moved on, he saw that four other robots were racing to complete their tasks.

The adjoining room was smaller and seemed to be the place where the communication pipes came in. He shone his torch on two big black trunk cables, the thickness of his fist, emerging out of a closed metal box and descending like tuberous roots into a trench that ran under his feet and up into some kind of switch array system. Both sides of the aisle were protected by heavy metal cages. He already knew that the fibre-optic pipes GVA-1 and GVA-2 both passed close to Geneva airport en route to Germany from the fibre landing site at Marseilles in southern France. Data could be transmitted to and received from New York at a fraction below the speed of light. VIXAL was astride the fastest communications link in Europe.

The beam of his torch traced other cables running along the wall at shoulder height, partly housed in galvanised metal, emanating from beside a small door. It was padlocked. He fitted the crowbar into the U-shape loop and used it as a lever to wrench the shackle free of its housing. It came away with a shriek, the door swung open and he shone his light into some kind of power control room—electricity meters, a big fuse box the size of a small cupboard and a couple of trip switches. Yet another video camera regarded him steadily. He quickly flipped the handles on the trip switches down to OFF. For an instant, nothing happened, and then somewhere in the big building a diesel generator shuddered into life and, bizarrely, all the lights came on. Hoffmann, in a fury of frustration, took a swing at the camera lens with the end of his crowbar, poking his tormentor in the eye, smashing it to a satisfactory number of pieces, then set about the fuse board, splintering the plastic casings, only finally giving up when it was obvious he was having no effect.

He turned off the torch and retraced his steps to the communications room. At the far end he presented his face to the sensor and the door to the next room opened onto a huge open space with a high ceiling, digital clocks to mark the different time zones and large TV screens, obviously modelled on the trading floor at Les Eaux-Vives. There was a central control unit consisting of a six-screen array and separate monitors. In front of it, where the quants would have sat, there were ranks of motherboards, all processing at maximum capacity to judge by their rapidly flickering LEDs.

This must be the cortex, thought Hoffmann. He stood for a while in wonder. There was something about the independent purposefulness of the scene that he found unexpectedly moving, as he supposed a parent might be moved by witnessing a child for the first time unselfconsciously at large in the world. That VIXAL possessed no emotion or conscience; that it had no purpose other than the self-interested pursuit of survival through the accumulation of money; that it would, if left to itself, in accordance with Darwinian logic, seek to expand until it dominated the entire earth—this did not detract for Hoffmann from the stunning fact of its existence. He even forgave it for the ordeal it had subjected him to: after all, that had been for the purposes of research. It was simply behaving like a hedge fund.

Briefly he forgot that he had come to destroy it and bent over the screens to examine the trades that it was putting on. They were being processed at ultra-high frequency in tremendous volumes—millions of shares all held for only fractions of a second—submitting and instantly cancelling orders, probing the markets for hidden pockets of liquidity. But he had never seen it done on such a scale before. There could be little or no profit in it and he wondered briefly what VIXAL was aiming to achieve. Then an alert flashed onto the screen.

The CBOE has declared Self Help against the NYSE/ARCA as of 1.30 CT. The NYSE/ARCA is out of NBBO and unavailable for linkage. All CBOE systems are running normally.

The jargon masked the scale of the problem, took the heat out of it, as jargon is designed to do. But Hoffmann knew what it meant. The CBOE is the Chicago Board Options Exchange, which trades around one billion contracts a year in options on companies, indices and tradable funds—the VIX among them. 'Self Help' is what one US exchange is entitled to declare against another if its sister-exchange starts taking more than a one-second time period to respond to orders. The system is entirely automated and operates at a speed of thousandths of a second. To a professional such as Hoffmann, the CBOE Self Help alert gave warning that the New York electronic exchange ARCA was experiencing a serious system breakdown.

When Hoffmann saw the alert, he didn't immediately connect it with VIXAL. But when he looked up in puzzlement from the screen and ran his eye over the flickering lights of the CPUs; when he sensed, almost physically, the phenomenal volume and speed of the orders they were processing, and remembered the immense unhedged one-way bet VIXAL was taking on a market collapse—at that moment, he saw what the algorithm was doing.

He set off back towards the loading bay.

A NOISY CORTÈGE of eight patrol cars of the Geneva Police Department swept down the deserted Route de Clerval, slammed to a halt beside the perimeter of the processing facility, and sprouted along its length a dozen open doors. Leclerc was in the first car with Quarry. Genoud was in the second. Gabrielle was four cars back.

Leclerc's immediate impression, as he hauled himself out of the back seat, was that the place was a fortress. He took in the high metal fence, the razor wire, the surveillance cameras, and the sheer steel walls of the structure itself, rising like a silvery castle keep in the fading light. Behind him armed police were disgorging from the patrol cars, pumped up, ready to go. Leclerc could see that if he were not very careful, this could only end one way.

'He isn't armed,' he said as he passed among the deploying men, clutching a walkie-talkie. 'Remember that—he has no weapon.'

'A hundred litres of petrol,' said one gendarme. 'That's a weapon.'

'No, it isn't. No one tries to go in without my orders, and absolutely nobody shoots—understood?'

Leclerc reached the car containing Gabrielle. The door was open. She was still in the back seat, clearly in a state of shock. 'Madame Hoffmann,' he said, 'I know this is an ordeal for you, but would you mind . . .?' He offered her his hand. She looked at him blankly for a moment, then took it.

Emerging into the cold night seemed to wake her from her trance, and she blinked in amazement at the sight of the force assembled. She said, 'All this just for Alex?'

'I'm sorry. There is a standard procedure for cases such as this. Let's just make sure it ends peacefully. Will you help me?'

'Yes, of course. Anything.'

He led her to the front of the column, where Quarry was standing with Genoud. The company's head of security practically jumped to attention as he approached. *What a weasel he is*, Leclerc thought. Nevertheless, he made an effort to be polite to him; it was his style.

'Maurice,' he said, 'I understand you know this place. What are we dealing with exactly?'

'Three floors, separated by timber-framed partitions. It's a modular structure, each module filled with computer equipment.'

'Access?'

'Three entrances. One is a big unloading bay. There's an internal fire escape down from the roof.'

'How do the doors unlock?'

'Four-digit code here; face recognition inside.'

'What about power? Could we cut it off?'

Genoud shook his head. 'There are diesel generators around the back on the ground floor with enough fuel for forty-eight hours.'

'Security?'

'An alarm system. It's all automatic. No personnel on the premises.'

'How do we open the gates?'

'The same code as the doors.'

'Very well. Open them, please.'

He watched as Genoud keyed in the number. The gates did not respond. Genoud, grim-faced, tried a couple more times, with the same result. He sounded mystified. 'This is the right code, I swear.'

Leclerc took hold of the bars. The barrier didn't budge a millimetre. You could ram a truck at it and it would probably hold.

Quarry said, 'Maybe Alex couldn't get in either, in which case he won't be there.'

'Possibly, but it's more likely he's changed the code.' A man with death fantasies locked in a building with 100 litres of petrol! Leclerc called out to his driver: 'Make sure the fire department are bringing cutting equipment. Madame Hoffmann, will you see if you can speak to your husband and ask him not to do anything foolish?'

'I'll try.'

She pressed the entry buzzer. 'Alex?' she said softly. 'Alex?' She held her finger on the metal button, willing him to answer.

HOFFMANN HAD JUST finished dousing the CPU room, the tape-robot cabinets and the fibre-optic trench with petrol when he heard the buzzer on the control console. He had a jerry can in either hand. His arms ached with the weight. Fuel had slopped over his boots and jeans. On CNBC, the headline was: DOW DOWN MORE THAN 300 POINTS. He set the canisters beside the console and inspected the security monitors. By moving the mouse and clicking on individual shots, he was able to take in the entire scene at the gate—the gendarmes, Quarry, Leclerc, Genoud and Gabrielle, whose face when he brought it up occupied the entire screen. She looked shattered. His finger hovered over the button for a few seconds.

'Gabby . . .'

It was strange to watch on screen her reaction to the sound of his voice, the look of relief.

'Thank God, Alex. We're all so worried about you. How's it going in there?'

He glanced around. He wished he had the words to describe it. 'It's—unbelievable.'

'Is it, Alex? I bet it is.' She stopped, glanced to one side then moved her face closer to the camera, and her voice became quieter, confiding. 'Listen, I'd like to come and talk to you. I'd like to see it, if I may. All these others would stay back here.'

'You say that, Gabby, but I don't think they would. I'm afraid there's been a lot of misunderstanding.'

She said, 'Hang on a minute, Alex,' and then her face disappeared from the screen. He heard a discussion start, but she had put her hand over the entry speaker and the words were too muffled for him to make out. He glanced over at the TV screens. The CNBC headline was: DOW DOWN MORE THAN 400 POINTS.

Hoffmann said, 'I'm sorry, Gabby. I'm going to have to go now.'

She cried, 'Wait!'

Leclerc's face suddenly appeared on camera. 'Dr Hoffmann, it's me—Leclerc. Open the gates and let your wife in. You need to talk to her. My men won't make a move, I promise you.'

Hoffmann hesitated. It struck him, oddly, that the policeman was right. He did need to talk to her. Or at least show her—let her see it all before it was destroyed. It would explain everything far better than he ever could.

He pressed the buzzer to let her in.

14

As soon as there was enough of a gap, Gabrielle slid around the gate and set off across the car park. She had not gone far when she heard shouting behind her and turned to see Quarry breaking free of the group and striding after her.

'Not going to let you do this alone, Gabs,' he said as he drew level with her. 'My fault this, not yours. I got him into it.'

'It's nobody's fault, Hugo,' she said without looking at him. 'He's ill.'

'Still—you don't mind if I tag along?'

She ground her teeth. *Tag along*—as if they were on a stroll.

But when they rounded the corner and she saw her husband standing in the open entrance of the loading bay, she was glad she had someone beside her, even Quarry, because Alex had a long iron bar in one hand and a big red jerry can in the other, and everything about him was disturbing—the way he stood perfectly still, the blood and oil on his face and in his hair, the fearful staring expression on his face.

He said, 'Quickly, come on, it's really getting started now,' and before they had even reached him he had turned and disappeared back inside. They hurried after him, past the BMW, through the loading bay, past the motherboards and the tape robots. It was hot. The petrol was vaporising, making it difficult to breathe.

Quarry cried after him in a panic, 'Jesus, Alex, this place could explode!'

They emerged into a much larger room that was filled with cries of panic. Hoffmann had pumped up the sound on the big TV screens. Aside from the noise of these, a man was ranting somewhere like a commentator in the final furlong of a big race: the live audio feed from the pit of the S&P 500 in Chicago.

'Here they come to sell 'em again! Nine-halves trade now, twenties trade now, evens trade now, guys, eight-halves trading as well . . .'

In the background, people were screaming as if they were witnessing a disaster. On one of the TV screens Gabrielle took in a caption: DOW, S&P 500, NASDAQ HAVE BIGGEST ONE-DAY DROPS IN OVER A YEAR.

Another man was talking over pictures of a night-time riot: 'Hedge funds are gonna try to break Italy, they're going to try to break Spain. There is no resolution . . .'

Quarry stood transfixed. 'Don't tell me *we're* doing that.'

Hoffmann was upending the big jerry can and pouring petrol over the CPUs. 'We started it. Attacked New York. Set off an avalanche.'

NINETEEN-POINT-FOUR billion shares were traded on the New York Stock Exchange during the course of that day: more than were traded in the whole decade of the 1960s. Events were denominated in milliseconds, far beyond the speed of human comprehension. They could only be reconstructed later, when the computers yielded their secrets.

OUTSIDE, THREE TRUCKS from the Geneva Fire Service had pulled up next to the patrol cars. So many men; so many lights. Leclerc told them to get started. The jaws of the hydraulic cutters, once they were in place, reminded him of giant mandibles, chomping through the heavy iron fence posts one by one as if they were blades of grass.

GABRIELLE was pleading with her husband: 'Come on, Alex, please. Leave it now and come away.'

Hoffmann finished emptying the last jerry can and dropped it. With his teeth he began tearing at the packet of cleaning cloths. 'You two go. I'll be right behind.' He looked at her and for an instant he was the old Alex. 'I love you. Now go, please.' He wiped the cloth in the petrol that had pooled on the cover of a motherboard, thoroughly soaking it. In his other hand he held a cigarette lighter. 'Go,' he repeated, and there was such desperation in his voice that Gabrielle began to back away.

On CNBC the commentator said: 'This is capitulation really, this is classic capitulation; there is fear in this . . .'

Quarry, at the trading screen, could barely credit what he was seeing. In seconds the Dow had slipped from minus 800 to minus 900. The VIX was up by forty per cent—that was close on a half-billion-dollar profit he was looking at right there on that one position . . .

The hysterical voice from the Chicago pit continued to rant, a sob in his throat: '. . . seventy-five even offer here right now, guys, seventy even bid and here comes Morgan Stanley to sell . . .'

Quarry heard a *wumph!* and saw Hoffmann with fire coming out of his fingers. *Not now*, he thought, *don't do it yet—not till VIXAL has finished its trades*. Beside him Gabrielle screamed, 'Alex!' Quarry flung himself towards the door. The fire left Hoffmann's hand, seemed to dance in the air for an instant, and then expanded into a brilliant bursting star.

TIME-CODED RECORDINGS of the open channels of the police radios establish that at precisely the moment the Chicago market froze—8:45:28 p.m.—an explosion was heard inside the processing facility. Leclerc was running towards the building, lagging behind the gendarmes, when the bang stopped him dead and he crouched down, his arms clasped over his head—an undignified posture for a senior police officer, he reflected afterwards. Some of the younger men, with a fearlessness born of inexperience, never paused, and by the time Leclerc was back on his feet, they were already running back from round the corner of the building, hauling Gabrielle and Quarry along with them.

Leclerc shouted, 'Where's Hoffmann?'

From the building came a roaring sound.

THE CAMERAS RECORD dispassionately, scientifically, Hoffmann as he recovers consciousness in the large central room. The screens are all blown out. The motherboards are dead, VIXAL extinct. There is no sound except the noise of the flames moving from room to room as they take hold of the wooden partitions, the false floors and ceilings, the kilometres of plastic cable, the plastic components of the CPUs.

Hoffmann gets up on all fours, rises to his knees then lumbers to his feet. He stands swaying. He wrenches off his jacket and holds it in front of him for protection, then runs into the inferno of the fibre-optic room, past the smouldering robots, through the darkened CPU farm and into the loading bay. He sees the steel shutter is down. He hits the button with the heel of his hand to open it. No response. He repeats the motion frantically, as if hammering it into the wall. Nothing. All the lights are out: the fire must have shorted the circuits.

Hoffmann has a choice now. He can either stay where he is and risk being trapped and burned to death. Or he can try to go back into the flames and reach the fire escape in the tape-robot suite. The calculation in his eyes . . .

He goes for the latter. The heat has become much more intense in the last few seconds. One of the robots has ignited and is melting in its central section, so that as he rushes past it, the automaton topples forwards at the midriff in a fiery bow and crashes to the floor behind him.

The ironwork of the staircase is too hot to touch. He can feel the heat of the metal even through the soles of his boots. The steps don't run all the way up to the roof but only to the next floor, which is in darkness. By the crimson glow of the fire behind him he can make out a large space with three doors leading off it. A noise like a strong wind in a loft is shifting around up here. Somewhere in the distance he hears a crash as a section of the floor gives way. He puts his face in front of the sensor to unlock the first door. When it doesn't respond, he wipes his face on his sleeves: there is so much sweat and grease on his skin it is possible the sensors can't recognise him. But even when his face is cleaner it doesn't respond. The second door does open and he steps into utter darkness. The night-vision cameras record him groping blindly around the walls for the next exit, and so it goes on, from room to room, as Hoffmann seeks to escape the maze of the building, until, at last, at the end of a passage, he opens a door on to a furnace. A tongue of fire races towards the fresh supply of oxygen like a hungry living thing. He turns and runs. The flames seem to pursue him, lighting ahead the gleaming metal of a staircase. He passes out of camera shot. The fireball reaches the lens a second later. The coverage ends.

To the people viewing it from the outside, the processing facility resembles a pressure cooker. No flames are visible, only smoke issuing from the seams and vents of the building, accompanied by this incessant roar. The fire service plays water on the walls from three different directions to try to cool them. The infrared equipment keeps detecting shifting black pockets inside the structure where the heat is less intense and where someone might have survived. A team wearing heavy protective gear is preparing to go in.

Gabrielle has been moved back with Quarry to inside the perimeter fence. Someone has put a blanket round her shoulders. They both stand watching. Suddenly, from the flat roof of the building, a jet of orange flame shoots into the night sky. From its base something detaches. It takes a moment for them all to realise that it is the fiery outline of a man. He runs to the edge of the roof, his arms outstretched, then leaps and falls like Icarus.

15

The gendarmes had gone from the office building. One elevator was cordoned off by black-and-yellow tape and had a sign stuck to it— DANGER: NOT WORKING—but the other was operational and, after a brief hesitation, Quarry stepped into it.

Van der Zyl and Ju-Long were waiting for him in Reception. They rose as he came in. Both looked badly shaken.

Van der Zyl said, 'It's just been on the news. They had shots of the fire, this place—everything.'

Quarry swore, looked at his watch. 'I'd better start emailing the major clients straight away.' He noticed that van der Zyl and Ju-Long were looking at one another. 'Well, what is it?'

Ju-Long said, 'Before you do, there's something you ought to see.'

He followed them onto the trading floor. To his amazement, none of the quants had gone home. They rose as he came in and stood in complete silence. He wondered if it was meant as some sort of mark of respect. Out of habit he glanced up at the business channels. The Dow had recovered almost two thirds of its losses to close down 387; the VIX was up sixty per cent. The imminent UK election results were being forecast from a nation-wide exit poll: NO OVERALL CONTROL. *That just about sums it up*, he thought. He checked the nearest screen for the day's P&L, blinked at it and read it again, then turned in wonderment to the others.

'It's true,' said Ju-Long. 'We made a profit out of the crash of four-point-one billion dollars.'

'And the beauty of it is,' van der Zyl added, 'that that represents only zero-point-four per cent of total market volatility. No one will ever notice, except us.'

'Jesus wept . . .' Quarry quickly did the calculation in his head of his personal net worth. 'That must mean VIXAL managed to complete all the trades before Alex destroyed it.'

Ju-Long said quietly, 'It's still trading.'

'But it can't be. I just saw all the hardware burned to the ground.'

'Then it must have other hardware we don't know about. Something quite miraculous appears to have taken place. Have you seen the intranet? The company slogan has changed.'

Quarry looked at the faces of the quants. They seemed to him to be both blank and radiant at the same time, like members of a cult. It was eerie. Several of them nodded at him encouragingly. He bent to examine the screensaver.

THE COMPANY OF THE FUTURE WILL HAVE NO WORKERS
THE COMPANY OF THE FUTURE WILL HAVE NO MANAGERS
THE COMPANY OF THE FUTURE WILL BE A DIGITAL ENTITY
THE COMPANY OF THE FUTURE WILL BE ALIVE

IN HIS OFFICE, Quarry was writing an email to the investors:

My dear friends, by the time you read this you will probably have begun to hear the tragic story of what happened to Alex Hoffmann yesterday. I will call you all individually later today to discuss the situation. For now I just wanted you to know that he is receiving the very finest medical care. Of course it is too early to talk of the future of the company he founded, but I did want to reassure you that he has left systems in place which mean that your investments will not only continue to prosper, but will, I am confident, go from strength to strength. I will explain in more detail when I speak with you.

The quants had taken a vote on the trading floor and agreed to keep what had happened confidential. In return, each would receive an immediate cash bonus of $5 million. There would be further payments in the future, dependent on VIXAL's performance. No one had dissented: they had all seen what had happened to Rajamani.

There was a knock at the door. Quarry shouted, 'Come!' It was Genoud. 'Hello, Maurice, what do you want?'

'I've come to take out those cameras, if that's all right with you.'

Quarry considered VIXAL. He pictured it as a kind of glowing celestial digital cloud, occasionally swarming to earth. It might be anywhere—in some sweltering, industrial zone stinking of aviation fuel and resounding to the throb of cicadas beside an international airport in Southeast Asia; or in a cool and leafy business park in the soft, clear rain of New England or the Rhineland; or occupying a darkened floor of a brand-new office block in the City of London or Mumbai or São Paulo; or even roosting undetected on 100,000 home computers. *It is all around us*, he thought, *in the very air we breathe*. He looked up at the hidden camera and gave the slightest bow of obeisance.

'Leave them,' he said.

GABRIELLE WAS BACK where her day had begun, sitting in the University Hospital, only this time she was beside her husband's bed. He had been put into his own room at the end of a darkened ward on the third floor. There were bars on the windows and gendarmes outside. It was hard to see Alex under all the bandaging and tubing. He had been unconscious since he hit the ground. They told her he had multiple fractures and second-degree burns; they had just brought him out of emergency surgery and connected him to a drip and a monitor. The surgeon declined to offer a prognosis: he said only that the next twenty-four hours would be critical.

Alex cried out in his sedated sleep. He seemed terribly agitated by something. She touched his bandaged hand and wondered what was passing through that powerful mind. 'It's all right, darling. Everything's going to be all right now.' She laid her head on the pillow next to his. She felt strangely content, despite everything, to have him beside her at last. Beyond the barred window a church clock was striking midnight. Softly she began singing to him a baby's lullaby.

robert **harris**

Profile

Born:
March 1957, Nottingham.
Education:
Read English Literature at
Selwyn College,
Cambridge.
First job:
At the BBC, working on
Panorama and *Newsnight*.
Likes:
Fast cars, fine wines.

**Books that have been
filmed:**
Enigma, which starred
Kate Winslet and Dougray
Scott; *Archangel*, a Daniel
Craig TV drama and *The
Ghost*, which became *The
Ghostwriter*, with Ewan
McGregor and Pierce
Brosnan, directed by
Roman Polanski.

Robert Harris's novels do not fit neatly into any category. His first novel, *Fatherland*, a vision of an alternative future, in which he imagines Germany as it might have been had the Nazis won the Second World War, put him on the mass-market map, selling millions of copies worldwide. Other diverse best sellers followed, including *Enigma*, a code-breaking drama set in wartime Bletchley Park; *Pompeii*, based upon the historic eruption of Mount Vesuvius in AD 79, which buried an entire Roman community; and *The Ghost*, a gripping story about a former British prime minster and his ghostwriter.

Now, Harris's latest novel, *The Fear Index*, has captured the world's attention anew with its striking, almost prescient, topicality. It tells of a visionary scientist who develops a ground-breaking computer program that can potentially turn any investment into gold—ultimately at the expense of the world's financial security. The book is a parable for our times, in that it warns of the perils of unfettered greed and the obsession with making riches from financial markets at the press of a computer key. 'A dozen years ago I wanted to write a version of George Orwell's *1984*, in which the threat to the individual wasn't the state but rather corporations and computers,' Robert Harris explains. 'I got very interested in artificial intelligence. It was not until the financial crash [2008] that I realised I could marry finance and computers.'

He had little knowledge of how hedge funds and other investment tools operated, however, and had to ask 'a lot of very embarrassing questions of very busy people'. In particular, he turned to a good friend who works for a large banking organisation. 'I couldn't have told you what a hedge fund was before I started researching the book,' he admits. 'The term itself is so stupid I thought it was a bolt hole for the rich and slightly dim, but then I met a lot of hedge fund managers and, my God, they are seriously clever. Probably the smartest people you'll find outside the Large Hadron Collider.' What Harris learned during his research left him with a lasting impression. 'The US Security and Exchange Commission reports on the flash crash were total eye-openers,' he reveals. 'It was the first time I grasped the market's millisecond-by-millisecond nature and its sheer scale.'

Asked whether a trading algorithm or computer program could really run amok as he depicts, Harris answers: 'The financial world is at the cutting edge of high technology. There are wonderful things thrown up by this, but it's buckling and distorting all the values of the world around us. I think human ingenuity created this and human ingenuity will find a way of making it all work, but there may be some alarming hairpin bends along the way.'

Before he became a writer, Robert Harris was a self-confessed political junkie, who faithfully supported the Labour Party and hung out with Tony Blair and other left-leaning alumni. Politics, for Harris, was a passion that started early in life. At six, he apparently wrote an essay entitled 'Why me and my dad don't like Sir Alec Douglas-Home', criticising the then Conservative prime minister, and, later, aged sixteen, he stood as a candidate in mock elections at his secondary school. As an undergraduate at Cambridge, studying English, he edited the student newspaper, demonstrating his journalistic flair by bagging interviews with top political figures of the day. After graduating, he worked as a reporter for BBC's *Newsnight* and *Panorama*, and went on to hold the position of political editor at the *Observer*, subsequently writing regular columns for the *Sunday Times* and the *Daily Telegraph*. In 2003 he was named Columnist of the Year at the British Press Awards.

One thing's for sure, Robert Harris has come a long way from the council estate where he grew up as the son of a Nottinghamshire printer, educated at local state schools. 'We had very little money,' he remembers, 'but I had no sense whatsoever of being poor and had an extremely happy and culturally rich childhood. My father read Graham Greene and Georges Simenon and was a strong trades unionist and Labour supporter. There's a lot of moaning today about too many kids going to university, but my parents were bright people and I wish they'd had that opportunity.'

Harris's writing ambitions and hard work have paid off handsomely, and he now lives in a rambling, picturesque vicarage in Berkshire with his wife, writer Gill Hornby (sister of author Nick Hornby), and four children. Of his own talents, he says humbly, 'I write as well as I can. I'm a journalist at heart, so it's the story that matters. For me, the best thing is to go into my study in the morning and stay there and put words together.'

The House Of Silk

a Sherlock Holmes novel by

ANTHONY HOROWITZ

It is November 1890 and London is in the
grip of a merciless winter. Sherlock Holmes
and Dr Watson are enjoying tea by a roaring
fire when an agitated gentleman arrives at
221b Baker Street, begging for help and speaking
of a scar-faced man in a flat cap who has
been stalking him.

Intrigued, Holmes and Watson know that
the game's afoot once more—the game of
following a tantalising series of puzzling and sinister
clues through the fog-shrouded, gas-lit streets
of London . . .

Preface

I have often reflected upon the strange series of circumstances that led me to my long association with one of the most singular and remarkable figures of my age. If I were of a philosophical frame of mind I might wonder to what extent any one of us is in control of our own destiny, or if indeed we can ever predict the far-reaching consequences of actions that, at the time, may seem entirely trivial.

For example, it was my cousin, Arthur, who recommended me as Assistant Surgeon to the Fifth Northumberland Fusiliers, because he thought it would be a useful experience for me, and he could not possibly have foreseen that a month later I would be dispatched to Afghanistan. At that time the Second Anglo-Afghan War had not even commenced. And what of the Ghazi who sent a bullet hurtling into my shoulder at Maiwand? Nine hundred British and Indian souls died that day and it was doubtless his intention that I would be one of them. But his aim was awry, and although badly wounded, I was saved by Jack Murray, my loyal and good-hearted orderly, who managed to carry me back to British lines.

I was invalided home and devoted several months to a somewhat wasteful existence on the fringes of London society. At the end of that time, I was seriously considering a move to the South Coast, a necessity forced on me by my rapidly diminishing finances. But then we come to Henry Stamford, an acquaintance who had served as my dresser at St Bart's. Had he not been drinking the night before, he would not have had a headache and chosen to take the day off from the chemical laboratory where he was now employed. Lingering at Piccadilly Circus, he decided to stroll up Regent Street to Arthur Liberty's East India House to purchase a gift for his wife. Had he walked the other way, he would not have bumped into me as I came out of the Criterion Bar and as a result I might never have met Sherlock Holmes.

For it was Stamford who suggested that I might share rooms with a man whom he believed to be an analytical chemist and who worked at the same hospital as he. Stamford introduced me to Holmes, who was then experimenting with a method of isolating bloodstains.

This was the great turning point of my life. I had never had literary ambitions but I think I can say without flattering myself that I have become quite renowned for the way I have chronicled the adventures of the great man, presenting no fewer than sixty adventures to an enthusiastic public.

It was always Holmes's belief that I exaggerated his talents and the extraordinary insights of his brilliant mind. He accused me more than once of vulgar romanticism, and thought me no better than any Grub Street scribbler. But generally I think he was unfair. Although I cannot make any great claim for my own powers of description, I am prepared to say that they did the job and that he himself could have done no better.

I have, as I say, received some recognition for my literary endeavours, but more valuable to me was my long friendship with the man himself.

It is a year since Holmes was found at his home on the Downs, stretched out and still, that great mind forever silenced. When I heard the news, I realised that I had lost not just my closest companion and friend but, in many ways, the very reason for my existence. Two marriages, three children, seven grandchildren, a successful career in medicine and the Order of Merit might be considered achievement enough for anyone. But not for me. I miss him to this day and sometimes I fancy that I hear them still, those familiar words: 'The game's afoot, Watson!' They serve only to remind me that I will never again plunge into the swirling fog of Baker Street with my trusty service revolver in my hand. I think of Holmes often, waiting for me on the other side of that great shadow that must come to us all, and in truth I long to join him. I am alone. My old wound plagues me and, as a terrible and senseless war rages on the continent, I no longer understand the world in which I live.

So why do I take up my pen one final time? It could be that, like so many old men with their lives behind them, I am seeking some sort of solace. But there is another reason, too. The adventures of *The Man in the Flat Cap* and *The House of Silk* were, in some respects, the most sensational of Sherlock Holmes's career, but at the time it was impossible for me to tell them, for reasons that will become clear. The fact that they became inextricably tangled up meant that they could not be separated. And yet it has always been my desire to set them down, to complete the Holmes canon.

It was impossible before—the events that I am about to describe were simply too monstrous, too shocking to appear in print. They still are. When I am done, I will have this manuscript packed up and sent to the vaults of Cox and Co. in Charing Cross, where my private papers are stored. I will give instructions that for one hundred years, the packet must not be opened. Perhaps future readers will be more inured to scandal and corruption than my own would have been. To them I bequeath one last portrait of Mr Sherlock Holmes.

But I have wasted enough energy on my own preoccupations. I should have already opened the door of 221b Baker Street and entered the room where so many adventures began. I see it now, the glow of the lamp behind the glass and the seventeen steps beckoning me up from the street. How long ago since last I was there. There he is, with pipe in hand. He turns to me. He smiles. 'The game's afoot . . .'

ONE
The Wimbledon Art Dealer

'Influenza is unpleasant,' Sherlock Holmes remarked, 'but you are right in thinking that, with your wife's help, the child will recover soon.'

'I very much hope so,' I replied, then gazed at him in wide-eyed astonishment. 'But for heaven's sake, Holmes!' I exclaimed. 'You have taken the very thoughts from my head. I swear I have not uttered a word about the child nor his illness. You know that my wife is away—that much you might have deduced from my presence here. But I have not mentioned the reason for her absence and I am certain that there has been nothing in my behaviour that could have given you any clue.'

It was in the last days of November, the year 1890, when this exchange took place. London was in the grip of a merciless winter. Outside, people drifted along the pavements like ghosts, with their heads bowed and faces covered, while the growlers rattled past, their horses anxious to be home. And I was glad to be in, with a fire blazing in the hearth, the familiar smell of tobacco in the air and a sense that everything was in its right place.

I had telegraphed my intention to stay with Holmes for a short while, and I had been delighted to receive his acquiescence. I was temporarily alone. And I had it in mind to watch over my friend until I was certain that he was fully restored to health. For Holmes had deliberately starved himself for three days and nights in order to persuade a particularly cruel adversary that he was close to death. The ruse had succeeded triumphantly, and the man was now in the capable hands of Inspector Morton of the Yard. But I was still concerned about the strain that Holmes had placed upon himself.

I was therefore glad to see him enjoying a plate of scones with violet honey and cream, along with a pound cake and tea, which Mrs Hudson had served for the two of us. Holmes was lying at ease in his big armchair, with his feet stretched out in front of the fire. He had always been of a distinctly lean and even cadaverous physique, those sharp eyes accentuated by his aquiline nose, but at least there was some colour in his skin and everything about his manner pronounced him to be very much his old self.

He had greeted me warmly and, as I took my place opposite him, I felt the strange sensation that I was awakening from a dream. It was as if the past two years had never happened, that I had never met my beloved Mary, married her and moved to our home in Kensington. I could still have been a bachelor, living here with Holmes, sharing with him the excitement of the chase and yet another mystery.

And it occurred to me that he might well have preferred it thus. Holmes spoke seldom about my domestic arrangements. It would be unfair to say that the entire subject of my marriage was forbidden, but there was an unspoken agreement that we would not discuss it at any length. My happiness and contentment were evident to Holmes, and he was generous enough not to begrudge it. When I had first arrived, he had asked after Mrs Watson. But he had not requested any further information and I had provided none, making his remarks all the more unfathomable.

'Are you seriously telling me, Holmes, that you could deduce the sickness of a child you have never met, simply from my behaviour over a plate of scones?'

'That and more,' Holmes replied. 'I can tell that you have just returned from Holborn Viaduct. That you left your house in a hurry, but even so missed the train. Perhaps the fact that you are currently without a servant girl is to blame.'

'No, Holmes!' I cried. 'I will not have it! You are correct on every count. But how is it possible . . .?'

'It is a simple matter of observation and deduction, the one informing the other. Were I to explain it to you, it would seem painfully childish.'

'And yet I must insist that you do just that.'

'Well, I suppose I must oblige,' returned Holmes with a yawn. 'If my memory serves, we are approaching the second anniversary of your marriage, are we not?'

'Indeed so, Holmes. It is the day after tomorrow.'

'An unusual time, then, for you to separate from your wife. The fact that you have chosen to stay with me for a prolonged period would suggest that there was a compelling reason for her to part company with you. As I recall, Miss Mary Morston—as she once was—came to England from India and had no friends or family here. She was taken on as a governess, looking after the son of Mrs Cecil Forrester, in Camberwell, which is where you met her. Mrs Forrester was very good to her and I would imagine that the two of them have remained close.'

'That is indeed the case.'

'And so, if anyone were likely to call your wife away, it might well be her. I wonder then what reason might lie behind such a summons, and in this cold weather the sickness of a child springs to mind. It would, I am sure, be comforting for the afflicted lad to have his old governess back.'

'His name is Richard and he is nine years old,' I concurred. 'But how can you be so confident that it is influenza?'

'Were it more serious, you would have insisted upon attending yourself.'

'Your reasoning has so far been utterly straightforward but it does not explain how you knew that my thoughts had turned towards them at that precise moment.'

'You will forgive me if I say that you are to me as an open book, my dear Watson. I noticed your eye drift towards the newspaper on the table right beside you. You glanced at the headline and then turned it face down. Why? Perhaps the report on the train crash at Norton Fitzwarren disturbed you. The findings of the investigation into the deaths of ten passengers were published today and it was, of course, the last thing you would wish to read just after leaving your wife at a station.'

'That did indeed remind me of her journey,' I agreed. 'But the sickness of the child?'

'From the newspaper, your attention turned to the patch of carpet beside the desk and I distinctly saw you smile to yourself. It was there that you once kept your medicine bag and it was surely that association which reminded you of the reason for your wife's visit.'

'This is all guesswork, Holmes,' I insisted. 'You say Holborn Viaduct, for example. It could have been any station in London.'

'You know that I deplore guesswork. It is sometimes necessary to connect points of evidence with the use of imagination, but that is not the same thing. Mrs Forrester lives in Camberwell. The London Chatham and Dover Railway has regular departures from Holborn Viaduct. I would have considered that the logical starting point, even if you had not obliged me by leaving your own suitcase by the door. I can clearly see a label from the Holborn Viaduct Left Luggage Office attached to the handle.'

'And the rest of it?'

'The fact that you have lost your maid and that you left the house in a hurry? The smudge of black polish on the side of your left cuff clearly indicates both. You cleaned your own shoes and you did so rather carelessly. Moreover, in your haste, you forgot your gloves—'

'Mrs Hudson took my coat. She could also have taken my gloves.'

'In which case, when we shook hands, why would yours have been so cold? No, Watson, your entire bearing speaks of disarray.'

'Everything you say is right,' I admitted. 'But one last mystery, Holmes. How can you be so sure that my wife missed her train?'

'As soon as you arrived, I noticed a strong scent of coffee on your clothes. Why would you be drinking coffee before coming to me for tea? The inference is that you missed your train and were forced to stay with your wife for longer than intended. You stowed your case at the left luggage office and went with her to a coffee house.'

I burst into laughter. 'Well, Holmes,' I said. 'I can see that I had no reason to worry about your health. You are as remarkable as ever.'

'It was quite elementary,' returned the detective with a languid gesture of one hand. 'But perhaps something of greater interest now approaches. Unless I am mistaken, that is the front door . . .'

Sure enough, Mrs Hudson ushered in a man who walked into the room as if he were making an entrance on the London stage. He was formally dressed in a dark tail coat, wing collar and white bow tie with a black cloak around his shoulders. His dark hair was surprisingly long, his skin pale, his face a little too elongated to be truly handsome. His age, I would have said, would have been in the mid-thirties and yet the seriousness of his demeanour made him appear older. Our visitor waited in the doorway, looking anxiously around him, while Mrs Hudson handed Holmes his card.

'Mr Carstairs,' Holmes said. 'Please take a seat.'

'You must forgive me arriving in this manner—unexpected and unannounced.' He had a clipped way of speaking. His eyes still did not quite meet our gaze. 'In truth, I had no intention of coming here at all. I live in Wimbledon and have come into town for the opera—not that I'm in the mood. I have just come from my club where I met my accountant, a man I have known for many years. When I told him of the troubles I have been having, he urged me to consult you. By coincidence, my club is not far from here and so I resolved to come straight from him to you.'

'I am happy to give you my full attention,' Holmes said. 'Dr John Watson is my closest adviser. I can assure you that anything you have to say to me can be uttered in his presence.'

'Very well. My name, as you see, is Edmund Carstairs and I am a dealer in fine art. I have a gallery, Carstairs and Finch on Albemarle Street, which has been in business for six years. We specialise in the works of Gainsborough, Reynolds, Constable and Turner. Their paintings will be familiar to you, I am sure, and they command the very highest prices. Our clients include many members of the aristocracy.'

'Your partner, Mr Finch?'

'Tobias Finch is rather older than myself, although we are equal partners. He is more conservative than I. For example, I have a strong interest in new work from the continent. I refer to the *impressionistes*, such artists as Monet and Degas. My partner, alas, insists that such works are little more than a blur, and I cannot persuade him that he is missing the point. However, I will not tire you gentlemen with a lecture on art.'

Holmes nodded. 'Pray continue.'

'Two weeks ago I realised that I was being watched. Ridgeway Hall, my home, stands on a narrow lane, with a cluster of almshouses some distance away. These are our closest neighbours. From my dressing room I have a view of the village green and here, on a Tuesday morning, I became aware of a man standing with his legs apart and his arms folded. I was struck at once by his extraordinary stillness. He was wearing a long frock coat of a cut that was most certainly not English. I was in America last year and if

I were to guess I would say it was from this country that he originated. What struck me most forcefully, however, was that he was also wearing a flat cap of the sort that is sometimes called a cheese cutter.

'It was this and the way that he stood there that first attracted my attention. There was a light rain falling, but he didn't seem to notice it. His eyes were fixed on my window. I gazed at him for at least a minute, then went down to breakfast. However, before I ate, I sent the scullery boy out to see if the man was still there. He was not.'

'Ridgeway Hall is, I am sure, a fine building,' Holmes remarked. 'A visitor to this country might well have found it merited his examination.'

'And so I told myself. But a few days later, I saw him a second time, in London. My wife and I had just come out of the Savoy Theatre and there he was, on the other side of the road, wearing the same coat, again with the flat cap. He was unmoving and, with the crowds passing on either side of him, he could have been a solid rock in a fast-flowing river.'

'Did your wife see him?'

'No. And I did not wish to alarm her by making any mention of it.'

'This is most interesting,' Holmes remarked. 'The behaviour of this man makes no sense. It's as if he is making every effort to be seen and yet he makes no attempt to approach you.'

'He did approach me,' Carstairs replied. 'The very next day, when I returned early to the house shortly before three o'clock. It was as well that I did, for there was the rogue approaching my front door. I called out to him and he turned. At once, he began to run towards me and I lifted my walking stick to protect myself. But his mission was not one of violence. He came straight up to me and I saw his face: thin lips, dark brown eyes and a livid scar on his right cheek. I could smell spirits on his breath. He didn't utter a word but instead lifted a note into the air and pressed it into my hand. Then he ran off.'

'And the note?' Holmes asked.

'I have it here.'

The art dealer produced a square of paper, folded into four. Holmes opened it carefully. 'There was no envelope?'

'No.'

'I find that of the greatest significance. But let us see . . .'

There were just six words written in block capitals on the page.

ST MARY'S CHURCH. TOMORROW. MIDDAY.

'The paper is English,' Holmes remarked. 'Even if the visitor was not. He writes in capitals, Watson. What do you suggest his purpose might be?'

'To disguise his handwriting,' I said.

'It is possible. Although since the man had never written to Mr Carstairs, and is perhaps unlikely to write to him again, you would have thought his handwriting would have been of no consequence. Was the message folded when it was handed to you, Mr Carstairs?'

'No. I think not. I folded it myself later.'

'The picture becomes clearer by the minute. This church that he refers to, St Mary's. I assume it is in Wimbledon?'

'It is just a few minutes' walk from my home.'

'This behaviour is lacking in logic, do you not think? The man wishes to speak with you. He places a message to that effect in your hand. But he does not utter a word.'

'My guess was that he wished to talk to me alone. As it happened, my wife, Catherine, emerged from the house a few moments later. She had been standing in the breakfast room that looks out onto the drive and she had seen what had just occurred. "Who was that?" she asked.

'"I have no idea," I replied.

'"What did he want?"

'I showed her the note. "It's someone wanting money," she said. "I saw him out of the window just now—a rough-looking fellow. Edmund, you mustn't go."

'"I have no intention of meeting him," I replied.'

'You reassured your wife,' Holmes murmured. 'But you went to the church at the appointed time.'

'I did exactly that—and carried a revolver with me. He wasn't there. I paced the flagstones for an hour and then I came home. I have not seen him again, but I have been unable to get him out of my mind.'

'The man is known to you,' Holmes said.

'Yes, Mr Holmes. I believe I know his identity, although I confess I do not see the reasoning that has brought you to that conclusion.'

'It strikes me as self-evident,' Holmes replied. 'Nothing that you have described would suggest that this man is any threat to you, but you began by telling us of the sense of trouble and oppression that has brought you here and would not even meet him without carrying a gun. And you still have not told us the significance of the flat cap.'

'I know who he is. I know what he wants. I am appalled that he has followed me to England.'

'Mr Carstairs, your story is full of interest and, if you have time before your opera begins, I think you should give us the complete history of this affair. You mentioned that you were in America a year ago. Was this when you met the man in the flat cap?'

'I never met him. But it was on his account that I was there.'

'So tell us of your business on the other side of the Atlantic. An art dealer is not the sort of man to make enemies, I would have thought. But you seem to have done just that.'

'Indeed so. My foeman is called Keelan O'Donaghue and I wish to heaven that I had never heard the name.'

Holmes began to fill his pipe. Meanwhile, Edmund Carstairs drew a breath and this is the tale that he told:

'Eighteen months ago, I was introduced to Cornelius Stillman, who was in London at the end of a lengthy European tour. His home was on the East Coast of America and he was what is termed a Boston Brahmin, which is to say that he belonged to one of their most elevated families. He had made a fortune from mines and, in his youth, apparently had ambitions to become an artist. Part of the reason for his visit was to visit the museums and galleries of Paris, Florence and London.

'Like many wealthy Americans, he was imbued with a sense of civic responsibility. He had purchased land in the Back Bay area of Boston and had begun work on the construction of an art gallery called The Parthenon, which he planned to fill with the finest works, purchased on his travels. I found him to be a volcano of a man, brimming with energy and enthusiasm. His knowledge of art, his aesthetic sensibility, set him apart from many of his fellow citizens. The Parthenon, he said, would be a temple to art and to civilisation.

'I was overjoyed when Mr Stillman agreed to come to my gallery. Mr Finch and I spent many hours in his company in Albemarle Street, showing him some of the purchases we had recently made. The long and the short of it was that he bought from us a series of four landscapes by John Constable that were quite the pride of our collection. These were views of the Lake District, painted in 1806, and unlike anything else in the artist's canon. Mr Stillman promised that they would be exhibited in a room which he would design specifically for them. We parted on excellent terms and I banked a substantial sum of money. Indeed, Mr Finch remarked that this was undoubtedly the most successful transaction of our lives.

'The works were dispatched with the White Star Line from Liverpool to New York. We had intended to send them directly to Boston but we missed the RMS *Adventurer* by a matter of hours and so chose another vessel. Our agent, James Devoy, met the package in New York and travelled with it on the railroad—a journey of one hundred and ninety miles.

'But the paintings never arrived.

'There were, in Boston at this time, a number of gangs operating particularly in the south of the city and the police had been unable to bring them to justice. One of the most dangerous groups was known as the Flat Cap Gang, headed by a pair of twins—Rourke and Keelan O'Donaghue, originally from Belfast. The two of them were never seen apart. Although they were identical when they were born, Rourke was the larger, square-shouldered and barrel-chested with heavy fists. It is said that he beat a man to death when he was barely sixteen. By contrast, his twin was smaller and quieter. He seldom spoke—there were rumours that he was unable to. Rourke was bearded, Keelan clean-shaven. Both wore flat caps and it was this that gave the gang its name. It was also widely believed that they carried each other's initials tattooed on their arms, and that in every aspect of their lives they were inseparable.

'Of the other gang members, their names tell you perhaps as much as you would wish to know. There was Frank "Mad Dog" Kelly and Patrick "Razors" Maclean. Another was known as "The Ghost" and was feared as much as any supernatural being. They were involved in robberies, burglaries and protectionism. And yet they were held in high regard by many of the poorer inhabitants of Boston. They were the underdogs, waging war on an uncaring system. There was a belief that they would never be caught, that they could get away with anything.

'I had never heard of the Flat Cap Gang when I sent off the paintings at Liverpool but somehow, at exactly the same time, they were tipped off that a large amount of currency was about to be transferred from New York to the First National Bank in Boston, travelling on the Boston and Albany Railroad. Some say that Rourke was the brains behind their operation. Others believe that Keelan was the mastermind. In any event, they arrived at the idea of holding up the train and making off with the cash.

'Train robberies were still prevalent in the western frontiers of America, but for such a thing to take place on the more developed eastern seaboard was almost inconceivable and that is why the train left the Grand Central Terminal in New York with only one armed guard in the mail car. The bank-notes were contained in a safe. And by some wretched chance, the paintings were travelling in the same compartment. Our agent, James Devoy, had taken a seat as close to the mail car as possible.

'Just outside Pittsfield the track climbed steeply upwards before crossing the Connecticut River. A tunnel ran for two thousand feet and, according to railway regulations, the engineer was obliged to test his brakes at the exit. The train was therefore travelling very slowly as it emerged and Rourke and Keelan O'Donaghue jumped down onto the roof of one of the wagons. They climbed over the tender and, to the astonishment of the driver and his brakeman, suddenly appeared in the engine cab with guns drawn.

'They ordered the train to a halt in a forest clearing where Kelly, Maclean and the other gang members were waiting with horses—and with dynamite. Rourke struck the driver with the side of his revolver, concussing him. Keelan tied the brakeman to a metal stanchion. Meanwhile, the rest of the gang boarded the train. Ordering the passengers to remain seated, they approached the mail car and began to set charges around the door.

'James Devoy had seen what was happening and must have guessed that the robbers were here for reasons other than the Constables. While the other passengers cowered around him, Devoy left his seat and climbed down, meaning to plead with the gang. At least, I assume that was his intention. Before he could say a word, Rourke gunned him down. Devoy was shot three times in the chest and died in a pool of his own blood. A moment later, a huge explosion rent the air and the entire wall of the mail car was blown apart. The guard was killed instantly. The safe with the money was exposed.

'A second, smaller charge sufficed to open it and now the band discovered that they had been misinformed. Only two thousand dollars had been sent, immeasurably less than they had expected. Even so, they snatched up the notes with cries of exaltation, unaware that they had destroyed four canvases that alone were worth twenty times what they had taken. Even now I have to remind myself that two men died that day, but I would be lying to you if I did not say that I mourn the loss of those paintings just as much.

'Finch and I heard the news with horror. How bitterly we regretted the route we had chosen and blamed ourselves for what had occurred. There were also financial considerations. Mr Stillman had paid a deposit for the paintings but, according to the contract, we were responsible for them until they were delivered into his hands. It was fortunate that we were insured with Lloyd's of London or else we would have been wiped out. There was also the matter of James Devoy's family. I learned that he had a wife and a young child. Someone would have to take care of them.

'It was for these reasons that I travelled to America. I met Mrs Devoy in New York and promised her that she would receive some compensation. Her son was nine years old and a sweeter, more good-looking child would be hard to imagine. I then travelled to Boston and from there to Providence, where Cornelius Stillman had built his summer house. Shepherd's Point was huge, constructed in the style of a French chateau. The gardens alone stretched out for thirty acres and the interior displayed an opulence that I will never forget. The magnificent wooden staircase that dominated the Great Hall, the library with its five thousand volumes, the chapel with its ancient organ once played by Purcell . . . And as for the art! I counted works by Titian, Rembrandt and Velasquez before I had even reached the drawing room. It was while I was considering all this wealth, the limitless funds on which my host must be able to draw, that an idea formed in my mind.

'Over dinner that night I raised the subject of Mrs Devoy and her child. Stillman assured me that even though they were not resident in Boston, he would alert the city fathers who would take care of them. Encouraged by this, I asked if there was any way he could help bring the Flat Cap Gang to justice. Might it not be possible to offer a sizable reward for information and, at the same time, to hire a private detective agency to apprehend them on our behalf? In this way we would simultaneously avenge the death of Devoy and punish them for the loss of the Constable landscapes.

'Stillman seized on my idea with enthusiasm. "You're right, Carstairs!" he cried. "I'll show these bums it was a bad day that they chose to hornswoggle Cornelius T. Stillman!" He even insisted on funding the full cost of the detectives and the reward, although I offered to make a contribution. We shook hands on it and he suggested that I stay with him while the arrangements were made, an invitation I was glad to accept. There was enough in Stillman's summer home to keep me entranced for months.

'But events took a swifter course. Mr Stillman contacted Pinkerton's and engaged a man called Bill McParland. I did not meet him myself but I knew enough of McParland's reputation to be sure that he was a formidable investigator who would not give up until the Flat Cap Gang had been delivered into his hands. Advertisements were placed offering a reward of $100 for information leading to the arrests of Rourke and Keelan O'Donaghue and all those associated with them. I was glad to see that Mr Stillman had included my name along with his own beneath the announcement, even though the money was entirely his.

'I spent the next few weeks at Shepherd's Point and in Boston and travelled to New York a few times to spend several hours at the Metropolitan Museum of Art. I also visited Mrs Devoy and her son. While I was in New York I received a telegram from Stillman, urging me to return. McParland had been given a tip-off. The net was closing in on the Flat Cap Gang.

'I returned at once to hear from Cornelius Stillman what had occurred. The tip-off had come from the owner of a dram shop—what the Americans call a saloon—in the South End, home to a large number of Irish immigrants. The O'Donaghue twins were holed up in a tenement house close to the Charles River, a squalid building on three storeys with dozens of rooms clustered together. A rough construction of timber had been added at the back and this the twins had managed to make their own. Keelan had one room to himself. Rourke shared another with two men and a third was occupied by the rest of the gang.

'As the sun set that evening, they were crouched around the stove, drinking gin and playing cards. They had no lookout and so they were oblivious to the approach of McParland, who was closing in on the tenement accompanied by a dozen armed men.

'When his men were in position, McParland took up his bullhorn and called out a warning. But if he had hoped that the Flat Cap Gang would surrender quietly, he was disillusioned a moment later by a volley of shots. The twins were not going to give up without a fight, and a cascade of lead poured out into the street. Two of the Pinkerton men were gunned down and McParland himself was wounded, but the others gave as good as they got, emptying their six-shooters directly into the structure. Hundreds of bullets tore through the flimsy wood. There was nowhere to hide.

'When it was all over, they found five men lying in the smoke-filled interior, their bodies shot to pieces. Keelan O'Donaghue had escaped. At first it seemed impossible, but one of the floorboards was pulled aside to reveal a narrow drainage ditch that continued all the way to the river. It must have been the devil of a tight squeeze for the pipe was barely large enough to contain a child. McParland led some of his men down to the river but by then it was pitch dark and he knew any search would be fruitless. The Flat Cap Gang was destroyed but one of its ringleaders had got away.

'This was the outcome that Cornelius Stillman described to me in my hotel that night, but it is not the end of the story. I remained in Boston another week, partly in the hope that Keelan O'Donaghue might be found. A slight concern had risen in my mind. Stillman had made public the fact that I had been party to the reward and to the posse that had been sent after the Flat Cap Gang. It now occurred to me that to have killed one twin and to have left the other alive might make me a target for revenge, particularly in a place where the very worst criminals could count on the support of so many friends and admirers. I did not stray into the rougher parts of the city. And I certainly didn't go out at night.

'Keelan O'Donaghue was not captured and there was some doubt that he had survived. He could have been wounded and died of blood loss. He could have drowned. Stillman had persuaded himself that this was the case by the time we met for the last time. I had booked passage back to England on the SS *Catalonia*. I was about to board the ship when I heard the news being shouted out by a newsboy and there it was, on the front page.

'Cornelius Stillman had been shot dead while walking in the rose garden of his home in Providence. With a shaking hand, I read that a young man wearing a flat cap had been seen fleeing from the scene. According to the report, Bill McParland was assisting the police and there was a certain irony in this, as he and Stillman had fallen out before Stillman's death. Stillman had held back half the fee, arguing that the job would not be fully completed until the last body had been recovered. Well, that last body was up and walking, for there could be no doubt at all as to the identity of Stillman's assailant.

'I went directly to my cabin and remained there until the *Catalonia* slipped out of port. Only then did I return to the deck and watch as Boston disappeared behind me. I was hugely relieved to be away.

'That, gentlemen, is the story of the lost Constables and my visit to America. I of course told Mr Finch what had occurred and I have spoken of it with my wife. But I have never repeated it to anyone else. It happened more than a year ago. And until the man in the flat cap appeared outside my house, I thought—I prayed—that I would never have to refer to it again.'

Holmes had been listening with a look of intense concentration on his face. There was a lengthy silence. A coal tumbled and the sound of it seemed to draw him out of his reverie.

'What was the opera you intended to see tonight?' he asked.

It was the last question I had expected. It seemed to be of such trivial importance in the light of everything we had just heard that I wondered if he was being deliberately rude.

Carstairs must have thought the same. He started back, turned to me, then back to Holmes. 'I am going to a performance of Wagner—but has nothing I have said made any impression on you?'

'On the contrary, I found it of great interest.'

'And the man in the flat cap . . .'

'You evidently believe him to be this Keelan O'Donaghue. You think he has followed you to England in order to exact his revenge?'

'What other possible explanation could there be?'

'Offhand, I could perhaps suggest half a dozen. Any interpretation of a series of events is possible until all the evidence says otherwise and even then one should be wary before jumping to a conclusion. It might be that this man has crossed the Atlantic and found his way to your Wimbledon home. However, one might ask why it has taken him more than a year to make the journey and what purpose he had in inviting you to a meeting at the church. Why not just shoot you down where you stood, if that was his intent? Even more strange is the fact that he failed to turn up.'

'He is trying to terrorise me.'

'And succeeding.'

'Are you saying that you cannot help me, Mr Holmes?'

'At this juncture, I do not see that there is a great deal I can do. Your unwanted visitor has given us no clue as to how we may find him. If he should reappear, then I will be pleased to give you what assistance I can. But you can enjoy your opera in a tranquil state of mind. I do not believe he intends to do you harm.'

But Holmes was wrong. At least, that was how it appeared the very next day. For it was then that the man in the flat cap struck again.

THE TELEGRAM ARRIVED the next morning. O'DONAGHUE CAME AGAIN LAST NIGHT. MY SAFE BROKEN INTO AND POLICE NOW SUMMONED. CAN YOU COME? It was signed Edmund Carstairs.

'I was anticipating something very much like this,' Holmes said. 'It occurred to me that the so-called man in the flat cap was more interested in Ridgeway Hall than its owner.'

'You expected a burglary?' I stammered. 'But, Holmes, why did you not give Mr Carstairs a warning?'

'With no further evidence there was nothing I could hope to achieve. But now our unwanted visitor has generously decided to assist us. He has quite probably forced a window. He will have walked across the lawn, stood in a flowerbed and left muddy tracks across the carpet. From this we will learn his height, his weight, his profession and any peculiarities he may have in his gait. If he has taken jewellery, it will have to be disposed of. At least now he will have laid a track that we can follow. There are plenty of trains to Wimbledon. I take it you will join me?'

'Of course, Holmes. I would like nothing better.'

My first impression of Ridgeway Hall was that it was a perfect jewel of a house and one well suited to a collector of fine art. Two gates, one on each side, opened from the public lane with a gravel drive, shaped like a horseshoe, sweeping up to the front door. The house itself was what I would have termed a villa, built in the classic Georgian style, perfectly square, with elegant windows placed symmetrically on either side of the front entrance. This symmetry even extended to the trees, planted so that one side of the garden almost formed a mirror image of the other. And yet, an Italian fountain with cupids and dolphins playing in the stone had been positioned slightly out of kilter. It was impossible to see it without wishing to pick it up and carry it two or three yards to the left.

It turned out that the police had already come and gone. The door was opened by a grim-faced manservant. He led us along a wide corridor, the walls hung with paintings and engravings, antique mirrors and tapestries. We were shown into the drawing room where Carstairs was sitting on a chaise longue, talking to a woman who was a few years younger than himself. He was wearing a black frock coat, a silver-coloured waistcoat and his long hair was neatly combed. He sprang to his feet the moment he saw us.

'You told me yesterday that I had no reason to fear Keelan O'Donaghue. And yet last night he broke into this house. He has taken fifty pounds and jewellery from my safe. But for the fact that my wife actually surprised him in the middle of his larceny, who knows what he might have done next?'

I turned my attention to the lady. She was a small, very attractive person of about thirty years of age with fair hair tied in a knot, a style that seemed designed to accentuate the elegance of her features. I guessed that she had a quick sense of humour, for it was there in her eyes and her lips, which were constantly on the edge of a smile. There was something about her that reminded me of my own dear Mary.

'Perhaps you should begin by introducing us,' Holmes remarked.

'Of course. This is my wife, Catherine.'

'And you must be Mr Sherlock Holmes. I am very grateful to you for replying so quickly to our telegram. I told Edmund to send it.'

'I understand that you have had an unsettling experience,' Holmes said.

'Indeed so. I was woken up last night and saw from the clock that it was twenty past three. There was a full moon shining through the window. I heard a sound from inside the house and I went downstairs.'

'It was a foolish thing to do, my dear,' Carstairs remarked.

'It didn't occur to me that there might be a stranger in the house. I thought it might be Mr or Mrs Kirby—or even Patrick. You know I don't completely trust that boy. Anyway, I looked briefly in the drawing room. Then, for some reason, I was drawn to the study.'

'You had no light with you?' Holmes asked.

'The moon was enough. I opened the door and there was a silhouette perched on the windowsill. He saw me and the two of us froze. I didn't scream. I was too shocked. Then it was as if he simply fell backwards through the window and at that moment I raised the alarm.'

'I can tell from your accent that you are American,' Holmes said. 'Have you been married long, Mrs Carstairs?'

'Edmund and I have been married for almost a year and a half.'

'I should have explained to you how I met Catherine,' Carstairs said. 'The only reason that I chose not to do so was because I thought it had no relevance.'

'Everything has a relevance,' remarked Holmes. 'The most immaterial aspect of a case can be its most significant.'

'We met on the *Catalonia* the very day that it left Boston,' Catherine Carstairs said. She reached out and took her husband's hand. 'I was travelling alone, apart, of course, from a girl whom I had employed to be my companion. I saw Edmund as he came on board and it was obvious from his face that something dreadful had happened. And by a stroke of good fortune we found ourselves seated next to each other at dinner.'

Carstairs continued the tale. 'I have always been of a nervous disposition and the loss of the paintings, the death of Cornelius Stillman, the terrible violence . . . it had all been too much for me. I was quite unwell. But from the first Catherine looked after me. I have always sneered at the concept of "love at first sight", Mr Holmes. Nonetheless, that is what occurred. By the time we arrived in England, I knew that I had found the woman with whom I wished to spend the rest of my life.'

'And what was the reason for your visit to England?' Holmes asked, turning to the wife.

'I was married briefly in Chicago. My husband was well respected but he was never kind to me. He had a dreadful temper and there were times when I feared for my safety. Then, quite suddenly, he became ill with tuberculosis and died. His house and much of his wealth went to his two sisters. I was left with little money, no friends and no reason to stay in America. I was coming to England for a new start.' She glanced down and added, 'I had not expected to come across it so soon, nor to find the happiness that had for so long been missing from my life.'

'You mentioned a companion on the *Catalonia*,' Holmes remarked.

'I hired her in Boston and she left my employ soon after we arrived.'

In the corridor, the clock chimed the hour. Holmes sprang to his feet with a smile on his face and that sense of energy and excitement that I knew so well. 'We must waste no further time!' he exclaimed. 'I wish to examine the safe and the room in which it is contained.'

But before we could make a move, another woman came into the room, as different from Catherine Carstairs as could be imagined. She was plain and unsmiling, dressed in grey. From her dark eyes, her pale skin and the shape of her lips, I surmised that she must be related to Carstairs.

'What now?' she demanded. 'First I am disturbed in my room by police officers asking absurd questions. And that is not enough? Are we to invite the whole world in to invade our privacy?'

'This is Mr Sherlock Holmes, Eliza,' Carstairs stammered. 'I told you that I consulted with him yesterday.'

'And much good did it do you. There was nothing he could do; that was what he told you. We could all of us have been murdered in our beds.'

Carstairs glanced at her fondly but with exasperation. 'This is my sister, Eliza.'

'You reside in this house?' Holmes asked her.

'I reside here, but I am not part of this family. You might as well speak to the servants as to me.'

'You know that's not fair, Eliza,' Mrs Carstairs said.

Holmes turned to Carstairs. 'Perhaps you might tell me how many people there are in the house.'

'Apart from myself and Catherine, Eliza occupies the top floor. We have Kirby, who is our footman and man-of-all-work. He showed you in. His wife acts as our housekeeper and the two of them have a nephew, Patrick, who came to us recently from Ireland and acts as the kitchen boy, and there is a scullery maid, Elsie. In addition, we have a coachman and groom, but they live in the village.'

'A large household and a busy one,' Holmes remarked. 'But we were about to examine the safe.'

Eliza Carstairs remained where she was. The rest of us went down the corridor and into Carstairs's study, which was at the back of the house. This turned out to be a well-appointed room with a desk framed by two windows, a handsome fireplace and some landscapes that, from the almost haphazard way the paint had been applied, I knew must belong to the Impressionist school of which Carstairs had spoken. The safe was tucked away in one corner, still open.

'The police have examined it,' Carstairs said. 'But I felt it best to leave it open until you arrived.'

'You were right,' Holmes said. He glanced at the safe. 'The lock does not appear to have been forced, which would suggest that a key has been used.'

'There was only one key,' Carstairs returned, 'although I asked Kirby to make a copy of it six months ago. Catherine keeps her jewellery in the safe and she felt she should have a key of her own.'

'I lost it,' Mrs Carstairs said. 'Edmund and I have been through this. The last time I used it was on my birthday, in August. I have no idea what happened to it after that.'

'Could it have been stolen?'

'I kept it in a drawer beside my bed and nobody comes into the room apart from the servants.'

Holmes turned to Carstairs. 'You did not replace the safe.'

'It was in my mind to do so but if the key had been dropped in the garden or the village, nobody could know what it opened. Anyway, we cannot be sure that it was my wife's key that was used. Kirby could have had a second copy made.'

'How long has he been with you?'

'Six years.'

'You have had no cause to complain about him?'

'None whatsoever.'

'And what of the kitchen boy? Your wife says she mistrusts him.'

'My wife dislikes him because he is insolent. He has been with us for only a few months and we took him on only at the behest of Mrs Kirby. She will vouch for him and I have no reason to think him dishonest.'

Holmes had taken out his glass and examined the safe, paying particular attention to the lock. 'You say that some jewellery was stolen?'

'It was a necklace belonging to my late mother. Three clusters of sapphires in a gold setting. I imagine it would have little financial value to the thief but it had great sentimental value to me. She lived with us here until a few months ago when . . .' He broke off and his wife went over to him and laid a hand on his arm. 'She had a gas fire in her bedroom. Somehow the flame blew out and she was asphyxiated in her sleep.'

'She was very elderly?'

'She was sixty-nine. She always slept with the window closed. Otherwise she might have been saved.'

Holmes went over to the window. I joined him there as he examined the sill, the sashes and the frame. As was his habit, he spoke his observations aloud. 'No shutters. The window is snibbed and some distance from the ground. It has evidently been forced from the outside.' He seemed to be making a calculation. 'I would like to speak to your man, Kirby. And after that I will walk in the garden, although I imagine the police will have trampled over anything that might have furnished me with any clue as to what has taken place. Did they give you any idea of their line of investigation?'

'Inspector Lestrade returned and spoke to us shortly before you arrived.'

'What? Lestrade? He was here?'

'Yes. He had already ascertained that a man with an American accent took the first train from Wimbledon to London Bridge at five o'clock this morning. From the way he was dressed and the scar on his right cheek, we are certain that it is the same man that I saw.'

We retraced our footsteps to the front door where Kirby was waiting for us. He was from Barnstaple originally, his wife from Belfast. Holmes asked him if the house had changed much during his time there.

'Oh yes, sir,' came the reply. 'Old Mrs Carstairs was very fixed in her ways. The new Mrs Carstairs could not be more different. She has a very cheerful disposition. My wife considers her a breath of fresh air.'

'You were glad that Mr Carstairs married?'

'We were delighted, sir, as well as surprised.'

'Surprised?'

'Mr Carstairs had formerly shown no interest in such matters, being devoted to his family and to his work. Mrs Carstairs rather burst in on the scene but we are all agreed that the house has been better for it.'

'You were present when old Mrs Carstairs died?'

'I was, sir. In part I blame myself. The lady had a fear of draughts, as a result of which I had stopped up every crevice by which air might enter the room. The gas, therefore, had no way of escaping.'

'Was the kitchen boy, Patrick, in the house at the time?'

'Patrick had arrived from Belfast just one week before.'

'He is your nephew, I understand.'

'On my wife's side, yes, sir. We had hoped to give him a good start in life but he has yet to learn the correct attitude for one befitting his station. He is not such a bad young man and I hope that in time he will prosper.'

'Thank you, Kirby.'

Out in the garden, Holmes strode across the lawn. 'This is a wholly remarkable case, do you not think?'

'It strikes me as quite trivial,' I replied. 'The sum of fifty pounds has been taken along with an antique necklace. I can't call this the most testing of your challenges, Holmes.'

'I find the necklace particularly fascinating. You have already arrived, then, at the solution?'

'I suppose it hinges on whether the unwanted visitor to this house was the twin brother from Boston.'

'And if I were to assure you that he was almost certainly not?'

'Then I would say that, not for the first time, you are being thoroughly perplexing.'

'Dear old Watson. How good it is to have you at my side. But I think this is where the intruder arrived last night . . .' We had come to the bottom of the garden where the drive met the lane. The cold weather and the well-tended lawn had created a perfect canvas on which all the comings and goings of the preceding twenty-four hours had been, in effect, frozen. 'There, if I am not mistaken, goes the thorough and efficient Lestrade.' Holmes pointed to one set of footprints in particular.

'You cannot possibly know they are his.'

'No? The length of the stride would suggest a man of about five foot six inches in height, the same as Lestrade. The most damning evidence is that they are heading in quite the wrong direction. He has entered and left by the gate on the right, the first gate that you come to on approaching the house. The intruder, however, surely came in the other way.'

'Both gates seem identical to me, Holmes.'

'But the one to the left is less conspicuous due to the position of the fountain. If you were to approach the house without wishing to be seen, this is the one you would choose and we have only one set of footprints here with which to concern ourselves. Halloa! What have we here?' Holmes crouched down and seized hold of the butt of a cigarette. 'An American cigarette, Watson. There is no mistaking the tobacco. You will notice that there is no ash. Meaning that although he was careful not to be seen, he did not linger long. Do you not find that significant?'

'It was the middle of the night, Holmes. He had no fear of being noticed.'

'Even so . . .' We followed the tracks round the side of the house to the study. Holmes examined the window that we had already examined from within. 'He must have been a man of uncommon strength.'

'The window would not have been so difficult to force.'

'Indeed not, Watson. But consider the height of it. There is no sign of a ladder, nor even a garden chair. It is just possible that he could have found a toehold on the wall. But he would still have had to use one hand to cling to the sill while he jemmied open the window with the other. We must also ask ourselves if it was a coincidence that he chose to break into the room in which the safe was contained.'

'Surely he came round the back of the house because it was more secluded and chose a window at random?'

'In which instance he was remarkably fortunate.' Holmes had concluded his examination. 'But a necklace with three clusters of sapphires in a gold setting should not be hard to trace, and that should lead us to our man. Lestrade has at least confirmed that he took the train to London Bridge. We must do the same.'

We made our way across the front of the house, but before we could reach the lane, the front door of Ridgeway Hall opened and Eliza Carstairs, the art dealer's sister, hurried out.

'Mr Holmes!' she cried. 'I was rude to you inside and for that you must forgive me. But I must tell you now that nothing is what it seems and that unless you help us, unless you can lift the curse that has fallen on this place, we are doomed.'

'I beg of you, Miss Carstairs, to compose yourself.'

'She is the cause of all this!' The sister flung an accusatory finger in the direction of the house. 'Catherine Marryat—for that was her name by her first marriage. She came upon Edmund when he was at his lowest ebb. He was exhausted, infirm and—yes, in need of someone to take care of him. Out at sea, with days on board that ship, she spun a web around him so that when he returned home, it was too late. We could not dissuade him.'

'You would have looked after him yourself.'

'I love him as only a sister can. My mother too. And do not believe for a single minute that she died as a result of an accident. When Edmund announced his determination to ally himself with Mrs Marryat, it broke my mother's heart. Of course we would have liked to see Edmund married. But how could he marry her? A foreign adventuress who was clearly interested only in his wealth. My mother killed herself. She could not live with the shame and the unhappiness of this accursed marriage and so she turned on the gas tap and lay on her bed until the fumes had done their work.'

'Did your mother communicate her intentions to you?' Holmes asked.

'She didn't need to. I knew what was in her mind. This has not been a pleasant household from the day that the American woman arrived, Mr Holmes. And this intruder who has stolen Mama's necklace is all part of the same evil business. How do we know that this stranger has not come here on her account? Perhaps he is an old acquaintance who has followed her here. So long as this marriage continues, we will none of us be safe.'

'Your brother seems perfectly content,' Holmes responded. 'What would you have me do?'

'You can investigate her.'

'It is none of my business, Miss Carstairs.'

Eliza Carstairs gazed at him with contempt. 'I have read of your exploits, Mr Holmes, and I have always considered them to be exaggerated. For all your cleverness, you have always struck me as someone with no understanding of the human heart. Now I know that to be true.' And with that, she went back into the house.

Holmes watched her until the door had closed. 'Most singular,' he remarked. 'This case becomes increasingly curious and complex.'

'I have never heard a woman speak with such fury,' I observed.

'Indeed, Watson. But there is one thing I would particularly like to know, for I am beginning to see great danger in this situation.' He glanced at the fountain. 'I wonder if Mrs Catherine Carstairs is able to swim?'

HOLMES SLEPT IN LATE the next morning and I was sitting on my own, reading *The Martyrdom of Man*, by Winwood Reade, a book that he had recommended to me but which, I confess, I had found heavy going. The morning post had brought a letter from Mary. All was well in Camberwell; Richard Forrester was not so ill that he could not take delight in seeing his old governess again, and she was enjoying the companionship of the boy's mother.

I had picked up my pen to reply to her when there was a loud ring at the front door, followed by the patter of many feet on the stairs. It was a sound that I remembered well, so I was fully prepared when about half a dozen street Arabs burst into the room.

'Wiggins!' I exclaimed, for I remembered the oldest of them.

'Mr 'olmes sent us a message, sir, summoning us on a matter of the greatest hurgency,' Wiggins replied.

Sherlock had once named them the Baker Street division of the detective police force. At other times he referred to them as the Irregulars. A more ragged bunch would be hard to imagine, boys between the ages of eight and fifteen, held together by dirt and grime. Several of the boys were barefooted. One, I noted, was a little smarter and better fed than the others and I wondered what wickedness—pickpocketing, perhaps, or burglary—had furnished him with the means to prosper. He could not have been more than thirteen years old and yet he was already quite grown up. Childhood, after all, is the first precious coin that poverty steals from a child.

A moment later, Sherlock Holmes appeared and with him, Mrs Hudson. I could see that our landlady was out of sorts. 'Please calm yourself, my good Mrs Hudson,' Holmes laughed. 'Wiggins! I've told you before. I will not have the house invaded in this way. In future, you alone will report to me. But since you are here, listen carefully. Our quarry is an American man in his mid-thirties who occasionally wears a flat cap. He has a scar on his right cheek and has in his possession a gold necklace set with three clusters of sapphires. Now, where do you think he would go to dispose of it?'

'Fullwood's Rents!' one boy shouted out.

'Flower Street,' cried another.

'The pawnbrokers!' interjected the better-dressed boy.

'The pawnbrokers!' Holmes agreed. 'What's your name, boy?'

'Ross, sir.'

'Well, Ross, you have the makings of a detective. The man that we seek is new to the city and will not know Flower Street or Fullwood's Rents or any of the more esoteric corners. He will go to the most obvious place so that's where I want you to begin. He arrived at London Bridge, and let us assume that he chose to reside close to there. You must visit every pawn-broker in the district, describing the man and the jewellery.' Holmes reached into his pocket. 'My rates are the same as always. A shilling each and a guinea for whoever finds what I'm looking for.'

Wiggins snapped a command and, with a great deal of noise and bustle, our unofficial police force marched out, watched by a hawk-eyed Mrs Hudson. As soon as they had gone, Holmes sank into a chair.

'Do you not think that Lestrade will also be enquiring at the pawn-brokers?' I said.

'I somehow doubt it. It is so obvious that it will not have crossed his mind. However, we have the whole day ahead of us and nothing to fill it, so let's take lunch together at Le Café de l'Europe beside the Haymarket Theatre. After that, I have it in mind to visit the gallery of Carstairs and Finch in Albemarle Street. It might be interesting to acquaint ourselves with Mr Tobias Finch. Mrs Hudson, should Wiggins return, you might direct him there.'

We left the house and strolled down to the Haymarket. Although very cold, it was another brilliant day with crowds of people pouring in and out of the department stores and street sellers calling out their wares. We ate at Le Café de l'Europe, where we were served an excellent game pie and Holmes was in an effusive mood.

It was but a short distance to the gallery, and once again we strolled together. I have to say that I took an immense satisfaction in these moments of quiet sociability. It was about four o'clock and the light was already fading when we arrived at the gallery. A low door led into a rather gloomy interior with two sofas, a table and a single canvas mounted on an easel. As we entered, we heard two men arguing in the adjoining room. One voice belonged to Edmund Carstairs.

'It's an excellent price,' he was saying. 'These works are like good wine. Their value can only rise.'

'No, no, no!' replied the other voice in a high-pitched whine. 'It's a waste of money, Edmund.'

'Six works by Whistler—'

'Six works we shall never be rid of!'

I was standing at the door and closed it more heavily than was strictly necessary, wishing to signal our presence. It had the desired effect. The conversation broke off and a moment later a thin, white-haired individual, immaculately dressed in a dark suit with a wing collar and black tie, appeared from behind a curtain. He must have been at least sixty years old, but there was still a spring in his step.

'I take it you are Mr Finch,' Holmes began.

'Yes, sir. That is indeed my name. And you are . . .?'

'I am Sherlock Holmes.'

'Mr Holmes!' Carstairs had also come into the room. The contrast between the two men was striking: the one, belonging almost to another age, the other younger and more dandified. 'This is Mr Holmes, the detective I was telling you about,' he explained to his partner.

'Yes, yes. I know. He has just introduced himself.'

'I did not expect to see you here,' Carstairs said.

'I came because it interested me to see your professional place of work,' Holmes explained. 'But I also have a number of questions for you, relating to the Pinkerton's men who you employed in Boston.'

'A dreadful affair!' Finch interjected. 'I won't recover from the loss of those paintings, not until the end of my days. If only we had sold him a few of your Whistlers, Edmund. They could have been blown to pieces and no one would give a jot!' Once the old man had started, there seemed to be no stopping him. 'Picture dealing is a respectable business, Mr Holmes. I would not wish it to be known that we have been involved with gunmen and murder!' The old man's face fell as he saw he was involved with more besides, for the door had just opened and a boy had rushed in. I at once recognised Wiggins, but to Finch it was as if the worst assault were being committed. 'Get out of here!' he exclaimed. 'We have nothing for you.'

'You need not concern yourself, Mr Finch,' Holmes said. 'I know the boy. What is it, Wiggins?'

'We've found 'im, Mr 'olmes!' Wiggins cried, excitedly. 'The cove you was looking for. Me and Ross was about to go in the jerry shop on Bridge Lane—Ross knows the place for 'e's in and out of there often enough 'imself—when the door opens and there 'e is, 'is face cut livid by a scar.'

'Where is he now?' Holmes asked.

'We followed 'im to 'is 'otel, sir. Will it be a guinea each if we take you there?'

'I have always played you fair, Wiggins,' replied Holmes. 'Tell me, where is this hotel?'

'In Bermondsey, sir. Mrs Oldmore's Private 'otel. Ross will be there now. I left 'im there to act as crow while I 'iked all the way to your rooms and then 'ere to find you. Are you going to come back with me, Mr 'olmes? Will you take a four-wheeler? Can I ride with you?'

'You can sit up with the driver.'

Holmes turned to me. 'We must leave at once. By a lucky chance, we have the object of our investigation in our grasp. We must not let him slip between our fingers.'

'I will come with you,' Carstairs announced.

'Mr Carstairs, for your own safety—'

'I have seen this man. If anyone can be sure that these boys have correctly identified him, it is I. And if this man is who I believe he is, then I am the cause of his presence here and it is only right I see it to the end.'

'Very well,' Holmes said. 'The three of us will leave together.'

And so we hurried out of the gallery, leaving Mr Finch gaping after us. A four-wheeler was located and we climbed in, Wiggins scrambling up beside the driver. With a crack of the whip we were away, as if something of our urgency had communicated itself to the horses. It was almost dark and the city had once again turned cold and hostile. The shoppers and the entertainers had gone home and their places had been taken by shabby men and gaudy women, who needed shadows in which to conduct their business and whose business, in truth, carried shadows of its own.

The carriage took us over Blackfriars Bridge where the wind cut into us like a knife. Holmes had not spoken since we had left, and I felt that in some way he'd had a presentiment of what was to come. This was not something he ever admitted and had I ever suggested it I know he would have been annoyed. No soothsayer he! For him it was all intellect, all systematised common sense, as he once put it. Yet still I was aware of something that defied explanation and which might even be considered supernatural. Like it or not, Holmes knew that the evening's events were going to provide a turning point after which his life—both our lives—would never be quite the same.

Mrs Oldmore's Private Hotel was a mean, dilapidated building close to the river. Lamps burned behind the windows, but the glass was so dirt-encrusted that barely any light seeped through. Ross was waiting for us, shivering with cold. As Holmes and Carstairs climbed out of the carriage, he stepped back and I saw that something had greatly frightened him. His eyes were filled with alarm and his face, in the glow of the streetlamp, was ashen white. But then Wiggins leaped down and grabbed hold of him and it was as if the spell was broken.

'It's all right, my boy!' Wiggins cried. 'We are both of us to 'ave a guinea. Mr 'olmes 'as promised it.'

'Tell me what has happened,' Holmes said. 'Has the man you recognised left the hotel?'

'Who are these gentlemen?' Ross pointed first at Carstairs, then at me. 'Why are they 'ere?'

'It's all right, Ross,' I said. 'I am John Watson, a doctor. You saw me this morning when you came to Baker Street. And this is Mr Carstairs who has a gallery in Albemarle Street. We mean you no harm.'

'Albemarle Street in Mayfair?' The boy was so cold that his teeth were chattering. He had been standing out here for at least two hours on his own.

'What have you seen?' Holmes asked.

'I ain't seen nothin',' Ross replied. There was something about his manner now that might almost have suggested that he had something to hide. 'I been 'ere, waitin' for you. 'e ain't come out. No one 'as gone in. And the cold, it's gone right through my bones.'

'Here is the money that I promised you.' Holmes paid both the boys. 'Now take yourselves home. You have done enough tonight.' The boys ran off together, Ross casting one last look in our direction. 'I suggest we enter the hotel and confront this man,' Holmes went on. 'That boy, Watson. Did it occur to you that he was dissembling?'

'There was certainly something he was not telling us,' I concurred.

'Let us hope that he has not acted in some way so as to betray us. Mr Carstairs, please stand well back. It is unlikely that our target will attempt violence, but we have come here without preparation. We must live on our wits. Come on!'

The three of us entered the hotel. A few steps led up to the front door, which opened into a public hallway with a small office to one side. An elderly man was sitting there, half asleep, but he started when he saw us.

'God bless you, gentlemen,' he quavered. 'We can offer you single beds at five shillings a night—'

'We are not here for accommodation,' Holmes replied. 'We are in pursuit of a man who has recently arrived from America. He has a scar on one cheek. If you do not wish to land yourself in trouble with the law, you will tell us where he can be found.'

'You must be referring to Mr Harrison from New York. He has the room at the end of the corridor on this floor. Number six.'

We set off at once, down a bare corridor with gas-jets turned so low that we had almost to feel our way through the darkness. Number six was indeed at the end. Holmes raised his fist to knock, then stepped back, a single gasp escaping from his lips. I looked down and saw a streak of liquid, almost black in the half-light, curling out from beneath the door and forming a small pool against the skirting. I saw Carstairs recoiling.

Holmes tried the door. It wouldn't open. Without saying a word, he brought his shoulder up against it and the flimsy lock shattered. Leaving Carstairs in the corridor, the two of us went in and saw at once that the crime had taken a turn for the worse. The window was open. The room was ransacked. And the man we had been pursuing was curled up with a knife in the side of his neck.

QUITE RECENTLY I saw George Lestrade again and we spent the afternoon together, reminiscing. My readers will hardly be surprised to learn that it was the subject of Sherlock Holmes that occupied much of our discourse, and I felt a need to apologise to Lestrade on two counts. First, I had never described him in the most glowing terms. The words 'rat-faced' and 'ferret-like' spring to mind. Unkind as it was, it was at least accurate, for Lestrade himself had once joked that Mother Nature had given him the looks of a criminal rather than a police officer and that he might have made himself a richer man had he chosen that profession.

But where I perhaps did Lestrade an injustice was in suggesting that he had no investigative skill whatsoever. It's fair to say that Sherlock Holmes occasionally spoke ill of him, but then Holmes was equally disparaging about almost every police officer he encountered. Next to Holmes, any detective would have found it nigh on impossible to make his mark and even I sometimes had to remind myself that I was not a complete idiot. But Lestrade was in many ways a capable man. Were you to look in the public records you would find many successful cases that he investigated quite independently. Even Holmes admired his tenacity. And, when all is said and done, he did finish his career as Assistant Commissioner in charge of the CID, even if a large part of his reputation rested on the cases that Holmes had, in fact, solved, but for which he took the credit.

At any event, it was Lestrade who arrived at Mrs Oldmore's Private Hotel the next morning. After Holmes had alerted the constables in the street, the room had been closed off and kept under police guard until the cold touch of light could dispel the shadows and lend itself to a proper investigation.

'Well, well, Mr Holmes,' he remarked with a hint of irritation. 'They told me you were expected when I was at Wimbledon and here you are again.'

'We have both been following in the footsteps of the unfortunate wretch who has ended his days here,' retorted Holmes.

Lestrade took one look at the body. 'This would indeed seem to be the man we have been seeking. How did you come to find him?'

'It was absurdly simple. I knew, thanks to the brilliance of your own inquiries, that he had returned on the train to London Bridge. Since then, my agents have been scouring the area and two of them were fortunate enough to come across him in the street.'

'I assume that you are referring to that gang of urchins you have at your beck and call. They're all thieves and pickpockets when they are not being encouraged by you. Is there any sign of the necklace?'

'No obvious sign—no. But then I have not yet had a chance to search the room in its entirety.'

'Then maybe we should start by doing just that.'

It was a dismal place with tattered curtains, a mouldering carpet and a bed that looked more exhausted than anyone who might have attempted to sleep in it. The window looked over a narrow alley to a brick wall opposite. Lestrade turned his attentions to the dead man. The knife that had killed him had buried itself up to the hilt, penetrating the carotid artery. My training told me that he would have died instantly. Now that I was able to scrutinise him more carefully, I saw that he was in his early forties, well built, with muscular arms. He had close-cropped hair that had begun to turn grey. Most striking of all was the scar that began at the corner of his mouth and slanted over his cheekbone. He had come close to death once. He had been less fortunate the second time.

'Can we be sure that this is the same man who imposed himself on Mr Edmund Carstairs?' Lestrade asked.

'Indeed so. Carstairs was able to identify him.'

'He was here?'

'Briefly.' Holmes smiled to himself and I recalled how we had been compelled to bundle Edmund Carstairs into a cab and send him on his way. He had barely glimpsed the body but it had been enough to send him into a fainting fit and I had understood how he must have been on board the *Catalonia* following his experiences with the Flat Cap Gang in Boston.

'Here is further evidence if you need it.' Holmes gestured at a flat cap, lying on the bed.

Lestrade had meanwhile turned his attention to a packet of cigarettes lying on a table nearby. He examined the label. 'Old Judge . . .'

'Manufactured, I think you will find, by Goodwin and Company of New York. I found the stub of one such cigarette at Ridgeway Hall.'

'Did you now?' Lestrade said. 'Well, I suppose we can discard the idea that our American friend was the victim of a random attack? Though it is always possible that he returned to his room and surprised someone as they were ransacking the place. A fight ensued. A knife was drawn . . .'

'I think it unlikely,' Holmes said. 'What happened in this room can only be a direct result of his activities in Wimbledon. And then there is the position of the body and the angle at which the knife was driven into his neck. It seems to me that the attacker was waiting for him beside the door. He walked in and was seized from behind. Looking at him, you can see that he was a powerful man, capable of taking care of himself. But in this instance he was taken by surprise and killed with a single blow.'

'Theft might still be the motive,' Lestrade insisted. 'If the fifty pounds and the necklace are not here, where are they?'

'I have every reason to believe you will find the necklace in a pawn-broker on Bridge Lane. Our man had just come from there. It would appear that whoever killed him took the money, but I would suggest that was not the primary reason for the crime. Perhaps you should ask yourself what else was taken. You would think that a visitor from America might have a passport or letters of introduction. His wallet, I notice, is absent. You know what name he used on entering the hotel?'

'He called himself Benjamin Harrison.'

'Which is of course the current American president.'

'The American president? Of course. I was aware of that.' Lestrade scowled. 'But whatever name he chose, we know he is Keelan O'Donaghue, late of Boston. You see the mark on his face? That's a bullet wound.'

Holmes turned to me. 'It is certainly a gun wound,' I said. I had seen many similar injuries in Afghanistan. 'I would say it is about a year old.'

'Which ties in with what Carstairs told me,' Lestrade concluded. 'It seems to me that we have come to the end of this whole sorry episode. O'Donaghue was injured in the shoot-out at the Boston tenement. At the same time, his twin brother was killed and he came to England on a mission of revenge. That much is as plain as a pikestaff.'

'It could hardly be less plain if a pikestaff had been used as the murder weapon,' Holmes demurred. 'Perhaps you can explain then: who killed Keelan O'Donaghue—and why?'

'Well, the most obvious suspect would be Edmund Carstairs himself.'

'Except that Mr Carstairs was with us at the time of the murder. Besides, he did not know where his victim was staying. I might also ask why, if this really is Keelan O'Donaghue, he has a cigarette case with the initials WM?'

'What cigarette case?'

'It is on the bed, partly covered by the sheet. That would doubtless explain why the killer missed it, too.'

Lestrade examined the object in question. 'O'Donaghue was a thief. There is no reason why he might not have stolen this.'

'Is there any reason why he would have stolen it? It is not a valuable item. It is made of tin with the letters painted on.'

The case was empty. Lestrade snapped it shut. 'The trouble with you, Holmes, is that you have a way of complicating things. If O'Donaghue did visit this pawnshop of yours, then we will know him to be the thief who broke into Carstairs's safe. Doubtless he would have had other criminal contacts here in London. He may well have recruited one to help him in his vendetta. The two of them fell out. The other pulled a knife. This is the result!'

'You are certain of that?'

'I am as certain as I need to be.'

'Well, we shall see. Perhaps the owner of the hotel will be able to enlighten us.'

But Mrs Oldmore, a grey-haired, sour-faced woman who was waiting in the small office, had little to add.

''e took the room for the week,' she said. 'It was 'is first time in London.

'e 'ad no idea 'ow to find 'is way around. 'e asked me 'ow to get to Wimbledon. "I will go there tomorrow," 'e said. "There is someone who owes me somethin' and I means to collect it." From the way 'e talked, I could tell 'e was up to no good. And now this Mr 'arrison is murdered! It's the world we live in, where a respectable woman can't run an 'otel without 'aving corpses spread out on the floorboards.'

We left her sitting in misery and Lestrade took his leave. 'If you need me, you know where to find me, Mr Holmes,' he said.

'If I should ever find myself in need of Inspector Lestrade,' Holmes muttered after he had gone, 'then things will have come to a pretty pass.'

We went out into the street and then entered the alleyway that ran past the room in which the American had met his end. The window was about halfway down, with a wooden crate set just beneath it. It was evident that the killer had used this as a step to gain entrance. The window would have opened easily from outside. Together we followed the alley to the point at which it ended with a high wooden fence. By now, Holmes was deep in thought and I could see the unease in his pale, elongated face.

'You remember the boy—Ross—last night?' he said.

'You thought that there was something he was holding back.'

'And now I am certain of it. From where he was standing, he had a clear view of both the hotel and the alleyway, the end of which, as we have both seen, is blocked. The killer can have entered, therefore, only from the road, and Ross may well have had a sight of who it was.'

'But if he saw something, Holmes, why did he not tell us?'

'Because he had some plan of his own, Watson. If Ross thought that there was money to be made, he would take on the devil himself! And yet, what is it that this child could have seen? A figure flitting down a passageway and disappearing from sight? Perhaps he hears a cry as the blow is struck. Moments later, the killer appears a second time, hurrying away into the night. Ross remains where he is and a short while later the three of us arrive.'

'He was afraid,' I said. 'He mistook Carstairs for a police officer.'

'It was more than fear. I would have said the boy was in the grip of something close to terror, but I assumed . . .' He struck a hand against his brow. 'We must find him. I hope I have not been guilty of a grave miscalculation.'

We stopped at a post office on the way back to Baker Street. Holmes sent another wire to Wiggins but, twenty-four hours later, there was still no report from him. And then we heard the worst possible news. Ross had disappeared.

TWO
The White Ribbon

In 1890, the year of which I write, there were some five and a half million people in the 600 square miles of the Metropolitan Police District of London and then, as always, those two constant neighbours, wealth and poverty, were living uneasily side by side. It is necessary to reflect upon the lower depths of the great cauldron of London to understand the impossibility of the task that faced us. We had to find one child among so many, and if Holmes was right, if there was danger abroad, we had no time to spare. Where to begin? There were tens of thousands of children out on the street, begging, pickpocketing and pilfering or, if they were not up to the mark, quietly dying unknown and unloved, their parents indifferent, if indeed those parents were themselves alive. There were children who slept on rooftops, in pens at Smithfield Market, down in the sewers and even, I heard, in holes scooped out of the dust-heaps on Hackney Marshes.

Holmes had been in a mood of constant disquiet from the moment we had left Mrs Oldmore's Hotel. During the day, he had paced up and down the room like a bear. Although he had smoked incessantly, he had barely touched his lunch or dinner. I do not think he slept at all. Late into the night, I heard him picking out a tune on his Stradivarius, but the music was full of discords and I could tell that his heart wasn't in it. I understood all too well the nervous energy that afflicted my friend. He had spoken of a grave mis-calculation. The disappearance of Ross suggested that he had been proved right and, if this were the case, he would never forgive himself.

I thought we might go back to Wimbledon. From what he had said at the hotel, Holmes had made it clear that the adventure of the man in the flat cap was over, the case solved, and all that remained was for him to launch into one of those explanations that would leave me wondering how I could have been so obtuse as to have not seen it for myself. However, breakfast brought a letter from Catherine Carstairs, informing us that she and her husband had gone away for a few days. Edmund Carstairs, with his fragile nature, needed time to regain his composure and Holmes would never reveal what he knew without an audience. I would therefore have to wait.

It was another two days before Wiggins returned to 221b Baker Street, this time on his own. He had been searching for Ross, but without success.

''e came to London at the end of the summer,' Wiggins explained.

'Came to London from where?'

'I've no idea. When I met 'im 'e was sharing in King's Cross with a family but they ain't seen 'im since that night at the 'otel. It sounds to me like 'e's lying low.'

'I want you to tell me what happened that night,' Holmes said, sternly. 'The two of you followed the American from the pawnbroker to the hotel. You left Ross watching the place while you came for me. He must have been alone there for a couple of hours. Finally, we returned, Mr Carstairs, Dr Watson, you and I. Ross was still there. I gave you both money and dismissed you. You left together.'

'We didn't stay together long,' Wiggins replied. ''e went 'is way and I went mine.'

'Did he say anything to you? Did the two of you speak?'

'Ross was in a strange mood. There was something 'e'd seen . . . A man. It put the wind up 'im. 'e was shook to the core.'

'He saw the killer!' I exclaimed.

'I don't know what 'e saw but I can tell you what 'e said. "I know 'im and I can make something from 'im. More than the guinea I got from bloody Mr 'olmes." Them were 'is words exactly. 'e was in an 'urry to be off. I don't know where 'e went.'

Holmes moved closer to the boy and crouched down. Wiggins seemed very small beside him. 'Listen to me,' Holmes said. 'It seems to me that Ross could be in great danger. You must tell me what you know of his past. Where did he come from before you met him? Who were his parents?'

''e never 'ad no parents. They were dead, long ago. 'e never said where 'e come from and I never asked.'

'Think, boy. If he found himself in trouble, is there anyone he would turn to, any place where he might seek refuge?'

Wiggins shook his head, then seemed to think again. 'Is there another guinea in it for me?'

Holmes's eyes narrowed. 'Is the life of your compatriot worth as little as that?' he demanded.

''e was nothing to me, Mr 'olmes. Why would I care if 'e lived or died?' Holmes was still glaring at him and Wiggins suddenly softened. 'All right. There was a charity what took 'im in. Chorley Grange, up 'amworth way. 'e told me that 'e'd been there but 'e 'ated it and ran away. That was when 'e set up in King's Cross. I suppose, if someone was after 'im, maybe 'e could have gone back. Better the devil you know . . .'

Holmes straightened up. 'Thank you, Wiggins,' he said. 'I want you to keep looking for him.' He handed over a coin. 'If you find him, you must bring him here at once. Do you understand me?'

'Yes, Mr 'olmes.'

'Good. Watson, I trust you will you accompany me? We can take the train from Baker Street.'

One hour later, a cab dropped us off in front of three handsome buildings on a narrow lane that climbed steeply from the village of Roxeth up to Hamworth Hill. The largest of these, at the centre, resembled an English gentleman's country home of perhaps a hundred years ago, with a red-tiled roof and a verandah running its full length at the level of the first floor. The entire habitation was surrounded by farmland, with a lawn slanting down to an orchard. The buildings on each side were either barns or brewhouses but had presumably been adapted to the school's needs. There was a fourth structure on the other side of the lane, surrounded by an ornate metal fence with an open gate. It gave the impression of being empty. A wooden sign read: *Chorley Grange Home for Boys.*

We rang the front doorbell and were admitted by a man in a dark grey suit who listened in silence as Holmes explained who we were. 'Very good, gentlemen. If you would like to wait here . . .' He left us standing in an austere, wood-panelled hall. A long corridor with several doors stretched into the distance. Not a sound came from within. It struck me that the place was more like a monastery than a school.

Then the servant returned, bringing with him a short, round-faced man. He was about forty years old, bald, dressed in the manner of a clergyman, complete with dog collar. As he walked towards us, he beamed and spread his arms in welcome.

'Mr Holmes! You do us a great honour. The greatest detective in the country, here at Chorley Grange! It is really quite remarkable. And you must be Dr Watson. We have read your stories in class. The boys will not believe that you are here. You must forgive me, gentlemen, but I cannot contain my excitement. I am the Reverend Charles Fitzsimmons. Vosper tells me that you are here on serious business. Please, come with me to my study. You must meet my wife and perhaps we can offer you some tea?'

We followed the little man down a second corridor and into a room too large to be comfortable even though some effort had been made with a sofa and several chairs arranged around a fireplace. It had been cold in the corridor, and it was colder here, despite the fire in the grate. Rain was hammering now against the windows and running down the glass. Although it was only the middle of the afternoon, it could just as well have been night.

'My dear,' exclaimed our host. 'This is Mr Sherlock Holmes and Dr Watson. Gentlemen, may I present my wife, Joanna?'

I had not noticed the woman sitting in an armchair in the darkest corner of the room. The two of them made an odd couple, for she was remarkably tall and several years older than him. She was dressed entirely in black, her hair was tied in a knot behind her and her fingers were long and thin. Were I a boy, I might have thought her witchlike. I had the perhaps unworthy thought that I could understand why Ross had chosen to run away.

'Will you have some tea?' the lady asked. Her voice was as thin as the rest of her, her accent deliberately refined.

'We will not inconvenience you,' Holmes replied. 'As you are aware, we are here on a matter of some urgency. We are looking for a boy who we know only by the name of Ross.'

'Ross?' The reverend searched in his mind. 'Ah yes! Poor young Ross! We have not seen him for a while, Mr Holmes. He did not stay with us long.'

'He was a difficult and a disagreeable child,' his wife cut in. 'He refused to conform.'

'You are too hard, my dear. But it is true, Mr Holmes, that Ross did not settle into our ways. He had been here for only a few months before he ran away. That was last summer . . . July or August. May I ask why you are looking for him? I hope he has not done something amiss.'

'Not at all. A few nights ago he was the witness to certain events in London. I merely wish to know what he saw.'

'It sounds most mysterious, does it not, my dear? I will not ask you to elucidate further. We do not know where he came from. We do not know where he has gone.'

'Then I will not take up your time.' Holmes turned to the door, then seemed to change his mind. 'Though perhaps you might like to tell us something about your work here. Chorley Grange is your property?'

'Not at all, sir. My wife and I are employed by the Society for the

Improvement of London's Children. We have thirty-five boys here, all taken from the streets of London. We give them food and shelter and, more important than either, a good Christian education. The boys are taught shoemaking, carpentering and tailoring. In addition, they learn how to breed pigs and poultry. When they leave, many of them will go to Canada, Australia and America to begin a new life. We are in contact with a number of farmers who will be pleased to give them a fresh start.'

'How many teachers do you have?'

'Just the four of us, along with my wife. You met Mr Vosper at the door. He is the porter and teaches maths and reading. You have arrived during lessons and my other two teachers are in class.'

'How did Ross come to be here?'

'The society has volunteers who work in the city and who bring the boys to us. I can make enquiries if you wish, although it has been so long since we had any news of him that I doubt we can be of any help.'

'We cannot force the boys to stay,' Mrs Fitzsimmons said. 'The majority will choose to do just that, and will grow up to be a credit to the school. But there are the occasional boys with no gratitude whatsoever.'

'We have to believe in every child, Joanna.'

'You are too soft-hearted, Charles. They take advantage of you.'

'Ross cannot be blamed for what he was. His father was a slaughterman who came into contact with a diseased sheep and died. His mother turned to alcohol. She's dead too. Ross was looked after by an elder sister but we don't know what became of her. Ah yes! I remember how he came here. Ross was arrested for shoplifting. The magistrate handed him to us.'

'So you have no idea at all where we might be able to find him?'

'I am sorry you have wasted your time, Mr Holmes. We do not have the resources to search for boys who have chosen to leave us. Can you tell us why it is so important for you to find him?'

'We believe him to be in danger.'

'All these homeless boys are in danger.' Fitzsimmons clapped his hands together as if struck by a sudden thought. 'Might it help you to speak to some of his former classmates? It is always possible that he may have told one of them something. And if you would like to accompany me, it will give me an opportunity to show you the school.'

'That would be most kind of you, Mr Fitzsimmons.'

We left the study. Mrs Fitzsimmons did not join us.

'You must forgive my wife,' the Reverend Fitzsimmons muttered. 'I can assure you that she lives for these boys. She teaches them divinity, helps with the laundry, nurses them when they are ill.'

'You have no children of your own?' I asked.

'We have thirty-five children of our own, Dr Watson, for we treat them exactly as if they were our flesh and blood.'

He took us into one of the rooms. Here were eight or nine boys, all clean and well groomed, dressed in aprons, silently concentrating on the shoes that were laid out in front of them while the man we had met at the door, Mr Vosper, watched over them. They rose as we came in and stood in respectful silence but Fitzsimmons waved them down cheerfully. 'Sit down, boys! This is Mr Sherlock Holmes, who has come to visit us. All well, Mr Vosper?'

'Indeed so, sir.'

'Good! Good!' Fitzsimmons positively beamed with approval. He set off again, this time leading us upstairs to show us a dormitory, a touch spartan but decidedly clean and airy. We saw the kitchens, the dining room, a workshop and finally came to a classroom with a lesson in progress. A young man sat marking a copybook while a twelve-year-old boy stood reading to his fellows from a well-worn Bible. The boy stopped the moment we walked in. Fifteen students stood up respectfully, gazing at us with pale, serious faces.

'Sit down, please!' exclaimed the reverend. 'Forgive the interruption, Mr Weeks.' He gestured at the teacher, who was in his late twenties, with a strange, twisted face and a tangle of brown hair. 'This is Robert Weeks, a graduate of Balliol College. Mr Weeks was building a successful career in the city but has chosen to join us for a year to help those less fortunate than himself. Do you remember the boy Ross, Mr Weeks?'

'Ross? He was the one who ran away.'

'This gentleman here is Mr Sherlock Holmes, the well-known detective.' This caused a certain tremor of recognition among some of the boys. 'He is afraid that Ross may have got himself into trouble.'

'Not surprising,' muttered Mr Weeks. 'He was not an easy child.'

'Well, surely there must be someone in this room who can now help us find him? I beseech you all to consider the matter.'

'My desire is only to help your friend,' Holmes added.

There was a brief silence. Then a fragile, fair-haired boy in the back row put up his hand. 'Are you the man in the stories?' he asked.

'That's right. And this is the man who writes them.' It was rare for me to hear Holmes introduce me in this manner and I have to say I was extremely pleased to hear it. 'Do you read them?'

'No, sir. There are too many long words. But sometimes Mr Weeks reads them to us.'

'We must let you return to your studies,' Fitzsimmons said and began to usher us towards the door.

But the boy had not finished. 'Ross has a sister, sir,' he said.

Holmes turned. 'In London?'

'I think so, sir. He spoke of her once. Her name is Sally. He said that she worked at a public house, The Bag of Nails.'

For the first time, the Reverend Fitzsimmons looked angry. 'Why did you not tell me before, Daniel? This is very wrong of you.'

'I had forgotten, sir.'

'Had you remembered, we might have been able to find him.'

'I'm sorry, sir.'

'We'll say no more of it. Come, Mr Holmes.'

The three of us walked back towards the main door. I was glad Holmes had paid the cab driver to wait for it was still raining.

'The school does you credit,' Holmes said. 'I find it remarkable how quiet and well disciplined the boys seem to be.'

'My methods are simple, Mr Holmes. The stick and the carrot. When the boys misbehave, I flog them. But if they work hard and abide by our rules, then they find that they are well fed. In the six years that my wife and I have been here, Ross is the only one who has run away. When you find him, I hope you will prevail upon him to return.'

'One last question, Mr Fitzsimmons. The building opposite. That is part of the school?'

'Indeed so. We use it for public performances. Did I mention to you that every boy in the school is a member of a band?'

'You have had a performance recently.'

'Two nights ago. You have doubtless noticed the many wheel tracks. I would be honoured if you came to our next recital, Mr Holmes—and you, Dr Watson. Indeed, might you consider becoming benefactors of the school?'

'I will certainly consider it.' We shook hands and left. 'We must go straight to The Bag of Nails,' Holmes said the moment we had climbed into the cab. 'There is not a second to be lost.'

'You really think . . .?'

'The boy, Daniel, told us what he had refused to tell his masters because he knew who we were and thought we could save his friend. What is it, I wonder, that gives me such cause for alarm? Driver, take us to the station! And let us just pray that we're not too late.'

HOW DIFFERENTLY things might have turned out had there not been two public houses in London with the name The Bag of Nails. We knew of one in Edge Lane in Shoreditch and made our way directly there. It was a small, squalid place, yet the landlord was amicable enough.

'There's no Sally working in this place,' he said, after we had introduced ourselves. 'I know no Ross, neither. There's a Bag of Nails over in Lambeth. Maybe you should try your luck there.'

We were soon crossing London in a hansom, but by the time we reached the lower quarter of Lambeth it was almost dark. The second Bag of Nails was more welcoming than the first, but conversely, its landlord was less so, a surly, bearded fellow.

'Sally Dixon? Is that the girl you want? You'll find her round the back but you'll tell me what you want with her first.'

'We wish only to speak with her,' Holmes replied. Once again, I could feel the tension burning within him. There was never a man who felt it more when circumstances conspired to frustrate him. He slid a few coins onto the bar. 'This is to recompense you for her time.'

'She'll be in the yard,' returned the landlord. 'I doubt you'll get much from her. She's not the most talkative of girls.'

There was a courtyard behind the building, filled with scrap. A pile of broken crates stood on one side, coal bags stuffed with Lord knows what on the other. In the middle, barefoot and in a dress too thin for this weather, a girl of about sixteen, with arms as thin as sticks, swept what space was available. I recognised in her the same looks as her younger brother. Her hair was fair, her eyes blue and, but for the circumstances in which she found herself, I would have said she was pretty. When she looked up, her face showed only suspicion. Sixteen! What had her life been to bring her here?

'Miss Dixon?' Holmes asked. The brushes of the broom swept back and forth, the rhythm unbroken. 'Sally?'

She slowly raised her head, examining us. 'Yes?' I saw that her hands had closed round the broom handle, clutching it as if it were a weapon.

'We don't wish to alarm you,' Holmes said. 'We mean you no harm.'

'What do you want?' Her eyes were fierce. 'Who are you?'

'We wish to speak to your brother, to Ross.'

Her hands tightened. 'Are you from the House of Silk? Ross is not here. He has never been here—and you will not find him.'

'We want to help him.'

'Of course, you would say that. You can both go away! You make me sick. Go back where you came from.'

Hoping to be of service, I took one step towards the girl. I had thought I would reassure her but I had made a grievous mistake. I saw the broom fall and heard Holmes cry out. Then the girl seemed to punch the air in front of me and I felt something white-hot slice across my chest. I pressed my hand against the front of my coat. When I looked down, I saw blood trickling between my fingers. So shocked was I, it took me a moment to realise that I had been stabbed. For a moment, the girl stood in front of me, snarling like an animal, her eyes ablaze. Holmes rushed to my side. 'My dear Watson!'

'What's going on here?' The landlord had appeared. The girl let out a howl, then fled through a narrow archway leading out into the street.

I was in pain, but I already knew that I had not been seriously injured. The thickness of my coat had protected me from the worst of what the blade might have achieved, and later that evening I would dress and disinfect a relatively minor wound.

'Watson?'

'It's nothing, Holmes. A scratch.'

'What's happened?' the landlord demanded. He was staring at my blood-stained hands. 'What did you do to her?'

'You might ask what she has done to me,' I grunted, although I was unable to feel any rancour towards this poor child who had struck out at me in fear and incomprehension and who had not really wished me any harm.

'Come inside,' Holmes said. 'You need to sit down.'

'No, Holmes. I assure you, it is not as bad as it seems.'

'Thank heaven for that. Landlord, it was the girl's brother that we came here to find. A boy of thirteen, shorter than her and better fed.'

'You mean Ross? He has been working here with her. You should have asked for him in the first place.'

'Is he here now?'

'No. He came a few days ago, needing a roof above his head. I said he could share with his sister in return for work in the kitchen. But the boy was more trouble than he was worth, never around when he was needed. I don't know what he was up to, but he had some sort of business in his mind, that I can tell you. He hurried out just before you arrived.'

'Do you have any idea where he went?'

'No. The girl might have told you. But now she's gone too.'

'Should either of them return, it is urgent that you send a message to my lodgings at 221b Baker Street. Here is further money for your pains. Come, Watson. Lean on me. I think I hear an approaching cab . . .'

And so the day's adventure ended with the two of us sitting by the fire, I with a restorative brandy and soda, Holmes smoking furiously. I took a moment to reflect on the circumstances that had brought us to this point. We had strayed a great distance from the man with the flat cap or the identity of the person who had killed him. Was this the person that Ross had seen outside Mrs Oldmore's Private Hotel? Somehow, that encounter had led him to believe that he could make some money for himself, and since then he had vanished. He must have told his sister something of his intentions, for she had been afraid on his behalf, almost as if she had been expecting us. Why else would she have been carrying a weapon? And then there were those words of hers: 'Are you from the House of Silk?' On our return Holmes had searched through the various encyclopedias that he kept on his shelves, but we were none the wiser as to what she had meant. We would just have to wait to see what the next day would bring.

What it brought was a police constable knocking at our door just after breakfast.

'Inspector Lestrade sends his compliments, sir. He is at Southwark Bridge and would be most grateful if you could join him.'

We put on our coats and left at once, taking a cab over Southwark Bridge, crossing the three great cast-iron arches that spanned the river from Cheapside. Lestrade was waiting for us on the south bank, standing with a group of policemen clustered around what looked like a small heap of discarded rags. We descended a spiral staircase that twisted down from the road and walked over the mud and shingle. It was low tide and the river seemed to have shrunk back, as if in distaste at what had happened here.

'Is he the boy you were looking for?' Lestrade asked.

Holmes nodded. Perhaps he did not trust himself to speak.

The boy had been beaten brutally and his throat cut. I had seen dead bodies before, but I found it far beyond understanding that any human being could have done this to a thirteen-year-old boy.

'It's a bad business,' Lestrade said. 'What can you tell me about him, Holmes? Was he in your employ?'

'His name was Ross Dixon,' Holmes replied. 'I know very little about him. You might ask at the Chorley Grange School for Boys in Hamworth, but there may not be much that they are able to add. He has a sister who worked until recently at The Bag of Nails public house in Lambeth. You may yet find her there. Have you examined the body?'

'His pockets were empty. But there is something strange that you should see, though heaven knows what it signifies.'

Lestrade nodded and a policemen knelt down and took hold of one of the small arms. The sleeve of his shirt fell back to reveal a white ribbon, knotted round the boy's wrist. 'It's a good-quality silk from the look of it,' Lestrade said. 'And it is untouched by blood or by any of this Thames filth. I would say, therefore, that it was placed on the boy after he was killed, as some sort of sign.'

'The House of Silk!' I exclaimed.

'Does it mean anything to you, Lestrade?' Holmes asked.

'The House of Silk? Is it a factory? I've never heard of it.'

'But I have.' Holmes stared into the distance, his eyes filled with horror and self-reproach. 'The white ribbon, Watson! I have seen it before.' He turned back to Lestrade. 'Thank you for informing me of this.'

'I hoped you might be able to shed some light on the matter. After all, this may be your fault.'

'Fault?' Holmes jerked round as though he had been stung.

'You employed the boy. You set him on the trail of a known criminal. I grant you, he may have had his own ideas but this is the result.'

I cannot say if Lestrade was being deliberately provocative but his words had an effect on Holmes on the journey back to Baker Street. He had sunk into the corner of the hansom and sat in silence, refusing to meet my eyes. He appeared more gaunt than ever, as if he had been struck down by some virulent disease. I watched and waited as he brought that enormous intellect of his to bear on the terrible turn that this adventure had taken.

'It may be that Lestrade is right,' he said at length. 'I have used my Baker Street Irregulars without much thought but I have never wantonly put them in harm's way. It never occurred to me that this horror might be the result of my actions. Would I have allowed a young boy to stand alone outside a hotel in the darkness had it been your son or mine? And the logic of what has taken place seems inescapable. The child saw the killer enter the hotel. He thought he could turn the situation to his advantage. He attempted to do so and he died. For that I must hold myself responsible.

'And yet! How does the House of Silk fit into this conundrum and what are we to make of the strip of silk around the boy's wrist? Once again I am blameworthy. I was warned! Honestly, Watson, there are times when I wonder if I shouldn't leave this profession and seek my fortune elsewhere. Certainly, on the strength of my achievements so far in this case, I have no right to call myself a detective. A child is dead. How am I to live with that?'

'My dear chap . . .'

'Say nothing. There is something I must show you. I was forewarned. I could have prevented it . . .'

We had arrived back. Holmes plunged into the building, taking the stairs two at a time. I followed more slowly, for the wound I had sustained the day before was hurting. As I arrived in our sitting room, I saw him seize hold of an envelope. 'Here it is!' he announced. 'It was hand delivered.'

I opened the envelope and, with a shiver, drew out a short length of white silk ribbon. 'What is the meaning of this, Holmes?' I asked.

'I asked myself the same thing when I received it. In retrospect, it would seem to have been a warning.'

'When was it sent?'

'Seven weeks ago. I examined the contents and tried to work out their significance but, being otherwise engaged at the time, I set it aside. Now, as you can see, it has come back to haunt me.'

'But who would have sent it to you? And to what purpose?'

'I have no idea, but for the sake of that murdered child, I intend to find out.' Holmes took the strip of silk from me and held it in front of him, examining it in the way that a man might a poisonous snake. 'If this was directed to me as a challenge, it is one I now accept. And I tell you, Watson, that I shall make them rue the day that it was sent.'

SALLY HAD NOT RETURNED to her place of work that night nor the following morning. The landlord of The Bag of Nails knew that Ross was dead—he had already been visited by Lestrade and he was even less pleased to see us than he had been the day before.

'Have you not caused enough trouble already?' he demanded. 'That girl may not have amounted to much but she was still a good pair of hands. I wish the two of you had never shown up.'

'It was not we who brought the trouble, Mr Hardcastle,' Holmes replied, for he had read the landlord's name—Ephraim Hardcastle—above the door. 'It was here already. It seems you were the last person to see the boy alive. Did he tell you nothing before he left?'

'Why would he speak to me or I to him?'

'But you said that he had some business on his mind.'

'I knew nothing of that.'

'Mr Hardcastle, I have sworn to find his killer and bring him to justice. I cannot do so if you refuse to help.'

The landlord nodded slowly and spoke in more measured tones. 'Very well. The boy turned up three nights ago needing a crib until he could sort himself out. Sally asked my permission and I gave my assent. There's a whole load of rubbish to be cleared out of the yard and I thought he could help. He did a little work on that first day, but in the afternoon he went out, and when he came back, he was very pleased with himself.'

'Did his sister know what he was doing?'

'She might have, but she said nothing to me.'

'Pray continue.'

'I have little to add. I saw him only once more before you arrived. He came into the public bar and asked me the time.'

'Then he was on his way to a fixed appointment. What use would a child such as Ross have with the time unless he had been asked to present himself in a certain place at a certain time? You said that he spent three nights here with his sister.'

'He shared her room.'

'I would like to see it.'

'The police have already been there. They found nothing.'

'I am not the police.' Holmes placed a few shillings on the bar. 'This is for your inconvenience.'

'Very well. But I will not take your money. You are on the trail of a monster and it will be enough if you make sure he can't hurt anyone else.'

A flight of stairs led down to the cellars and, lighting a candle, the landlord took us to a windowless room where Sally slept on a mattress on the bare wooden floor. Two objects lay in the middle of this makeshift bed. One was a knife, the other a doll that she must have rescued from some rubbish tip. A chair and a small table with a candle stood in one corner. The doll and the knife aside, Sally had nothing she could call her own beyond her name.

Holmes swept his eyes across the room. 'Why the knife?' he murmured.

'To protect herself,' I suggested.

'The weapon that she used to protect herself she carried with her, as you know. This second knife is almost blunt. The candle, I think, is of interest.'

It was the unlit candle on the table to which Holmes referred. He picked it up, then crouched down and began to shuffle along the floor. It took me a moment to realise that he was following a trail of melted wax droplets. They led him to the corner farthest away from the bed. 'She carried it to this far corner . . . to what purpose? Unless . . . The knife please, Watson.' I handed it to him and he pressed the blade into one of the cracks between the wooden floorboards. One of the boards was loose and he used the knife to prise it up, then reached inside and withdrew a bunched-up handkerchief. 'If you could be so kind, Mr Hardcastle . . .'

The landlord brought over his own candle. Holmes unfolded the handkerchief and, by the light of the flickering flame, we saw that there were several coins inside—three farthings, two florins, a crown, a gold sovereign and five shillings.

'This is Ross's,' Holmes said. 'The sovereign, I gave him.'

'My dear Holmes! How can you be sure it's the same sovereign?'

Holmes held it to the light. 'St George rides his horse but has a gash across his leg. I noticed it as I handed it over. But what of the rest of it?'

'He got it from his uncle,' Hardcastle muttered. Holmes turned to him. 'When he came here, he said he could pay for the room and that he had been given money by his uncle. I didn't believe him and said he could work in the yard instead.'

'The thing takes shape. The boy decides to use the information that he has gleaned from Mrs Oldmore's Hotel. He presents himself and makes his demands. He is invited to a meeting. It is at this meeting that he will be killed. But he has left his wealth behind with his sister. She hides it beneath the floorboards. One last question for you, Mr Hardcastle. Did Sally ever mention the House of Silk?'

'No. I have never heard of it. What am I to do with these coins?'

'Keep them. The girl has lost everything. Perhaps one day she will come to you, needing help, and you will be able to give them back.'

From The Bag of Nails we headed towards Bermondsey. I wondered aloud if Holmes intended to revisit the hotel. 'Not the hotel, Watson,' he said. 'But nearby. We must find the source of the boy's wealth.'

'He got it from his uncle,' I said.

Holmes laughed. 'You surprise me, Watson. Are you really so unfamiliar with the language of at least half the population of London? Every week thousands of itinerant workers visit their uncles, by which they mean the pawnbrokers. The only question is—what did Ross sell to receive his florins and shillings?'

'And where did he sell it?' I added. 'There must be hundreds of pawnbrokers in this part of London.'

'You will recall that Wiggins mentioned that Ross was frequently in and out of a pawnbroker in Bridge Lane. Perhaps that is where his "uncle" is to be found.'

What a place of broken promises and lost hopes the pawnbroker proved to be! Every class, every profession, every walk of life was represented in its grubby windows, the detritus of so many lives pinned like butterflies behind the glass. Overhead, a wooden sign with three red balls on a blue background hung on rusty chains. '*Money advanced on plate, jewels, wearing apparel and every description of property*' read the notice below, and so it was, for even Aladdin would have been unlikely to stumble on such a treasure trove.

I followed Holmes into a darkened interior where a man of about fifty was perched on a stool, reading a book with one hand, while the other rested on the counter, the fingers rolling slowly inwards as if turning some invisible object over in his palm. There was something neat and meticulous in his manner that put me in mind of a watchmaker.

'How may I help you, gentlemen?' he enquired. 'It looks to me as if you are here on official business. Are you from the police? If so, I know nothing about my customers. It is my practice never to ask questions.'

'My name is Sherlock Holmes.'

'The detective? I am honoured. What brings you here? Perhaps it has something to do with a gold necklace, set with sapphires? I paid five pounds for it and the police took it back again, so I gained nothing at all.'

'We have no interest in the necklace,' said Holmes. 'Nor in the man who brought it here.'

'Which is just as well, for the man who brought it here is dead, or so the police tell me.'

'We are interested in another customer, a child by the name of Ross.'

'I hear that Ross has also left this vale of tears. Poor odds, would you not say, to lose two pigeons in so short a space of time?'

'You paid Ross money recently.'

'Who told you so?'

'Do you deny it?'

'I do not deny it nor do I affirm it. I merely say that I would be most grateful if you would leave.'

'What is your name?'

'Russell Johnson.'

'I will make you a proposition, Mr Johnson. Whatever Ross brought to you, I will purchase, but only on the condition that you play fair with me. I know a great deal about you and if you attempt to lie, I will return with the police and take what I want and you will have made no profit at all.'

Johnson smiled. 'You know nothing about me at all, Mr Holmes.'

'No? I would say you were brought up in a wealthy family and were well educated. You might have been a successful pianist. Your downfall was due to an addiction, probably gambling, quite possibly dice. You were in prison earlier this year for receiving stolen goods and were considered troublesome by the warders. You served a sentence of at least three months but were released in September and since then you have done brisk business.'

'Who told you all this?'

'I did not need to be told, Mr Johnson. It is all painfully apparent. And now, if you please, what did Ross bring you?'

Johnson considered then nodded slowly. 'I met Ross two months ago. He was brought here by a couple of other street boys. He seemed better dressed than the others and carried with him a gentleman's pocket watch. He came in a few times after that, but he never brought in anything as good again.' Johnson went over to a cabinet and produced a watch on a chain, set in a gold casing. 'This is the watch, and I gave the boy five shillings for it although it's worth at least ten pounds. You can have it for what I paid.'

'And in return?'

'You must tell me how you know so much about me.'

'Very well, Mr Johnson. Your education is obvious from your speech. I also note the copy of Flaubert's letters to George Sand, untranslated, which you were reading as we came in. It is a wealthy family that gives a child a solid grounding in French. The fingers of a pianist are easily recognised.

That you should find yourself working in this place suggests the rapid loss of your wealth and position. There are not so many ways that could have happened: alcohol, drugs, a poor business speculation perhaps. But you speak of odds and refer to your customers as pigeons, a name often given to novice gamblers, so that is the world that springs to mind. You have a nervous habit, I notice. The way you roll your hand suggests the dice table.'

'And the prison sentence?'

'You have been given what I believe is called a terrier crop, a prison haircut, although you are displaying a further growth of about eight weeks, suggesting that you were released in September. There are marks on both your wrists that tell me you wore shackles while you were in jail and that you struggled against them. The receipt of stolen goods is the most obvious crime for a pawnbroker. The fact that you have been absent for a lengthy period is apparent from the books in the window, which have faded in the sunlight, and from the dust on the shelves. At the same time, I notice many objects that are dust-free and so have been added recently, indicating a brisk trade.'

Johnson handed over the prize. 'Thank you, Mr Holmes,' he said. 'You are quite correct in every respect. I come from a good family in Sussex and did hope once to be a pianist. I went into the law and might have prospered except that I found it so damnably dull. Then a friend took me to the Franco-German Club in Charlotte Street and I was introduced to baccarat, to roulette, to hazard and, yes, to dice. Sometimes I won. More often I lost. Five pounds one night. Ten pounds the next. My work became careless. I was sacked from my job. With the last of my savings I set myself up in these premises. I still go back, night after night. I cannot prevent myself.'

Holmes paid him the money and together we returned to Baker Street. He examined the watch in the cab. It was a minute repeater with a white enamel face in a gold case manufactured by Touchon & Co of Geneva. On the reverse he found an engraved image: a bird perching on a pair of crossed keys.

'A family crest?' I suggested.

'Watson, you are scintillating,' replied he. 'That is exactly what I believe it to be. Hopefully my encyclopedia will enlighten us further.'

Sure enough, the pages revealed a raven and two keys to be the crest of the Ravenshaws, one of the oldest families in the kingdom with a manor house just outside the village of Coln St Aldwyn in Gloucestershire. Lord

Ravenshaw had recently died at the age of eighty-two. His son, the Honourable Alec Ravenshaw, had now inherited both the title and the family estate. Holmes insisted on leaving London at once.

I just had time to pack a few things for an overnight stay, and by the time the sun had set we found ourselves in a pleasant inn, dining on a leg of lamb and a pint of quite decent claret. I forget now what we talked about over the meal, although the time passed in the easy conviviality that the two of us had so often enjoyed. Inwardly, I could tell, Holmes was still uneasy. The death of Ross preyed on him and would not let him rest.

Before he had even taken breakfast, Holmes had sent his card up to Ravenshaw Hall, asking for an audience, and the reply came soon enough. The new Lord Ravenshaw had some business to take care of, but would be pleased to see us at ten o'clock.

We were there on the hour, walking up the driveway to a handsome Elizabethan manor house surrounded by lawns that sparkled with the morning frost. Our friend, the raven with two keys, appeared in the stonework beside the main gate and again in the lintel above the front door. There was a carriage parked outside, and suddenly a man came hurrying out of the house, climbed into it and swung the door shut behind him. A moment later he was gone, rattling past us on the drive. But I had already recognised him.

'Holmes,' I said. 'I know that man!'

'Mr Tobias Finch, was it not? A singular coincidence, do you not think?'

'It certainly seems very strange.'

'We should broach the subject with a certain delicacy. If Lord Ravenshaw is finding it necessary to sell off some of his family's heirlooms—'

'He could be buying.'

'That is also a possibility.'

We were admitted by a footman who led us through the hall and into a drawing room of truly baronial proportions. Some chairs and sofas had been arranged around a massive stone fireplace—there was the raven once again, carved into the lintel—with green logs crackling in the flames. Lord Ravenshaw was standing there, warming his hands. His eyes protruded conspicuously and it struck me that this might be due to some abnormality of the thyroid gland. He was wearing a riding coat and leather boots and carried a crop tucked under his arm. Even before we had introduced ourselves, he seemed keen to be on his way.

'Mr Sherlock Holmes,' he said. 'Yes, yes. I think I have heard of you.

A detective? I cannot imagine any circumstances in which your business would connect with mine.'

'I have something that I believe may belong to you, Lord Ravenshaw.' Holmes took out the watch.

For a moment Ravenshaw weighed it in his hand. Slowly, it dawned on him that he recognised it. He wondered how Holmes had found it. He was pleased to have it back. He spoke not a word but all these emotions passed across his face and even I found them easy to read.

'I am very much obliged to you,' he said, at length. 'I am very fond of this watch. I never thought I would see it again.'

'I would be interested to know how you lost it, Lord Ravenshaw.'

'I can tell you exactly, Mr Holmes. I was in London in June for the opera. As I climbed out of my carriage, a young street urchin ran into me. I thought nothing of it at the time, but during the interval I discovered that I had been pickpocketed.'

'Did you report the incident to the police?'

'I do not quite understand the purpose of these questions. For that matter, I'm rather surprised that a man of your reputation should have come all this way from London to return it. I take it you are hoping for a reward?'

'Not at all. The watch is part of a wider investigation and I hoped you might be able to help.'

'Well, I'm afraid I must disappoint you. I know nothing more. And I didn't report the theft, doubting that there was anything the police would be able to do. I am very grateful to you for returning the watch to me and am perfectly happy to pay your expenses. Other than that, I must wish you a good day.'

'Just one last question, Lord Ravenshaw,' Holmes said, with equanimity. 'There was a man leaving here as we arrived. Was I right in recognising an old friend of mine, Mr Tobias Finch?'

As Holmes had suspected, Lord Ravenshaw was not pleased to have been discovered in the company of the art dealer. 'Yes, it was he. You might as well know that my father had execrable taste in art and it is my intention to rid myself of at least part of his collection. I have been speaking to several galleries in London. Carstairs and Finch is the most discreet.'

'And has Mr Finch ever mentioned to you the House of Silk?'

Holmes asked the question and the silence that ensued happened to coincide with the snapping of a log in the fire so that the sound came almost as a punctuation mark.

'You said you had one question, Mr Holmes. That is a second and I have had enough, I think, of your impertinence. Am I to call for my servant or will you now leave?'

'I am delighted to have met you, Lord Ravenshaw.'

'I am grateful to you for returning my watch, Mr Holmes.'

I was glad to be out of that room, for I had felt almost trapped in the midst of so much wealth and privilege. As we stepped onto the path and began to walk back down to the gate, Holmes chuckled. 'Well, there's another mystery for you, Watson.'

'He seemed unusually hostile, Holmes.'

'I refer to the theft of the watch. If it was taken in June, Ross could not have been responsible for he was at Chorley Grange at that time. According to Johnson, it was pawned in September. So what had happened to it in the months in between? If it was Ross who stole it, why did he hold on to it for so long?'

We had almost reached the gate and I glanced back at the hall. Lord Ravenshaw was standing at the window, watching us leave. And although I could have been mistaken, for we were some distance away, it seemed to me his face was filled with hate.

'THERE IS NO HELPING IT,' Holmes said with a sigh of irritation. 'We are going to have to call upon Mycroft.'

When I first heard that Holmes had a brother, it humanised him—or at least, it did until I met the brother. Mycroft was, in many ways, as peculiar as he: unmarried, unconnected, existing in a small world of his own creation. He was to be found every day from a quarter to five until eight o'clock in the Diogenes Club in Pall Mall, which catered to the most unsociable and unclubbable men in town. Nobody ever spoke to anyone else. In fact, talking was not allowed at all, except in the Stranger's Room. The dining room had all the warmth and conviviality of a Trappist monastery, although the food was at least superior as the club employed a French chef.

That Mycroft enjoyed his food was evident from his frame, which was excessively corpulent. It was always disconcerting to meet him, for I would glimpse in him, just for a moment, some of the features of my friend: the light grey eyes, the same sharpness of expression, but they would seem strangely out of place in this animated mountain of flesh. I did sometimes wonder what the two of them might have been like as boys. It was impossible to imagine, for they had grown up to become the sort of men who would like you to think that they had never been boys at all.

When Holmes first described Mycroft to me, he had said that he was an auditor, working for a number of government departments. But I later learned that his brother was much more important and influential. Holmes admitted to me that he was a vital figure in government circles, the man every department consulted when something needed to be known. It was Holmes's opinion that, had he chosen to be a detective, he might have been his equal or even, I was astonished to hear, his superior. But Mycroft suffered from a streak of indolence so ingrained that it would have rendered him unable to solve any crime, for the simple reason that he would have been unable to interest himself in it.

'Is he in London?' I asked.

'He is seldom anywhere else. I will inform him that we intend to visit.'

The Diogenes was one of the smaller clubs on Pall Mall, designed rather like a Venetian palazzo in the Gothic style, with highly ornate, arched windows and small balustrades. This had the effect of making the interior rather gloomy. Visitors were permitted only on the ground floor. Mycroft received us, as always, in the Stranger's Room.

'My dear Sherlock!' Mycroft exclaimed as he waddled in. 'How are you? You have recently lost weight, I notice.'

'And you have recovered from influenza.'

'A mild bout. I enjoyed your monograph on tattoos. Written during the hours of the night, evidently. Have you been troubled by insomnia?'

'The summer was unpleasantly warm. You did not tell me you had acquired a parrot, Mycroft.'

'Not acquired, Sherlock. Borrowed. Dr Watson, a pleasure. Mrs Hudson has been away?'

'She returned last week. You have a new cook.'

'The last one resigned.'

'On account of the parrot.'

'She always was highly strung.'

This exchange took place with such rapidity that I felt myself to be a spectator at a tennis tournament. Mycroft waved us to the sofa and settled his own bulk on a chaise longue. 'I was very sorry to hear of the death of the boy, Ross,' he said, suddenly more serious. 'You know, I have advised you against the use of these street children, Sherlock. I hope you didn't place him in harm's way.'

'It is too early to say. You read the newspaper reports?'

'Of course. This business of the white ribbon, though, I find most disturbing. I would say that it was placed there as a warning. You should be asking yourself whether that warning was a general one, or directed towards you.'

'I was sent a piece of white ribbon seven weeks ago.' Holmes had brought the envelope with him. He handed it to his brother.

'The envelope tells us little,' he said. 'It was pushed through your letter box in a hurry for the end is scuffed. Your name written by a right-handed, educated man.' He drew out the ribbon. 'This silk is Indian. It was purchased from a milliner's and then cut into two pieces of equal length, for although one end has been cut professionally with sharp scissors, the other was sliced roughly with a knife. I cannot add much more than that, Sherlock.'

'I did wonder if you might be able to tell me what it signifies. Have you heard of a place or an organisation called the House of Silk?'

Mycroft shook his head. 'The name means nothing to me. It sounds like a shop. Indeed, I seem to remember there being a gentleman's outfitter of that name in Edinburgh.'

'We heard it first mentioned by a girl who had probably lived her whole life in London. It filled her with such fear that she struck out at Dr Watson here, inflicting a knife wound on his chest.'

'Goodness!'

'I mentioned it also to Lord Ravenshaw—'

'The son of the former Foreign Minister?'

'The very same.'

Mycroft's reaction, I thought, was one of alarm, although he did his best not to show it. 'I can ask a few questions for you, Sherlock. Would it trouble you to call on me at the same time tomorrow?' He gathered the white ribbon into his pudgy hand.

In fact we did not have to wait twenty-four hours. The following morning, at about ten o'clock, we heard the rattle of approaching wheels. Holmes glanced outside. 'It's Mycroft!' he said.

I realised at once that this was a remarkable occurrence, for Mycroft had never visited us at Baker Street before. Holmes had fallen silent and there was a sombre expression on his face, from which I understood that something sinister must have introduced itself into the affair to have caused such a momentous event. We had to wait some time for Mycroft to join us. The stairs were narrow and steep, doubly unsuited to a man of his bulk. Eventually he appeared in the doorway and sat down in the nearest chair.

'Can I offer you some tea?'

'No, Sherlock. I do not intend to stay long.' Mycroft handed him the envelope. 'This is yours. I am returning it to you with some advice.'

'Pray continue.'

'I do not have the answer to your question or any idea what the House of Silk is or where it may be found. Believe me, I wish it were otherwise, for then you might have more reason to accept what I am about to say. You must make no further enquiries. Forget the House of Silk, Sherlock.'

'You know I cannot do that.'

'I know your character. It is the reason why I have come to you personally. I am concerned that you are putting yourself into the gravest danger, and Dr Watson too. Let me explain. I approached one or two people in certain government departments. I assumed that this House of Silk must refer to some sort of criminal conspiracy and I wished to discover if anyone in the police or one of the intelligence services was investigating it. The people I spoke to were unable to help. At least, that is what they said.

'What happened next came as a very unpleasant surprise. As I left my lodgings this morning, I was greeted by a carriage and taken to an office in Whitehall where I met a man whom I cannot identify, but who works in close association with the prime minister. This is a person whose wisdom and judgment I would never question. He came straight to the point, asking me why I had been asking about the House of Silk and what I meant by it. I decided at once not to mention your name—otherwise it might not be me knocking at your door. Having said that, my relationship with you is well known and you may already be suspected. I told him merely that one of my informers had mentioned it in relation to a murder in Bermondsey and that it had piqued my curiosity. He asked for the name of the informer and I made something up, trying to give the impression that it was a trivial affair and that my original enquiry had been nothing more than casual.

'He seemed to relax a little, although he continued to weigh his words with great caution. He told me that the House of Silk was indeed the subject of a police investigation. Things were at a delicate stage and any intervention from an outside party could do untold damage. I don't think a word of

this was true, but I pretended to acquiesce. After an exchange of pleasantries, I took my leave. But the point is, Sherlock, that politicians at this
very senior level have a way of saying a lot while giving away very little
and this gentleman managed to impress upon me what I am now trying to
tell you. You must leave it alone! Whatever the House of Silk is, it is a
matter of national importance. The government is aware of it and is dealing
with it and you have no idea of the damage you may do and the scandal you
may cause if you continue to be involved. Do you understand me?'

'You could not have been more lucid.'

'And will you heed what I have said?'

'I cannot promise that,' Holmes said. 'While I feel myself responsible for
the death of the child, I owe it to him to do all I can to bring his killer to
justice. His task was simply to watch over a man in a hotel. But if this inadvertently drew him into some wider conspiracy, then I fear I have no choice
but to pursue the matter.'

'I suppose your words do you credit, Sherlock. But let me add this.'
Mycroft got to his feet, anxious to be on his way. 'If you go ahead with this
investigation, and if it does lead you into peril, you cannot come back to me
for there will be nothing I can do to help you. The very fact that I have
exposed myself by asking questions on your behalf means that my hands
are now tied. I urge you once more to think again. This is not one of your
petty puzzles of the police court. If you upset the wrong people, it could be
the end of your career . . . and worse.'

There was nothing more to be said. Mycroft bowed slightly and left.

'Well, Watson,' Holmes exclaimed. 'What do you make of that?'

'I hope you will consider what Mycroft had to say,' I ventured.

'I have already considered it.'

'I rather feared as much.'

Holmes laughed. 'You know me too well, my boy. And now I have an
errand to run and must hurry if I am to make the evening editions.'

He rushed out, leaving me alone with my misgivings. At lunch time he
returned but did not eat, a sure sign that he was engaged upon some stimu-
lating line of enquiry. I had seen him so often like this. Just as an animal
will devote its entire being to one activity, so could he allow events to
absorb him to the extent that even the most basic needs—food, water,
sleep—could be set aside. The arrival of the evening newspaper showed me
what he had done. He had placed an advertisement in the personal columns.

£20 REWARD—Information relating to the House
of Silk. To be treated in the strictest confidence.
Apply 221b Baker Street.

'Holmes!' I exclaimed. 'You have done the very opposite of what your
brother suggested. You could at least have proceeded with discretion.'

'Discretion will not help us, Watson. It is time to seize the initiative.
Mycroft inhabits a world of whispering men in darkened rooms. Well, let us
see how they react to a little provocation.'

'You believe you will receive an answer?'

'Time will tell. But we have at least set our calling card on this affair, and
even if nothing comes of it, no harm has been done.'

Those were his words. But Holmes had no idea of the type of people
with whom he was dealing. Harm, in the worst possible way, was to come to
us all too soon.

'HA, WATSON! It would appear that our bait, cast though it was over
unknown waters, may have brought in a catch!'

So spoke Holmes a few mornings later, standing at our bow window in
his dressing gown. I joined him and looked down into Baker Street, at the
crowds passing on either side.

'Who do you mean?' I asked. 'I see a great many people.'

'But in this cold weather few of them wish to linger. There is one man,
however, who is doing precisely that. There! He is looking our way.'

The man in question was wrapped in a coat and a scarf with a black felt
hat. He seemed to be rooted to the spot, unsure whether to continue or not.

'I noticed him first fifteen minutes ago, walking up from the
Metropolitan Railway. Since he arrived, he has barely moved. He is making
sure that he is not observed. Ah! Finally, he has made up his mind!' As we
watched him, the man crossed the road. 'He should be with us in a
moment,' Holmes said, returning to his seat.

Sure enough, the door opened and Mrs Hudson introduced our new visitor, who peeled off the hat, the scarf and the coat to reveal a strange-looking
young man. He could not have been past thirty yet his hair was thin, his skin
grey and his lips cracked, all of which made him seem much older. His
clothes were expensive but dirty. He seemed nervous, yet regarded us with a
bullish self-confidence that was almost aggressive. I was unsure whether

I was in the presence of an aristocrat or a ruffian of the lowest sort.

'Please take a seat,' said Holmes, at his most congenial. 'Would you like some hot tea?'

'I'd prefer a tot of rum,' he replied. His voice was hoarse but educated.

'We have none. But some brandy?' Holmes nodded at me and I poured a good measure into a glass and handed it over.

The man drained it at once. 'Thank you, I've come for the reward. I shouldn't have. The people I deal with would cut my throat if they knew I was here, but I need the money and twenty pounds will keep the demons away for a good while. Do you have it here?'

'You will have the payment when we have your information,' Holmes replied. 'I am Sherlock Holmes. And you . . .?'

'You may call me Henderson, which is not my real name. You see, Mr Holmes, I have to be careful. You placed an advertisement asking for information about the House of Silk, and from that moment this house will have been watched. One day you may be asked to provide the names of all your visitors. You will understand if I hide my identity.'

'You are a teacher are you not?'

'What makes you say that?'

'There is chalk dust on the edge of your cuff and I notice a red ink stain on the inside of your third finger.'

Henderson smiled briefly. 'I am sorry to correct you but I am a tidewaiter, although I use chalk to mark the packages before they are unloaded and enter the numbers in a ledger using red ink. I used to work with the customs officer at Chatham but came to London two years ago. I thought a change of scene would help my career, but it has almost ruined me. I would sell my mother for twenty pounds, Mr Holmes. There is nothing I would not do.'

'And what is the cause of your undoing, Mr Henderson?'

'Opium,' he said. 'I used to take it because I liked it. Now I cannot live without it. Here is my story. I left my wife in Chatham until I had established myself and took up lodgings in Shadwell to be close to my new place of work. It's a colourful neighbourhood and there are enough temptations to part any fool and his money. It was twelve months ago that I paid my first fourpence for the little pellet of brown wax to be drawn from the gallipot. The pleasure it gave me was beyond anything I had experienced. Of course I went back. First a month later, then a week, then suddenly it was every day. My true friends fell away. My false ones encouraged me to smoke more. My employers have threatened to dismiss me, but I no longer care. The desire for opium fills my every waking moment. Give me the reward so that I can again lose myself in the mists of oblivion.'

I looked on the man with horror and pity. Henderson was being destroyed, slowly, from within.

Holmes was grave. 'The place where you go to take this drug—is it the House of Silk?' he asked.

Henderson laughed. 'Do you really think I would have taken so many precautions if the House of Silk were merely an opium den?' he cried. 'Do you know how many opium dens there are in Shadwell and Limehouse? You can stand at a crossroads and find one whichever direction you take. There's Mother Abdullah's and Creer's Place and Yahee's. I'm told you can buy the stuff in the Haymarket and Leicester Square.'

'Then what is it?'

'The money!'

Holmes hesitated then passed across four five-pound notes. Henderson snatched them up. 'Where do you think the opium comes from? Where do Creer or Yahee go when their stocks run low? Where is the centre of the web that stretches across the entire country? That is the answer to your question, Mr Holmes. The House of Silk! It is a criminal enterprise that operates on a massive scale. I have heard it said that it has friends in the very highest places, that its tentacles ensnare government ministers and police officers. We are talking of an import and export business, if you like, but one worth many thousands of pounds a year. The opium comes in from the east. It is transported to this central depot and distributed at a much-inflated price.'

'Where is it to be found?'

'In London. I do not know exactly where.'

'Who runs it?'

'I have no idea.'

'Then you have hardly helped us, Mr Henderson. How can we even be sure that what you say is true?'

'Because I can prove it. I have long been a customer at Creer's Place. It's done up to be Chinese, but the man who runs it is as English as you or I and a more vicious sort you wouldn't want to meet. Black eyes and a head like a dead man's skull. Even so, he and I rub along well enough. He has a little office off the main room and sometimes he'll invite me in. He likes to hear stories about life at the docks. He uses boys to bring in supplies and—'

'Boys?' I interrupted. 'Was one of them called Ross?'

'They have no names. But I was there a few weeks ago and one of these lads came in late. Creer had been drinking and knocked him to the ground. "Where have you been?" he demanded.

'"The House of Silk," the boy replied.

'"And what do you have for me?"

'The boy handed over a packet and slunk out of the room. "What is the House of Silk?" I asked. That was when Creer told me what I have told you now. Had it not been for the whisky, he would not have been so loose-tongued. When he realised what he had done he opened a bureau beside his desk and the next thing I knew, he was pointing a gun at me. "Why do you want to know?" he cried. "Why do you ask me these questions?"

'"I was making idle conversation. That's all," I assured him.

'"There is nothing idle about it, my friend. You repeat a word of what I have just said to anyone, they'll be hauling your remains out of the Thames. Do you understand? If I don't kill you, they will." Then he lowered the gun, and when he spoke again it was in a softer tone of voice. "Never mention the subject again. Do you hear me?"

'And that was the end of it. If he knew I had come to you, I have no doubt he would be as good as his word. But if you are seeking the House of Silk, you must begin with his office for he can lead you there.'

'Where is it to be found?'

'In Bluegate Fields on the corner of Milward Street, a low, dirty place with a red light burning in the doorway.'

'Will you be there tonight?'

'Thanks to your beneficence I will be there for many nights to come.'

'Does this man, Creer, ever leave his office?'

'Frequently. He goes out to take the air.'

'Then you may see me tonight. And if I find what I am looking for, I will double your reward.'

'Do not say you know me. Do not acknowledge my presence.'

'I understand.'

When Henderson left, Holmes turned to me, a gleam in his eyes. 'An opium den! That does business with the House of Silk. What do you think, Watson?'

'I don't like it one bit, Holmes. I think you should stay well away.'

'Pshaw! I think I can look after myself.' Holmes strode over to his desk, opened a drawer and took out a pistol. 'I'll go armed.'

'Then I shall go with you.'

'My dear Watson, as much as I am grateful to you, the two of us together would look anything but the sort of customers who might be seeking out an East London opium den.'

'Holmes, I insist. I will remain outside. Then, if you are in need of assistance, a single shot will bring me to the scene. Creer may have other thugs working for him. And can we trust Henderson not to betray you?'

'Very well. Where is your revolver?'

'I did not bring it with me.'

'No matter. I have another.' Holmes smiled with relish. 'Tonight we shall pay Creer's Place a visit and we shall see what we shall see.'

THERE WAS ANOTHER FOG that night. I would have urged Holmes to postpone his visit to Bluegate Fields but I could see from his face that he would not be deterred. Although he had not said as much, I knew that it was the death of the child, Ross, that compelled him. For as long as he held himself even partly responsible for what had occurred, he would not rest.

And yet how oppressed I felt as the cab dropped us beside an alleyway near the Limehouse Basin. The fog, thick and yellow, deadened every sound. It seemed like some evil animal snuffling through the darkness in search of its prey and it was as if we were delivering ourselves into its very jaws. We were by a canal and a rat, or some other creature, scuttled in front of us and slipped into the black water with a splash. A dog barked. We walked past a barge, tied to one side, chinks of light just visible behind the curtained windows. We turned a corner and all of this was swallowed up immediately by the fog, which fell like a curtain behind us. Ahead, too, there was nothing, and if we had been about to step off the edge of the world, we would have been no wiser. But then we heard the jangle of a piano, one finger picking out a tune. And finally, in front of us, I saw the windows of a public house, The Rose and Crown.

'We are here, Watson,' Holmes whispered. He pointed. 'There is Milward Street, and I would imagine that to be Creer's Place. You see the red light in the doorway.'

'Holmes, I beg of you one last time to let me accompany you.'

'No, no. It is better for one of us to remain on the outside for if it turns out I am expected, you will be in the stronger position to come to my aid.'

'You think Henderson was lying to you?'

'His story struck me as in every way improbable.'

'Then, for heaven's sake, Holmes—'

'I cannot be entirely certain, not without entering. It is just possible that Henderson spoke the truth. But if this is a trap, we will spring it and see where it takes us.' I opened my mouth to protest but he continued, 'We have touched something very deep, old friend. We will not get to the bottom of it if we refuse to take risks. Wait for me for one hour. Then you must come after me but take the greatest care. And if you hear gunfire, come at once.'

'Whatever you say, Holmes.'

It was with the gravest misgivings that I watched him cross the road to stand in the glow of the red light. I heard a clock strike the hour, the bell sounding eleven times. Before the first chime had faded, Holmes had gone.

Even in my greatcoat, it was too cold to stand outside for an hour and I pushed open the door of The Rose and Crown. I found myself in a single room divided in two by a narrow bar. Between fifteen and twenty people were huddled together at tables, playing cards, drinking and smoking. A worn-out piano stood next to the door and a woman in front of it idly prodded the keys. This was the music I had heard outside.

An old, grizzled man poured me a glass of ale for a couple of pence and I stood there, not drinking, ignoring my own worst imaginings. None of the sailors and dock workers took any notice of me, and for that I was glad. A clock on the wall showed the passing hour and it seemed to me that the minute hand was deliberately dragging itself. I will never forget the fifty-minute vigil that I spent in that little room with the slap of the cards against the table and the out-of-tune notes picked out on the piano.

Fifty minutes exactly, for it was at ten to midnight that the night was shattered by two gunshots and, almost immediately, by the shrill cry of a police whistle and voices shouting out in alarm. I was instantly out in the street. That Holmes had fired the shots I never doubted. But had he fired them as a warning, for me, or was he in some sort of peril, forced to defend himself? I hurled myself across the street and up to the entrance of Creer's Place. The door was unlocked. Drawing my weapon, I rushed in.

The dry, burning smell of opium greeted my nostrils. I was standing in a dank, gloomy room decorated in the Chinese style as Henderson had described. Of the man himself there was no sign. Four other men lay stretched out on mattresses. Three of them were unconscious and the last was gazing at me with unfocused eyes. One mattress was empty.

A man came rushing towards me and I knew that this must be Creer himself. He was completely bald with black, deep-set eyes. I could see that he was about to challenge me, then he saw my revolver and fell back.

'Where is he?' I demanded.

'Who?'

'You know who I mean!'

My eyes travelled past him to an open doorway and a corridor, lit by a gas lamp, beyond. Ignoring Creer, I pushed my way forward. There was another door at the far end of the corridor and, as Holmes could not have possibly left by the front, he must surely have come this way. I forced it open and felt the rush of cold air. I was at the back of the house. I heard more shouting, the clatter of a horse and carriage, the blast of a police whistle. Where was Holmes? Had he been hurt?

I ran down a narrow street, through an archway and into a courtyard. A small crowd had gathered here. I saw a man in evening dress, a police constable, two others. They were all staring at a tableau in front of them, none of them daring to move forward and take charge. I pushed my way through them. And never will I forget what I then saw.

There were two figures. One was a young girl who I recognised at once. Sally Dixon had been shot twice, in the chest and in the head. She was lying on the cobblestones in a pool of blood. I also knew the man who lay unconscious in front of her, one hand stretched out, still holding the gun that had shot her.

It was Sherlock Holmes.

THREE
Under Arrest

Sitting here twenty-five years later, I still have every detail of that night printed on my mind. Poor Holmes. I see him now, recovering consciousness to find himself surrounded, under arrest and unable to explain to himself or to anyone else what had just taken place. It was he who had chosen, willingly, to walk into a trap. This was the unhappy result.

A constable had arrived. He was young and nervous but went about his business with commendable efficiency. First, he checked that the girl was dead, then turned his attention to my friend. Holmes looked dreadful. Although his eyes were open he seemed unable to see clearly . . . he certainly didn't recognise me. Matters were not helped by the crowd, and I asked myself how they could have chosen such a night to congregate here. A tall, elegantly dressed man gesticulated with his stick.

'Take him up, officer! I saw him shoot the girl.' He had a thick Scottish accent. 'God help her, the poor creature. He killed her in cold blood.'

'Who are you?' the constable demanded.

'My name is Thomas Ackland. I saw exactly what happened.'

I pushed my way forward and knelt beside my stricken friend. 'Holmes!' I cried. 'Can you hear me? For God's sake tell me what has happened.'

But Holmes was still incapable of reply and now I found the constable examining me. 'You know this man?' he demanded.

'Indeed I do. He is Sherlock Holmes. My name is John Watson and I am a doctor. Officer, you must allow me to attend upon my friend. However the facts may appear, I can assure you that he is innocent of any crime.'

'That is not true. I saw him shoot the girl.' Ackland took a step forward. 'I, too, am a doctor,' he continued. 'And I can tell you that this man is under the influence of opium. It is evident from his eyes and from his breath and you need seek no further motive for this vile and senseless crime.'

Was he right? Holmes was certainly in the grip of some sort of narcotic. Yet there was something about the diagnosis that puzzled me. Although I would have had to agree that the pupils of Holmes's eyes were dilated, they lacked the ugly pinpricks of light that I would have expected to find. I felt his pulse and found it almost too sluggish, suggesting that he had just been aroused from a deep sleep rather than involved in the strenuous activity of chasing and shooting his victim. And since when had opium ever caused an event such as this? Never had I heard of a user being driven to acts of violence. Even had Holmes been in the grip of the most profound paranoia, what possible motive could his muddled consciousness have come up with for killing the one girl he had been most eager to find and protect? How, for that matter, had she come to be here? Finally, I doubted that Holmes would have been able to shoot with any accuracy had he been under the influence of opium. He would have had difficulty even holding the gun steady.

'Did you accompany this person here tonight?' the constable asked me.

'Yes. But we were briefly apart. I was at The Rose and Crown.'

'And he?'

'He . . .' I stopped myself. I could not reveal where Holmes had been. 'My friend is a celebrated detective in pursuit of a case. Call for Inspector Lestrade who will vouch for him. As bad as this looks, there must be another explanation.'

'There is no other explanation,' Dr Ackland interjected. 'The girl was in the street, begging. He took out a gun and he shot her.'

'There is blood on his clothing,' the constable agreed. 'He was evidently close to her when she was killed. And when I arrived in this courtyard, there was nobody else in sight.'

'Did you see the shot fired?' I asked.

'No. But I arrived moments later. And nobody ran from the scene.'

'He did it!' somebody shouted in the crowd and this was followed by a murmur of assent.

'Holmes!' I cried, kneeling beside him. 'Can you tell me what happened?'

Holmes made no response and I became aware of another man who was now standing over me. 'Please will you get to your feet,' he demanded, in a voice as cold as the night itself.

'This man is my friend—' I began.

'And this is the scene of a crime. Stand up and move back. Thank you. Now, if anyone here saw anything, give your name and address to the officer. Otherwise, return to your homes. Officer? What's your name? Perkins! This is your beat?'

'It is, sir.'

'Can you tell me what you know? Try to keep it concise.' He stood in silence as the constable gave his version of events, which added up to little more than I already knew. He nodded. 'Very well, Constable Perkins. Write down these people's details in your notebook. I'll take charge now.'

This new arrival was one of the most reptilian men I have ever encountered, with eyes too small for his face, thin lips and skin so smooth as to be almost featureless. His most prominent feature was a thick mane of hair of a most unnatural white. It was not as if he was old—he could not have been more than thirty or thirty-five. The hair was in complete contrast to his wardrobe, which consisted of black overcoat, black gloves and scarf. Although he was not a large man, he had a certain presence, even an arrogance. He spoke softly, but his voice had an edge that left you in no doubt that he was used to being obeyed. But it was his mercurial quality that most unnerved me, his refusal to connect emotionally with anyone at all. That was what put me in mind of a snake. From the moment I had first spoken to him, I felt him slithering around me.

'So your name is Dr Watson?' he said.

'Yes.'

'And this is Sherlock Holmes! Well, I rather doubt we'll be reading of this in one of your famous chronicles, unless it comes under the heading of *The Adventure of the Psychotic Opium Addict*. Your colleague was at Creer's Place tonight?'

'He was pursuing an investigation.'

'Pursuing it with a pipe and a needle it would seem. A rather unorthodox method of detection, I would have said. A pretty business we have here! This girl can't be more than sixteen or seventeen years old.'

'Her name is Sally Dixon. She was working at a public house called The Bag of Nails in Lambeth.'

'She was known to her assailant?'

'Mr Holmes was not her assailant!'

'There are witnesses who have a different point of view.' He glanced at the Scottish man. 'You are a doctor? You saw what happened here tonight?'

'The girl was begging. This man came from that building over there. He followed the girl into this square and he killed her with a revolver. It's as plain as that.'

'In your opinion, is Mr Holmes well enough to travel with me to Holborn police station?'

'He cannot walk but there is no reason why he should not travel in a cab.'

'There is one on the way.'

The white-haired man walked over to Holmes, who still lay on the ground. 'Can you hear me, Mr Holmes?'

'Yes.' It was the first word he had spoken.

'My name is Inspector Harriman. I am arresting you for the murder of this young woman, Sally Dixon. You are not obliged to say anything unless you desire to do so, but whatever you do say I shall take down in writing and it may be used as evidence against you hereafter. Do you understand?'

'This is monstrous!' I cried. 'Sherlock Holmes had nothing whatsoever to do with this crime. Your witness is lying. This is some conspiracy—'

'If you do not wish to find yourself arrested for obstruction and quite possibly sued for slander, then I suggest you remain silent. Step aside and leave me to get on with my business.'

'Do you have no idea who this is and to what extent the police force in this city and, indeed, in this country, are indebted to him?'

'I know very well who he is and I cannot say that it makes any difference to the situation as I find it. We have a dead girl. The murder weapon is in his hand. We have a witness. I think that's enough to be getting on with.'

There was nothing more I could do except stand and watch as Constable Perkins, with the help of the doctor, lifted Holmes to his feet and dragged him away.

As he was being helped into the cab, our eyes met and I was relieved to see that some of the life had returned to them. More policemen had arrived and I saw Sally carried away on a stretcher. Before I knew it, I was on my own and I hurriedly made for home.

I HAD A VISITOR, early the next morning. It was the one man I most wanted to see—Inspector Lestrade. As he came striding in, interrupting me at my breakfast, my first thought was that he brought news that Holmes had already been released. One look at his face, however, was enough to dash my hopes. He was grim and unsmiling. Without asking permission, he sat down heavily at the table.

'Will you have some breakfast, Inspector?' I ventured.

'I am certainly in need of something to restore me. This business beggars belief. Have these people forgotten how much of a good turn we owe Sherlock Holmes at Scotland Yard? It doesn't look good, Dr Watson.'

I poured him a cup of tea and Lestrade sipped noisily. 'Where is Holmes?' I asked.

'They held him overnight at Bow Street.'

'Have you seen him?'

'They wouldn't let me! As soon as I heard what had happened, I went straight round. But this man, Harriman, he's a queer one. Most of us at Scotland Yard muddle along together as best we can. But not him. He has no friends and no family that I know of. I've never spoken more than a few words to him. This morning I asked to visit Mr Holmes but he just walked right past me. A little common courtesy wouldn't have hurt, but that's the man we're up against. He's with Holmes now, interviewing him. As far as I can tell, Harriman's already made up his mind, but of course it's all non-sense. I've come here, hoping you can shed some light on this matter. Is it true that Mr Holmes visited an opium den?'

'He went there, but not to indulge in that hateful practice. He is still investigating the deaths of the man in the flat cap and the child, Ross. That was what took him to East London.'

Lestrade took out his notebook. 'I think you had better tell me what progress you and Mr Holmes had made. If I am going to fight on his behalf then the more I know the better. I ask you to leave nothing out.'

It was strange, really, for Holmes would, in normal circumstances, have told the police none of the details of his investigation. On this occasion, though, I had no choice but to acquaint Lestrade with everything, starting with our visit to Chorley Grange School for Boys, which had led us to Sally Dixon and The Bag of Nails. I told him of her attack on me, our discovery of the stolen pocket watch, our unhelpful interview with Lord Ravenshaw, and Holmes's decision to place an advertisement in the evening papers. Finally, I described the visit of the man who called himself Henderson.

'He was a tidewaiter?'

'That was what he said, Lestrade, but I fear he was dissimulating, as in the rest of his story. I believe this was a deliberate trap to incriminate Holmes and to bring an end to his investigation.'

'But what is this House of Silk? Why would anyone go to such lengths to keep it secret?'

'I cannot say.'

Lestrade shook his head. 'All this seems a long way from the point where we started—a dead man in a hotel room. That man, as far as we know, was Keelan O'Donaghue, a hoodlum from Boston, who came to England on a mission of revenge against the picture dealer, Mr Carstairs of Wimbledon. So how do you get from there to the deaths of two children, the business of the white ribbon, this mysterious Henderson and all the rest of it?'

'That was exactly what Holmes was trying to discover. Can I see him?'

'Until Mr Holmes has been formally charged, nobody will be allowed to speak with him. They are taking him to a police court this afternoon.'

'We must be there.'

'You understand that no defence witnesses will be called at this stage. Even so, I will try to speak for him and attest to his good character.'

'Will they keep him at Bow Street?'

'For the time being, but if the judge thinks there's a case to answer—and I can't see him thinking otherwise—he will be put in prison.'

'What prison?'

'I can't say, Dr Watson. In the meantime, is there anyone to whom you can apply? Perhaps among Mr Holmes's clients there is someone of influence to whom you can turn.'

My first thought was of Mycroft. Would he agree to see me? He had issued a warning in this very room, and he had been adamant that he would be powerless if it was ignored. Even so, I made the decision to present myself at the Diogenes Club as soon as the opportunity arose.

Lestrade rose to his feet. 'I will call for you at two o'clock.'

'Thank you, Lestrade.'

'Don't thank me yet, Dr Watson. Harriman wants to try Mr Holmes for murder and I think you should prepare yourself for the worst.'

NEVER BEFORE had I attended a police court and yet, as I approached that solid and austere building on Bow Street in the company of Lestrade, I felt a strange sense of familiarity.

Lestrade smiled mournfully. 'I don't suppose you expected to find yourself in a place like this, eh, Dr Watson?' I told him that he had taken the very thought from my head. 'Well, you have to wonder how many other men have passed this way thanks to you and Mr Holmes.' He was quite right. This was the end of the process that we had so frequently begun, the first step on the way to the Old Bailey and then perhaps the gallows.

The courtroom was square and windowless, with wooden benches and barriers and the royal arms emblazoned on the far wall. This is where the magistrate sat, a stiff, elderly man. There was a railed-off platform in front of him and it was here that the prisoners were brought one after the other, for the process was rapid. Lestrade and I took our places in the public gallery and we watched as a forger, a burglar and a magsman were all remanded in custody to await trial. And yet the magistrate could also be compassionate. Two children, no more than eight or nine years old, brought in for begging, were handed over to the Police Courts Mission with the recommendation that they should be looked after either by the Waifs and Strays Society, by Dr Barnardo's orphanage or by the Society for the Improvement of London's Children. It was odd to hear the last of these three named for this was the organisation responsible for Chorley Grange.

Now Lestrade nudged me and I became aware of a new sense of gravity in the courtroom. More uniformed policemen and clerks took their places. Two men that I recognised sat down a few feet apart on one of the benches.

One was Dr Ackland, the other a red-faced man who might have been in the crowd outside Creer's Place. Behind them, sat Creer himself. They were all here, I saw at once, as witnesses.

And then Holmes was brought in, wearing the same clothes in which he had been arrested. He had clearly not slept. I tried not to imagine the various indignities that must have been heaped upon him. But as he was led into the dock he looked at me and I saw a glint in his eye which told me that the fight was not over yet and reminded me that Holmes had always been at his most formidable when the odds seemed to be stacked against him.

A barrister presented himself, a well-rounded, diminutive sort, and it soon became clear that he had assumed the role of prosecutor.

'The accused is a well-known detective,' he began. 'Mr Sherlock Holmes has achieved public renown through a series of stories that, though gaudy and sensational, are based at least partly on truth.' I bristled at this and might even have protested had Lestrade not tapped me gently on the arm.

'That said, I will not deny that there are one or two less capable officers at Scotland Yard who owe him a debt of gratitude in that, from time to time, he has helped direct their investigations.' Hearing this, it was Lestrade's turn to scowl. 'But even the best of men have their demons and in the case of Mr Holmes it is opium that has turned him from a friend of the law into the basest malefactor. Last night he entered Creer's Place, an opium den in Limehouse. My first witness is the owner of the establishment, Isaiah Creer.'

Creer took the witness stand. Prompted by the prosecutor, he told the following tale. Yes, the accused had entered his house—a private and legal establishment, My Lord—just after eleven o'clock. He had demanded a dose of the intoxicant and smoked it immediately. Half an hour later, he had asked for a second. Mr Creer had been concerned that Mr Holmes had become agitated. Mr Creer had suggested that a second dose might be unwise but the gentleman had disagreed in the strongest terms and, in order to maintain the tranquillity for which his establishment was noted, he had provided the essentials. Mr Holmes had smoked the second pipe and his sense of delirium had increased to the extent that Creer had sent a boy out to find a policeman, fearing there might be a breach of the peace. He had attempted to calm Mr Holmes down, but without success. Beyond control, Mr Holmes had insisted that there were enemies in the room, that he was being pursued, that his life was in danger. He had produced a revolver, at which point Mr Creer had insisted that he leave.

'My only thought was to have him out of the house,' he told the court. 'But I see now that I should have let him remain until help arrived in the shape of Constable Perkins. For when I released him onto the street he was out of his mind. I have seen this happen before, Your Honour. It is a rare side effect of the drug. I have no doubt that when Mr Holmes gunned down that poor girl, he believed he was confronting some monster.'

The story was corroborated in every respect by a second witness, the red-faced man I had already noticed. He was a languid aristocratic type of not more than thirty and dressed in the latest fashion. He repeating almost verbatim what Creer had said. He had, he said, been stretched out on a mattress on the other side of the room and swore that he was perfectly conscious of what had been taking place. 'Opium, for me, is an occasional indulgence,' he concluded. 'It provides a few hours in which I can retreat from the anxieties and the responsibilities of my life. I see no shame in it. But then I,' he added, pointedly, 'am able to handle it.'

It was only when the magistrate asked him his name for the record that the young man created a stir in the court. 'Lord Horace Blackwater.'

The magistrate stared at him. 'Do I take it, sir, that you are part of the Blackwater family of Hallamshire?'

'The Earl of Blackwater is my father.'

I was as surprised as anyone. It seemed shocking that the scion of one of the oldest families in England should have found his way to a sordid drug den in Bluegate Fields. At the same time, I could imagine the weight that his evidence would add to the case against my friend. This was not just some low-life, it was a man who could quite possibly ruin himself by even admitting he had been at Creer's Place. He was fortunate that there were no journalists present. The same, I hardly need add, would be true for Holmes.

His place was taken by the constable who I had encountered on the night. Perkins had the least to say, but much of the story had already been told for him. He had been asked to come to the house on the corner of Milward Street. He had been on his way when he had heard two gunshots and had rushed to Coppergate Square to discover a man, unconscious with a gun, and a girl lying in a pool of blood. He had taken charge of the scene as a crowd had gathered. He described how I had arrived and identified the unconscious man as Sherlock Holmes.

'I couldn't believe it,' he said. 'To think that Mr Sherlock Holmes might be involved in this sort of thing . . . well, it beggared belief.'

Perkins was followed by Inspector Harriman. From the way he spoke, with every word measured and carefully delivered, it could be imagined that he had been rehearsing this speech for hours. He did not even attempt to keep the contempt out of his voice. The imprisonment, and indeed the execution of my friend, might have been his only mission in life.

Thus he began. 'I had been called to a break-in at a bank on the White Horse Road, a short distance away. As I was leaving, I heard the sound of gunshots and turned my way south to see if I could assist. By the time I arrived, Constable Perkins was in command, doing an admirable task. He informed me of the identity of the man who now stands before you. That Mr Holmes murdered Sally Dixon is beyond question. At the scene of the crime I observed that the gun in his hand was still warm, that there were residues of powder-blackening on his sleeve and several small bloodstains on his coat that could have arrived there only if he had been standing in close proximity to the girl when she was shot. Mr Holmes offered no defence. When I placed him under arrest, he made no attempt to persuade me that the circumstances were anything other than what I have described.

'It was only this morning that he came up with a cock-and-bull story proclaiming his innocence. He told me that he had visited Creer's Place because he was investigating a case, the details of which he refused to share with me. He said that a man, known to him as Henderson, had sent him to Limehouse in pursuit of some clue, but that as soon as he had entered the den he had been overpowered and forced to consume some narcotic. Speaking personally, I find it a little strange when a man visits an opium den and then complains that he has been drugged. But we know that this is a barrel of lies. We have already heard from a distinguished witness who saw Mr Holmes smoke one pipe and then demand a second. Mr Holmes also claims that the murdered girl was part of this mysterious investigation. It may well be that he had met her before and in his delirium he confused her with some imaginary criminal. He had no other motive for killing her.

'Mr Holmes now insists that he is part of a conspiracy that includes me, Constable Perkins, Isaiah Creer, Lord Horace Blackwater and, quite possibly, Your Honour yourself. I would describe this as delusional, but actually it's a deliberate attempt to extricate himself from the consequences of the delusions he was suffering last night. How unfortunate for Mr Holmes that we have a second witness who saw the killing itself. His testimony will, I am sure, bring an end to these proceedings. For my part, I can say only that in my fifteen years with the Metropolitan Police, I have never encountered a case where the guilty party was more obvious.'

The final witness was Dr Thomas Ackland who struck me as an unattractive man with curls of bright red hair, dark freckles and watery blue eyes. It is possible that I exaggerate his appearance for, as he spoke, I felt a deep loathing for a man whose words seemed to place the final seal on my friend's guilt. I have gone back to the official transcripts so that it cannot be claimed that my own prejudices distort the record.

The Prosecutor: Dr Ackland, could you please tell the court how you happened to be in the vicinity of Milward Street and Coppergate Square?
Witness: I had been to visit one of my patients. I left his house at eleven o'clock, intending to walk home. I became lost in the fog and it was by chance that I entered the square a little before midnight.
The Prosecutor: And what did you see?
Witness: There was a girl, no more than fourteen or fifteen years old. I shudder to think what she might have been doing out in the street at this hour . . . When I first noticed her, her hands were raised and she was clearly terrified. She uttered one word. 'Please . . .!' Then there were two shots and she fell to the ground. The second shot had penetrated the skull and would have killed her instantly.
The Prosecutor: Did you see who fired the shots?
Witness: Not at first. It was very dark and I was in fear of my life, for it occurred to me that there must be some madman on the loose. Then I made out a figure standing a short distance away, holding a gun that was still smoking. As I watched, he fell to his knees. Then he sprawled, unconscious, on the ground.
The Prosecutor: Do you see that figure today?
Witness: Yes. He is standing in front of me in the dock.

There was a stir in the public gallery for this was the most damning evidence of all. Next to me, Lestrade had become very still and it occurred to me that the faith in Holmes that had done him such credit must surely be shaken to the core. And what of me? I was in turmoil. It was, on the face of it, inconceivable that my friend could have killed the one girl he most wanted to interview, for there was still a chance that Sally Dixon could have been told something by her brother that might have led us to the House of

Silk. And then there was still the question of what she was doing in Coppergate Square to begin with. Had she been held prisoner before Henderson even visited us and could he have deliberately led us into a trap with this end in mind? That seemed to me to be the only logical conclusion. But I recalled something Holmes had said to me many times, namely that when you have eliminated the impossible, whatever remains, however improbable, must be the truth. I might be able to dismiss the evidence given by Isaiah Creer. But it was impossible to suggest that an eminent Glaswegian doctor, a senior police officer from Scotland Yard and the son of the Earl of Blackwater should come together to incriminate a man that none of them had ever met.

Either all four of them were lying. Or Holmes, under the influence of opium, had indeed committed a terrible crime.

The magistrate needed no such deliberation. Having heard the evidence, he called for the Charge Book and entered Holmes's name and address, his age and the charge that had been preferred against him. Holmes, who had not uttered a word throughout the entire procedure, was then informed that he would have to remain in custody until the coroner's court, which would be convened after the weekend. After that, he would proceed to trial. And that was the end of the business. I watched as Holmes was led away.

'Come with me, Watson!' Lestrade said. 'Move sharp, now.'

I followed him down a flight of stairs and into a basement area that was utterly without comfort. He led me into the Prisoners' Waiting Room.

There was a movement at the door and Holmes appeared, escorted by a uniformed officer. I rushed towards him and my voice broke as I addressed him. 'Holmes! I do not know what to say. The injustice of your arrest, the way you have been treated . . . it is beyond any imagining.'

'It is certainly most interesting,' returned he. 'How are you, Lestrade? A strange turn of events, do you not think? What do you make of it?'

'I really don't know what to think, Mr Holmes,' Lestrade muttered.

'Well, that's nothing new. It seems that our friend, Henderson, led us a pretty song and dance, hey, Watson? However, he has still proved useful. Before, I suspected that we had stumbled on to a conspiracy that went far beyond a murder in a hotel room. Now I am certain of it.'

'But what good is it to know these things if you are to be imprisoned and your reputation destroyed?' I replied.

'I think my reputation will look after itself,' Holmes said. 'If they hang me, Watson, I shall leave it to you to persuade your readers that the whole thing was a misunderstanding.'

'I should warn you that we have very little time,' growled Lestrade. 'And the evidence against you seems unarguable.'

'What did you make of the evidence, Watson?'

'I don't know what to say, Holmes. These men don't appear to know each other. They have come from different parts of the country. And yet they are in complete agreement about what occurred.'

'Then let me tell you at once that what I have told Inspector Harriman is the true version of events. After I entered the opium den, I was approached by Creer and greeted as a new customer. There were four men lying on the mattresses and one of them was indeed Lord Horace Blackwater, although of course I did not know him at the time. I pretended that I had come for my fourpenny worth and Creer insisted that I follow him into his office to make the payment. I did as he asked and two men sprang on me, seizing hold of my neck and pinioning my arms. One of them was Henderson. I was unable to move. "You have been very unwise, Mr Holmes, to believe that you could take on people more powerful than yourself," Henderson said. At the same time, Creer approached me carrying a small glass filled with some foul-smelling liquid and there was nothing I could do as it was forced between my lips. There were three of them and only one of me. I could not reach my gun. The effect was almost immediate. The strength went out of my legs. They released me and I fell to the floor.'

'The devils!' I exclaimed.

'And then?' Lestrade asked.

'I remember nothing more until I awoke with Watson beside me.'

'That's all very well, Mr Holmes,' said Lestrade, 'but how do you explain the testimonies we have heard from Dr Ackland, from Lord Horace Blackwater and from my colleague, Harriman?'

'They have colluded.'

'But why? These are not ordinary men.'

'Were they ordinary I would be more inclined to believe them. Does it not strike you as strange that three such remarkable specimens should have emerged, out of the darkness, at exactly the same time?'

'What they said made sense. There was not a single questionable word spoken in this court.'

'I beg to differ, Lestrade, for I heard several. Did you not find it surprising that although Dr Ackland said it was too dark for him to see who fired the shot, in the same breath he testified that he could see smoke rising from the gun? And then there's Harriman. You might find it worthwhile to confirm that there really was a break-in at a bank on the White Horse Road.'

'Why?'

'Because if I were to rob a bank, I would wait until after midnight when the streets were a little less populated. I might also head for Mayfair, Kensington or Belgravia—anywhere where the local residents might have deposited enough money to be worth stealing.'

'And what of Perkins?'

'Constable Perkins was the only honest witness. Watson, I wonder if I could trouble you . . .?'

Before Holmes could continue, Harriman appeared in the doorway. 'What the devil is going on here?' he demanded. 'Who are you, sir?'

'I am Inspector Lestrade.'

'Lestrade! This is my case. Why are you interfering?'

'Mr Sherlock Holmes is well known to me—'

'Mr Sherlock Holmes is well known to a great many people. Are we going to invite them all in?' Harriman turned to the policeman who had brought Holmes from the courtroom. 'Officer! You'll hear more of this in due course. For the present, you can escort Mr Holmes to the back yard where a van is waiting to take him to his next place of residence.'

'And where is that?' Lestrade demanded.

'He is to be held at the House of Correction at Holloway.'

I blanched at this, for all of London knew the conditions that prevailed at that grim and imposing fortress. 'Holmes!' I said. 'I will visit you—'

'It distresses me to contradict you, but Mr Holmes will not be receiving visitors until my investigation is complete.'

There was nothing more that Lestrade or I could do. Holmes allowed the policeman to lead him from the room. Harriman followed and the two of us were left alone.

ALL THE NEWSPAPERS had reported on the death of Sally Dixon and the subsequent trial. I need hardly say that this made unpleasant reading at the breakfast table on the Monday following Holmes's arrest. The weekend had been and gone. Two days in which I could do little but fret and wait for news. I had sent fresh clothes and food to Holloway, but could not be sure that

Holmes had received them. From Mycroft I had heard nothing, although he could not possibly have missed the stories in the newspapers and, besides, I had sent repeated messages to the Diogenes Club. I did not know whether to be indignant or alarmed. Although it was true that he had warned us against precisely the course of action we had taken, surely he would not have hesitated to use his influence, given the seriousness of the situation.

I had resolved to present myself in person at the club when the doorbell rang and, after a short pause, Mrs Hudson introduced a beautiful woman, dressed with simple elegance and charm. So absorbed was I with my thoughts that it took me a few moments to recognise Mrs Catherine Carstairs, the wife of the Wimbledon art dealer whose visit to our office had set in motion these unhappy events. Here was a paradox indeed. On the one hand, the discovery of the dead man in Mrs Oldmore's Private Hotel had been the cause of everything that had happened but on the other it didn't seem to have anything to do with it. I might have said that it was as if two of my narratives had somehow got muddled together so that the characters from one were unexpectedly appearing in the other. Such was my sense of confusion on seeing Mrs Carstairs. And there she was, standing in front of me sobbing while I simply stared at her like a fool.

'My dear Mrs Carstairs!' I exclaimed, leaping to my feet. 'Please, do not distress yourself. Sit down. May I get you a glass of water?'

I led her to a chair and she produced a handkerchief, which she used to dab at her eyes. 'Dr Watson,' she murmured at last. 'You must forgive me coming here.'

'Not at all. Have you further news from Ridgeway Hall?'

'Yes. Horrible news. But is Mr Holmes away?'

'You have not heard? Have you not seen a newspaper?'

She shook her head. 'I don't interest myself in the news.'

'I'm afraid Mr Sherlock Holmes is indisposed,' I said. 'And is likely to be for some time.'

'Then I have no one else to turn to.' She bowed her head. 'Edmund does not know I have come here today. In fact, he counselled strongly against it. But I swear to you, I will go mad, Dr Watson.'

She began to cry afresh and I sat, helpless, until the tears abated. 'Perhaps it might help if you tell me what has brought you here,' I suggested.

She suddenly brightened. 'Of course! You're a doctor! We've seen doctors already but maybe you'll be different. You'll understand.'

'Is your husband ill?'

'Not my husband. My sister-in-law, Eliza. When you first met her, she was complaining of headaches and various pains, but since then her condition has worsened. Edmund thinks she may be dying.'

'What made you think you might find help here?'

Mrs Carstairs straightened herself in her chair. Suddenly I was aware of the strength of spirit that I had noticed when we first met. 'There is no love between my sister-and-law and I,' she said. 'I'll not pretend otherwise. From the very start, she thought me an adventuress who planned only to profit from her brother's wealth. Forget the fact that I came to this country with enough money of my own. She and her mother would have hated me, no matter who I was, and they never gave me a chance. Edmund had always belonged to them, and they could never bear the idea of his finding happiness with anyone else. Eliza even blames me for the death of her mother. What was a tragic domestic accident became in her mind a suicide, as if the old lady preferred to die than to see me as the new mistress of the house. Why could they never accept the fact that Edmund loves me and be glad for us?'

'And this new illness . . .?'

'Eliza thinks she is being poisoned. Worse than that, she insists that I am responsible. Don't ask me how she has arrived at this conclusion.'

'Does your husband know of this?'

'Of course he does. She accused me while I was there with them in the room. Poor Edmund! He didn't know how to respond—for if he had taken my side against her, who knows what it would have done to her state of mind. The moment we were alone he begged my forgiveness. Edmund takes the view that her delusions are part of the sickness. Even so, the situation has become intolerable. All her food is now prepared separately in the kitchen and carried straight up to her room by Kirby, who makes sure that it never leaves his sight. Edmund actually shares the dish with her. For a week now he has eaten everything that she has eaten and he is in perfect health, while she becomes sicker and sicker.'

'What do the doctors believe to be the cause of her illness?'

'They are baffled. First they thought it was diabetes, then blood poisoning. Now they are treating her for cholera.' Her eyes were full of tears. 'I will tell you a terrible thing, Dr Watson. Part of me wants her to die. Sometimes I find myself thinking that if Eliza were to go, at least Edmund and I would be left in peace. She seems intent on tearing us apart.'

'Would you like me to come with you to Wimbledon?' I asked.

'Would you?' Her eyes brightened. 'Edmund did not want me to see Sherlock Holmes. There were two reasons. The man from Boston is dead and there seems nothing more to be done. And were we to bring a detective to the house, he feared it would only persuade Eliza that she was right.'

'Whereas you thought . . .?'

'I hoped Mr Holmes would prove my innocence.'

'I should warn you that I am only a general practitioner but my long collaboration with Sherlock Holmes has given me an eye for the unusual and I may notice something that your other advisers have missed.'

'I would be so very grateful, Dr Watson. I still sometimes feel such a stranger in this country that it's a blessing to have anyone on my side.'

We left together. I had no wish to leave Baker Street but I could see that there was nothing to be gained by sitting there on my own. I had yet to be given permission to visit Holmes at Holloway. Mycroft would not arrive at the Diogenes Club until the afternoon. And despite what Mrs Carstairs had said, the mystery of the man in the flat cap was far from resolved.

Carstairs was not at first pleased to see me when I presented myself in the hallway of his home. He had been about to leave for lunch. 'Dr Watson!' he exclaimed. He turned to his wife. 'I thought we had agreed that we would not be resorting to the services of Sherlock Holmes.'

'I am not Holmes,' I said.

'Indeed not. I was just reading in the paper that Mr Holmes has fallen into the most disreputable circumstances.'

'He did so in pursuit of the business that you brought to his door.'

'A business that has now been concluded.'

'He does not think so.'

'Come, Edmund,' Mrs Carstairs cut in. 'Dr Watson has kindly agreed to see Eliza and give us the benefit of his opinion.'

'Eliza has already been seen by several doctors.'

'And one more opinion can't hurt.' She took his arm. 'Please, my dear. Let him see her. It may help her, too, even if it's only to have someone else to whom she can complain.'

Carstairs relented. 'Very well. But I heard my sister drawing a bath. Elsie is with her now. It will be at least thirty minutes before she is presentable.'

'I am quite happy to wait,' I said. 'But I will use the time, if I may, to examine the kitchen. If your sister persists in her belief that her food is being tampered with, it may prove useful to see where it is prepared.'

'Of course, Dr Watson. And you must forgive my rudeness just now. I wish Mr Holmes well and I am glad to see you. It's just that this nightmare never seems to stop. First Boston, then my poor mother, that business at the hotel, now Eliza.'

We went downstairs into a large, airy kitchen. There were three people in the room. I recognised the manservant, Kirby, who was sitting at the table, buttering some bread. A small, ginger-haired pudding of a woman was standing at the stove, stirring a soup. The third person was a sly-looking young man, sitting in the corner, idly polishing the cutlery. Although Kirby had risen to his feet the moment we entered, I noticed that the young man remained where he was. I remembered Carstairs telling Holmes and me that Kirby's wife had a nephew, Patrick, who worked below stairs.

Carstairs introduced me. 'This is Dr Watson, who is trying to determine the cause of my sister's illness. He may have some questions for you and I would be glad if you would answer them as candidly as you can.'

I began with the cook, who seemed the most approachable of the three. 'You prepare all the food, Mrs Kirby?' I asked.

'Everything is prepared in this kitchen, sir, by me and by my husband. All the food passes through my hands and if there is anything poisoned in this house, Dr Watson, you won't be finding it here. My kitchen is spotless, sir. We scrub it with carbolate of lime once a month.'

'It's not the food that's the cause of Miss Carstairs's illness,' muttered Kirby with a glance at the master of the house. 'You and Mrs Carstairs have had nothing different from her and you're both well.'

'If you ask me, there's something strange what's come into this house,' Mrs Kirby said.

'What do you mean by that, Margaret?' Mrs Carstairs demanded.

'I don't mean anything by it, ma'am. We're all worried to death on account of poor Miss Carstairs and it's as if there's something wrong about this place. But whatever it is, my conscience is clear and I would pack my bags tomorrow if anyone suggested otherwise.'

'Nobody is blaming you, Mrs Kirby.'

'She's right, though. There is something wrong in this house.' It was the kitchen boy, speaking for the first time.

'Your name is Patrick, is it not?' I asked.

'That's right, sir.'

'And where are you from?'

'From Belfast, sir.'

It was surely a coincidence but Rourke and Keelan O'Donaghue had also come from Belfast.

'How long have you been here, Patrick?' I asked.

'Two years. I came here just before Mrs Carstairs.' The boy smirked.

Everything about his behaviour—the way he slouched on his stool and the manner of his speech—struck me as purposefully disrespectful.

'How dare you speak to us like that, Patrick,' said Mrs Carstairs. 'If you're insinuating something, you should say it. And if you're unhappy here, you should leave.'

'I like it well enough, Mrs Carstairs, and I wouldn't say there was any-where else I would want to go.'

'Such insolence! Edmund, will you not speak to him?'

Carstairs hesitated, and in that brief pause there was a jangle. Kirby looked at the row of servants' bells. 'That's Miss Carstairs, sir.'

'She must have finished her bath,' Carstairs said. 'We can go up to her. Unless you have any more questions, Dr Watson?'

'Not at all,' I replied. The few questions I had asked had been futile and I was suddenly dispirited. Had Holmes been present, he would probably have solved the entire mystery by now.

We went all the way to the top floor. Carstairs knocked gently at the door, then entered his sister's bedroom to see if she would receive a visit from me. I waited outside with Mrs Carstairs. 'I will leave you here, Dr Watson,' said she. 'It will only distress my sister-in-law if I go in. Thank you again for coming. I feel so relieved to have you as my friend.'

She swept away just as Carstairs invited me in. I entered a close, plushly furnished bedroom built into the eaves. I noticed that a second door opened into an adjoining bathroom and the smell of lavender bath salts was heavy in the air. Eliza Carstairs was lying in bed, propped up with pillows. I could see at once that her health had deteriorated rapidly since my last visit. She had the pinched, exhausted quality that I had all too often observed in my more serious patients.

'Dr Watson!' she greeted me. 'Why have you come to visit me?'

'Your sister-in-law asked me, Miss Carstairs,' I replied.

'My sister-in-law wants me dead.' Her voice rasped in her throat.

'That is not the impression she gave. May I take your pulse?'

'You may take what you wish. I have nothing more to give. And when I am gone, take my word for it, Edmund will be next.'

'Hush, Eliza! Don't say such things,' her brother scolded her.

I held her pulse, which was beating too rapidly. Her skin had a slightly bluish tinge that, along with the other symptoms, made me wonder if her doctors might be right in suggesting cholera. 'You have abdominal pain?' I asked.

'Yes.'

'And aching joints?'

'I can feel my bones rotting away.'

'You have doctors in attendance. What drugs have they prescribed?'

'My sister is taking laudanum,' Carstairs said.

I released her. 'You might open the windows to allow the air to circulate, and cleanliness, of course, is of the first importance.'

'I bath every day.'

'It would help to change the bed linen every day too. But above all, you must eat. I have visited the kitchen and seen that your meals are well prepared. You have nothing to fear.'

'I am being poisoned.'

'If you are being poisoned, then so am I!' Carstairs exclaimed.

The sick woman fell back, closing her eyes. 'I thank you for your visit, Dr Watson. Open the windows and change the bed clothes! I can see that you must be at the very pinnacle of your profession!'

Carstairs ushered me out and the two of us parted company at the front door. 'Thank you for your visit, Dr Watson,' he said. 'I very much hope that Mr Holmes will be able to extricate himself from his difficulties.'

I was about to leave and then I remembered. 'There is just one other thing, Mr Carstairs. Is your wife able to swim?'

'What an extraordinary question! Why do you wish to know?'

'I have my methods . . .'

'Well, as a matter of fact, Catherine cannot. She will not enter the water under any circumstances.'

The door closed. I had received an answer to the question Holmes had put to me. Now all I needed to know was why I had asked it.

A NOTE FROM MYCROFT awaited me on my return. He would be at the Diogenes Club early that evening and would be pleased to see me. Mrs Hudson had laid out a late lunch, which I ate before falling asleep in my chair. The sky was already darkening when I set out and caught a cab to Pall Mall.

He met me once again in the Stranger's Room but this time his manner was more formal than it had been when I was there with Holmes. He began without any pleasantries. 'This is a very bad business. I told my brother that no good would come of it—but that was his character, even when he was very young. He was impetuous.'

'Can you help him?'

'You already know the answer, Dr Watson. There is nothing I can do.'

'Would you see him hanged for murder?'

'It will not come to that. I am working behind the scenes, and although I am finding a surprising amount of interference and obfuscation, he is well known to too many people of importance for that possibility to arise.'

'What can you tell me of Inspector Harriman?'

'A good police officer, a man of integrity, with not a spot on his record.'

'And what of the other witnesses?'

Mycroft gave himself pause for thought. 'I have investigated the backgrounds of both Dr Thomas Ackland and Lord Horace Blackwater, and as far as I can see they are both of good families, both single, both wealthy men. They do not club together. They did not go to the same school. Beyond the coincidence of their both being in Limehouse at the same time of night, there is nothing that connects them.'

'Unless it is the House of Silk.'

'Exactly.'

'And you will not tell me what it is.'

'I will not tell you because I do not know. If there is a society or fellowship at the heart of government that is so secret that even to mention its name has me summoned to certain offices in Whitehall, then my instinct is to look the other way, not to place damn fool advertisements in the national press! I told my brother as much.'

'So what will happen? Will you allow him to stand trial?'

'I fear you place too high a value on my influence.' Mycroft produced a tortoiseshell box and took a pinch of snuff. 'I can be his advocate, no more and no less. If it becomes necessary, I will appear as a character witness.' Mycroft put the snuff away and rose to his feet. 'Do not be disheartened, Dr Watson. My brother is a man of considerable resource and even in this, his darkest hour, he may yet surprise you.'

'They will not let me see him.'

'Re-apply tomorrow. Eventually, they must let you in.' He walked with me to the door. 'My brother is very fortunate to have a staunch ally as well as such a fine chronicler,' he remarked.

'I hope I have not written his last adventure.'

'Goodbye, Dr Watson. I would be obliged if you did not communicate with me again except, of course, in the most urgent circumstances. I wish you a good evening.'

It was with a heavy heart that I returned to Baker Street, for Mycroft had been even less helpful than I had hoped and I wondered what circumstances he could have been referring to if these were not urgent already. At least he might have gained me admittance to Holloway so the journey had not entirely been wasted. As I left my cab and walked to the front door, I found my path blocked by a short man with black hair.

'Dr Watson?' he asked.

'Yes.'

'I wonder if I might ask you, Doctor, to come with me?'

'On what business?'

'On a matter that relates to your friend, Mr Sherlock Holmes.'

I examined him more closely. I would have taken him for a tradesman, perhaps a tailor or even an undertaker, for there was something almost studiously mournful about his face. From the way he was standing, poised on the balls of his feet, I expected him to whip out a tape measure at any moment. But to measure me for what? A new suit or a coffin?

'What information do you have that you cannot tell me here?'

'I have no information at all, Dr Watson. I am merely the humble servant of one who does, and it is this person who has sent me here to request you to join him.'

'To join him where? Who is he?'

'I regret that I am not at liberty to say.'

'Then you're wasting your time. I am in no mood to go out tonight.'

'You do not understand, sir. The gentleman for whom I work is not inviting your presence. He is demanding it. Could I ask you to look down, sir? There! Do not start. Now, if you would be kind enough to come this way . . .'

On doing as he had asked, I had seen that he was holding a revolver, aimed at my stomach. It was as if he had performed some unpleasant magic trick and the weapon had suddenly materialised.

'You will not shoot me in the middle of the street,' I said.

'On the contrary, Dr Watson. I do not wish to kill you any more than you, I am sure, wish to die. We mean you no harm. After a while, all will be explained and you will understand why these precautions are necessary.'

He had an extraordinary manner of speaking, both obsequious and threatening. He gestured with the gun and I observed a black carriage standing by. It was a four-wheeler with windows of frosted glass, and I wondered if the man who had demanded to meet me was sitting inside. I opened the door. The interior was empty. 'How far are we travelling?' I asked. 'My landlady is expecting me for dinner.'

'You'll get dinner where we're going.'

Would he really have shot me down outside my own home? I quite believed he would. At the same time, were I to climb into this carriage, I might be carried away and never seen again. Suppose he had been sent by the same people who had killed Ross and his sister and who had dealt so cunningly with Holmes? But I reminded myself that the man had said that he represented someone with information. Whichever way I looked at it, it seemed to me I had no choice. I climbed in. The man followed me and closed the door whereupon I saw that the opaque glass stopped me looking out.

As we set off all I could see was the passing glow of the gas lamps and even those fell away once we left the city. A blanket had been placed on the seat for me and I drew it over my knees for the night had become very cold. My companion said nothing and seemed to have fallen asleep. But when, after about an hour, I reached out to open the window, wondering if I might see something in the landscape that would tell me where I was, he jerked up and shook his head. 'Really, Dr Watson, I would have expected better of you. My master has taken great pains to keep his address from you. I would ask you to keep your hands to yourself and the windows closed.'

'For how long are we going to travel?'

'For as long as it takes.'

'Do you have a name?'

'I fear that I am not at liberty to reveal it to you.'

'And what can you tell me of the man who employs you?'

'I could talk my way to the North Pole on that subject, sir. But he would not appreciate it. All in all, the less said the better.'

The journey lasted two hours, but there was nothing to tell me in which direction we were going nor how far, and it had occurred to me that we might well be going round and round in circles. I felt swallowed up by the darkness and finally dozed off, for the next thing I knew we had come to a shuddering halt and my travelling companion was opening the door.

'We will go straight into the house, Dr Watson,' he said. 'It is a nasty night. If you do not go straight in, I fear it might be the death of you.'

I glimpsed only a massive, uninviting house, the front draped in ivy. The building itself put me in mind of an abbey with crenulated windows, gargoyles and a tower stretching above the roof. A door stood open beneath the porch. Urged on by my fellow passenger, I hurried in.

'This way, sir.' I followed him down a passageway, past windows of stained glass, oak panelling, faded paintings. We came to a door. 'In here. I will let him know you have arrived. Touch nothing.'

I was in a library with a log fire burning in a stone fireplace and candles arranged on the mantel. A round table of dark wood with several chairs occupied the centre of the room. Shelves rose from the floor to the ceiling. I took a candle and examined some of the covers. Whoever owned this house must be well versed in French, German and Italian, for all three languages were evident as well as English. There were no works of fiction as far as I could see. Indeed, the selection of books put me very much in mind of Sherlock Holmes, for they seemed accurately to reflect his tastes. I sat down on one of the chairs and stretched my hands in front of the fire. I was grateful for the warmth for the journey had been merciless.

A second door opened suddenly to reveal a man so tall and thin that he seemed out of proportion to the frame that surrounded him. As he entered, I saw that he was almost bald, with a high forehead and deep, sunken eyes. I noticed that the library connected with a chemical laboratory and that was where he had been occupying himself while I waited. The man himself smelled strongly of chemicals, and although I wondered about the nature of his experiments, I thought it better not to ask.

'Dr Watson,' he said. 'I must apologise for keeping you waiting. Have you been offered wine? No? Underwood, assiduous in his duties though he undoubtedly is, cannot be described as the most considerate of men. I trust that he looked after you on the long journey here.'

'He did not even tell me his name.'

'That is hardly surprising. I do not intend to tell you mine. But it is already late and we have business to attend to. I am hoping you will dine with me.'

'It is not my habit to take dinner with men who refuse even to introduce themselves.'

'Perhaps not. But I would ask you to consider this: anything could happen to you in this house. To say that you are completely in my power may sound silly and melodramatic, but it happens to be true. Nobody saw you come here. If you were never to leave, the world would be none the wiser. So I would suggest that, of the options open to you, a dinner with me may be one of the more preferable. The food is frugal but the wine is good. The table is laid next door. Please come this way.'

He led me across to a dining room with a minstrel's gallery at one end and a huge fireplace at the other. A refectory table ran the full distance between the two, with room enough for thirty people, but tonight it was empty. A single shaded lamp cast a pool of light over a few cold cuts, bread, a bottle of wine. It appeared that the master of the house and I were to eat alone, hemmed in by the shadows, and I took my place with a sense of oppression and little appetite.

'I have often wanted to meet you, Dr Watson,' my host began. 'It may surprise you to learn that I am a great admirer of yours. I have just finished *The Adventure of the Copper Beeches*, and I think it very well done.' Despite the bizarre circumstances of the evening, I could not help but feel a certain satisfaction. 'As always, I was most gripped by your depiction of Mr Sherlock Holmes and his methods. You have opened the workings of a great mind to the public and for that we should all be grateful. Some wine?'

'Thank you.'

He poured two glasses, then continued. 'It is a shame that Holmes does not devote himself exclusively to domestic crime. It is when your friend turns his attention to business enterprises organised by people such as myself that he becomes an annoyance. I rather fear that recently he has done precisely that, and if it continues it may well be that the two of us have to meet, which, I can assure you, would be not at all to his advantage.'

There was an edge to his voice that caused me to shudder. 'You have not told me who you are,' I said. 'Will you explain what you are?'

'I am a mathematician, Dr Watson. I am also what you would doubtless term a criminal, although I would like to think that I have made a science out of crime. I try not to dirty my own hands. I am an abstract thinker. Crime in its purest form is, after all, an abstract, like music. I orchestrate. Others perform.'

'And what do you want with me? Why have you brought me here?'

'I wish to help Mr Sherlock Holmes. It was a pity that he did not pay attention to me two months ago when I sent him a certain keepsake, inviting him to look into the business that has now caused him such grief. Perhaps I should have been a little more direct.'

'What did you send him?' I asked, but I already knew.

'A length of white ribbon.'

'You are part of the House of Silk!'

'I have nothing to do with it!' For the first time he sounded angry.

'But you know what it is.'

'I know everything. Any act of wickedness that takes place in this country is brought to my attention. I have agents in every street.' I waited for him to continue, but when he did so, it was on another tack. 'You must swear on everything sacred to you that you will never tell Holmes, or anyone else, of this meeting. You must never write about it. You must never mention it.'

'How do you know I will keep such a promise?'

'You are a man of your word.'

'And if I refuse?'

He sighed. 'Let me tell you now that Holmes's life is in great danger. He will be dead within forty-eight hours unless you do as I ask. I alone can help you, but will do so only on my terms.'

'Then I agree.'

'You swear?'

'Yes.'

'On what?'

'On my friendship with Holmes.'

He nodded. 'Now we understand each other.'

'Then what is the House of Silk? Where will I find it?'

'I cannot tell you. I fear Holmes must discover it for himself. Why? Well, in the first instance because it will interest me to study his methods. There is also a broader point of principle at stake. I have admitted to you that I am a criminal, but what does that mean? Simply that there are certain rules that govern society but which I choose to ignore. I have met perfectly respectable bankers and lawyers who would say exactly the same. But I am not an animal, Dr Watson. I do not murder children. I consider myself a civilised man and there are other rules that are, to my mind, inviolable.

'So what is a man like myself to do when he comes across a group of people whose behaviour he considers to be beyond the pale? I could tell you who they are. I could have already told the police. Alas, such an act would cause considerable damage to my reputation among many of the people I employ who are less high-minded than me. There is such a thing as a criminal code. What right have I to judge my fellow criminals? I would certainly not expect to be judged by them.'

'You sent Holmes a clue.'

'I acted on impulse, which is very unusual for me and shows how annoyed I had become. Even so, it was a compromise, the least I could do in the circumstances. If it did spur him into action, I could console myself with the thought that I had done little and was not really to blame. If he chose to ignore it, no damage had been done, and my conscience was clear. That said, I was very sorry that he chose the latter course of action—or inaction, I should say. It is my sincere belief that the world would be a much better place without the House of Silk. It is still my hope that this will come to pass. That is why I invited you here tonight.'

'If you cannot give me information, what can you give me?'

'I can give you this.' He slid something across the table towards me. I looked down and saw a small metal key.

'What is this?' I asked.

'It is the key to his cell.'

'What?' I almost laughed aloud. 'You expect Holmes to escape?'

'Let me assure you that there is no possible alternative.'

'There is the coroner's court. The truth will come out.'

His face darkened. 'I begin to wonder if I'm not wasting my time. Let me make it clear to you: Sherlock Holmes will never leave the House of Correction alive. The coroner's court has been set for next Thursday, but Holmes will not be there. His enemies plan to kill him while he is in jail.'

I was horrified. 'How?'

'That I cannot tell you. There are a hundred accidents they could arrange. Doubtless they will find a way to make the death appear natural. But trust me. The order has already been given. His time is running out.'

I picked up the key. 'How did you get this?'

'That is immaterial.'

'Then tell me how I am to get it to him. They won't let me see him.'

'That is for you to arrange. You have Inspector Lestrade on your side. Speak to him.' He stood up suddenly, pushing his chair back from the table.

'There is nothing more to be said, I think. You have no idea how keenly I have felt the pleasure of making your acquaintance. Indeed, I quite envy Holmes having such a staunch biographer at his side. I, too, have certain stories of interest to share with the public and I wonder if I might one day call on your services. No? Well, it was an idle thought. But this meeting aside, I suppose it is always possible that I may turn up as a character in one of your narratives. I hope you will do me justice.'

At that moment the door opened and Underwood appeared. Taking the key, I stood up. 'Thank you,' I said.

He did not reply. At the door, I took one look back. My host was sitting on his own at the head of that huge table, poking at his food in the candle-light. Then the door closed. And, apart from one brief glimpse at Victoria Station a year later, I never saw him again.

MY RETURN TO LONDON was, in some respects, even more of an ordeal than my departure. Holmes was to be murdered! The metal key that I had been given was clutched so tightly in my hand that I could have made a duplicate from the impression squeezed into my flesh. My only thought was to reach Holloway, to warn Holmes of what was afoot and to assist in his immediate exit from that place. And yet how was I to reach him?

With these thoughts raging in my mind, the journey seemed to stretch on for ever. It was particularly vexing to reflect that had Holmes been in my place, he would have taken note of all the different elements—the blast of a steam whistle, the smell of stagnant water, the changing surfaces beneath the wheels—and drawn a detailed map of our journey at the end of it. But I could only wait for the slowing down of the horses and the jolting halt that signalled we were at the end of our journey. Sure enough, Underwood threw open the door and there, across the road, were my familiar lodgings.

'Safely home, Dr Watson,' said he.

'I will not forget you easily, Mr Underwood,' I replied.

He raised his eyebrows. 'My master has told you my name?'

'Perhaps you would care to tell me his.'

'Oh no, sir. My life is of little significance in comparison with his great-ness but nonetheless I would wish it to continue for a while yet.'

I climbed down and watched as the carriage rattled away, then hurried in.

But there was to be no rest for me that night. I had already begun to for-mulate a plan by which the key might safely be delivered to Holmes, along with a message alerting him to the danger he was in even if, as I feared, I was not permitted to visit him myself. A straightforward letter would do no good. Our enemies were all around and there was every chance that they would intercept it. But I could still send him a message—and some sort of code was required. The question was, how could I indicate that it was there to be deciphered? There was also the key. How could I deliver it into his hand? Casting my eye around the room, I fell upon the answer: *The Martyrdom of Man* by Winwood Reade. What could be more natural than to send my friend something to read while he was confined?

Upon examining the volume, I saw that it would be possible to slip the key into the space between the spine and the bound edges of the pages. This I did and carefully poured liquid wax into the two ends, in effect gluing it in place. I then wrote the name, Sherlock Holmes, on the frontispiece and, beneath it, an address: 122b Baker Street. Holmes would recognise my hand at once and see that the number of our lodgings had been inverted. Finally, I turned to page 122 and, using a pencil, placed a series of tiny dots under certain letters in the text so that a new message was spelled out: YOU ARE IN GREAT DANGER. THEY PLAN TO KILL YOU. USE KEY TO CELL. I AM WAITING. JW.

I awoke early the next day and sent a message to Lestrade, urging him once again to help arrange a visit to Holloway. To my surprise, I received a reply informing me that I could enter the prison at three o'clock that afternoon, that Harriman had concluded his preliminary investigation and that the coroner's court had indeed been set for Thursday, two days hence. On first reading this struck me as good news but then I was struck by a more sinister explanation. If Harriman was part of the conspiracy, he might well have stood aside for a different reason. My host of the night before had insisted that Holmes would never be allowed to stand trial. Suppose the assassins were preparing to strike! Could Harriman know that it was already too late?

I arrived at Camden Road before the clocks had struck the half-hour. The coachman left me in front of the outer gate and hurried away. I couldn't blame him. This wasn't a place where any Christian soul would have chosen to linger. Holloway Prison stood on the site of a former cemetery, and the whiff of death and decay still clung to the place, damning those who were inside, warning those without to stay away.

It was as much as I could bear to wait thirty minutes with my breath frosting and the cold spreading upwards through my feet. At last I walked forward, clutching the book, and as I entered the prison it occurred to me that were I to be discovered, this horrid place could well become my home.

The door was opened almost at once by a surprisingly jovial officer. 'Come in, sir. It's more pleasant in than out and there's not many days you could say that with any truth.' I watched him lock the door behind us, then followed him across a courtyard to a second gate, smaller, but no less secure, than the first. I was already aware of an eerie silence inside the prison. The light was fading rapidly but as yet no lamps had been lit.

I was taken into a small room with a desk, two chairs and a single window looking directly onto a brick wall. A large clock faced me and a man sat beneath it. He was elderly, with grey hair cut short and steely eyes. As he saw me, he came round from behind the desk.

'Dr Watson, my name is Hawkins. I am the chief warder. You have come to see Mr Sherlock Holmes?'

'Yes.' I uttered the word with a sudden sense of dread.

'I am sorry to inform you that he was taken ill this morning. His illness came suddenly and he was given treatment at once.'

'What is wrong with him?'

'We have no idea. He took his lunch at eleven o'clock and rang the bell for assistance immediately after.'

I felt an ice-cold tremor in the very depths of my heart. It was exactly what I had been fearing. 'Where is he now?' I asked.

'He is in the infirmary. Our medical officer, Dr Trevelyan, has a number of private rooms that he reserves for desperate cases.'

'I must see him at once,' I said. 'I am a medical man myself.'

'Of course, Dr Watson. I have been waiting to take you there.'

But before we could leave, a man that I knew all too well appeared, blocking our way. Inspector Harriman was dressed in black as always, carrying a black walking stick. 'So what's this all about, Hawkins?' he asked. 'Sherlock Holmes ill?'

'Seriously ill,' Hawkins declared.

'You're sure he's not deceiving you? When I saw him this morning, he was in perfect health.'

'I assure you, sir, that he is gravely stricken. We are just on our way to see him.'

'Then I will accompany you.'

The three of us set off through the depths of the prison. My overall impressions were of heavy flagstones, of gates that creaked as they were unlocked, of barred windows too small and so many doors, each identical, each sealing up some small facet of human misery.

'If Holmes has been poisoned, he must be sent immediately to a hospital,' I said.

'Who said anything about poison?' Harriman had overheard me.

'Dr Trevelyan is a good man,' returned Hawkins. 'He will have done everything within his power . . .'

We had reached the end of the central block and found ourselves in what must be a recreation area, with a gallery that ran the full length of the room above. A net had been stretched across our heads so that nothing could be thrown down. We passed through an archway and up a matted staircase. By now I had no idea where I was. I thought of the key that I was carrying, concealed in the book. Even if I had been able to deliver it into Holmes's hands, what good would it have been? He would have needed a dozen keys and a detailed map to get out of this place.

There was a pair of glass-panelled doors ahead of us. These had to be unlocked, but then swung open into a bare room with eight beds, facing each other in two rows of four. Only two of the beds were occupied.

A man dressed in a patched frock coat rose from where he had been working and came to greet us. From the very first I thought I recognised him, just as—it occurred to me now—his name had also been familiar.

'Mr Hawkins,' he said, addressing the chief warder. 'I have nothing further to report to you, sir, except that I fear the worst.'

'This is Dr John Watson,' Hawkins said.

'Dr Trevelyan.' He shook my hand. 'It is a pleasure to make your acquaintance, although I would have asked for happier circumstances.'

I was certain I knew the man. But from the way he had spoken, he was making it clear that, even if we were not meeting for the first time, this was the impression he wished to give.

'Is it food poisoning?' Harriman demanded.

'I am positive that poison of one sort or another is responsible,' the doctor replied. 'As to how it came to be administered, that is not for me to say.'

'Are you suggesting foul play?'

'I have said what I have said, sir.'

'Well, I don't believe a word of it. I can tell you, Doctor, that I was rather expecting something of this sort. Where is Mr Holmes?' Harriman barked.

Trevelyan hesitated and the warder stepped forward. 'This is Inspector Harriman, Dr Trevelyan. He is in charge of your patient.'

'I am in charge of my patient while he is in my infirmary,' the doctor retorted. 'But there is no reason why you should not see him. I gave him a sedative and he may well be asleep. He is in a side room.'

'Then let us waste no more time.'

'Rivers!' Trevelyan called out to a lanky, round-shouldered fellow sweeping the floor in one corner. He was wearing the uniform of a male nurse rather than that of a prisoner. 'The keys . . .'

'Yes, Dr Trevelyan.' Rivers took up a key-chain and carried it to an arched door on the far side of the room. He was sullen and rough-looking, with unruly ginger hair spilling down to his shoulders. He fitted a key into the lock.

'Rivers is my orderly,' Trevelyan explained. 'He's a good man, but simple.'

'Has he been in communication with Holmes?' Harriman asked.

'Rivers is seldom in communication with anyone, Mr Harriman. Holmes himself has not uttered a word since he was brought here.'

I heard the tumblers fall as the lock connected. There were also two bolts on the outside that had to be drawn back before the door could be opened to reveal a small room with a square window, a bed and a privy.

The bed was empty.

Harriman plunged inside. He tore off the covers. He knelt down and looked under the bed. There was nowhere to hide. The bars on the window were still in place. 'Is this some sort of trick?' he roared. 'Where is he?'

I looked in. There could be no doubt. Sherlock Holmes had disappeared.

FOUR
The House of Silk

Harriman rose to his feet and almost fell upon Dr Trevelyan. For once his carefully cultivated sang-froid had deserted him. 'What game is going on here?' he cried.

'I beg of you to show some restraint, Inspector Harriman.' The chief warder imposed himself between the two men, taking charge. 'Mr Holmes was in this room?'

'Yes, sir,' Trevelyan replied.

'And it was locked and bolted, as I saw just now, from the outside?'

'Indeed so, sir. It is a prison regulation.'

'Who was the last to see him?'

'Rivers took him a mug of water, upon my request.'

'I took it but he didn't drink it,' the orderly grumbled. 'He didn't say nothing, neither. He just lay there.'

Harriman walked up to Dr Trevelyan until the two of them were but inches apart. 'Are you really telling me he was ill, Doctor, or was he dissembling—first so that he would be brought here, second so that he could choose his moment to walk out?'

'As to the first, he was most certainly ill,' replied Trevelyan. 'He had a high fever, his pupils were dilated and the sweat was pouring from his brow. As to the second, he could not possibly have walked out. Look at the door, for heaven's sake! It was locked from the outside. There are the bolts, which were fastened until Rivers drew them back just now. And even if Mr Holmes had been able to leave the cell, where do you think he would go? The door through which you three gentlemen entered was locked. And there must be a dozen more locks and bolts between here and the front gate.'

'Nobody can leave this place,' muttered Rivers, and he seemed to smirk as if at some private joke. 'Unless his name is Wood. Now, he left here only this afternoon. Not on his own two legs though, and I don't think anyone would have had a mind to ask him where he was going.'

'Wood? Who is Wood?' Harriman asked.

'Jonathan Wood was here in the infirmary,' Trevelyan replied. 'He died last night and was carried out in a coffin not an hour ago.'

'Are you telling me that a closed coffin was taken from this room?' I could see the detective working things out and realised, as did he, that it presented the most obvious method for Holmes's escape. He turned on the orderly. 'Was the coffin here when you took in the water?' he demanded.

'It might have been.'

'Did you leave Holmes on his own, even for a few seconds?'

'No, sir. Not for one second.' The orderly shuffled on his feet. 'Well, maybe I attended to Collins when he had his fit.'

'What are you saying, Rivers?' Trevelyan cried.

'I opened the door. I went in. He was sound asleep on the bed. Then Collins began his coughing. I put the mug down and ran out to him.'

'And what then? Did you see Holmes again?'

'No, sir. I settled Collins. Then I went back and locked the door.'

'Where is the coffin?' Harriman exclaimed.

'There will be a wagon waiting to carry it to the undertaker in Muswell Hill,' Trevelyan replied. He grabbed his coat. 'It may not be too late. If it's still there, we can intercept it before it leaves.'

Hawkins went first with a furious Harriman at his side. Trevelyan and Rivers came next. I followed last, the book and the key still in my hand. How ridiculous they seemed now. The doors were unlocked and swung open, one after another. Nobody stood in our way. We took a different path from that which I had used originally, finally crossing a grassy courtyard and arriving at a side entrance.

As we went, I found myself reflecting on the number of strange circumstances that had come together to effect my friend's escape. He had managed to fool a trained doctor. Well, that was easy enough. He had done much the same to me. But he had inveigled himself into a room in the infirmary at exactly the same time as a coffin had been delivered and had, moreover, been able to count on an open door, a coughing fit and the clumsiness of a mentally backward orderly. It all seemed too good to be true. Not, of course, that I cared one way or another. But I was sure that we had leaped to a false conclusion and, perhaps, that was exactly what he had intended.

We found ourselves in a broad, rutted avenue that ran along the side of the prison. Harriman let out a cry and pointed. A wagon stood waiting while two men loaded a makeshift coffin into the back.

'Hold there!' cried Harriman. He strode up to the two men who were about to lever the box into the wagon. 'Lower the coffin back to the ground! I wish to examine it.' The men glanced at each other quizzically before they obeyed. The coffin lay flat upon the gravel. 'Open it!'

This time the men hesitated—to carry a dead body was one thing but to look on it quite another.

'It's all right,' Trevelyan assured them, and at that very moment I realised how I knew him.

His full name was Percy Trevelyan and he had come to our Baker Street lodgings six or seven years before, urgently in need of my friend's services. There had been a patient who had been found hanged in his room . . . the police had assumed that it was suicide, an opinion with which Holmes had at once disagreed. It was strange that I had not recognised Trevelyan immediately for I had studied his work on nervous diseases—he had won the Bruce Pinkerton prize, no less. Circumstances had not been kind to him then, and his health had clearly deteriorated. But it was certainly he, reduced to the role of prison doctor, a position well beneath a man of his capabilities, and it occurred to me that he must have colluded in this attempted escape. He certainly owed Holmes a debt of gratitude and why else would he have pretended not to know me? Now I understood how Holmes had got into the coffin in the first place. Trevelyan had placed his orderly in charge quite deliberately. Why else would he have trusted a man who was evidently unfit for any such responsibility? The coffin would have been placed nearby. Everything would have been planned in advance. The pity of it was that the two labourers had been so slow in their work. They should have been halfway to Muswell Hill by now. Trevelyan's assistance had been to no avail.

One of the labourers had produced a crowbar and the lid of the coffin was torn free, the wood splintering. As one, Harriman, Hawkins, Trevelyan and I moved closer.

'That's him,' Rivers grunted. 'That's Jonathan Wood.'

It was true. The corpse was definitely not Sherlock Holmes.

Trevelyan was the first to recover. 'I told you, it's Wood. He died in the night—a coronary infection.' He nodded at the undertakers. 'You may close the coffin and take him up.'

'But where is Sherlock Holmes?' Hawkins cried.

'He cannot have left the prison!' Harriman replied. 'He must still be inside, awaiting his opportunity. We must raise the alarm and search the place from top to bottom.'

'But that will take all night!'

Harriman's face was as colourless as his hair. 'I don't care if it takes all week! The man must be found.'

HE WASN'T. Two days later, I was alone in Holmes's lodgings, reading a report of the events that I had myself witnessed:

Police are unable to explain the mysterious disappearance of the well-known consulting detective, Sherlock Holmes, who was being held at Holloway Prison in connection with the murder of a young woman in Coppergate Square. Inspector J. Harriman who is in charge of the inquiry

has accused the prison authorities of a dereliction of duty, a charge that
has been strenuously denied. The fact remains that Mr Holmes somehow
managed to spirit himself out of a locked cell and through a dozen
locked doors in a manner that would appear to deny the laws of nature.
The police are offering a reward of £50 to anyone who can supply
information leading to his apprehension.

Mrs Hudson had spoken but one brief sentence when she had served my
breakfast. 'It's a lot of nonsense, Dr Watson.' She seemed personally offended
and it is somehow comforting to me, all these years later, to reflect that she
had complete faith in her most famous lodger.

My sojourn was interrupted by the arrival of that lady, and another visitor. I was unprepared for the arrival of the Reverend Charles Fitzsimmons,
the principal of Chorley Grange School, and I greeted him, I am afraid,
with a look of blank puzzlement. The fact that he was wrapped in a thick
black coat with a hat and scarf did help to make a stranger of him.

'You will forgive me interrupting you, Dr Watson,' he said, divesting himself of these outer garments and revealing the clerical collar that would have
at once jogged my memory. 'I was unsure whether to come but felt I must . . .
But first, this extraordinary business with Mr Sherlock Holmes, is it true?'

'It is true that Holmes is suspected of a crime of which he is completely
innocent,' I replied.

'But I read now that he has escaped. Do you know where he is?'

'I have no idea.'

'And the child, Ross, do you have any news of him?'

'In what sense?'

'Have you found him yet?'

Evidently, Fitzsimmons had somehow missed the reports of the boy's
death—although, it occurred to me, Ross had not actually been named.
'I am afraid we were too late. We did find Ross, but he was dead.'

'Dead? How did it happen?'

'He was left to die by the river, close to Southwark Bridge.'

'Dear God in heaven!' he exclaimed. 'What wickedness is there in this
world? Then my visit to you is redundant, Dr Watson. I thought I might be
able to help you find him. I had come upon a clue. I brought it to you in the
hope that you might know the whereabouts of Mr Holmes and pass it to him
and that even given his own exigencies, he might . . .' His voice trailed off.

'What is this clue?' I asked.

'My wife found it in the dormitory. The bed occupied by Ross is now taken by another child, but there was a copybook concealed there.' Fitzsimmons took out a thin book, faded and crumpled. There was a name written in a childish hand on the front.

'Each child in the school is given a copybook and a pencil. You will see inside his that he seems to have passed much of his time scribbling. But on examining it, we discovered this.'

He had opened the book in the middle to show a sheet of paper, neatly folded and slipped inside as if the intention had been deliberately to conceal it. It was an advertisement, the text decorated by images of a snake, a monkey and an armadillo. It read:

DR SILKIN'S HOUSE OF WONDERS
MIDGETS, JUGGLERS, THE FAT LADY
AND THE LIVING SKELETON
A cabinet of curiosities from the four corners of the globe
ONE PENNY ENTRANCE
Jackdaw Lane, Whitechapel

'I would, of course, discourage my boys from ever entering such a place,' the Reverend Fitzsimmons said. 'It may be that Ross concealed this advertisement for no other reason than that he knew it was against the very spirit of Chorley Grange. He was, as my wife told you, a very wilful boy—'

'But it may also have a connection for him,' I broke in. 'After he left you, he sought refuge with a family in King's Cross and also with his sister. But we have no idea where he was before. It could be that he fell in with this crowd.'

'I feel sure it is worthy of investigation.' Fitzsimmons got to his feet. 'Is there any possibility that you will be in communication with Mr Holmes?'

'I am still hoping that he will contact me in some way.'

'Then perhaps you will see what he makes of it. Thank you for your time, Dr Watson. I am very, very shocked about young Ross. We will pray for him in the school chapel this Sunday.'

He left the room and I stared at the page. I must have read it two or three times before I saw what should have been obvious to me from the start: Dr Silkin's House of Wonders.

I had just found the House of Silk.

MY WIFE RETURNED TO LONDON the following day and I was waiting for her at Holborn Viaduct when her train drew in. I would not have left Baker Street for any other reason. I was certain that Holmes would attempt to reach me and dreaded the idea of his making his way to his lodgings, with all the dangers that would entail, only to find me not in. But I owed it to Mary to explain what had happened while she had been away and to inform her that, regretfully, it might be a while yet before we could be permanently reunited. And I had missed her. I looked forward to seeing her again.

It was now the second week in December and the sun was out. Although it was very cold, everything was ablaze with a sense of prosperity and good cheer. The pavements were almost invisible beneath the bustle of families. The sweetmeat and grocer shops were gloriously festooned. Every window carried advertisements for goose clubs, roast beef clubs and pudding clubs and the air was filled with the aroma of burnt sugar and mincemeat. As I made my way into the station, I reflected on the circumstances that had alienated me from the day-to-day pleasures of London in the festive season. That was perhaps the disadvantage of my association with Sherlock Holmes. It drew me into dark places where, in truth, nobody would choose to go.

The station was no less crowded. Mary's train had already arrived and I was briefly unable to locate her. But then I saw her and, as she climbed down from her carriage, a man appeared, shuffling across the platform as if about to accost her. I could see him only from the back and, apart from an ill-fitting jacket and red hair, would have been unable to identify him again. He seemed to speak briefly to her, then disappeared from sight. But perhaps I was mistaken. She saw me and smiled and then I had taken her in my arms and together we were walking towards the entrance where I had told my driver to wait.

There was much that Mary wanted to tell me of her visit. Mrs Forrester had been delighted to see her and the two of them had become the closest of companions, their relationship of governess and employer being long behind them. Once he had begun to recover from his sickness, the boy, Richard, was charming company. He was also an avid reader of my stories! The whole visit had been a success, apart from a slight headache and sore throat that she had herself picked up in the last few days. When I pressed her, she complained of a sense of heaviness in the muscles of her arms and legs. 'But don't fuss over me, John. What is this extraordinary business I've been reading about with Sherlock Holmes?'

I blame myself for not examining Mary more closely but she made light of her illness. Even so, I have always had to live with the knowledge that I failed to recognise the early signs of the typhoid fever that would take her from me all too soon.

'Did you see that man just now?' she asked, just after we set off.

'At the train? Yes, I did see him. Did he speak to you?'

'He addressed me by name. And he pressed this into my hand.'

She produced a small cloth bag that she had been clutching all the time. Now she handed it to me. There was something heavy inside the bag, and, on pouring the contents into the palm of my hand, I found myself holding three solid nails.

'Did the man say nothing more?' I asked. 'Can you describe him?'

'Not really, I barely glanced at him. He had a dirty, unshaven face.'

'He said nothing else? Did he demand money?'

'I told you. He greeted me by name, nothing more.'

'But why would anyone give you a bag of nails?' The words were no sooner out of my mouth than I understood. 'The Bag of Nails! Of course! I believe, Mary, that you may have just met Holmes himself.'

'It looked nothing like him.'

'That is exactly the idea!'

'This bag of nails means something to you?'

It meant a great deal. Holmes wanted me to return to one of the two public houses that we had visited when we were searching for Ross. Both had been called The Bag of Nails, but which one did he have in mind? Surely not the one in Lambeth, for that was where Sally Dixon had worked and it was known to the police. The one in Edge Lane was more likely.

'My dear, I'm afraid I am going to have to abandon you the moment we are home,' I said.

'You are not in any danger are you, John?'

'I hope not.'

She sighed. 'Sometimes I think you are fonder of Mr Holmes than you are of me.' She saw the look on my face and patted my hand gently. 'I'm only being pleasant with you. And you don't need to come all the way to Kensington. We can stop at the next corner. Go to him, John. If he resorted to such lengths to send a message, then he must be in trouble and needs you. You cannot refuse.'

And so I parted company from her. I slipped out into the traffic in the

Strand, dodged between various carriages and looked carefully about me before turning back the way I had come. It had occurred to me that, if Holmes was afraid of being followed, I should be too. I arrived in Shoreditch about thirty minutes later. I remembered the public house well.

There was one man sitting in the saloon bar and it was not Sherlock Holmes. To my great surprise, I recognised Rivers, who had assisted Dr Trevelyan at Holloway Prison. He was no longer wearing his uniform, but his sunken eyes and unruly ginger hair were unmistakable.

'Mr Rivers!' I exclaimed.

'Sit down with me, Watson. It's very good to see you again.'

It was Holmes who had spoken—and in that second I understood how I had been deceived and how he had effected his escape from prison. I confess that I almost fell into the seat that he had proffered, seeing the smile that I knew so well, beaming at me from beneath the wig and the make-up. That was the wonderment of Holmes's disguises. He had a knack of metamorphosing into whatever character he wished to play and, if he believed it, you would believe it too, right up to the moment of revelation. And yet once you had seen it for what it was, it would never deceive you again. I had sat down with Rivers. But now it was obvious to me that I was with Holmes.

'Tell me—' I began.

'All in good time, my dear fellow,' he interrupted. 'First, assure me that you were not followed here. There were two men behind you at Holborn Viaduct. Doubtless policemen in the employ of our friend, Inspector Harriman.'

'I didn't see them. But I took great care leaving my wife's carriage when it was halfway down the Strand. I can assure you that if there were two men with me at the station, they are now in Kensington and wondering what became of me.'

'My trusty Watson!'

'But how did you even come to be at Holborn Viaduct at all?'

'I followed you from Baker Street, realised which train you must be meeting and managed to get ahead of you in the crowd.'

'That is only the first of my questions, Holmes. Let us start with Dr Trevelyan. I assume you recognised him and persuaded him to help you escape.'

'Exactly the case. It was a happy coincidence that our former client should have found employment at the prison, although I would like to think that any medical man would have been persuaded to my cause when it became clear that there was a plan to murder me.'

'You knew of that?'

Holmes glanced at me keenly, and I realised that if I were not to break the pledge I had given to my sinister host, two nights before, then I must pretend to know nothing at all. 'It was clear to me that the evidence would begin to fall apart as soon as I was allowed to speak and so, of course, my enemies would not permit it. I took particular care to examine my food. There are few poisons that are completely tasteless and certainly not arsenic. I detected it in a bowl of meat broth brought to me on my second evening . . . a foolish attempt, Watson, and one that I was grateful for, as it gave me the weapon that I needed.'

'Was Harriman part of this plot?' I asked.

'Inspector Harriman has either been paid well or is at the very heart of the conspiracy. I suspect the latter. I thought of going to Hawkins, the chief warder, who struck me as a civilised man. However, to have raised the alarm too soon might have been to precipitate a more lethal attack, and so I requested an interview with the medical officer. I was delighted to discover that we were already acquainted. I showed him the sample of the soup that I had kept back and explained to him that I had been falsely arrested and that it was my enemies' intention that I should never leave Holloway alive. Dr Trevelyan was horrified. He would have been inclined to believe me anyway for he still felt himself to be in debt to me.'

'How did he come to be in Holloway?'

'Needs must, Watson. Trevelyan is a brilliant man, but one who fortune has never favoured. We must try to help him one day.'

'Indeed so, Holmes. But continue . . .'

'His first instinct was to inform the chief warder, but I persuaded him that, although it was critical for me to regain my liberty, we could not risk involving anybody else. It was obvious that I could not physically force my way out. There was no question of digging a tunnel or climbing the walls. There were no fewer than nine locked doors between my cell and the outside world and, even with the best of disguises, I could not hope to walk through them unchallenged.

'And then Trevelyan mentioned Jonathan Wood, a poor wretch who was not expected to survive the night. Trevelyan suggested to me that when Wood died, I could be admitted to the prison hospital. He would conceal the body and smuggle me out in the coffin. I dismissed the idea. A dead body leaving the prison at such a time would be too obvious.

'But during my time in the hospital I had already taken note of the orderly, Rivers, and in particular his appearance. I saw at once that all the necessary elements—Harriman, the poison, the dying man—were in place and that it would be possible to devise an alternative scheme.

'Wood died shortly before midnight. Trevelyan came to my cell and told me personally what had come to pass, then returned home to collect the few items that I had requested. The following morning, I announced that my illness had worsened. Trevelyan admitted me to the hospital where Wood had already been laid out. I was there when his coffin arrived and even helped to lift him into it. Rivers, however, had been given the day off and Trevelyan produced the wig and the change of clothes that would allow me to disguise myself as him. The coffin was removed shortly before three o'clock and everything was in place. You must understand the psychology, Watson. We needed Harriman to do our work for us. First of all, we would reveal my disappearance from a securely locked cell. Then, we would inform him of a coffin and a dead body that had just left the place. I had no doubt that he would jump to the wrong conclusion, which is precisely what he did. So confident was he that I was in the coffin, that he did not take so much as a second glance at the slow-witted orderly who was responsible for what had occurred. He rushed off, in effect easing my passage out. It was Harriman who ordered the doors to be unlocked and opened. It was Harriman who undermined the very security that should have kept me in.'

'It's true, Holmes,' I exclaimed. 'I never looked at you. All my attention was focused on the coffin.'

'Your appearance was the one eventuality that I had never considered and I was afraid you might reveal your acquaintanceship with Dr Trevelyan. But you were magnificent, Watson. Having both you and the warder there made Harriman more determined to chase down the coffin before it left.'

I took this as a compliment, although I understood the role I had actually played. Holmes liked an audience as much as any actor and the more there were of us present, the easier he would have found it to play the part.

'But what are we to do now?' I asked. 'The very fact that you have chosen to escape will only help to persuade the world of your guilt.'

'You paint a bleak picture, Watson. For my part, I would say that circumstances have immeasurably improved since last week.'

'Where are you staying?'

'Have I not told you? I keep rooms all over London for eventualities just such as this. I have one nearby.'

'Even so, Holmes, it seems that you have made many enemies.'

'We have to ask ourselves what it is that unites such disparate bodies as Lord Horace Blackwater, Dr Thomas Ackland and Inspector Harriman. What do these three men have in common? The fact that they are all men is a start. They are all wealthy and well connected. When brother Mycroft spoke of a scandal, these are the very sort of people who might be damaged. I understand, by the by, that you returned to Wimbledon.'

I could not possibly conceive how Holmes could have heard this but I merely assented and told him of my last visit. He seemed particularly agitated by the rapid decline in Eliza Carstairs's health. 'We are dealing with a mind of unusual cunning and cruelty, Watson. It is imperative that we conclude this business so that we can visit Edmund Carstairs again.'

'Do you think that the two are connected?' I asked. 'I cannot see how the events in Boston and the murder of Keelan O'Donaghue here in London could possibly have led to the business with which we are now occupied.'

'That is only because you are assuming that Keelan O'Donaghue is dead,' replied Holmes. 'We shall have more news soon enough. While I was in Holloway, I was able to send a message to Belfast—'

'They permitted you to wire?'

'I had no need for the post office. There was a man in my wing, a forger, who I met in the exercise yard and who was released two days ago. He carried my enquiry with him and, as soon as I have a reply, you and I shall return to Wimbledon. In the meantime, you have not answered my question.'

'What connects the three men? It is obvious. The House of Silk.'

'And what is the House of Silk?'

'Of that I have no idea. But I think I can tell you where to find it.'

'Watson, you astonish me.'

'You do not know?'

'I have known for some time. Nonetheless, I will be fascinated to know your own conclusions—and how you arrived at them.'

I unfolded the advertisement and showed it to my friend, relating my recent interview with the Reverend Fitzsimmons. For a moment he seemed puzzled, then his face brightened. 'But of course. This is exactly what we have been looking for. I must congratulate you, Watson.'

'This was the address that you had expected?'

'Not exactly. Nonetheless, I am confident it will provide all the answers that we have been searching for. I would imagine we would do better to approach under cover of darkness. Would you be amenable to meeting me here again in four hours?'

'I would be happy to, Holmes.'

'I knew I could count on you. And I would suggest you bring your service revolver. I fear it is going to be a long night.'

THERE ARE, I THINK, occasions when you know that you have arrived at the end of a long journey, even though your destination is still concealed. That was how I felt as I approached The Bag of Nails a second time, with a chill, unforgiving darkness descending on the city. Mary had been asleep when I returned home and I had not disturbed her, but as I had stood in my consulting room, checking that my revolver was fully loaded, I wondered what a casual observer would make of the scene: a respectable doctor in Kensington arming himself to set out in pursuit of a conspiracy that had so far encompassed murder, kidnap and the perversion of justice.

Holmes was no longer in disguise, apart from a hat and a scarf which he had drawn across the lower part of his face. He had ordered two brandies to brace us against the bitterness of the night. We barely spoke, but I remember that as we set the glasses down he glanced at me, and I saw all the good humour and resoluteness that I knew so well, positively dancing in his eyes.

'So, Watson . . .?' he asked.

'Yes, Holmes,' I said. 'I am ready.'

'And I am very glad to have you once again at my side.'

A cab carried us east and we descended on the Whitechapel Road, walking the remaining distance to Jackdaw Lane, a narrow passageway with shops and warehouses rising three storeys on either side. An alleyway opened out about halfway down and it was here that a man had imposed himself, dressed in a frock coat and a top hat. He had the beard, the moustache and the bright eyes of a pantomime Mephistopheles.

'One penny entrance!' he exclaimed. 'Here you will see some of the wonders of the world from Negros to Esquimaux and more. Come, gentlemen! Dr Silkin's House of Wonders will astonish you.'

'You are Dr Silkin?' Holmes asked.

'I have that honour, sir. Dr Asmodeus Silkin, late of India, late of the

Congo. My travels have taken me all over the world and all that I have experienced you will find here for the sum of a single penny.'

We handed over two coins and were duly ushered through. The spectacle that awaited us took me quite by surprise. I suppose in the harsh light of the day it might have been revealed in all its tawdry shabbiness, but the night, held at bay by a ring of burning braziers, had lent it a certain exoticism so that if you did not look too closely you really could believe that you had been transported to another world . . . perhaps one in a storybook.

We were in a cobbled yard, surrounded by buildings in such a state of disrepair that they were partly open to the elements. Some of these entranceways had been hung with signs advertising entertainments that a further payment would provide. The man with no neck. The world's ugliest woman. The five-legged pig. I heard the crack of rifles. A shooting gallery had been set up inside one of the buildings; I could make out the gas flames jetting and the green bottles standing at the far end.

There were also Gypsy wagons parked in the courtyard itself, with platforms constructed between them for performances that would continue throughout the night. A pair of identical twins were juggling a dozen balls. A black man in a loincloth held up a red-hot poker and licked it with his tongue. A woman in a feathered turban read palms. And all around, a crowd laughed and applauded, wandering aimlessly from performance to performance while a barrel organ jangled ceaselessly.

'Do you still believe this to be the House of Silk?' Holmes asked.

'It seems unlikely, I agree. Are you telling me that you do not think it is?'

'I knew from the outset that there was no possibility of it so being.'

For once, I could not hide my irritation 'If you knew from the start, Holmes, that this was not the House of Silk, then why are we here?'

'Because we were invited. The advertisement was meant to be discovered, Watson. And you were meant to give it to me.'

I decided that, following his ordeal in Holloway prison, Holmes had returned entirely to his old self—secretive and thoroughly annoying. I was determined to prove him wrong. Surely it could not be a coincidence, the name of Dr Silkin on the advertisements, the fact that one had been found concealed beneath Ross's bed? If it was meant to be discovered, why place it there? I looked around me, searching for anything that might be worth my attention, but in the whirl of activity it was almost impossible to settle on anything that might be relevant.

But then my breath caught in my throat. The fortuneteller was sitting on a sort of raised platform in front of her caravan. She had been gazing in my direction and, as I caught her eye, she raised a hand in salutation, and there it was, tied round her wrist: a length of white silk ribbon.

My immediate thought was to alert Sherlock Holmes but I decided against it. I had been ridiculed enough for one evening. And so, without explanation, I climbed the few steps to the platform. The Gypsy woman was large and masculine with a heavy jaw and mournful, grey eyes.

'I would like to have my fortune told,' I said.

'Sit down,' she replied. There was a footstool opposite her in the cramped space and I lowered myself onto it.

'Can you see the future?' I asked.

'It will cost you a penny.'

I paid her the money and she took my hand, spreading it in her own so that the white ribbon was right before me. Then she began to trace the lines on my palm. 'A doctor?' she asked.

'Yes.'

'And married. Happily. No children.'

'You are quite correct on all three counts.'

'You have recently known the pain of a separation.'

Was she referring to my wife's sojourn in Camberwell or to the imprisonment of Holmes? And how could she possibly know of either? I am now, and was then, a sceptic.

'Have you come here alone?' she asked.

'No. I am with a friend.'

'Then I have a message for you. You will have seen a shooting range contained in the building behind us. You will discover all the answers that you seek in the rooms above it. Tread carefully, Doctor. You have a long lifeline but it has weaknesses.'

'Thank you.' I took my hand back as if snatching it from the flames. As sure as I was that the woman was a fake, there was something about her performance that had unnerved me. I had a sudden instinct that this was an evil place and that we should never have come. I climbed back down and told Holmes what had just transpired.

'So are we now to be guided by fortunetellers?' was his brusque response. 'Well, Watson, there are no other obvious alternatives. We must see this through to the end.'

The shooting gallery was before us, with a staircase twisting unevenly above. There was a volley of rifle shots. With Holmes leading the way, we climbed up, treading carefully. Ahead of us, an irregular gap in the wall loomed open, with only darkness beyond. I looked back and saw the Gypsy woman watching us with an evil eye, the white ribbon dangling from her wrist. Before I reached the top I knew that I had been deceived.

We entered the upper floor, which was empty. The dust was thick on every surface. The floorboards creaked beneath our feet. The music from the barrel organ seemed distant now and the murmur of the crowd had disappeared. There was still enough light reflecting from the torches that blazed all around the fair to illuminate the room but it cast distorted shadows and the farther we went in, the darker it would become.

'Watson . . .' Holmes muttered, and the tone of his voice was enough to tell me what he desired. I produced my gun.

'Holmes,' I said. 'We are wasting our time. There is nothing here.'

'And yet a child has been here before us,' replied he.

I looked beyond him and saw, lying on the floor in the far corner, a spindle top and a lead soldier with most of its paint worn away. Had the toys once belonged to Ross? I found myself drawn towards them, just as had been intended, for too late did I see the man step out from behind an alcove, nor could I avoid the cudgel that came sweeping through the air. I was struck on the arm below the elbow and felt my fingers jerk open in a blaze of white pain. The gun clattered to the ground. I lunged for it, but was struck a second time, a blow that sent me sprawling. At the same time, a voice came out of the darkness.

'Don't either of you move or I'll shoot you where you stand.'

Holmes ignored the instruction. He was already at my side, helping me to my feet. 'Watson, are you all right?'

I clasped my arm, searching for any break or fracture and knew at once that I had only been badly bruised. 'I'm not hurt.'

A man with an upturned nose and heavy shoulders stepped towards us, allowing the light from outside to fall across his face. I recognised Henderson, who had sent Holmes into the trap at Creer's opium den. He was holding a revolver. His accomplice picked up my own weapon and shuffled forward, keeping it trained on us. This second man was burly, with swollen ears and lips, like those of a boxer after a bad fight. His cudgel was actually a heavy walking stick, which still dangled from his left hand.

'Good evening, Henderson,' Holmes remarked. He could have been casually greeting an old acquaintance.

'You are not surprised to see me, Mr Holmes?'

'On the contrary, I had fully expected it.'

'And you remember my friend, Bratby?'

Holmes turned to me. 'This was the man who held me down in the office at Creer's Place, when the opiate was forced on me. I had rather hoped he might be here too.'

Henderson laughed. 'I am afraid you are all too easily gulled, Mr Holmes. You did not find what you were looking for at Creer's. You haven't found it here, either.'

'And what are your intentions?'

'I would have thought that would be obvious. We thought we'd dealt with you at Holloway Prison, so this time our methods are going to be a little more direct. I have been instructed to shoot you like a dog.'

'In that event, would you be so kind as to satisfy my curiosity on a couple of points? Was it you who killed the girl at Bluegate Fields?'

'As a matter of fact it was. She was stupid enough to return to the public house where she worked and it was easy enough to pick her up.'

'And her brother?'

'Little Ross? Yes, that was us. The boy stepped out of line and we had to make an example of him.'

'Thank you very much. It is exactly as I thought.'

'You're a cool enough customer, aren't you, Mr Holmes? I suppose you've got it all figured out, haven't you!'

'Of course. I assume you paid the fortuneteller to do your bidding?'

'Cross her palm with sixpence and she'd do anything.'

'Let's get it over with,' the man called Bratby urged.

'Not yet, Jason. Not quite yet.'

For once, I did not need Holmes to explain why they were waiting. When we had been climbing the stairs, there had been a crowd gathered around the shooting gallery with the shots ringing out below. Now, for the moment, it was silent. The two assassins were waiting for the crack of the rifles to recommence. The sound would mask two further gunshots up here.

'You might as well give yourselves up now,' Holmes remarked. He was utterly calm and I began to wonder if he had indeed known all along that the two men would be here.

'What?'

'The shooting gallery is closed. The fair is over. Do you not hear?'

For the first time, I realised that the barrel organ had stopped. The crowd seemed to have departed. Outside all was silent.

'What are you talking about?'

'It was expedient to walk into your trap the first time, Henderson, to see what you were planning. Do you really believe I would do the same a second time?'

'Put those guns down!' a voice cried out.

In the next few seconds, there was such a confusion of events that I was barely able to make any sense of them. Henderson brought his gun round to fire either at me or past me. I will never know, for at the same moment there was a fusillade of shots and he was thrown off his feet, a fountain of blood bursting from his head. Bratby spun round and a bullet hit him in the shoulder and another in the chest. I heard him cry out as he was thrown back, my gun flying out of his hand. Sobbing in pain, he crumpled to the ground.

There was a brief pause, the silence almost as shocking as the violence that had gone before.

'You left that very late, Lestrade,' Holmes remarked.

'I was interested to hear what the villain said,' the same replied. I looked round and saw Inspector Lestrade. Three police officers were already entering the room.

'You heard him confess to the murders?'

'Yes, indeed, Mr Holmes.' One of his men examined Henderson briefly and shook his head. 'I'm afraid he will not face justice for his crimes.'

'Some might say he already has.'

'I would have preferred him alive, if only as a witness. I've put my neck on the line for you, Mr Holmes, and this night's work could cost me dear.'

'It will cost you another commendation, Lestrade, and well you know it.' Holmes turned his attention to me. 'Are you hurt, Watson?'

'Nothing that a little embrocation and a whisky and soda won't cure,' I replied. 'But tell me, Holmes. You knew all along that this was a trap?'

'It seemed inconceivable to me that an illiterate child would keep an advertisement. As our late friend, Henderson, said, we had already been deceived once. I am beginning to learn how our enemies work.'

'Meaning . . .?'

'They used you to find me. The men who followed you to Holborn Viaduct were not police officers. They were in the employ of our enemies, who had provided you with what appeared to be an irresistible clue in the hope that you would know of my whereabouts and would deliver it to me.'

'But the name, Dr Silkin's House of Wonders?'

'Silkin is not so uncommon a name. They could have used Silkin the bootmaker in Ludgate Circus. It was necessary only to draw me into the open so that they could finally be rid of me.'

'What of you, Lestrade? How did you come to be here?'

'Mr Holmes approached me and asked me to come, Dr Watson.'

'You believed in his innocence!'

'I never doubted it from the start. Inspector Harriman said he was on his way from a bank robbery on the White Horse Road, but there was no such robbery. I visited the bank. If Harriman was prepared to lie about that in court, he might be prepared to lie about a few other things.'

'Whatever our differences,' Holmes cut in, 'we have collaborated too often to fall out over a false accusation. Is that not true, Lestrade?'

'Whatever you say, Mr Holmes.'

'And he is as eager as I to bring the true culprits to justice.'

'This one is alive!' exclaimed one of the police officers who had been examining our two assailants.

Holmes knelt beside Bratby. 'Can you hear me?' he asked. There was a silence, then a soft whining. 'There is nothing we can do for you but you still have time to make some amends before you meet your maker.'

Very quietly, Bratby began to sob.

'I know everything about the House of Silk. I know what it is. I know where it is to be found . . . indeed, I visited it last night but found it empty. For the good of your own salvation, tell me. When does it next meet?'

There was a long silence. Despite myself, I felt a surge of pity for this man, who was about to breathe his last, even though he had intended to kill me.

'Tonight,' he said. And died.

Holmes straightened up. 'At last fortune is on our side,' he said. 'Lestrade, do you have at least ten men with you? They will need to be resolute for they will not forget what we are about to reveal.'

'We're with you, Holmes,' Lestrade replied. 'Let's get this over with.'

Holmes pressed my gun into my hand, looking me in the eyes. I knew what he was asking. I nodded and together we set off.

WE RETURNED to Chorley Grange School for Boys. Where else could the investigation have taken us? It was from here that the flyer had come and it was obvious that somebody had placed it under the mattress of Ross's bed for the headmaster to find, knowing that he would bring it to us. It was possible that Charles Fitzsimmons had been lying and was part of the conspiracy, too. And yet, I found that hard to believe.

We travelled in four separate carriages, silently climbing the hill that seemed to rise endlessly from the northern edge of London. Lestrade was carrying a revolver, as were Holmes and I, but his men were unarmed, so if we were preparing for a confrontation, speed and surprise would be of the very essence.

Holmes gave the signal and the carriages stopped a short distance from our target, which was not the school itself, as I had imagined, but the square building on the other side of the lane. Fitzsimmons had told us it was used for musical recitals and there were several coaches parked outside. I could hear piano music coming from within.

We took up our positions behind a clump of trees where we could remain unobserved. It was half past eight and it had begun to snow. The ground was already white. I was in considerable pain from the blow that had been inflicted on me at the fair, my entire arm throbbing. But I was determined to show none of it. I had come this far and I would see it through to the end.

'What's the plan, Mr Holmes?' Lestrade asked.

'If you want to catch these people red-handed, then we must enter without raising the alarm.'

'We're going to break into a concert?'

'It is not a concert.'

I heard the soft rattle of yet another approaching carriage and turned to see a brougham pulled by a pair of fine, grey mares. The driver was whipping them on, for the hill was steep. I glanced at Holmes. There was a look in his face I would describe as a sort of cold satisfaction.

'Do you see, Watson?' he whispered.

Holmes pointed and, in the moonlight, I saw a symbol painted in gold on the side of the brougham: a raven and two keys, the family crest of Lord Ravenshaw. Was it possible that he was involved in this too? Lord Ravenshaw descended, clearly recognisable even at this distance. He walked to the front door and knocked on it. It was opened by an unseen figure, but as the yellow light spilled out, I saw him holding something that resembled a long strip of paper. It was a white silk ribbon. The new arrival was admitted. The door closed.

'It is exactly as I thought,' Holmes said. 'Watson, are you prepared to accompany me? I must warn you that what you will encounter on the other side of that door may cause you great distress. Well, there is no helping it. Your gun is loaded? A single shot, Lestrade. That will be the signal for you and your men to come in.'

We left the protection of the trees, our feet crunching on an inch of fresh snow. The house loomed up in front of us, the windows heavily curtained. We passed the line of carriages and reached the front door. Holmes knocked. The door was opened by a young man with arched eyebrows and a manner that was both supercilious and deferential. He was dressed in a vaguely military style with a short jacket, peg-top trousers and buttoned boots.

'Yes?' The house steward, if that was what he was, regarded us with suspicion.

'We are friends of Lord Horace Blackwater,' Holmes said, and I was astonished to hear him name one of his accusers at the police court.

'And your name?'

'Parsons. This is a colleague of mine, Mr Smith.'

'Did Sir Horace provide you with any token or means of identification? It is not normally our practice to admit strangers.'

'Most certainly. He told me to give you this.' Holmes withdrew a length of white silk ribbon.

The effect was immediate. The house steward bowed his head and opened the door a little wider, gesturing with one hand. 'Come in.'

We were admitted into a hallway that took me by surprise, for I had been expecting the gloomy nature of the school. I was surrounded by opulence, warmth and bright light. A black-and-white tiled corridor led into the distance, punctuated by elegant mahogany tables. Elaborate rococo mirrors with brilliant silver frames hung on the walls, which were draped with heavily embossed scarlet and gold wallpaper. There were flowers and potted plants everywhere, their scent heavy in the overheated air. The piano music was coming from a room at the far end. There was nobody else in sight.

'If you would like to wait in here, gentlemen, I will inform the master of the house that you are here.'

The servant led us through a door and into a drawing room as well appointed as the corridor outside.

'Can I offer you gentlemen a drink?' the house steward said. We both declined and he left the room and closed the door. We were alone.

'For heaven's sake, Holmes!' I cried. 'What is this place?'

'It is the House of Silk,' he replied, grimly. He had gone over to the door and was listening for anyone outside. He carefully opened it and signalled to me. 'We have an ordeal ahead of us,' he whispered. 'But we must see an end to it.'

We slipped outside and made our way down the corridor. Somewhere, far above us, I heard someone cry out very briefly and my blood froze, for I was sure it was the sound of a child. We reached a staircase and began to make our way up. Even as we took the first steps, I heard a door open and a man's voice, which I thought I recognised. It was the master of the house. He was on his way to see us.

We hurried forward, turning the corner just as two figures—the house steward and another—passed below.

'Onwards, Watson,' Holmes whispered.

We came to a second corridor. It was carpeted, with floral wallpaper and there were many doors. There was an odour in the air that was sweet and unpleasant. Even though the truth had still not fully dawned on me, my every instinct was to leave this place.

'We must choose a door,' Holmes muttered. 'But which one?'

He chose the one closest to him and opened it. We looked in. At the rug, the candles, the mirror, the bearded man we had never seen before dressed only in a shirt open at the collar, at the boy on the bed behind him.

I did not want to believe it. But nor could I disavow the evidence of my own eyes. For that was the secret of the House of Silk. It was a house of ill-repute, but one designed for men with a predilection for young boys. Their wretched victims had been drawn from those same schoolchildren I had seen at Chorley Grange, plucked off the London streets with no families or friends, ignored by a society to which they were little more than an inconvenience. They had been forced or bribed into a life of squalor, threatened with death if they did not comply. Ross had briefly been one of them. No wonder he had run away. And no wonder his sister had tried to stab me, believing I had come to take him back. What sort of country did I live in, that could so utterly abandon its young?

All these thoughts raced through my consciousness in the few seconds that we stood there.

Then the man noticed us. 'What the devil do you think you're doing?' he thundered.

Holmes closed the door. At that moment, there was a cry from downstairs as the master of the house entered the drawing room and found that we had gone. The piano music stopped. A door opened farther down the corridor and a man stepped out, his clothes in disarray. This time I knew him at once. It was Inspector Harriman.

He saw us. 'You!' he exclaimed.

Without a second thought, I took out my revolver and fired the single shot that would bring Lestrade and his men rushing to our aid. But I did not fire into the air as I could have done. I aimed at Harriman. For the only time in my life, I knew exactly what it meant to wish to kill a man.

My bullet missed. At the last second, Holmes must have seen what I intended and cried out. It was enough to spoil my aim. The bullet went wild. Harriman ran away, reaching a second staircase and disappearing down it. At the same time, more doors flew open and middle-aged men lurched into the corridor, their faces filled with panic. Down below, there was the crash of wood and the sound of shouting. I heard Lestrade calling out. There was a second gunshot. Somebody screamed.

Holmes was already moving forward, following Harriman. The Scotland Yard man had clearly decided that the game was up, but it seemed inconceivable that he would be able to escape. Yet, that was evidently what Holmes feared, for he had already reached the staircase and was hurrying down. I followed, and together we reached the ground floor. Here, everything was chaos. The front door was open, an icy wind blowing through the corridors. Lestrade's men had already begun their work. Lord Ravenshaw ran out of one of the rooms. He was seized by an officer.

'Get your hands off me!' he shouted. 'Don't you know who I am?'

It had not yet dawned on him that the whole country would soon know who he was, and would doubtless hold his name in revulsion. Other clients of the House of Silk were already being arrested, many of them weeping tears of self-pity. I saw Robert Weeks, the teacher who had been a graduate from Balliol College, dragged out of a room, his arm twisted behind his back.

The door at the back of the house was open. One of Lestrade's men was lying in front of it, blood pumping out of a wound in his chest. Lestrade was attending to him. Seeing Holmes he looked up, his face flushed with anger. 'Harriman fired as he came down the stairs.'

'Where is he?'

'Gone!' Lestrade pointed at the open door.

Without another word, Holmes plunged after Harriman. I followed out into the darkness and the swirling snow. We took a path round the side of the house. It was hard even to make out the buildings on the other side of the lane. Then we heard the crack of a whip and the whinny of a horse, and one of the carriages, a four-wheeler drawn by two horses, shot forward towards the gate. With a heavy heart, I realised that Harriman had got away.

But Holmes was having none of it. He leaped into the nearest vehicle, a flimsy dogcart with but one horse—and not the healthiest specimen at that. I managed to clamber into the back and then we were off in pursuit. We burst through the gates, then swept round into the lane. With Holmes whipping it on, the horse proved to have spirit and the little dogcart flew over the snow-covered surface. We might have one horse less than Harriman, but our vehicle was lighter and more agile. I could only cling on, thinking that if I fell off I would surely break my neck.

This was no night for a chase. The snow was sweeping down horizontally, punching at us in a series of continuous bursts. I could not understand how Holmes could see, but there was Harriman, no more than fifty yards ahead of us. I heard him cry out with vexation, heard the lash of his whip. Holmes was sitting in front of me, crouched forward, holding the reins with both hands, keeping his balance only with his feet. Every pothole threatened to throw him out. The slightest curve caused us to skid madly across the icy surface. In my mind's eye I saw catastrophe as our steed, excited by the chase, ended up dashing us to pieces. The hill was steep and it was as if we were plunging into a chasm.

Forty yards, thirty . . . somehow we were managing to close the gap. Harriman was aware of us now. I saw him glance back, his white hair a mad halo around his head. He reached for something. There was a flash of red, a gunshot that was almost lost in the cacophony of the chase. I heard the bullet strike wood. It had missed Holmes by inches. The closer we were, the easier a target we became. And yet still we hurtled down.

Harriman fired a second time. Our horse stumbled. The entire dogcart flew into the air, then came crashing down, jarring my spine. Fortunately, the animal had been wounded and not killed and, if anything, the near calamity only made it all the more determined. Thirty yards, twenty . . . In a few seconds we would overtake.

But then Holmes was dragging on the reins and I saw a sharp bend ahead—the lane veered round to the left, and if we tried to take it at this speed we would be killed. The dogcart sluiced across the surface. I tightened my grip, the whole world barely more than a blur. There was a sharp crack ahead of me—the sound of splintering wood. I opened my eyes to see that the curricle had taken the corner too quickly. It was on one wheel and the wooden frame broke apart even as I watched. Harriman was jerked out of his seat and into the air, the reins pulling him forward. For a brief second he was there. Then the whole thing toppled onto its side, with Harriman disappearing from sight. The horses had become separated from the carriage and took off into the darkness. The curricle slithered and spun, finally coming to a halt right in front of us, and for a moment I thought we would crash into it. But Holmes guided our horse round the obstacle, drawing it to a halt.

Our horse stood there, panting. There was a bloody streak along its flank and I felt as if my every bone had become dislocated.

'Well, Watson,' Holmes rasped, breathing heavily. 'Do you think I have a future as a cab driver?'

'You might have one indeed,' I replied. 'But don't expect too many tips.'

We climbed down—but one glance told us that the pursuit was over in every sense. Harriman's neck was broken, his face contorted by a hideous grimace of pain. His sightless eyes stared up at the sky. Holmes nodded. 'This was no more than he deserved,' he said.

'He was a wicked man, Holmes. These are all evil people.'

'You put it quite succinctly, Watson. Can you bear to return to Chorley Grange? Lestrade should by now have taken charge of the situation.'

Our horse was full of fire and resentment, its nostrils steaming in the night. With difficulty we managed to turn it round and drove slowly back up the hill. The journey down had been a matter of a few minutes. It took us more than half an hour to return. But the snow seemed to be gentler and the wind had dropped. I was glad to have time to collect myself.

'Holmes,' I said. 'When did you first know?'

'About the House of Silk? The first time we came to Chorley Grange you will recall how angry Fitzsimmons became when the child that we questioned mentioned that Ross had a sister who worked at The Bag of Nails. He tried to make us believe that he was annoyed that this information had not come to us sooner. But in fact he was furious that anything had been told to us at all. I was also puzzled by the nature of the building opposite the school. I could see at a glance that the wheel tracks belonged to a number of different carriages, including a brougham and a landau. Why should the owners of such expensive vehicles be coming to a musical recital by a group of deprived boys? It made no sense.'

'But you did not realise . . .'

'Not then. It was only when we discovered the body of poor Ross that I began to see that we had entered an arena different from anything we had formerly experienced. It was not just his injuries. It was the white ribbon tied round his wrist. Anyone who could have done such a thing to a dead child must have a mind that was utterly corrupt.'

'The white ribbon . . .'

'As you saw, it was the token by which these men would be allowed entrance to the House of Silk. By looping it round the child's wrist, they knew that it would be reported in the papers and would therefore act as a warning to anyone who dared cross their path.'

'And the name, Holmes. Is that why they called it the House of Silk?'

'I fear the answer has been in front of us all the time. You will recall the name of the charity that Fitzsimmons told us supported his work? The Society for the Improvement of London's Children. I rather think we have been pursuing the House of SILC—and not Silk. The charity could have been constructed precisely for these people. It gave them the mechanism to find the children and the mask behind which they could exploit them.'

We had reached the school. Lestrade was waiting for us at the door. 'Harriman?' he asked.

'He is dead. His cart overturned.'

'I can't say I'm sorry.'

'How is your officer, the man who was shot?'

'Badly hurt, Mr Holmes. But he'll live.'

We followed Lestrade back inside. It made me shudder to return, but I was aware that we still had unfinished business.

'I have sent for more men,' Lestrade told us. 'The children have been sent back to the school and I have two officers keeping an eye on them, for all the teachers in this horrible place are implicated and I have them under arrest. Two of them—Weeks and Vosper—I think you met.'

'What of Fitzsimmons and his wife?' I asked.

'They're in the drawing room and we'll see them shortly, although there's something I want to show you first.' We followed Lestrade upstairs, he talking all the while. 'There were another nine men here. They include Lord Ravenshaw and another who will be well known to you, a doctor by the name of Ackland. Now I can see why he was so keen to perjure himself.'

'And what of Lord Horace Blackwater?' asked Holmes.

'He was not present tonight, Mr Holmes, although I'm sure we'll find that he was a frequent visitor. But come this way.'

We walked along the corridor where we had encountered Harriman. The doors were now open, revealing bedrooms, all of which were luxuriously appointed. I found myself in a room draped in blue silk with a door leading into a bathroom with piped water. The opposite wall was taken up by a low cabinet on which stood a glass tank containing a number of rocks and dried flowers arranged in what amounted to a miniature landscape.

'My men continued along the corridor to the next room,' Lestrade explained. 'It is nothing more than a storage cupboard. Now, look here. This is what we found.'

He drew our attention to the tank and I realised that there was a small aperture cut into the wall behind it, perfectly concealed by the glass.

'A window!' I exclaimed. And then I grasped its significance. 'Anything that happened in this room could be observed.'

'Not just observed,' Lestrade muttered, grimly.

He took us back out into the corridor, then threw open the door of the cupboard. It was empty inside but for a table on which stood a mahogany box. Lestrade unfastened the box, which opened like a concertina, and I realised that it was a camera and that its lens was pressed against the other side of the window that we had just seen.

'A quarter-plate Le Merveilleux, manufactured by J. Lancaster and Son of Birmingham, if I am not mistaken,' Holmes remarked.

'Is this part of their depravity?' Lestrade demanded. 'That they had to keep a record of what took place?'

'I think not,' Holmes replied. 'But I now understand why my brother, Mycroft, was given such a hostile reception when he began his enquiries and why he was unable to come to my aid. You say you have Fitzsimmons downstairs? I think it is time we had our reckoning.'

The fire was still burning in the drawing room and the room was close. The Reverend Charles Fitzsimmons was sitting on the sofa with his wife and I was glad to see that he had exchanged his clerical garb for a black tie and dinner jacket. I do not think I could have borne any more of his pretence that he was part of the church. Mrs Fitzsimmons refused to meet our eyes and did not utter a word throughout the interview that followed.

'Mr Holmes!' Fitzsimmons sounded pleasantly surprised to see him. 'I must congratulate you, sir. You have proven yourself to be every bit as formidable as I was led to believe. Your disappearance from Holloway was extraordinary. And as neither Henderson nor Bratby have returned I will assume that you got the better of them at Jackdaw Lane?'

'They are dead,' Holmes said.

'They would have ended up being hanged anyway, so I suppose it makes no great difference.'

'Are you prepared to answer my questions?'

'I see no reason why not. I am not ashamed of what we have been doing here at Chorley Grange. Some of the policemen have treated us very roughly and . . .' He called out to Lestrade at the door, '. . . I can assure you I will be making an official complaint. We have only been providing what certain men have been requesting for centuries. I am sure you have studied the ancient civilisations of the Greeks, the Romans and the Persians? The cult of Ganymede was an honourable one, sir. Are you repulsed by the work of Michelangelo or even by the sonnets of William Shakespeare? Well, I'm sure you have no wish to discuss the semantics of the matter.'

'Was the House of Silk your idea?'

'It was entirely mine. I can assure you that the Society for the Improvement of London's Children has no knowledge of what we have been doing.'

'It was you who ordered the killing of Ross?'

'I am not proud of it, Mr Holmes, but it was necessary to ensure my own safety and the continuation of this enterprise. I am not confessing to the murder itself. That was carried out by Henderson and Bratby. And you would be deluding yourself if you thought of Ross as some innocent. He was a nasty piece of work and brought his end entirely upon himself.'

'I believe you have been keeping a photographic record of your clients.'

'It has been necessary from time to time.'

'I assume your purpose was blackmail.'

'Occasionally, and only when absolutely necessary. I have made a considerable amount of money from the House of Silk and had no need for any other form of revenue. It was more to do with self-protection. How do you think I was able to persuade Dr Ackland and Lord Horace Blackwater to appear in court? It was an act of self-preservation on their part. It is for this same reason that I can tell you now that my wife and I will never stand trial in this country. We know too many secrets about too many people, some of whom are in the highest positions, and we have the evidence tucked away. The gentlemen who you found here tonight were but a small selection of my grateful clients. We have ministers and judges, lawyers and lords. I could name one member of the noblest family in the country who has been a frequent visitor here, but of course he relies on my discretion, just as I can rely on his protection. You take my point, Mr Holmes? Six months from now my wife and I will begin again. Perhaps it will be necessary to look to the continent. But the House of Silk will re-emerge. You have my word on it.'

Holmes said nothing. He stood and together he and I left the room. He did not mention Fitzsimmons again that night and nor did he have anything further to say on the subject the following morning. But by then, we were busy again, for the entire adventure had begun at Wimbledon and it was to there that we now returned.

THE SNOWFALL of the night before had tranformed Ridgeway Hall, accentuating its symmetry and rendering it somehow timeless. As I approached it for the last time, in the company of Sherlock Holmes, it almost felt like an act of vandalism to scour the white driveway with our carriage wheels.

I had passed a wretched night, desperate to fall asleep in order to put out of my mind everything I had seen at Chorley Grange, yet unable to do so. I had come to the breakfast table and been irked to see Holmes restored in every way to his old self, greeting me in that precise way of his as if nothing untoward had occurred. It was he who had insisted on this visit, having already sent a wire to Edmund Carstairs before I had risen. He clearly placed great significance on Eliza Carstairs's sudden illness. He insisted on seeing her for himself, although how he might be able to help her when so many doctors had failed was beyond my comprehension.

The door was opened by Patrick, the Irish scullery boy. He looked blankly at Holmes, then at me. 'Oh, it's you,' he scowled. 'I wasn't expecting to see you back here again.'

'Patrick? Who is it?' Edmund Carstairs had appeared in the hallway and came forward, clearly agitated. He was as immaculately attired as he had been on every occasion that I had seen him, but the lines that days of anxiety had drawn were clearly visible on his face.

'You received my wire?' Holmes said.

'I did. But you evidently did not receive mine. I clearly stated that I had no further need of your services. I am sorry to say it, but you have not been helpful to my family, Mr Holmes. And I understood that you were in serious trouble with the law.'

'Those matters have been resolved. As to your wire, Mr Carstairs, I did indeed receive it, and read what you had to say with interest.'

'And you came anyway?'

'If you wish your sister to die, you will send me away. If not, you will invite me in and hear what I have to say.'

Carstairs hesitated but in the end his better sense prevailed. 'Please,' he said. 'Let me take your coats. I don't know what Kirby is doing.' We removed our outer garments and he gestured towards the drawing room.

'If you will permit me, I would like to see your sister before we sit down,' Holmes remarked.

'My sister is no longer able to see anyone. Her sight has failed her.'

'I wish merely to see her room. Is she still refusing to eat?'

'It is no longer a question of refusal. She is unable to consume solid food. It is the best I can do to make her take a little warm soup.'

'She still believes she is being poisoned?'

'In my view, it is this irrational belief that has become the main cause of her illness, Mr Holmes. As I told your colleague, I have tasted every single morsel that has passed her lips with no ill effect at all.'

We climbed back up to the attic room that I had been in before. As we arrived, the manservant, Kirby, appeared with a tray of soup, the plate untouched. We went in. I was at once dismayed by the sight of Eliza Carstairs. How long had it been since I had last seen her? Hardly more than a week and in that time she had visibly deteriorated. The shape of the body beneath the covers was tiny and pathetic. Her eyes stared at us but saw nothing.

Holmes examined her briefly. 'Her bathroom is next door?' he asked.

'Yes. But she is too weak to walk there. Mrs Kirby and my wife bathe her where she lies . . .'

Holmes entered the bathroom, leaving Carstairs and myself in an uneasy silence. At last he reappeared. 'We can return downstairs,' he said. Carstairs and I followed him out. The entire visit had lasted less than thirty seconds.

We went back down to the drawing room where Catherine Carstairs was reading in front of a cheerful fire. She rose quickly to her feet. 'Why, Mr Holmes and Dr Watson! You are the last two people I expected to see.' She glanced at her husband. 'I thought . . .'

'I did as we agreed, my dear. But Mr Holmes chose to visit us anyway.'

'I am surprised that you did not wish to see me, Mrs Carstairs,' Holmes remarked. 'Particularly as you came to consult me a second time.'

'I don't wish to be rude, Mr Holmes, but I have long since given up hope that you can be of assistance to us. If there is nothing you can do to help poor Eliza, then there is no reason for you to stay.'

'I believe I can save Miss Carstairs. It may still not be too late.'

'Save her from what?'

'From poison.'

Catherine Carstairs started. 'She is not being poisoned! There is no possibility of that. The doctors are all agreed.'

'Then they are all wrong. May I sit down? There is much that I have to tell you and I think we would all be more comfortable seated.'

The wife glared at him but this time the husband took Holmes's side. 'I will listen to what you have to say, Mr Holmes. But if I believe that you are attempting to deceive me, I will have no hesitation in asking you to leave.'

'My aim is not to deceive you,' returned Holmes. 'In fact, quite the contrary.' He sat down in the armchair farthest from the fire. I took the chair next to him. Mr and Mrs Carstairs sat together on the sofa opposite.

'You came to my lodgings, Mr Carstairs, because you were afraid that your life might be threatened by a man you had never met. You were on your way that evening to the opera, to Wagner, as I recall. But it was late by the time you left me. I imagine you missed the first curtain.'

'No. I arrived on time.'

'No matter. There were many aspects of your story that I found quite remarkable, the principal one being the strange behaviour of this vigilante, Keelan O'Donaghue. I could well believe that he had followed you all the way to London with the express purpose of killing you. You were, after all, responsible in part for the death of his twin brother. And he had already taken vengeance on Cornelius Stillman, the man who paid for the Pinkerton's agent who tracked down the Flat Cap Gang in Boston. Remind me, if you will, what is the name of the agent you employed?'

'It was Bill McParland.'

'Of course. As I say, it is no surprise that Keelan should have sought your death. So why did he not kill you? Once he had discovered where you lived, why did he not put a knife in you? Nobody knew he was in this country. He could have been on a ship back to America before you were even in the morgue. But, in fact, he did the exact opposite. He stood outside your house, wearing the flat cap that he knew would identify him. Worse, he appeared again when you were leaving the Savoy. What was in his mind, do you think?'

'He wished to frighten us,' Mrs Carstairs said.

'But on his third visit he pressed a note into your husband's hand asking for a meeting at your local church.'

'He did not show up.'

'Perhaps he never intended to. His final intervention came when he broke into the house and stole fifty pounds and jewellery from your safe. Not only does he know exactly which window to choose, he has somehow got his hands on a key lost by your wife several months before he arrived in the country. And he is now more interested in money than in murder, for he could climb the stairs and kill you both in your bed—'

'I woke up and heard him.'

'Indeed so, Mrs Carstairs. But by that time he had already opened the safe. I take it that you and Mr Carstairs sleep in separate rooms?'

Carstairs flushed. 'I do not see that our domestic arrangements have any bearing on the case.'

'But you do not deny it. Very well, let us stay with our strange intruder. He makes his getaway to a hotel in Bermondsey. But a second assailant catches up with Keelan O'Donaghue, stabs him to death, and takes not only his money but anything that might identify him, apart from a cigarette case which bears the initials WM.'

'What do you mean by all this, Mr Holmes?' Catherine Carstairs asked.

'I am merely making it clear, Mrs Carstairs, that this narrative makes no sense whatsoever—unless, that is, you start from the premise that it was not Keelan O'Donaghue who came to this house, and that it was not your husband with whom he wished to communicate.'

'But that's ridiculous. He gave my husband that note.'

'And failed to appear at the church. It may help if we put ourselves in the position of this mysterious visitor. He seeks a private interview with a member of this household but that is not such a simple matter. Apart from yourself and your husband, there is your sister, various servants . . .

'To begin with, he watches from a distance but finally he approaches with a note written in large letters and neither folded nor in an envelope. Clearly, his intention cannot be to post it through the door. But is it possible, perhaps, that he hopes to see the person for whom this correspondence is intended, to hold it up so that it can be read through the window of the breakfast room? No need to ring the bell. No need to risk the message falling into the wrong hands. However, Mr Carstairs returns unexpectedly early to the house, before our man has had the chance to achieve his aim. So what does he do? He raises the note high above him and hands it to Mr Carstairs. He knows he is being watched from the breakfast room and his meaning now is different. "Find me," he is saying. "Or I will tell Mr Carstairs everything I know. I will meet him in the church." Of course, he does not turn up at the assignation. He has no need to. The warning is enough.'

'But with whom did he wish to speak?' Carstairs demanded.

'Who was in the breakfast room at the time?'

'My wife.' He frowned as if anxious to change the subject. 'Who was this man, if he was not Keelan O'Donaghue?' he asked.

'The answer to that is perfectly simple, Mr Carstairs. He was Bill McParland, the Pinkerton's detective. Consider for a moment. We know that McParland was injured during the shoot-out in Boston and the man in the hotel room had a scar on his right cheek. We also know that McParland had fallen out with Cornelius Stillman, who had refused to pay him the amount of money he felt he was owed. He therefore had a grievance. And then there is his name. Bill, I would imagine, is short for William and the initials we found on the cigarette case were—'

'WM,' I interjected.

'Precisely, Watson. And now things begin to fall into place. Let us begin by considering Keelan O'Donaghue himself. You told us that Rourke and Keelan O'Donaghue were twins but that Keelan was the smaller of the two. They carried each other's initials, tattooed on their arms. Keelan was clean-shaven and taciturn. He wore a flat cap that would have made it difficult to see very much of his face. He was of slender build, able to squeeze through the gulley that led to the river and so effect his escape. But I was particularly struck by one detail. The gang lived together in the tenement in the South End of Boston—apart from Keelan who had the luxury of his own room. I wondered from the start why that might be.

'The answer, of course, is obvious, given all the evidence I have just laid out, and I am happy to say that I have had it confirmed by no less than Mrs Caitlin O'Donaghue who still lives in Sackville Street in Belfast. It is this. In the spring of 1865 she gave birth, not to twin brothers but to a brother and a sister. Keelan O'Donaghue was a girl.'

The silence that greeted this revelation was, in a word, profound. Even the flames in the fireplace seemed to be holding their breath.

'A girl?' Carstairs looked at Holmes in wonderment. 'Running a gang?'

'A girl who would have had to conceal her identity if she were to survive in such an environment,' Holmes returned. 'Anyway, it was her brother who ran the gang.'

'And where is this girl?'

'You are married to her, Mr Carstairs.'

I saw Catherine Carstairs turn pale.

'You do not deny it, Mrs Carstairs?' Holmes asked.

'Of course I deny it!' She turned to her husband and suddenly there were tears in her eyes. 'You're not going to allow him to speak to me in this way, are you, Edmund? To suggest that I might have some connection with a hateful brood of criminals and evildoers!'

'Your words, I think, fall on deaf ears, Mrs Carstairs,' Holmes remarked.

And it was true. Carstairs was gazing in front of him with an expression of horror.

'Please, Edmund . . .' She reached out to him, but Carstairs flinched and turned away.

'May I continue?' Holmes asked.

Catherine Carstairs was about to speak but then her shoulders slumped and it was as if a veil had been torn from her face. 'Oh yes, oh yes,' she snarled. 'We might as well hear the rest of it.'

'Thank you.' Holmes nodded in her direction, then went on. 'After the destruction of the Flat Cap Gang, Catherine O'Donaghue—for that was her given name—found herself alone, in America, wanted by the police. She had lost the brother who she must have dearly loved. Her first thoughts were of revenge. Still in disguise, she tracked Cornelius Stillman down to the garden of his house in Providence and shot him dead. But he was not the only person mentioned in the advertisement in the Boston press. Reverting to her female persona, Catherine followed his junior partner onto the *Catalonia*. It was time to return to her family in Belfast. Nobody would suspect her, travelling as a single woman, accompanied by a maid. She took with her what profits she had been able to save from her past crimes. And somewhere in the middle of the Atlantic she would come face to face with Edmund Carstairs. It is easy enough to commit murder on the high seas. Carstairs would disappear and her revenge would be complete.'

Holmes now addressed Mrs Carstairs directly. 'But something changed your mind. What was it, I wonder?'

The woman shrugged. 'I saw Edmund for what he was.'

'As I thought. Here was a man with no experience of the opposite sex apart from a mother and sister who dominated him. He was ill. He was afraid. How amusing it must have been to draw him into your net. How much sweeter this revenge than the one you had originally planned. You would play the part of the devoted wife, the charade made easier by the fact that you have chosen to sleep in separate rooms and, I fancy, have never allowed yourself to be seen in a state of undress. There was the inconvenience of that tattoo. Were you ever to visit a pleasure beach, you would naturally be unable to swim.

'All would have been well but for the arrival of Bill McParland. How had he picked up your trail and learned your new identity? We will never know, but he was a very good detective and doubtless had his methods. It was not your husband he was signalling outside this house and at the Savoy. It was you. He had come here for the money he was owed. He demanded money from you. If you paid him enough, he would let you keep your secret.'

'You have it all, Mr Holmes.'

'Not quite. You needed to give McParland something but had no access to resources of your own. It was therefore necessary to create the illusion of a burglary. You came down in the night and guided him to the correct window with a light. You opened that window from inside and opened the safe, using a key that you had never lost. As well as the money, you gave him a necklace that had belonged to the late Mrs Carstairs, which you knew had sentimental value to your husband. It seems to me that any chance you had to hurt him was irresistible and you seized it with alacrity.

'McParland made one mistake. The money that you gave to him was only a first payment. Foolishly, he gave you the name of the hotel where he was staying. You chose your moment, slipped out of the house and climbed into the hotel through a back window. You were waiting in McParland's room when he returned and you struck from behind, stabbing him in the neck. I wonder, incidentally, how you were dressed?'

'In my old style. Petticoats would have been a little cumbersome.'

'You silenced McParland and removed any trace of his identity, missing only the cigarette case. And with him gone, there was nothing to stand in the way of the rest of your scheme.'

'There is more?' Carstairs rasped.

'Indeed so, Mr Carstairs.' Holmes turned back to the wife. 'It was your intention to kill Edmund's family one at a time: his mother, his sister and then he. At the end of it, this house, the money, the art . . . all of it would be yours. It is hard to imagine the relish with which you went about your task.'

'It has been a pleasure, Mr Holmes. I have enjoyed every minute of it.'

'My mother?' Carstairs gasped the two words.

'The most likely explanation was that the gas fire in her bedroom blew out. But your manservant, Kirby, told us that your mother disliked draughts and he had stopped up every crevice in the room, so it was impossible a draught could have blown out the fire. The truth is, Catherine Carstairs entered the room and deliberately blew out the flame, leaving the old lady to perish.'

'And Eliza?'

'You told me that you have carefully examined everything she has eaten, which suggests that she is being poisoned in another way. The answer, Mr Carstairs, is the bath. Your sister insists on bathing regularly and I would say that a small measure of aconitine has been added, regularly, to her lavender bath salts. It has entered Miss Carstairs's system through her skin. Aconitine is a highly toxic alkaloid that is soluble in water and which would have killed your sister instantly if a large dose had been used. Instead, you have noted this slow but remorseless decline. It is a striking and innovative method of murder, Mrs Carstairs, and one that I am sure will be added to the annals of crime.'

'You devil!' Carstairs twisted away from her. 'How could you?'

'Mr Holmes is right, Edmund,' his wife returned and I noticed that her voice was harder, the Irish accent now prominent. 'I would have put all of you in your graves. First your mother. Then Eliza. And you have no idea what I was planning for you!' She turned to Holmes. 'And what now, clever Mr Holmes? Do you have a policeman waiting outside?'

'There is indeed a policeman waiting, Mrs Carstairs. But I have not finished yet.' Holmes drew himself up and I saw a coldness in his eyes that went beyond anything I had ever seen before. 'There is still the death of the child, Ross, to be accounted for.'

Mrs Carstairs burst out laughing. 'I know nothing about Ross,' she said.

'It is no longer you I am addressing, Mrs Carstairs,' Holmes replied and turned to her husband. 'My investigation into your affairs took an unexpected turn on the night that Ross was murdered, Mr Carstairs. I was following one line of investigation and it took me suddenly onto another. From the moment I arrived at Mrs Oldmore's Private Hotel, I had left the Flat Cap Gang behind me.

'Let us go back to that night, for you, of course, were with me. Ross was left to watch the hotel while his companion, Wiggins, came for me. We drove—you, me, Watson and Wiggins—over to Blackfriars. Ross saw us and I perceived the boy was terrified. He asked who you were. Watson attempted to reassure him and, in doing so, named you and gave the boy your address. That, I rather fear, was to be the death of him—though do not blame yourself, Watson, for the mistake was equally mine.

'I had assumed that Ross was frightened because of what he had seen at the hotel. I was convinced that he must have seen the killer. But I was wrong. What had frightened the boy was the sight of you, Mr Carstairs. The two of you had met at the House of Silk.'

Another dreadful silence.

'What is the House of Silk?' Catherine Carstairs asked.

'I will not answer your question, Mrs Carstairs. Nor do I need to address myself to you again except to say your entire scheme would have worked only with a man who wanted a wife to spite his family, to give him a certain standing in society, not for reasons of love or affection. As you put it, you knew him for what he was. I myself wondered exactly what sort of creature I was dealing with on the first day we met for it fascinates me to meet a man who tells me he is late for a Wagner opera on an evening when no Wagner is being played.

'Ross recognised you, Mr Carstairs. He had already stolen a gold watch from one of the men who had preyed on him. As soon as he got over the shock of encountering you, he must have seen the possibilities of considerably more. Did he threaten to expose you if you did not pay him a fortune? Or had you already scuttled off to Charles Fitzsimmons and his gang of thugs and demanded that they take care of the situation?'

'I never asked them to do anything,' Carstairs muttered.

'You went to Fitzsimmons and told him that you were being threatened. Acting on his instructions, you sent Ross to a meeting where he believed he would be paid for his silence. It was not Fitzsimmons or yourself that Ross met. It was the two thugs who called themselves Henderson and Bratby. And they made sure he would not trouble you again.' Holmes paused. 'Ross was murdered for his audacity, a white ribbon placed around his wrist as a warning. You may not have commanded it, Mr Carstairs, but I want you to know that I hold you personally responsible. You are a man as vile as any I have ever met.'

He rose to his feet. 'And now I will leave. It occurs to me that your marriage was not perhaps as ill-judged as might be thought. The two of you are made for each other. Well, you will find police carriages waiting outside for both of you. Ready, Watson? We will show ourselves out.'

Edmund and Catherine Carstairs sat motionless on the sofa together. Neither of them spoke. But I felt them watching us intently as we left.

Afterword

It is with a heavy heart that I draw to the end of my task. While I have been writing this, it is as if I have been reliving it, and although there are some details I would wish to forget, still it has been good to find myself back at Holmes's side. Would that there was more to tell, for once I am finished I will find myself alone once again.

Charles Fitzsimmons—I forbear to use the word Reverend—was quite correct. He never did come to trial. But on the other hand, he was not released as he had so fondly expected. He fell down a flight of prison stairs and was found with a fractured skull. Was he pushed? It would seem very likely for, as he had boasted, he knew some unpleasant secrets about a number of important people. Unless I misunderstood him, he went so far as to suggest that he might have connections with the royal family. I remember what Mycroft Holmes said to us, and from the way he behaved, it was evident that he had come under considerable pressure . . . But no, I will not even consider the possibility. Fitzsimmons was attempting to inflate his own importance and there's an end to it.

It is true that, in the weeks that followed, there was a series of resignations at the highest level that both astonished and alarmed the country.

I very much hope, though, that Fitzsimmons was not assassinated. He was a monster but no country can afford to throw aside the rule of law simply for the sake of expediency. This seems even more clear to me now, while we are at war. Perhaps his death was just a lucky accident.

Lestrade told me that Mrs Fitzsimmons went mad after the death of her husband and was transferred to a lunatic asylum. Again, this was a fortunate outcome, as there she could say what she liked and nobody would believe her. For all I know, she is still there to this day.

Edmund Carstairs was not prosecuted. He left the country with his sister, who remained an invalid for the rest of her life. Catherine Carstairs was tried under her maiden name and sentenced to life imprisonment. She was fortunate to escape the noose. Lord Ravenshaw blew his brains out with a revolver. There may have been one or two other suicides, too, but Lord Horace Blackwater and Dr Thomas Ackland both escaped justice. I suppose one has to be pragmatic about these things, but it still annoys me.

Then there is the strange gentleman who accosted me that night and gave me such an unusual supper. I never did tell Holmes about him. I had given my word and, as a gentleman, I felt I had no choice but to keep it. I am quite certain that my host was Professor James Moriarty, who was to play such a momentous role in our lives a short while later, and it was the devil's own work to pretend that I had never met him. To this day I believe that Moriarty genuinely wanted to help Holmes and see the House of Silk shut down. It offended his sensibilities, so he sent Holmes the white ribbon in the hope that his enemy would do his work for him. And that, of course, is what happened, although to the best of my knowledge Moriarty never sent a note of thanks.

I returned to my old lodgings in January to see how Holmes was bearing up after our adventure. It was during this time that one last incident took place which I must now record.

Holmes had been completely exonerated, and any record of the accusations made against him annulled. He was not, however, in an easy state of mind. It would have helped if he was on a case, but he was not and it was when he was idle that he became prone to depression. But this time, I realised, it was something more. He had not mentioned the House of Silk, but reading the newspaper one morning, he drew my attention to a brief article concerning Chorley Grange School for Boys, which had just been closed down.

'It's not enough,' he muttered.

One evening, after we had taken dinner, he suddenly announced that he was going out. January was as glacial as December had been, and though I had no desire at all for this late expedition, I nonetheless asked him if he would like me to accompany him.

'No, no, Watson. It's kind of you. But I think I would be better alone.'

'But where are you going at this late hour, Holmes? Any business you may have can surely wait until the day.'

'Watson, you are the very best of friends and I am aware that I have been poor company. What I need is a little time alone. But tomorrow I am sure you will find me in better spirits.'

And he was. We spent a companionable day visiting the British Museum and lunching at Simpson's, and it was only as we were returning home that I saw in the newspapers a report of the great fire on Hamworth Hill. A building that had once been occupied by a charitable school had been razed to the ground. I asked no questions. Nor had I remarked that morning that his coat, which had been hanging in its usual place, had carried about it the strong smell of cinders. That evening, Holmes played his Stradivarius for the first time in a while. I listened with pleasure to the soaring tune as we sat together on either side of the hearth.

I hear it still. As I lay down my pen and take to my bed, I am aware of the bow being drawn across the bridge and the music rises into the night sky. It is far away and barely audible but—there it is! A pizzicato. Then a tremolo. The style is unmistakable. It is Sherlock Holmes who is playing. It must be. I hope with all my heart that he is playing for me . . .

anthony **horowitz**

Profile

Born:
April 5, 1956, Stanmore, Middlesex.

Family:
Married to Jill. They have two sons.

Education:
Read English Literature at York University.

Favourite author:
Charles Dickens.

Favourite Sherlock Holmes story:
The Dying Detective.

Little-known facts:
Is a huge *Tintin* fan. Has been asked to write 'Tintin 2' film script. Spent a year working as a cowboy in Australia.

Website:
anthonyhorowitz.com

When Anthony Horowitz was asked if he'd write a new Sherlock Holmes novel true to the spirit of the original, classic mysteries by Sir Arthur Conan Doyle, it took him just ninety minutes, over a lunch with his London publisher, to agree. How did he decide so swiftly that he was capable of meeting this exciting request from Doyle's Estate? Where did his enthusiasm for the iconic detective come from?

'I've been reading nineteenth-century literature all my life and so it's a world I'm very comfortable in,' Horowitz recently said in an interview. 'I was quite surprised how easily I slipped into Holmes's Turkish slippers. The truth of the matter is that Doyle had already done a large part of the work for me in creating that relationship and that world, and a wonderful cast of minor characters to draw on.'

Anthony Horowitz, who lives in Clerkenwell, London, is the imagination and talent behind some of British TV's longest running and most popular television mystery dramas, including *Midsomer Murders*, *Foyle's War* and *Poirot*, based on the famous Belgian sleuth. He is also the creator of the very popular 'Alex Rider' boy-detective series for teenagers, which has sold millions of copies worldwide. A thirty-year career spinning mysteries and whodunnits did, in fact, make him the perfect person to take on this project.

Horowitz claims that the plot for the new novel fell into place very quickly. He knew he had to start with a question, which the book would then answer. 'The question here was "Why haven't we heard this story before?" At the end of that first lunch, I'd worked that out. I also knew that the Baker Street Irregulars would have to be there, too, because that fitted in with my children's writing, and I'd worked out how to get Moriarty in.' He decided to set *The House of Silk* just three days after a previous mystery by Conan Doyle, *The Dying Detective*, ends. Officially, therefore, as Watson's prologue explains, it is a 'missing case'; one which has only just come to light and which is in the process of being written up by him following Holmes's death.

The fact that Horowitz was already well acquainted with Conan Doyle's *oeuvre*—he was given a complete set of the stories when he was sixteen—helped him enormously. He was very familiar with the world of 221b Baker Street, as well as the famous cast of characters, which includes Sherlock's trusted sidekick, Dr Watson, housekeeper, Mrs Hudson, and arch enemy, Professor Moriarty. However, before starting to write, he decided to re-read the entire canon of fifty-six short stories and four novels, in order to ensure he got the tone exactly right. 'I realised that this would be the key. I had to become invisible, to find that extraordinary, authentic voice.'

The work flowed remarkably smoothly and the book was written in a few short months. 'Normally it takes me seven months to a year to write a novel . . . but with this one—well, I've never written anything like it. You know, Doyle believed very much in spiritualism, in communicating beyond the grave . . . and sometimes it was as though he was just standing watching me. I never had to search for language, I never had to worry about characters. It all just happened. It was like playing with the most fantastic train set in the world.' He adds, 'Holmes helped push me into murder-mystery writing. I do feel in a strange way that I've come full circle because this is where I began.'

So, why does Horowitz think Holmes's appeal has been so enduring? 'Well, he was the first, the father of all modern detectives, but I think that what makes him so unforgettable is his relationship with Watson. He is austere, irritating, aloof. Watson is warm, loyal, affable. Together they have the greatest friendship in literature.'

This revival of Sherlock Holmes's character coincides with wider interest in the iconic detective. A sequel to the first recently released Sherlock Holmes film starring Robert Downey, Jr. and Jude Law was released at the end of 2011, and a second series of the BBC TV drama, *Sherlock*, starring Benedict Cumberbatch and Martin Freeman, has recently been broadcast. Meanwhile, Anthony Horowitz is already thinking of another book to be set during the same period. This time, however, there will be only a fleeting appearance by Sherlock, at most. 'Trust me,' he says, 'it's going to be even better. I've got an idea for it in my head that makes me smile when I think of it.'

In the meantime, there are more Hollywood scripts and TV plays to write. The load appears somewhat exhausting. But Horowitz is undaunted and says confidently: 'You know what I think the best thing I can say about my work is? I've been writing for thirty-five years, and every day that I come up the stairs to this room to write—every day I still get the same thrill from writing.'

LETHAL

SANDRA BROWN

When her four-year-old daughter informs her a sick man is in their yard, Honor Gillette rushes out to help him. But that 'sick' man turns out to be Lee Coburn, a man accused of murdering seven people the night before. Dangerous, desperate, and armed, he claims that her beloved late husband possessed something extremely valuable that places Honor and her daughter in grave danger. And Coburn is there to retrieve it—at any cost.

Chapter 1

'Mommy?'

'Hmm?'

'There's a man in the yard.'

'What's that?'

The four-year-old came to stand at the corner of the kitchen table and gazed yearningly at the frosting her mother was applying to the top of the cupcake. 'Can I have some, Mommy?'

'*May* I have some. When I'm done, you can lick the bowl.'

'You made chocolate.'

'Because chocolate is your favourite, and you're my favourite girl. And I've got sprinkles to add as soon as I finish the icing.'

Emily beamed, then her face puckered with concern. 'He's sick.'

'Who's sick?'

'The man in the yard.'

Finally the innate mom-screen that filtered out unimportant chatter was penetrated. 'There's really a man outside?' Honor absently wiped her hands on a tea towel as she stepped round the child.

'He's lying down because he's sick.'

Emily trailed her mother as she made her way from kitchen to living room. Honor looked through the front window, but all she saw was the lawn sloping gradually down to the dock.

Beyond the dock's weathered wood planks the bayou waters moved indolently. The stray cat, who refused to take Honor seriously when she told him that this was *not* his home, was stalking unseen prey in her bed of brightly coloured zinnias. 'Em, there's not—'

'By the bush with the white flowers,' Emily said stubbornly.

Honor went to the door, unlocked it, stepped out onto the porch, and looked in the direction of the rose of Sharon shrub.

And there he was, lying face down, his left arm outstretched. He lay motionless. Quickly Honor gently pushed Emily back through the door. 'Sweetie, go into Mommy's bedroom. My phone is on the nightstand. Bring it to me, please.' She kept her voice calm, but then hurriedly ran across the dewy grass towards the prone figure.

When she got closer, she saw that his clothing was filthy, torn in places, and bloodstained. There were smears of blood on the exposed skin of his outstretched arm and hand. A clot of it had matted his dark hair.

Honor knelt down. 'Sir? Can you hear me? I'll call for help.'

He sprang up so quickly that she didn't have time to recoil. His left hand shot round her neck while his right jammed the blunt barrel of a handgun into her ribs. 'Who else is here?'

Her vocal cords were frozen with fear; she couldn't speak.

He squeezed her neck. '*Who else is here?*'

It took several tries before she stammered, 'My . . . my dau—'

'Anybody besides the kid?'

She shook her head.

His blue eyes cut like lasers. 'If you're lying to me . . .'

He didn't even have to complete the threat to coax a whimper from her. 'I'm not lying. I swear. We're alone. My daughter's only four years old. Don't hurt her. I'll do whatever you say, just don't—'

'Mommy?'

Honor shifted her eyes towards Emily, standing several yards away, blonde curls wreathing her sweet face. She was clutching the cellphone, her expression apprehensive.

Honor's heart clenched. She managed to say, 'It's OK, sweetheart.' Her eyes shifted back to the man. *Please*, her eyes silently implored. Then she whispered, 'I beg you.'

Those hard, cold eyes magnetised hers as he gradually eased the pistol away, placing it behind his thigh where Emily couldn't see it. He removed his hand from Honor's neck and turned towards Emily. 'Hi.'

Emily regarded him shyly. 'Hello.'

He extended his hand. 'Give me the phone.'

She didn't move. 'You didn't say please.'

Please appeared to be a foreign concept to him. But after a moment, he said, 'Please.'

Emily took a step towards him, then looked at Honor. Honor managed to form a smile. 'It's OK, sweetie. Give him the phone.'

Emily closed the distance between them, leaned far forwards, and dropped the phone into his blood-smeared palm. It closed around it. 'Thanks.'

'You're welcome. Are you gonna call Grandpa?'

His eyes shifted to Honor. 'Grandpa?'

'He's coming for supper tonight,' Emily announced happily. 'Mommy said I can have pizza for supper because it's a party.'

'Huh.' He slid Honor's cellphone into the front pocket of his jeans. 'Let's go inside. You can tell me about the party.' Keeping a grip on Honor's arm, he propelled her towards the house. Emily got distracted by the cat. She chased after him, calling, 'Here, Kitty,' as he slunk into a hedge on the far side of the yard.

As soon as Emily was out of earshot, Honor said, 'I've got some money. A couple of hundred dollars. Just please don't hurt my daughter.'

'Where's your boat?' He hitched his chin towards the dock.

She looked at him blankly. 'I don't have a boat.'

'Don't mess with me.'

'I sold the boat when . . . A couple of years ago.'

He seemed to weigh her honesty, then asked, 'Where's your car?'

'Parked in front.'

'Keys in it?'

'On a wall hook by the kitchen door.'

He started up the steps of the porch, pushing her in front of him. She turned her head, about to call out to Emily, but he said, 'Leave her for now.'

'What are you going to do?'

'First,' he said, opening the door, 'I'm going to make sure you aren't lying to me about anyone else being here. And then . . . we'll see.'

She could feel the tension in him as he propelled her from the empty living room then down the short hallway towards the bedrooms. 'There's no one here except Emily and me.'

He gave the door of Emily's bedroom a push and it swung open to a panorama of pink. No one was lying in wait. Still mistrustful, he shoved Honor towards the second bedroom.

Her room looked almost mockingly serene. Sunlight coming through the shutters painted stripes on the hardwood floor, the white comforter, the pale grey walls. He relaxed marginally when he glanced into the connecting bathroom and discovered it also empty.

They returned to the kitchen, where his eyes darted from point to point, taking it all in. When she saw his gaze alight on the wall hook with her car keys hanging from it, she said, 'Take the car. Just go.'

Ignoring that, he asked, 'What's in there?'

'Laundry room.'

He went to that door and opened it. Washing machine and dryer. A rack on which she dried her delicates—an array of lace in pastels, one black bra. When he came back, those Nordic eyes moved over her in a way that made her face turn hot even as her torso became cold and clammy with dread.

His entire aspect was menacing, starting with his chilling eyes and the pronounced bone structure of his face. He was tall and lean, the skin on his arms stretched over taut muscles. His clothes and hair had snagged twigs, moss, small leaves. Dried mud caked his jeans. He smelt of the swamp, of sweat, of danger.

Overpowering him would be impossible. He stood between her and the drawer where the butcher knives were stored. Even if she could outrun him and escape, she wouldn't leave Emily behind.

'I've answered all your questions truthfully, haven't I?' she said, her voice low and tremulous. 'I've offered you my money and—'

'I don't want your money.'

'Then what do you want?'

'Your cooperation.'

'With what?'

'Put your hands behind your back.'

'Please.' The word was spoken on a sob. 'My little girl—'

'I'm not going to ask you again.' He took another step closer.

She backed away and came up against the wall behind her.

One last step brought him to within inches of her. 'Do it.'

Her instinct was to scratch and claw and kick. But she clasped her hands together at the small of her back.

He leaned in close and placed his hand beneath her chin. 'You see how easy it would be for me to hurt you?' he whispered.

She looked into his eyes and nodded numbly.

'Well, I *won't* hurt you. Or your kid. But you gotta do what I say. OK?'

She might have derived some level of comfort from the promise, even if she didn't believe it. But she suddenly realised who he was, and that sent a bolt of terror through her. Breathlessly, she rasped, 'You're . . . You're the man who shot all those people last night.'

'COBURN. C-O-B-U-R-N. First name Lee, no known middle initial.'

Sergeant Fred Hawkins of the Tambour Police Department removed his hat and wiped sweat off his forehead. It had already gone greasy in the heat, and it wasn't even nine o'clock yet. Mentally he cursed the heat index of coastal Louisiana. The older he got, the more he minded it.

He was in a cellphone conversation with the sheriff of neighbouring Terrebonne Parish. 'Chances are that's an alias, but it's on his employee records. We lifted prints off his car . . . Yeah, that's the damnedest thing. You'd think he would've sped away from the scene, but his car is still parked in the employee lot. Maybe he thought it would be spotted too easily. Or, I guess if you kill seven people in cold blood, you're not thinking logically. Best we can tell, he fled on foot. I put his prints in the national pipeline.'

While the sheriff was assuring Fred of his department's capacity for finding men at large, Fred nodded a greeting to his twin brother Doral who joined him where he was standing outside his patrol car. It was parked on the shoulder of the two-lane state highway.

'You heard right, Sheriff. Bloodiest crime scene I've ever had the misfortune of investigating. Full-scale execution. Sam Marset was shot in the back of the head at close range.'

The sheriff expressed his disgust, then signed off with a pledge to be in touch if the murderous psycho was spotted in his parish.

Doral extended a Styrofoam cup. 'You look like you could use coffee.'

Fred removed the lid and took a sip. His head jerked back in surprise.

Doral laughed. 'Thought you could use a little pick-me-up.'

'We ain't twins for nothing. Thanks.' As Fred drank the bourbon-laced coffee, he surveyed the line of patrol cars parked along the state highway. Dozens of uniformed officers from various agencies milled about at the edge of the woods, some talking on cellphones, others studying maps.

'As City Manager, I came out to offer any help that I or the City of Tambour can provide.'

'As lead investigator on the case, I appreciate the city's support,' Fred said drolly. 'Now, tell me where you think he ran to.'

'You're the cop, not me.'

'You're the best tracker for miles around. We gotta catch this son of a bitch, Doral. You ready?'

'If you're waiting on me, you're backing up.'

The two joined the search party. As its appointed organiser, Fred gave the command. Officers fanned out and began picking their way through the tall grass towards the tree line that demarcated the dense forest. Trainers unleashed their dogs. They were commencing the search here because a motorist who'd been changing a flat on the side of the road late last night had seen a man running into the woods. It wasn't much to go on, but they didn't have any other leads.

Doral studied the ground. 'Is Coburn familiar with this territory?'

'Don't know. Could be he's never even seen a swamp.'

'Let's hope.'

'His employee application said his residence before Tambour was Orange, Texas. But I checked the address and it's bogus.'

'He's been here thirteen months. Somebody has to know where he's from,' Doral said.

'A checker at Rouse's who'd rung up his groceries a few times said he was pleasant enough, but definitely not a friendly sort. Paid in cash. We ran his Social Security number. No credit cards, debts, bank account. Cashed his pay cheques. Everyone in the apartment complex knew him by sight. Men said they knew better than to mess with him. Women thought he was attractive.'

'Girlfriends?'

'None that anybody knew of,' said Fred.

'You search his apartment?'

'Thoroughly. The man lived like a monk. A TV, but no cable hookup. No computer. No notepad, calendar, address book. Zilch.'

'What about his phone?'

Fred had found a cellphone at the murder scene that didn't belong to any of the bullet-riddled bodies. 'Recent calls, one to that lousy Chinese food place that delivers in town, and one came in to him from a telemarketer.'

'Well, damn.' Doral swatted at a biting fly.

'Right now, we know nothing about Lee Coburn except that we're gonna catch hell if we don't find him.' Lowering his voice, Fred added, 'Best thing for us? We find him floating in a bayou.'

'Townsfolk wouldn't complain. Marset was highly thought of.'

Sam Marset, owner of the Royale Trucking Company, had been president of the Rotary Club, an elder at St Boniface Catholic Church and a Mason. He'd been a pillar of the community, admired and liked.

He was now a corpse with a bullet hole in his head. His murder had warranted a press conference covered by newspapers and New Orleans television stations. The NOPD had loaned Tambour police a sketch artist, and Fred had filled television screens with the drawing: Caucasian male around six feet three inches tall, average weight, black hair, blue eyes, thirty-four years old. Fred had warned that Coburn was armed and dangerous.

'You laid it on,' Doral said. 'He hasn't a prayer of escaping.'

Fred's cellphone rang. He glanced at caller ID and smiled. 'Tom VanAllen. FBI to the rescue.'

COBURN GRADUALLY backed away from the woman, but even then, her fear of him was palpable. Good. Fear would inspire cooperation.

'They're searching for you,' she said. 'Police, troopers, volunteers. Dogs. You should keep running.'

'You'd like that, wouldn't you, Mrs Gillette?'

Her expression became even more stark with fear, so the significance of his knowing her name hadn't escaped her. He hadn't randomly selected her house in which to take refuge.

'Mommy, the kitty went into the bushes and won't come out.'

Coburn's back was to the door, but he'd heard the little girl come in from outside, had heard her sandals slapping against the floor as she approached the kitchen. But his gaze remained on her mother.

Her face had turned as white as chalk. But he gave her credit for keeping her voice light. 'That's what kitties do, Em. They hide.'

'How come?'

'The kitty doesn't know you, so maybe he's afraid.'

'That's silly.'

Coburn slid the pistol into the waistband of his jeans and tugged his T-shirt over it, then turned round. The kid was staring at him with curiosity.

'Does your boo-boo hurt?' She pointed to his head.

Reaching up, he touched congealed blood. 'No, it doesn't hurt.'

He stepped round her as he crossed to the table. His mouth was watering from the aroma of freshly baked cake. He stripped away the paper case of a cupcake, ravenously crammed it into his mouth and reached for another.

He hadn't eaten since noon yesterday, and he'd been slogging through the swamp all night. He was starving.

'You're supposed to wash your hands before you eat,' the kid said.

'Oh yeah?' He peeled the paper off the second cupcake.

The kid nodded solemnly. 'It's the rule.'

He shot a look at the woman, who had moved up behind her daughter and placed protective hands on her shoulders. 'I don't always go by the rules,' he said. Keeping an eye on them, he went to the fridge and took out a bottle of milk. He thumbed off the cap and tilted the bottle towards his mouth, drinking from it in gulps.

'Mommy, he's drinking from—'

'I know, darling. But it's OK just this once. He's very thirsty.'

The kid watched in fascination as he drank at least a third of the milk. She wrinkled her nose. 'Your clothes are dirty and stinky.'

'I fell in the creek.'

Her eyes widened. Nervously, the mother turned her towards the living room. 'Why don't you go watch Dora while I talk to our company.'

The child dug her heels in. 'You said I could lick the bowl.'

The mother handed her the spatula from the bowl of frosting. She took it happily and said to him, 'Don't eat any more cupcakes. They're for the birthday party.' Then she skipped out of the room.

The woman said nothing until they heard the TV show come on. Then, 'How do you know my name?'

'You're Eddie Gillette's widow, right? What's your first name?'

'Honor.'

'Well, Honor, I don't have to introduce myself, do I?'

'They said your name is Lee Collier.'

'Coburn. Pleased to meet you. Sit down.' He indicated a chair at the kitchen table.

She hesitated, then slowly lowered herself into it.

He worked a cellphone out of the front pocket of his jeans and punched in a number, then sat down, staring at her. She defiantly held his gaze. She was scared but trying not to show it, which was OK by him. He'd rather deal with a little determination than bawling and begging.

When his call was answered by an automated voicemail recording, he said, 'You know who this is. All hell's broke loose.'

As soon as he clicked off, she said, 'You have an accomplice?'

'You could say.'

'Was he there during the . . . the shooting? They said seven people were killed.'

'That's how many I counted.'

She wet her lips. 'Why did you kill them?'

'What are they saying on TV?'

'That you were a disgruntled employee.'

He shrugged. 'You could call me disgruntled.'

'You didn't like the trucking company?'

'No. Especially the boss.'

'Sam Marset. But the others were just shift workers, like you. Was it necessary to shoot them, too?'

'Yes. They were witnesses.'

His candour seemed to astonish and repel her. For a time, she remained quiet. Then she asked, 'How'd you know my husband?'

'Actually I never had the pleasure. But I've heard about him. Around Royale Trucking, his name pops up a lot.'

'He was born and raised in Tambour. Everybody loved Eddie.'

'Among other things, he was a cop, right?'

'What do you mean by "among other things"?'

'Your husband, the late, great Eddie the cop, was in possession of something extremely valuable. I came here to get it.'

Before she could respond, her cellphone, still in his pocket, rang, startling them both. Coburn pulled it out. 'Who's Stanley?'

'My father-in-law. If I don't answer—'

'Forget it.' He waited until the ringing stopped, then nodded towards the cupcakes. 'Whose birthday is it?'

'Stan's. He's coming over for dinner to celebrate.'

'What time?'

'Five thirty.'

He glanced at the wall clock. That was almost eight hours from now. He hoped to have what he was after and be miles away by then. A lot depended on how much Eddie Gillette's widow knew about her late husband's extra-curricular activities. He could tell her fear of him was genuine. But her fear could be based on any number of reasons, one of them being that she wanted to protect what she had and was afraid of him taking it away from her. Or she could be innocent, afraid only of the danger he posed to her and her kid.

She looked innocent enough. The white T-shirt and blue jean shorts were as wholesome as home-baked cupcakes. Her blonde hair was in a loose pony-tail. Her eyes were hazel veering towards solid green. She had the scrubbed appearance of the classic all-American girl next door, except that Coburn had never lived next door to anybody who looked as good as she did.

She said, 'You're in a lot of trouble, and you're only wasting time here. Eddie didn't own anything valuable. You can see for yourself how simply we live. When Eddie died, I had to sell his fishing boat to make ends meet until I could return to teaching.'

'Teaching.'

'Second grade. His pension isn't much so I support us on my salary.' She paused. 'You've been misinformed, Mr Coburn. Eddie had nothing valuable, and neither do I. If I did, I would gladly hand it over. I value Emily's life more than anything I could ever own.'

He looked at her thoughtfully. 'Nicely put, but I'm not convinced.' He stood and hauled her up. 'Let's start in the bedroom.'

Chapter 2

His street name was Diego.

That's all he'd ever been called, and, as far as he knew, that was the only name he had. His earliest memory was of a skinny black woman asking him to fetch her cigarettes. He didn't know if she was his mother or not. The woman had operated a hair-braiding salon when she felt like it. If she needed quick cash, she sent Diego out to solicit clients off the streets. One day he found her dead on the floor, and after that, he'd fended for himself. He was seventeen years old and wise beyond his years.

His eyes showed it as he looked at the read-out on his vibrating cell-phone. *Private caller.* Which translated to The Bookkeeper. He answered with a surly, 'Yeah?'

'You sound upset, Diego.'

Pissed, more like it. 'You should have used me to take care of Marset. But you didn't. Now look at the mess you've got.'

'So you've heard about the warehouse and Lee Coburn?'

'I got a TV. Flat screen.'

'Thanks to me.'

Diego let that pass without comment. The Bookkeeper didn't need to know that their working relationship wasn't exclusive.

'Guns,' he said scornfully. 'They're noisy. Why shoot up the place? I would have taken out Marset silently, and you wouldn't have a circus going on down there in Tambour.'

'I needed to send a message.'

Don't mess with me, or else. Diego supposed that anyone who'd crossed The Bookkeeper was looking over his shoulder this morning. 'They haven't found Lee Coburn,' he said, almost as a gibe.

'I hope they find him dead. If not, he'll have to be taken out.'

'That's why you're calling me.'

'It will be tricky to get close to someone in police custody.'

'I specialise in tricky. I can get close. I always do.'

'Which is why you're the man for this job, should it become necessary. I want no loose ends. Be ready.'

No loose ends. No mercy. The Bookkeeper's mantra.

Diego slid his hand into his pocket and fondled the straight razor for which he was famous. 'I stay ready,' he said.

ENGROSSED IN HER TV programme, Emily didn't notice Honor and Coburn as they passed through the living room.

When they reached Honor's bedroom, she jerked her arm free from his grip. 'The manhandling is unnecessary.'

'That's for me to decide.' He nodded towards the computer on the writing desk. 'Boot it up.'

He just stood there, looking dangerous, until she went to the desk and sat down. She typed in her password. He reached over her shoulder and, manoeuvring the mouse, began navigating through her emails and documents.

Finally it was clear that the files were useless to him. 'Eddie's password?'

'We used the same one, and the same email address.'

'I didn't see any emails to or from him.'

'They've been deleted.'

'Why?'

'He's been gone for two years. Why would I keep them?' she snapped. She stood and moved away. 'I'm just going to check on Emily.'

'Stay where you are.'

His eyes made a sweep of the room and did a double take when a picture frame on top of the dresser grabbed his attention. He picked up the picture, then thrust it into her hands. 'Who are these guys?'

'The oldest one is Stan, Eddie's father. That's Eddie standing next to him.'

'The other two? Twins?'

'Fred and Doral Hawkins. Eddie's best friends. They'd gone on an overnight fishing trip. They posed on the pier with their catch and asked me to take this picture.'

'Is that the boat you sold?'

'No, that was Doral's charter boat. Hurricane Katrina took it. Now he's our city manager. Fred and Eddie enrolled in the police academy together. Fred is spearheading the manhunt for you.'

He absorbed that. 'They seem like a real chummy quartet.'

'The three boys were friends in school. Stan practically raised the twins along with Eddie. They've been a great help since he died.'

'How'd Eddie die?' he asked. 'What killed him?'

'Car accident.'

'What happened?'

'It's believed he swerved to miss hitting an animal or something. He lost control and went headlong into a tree.' She looked wistfully at her husband's face. 'He was on his way home from work.'

'Where's his stuff? You're bound to have kept his personal belongings.'

She met his cold eyes head-on. 'You're a cruel son of a bitch.'

His eyes were implacable. 'I need to see his stuff. Either you hand it over to me, or I'll tear your house apart looking for it.'

'Be my guest. But I'll be damned before I'll help you.'

'Oh, I doubt that.'

Her gaze swung towards the living room, where Emily was still enjoying one of her favourite shows.

'Your kid is all right so long as you don't play games with me.' He spoke softly, malevolently, and his point was made.

Furious with him, she said coolly, 'It would be helpful if you told me what you're looking for. Gold bars? Stock certificates? Precious stones? If I had something like that, don't you think I'd have liquidated it by now?'

'You wouldn't make it obvious. If you were suddenly flush with cash, people would be onto you.'

'People? What people? Onto me? I don't understand.'

'I think you do. Where's Eddie's stuff?'

She defied him with her glare. Telling him to go to hell was on the tip of her tongue. But then Emily giggled.

In her sweet, piping voice she addressed something to the characters on the programme, then clapped her hands in delight.

Honor's bravado evaporated. 'There's a box. Under the bed.'

It wasn't a long commute between Tom VanAllen's home and the FBI's field office in Lafayette. Often, he considered it not long enough. It was the only time of his day in which he could think of nothing more complicated than to drive within the speed limit.

He wheeled into his driveway and acknowledged that his house looked a little tired and sad compared to others in the neighbourhood. But when would he have time to do repairs or repaint?

Janice heard him come in and hurried to the door, cellphone in hand. 'I was just about to call you to ask if you'd be home for lunch.'

'I didn't come home to eat. That multiple murder in Tambour—'

'It's all over the news. The guy hasn't been caught yet?'

He shook his head. 'I've got to go down there myself.'

'Why must you? You dispatched agents early this morning.'

Royale Trucking Company conducted interstate trade. When the carnage was discovered inside the warehouse, Tom, as agent in charge of the field office, had been notified. 'It's politick for me to review the situation in person. How's Lanny today?'

'Like he is any other day.'

Tom pretended not to hear the bitterness in her voice as they headed to the room where their thirteen-year-old son was confined.

In fact, where he and Janice were confined. Sadly, this room was at the epicentre of their lives, their marriage, their future. An accident at birth had cut off their son's oxygen and left him with severe brain damage. He didn't speak, walk, or sit alone. His responses to stimuli were limited to blinking his eyes on occasion, and to making guttural sounds neither Tom nor Janice could interpret.

'He's soiled himself,' Tom said upon entering the room.

'I checked him five minutes ago,' Janice said defensively.

'I'll take care of this.'

'You're in a hurry to get away.'

'Five minutes won't matter. Will you fix me a sandwich, please? I'll eat it on the way down to Tambour.'

After seeing to Lanny, he went into their bedroom and changed out of his suit and into outdoor clothes. He had little to contribute to the manhunt, but he'd make the gesture.

When he walked into the kitchen, Janice was preoccupied with making his sandwich. He studied her without her being aware of it.

She hadn't retained the prettiness she'd had when they first met. The years since Lanny's birth had taken a toll. Her slender young body was gaunt now and worry had etched lines around her eyes.

Tom didn't blame her for these changes. The changes in him were just as disagreeable. Unhappiness and hopelessness were stamped on their faces. Worse, their love for each other had been drastically altered by the ongoing tragedy their life had become.

Every day Tom asked himself how long they could go on in their present state. Something must change. Tom knew it. He figured Janice did, too. But neither wanted to be the first to suggest doing what they had pledged never to do, which was to place Lanny in a special care facility. Tom was afraid she'd talk him out of it. And equally afraid she wouldn't.

Sensing his presence, she glanced over her shoulder. 'Do you plan to stay away overnight?'

'I can't leave you alone with Lanny for that long.'

'I would manage.'

Tom shook his head. 'I'll come back. Fred Hawkins will share all his case notes.'

'You mean the oracle of the Tambour Police Department?' She considered everyone in Tambour a hick, starting with Fred Dawkins and his twin, Doral.

'Everybody wants the head of Sam Marset's killer on a pike, and they're breathing down Fred's collar to get it,' Tom told her. He glanced at the clock on the microwave oven. 'Twelve hours into the investigation, and Fred doesn't have any substantial leads.'

Janice winced. 'The scene was described as a blood bath. What was the owner of the company doing in the warehouse at that time of night?'

'Fred thinks that maybe Coburn got into a fight with a co-worker, something serious enough for the foreman to call Marset.'

'Is Lee Coburn a habitual troublemaker?'

'His employment record didn't indicate that. But no one claims to know him well. His prints haven't turned up any prior arrests.'

Janice frowned. 'He's probably one of those wackos who slips through the cracks of society until he does something like this.'

Tom took a canned drink from the fridge. 'I'd better be off. I turned Lanny, so you don't have to do that for a while.'

'Don't worry about us, Tom. Go. Do your job. I'll handle things till you get home.'

He wished he could think of something to say that would brighten her day, wished there *was* something to say. But he knew there wasn't, so he trudged from his house, feeling the burden of their lives weighing heavily on his shoulders because he didn't know how to make it better. He felt no more confident about improving the situation in Tambour.

HONOR RETRIEVED the sealed rubber box from under her bed.

Coburn dumped the contents of the box onto her white comforter and began pawing through Eddie's personal effects. First were Eddie's diplomas from high school, LSU and the police academy. He removed the first from its leather folder and ripped the lining.

'There's no need to do that!' Honor protested.

'I think there is.' He reached for another, subjecting it to the same vandalism. Then, he examined Eddie's death certificate. 'Broken neck?'

'He died instantly. Or so I was told.'

After perusing the death certificate, Coburn thumbed through the guest book for the funeral service. It was breaking her heart to see items precious to her handled by a man with blood on his hands. She was especially incensed when he picked up Eddie's ring and memorised the wedding date and initials. He went through Eddie's wallet several times. He questioned her about each article arrayed on her comforter. It was an exercise in futility.

'Whatever you're looking for isn't here, Mr Coburn,' she said.

'It's here. And you can drop the mister. Just plain Coburn will do.' He looked around the room. 'Bank statements, tax records. Where's all that?'

She pointed overhead. 'In the attic. The access is in the hall.'

He dragged her along behind him, pulled down the trap door, then unfolded the ladder and motioned to her. 'Up you go.'

She climbed the ladder. The file storage boxes were right where she knew they would be. She picked up the first one. Coburn waited in the narrow opening to take it from her and carry it down. They repeated the procedure until all had been removed from the attic.

'This is pointless,' she said as she dusted her hands.

'Wait a minute. What about those?' He'd spied the boxes which Honor had hoped would escape his notice. 'What's in those?'

'Christmas decorations.'

'Ho-ho-ho. Hand them down.'

One by one, she handed the boxes down to him.

By the time she had descended the ladder, he was stripping the sealing tape off one of the boxes. When he pulled back the flaps, it wasn't tinsel that blossomed out, but a man's shirt.

He looked up at her, the obvious question in his eyes. 'He's been dead how long?'

She refused to explain to a criminal that Eddie's clothing brought back happy memories. Giving it away would be tantamount to letting go of the memories themselves. She was spared from having to discuss this with Coburn when Emily appeared.

'Dora's over and so's Barney, and I'm hungry. Can we have lunch?'

THE KID'S QUESTION reminded Coburn that he hadn't eaten anything in twenty-four hours except two cupcakes. He motioned the widow into the kitchen. She fixed the kid a peanut butter and jelly sandwich. He asked for one and watched her make it.

'You gotta wash your hands this time.' The kid placed a step stool in front of the sink. 'You can use my Elmo soap.'

She handed him a plastic bottle with a bug-eyed, red character grinning from the label. He and the kid washed their hands. She asked him, 'Do you have an Elmo?'

He took the towel from her. 'No, I don't have . . . an Elmo.'

'Who do you sleep with?'

Involuntarily, his gaze darted to Honor and made a connection that was almost audible, like the clack of two magnets. 'Nobody.'

'Does your mommy read you stories before you go to sleep?'

'Stories? No, my mom, she's . . . gone.'

'So's my daddy. He's in heaven. Are you scared of the dark?'

'Emily,' Honor interrupted. 'Come and have your lunch.'

They gathered round the table. The widow looked ready to jump out of her skin if he so much as said boo. Truth be told, he was as discomfited by this domestic scene as she was. Since being a kid, he'd never talked to one. It was weird, carrying on a conversation with such a little person. He scarfed the sandwich, then took an apple from the basket of fruit on the table. The kid dawdled over her food.

'Emily, you said you were hungry,' her mother admonished.

But he was a distraction. The kid never took her eyes off him. She studied everything he did. When he took the first crunching bite of the apple, she said, 'My grandpa can peel an apple from the top to the bottom without it breaking. Mommy can't. She doesn't have a magic knife like Grandpa's.'

'You don't say. What kind of magic knife does he have?'

'Big. He carries it in a belt round his ankle.'

Honor scraped back her chair. 'Time for your nap, Em.'

The child climbed down from her chair and headed out of the kitchen. Coburn left the remainder of the apple on his plate and followed them.

In the frilly pink bedroom, the kid got up onto the bed and laid her head on the pillow. She reached for a faded cotton quilt and tucked it beneath her chin, and then addressed Coburn. 'Would you hand me my Elmo, please?'

He followed her gaze and saw a red stuffed toy. He recognised the grinning face from the bottle of soap. He picked it up. The thing began to sing, startling him. He quickly handed it to her.

'Thank you.' She cradled it against her chest and sighed happily.

Honor bent down and kissed her forehead. As they left the bedroom, the toy was still singing a silly little song about friends.

He took Honor's cellphone from his pocket and handed it to her. 'Call your father-in-law with the big, magic knife. Tell him the party's off.'

Chapter 3

The Royale Trucking Company's warehouse was cordoned off with crime scene tape. The vicinity just outside the barrier was jammed with official vehicles and gawking onlookers. They were collected in groups, exchanging the latest rumours surrounding the mass murder and the man who had committed it.

Allegedly committed it, Stan Gillette reminded himself as he parked his car and got out. Before leaving his house, he'd run his hand over his closely cropped hair, adjusted his starched collar, checked the crease in his trouser legs, the shine on his shoes. He'd never resented the US Marine Corps' near-impossible standards. He cut an authoritative figure, which was why no one challenged him as he made his way up to the yellow tape.

Inside it and several yards away, Fred Hawkins was engrossed in conversation with a handful of other men, Doral among them. Stan caught Doral's eye, and he jogged over.

Doral lit a cigarette. Noticing Stan's frown of disapproval, he said, 'I know, but this situation . . . And I was two weeks into being a non-smoker.'

'I'm sixty-five today, and I ran five miles before dawn.'

'You run five miles before dawn every day,' said Doral.

'Unless there's a hurricane blowing.'

Doral rolled his eyes. 'And then you only run two and a half.'

It was an old joke between them. Doral angled his exhale away from Stan. 'I figured wild horses couldn't keep you away for long.'

'There's nothing like being in the thick of it.' He was watching Fred who was gesturing as he talked to the men around him.

Following the direction of Stan's gaze, Doral nodded at the tall, skinny man who was giving Fred his undivided attention. 'Tom VanAllen just got here. Fred's filling him in.'

'What's your take on him?'

'He's the best kind of feeb agent. Not too bright. Not too ambitious.'

Stan chuckled. 'So if this investigation goes south . . .'

'He catches the flack. That's the idea, anyway. Shift the heat off Fred and onto the Feds. 'Course we'll be keeping close watch.'

'Give me the behind-the-scenes details.'

Doral talked for several minutes, but didn't tell Stan much that he didn't already know. Stan asked, 'No eyewitnesses?'

'Nope.'

'Then how's it being laid on this Coburn?'

'Only seven employees clocked in last night. Count Sam, and that's eight. Coburn's the only one unaccounted for. At the very least he's a person of interest. He'd locked horns with the boss.'

'Fact or conjecture?'

Doral shrugged. 'Fact. Until somebody says otherwise.'

'What do you know about the man?'

'Well, we know he ain't caught yet,' Doral said with exasperation. 'Men and dogs have been all over that area where it's believed he ran into the woods. Lady around there says her rowboat's missing . . .'

'Why aren't you out searching? If anybody can find him—'

'Fred wanted to escort VanAllen out there, make sure he got seen on TV, establish that the Feds are on the case. As city manager I personally welcomed VanAllen into the fray.' Doral noticed his brother waving at them. 'That's my cue to come rescue him.'

Stan said, 'Tell Fred I'll join the volunteers later. Honor's cooking me a birthday dinner. I'll get there as soon as I can without disappointing Emily.'

'Give her a hug from Uncle Doral.'

COBURN FIGURED Honor Gillette would jump at the chance to speak to her father-in-law, but she put up an argument. 'He's not due here until five thirty. You'll be gone by then.'

He hoped so, too. But he didn't want the old man showing up early. He nodded at the phone in her hand. 'Convince him not to come.'

She used speed dial to place the call.

'Don't try anything cute,' Coburn warned. 'Put it on speaker.'

Honor did as he asked, so he heard Stan's crisp voice when he answered. 'Honor? I tried to call you earlier.'

'I'm sorry. I couldn't get to the phone.'

Immediately he asked, 'Is something wrong?'

'I'm afraid the party has to be postponed. Em and I both came down with a bug. A stomach virus. I'd heard that one was going around.'

'I'm on my way.'

'No, Stan,' she said quickly. 'There's no sense in your getting it, too.'

'I never catch these things.'

'Well, I'd feel awful if you did. Besides, we're fine.'

'I could bring you Gatorade, soda crackers.'

'I've got all that. And the worst is past. Em's been able to keep down some Sprite. She's napping. We're feeling a little wrung out, but I'm sure this is one of those things that runs its course in twenty-four hours. We'll have your party tomorrow evening.'

'I hate to postpone it. Emily's going to love her present.'

She smiled wanly. 'It's *your* birthday.'

'Which entitles me to spoil my granddaughter if I've a mind to.'

Background noise, which had been loud during their conversation, turned into a racket.

'What's all the noise? Where are you?' Honor asked.

'Just leaving Royale's warehouse. If you've been sick you might not have heard about what happened here last night.' He capsulised it. 'Fred's in charge of the posse. Doral briefed me.'

Her eyes on Coburn's, she said, 'This man sounds dangerous.'

'He should be scared silly. Regardless of the holiday, every badge in five parishes is on the lookout. They'll run him to ground soon enough, and he'll be lucky if they don't string him up in the nearest tree. Everybody wants to avenge Sam Marset.'

'Any fresh leads?'

'A woman's boat was stolen overnight. They're checking that out now. And the FBI is on board.'

Honor gave an appropriate murmur. Stan Gillette must have taken it to mean that she was weary.

'Rest while you can. If you need anything—'

'I'll call, I promise.'

They exchanged goodbyes and Stan Gillette clicked off. Coburn extended his hand and, with reluctance, Honor dropped her cellphone into it. He used his own phone to redial the number he'd called earlier. He got the same recorded message. 'What holiday is it?'

'Yesterday was the Fourth. Since it fell on Sunday—'

'Today's the national holiday. Hell. I didn't think of that. How long will the kid sleep?'

'An hour. Sometimes a little longer.'

'OK, into the bedroom.'

'Why? I thought you wanted to go through the files.'

'I will. After.'

Her expression went slack with fear. He nudged her towards the bedroom. Her heart was hammering as she entered.

'Sit on the bed.'

She turned to face him and defiantly asked, 'Why?'

He'd removed the pistol from the waistband of his jeans. He wasn't pointing it at her, but tapping his thigh with the barrel was threat enough.

She sat down.

He backed up through the doorway and into the hall. Keeping his eyes on her, he used his foot to push the opened box of clothing from the hallway into the bedroom.

'Pick out clothes I can wear. I don't want to defile some sacred garment.'

It took her a moment to comprehend that she wasn't about to be raped. But he wanted clothing. She knelt beside the box and rifled through the garments, choosing a worn pair of jeans and an LSU Tigers T-shirt.

'OK, bring the clothes with you into the bathroom.'

'Into the bathroom? What for?'

'A shower. I'm sick of my own stink.' He flicked the barrel of the pistol towards the bathroom.

Slowly she stood up and walked towards it. He motioned for her to sit on the lowered toilet lid, which she did, watching with dread as he closed the door and flipped the lock.

He opened the shower stall door and turned on the water, then set the pistol on a shelf well out of her reach and tugged off his cowboy boots. Socks came next. He tossed his T-shirt to the floor.

She stared at the tiled floor, but within her peripheral vision she could see a lean torso with a barbed-wire tattoo banding the left biceps.

She hoped he would forget the cellphones, but he set them beside the pistol. A wad of currency and a piece of folded paper also went onto the shelf. Without any compunction, he stepped out of his jeans and undershorts.

Honor had forgotten, or rather hadn't allowed herself to remember, the particular essence of a naked man. She was acutely aware of Coburn's nakedness as he stood inches from her emanating a primitive masculinity.

In her determination not to be cowed, she'd kept her eyes open, but now they seemed to shut of their own volition. After what seemed like an eternity, she sensed him stepping into the shower stall. He didn't close the door. When the spray of hot water hit him, he actually sighed with pleasure.

That was the instant she'd been waiting for. She shot to her feet, dumping the garments to the floor, and lunged for the shelf. Only to find it empty.

'I figured you would try.'

Angrily, she spun towards the stall. He was casually working the bar of soap into a lather in his hands, water sluicing over him. With a smug smile, he tipped his head towards the narrow window high in the shower wall. On the tiled ledge, safe and dry, were the pistol, the cellphone, the money and the folded piece of paper.

With a strangled cry of despair, she launched herself at the door and turned the lock. She even managed to yank the door open before a soapy hand slammed it shut. He placed his other hand at her hip, the heel of it pressing against the bone, his palm and fingers tightly fitting themselves to the curve of her belly. She froze with fear.

His breath was rapid and hot against her neck. He said, 'We had a deal. You cooperate, you don't get hurt.'

'I didn't trust you to keep to the agreement.'

'Then we're even, lady. You just lost all trust privileges.' He released her. 'Sit down and stay there, or so help me God . . .'

Her knees gave way just as she sat down heavily. He got back in the stall and although she didn't look, she sensed him washing and rinsing.

When they left the bathroom, she said, 'While we were in there, someone could have come searching. You'd have been trapped.'

'I know where they're searching. Thanks to your father-in-law.'

'Where you stole the boat?'

'It's miles from here. It'll take them a while to pick up my scent again.'

'ARE YOU *SURE*?' Mrs Arleeta Thibadoux squinted doubtfully. ''Cause they're crazy, mean kids, always into trouble.'

Tom VanAllen had yielded the floor to Fred Hawkins, letting the police officer interview the owner of the small boat that had gone missing in the area where Lee Coburn was thought to have last been seen. The trio of boys of questionable repute, who lived a quarter of a mile from Mrs Thibadoux, had been interrogated and dismissed as the suspected thieves. Last night, they'd been in New Orleans with friends.

'Their friends can vouch for their whereabouts,' Fred told her.

'Hmm. Well.' She sniffed. 'That boat weren't worth much, anyhow. It'll be worth more money now if that killer got away in it. If you find it, don't let nobody do nothing to it.'

'No, ma'am, we won't.' Fred tipped his hat to her and made his way past the bird dogs sprawled on her porch.

Tom waved at a swarm of gnats. 'You think Coburn took her boat?'

'We gotta assume it was Coburn,' Fred said.

'My office called while you were talking to her,' Tom said. 'The search of the trucks hasn't yielded anything.'

The first thing he'd done last night, after being alerted to the multiple murder, was to order that all the trucks in the Royale fleet be stopped along their routes and thoroughly searched.

'Didn't expect it to,' Fred said. 'If Coburn had an accomplice who whisked him away in a company truck, he could have been dropped anywhere.'

'I'm aware of that,' Tom said testily. 'But the drivers are being questioned all the same.'

Fred shrugged as though to say it was the federal government's time and manpower that was being wasted. 'He's still in the area.'

'What makes you so sure?'

'I can feel him like hairs on the back of my neck standing on end.'

Tom didn't argue. He could hear the search helicopter hovering not too far away. 'Chopper might spot the boat.'

'But probably won't. It's been up there going on two hours. Coburn's too smart to let himself be sighted that easily. It's not like that chopper can sneak up on him. Meanwhile we've got police boats trolling miles—'

A whistle drew their attention to the ramshackle dock fifty yards from Mrs Thibadoux's dwelling. Doral was waving his arms high above his head.

VanAllen and Fred jogged down the grassy bank of the bayou. 'What have you got, brother?' Fred asked.

'Partial footprint. Blood.' Doral pointed out blood spatters near a depression in the mud. 'Looks like the heel of a cowboy boot.'

Fred grinned. 'A lady in Royale's offices said she never saw Coburn in anything except cowboy boots.'

'What do you make of the blood?' Tom asked.

'It's a few drips, so he couldn't be hurt too bad.' Fred turned to an officer. 'Get the lab boys from the sheriff's office down here.'

Doral stared out over the sluggish water. 'I hate to throw a wet blanket over this, but if Coburn put into the bayou here—'

'We're screwed,' Fred said, catching his twin's meaning.

'What I was thinking,' Doral said unhappily.

Tom hated to show ignorance, but had to ask. 'What were you thinking?'

'Well,' Doral said, 'from here Coburn could've gone in any one of five directions.' He pointed out the tributaries that converged into the widest section of the bayou behind the Thibadoux property. 'All five channels branch off into others, and those into others. It's miles of waterways and swamp to cover.'

Fred's elation had rapidly dissipated. 'Damn. We should have had this son of a bitch in custody by now. He worked on the loading dock. How smart can he be?'

Tom said, 'It's like he chose this point on purpose, isn't it? Like he knew that these creeks came together at this spot.'

'How could he know that if he's not from around here?' Doral asked.

Tom's cellphone vibrated. 'My wife,' he told the two men.

'You'd better take it,' Fred said.

Tom didn't talk about his circumstances at home, but he was certain people talked about them behind his back. Lanny was never mentioned, but everybody knew about him. Tom turned his back and answered the call. 'Is everything OK?'

'Fine,' Janice replied. 'I'm just calling to check on you. How's it going?'

'We just got a breakthrough, actually.' He shared it with her.

'How long will you be?'

'I was about to head back. How's Lanny?'

'You always ask that.' She sighed. 'He's fine.'

'I'll see you in a while,' he said and disconnected.

Finding the footprint and blood had galvanised the flagging officers involved in the manhunt. Fresh search dogs had been sent for. Fred and Doral were reorganising responsibilities. Tom figured this would be a good time to slip away. He knew he wouldn't be missed.

DARKNESS WOULD IMPEDE the search for Coburn. Which made The Bookkeeper unhappy to see that the sun was going down.

Sam Marset's execution had required an entire week of planning, and The Bookkeeper had braced for its repercussions. A backlash was to be expected, even hoped for, because the louder the communal gasp over such a bloody deed, the stronger the impact was on those who had to be taught a lesson.

The Bookkeeper had set out to build an empire. Not one of industry or art, nor of finance or real estate, but of corruption. The business had flourished, but to succeed, one had to be ruthless. One left no loose ends, and extended no mercy to traitors. The last person to have learned The Bookkeeper's policy the hard way was Sam Marset. But Marset had been the township of Tambour's favourite son.

So, as darkness encroached, The Bookkeeper acknowledged that the ripples of killing him had taken on the proportions of a tidal wave. All because of Lee Coburn.

Who *must* be found. Silenced. Exterminated.

The Bookkeeper was confident of that happening. No matter how clever the man believed himself to be, he couldn't escape The Bookkeeper's net. If Coburn wasn't killed by his eager but clumsy pursuers, Diego would be called upon to eliminate the problem. Diego was excellent at stealth. He would find a way to get to Coburn in an unguarded moment. He would apply his razor deftly and feel the hot gush of Coburn's blood on his hands.

The Bookkeeper envied him that.

BY SUNDOWN, Honor's house looked like storm damage.

Emily had woken from her nap on schedule. A juice box, a packet of raisins, and unlimited TV had kept her pacified. But even her favourite Disney DVDs didn't altogether distract her from their visitor.

She tried to maintain a running dialogue with Coburn, pestering him with questions until Honor shushed her, afraid her chatter would irritate him. While he was tearing through every book on the living-room shelves, she told Emily he was on a treasure hunt. Emily looked doubtful, but returned to her movie without argument.

The afternoon wore on, the longest of Honor's life. As Coburn upended furniture to search the undersides, she clung to a single ray of hope: he hadn't killed them immediately. She supposed they'd been spared because he thought she could be useful to his search. But if he became convinced that she knew nothing, what then?

Dusk claimed the last of the sunlight, and Honor's hope went with it.

Coburn switched on a table lamp and surveyed the havoc he'd wreaked. His eyes were bloodshot, making the blue irises look almost feral. He was a man whose frustration had reached a breaking point.

'Come here.'

Keeping her expression impassive, Honor approached him.

'Next I'll start tearing into the walls and ceilings, pulling up floors. Is that what you want?'

'That would take a lot of time. Now that it's dark, you should leave.'

'Not till I get what I came for.'

Before she could address that, Emily was standing beside her, clutching Elmo. 'Mommy, when is Grandpa coming?'

Honor rubbed her hand along the child's back. 'Grandpa's not coming tonight after all, sweetheart. We're going to have the party tomorrow.

Which will be even better,' she said quickly in order to prevent the protest she saw forming on Emily's lips. 'Because, silly me, I forgot to get party hats. We can't have Grandpa's party without hats. And, Grandpa told me he has a surprise present for you.'

'What is it?'

'I don't know. If he'd told me, it wouldn't be a surprise, would it?'

Emily's eyes were shining. 'Can I still have pizza for supper?'

'Sure. Plus a cupcake.'

'Yeah!' Emily raced towards the kitchen.

Honor turned to face Coburn. 'Her dinner is past due.'

'Make it quick.'

Which wouldn't be a problem, because by the time they entered the kitchen, Emily had already taken her small pizza from the freezer. Honor cooked it in the microwave and set it in front of her.

Coburn asked, 'You got any more of those?'

She heated him a pizza and he ate as greedily as he had at lunch.

'What are you eating, Mommy?'

'I'm not hungry.'

Arching an eyebrow, Coburn went to the freezer and helped himself to another pizza. He was jumpy, his nerves rubbed raw by exhaustion. The set of his shoulders was evidence of weariness. Honor caught him several times blinking rapidly as though trying to stave off sleep. To make a move, she needed only one second when his guard was down.

The problem was, she was exhausted too. Terror and rage had left her totally depleted. Emily's bedtime came as a relief.

Honor changed her into pyjamas. While she was using the bathroom, Honor said to Coburn, 'She can sleep in my bed. If she's with me, you can watch both of us at the same time.'

He gave one firm negative shake of his head. 'She can sleep in her bed.' She wouldn't leave the house without Emily, and he knew that. Separating them ensured that she wouldn't try to escape.

While Honor read a bedtime story, Coburn searched Emily's closet, pushing aside the hangers and tapping the floor and back wall.

He squeezed every stuffed toy in Emily's menagerie, which caused her to giggle. 'Don't forget to hug Elmo,' she said, and trustingly handed the toy up to him.

He turned it over and ripped open the Velcro on the back seam.

LETHAL | 325

'No!' Honor cried.

He shot her a look filled with suspicion.

'That's just access to the battery,' Honor said, knowing that Emily would be traumatised to see Elmo disembowelled. 'Please.'

He examined the inside of the toy, but eventually closed it up and returned it to Emily.

Honor listened to Emily's bedtime prayer, kissed her cheeks, and hugged her extra close. But eventually she had to let go. She eased Emily back onto her pillow and forced herself to leave and shut the door. Coburn was lurking in the hallway. She looked up into the unfeeling mask of his face. 'If you . . . do something to me, please don't let her see. No purpose would be served by harming her.'

A cellphone rang.

Determining that it was hers, he took it from his pocket, glanced at the read out, and passed it to her. 'Same as before. Put it on speaker. Find out what you can about the hunt for me.'

She answered with, 'Hi, Stan.'

'How are you feeling? Emily OK?'

'You know kids. They bounce back quicker than adults.'

'The party still on for tomorrow night, then?'

'Of course. Any news about the fugitive?'

'He's still out there, but it's going on twenty-four hours. He's either already dead or weakened to the point of being easy prey.' He told her about the place at which Coburn had launched the stolen boat. 'Dozens of boats are searching the waterways and will be through the night. The whole area's crawling with lawmen.'

He said good night and signed off. As Coburn took the phone from her, Honor heard the throaty growl of a small motor, getting closer. She spun away from Coburn and bolted towards the living room.

But he was on her before she got halfway across the room. One arm closed around her waist as his other hand clamped hard over her mouth. 'Don't go stupid on me,' he said. 'Get out there before they reach the porch. Talk loud enough for me to hear. If I sense that you're trying to send them a signal, I won't hesitate to act. Think about me standing over your daughter's bed.'

The boat's motor was idling. She saw lights through the trees.

'You got it?'

She nodded.

Gradually he released her and withdrew his hand from her mouth. She turned round to face him. She gasped, 'I beg you, don't hurt her.'

'It's up to you.' He prodded her with the pistol. 'Go.'

Her legs were shaking. She opened the door, stepped out onto the porch, and went down the steps.

Two sheriff's deputies came up from the dock, sweeping her property with the beams of their flashlights. They produced identification, rattled off a physical description of Coburn, and asked if she'd seen him. She told them she hadn't seen anyone.

They walked away and in seconds were out of sight. She went up the steps and re-entered the house. Coburn stood in the hallway.

She closed the door and pressed her forehead against the smooth wood. 'Good girl,' he said. 'Emily's safe and sound.'

His smug inflection was the final straw. The emotions that had been building all day reached a boiling point. Without thinking, she spun round and glared at him. 'I'm sick of your threats. I don't know why you came here or what you want, but I won't go along any more.' Reaching behind her, she pulled open the door. 'Get out of my house!'

He reached out to close the door. Seizing the opportunity, Honor jerked the pistol from the waistband of his jeans. He gave her wrist bone a hard chop. She cried out in pain as the pistol fell and slid across the floor.

Both of them went for it at once. He kicked it out of her reach. She scrambled after it. All she needed was to get hold of it long enough to pull the trigger once. The deputies would hear the shot.

She touched the metal, but instead of getting a grip, her fingers nudged the pistol farther away. Coburn was crawling over her, trying to get hold of the gun before she did. Her hand closed around the barrel. But he pinned her wrist to the floor with fingers that seemed made of steel. 'Let it go.'

'Go to hell.'

She yanked on her hand hard, wrenching it free of his grip. He cursed profusely as she drew the pistol under her, clutching it tightly. Honor lay as flat as possible, but he worked his hands beneath her to prise the weapon from her. She was gasping for air by the time he yanked it out. Moaning in defeat, she went limp and wept.

He flipped her over and straddled her. His face was contorted with fury. And she thought, *This is it. This is the moment I die.*

But to her astonishment, he tossed the pistol aside, placed both hands on her shoulders and leaned down on her heavily. 'What the fuck . . .? It could have discharged and blown a hole right through you. Stupid, idiotic thing to do, lady. Don't you know what . . .' Seemingly at a loss for words, he gave her shoulders a hard shake. 'Why'd you do that?'

Why was he asking such a dumb question? 'Just tell me—and please make it the truth—are you going to kill us?'

'No.' His eyes bored into hers. '*No.*'

She wanted desperately to believe him. 'Then why should I pay any attention to your threats? Why do anything you say?'

'Because you have a vested interest.'

'Me? I don't even know what you're looking for! Whatever it is, this *thing* you're after—'

'Is the *thing* that got your husband killed.'

IT WAS WELL PAST the dinner hour when Tom returned home. He found Janice in Lanny's room giving him his sponge bath before changing him into pyjamas. 'Honey, why didn't you wait for me?'

'I wanted to get him settled for the night so I could put my feet up.'

'Sit down. I'll finish.' He kissed his son's forehead. 'Hi, Lanny.'

Lanny's eyes remained fixed. Filled with a familiar despair, Tom dipped the sponge in the bowl of warm water.

'How's the crisis in Tambour?' Janice asked.

'The suspect is still at large. I think he'd be a fool to hang around here. It seems to me that he'd hitch a ride with a truck-driving pal and get as far away from southern Louisiana as possible.'

'Is there such a person as a truck-driving pal?'

'None identified as yet.' He smiled. 'Fred Hawkins thinks Coburn is still in the area. He feels him like standing hairs on the back of his neck.'

'What's next?' she scoffed. 'Reading chicken innards? Is Fred Hawkins up to the task?'

Tom washed Lanny's legs. 'He's certainly motivated. Mrs Marset made a personal call to the superintendent of police and put the squeeze on him, which he passed along through the ranks. Fred's starting to feel the heat.'

'I'll go fix dinner. Omelettes OK?'

Ten minutes later they sat down to their omelettes, exchanging brief snippets of forced conversation. Tom remembered times past when they couldn't say enough to each other about the events of the day.

When he finished his meal, he carried his plate to the sink and ran water over it, then turned to his wife. 'Janice, let's talk.'

She set her fork on the rim of her plate. 'About what?'

'Lanny. It may be time to readjust our thinking about his care.'

There, he'd said it. Lightning didn't strike him. Janice just stared up at him with an expression as closed as a storm shutter.

He pressed on. 'I think we should revisit the possibility—just the possibility—of placing him in a facility.'

She looked away. 'We made promises to him, and to each other, Tom.'

'We did,' he said sombrely. 'But we nursed a kernel of hope that he'd develop to some extent. I don't think that's going to happen.' Saying it out loud caused his voice to crack with emotion.

'All the more reason why he needs the best of care.'

'That's just it. I'm not sure we're providing it. Your patience and endurance amaze me. Truly. But caring for him is killing you. We're eroding as human beings. And how do we know that we're doing what's best for him? There are specialists for patients like Lanny.'

She stood up and wandered the kitchen as though looking for a means of escape. 'Even if we agreed that it would be best, we can't afford the private facilities. As for some modern-day Bedlam operated by the state, forget it. I'd never put him in a place like that.'

'We owe it to ourselves, and to him, to visit some of the better places. Would you be open to doing that if finances weren't a consideration?'

'But they are. Are you planning on winning the lottery?'

He'd said enough for one night. He'd known that broaching this subject would make him out to be the bad guy, but one of them had to be, and it wasn't going to be Janice.

She'd been valedictorian of her high-school class, an honour-graduate from Vanderbilt, a rising star in an investments firm. Then fate cruelly intervened. She'd had to sacrifice everything for Lanny, which made admitting defeat untenable to her.

He sighed. 'I'd better get to bed and sleep while I can. The agents I left in Tambour know to call me with any developments.' He paused at the door. 'You look done in, too. Coming soon?'

'Not yet. I'm tired but not sleepy. I'll stay up for a while.'

'Playing your word game with your cellphone friend in Japan?'

'Singapore.'

He smiled. Playing the games was her one form of recreation, and it had become almost an addiction. 'I hope you win.'

'I'm leading, but I've got a letter j that's challenging me.'

'You'll come up with a word,' he said. 'Don't stay up too late.'

Two hours later, Tom was still alone in bed. He got up and padded down the hall. Janice was in the den, staring into the screen of her cellphone, totally engrossed in a pastime apparently much more enjoyable than sleeping with him. He turned away and retraced his steps to their bedroom.

COBURN GRADUALLY WITHDREW his hands from Honor's shoulders. She lay perfectly still on the floor, and for one panicked moment, he wondered if she'd been injured during their struggle.

He wondered why he cared. 'Are you all right?'

She nodded.

He turned away and looked at the mess he'd made of her house. And he had nothing to show for his ransacking. Dead end.

Which more or less summarised the life and times of Lee Coburn, who would leave the world with seven murders as his only legacy. He swore beneath his breath. He was tired. No, more than tired. Weary. Weary of loading and unloading those damn trucks. Weary of the sad, one-room apartment that he'd been living in for the past thirteen months. Weary of life in general. 'Get up.'

She pushed herself into a sitting position. 'What did you mean?'

Her voice was breathless and shaky, but he knew what she was referring to. Instead of addressing the question, he propelled her towards the hallway and into her bedroom. He whipped back the comforter. 'I gotta lie down, which means you gotta lie down.'

She stood where she was, looking at him. 'What you said about Eddie . . . What did you mean?'

'What did I say? I don't remember.'

'You said that the thing you're after got him killed.'

'I never said that. You must've heard me wrong.'

'I didn't hear you wrong! Eddie's death was an accident.'

'If you say so.' He bent down to pick up a pair of black stockings that were in a heap of clothes he'd tipped onto the floor.

'Please,' she said. 'If his death wasn't an accident, as you imply, I'd like to know why he died and who was responsible.'

Her eyes were shades of green that were constantly changing. He'd seen them spark with anger. Now they glistened with unshed tears.

He hesitated, then shook his head.

'You think someone caused the crash and made it look like an accident?' He didn't say anything.

'He was killed because of something he had.'

'That someone else wanted.'

'Something valuable?' she said.

'The people who wanted it thought so.'

'Like cash?'

'Possibly. But I don't think so. More like the combination to a lock. Account number in a bank. Something like that.'

She shook her head with perplexity. 'Eddie wouldn't have had anything like that. Unless he was holding it for evidence.'

'Or . . .'

His insinuation sank in and she recoiled from it. 'Eddie wasn't party to any criminal activity. He was as honest as the day is long.'

'Maybe. But he got caught up with the wrong person.'

'Who?'

'The Bookkeeper.'

'Who?'

'Did Eddie know Sam Marset?'

'Yes, of course. Before we got married, Eddie moonlighted as a security guard at Mr Marset's company for several months.'

'How well did you know him?'

'Sam Marset? Only casually. He was an elder at our church.'

'Church elder,' he snorted. 'He was an unscrupulous son of a bitch.'

'Who deserved to be shot in the head.'

He raised one shoulder. 'Quick and painless.'

The statement and his matter-of-fact tone seemed to repel her. She tried to back away from him. He reached for her hand and began wrapping the black stockings around her wrists and the iron headboard.

Weariness swept over him. 'I've got to sleep,' he said. 'And you've got to lie beside me.'

For a long moment he looked at her. Her mouth, her breasts.

'I'll leave you alone,' he said gruffly. 'But I've got to tie your hands together. If you try to get away, there'll be all hell to pay.'

Chapter 4

When Honor woke up at dawn, she was alone in the bed and her hands were untied. She hadn't expected to fall asleep and was amazed that she had.

She vaulted off the bed and raced to Emily's room. Emily was sleeping peacefully, her plump hand clutching Elmo.

Honor rushed through the living room and into the kitchen beyond. The rooms were empty, dim and silent. Her keys were missing from the hook and when she looked through the window, she saw that her car wasn't parked out front. Coburn was gone.

'Thank God,' she whispered. Relief made her weak.

But only for a moment. She must alert the authorities. They could pick up his trail. They—

The surge of thought was rudely interrupted by a new realisation. How would she notify anyone? Without a phone, car or boat—

Boat. That's what had woken her!

She ran to her front door, unbolted it, and practically leapt down the steps, then scrambled down the slope to the dock.

'Honor!' Fred Hawkins steered from beneath the leafy cover of a willow.

'Fred! Thank God!'

He goosed the motor and reached the dock within seconds. Honor was so glad to see him, she almost missed the rope he tossed her. She knelt down and wound it around a metal cleat.

Fred had barely got his footing on the dock when Honor flung herself against him. His arms went around her. 'Honor, what's wrong?'

She gave his large torso a squeeze, then let him go and stepped back. 'He's been here. Coburn.'

'Son of a—Are you OK? Emily?'

'We're fine. Fine. He . . . he didn't hurt us, but he—' She gulped air. 'He took my car. My phone. I thought I heard a boat. I—'

'You're sure it was Coburn who stole—'

'Yes, yes.' She nodded. 'He showed up yesterday. He was here all night. I woke up just a few minutes ago. He was gone.'

Fred placed a hand on her shoulder. 'All right, slow down. Catch your breath and tell me everything that happened.'

In stops and starts, she described the day-long ordeal.

'I was so afraid, Fred. You have no idea. He knew who I was. He knew who Eddie was. He came here for a reason. He . . . he . . .'

'OK. You're all right now.' He muttered words of concern sprinkled with profanities. 'I've got to call this in. Let's go inside.'

Honor leaned against him as they made their way up the slope. With the arrival of help, the courage it had taken to protect herself and Emily abandoned her. She was trembling.

'He ransacked the house,' she said as they approached the porch. 'He said Eddie died with something valuable in his possession.'

'Not the Eddie I knew. What was he looking for? Money?'

'No. I don't know. *He* didn't know. But he insisted that I had something that Eddie had died protecting.'

'Eddie died in a car wreck.'

Stepping up onto the porch, she looked at him and shrugged. 'That didn't sway Coburn.'

Fred drew up short when they entered the living room and he saw the damage Coburn had done. 'Criminy. You weren't kidding.' He took a cellphone off his belt. 'I gotta let the others know.'

'I'm going to check on Emily.'

She tiptoed down the hall. Emily was still asleep.

As she re-entered the living room, Fred was where she'd left him, holding his cellphone to his ear. 'We don't know how much of a head start he's got or which direction he's moving in. But he's in her car. Hold on.' He covered the mouthpiece. 'What's your tag number?'

She recited it to him, and he repeated it into the phone, then described the make and model of her car.

'Put out an APB. Tell the superintendent that I need every officer available.' After clicking off, he smiled at her with regret. 'Cops are gonna be swarming this house inside and out. It's gonna get even more torn up.'

'It doesn't matter, so long as you catch him.'

He replaced his phone in his belt holster. 'We will. He couldn't be far.'

No sooner had he said the words than the front door burst open and Coburn barged in. He was holding the pistol, and the muzzle was aimed at the back of Fred's skull. 'Don't move!' he yelled.

Then, a bright red starburst exploded out of the centre of Fred Hawkins's forehead. Honor clamped her hands over her mouth and watched in horrified astonishment as Fred's body fell to the floor.

Coburn stepped over it and strode towards her.

On an adrenaline surge, she spun round and bolted down the hallway. He grabbed her arm and she swung her other fist at his head.

Cursing liberally, he caught her, pinned her arms, and backed her into the wall. 'Listen! Listen to me!' he said.

She fought like a wildcat to get free, but when her limbs proved useless, she tried to bang her forehead against his. He jerked back in the nick of time. 'I'm a federal agent!'

She went perfectly still and gaped at him.

'Hawkins—that's his name? He was the shooter at the warehouse. Him and his twin. Got it? He was the bad guy, not me.'

Honor stared at him with incredulity. 'Fred is a police officer.'

'Not any more.'

'He was—'

'A murderer. I watched him shoot Marset in the head.'

'I watched you shoot Fred!'

'I had no choice. He already had his gun in his hand to—'

'He didn't even know you were here!'

'—to kill *you*.'

She sucked in a breath and exhaled. 'That's impossible.'

'I saw him headed this way. I doubled back. If I hadn't, you'd be dead, and so would your kid. I'd be accused of two more murders.'

'Why would . . . why would . . . ?'

'Later. I'll tell you all of it. Right now, just believe me, OK?'

'I don't believe you. You can't be a cop.'

'Not a cop. FBI.'

She gazed into his hard, cold eyes. 'Show me your ID.'

'Undercover. Deep cover. No ID. You have to take my word for it.'

'You spent the last twenty-four hours terrifying me.'

'I had to be convincing. Think about it. If I was a killer on the run, you'd have been dead this time yesterday. Your little girl too.'

Tears of confusion and fear blurred her vision. 'I don't understand what I have to do with any of this.'

'Not you. Your late husband.' He let go of her with one hand and dug into the front pocket of his jeans, producing the folded sheet of paper she'd noticed the day before. 'He was somehow linked to that killing in the warehouse. This might help convince you.' He shook out the paper. 'Your husband's name, circled and underlined and with a question mark beside it.'

'Where did you get it?'

'Marset's office. I sneaked in there one night. Found this entry in an old day planner. Check the date.'

'Two days before Eddie died,' she murmured. She looked at Coburn with bewilderment, then tried to snatch the paper from him.

'Uh-uh.' He stuffed it back into his pocket. 'I might need that for evidence. Right now, we gotta get you out of here.'

'But the police are on their way. Fred told them you were here.'

He released her suddenly, then in seconds was back, a cellphone in each hand. 'His official phone,' he said, holding it up for her to see. 'Last call, an hour ago.' He tossed it to the floor. 'This phone. His burner.' His thumb worked the keypad. 'Last number called three minutes ago. Not the police.' He depressed the redial icon and Doral answered, 'Everything OK?'

Coburn disconnected. 'So now he knows everything's not OK.' The phone began ringing. Coburn turned it off and crammed it in his pocket. 'Get the kid.'

'I can't just—'

'You want you and your little girl to die?'

She recoiled. 'If what you say is true, why don't you arrest Doral?'

'I can't blow my cover yet. And I can't turn you over to the police because the whole damn department is dirty.'

'The Hawkins twins were my husband's best friends. Stan practically raised them. They have no reason to kill me.'

His chest was rapidly rising and falling with agitation. 'Did you tell Fred I came here looking for something?'

She hesitated before giving one bob of her head.

'That's why Fred would have killed you. The Bookkeeper would have ordered it.'

'You mentioned this bookkeeper last night. Who is it?'

'I wish I knew. But there's no time to explain that now. You just gotta believe that since Fred can no longer kill you, Doral will.'

Still she hesitated. 'That can't be true. He wouldn't hurt me.'

'The hell he wouldn't. If Doral thinks you've got information, he'd hurt you plenty, you or your kid. And then, whether you'd told him anything useful or not, he'd kill you.'

'You're telling me you're the good guy, and I'm supposed to believe it?' Her voice had gone raw and ragged. 'I know these men. I trust them. But I don't know *you*!'

He stared at her for several beats, then put his hand round the front of her neck to hold her head still. He moved his face close to hers and whispered, 'You know me. You know I'm who I say.'

Her pulse beat rapidly against his strong fingers, but it was his piercing gaze that held her pinned to the wall behind her.

'Because if I wasn't, I would have taken advantage of you last night.' He dropped his hand. 'Are you coming or not?'

DORAL HAWKINS HURLED an armchair against the wall. Then he clasped a handful of his thinning hair and pulled hard as though wanting to rip it from his scalp. He was in a state. Part agonising anguish, part sheer animal rage.

His twin lay dead on the floor of Honor's house with a bullet hole through his head. It had to be Coburn, that son of a bitch.

During their last phone conversation, Fred had told him that their quarry had torn up Honor's house and taken her car. 'She said he was after something that Eddie had died protecting.'

After a short pause, Doral had asked, 'What are you gonna do?'

'Go after him.'

'I mean about Honor.'

Fred's sigh had come loudly through the cell connection. 'The Bookkeeper didn't leave me a choice. When I called in that I was going to check out Eddie's place . . . Well, you know.'

Yes, Doral knew. The Bookkeeper took no prisoners, and it wouldn't matter if it was a family friend, or a woman and child.

They'd ended their call with the understanding that Fred would take care of the problem, so that by the time Doral joined him at the Gillette place, they could report to the sheriff's office the horrifying double murder of Honor and Emily. They'd chalk up the homicides to Coburn. It had been a good plan, now shot to hell.

Doral spent a critical ten minutes in rage and grief. But, his fit having subsided, he wiped the tears from his face and forced himself to evaluate the present situation. Which sucked. Big time.

Most troubling was that Fred's body was the only one in evidence. There was no sign of Honor and Emily. If his brother had dispatched them, he'd hidden their bodies very well.

Or Coburn had popped Fred before he'd had a chance to dispatch Honor and her daughter. If that was the case, where were they *now*? Hiding? Possibly. But that meant that as soon as he found them, he'd have to kill them.

There was also a third possibility, and it was the worst-case scenario: Coburn and Honor had escaped together. Doral gnawed on that. It portended all kinds of trouble, but he didn't know what to do about it. He'd let The Bookkeeper figure it out.

Like the Godfather in the movie, The Bookkeeper insisted on hearing bad news right away. Doral placed the call and it was answered on the first ring. 'Have you found Coburn?'

'Fred's been killed.'

He waited for a reaction, but didn't really expect one and didn't get it. He passed along everything that Fred had told him before he was shot. 'I got one more call from his cell, but when I answered, it was cut off. When I dial his number now, I get nothing. The phone's missing, there's no sign of Honor and Emily, and Fred's pistol is gone. And . . . the house is torn up all to hell. Honor told Fred that Coburn came here looking for something he thought Eddie had squirrelled away.'

The silence that followed was deafening. Doral tried to keep his gaze from wandering to his brother's corpse.

'Did Coburn find what he was looking for?'

This was the question Doral had most dreaded. 'Who's to say?'

'*You're* to say, Doral. Find them. Learn what they know, then dispatch them. There's no room for another mistake. Not when we're on the brink of opening up a whole new market.'

For months, The Bookkeeper had been obsessed with sealing a deal with a new cartel out of Mexico that needed protection as they trafficked goods across Louisiana. Drugs one way, guns the other. They were big players, willing to pay substantial sums. But it wasn't going to happen unless reliability was guaranteed. Killing Sam Marset was supposed to have been a swift resolution to a problem. But the mass murder had opened up a hornets' nest and they were now in damage-control mode.

Doral and Fred had had a patsy in place to frame for the warehouse murders. But the dock worker who'd escaped the blood bath, this Lee Coburn, had made himself an even better suspect. They'd counted on finding him within an hour of the killings, hunkered down somewhere, shaking in his boots. Later, they planned to attest that he'd been fatally shot while trying to escape arresting officer Fred Hawkins.

But Coburn had proved to be smarter than expected. He'd eluded Fred and him. And even when being tracked by armed men and bloodhounds, he'd run to Honor's house and spent a lot of valuable time searching it. You didn't have to be a rocket scientist . . .

'You know, I've been thinking.'

'I don't pay you to think, Doral.'

The insult stung, but he pressed on. 'This guy Coburn worked his way into Sam Marset's confidence. I'm beginning to think he's no ordinary loading-dock worker. He seems—what's the word? *Overqualified.* Not your average trucking company employee.'

After another weighty silence, The Bookkeeper said bitingly, 'Did you figure that out all by yourself, Doral?'

SINCE HONOR'S HOUSE was outside city limits, the sheriff's office had jurisdiction. The deputy, who was that department's singular homicide investigator, was a man named Crawford. Doral had failed to catch his first name.

Doral was retelling how he'd come to find the body of his brother, when Crawford looked beyond his shoulder and muttered, 'Dammit, who's that? Who let him in here?'

Doral turned. 'That's Stan Gillette, Honor's father-in-law.'

Stan made a beeline towards Doral. 'It's true? Honor and Emily have been kidnapped?' he barked. 'What are you doing here? Why aren't you out looking for them?'

'I will be, soon as Deputy Crawford frees me to go.' Doral made a cursory introduction. 'He's investigating—'

'With all due respect to your investigation,' Stan said, interrupting Doral and addressing the deputy, 'it can wait. Fred is dead and nothing can bring him back. Meanwhile two innocent people are missing, most likely kidnapped by a ruthless murderer.'

Crawford was several inches shorter than Stan and Doral, and physically unimposing, but he stood his ground. 'Mr Gillette, talking down to me and issuing orders won't get you anywhere except escorted off the premises, and if you resist, you'll be arrested.'

Doral could tell that Stan was about to blow a gasket. 'Cut him some slack, Crawford. Let me have a word with him. OK?'

The deputy shifted his gaze from one man to the other, then said, 'Coupla minutes while I'm talking to the coroner,' and moved away. But suddenly he came back around. 'Who notified you? How'd you get here so fast?'

Stan rocked forward and back on the balls of his feet. Finally he said, 'Yesterday Honor told me that she and Emily were sick. This morning, I was worried about them and decided to drive out.'

Crawford sized him up again, then turned away to consult the coroner.

Doral nudged Stan's arm. 'Back here.'

They moved down the hallway and into Honor's bedroom.

'Stan,' Doral said, needing to get this out before Deputy Crawford reappeared. 'Crawford noticed something and commented on it.'

'What?'

Doral indicated the bed. 'Looks like two people slept there last night. I'm not making anything of it,' he added hastily. 'I'm just telling you that Crawford remarked on it.'

'Suggesting what?' Stan asked. 'That my daughter-in-law slept with a man wanted for seven murders?'

'Is there a chance, Stan, the smallest chance, that she, you know, had met this guy before he showed up here yesterday?'

'No. If Honor is with Lee Coburn,' Stan said, his voice vibrating with anger, 'she was taken against her will.'

'Well, there's something else you should be aware of, Stan. Before you got here, Crawford was asking a lot of questions about Eddie.'

Stan was taken aback, instantly wary. 'What kind of questions?'

'Leading questions. He noticed that Eddie's clothes were strewn all over the place. Old files had been rifled through. The photo of the four of us, taken after the fishing trip? It had been removed from the frame. Crawford bagged the whole kit and caboodle as evidence. He said it looked like Coburn was after something that had belonged to Eddie.'

'Did you challenge him about it?'

Doral shook his head. 'Just thought you should know.'

'This isn't my car,' said Honor.

Coburn took his eyes off the rearview mirror to glance over at her. 'I ditched yours a few miles from your house where I picked up this one.'

'It's stolen?'

'No, I knocked on the door and asked if I could borrow it.'

She ignored the sarcasm. 'The owners will report it.'

'I switched the plates with another car.'

'You did all this between leaving my house and coming back to head off Fred?'

'I work fast.'

She absorbed all that. 'You said you saw Fred in a boat.'

'The road follows the bayou. I was driving without headlights. I saw the light on his boat, pulled off the road to check it out. Saw him and recognised him instantly. Figured what he would do if you repeated to him anything of what I'd told you. Went back. Lucky for you I did.'

She still didn't look convinced, and he couldn't say he blamed her. Yesterday she'd been icing cupcakes for a birthday party. Since then he'd threatened her at gunpoint, manhandled her, and wrecked her house. Now he was supposed to be the good guy.

She was nervously running her hands up and down her thighs, now clothed in jeans instead of yesterday's shorts. Occasionally she would glance at the little girl, who was in the back seat playing with that red thing. It and the ratty quilt she called her 'bankie', along with Honor's handbag, were all he'd allowed them to bring.

In a whisper, Honor asked, 'Do you think she saw?'

'No.'

On their race through the house, Honor had created a game requiring Emily to keep her eyes shut until they were outside. Coburn had carried her from her room to the car. He'd kept his hand on the back of her head, her face pressed into his neck, just in case she cheated and opened her eyes, in which case she would have seen Fred Hawkins's body on the living-room floor.

'Why didn't you tell me yesterday that you were an FBI agent?'

'I didn't trust you.'

She looked at him with a bewilderment that seemed genuine.

'You're Gillette's widow,' he explained. 'Reason enough for me to harbour doubts about you. Then when I saw that photo, saw him and his dad being chummy with the two guys I'd seen kill those seven in the warehouse, what was I supposed to think? In any case, I was and am convinced that whatever Eddie had, you have now.'

'But I don't.'

'Maybe. Or maybe you do have it and just don't know that you do. Anyway, I no longer think you're holding out on me. Even if you'd been crooked, I think you'd have given me anything I wanted if I didn't hurt your little girl.'

'You're right.'

'I came to that conclusion just before dawn and figured I'd leave you in peace. Then I saw Hawkins on his way to your house.'

'Am I truly to believe that Fred killed Sam Marset?'

'I witnessed it.' He glanced at her; her expression invited him to elaborate. 'There was a meeting scheduled for Sunday midnight at the warehouse between Marset and The Bookkeeper.'

She rubbed her forehead. 'What are you talking about?'

He took a breath. 'Interstate 10 cuts through Louisiana, north of Tambour. It's the southernmost coast-to-coast interstate, and its proximity to Mexico and the Gulf make it a pipeline for drug dealers and gunrunners.'

She nodded. 'OK.'

'Any vehicle you pass on it—everything from a semi-trailer, to a pick-up, to a family van—might be transporting street drugs, pharmaceuticals, weapons.' He looked over at her. 'You still following me?'

'Sam Marset owned Royale Trucking Company.'

'You get a gold star.'

'You're actually saying that Sam Marset's drivers were dabbling in this illegal transport?'

'Not his drivers. Sam Marset, your church elder. And not dabbling. He's big time. *Was*.'

She thought that over. 'Where do you factor in?'

'I was assigned to get inside Marset's operation, find out who he did business with. It took me months just to gain the foreman's trust. Then, only after Marset gave his approval, I was entrusted with the manifests. His company ships a lot of legal goods, but I also saw plenty of contraband. I just didn't have enough proof to catch the big fish.'

'Like Marset.'

'Him and bigger. But the real prize would be The Bookkeeper.'

'Who is that?'

'Good question. The bureau didn't even know about him until I got down here and realised that somebody is greasing the palms. The Bookkeeper is a facilitator. He goes to the people who're supposed to be preventing all this illegal trafficking, then bribes them. Police, state troopers, agents at the state weigh stations, the man guarding impounded vehicles. The Bookkeeper pays them off, then takes a hefty commission from the smuggler for guaranteeing his cargo safe passage.'

She ruminated on that. 'But you didn't learn his identity.'

'No. I'm missing a key element.' He gave her a hard look.

'Which you came to my house in search of.'

'Right. The Department of Justice isn't going to make a case until it knows it can't lose in court. We might make a deal with someone to testify against The Bookkeeper in exchange for clemency, but we also need phone records, cancelled cheques, deposit slips, names, dates. Hard evidence. I think that's what your late husband had.'

'You think Eddie was involved in this?' she asked. 'Drugs? Guns? You are so wrong, Mr Coburn.'

'Truth is, I don't know what side of the business your husband was working. But he was blood brothers with the twins, and in my book that makes him damn suspicious. And being a cop would be an asset.'

'Eddie was an *honest* cop.'

'You'd think that, wouldn't you? You're his widow. But I saw his bosom buddies mow down seven people in cold blood. I would have been victim number eight if I hadn't got away.'

'How did you manage that?'

'I was expecting something to happen. The meeting was supposed to be peaceful, no weapons. But I was on high alert because The Bookkeeper is reputed to be a ruthless son of a bitch.'

'Do you think this Bookkeeper is a public official?'

'Could be. I was hoping to learn his identity on Sunday night,' he said. 'Something big is brewing. I think The Bookkeeper is courting a new client. Scary people with a zero tolerance for screw-ups.'

'I refuse to believe that Eddie was involved in anything relating to this. I can't believe it of Sam Marset, either.'

'Marset was in it strictly for the money. He wasn't violent. And that was one grievance he held against The Bookkeeper. He demanded that they sit down together, hash out their differences.'

'But The Bookkeeper pulled a double-cross.'

'To put it mildly. Instead of The Bookkeeper, it was the Hawkins twins who showed up. Before Marset could even voice his outrage over the switcheroo, Fred popped him. Doral opened fire on the others with an automatic rifle. I slipped behind some crates, but when the others were down, they came after me. I made it out to an abandoned building, hid in the crawl space, then hightailed it to the river.' He looked over at her. 'You more or less know the rest.'

'So what now? Where are we going?'

'I have no idea. I didn't plan that far ahead. Actually I didn't count on living through that first night.' He glanced into the back seat. 'I sure didn't count on having a woman and kid in tow.'

'Well, I'm sorry for the inconvenience we've imposed,' Honor said. 'You can drop us at Stan's house and go about your business.'

He gave a short laugh. 'Don't you get it? If Doral Hawkins or The Bookkeeper think you know something that could help convict them, your life's not worth spit.'

'I *do* understand. Stan will protect us until—'

'Stan, the man in the photo with your late husband and the Hawkins twins? *That* Stan?'

'Stan would protect Emily and me with his dying breath.'

'Maybe. I don't know yet. Until I do, you contact nobody.'

'But we can't just keep driving around in a stolen car. What are you going to do with us?'

'I'm about to find out.'

He checked the clock in the car's dashboard and saw that it would be past nine on the east coast. He took the next turn off the main road. The blacktop soon gave way to gravel and gravel to rutted dirt, and the road finally came to a dead end at a stagnant creek.

He had three phones. Fred's he would keep. They couldn't use Honor's because the authorities could locate it using triangulation. Which left Coburn's burner, the disposable he'd never used until yesterday. He turned it on, saw that he was getting a signal, and punched in a number with the hope that today his call would be answered.

He was about to disconnect and try again when a woman said, 'Deputy Director Hamilton's office. How can I direct your call?'

'Put Hamilton on.'

'Whom may I say is calling?'

'Coburn. Lee Coburn.'

'That's impossible. Agent Coburn died more than a year ago.'

Chapter 5

Diego's cellphone vibrated, but just to be ornery, he waited several seconds before answering it. 'Who's this?'

'Who were you expecting?' The Bookkeeper asked snidely.

'So is the guy caught yet, or what?'

'No. He got Fred Hawkins.'

Diego was surprised by that, but withheld comment.

'Now everyone is really up in arms. If Coburn survives his *arrest*, I want you to be ready to move.'

'I've been ready.'

'I also may need you to take care of a woman and child.'

'That'll cost you extra.'

'I'm prepared for that. I'll be in touch.'

The call ended without another word.

Diego slipped the cellphone into the holster on his belt, and pushed his hands deep into the pockets of his jeans. The fingers of his right hand closed securely around his razor.

'Tori, you might want to look at this.'

Her receptionist knew better than to interrupt her when she was with a client, especially one as overweight as Mrs Perkins. She gave Amber a withering look, then said to her client, 'Six more of those, please.' Groaning, the woman went into a deep squat.

Tori turned to her receptionist and said, 'Well. What?'

Amber pointed to the flat-screen TVs in front of the treadmills. On one, a New Orleans station was broadcasting late-breaking news.

Tori watched for a few seconds. 'You interrupted me to watch an update on the Royale Trucking Company shootings? Unless the fugitive is presently in the women's sauna without a towel, why is this my problem?'

'It's your friend,' Amber said. 'They think she's been kidnapped.'

Tori looked quickly at Amber, then back at the screen. That's when she recognised Honor's house behind the reporter. Astonished, she turned up the volume and listened with mounting incredulity and anxiety.

'Police and FBI agents are on the scene, conducting a thorough investigation. No ransom demand has been received at this time. The body of police
officer Fred Hawkins was found in the—'

'Oh my God,' Tori gasped, slapping her hand to her chest.

'No information has been forthcoming except that it looked like an
execution-style killing. Police have asked citizens to be on the lookout for
the suspect and his supposed hostages.' The photograph that Honor had
sent with last year's Christmas card filled the screen.

Tori muted the sound and said to Amber, 'Take over with Mrs Perkins.
She's got fifteen more minutes of cardio. Call Pam and tell her to cover my
spin class. Don't call me unless there's an emergency.'

'Where are you going?'

Tori didn't bother answering. She was in her office for no longer than it
took to grab her cellphone and handbag. Then she left the health club, got
in her Corvette, and roared from the parking lot.

As she drove, she punched in Honor's cellphone number. It went to
voicemail. She scrolled her contact list and called Stan Gillette. Same
thing. Reaching the driveway of her condo, she brought the Vette to a
screeching halt and went inside.

'What the—' She spun round.

Leering at her from behind her door was Doral Hawkins.

'You scared the hell out of me, Doral!'

'That was the plan.'

'You always were a jerk. What are you doing here?'

'I called your club. The bimbo who answered the phone told me you'd
just left. I was only a coupla blocks away.'

'You couldn't have waited for me outside like a normal person?'

'I could have.'

She rolled her eyes. 'You know about Fred, right?'

'I found his body.'

'Oh. That's awful.'

'I have some questions to put to Honor.'

'Honor?'

'*Honor?*' he mimicked. Dropping the amicable pose, he advanced on her,
took her face between his hands, and mashed her features together until
they were distorted. 'You'd better tell me where she is.'

Tori didn't frighten easily, but she wasn't a fool. She was well acquainted with Doral's reputation. Since losing his charter boat to Hurricane Katrina, he had no visible means of support beyond the small stipend the city paid him. Yet he lived very well. She suspected that he was participating in something illegal; he and Fred had been committing petty crimes by high school. And the pair had a propensity for meanness. Doral looked mean now, and dangerous, and he was hurting her.

She shoved her knee into his crotch.

He yelped, and hopped backwards out of harm's way.

'Don't touch me again, Doral. What makes you think I know where Honor is?'

'I'm not screwing around, Tori.' He pulled a handgun from a holster at the small of his back.

'Oh, no, a gun!' she said in a high falsetto. 'Is this where I'm supposed to faint? Put that thing away before you hurt somebody.'

'I want to know where Honor is.'

'Well join the club! Everybody wants to know. It appears she's been taken hostage by a killer. I heard about it on TV and came straight here from the club.'

'What for? You expect to hear from her.' He made it sound like an accusation. 'Has she talked to you recently about Eddie? Did she share a secret about him?'

'No! What are you talking about? What kind of secret?'

He studied her for a moment, then muttered, 'Never mind.'

'No, not never mind. The same guy who shot your brother took Honor and Emily. Why aren't you out looking for them?'

'I'm not sure he *took* them.'

That stunned her. 'What do you mean?'

'You and Honor are close. If she knew this guy—'

'Where would she have met a freight worker turned mass murderer? What are you getting at? That the kidnapping is some kind of hoax?'

'I'm not getting at anything. But if you hear from your pal Honor, you'd do well to let me know. Or I'll hurt you, Tori. I'll hurt you bad.'

'SON OF A BITCH!'

Coburn hissed the profanity under his breath out of deference to the kid. Her mother was now staring at him.

He waggled the cellphone. 'I guess you heard that.'

'That Lee Coburn has been dead for over a year? Yes, I heard.'

'Obviously she hasn't got her facts straight.'

Honor frowned. 'Or I bought into your lies and now I'm—'

'Look, you want to go back to your house, take your chances with Doral Hawkins and anybody else who's in The Bookkeeper's pocket? Fine.'

It wasn't fine, of course, and he wouldn't let her go even if she chose to. He'd been described as cold and heartless, but even he would be uncomfortable sending a woman and a four-year-old to certain death. Besides, she probably knew a whole lot more than she was aware of. Until he'd wrung every last ounce of information from her, she stayed. 'Whether you know it or not, you hold the key that will bust open The Bookkeeper's crime ring.'

'For the umpteenth time—'

'You've got it. We just have to figure out what it is and where to find it.'

'Then drive to the nearest FBI office. We'll all look for it together.'

'I can't blow my cover. Hawkins and The Bookkeeper think that I'm just the freight dock worker who got away. An eyewitness to the murder. Which is bad. But if they discover I'm an undercover federal agent, the target on my back gets bigger.'

'But the FBI would protect you.'

'Like Fred Hawkins of the Tambour PD was going to protect you?'

'The Bookkeeper has local FBI agents on his payroll?'

'I'm not willing to bet my life against it, are you? You wouldn't be sitting there if you didn't believe at least some of what I've told you.'

'I'm sitting here because I believe that if you'd intended to hurt us, you would have done so as soon as you arrived yesterday. Also, if everything you've told me is true, then our lives, mine and Emily's, are in danger.'

'You're right so far.'

'But the main reason I came with you has to do with Eddie. You've raised two questions I want answered. One, was his death really an accident?'

'It was made to look like it, but I don't think it was.'

'If someone did cause the crash, I want them punished for it.'

'Fair enough. What's the second question?'

'Was Eddie a bad cop or a good cop? I know the answer to that one. I want you convinced of it, too.'

'I don't care one way or the other. All I care about is identifying The Bookkeeper and putting him out of business. The rest of it, including your dead husband's reputation, makes no difference to me.'

'Well it makes a difference to me. And it will to Stan.' She gestured to the phone still in his hand. 'I should tell him we're OK. He'll be beside himself.'

He shook his head. 'No. I don't trust him. I don't trust anyone.'

'You dragged me along. You trust me.'

He looked at her askance. 'What gave you that idea?'

'Mommy?'

Honor dragged her vexed gaze off him. 'What, sweetheart?'

'Is Coburn mad?'

Honor lied through her teeth. 'No, he's not mad.'

'He looks mad.'

Coburn did his earnest best not to look angry. 'I'm not mad.'

The kid didn't buy it, but she switched subjects. 'Can I ride in front? I don't have my car seat.'

'No, you can't.' Honor shot a condemning glance at Coburn for abandoning the seat along with her car. 'We'll break the rule just this once.'

'Do you know of someplace we can go?' Coburn asked her. 'We've gotta stay out of sight until I get through to Hamilton.'

She nodded thoughtfully. 'I know where we can go.'

TOM VANALLEN WAS WOKEN early that morning with the startling news that Fred Hawkins was dead and that Honor Gillette and her child were missing. Both the murder and the kidnapping were attributed to Lee Coburn.

He shared this with Janice, telling her about Doral's finding the body.

'That's horrible. They were so close.' After a moment she asked, 'What were they doing at Honor Gillette's house?'

'Fred went to check on her. According to Doral, when Fred arrived he found that the house had been tossed. Coburn apparently came up behind him. Anyway, I need to go, see it for myself.'

He hated having to leave before helping her with the arduous morning routine of getting Lanny cleaned, dressed and tube-fed. Janice, however, told him not to worry. 'This is a crisis situation. You're needed.' As she saw him off, she kissed his cheek.

He found the Gillette place just as Deputy Sheriff Crawford was leaving. They introduced themselves and Crawford brought him up to speed. 'Our CSU's got their hands full with this one. Your agents have come and gone. They're meeting me back in town, where we'll organise a task force. Tambour PD has offered us space for a command centre.'

'What does Doral Hawkins make of the mess in the house?'

'Same thing I do. Coburn was searching for something. Nobody seems to know what.'

The investigator took his leave, but gave Tom permission to walk through the house. He was in and out in minutes, and then drove back to Lafayette.

No sooner had he sat down at his desk than the office line rang. He depressed the blinking intercom button. 'Yes?'

'Deputy Director Hamilton is calling from Washington.'

Tom swallowed and depressed the other blinking button. 'VanAllen.'

'Tom, you've got a dung heap of trouble down there. Fill me in.'

Tom talked for five minutes without interruption. When he finished, Hamilton remained quiet.

Finally Hamilton spoke. 'This Coburn, was he an agent working under-cover for you to investigate Sam Marset's trucking interests?'

'I never heard of him until I went to the crime scene at the warehouse and Fred Hawkins told me the name of the suspect.'

'Sam Marset would have been in a perfect position to engage in illegal interstate trafficking. Has any such connection been drawn?'

'Not so far. I've assigned agents to track down anyone we can place in and around that warehouse in the last thirty days, but so far no illegal contraband has been discovered.'

'What motive did the suspect have for the killings?'

'We're trying to ascertain that, sir. But Coburn's lifestyle is making it difficult. Nobody knew him well. People—'

'Give it a shot, Tom. Take a guess. Why'd he kill them?'

'He was a disgruntled employee.'

'A disgruntled employee.' Hamilton said it without enthusiasm. 'Then why'd he go to the house of a dead cop and turn it upside-down? Why'd he take the widow and child?'

Tom had worked in the Lafayette office with Hamilton briefly, and when the man was bumped up to Washington, he'd recommended Tom as his successor. Tom felt pride in succeeding such a revered agent. He also panicked that he wouldn't live up to his standards. 'I've asked those questions myself, sir. They're unsettling.'

'To say the least. They imply that this was no ordinary shoot 'em up by some nutcase. Which means that you've got your work cut out. Find them.'

'Yes, sir.'

FOLLOWING THE DIRECTIONS Honor gave him, Coburn drove the stolen car down the dirt lane. He rolled to a stop and stared in dismay at the derelict shrimp boat, then turned and looked pointedly at Honor.

Defensively she asked, 'Do you have a better idea?'

'Yeah, we don't launch it. Who does it belong to?'

'To me. I inherited it when my dad died.'

'He shrimped in that thing?'

'He lived on it.'

The boat sat half in, half out of a sluggish channel that Honor claimed eventually fed into the Gulf. Vines had overtaken the hull. Windowpanes that weren't missing were so coated with grime they barely resembled glass. 'Who knows it's here?' he asked.

'No one. Dad brought it here to ride out Hurricane Katrina, then kept it here through Hurricane Rita. After that, he got sick and went downhill fast. I moved him into a hospice. He was there less than a week when he died.'

'Your mother?'

'Died years before. That's when dad sold the house, moved onto the boat.'

'Does your father-in-law know it's here?'

She shook her head. 'Stan didn't exactly approve of my dad's way of life, which was rather . . . bohemian. Stan discouraged visits with him. He especially didn't like Emily being exposed to him.'

'The more I hear about your father-in-law, the less I like him.'

'He's probably thinking the same of you. Stan means well.'

Coburn got out and opened the door to the back seat. Emily had already unbuckled her seat belt and was holding her arms up to him. He lifted her out, then passed her to Honor.

Emily turned to him. 'Coburn? Are we still on a 'venture?'

'I guess you could call it that.'

'Can we be on it for a long time?' she chirped. 'It's fun.'

Yeah, this is a blast, he thought as he went to the boat. The sides of the hull were shallow. He stepped aboard easily. Forest detritus was evidence that the deck hadn't been disturbed for some time.

Satisfied that they were alone, he cleared a spot for Emily when Honor passed her to him. He set her down on the deck.

He extended his hand to Honor, and helped her up. Once aboard, she surveyed the littered deck. Coburn noticed a sadness in her expression before she shook it off and said briskly, 'This way.'

She took Emily's hand and led them to the wheelhouse. The interior was in no better condition than the deck. The control panel was covered with a littered tarp that had collected small lakes of scummy rainwater. A tree branch had broken through a window. Honor pointed to a narrow passage with steps leading down.

Coburn descended carefully, ducking through an opening into a low-ceilinged cabin. It smelt of mildew, dead fish and motor oil and had a propane stove that was ghosted over with cobwebs. The door of the small refrigerator stood open.

'Electricity?' Coburn asked.

'There's a generator. I don't know if it still works.'

Doubtful, Coburn thought. There were two bunks separated by an aisle. He pointed to a door at the back of the cabin. 'The head?'

'I don't recommend it. I didn't even when Dad lived here.'

In fact, there was nothing to recommend the boat except that it seemed watertight. The floor was a mess, but it was dry.

He went to one of the bunks and peeled back the bare mattress, checking for varmints. Finding none, he held his hands out for Emily. Honor handed her over. He deposited her on the mattress.

She wrinkled her nose. 'It smells bad.'

'Tough,' Coburn said. 'Sit there and don't get down.'

Emily looked at him blankly. She held her bankie close and turned on Elmo, who broke into cheerful song.

'Coburn, we've got to get food and water at least,' Honor whispered.

'By we you mean me.'

She had the grace to look chagrined. 'I did, yes. I'm sorry. I haven't been here since I buried Dad. I didn't realise . . .' She looked at him with helplessness. 'Please let me call Stan.'

Rather than go through that tired routine, Coburn opened a narrow closet and found a broom, which he handed to her. 'Do your best. I'll be back as soon as I can.'

'COBURN!' EMILY CRIED, launching herself across the deck and wrapping her arms around his knees. 'Mommy said you were bringing me some lunch.'

Honor's heart was in her throat. He was standing on the deck, but she hadn't heard a sound to signal his approach. He was wearing a baseball cap and sunglasses. His boots and his jeans from mid-calf down were wet.

'I came along the creek bank,' he said. He fished a Tootsie Pop from the pocket of his jeans and handed it to her. She ripped off the wrapper.

'Thank you, Coburn. I love grape. Grape's my favourite.' Emily stuck the lollipop into her mouth.

'Why come by the creek? Where's the car?' Honor said.

'I left it back a piece. Someone could have found you. I didn't want to drive into a trap.' He stepped off the boat and began walking towards the road. In a few minutes, he returned, driving an old black pick-up truck. He handed her several bags from the bed, and hid the truck. By the time he came aboard, she'd made peanut butter sandwiches. She and Emily sat on one bunk, he on the other.

'Is this a picnic?' Emily asked.

'Sort of,' Honor said.

The bags Coburn had carried in contained foods that didn't require refrigeration. He'd also brought bottled water, a battery-operated lantern and hand sanitiser.

Once she'd been fed, Emily yawned. She protested when Honor suggested that she lie down and rest, but she was soon asleep.

'Were you able to reach your man? Hamilton?' she asked.

'I tried. Same woman insisted I was dead.' He shrugged and bit into a cookie. 'Hamilton doesn't want to talk to me yet.'

'You're not worried?'

'I don't panic unless I have to. Wastes energy.'

'Did you check the numbers in Fred's cellphone?'

'There were none, which is what I expected. And only one call in his log, that last one to his brother. The phone was a throw down.'

'A burner,' she said, remembering the term he'd used before.

'No records. Disposable. Virtually untraceable. If I ever get it to the techies, they can see if there's any intel to be had.'

Forty-eight hours ago, she wouldn't have imagined herself having a conversation about intel and burners. Nor would she have imagined a man like Coburn. She didn't know what to make of him, and it was disturbing that she wanted to make anything of him at all.

Changing the subject, she asked? 'Where'd you get the truck?'

'I got lucky. I spotted a rural mailbox with lots of mail in it, a dead giveaway that the residents are away. House sits way back off the road. The truck keys were on a peg inside the back door.'

'I assume you switched the licence plates.'

'SOP. Standard Operating Procedure. Remember that if you decide to pursue a life of crime.'

'I don't think I'm cut out for living on the edge.'

He gave her a slow once-over. 'You may surprise yourself.' His gaze reconnected with hers, hot and intense.

Uncomfortably, she looked away. 'Did you steal the groceries?'

'Bought. The cap and sunglasses were in the truck.' Coburn checked his wristwatch. 'I'll try Hamilton again.'

He dialled, and Honor heard a man answer. 'Hamilton.'

'You son of a bitch. Why are you messing with me?'

He replied blandly, 'A man in my position can't be too careful, Coburn. If the caller ID says Blocked, I don't answer.'

'I identified myself.'

'After I heard the news, I would have known it was you anyway. Mass murder. Kidnapping. You've outdone yourself, Coburn.'

'Like I need you to tell me that. If I wasn't in trouble, I wouldn't be calling.'

'Is speculation correct? Do you have the woman?'

'And her kid. They're fine. We've been picnicking. You want to talk to her yourself?' He passed the phone to Honor.

Her hands were trembling as she raised it to her ear. 'Hello?'

'Mrs Gillette? My name is Clint Hamilton. Please don't underestimate the importance of what I'm about to tell you. You, Mrs Gillette, are in the company of a dangerous man.'

Chapter 6

Tori had slammed her front door hard behind Doral, flipped the deadbolt. But even after he'd left, his threat echoed. She wasn't as afraid for herself, however, as she was for Honor.

Tori was accustomed to taking care of herself. But she wasn't above asking for help if she deemed it necessary. She placed a call.

'Tori, sweetheart. I was just thinking about you.'

His voice immediately soothed her raw nerves. 'What were you thinking?' she asked.

'I was just daydreaming.' He gave a chuckle. He was thirty pounds overweight and had imbibed oceans of bourbon over the course of his fifty-eight years. But he could afford to drink the best.

His name was Bonnell Wallace, and he had more money than God. His beloved wife of thirty years had died a year ago, and Bonnell had cut back to five drinks a day, and joined Tori's health club.

'Will you do something for me, Bonnell?'

'You name it, sugar.'

'A friend of mine is in danger. I may need some money.'

'How much?'

Just like that. No questions asked. Her heart swelled with affection. 'Don't agree so fast. I'm talking like a million or more.' Tori wondered what the going rate was for a ransom.

'I'm good for it. Tell me what's going on.'

'Have you heard about the woman and child who were kidnapped this morning?'

He had. Tori filled him in. 'I don't know what to do, but with your help, I can at least have cash on standby if her father-in-law gets a ransom call.'

'You just let me know what you need and it's yours.'

In a voice choked with emotion, she said, 'Have I told you what a sweetheart you are? How important you are to me?'

'You mean it?'

'I do,' she said, speaking with an honesty that surprised her.

'Well, that's good. Because I feel the same.'

They disconnected reluctantly.

Clutching the phone to her chest, her smile lingered. But when her doorbell rang, she dropped her phone, bolted to the door and flung it open.

On her threshold stood Stan Gillette. Tori didn't like Honor's father-in-law, and the dislike was returned. The only thing they had in common was their love for Honor and Emily, and only that love could have brought Stan to her doorstep.

Her heart practically stopped. 'Oh God. They're dead?'

'No. At least I hope not. May I come in?' he asked.

Weak with relief, she stood aside. He marched—the only word to describe his tread—across her threshold.

'How did you hear?'

'I saw it on the news.'

'You haven't heard from Honor?'

'Why does everyone keep asking me that?' said Tori.

His eyes narrowed on her. 'Who else asked you that?'

'Doral. He was here when I got home from the club.'

He paced around her living room, looking ill at ease.

'Something is bothering you. What?' she asked.

He turned to her. 'It may be nothing. But, have you ever tucked Emily in for the night?'

'As recently as two weeks ago. Honor had me out for burgers and we put Emily down, then killed a bottle of wine,' she said.

'Emily always sleeps with two things.'

'Her bankie and Elmo,' said Tori.

'They weren't in her bed this morning. They weren't anywhere.'

Tori processed this. 'A kidnapper who let Em take her bedtime pals along? Hmm.' She thought back to Doral's insinuation that the supposed kidnapping might not have been that at all.

Stan said, 'Victoria, if Honor has confided to you—'

'That she's involved with a man named Lee Coburn? Is that what you're waltzing around, Stan? The answer is no. If she knew this man at all, I swear to you that I'm unaware of it.'

He received her answer with characteristic stoicism.

Tori folded her arms. 'Just so you know, I've made arrangements to have a large sum of cash available if you get a ransom demand. Nobody has to know it came from me.'

'Thank you,' he said. 'I'll let you know.'

HONOR'S EYES REMAINED FIXED on Coburn as the man on the phone repeated how dangerous he was. When she didn't respond, Hamilton prompted her. 'Mrs Gillette?'

'Yes,' she said hoarsely. 'I'm listening.'

'Coburn is lethal. He's been trained to be. But the fact that he abducted you instead of killing you—'

'He didn't abduct me, Mr Hamilton. I came voluntarily.'

Several seconds ticked by before Hamilton said anything. Then he politely asked if Coburn was treating Emily and her well.

She thought of the threats and the strong-arming, and the battle over the pistol, but she also remembered his snatching up Emily's bankie and Elmo as they fled the house. She also thought of him risking capture to buy them food and water. 'We're all right.'

'I'm glad to hear it. Put Coburn back on.'

She passed him the phone. He told Hamilton everything that had transpired and ended by saying, 'I had no choice but to get her and the kid out of there. They'd be dead if I hadn't.'

Hamilton expelled a deep breath. 'OK. Except for the warehouse killer's identity, and the misconception that Mrs Gillette was kidnapped, that matches everything VanAllen told me.'

'Who's VanAllen?'

'My successor down there.'

'You talked to this VanAllen before taking my call?'

'I wanted to get his perspective. I wanted it unfiltered. I even asked him if you were an agent from his office working undercover.'

'Gee, you're a stitch.'

'I needed to know what he knew or suspected.'

'I'm kinda interested in that myself.'

'As far as local law enforcement is concerned, you're a friendless dock worker who went mad and shot up the place. That's good. Now that I've talked to you, I'll admit to VanAllen that I tricked him in order to get his unbiased assessment, and then I'll enlist him to help bring you and Mrs Gillette in. Once you, she and the child are safe, we'll figure out how to go in and mop up.'

Coburn frowned. 'Negative. I don't want to come in yet.'

'Don't worry about your cover. The official word will be that you died of a self-inflicted gunshot wound during a stand-off with federal agents. You'll be reassigned to another part of the country.'

'Sounds swell. Except that I haven't finished the job here.'

'You've done well, Coburn,' Hamilton said. 'You've fingered some key people in The Bookkeeper's organisation. I'm satisfied.'

'I'm not. Something big is about to happen. I want to put him out of commission before it does.'

'Something big, like what?'

'A new client. A Mexican cartel would be my guess. I think that's why Sam Marset was bumped. He was whining over a couple of his trucks getting stopped and searched. Those two weren't hauling anything except potting soil, but it spooked Marset, because he was guaranteed that none of his trucks would be subject to search. The Bookkeeper wanted to shut him up. He doesn't need a complaint department at any time, but especially not now.'

Hamilton mulled it over. 'We'll go with what we've got. With or without this pending arrangement, you've built a case. It's enough.'

'No federal prosecutor is going to touch this unless he's got a smoking gun or an eyewitness who'll swear his life away. It would also be a PR nightmare for the bureau. Sam Marset is just a name to you, but in these parts he was looked upon as a saint. Drag his name through the mud without absolute proof and all you'll do is cause resentment among the law-abiding population and put the offenders on red alert. Then the DEA will blame us for sending every dealer underground. Everybody will back off stings they had planned, and we'll all slink back to square one.'

'OK, Coburn. I hear you. You stay. But as good as you are, you can't clean this up by yourself. VanAllen will provide back-up.'

'Nix. The Bookkeeper has informers in every police department, sheriff's office, and city hall. Everybody's on the take.'

'You're saying you think VanAllen—'

'I'm saying give me forty-eight hours. I'm onto something that could blow the top off.'

'What is it?'

'I can't say.'

'Dammit. This *something* involves Mrs Gillette, doesn't it?'

Coburn said nothing.

'Coburn, you don't expect me to believe that you chose her house, out of all the houses in coastal Louisiana, to hide in, and that while you were there, you just up and decided to ransack the place. Or that without some uber-strong motivating factor she came with you of her own free will after watching you fatally shoot a family friend in her living room. And you certainly can't expect me to believe that you've taken a widow and child under your wing out of the goodness of your heart.'

'Aw now, that really hurts my feelings.'

'I know Mrs Gillette's late husband was a police officer and the recently deceased Fred Hawkins was his best friend. Call me crazy, but the coincidence of that has got my gut instinct churning.'

Coburn dropped the sarcasm. 'You're not crazy.'

'OK. Does she know who The Bookkeeper is?'

Coburn stared hard at Honor. 'No.'

'Then what's she sitting on?'

'I don't know.'

Hamilton swore under his breath. 'Fine, don't tell me. I'll supply VanAllen with whatever it takes to find you and bring you in, for the safety of the woman and child.'

Coburn's jaw turned to iron. 'You do that, and they'll die.'

'Look, I know VanAllen. I grant you, he's no dynamo, but—'

'Then what is he?'

'A bureaucrat.'

'That's a given. What's he like?'

'Mild-mannered. Beleaguered. He's got a special-needs son, a tragic case who ought to be in a perpetual care home but isn't.'

Coburn pulled a thoughtful frown. 'Give me forty-eight hours. During that time, you check out VanAllen. If you can convince me that he's honest, I'll come in. With luck, I'll have the goods on The Bookkeeper by then.'

'In the meantime, what will you do with Mrs Gillette and the child?'

'I don't know.'

'Let me talk to her again.'

Coburn handed the phone to Honor. 'I'm here, Mr Hamilton.'

'Mrs Gillette, what's your take on everything that's been discussed?'

'Is Lee Coburn his real name?'

Hamilton seemed surprised by the question, then replied in the affirmative.

'Why did the woman in your office say that he was dead?'

'She was under my orders to. For Coburn's protection. He's been in a precarious situation down there. I couldn't risk someone suspecting him of being an agent and calling an FBI office and inadvertently getting verification of it. So I put it through the bureau pipeline that he'd been killed.'

'You're the only person who knows he's alive?'

'Me and my assistant who answered the phone.'

'And now me.'

'That's right.'

'So if something happened to him, any information that he'd passed to me regarding Sam Marset and The Bookkeeper, or anything that I'd picked up inadvertently, would be valuable to the FBI and the Justice Department?'

'Yes,' he said. 'Tell me. What have you got? What's Coburn after?'

'Even I don't know, Mr Hamilton.'

'Then help me get other agents to you. You need to be brought in so I can protect you. Tell me where you are.'

She held Coburn's gaze for several long moments while her common sense waged war with something deeper. 'Didn't you hear what Coburn told you, Mr Hamilton? If you send other agents in after us now, you'll never get The Bookkeeper.' Before Hamilton could respond, she returned the phone to Coburn.

He took it from her and said, 'Too bad, Hamilton. No sale.'

'Have you brainwashed her? At least give me a phone number.'

'Forty-eight hours.'

'All right, dammit! I'll give you thirty-six. *Thirty-six*, and that's—'

Coburn disconnected, then asked Honor, 'Will this tub float?'

WHEN TOM GOT HOME, Janice was deep into a word game on her cellphone. She didn't know he was there until he spoke her name, then she nearly jumped out of her skin. 'Tom! Don't do that!'

'Sorry I startled you. I thought you'd have heard me come in.'

He tried but failed to keep his bitterness from showing. She was playing word games with someone she'd never met who lived on the other side of the world, while his world was crumbling.

Of course it wasn't her fault he was having a bad day. But he felt resentful, so rather than saying something that would set off a quarrel, he left his briefcase in the den and went to Lanny's room.

The boy's eyes were closed. He kissed Lanny's forehead.

When he entered the kitchen, Janice served him a meal at the kitchen table. Although the shrimp salad and sliced melon had been artfully arranged on the plate, he had no appetite.

'Would you like a glass of wine?'

He shook his head. 'I've got to go back to the office.'

Janice sat down across from him. 'You look done in.'

'I feel done in.'

'Nothing new on the kidnapping?'

'Nothing, and everyone including the dog catcher is out looking for them. Or their bodies.'

Janice reached across the table and covered his hand. 'I don't think he'll kill them, Tom.'

'Then why did he take them?'

'Ransom?'

'I don't think this is about ransom. Coburn doesn't fit the profile of a guy who shoots up his place of employment. Even Hamilton picked up on it.'

'Clint Hamilton? I thought he was in Washington now.'

'He is. But he called me today, wanted to know what the hell is going on down here and what I'm doing about it.'

She made a small sound of dismay. 'He was checking up on you?'

'Essentially. I don't know where Hamilton got his information, but he must have noticed the same discrepancies in Coburn's MO that I did. He even asked me if Coburn was an agent from my office working undercover at the trucking company.'

She sputtered a laugh, then sobered quickly. 'Was he?'

Tom gave her a crooked smile. 'Someone in New Orleans who outranked me could have placed him there, I suppose.'

'Without informing you?'

He shrugged, not wanting to admit that he was inconsequential.

He pushed back his chair and stood up. 'I'd better get back.'

She placed a hand on his arm. 'You're doing a good job, Tom. Don't let Hamilton browbeat you into thinking otherwise.'

He gave her a weak smile. 'I won't. The hell of it is, he's right. Any fool would realise it's no ordinary kidnapping. In all likelihood, Mrs Gillette witnessed Coburn shooting Fred Hawkins. Murderers don't leave eye-witnesses. He has a reason for keeping her alive.'

DORAL NAVIGATED the winding back roads at a high speed. He'd travelled them all his life and knew them intimately. He and Fred. He and Eddie.

Thoughts of Eddie called to mind the fishing trip that had been captured in the photo that Crawford had bagged as evidence. Doral remembered that excursion as one of the best times the four of them had had together.

From thoughts of that day, his mind drifted to his fishing boat and his pre-Bookkeeper years. For years, he'd run charters into the Gulf, putting up with groups of rich, drunken doctors, lawyers and stockbrokers. In a way, he'd been grateful to Hurricane Katrina for destroying his boat and putting an end to it. That's when The Bookkeeper had approached him and Fred with a moneymaking idea. The work was going to be a lot more lucrative than any enterprise they could have dreamed up on their own.

Doral enjoyed the inside joke of being a public official by day and something else entirely by night. He had a natural propensity for stalking and hunting. The only difference was that now the prey was human. So here he was speeding along back roads, his prey Lee Coburn. And his best friend's widow and child.

When his cellphone rang, he slowed down only marginally in order to answer the call, but after hearing the urgent message the caller imparted, he skidded to a stop. 'Are you kidding me?'

There was background noise, but the whispering caller made himself heard. 'I thought you should know so you could tell The Bookkeeper.'

'Thanks for nothing,' Doral muttered. He disconnected and pulled his car off the road, then called The Bookkeeper.

He skipped traditional greetings. 'It's rumoured that Coburn is an undercover federal agent.'

The Bookkeeper breathed deeply. 'When did you hear this?'

'Ten seconds before I called you. One of our plants in the PD heard it from a feeb agent who's working on the kidnapping.'

'Well, as you so astutely pointed out this morning, he does seem unusually smart for a dock worker. I only wish you'd realised that before you let him escape.'

Doral's gut clenched tight, but he didn't say anything.

'What about Honor's friend? Anything since this morning?'

'Tori hasn't left her house. One thing I found out, she's got a new boyfriend. Bigwig banker in New Orleans name of Bonnell Wallace.'

After a lengthy silence, The Bookkeeper said, 'Good information to hold in reserve in case we need it. Unfortunately, it hasn't moved you any closer to locating Coburn, has it?'

'No.'

'You and Fred left us with a mess, Doral. Coburn should have been killed along with the others. I haven't forgotten who let him get away. Find him. Kill him. Don't disappoint me again.'

'How were Fred and I to know—'

'It's your business to know.' The Bookkeeper's tone sliced to the bone. 'You've heard me speak highly of Diego and his razor.'

Goosebumps broke out on Doral's sweat-dampened arms.

'The only problem with using Diego is that it's over too quickly. The person who failed me doesn't suffer long enough.'

Honor's protests fell on deaf ears.

Within minutes of hanging up on Hamilton, Coburn was in the wheel-house, flinging back the tarp that had been placed over the control panel. 'Do you know how to start the engine?' He asked impatiently.

'Yes, but we'd have to get it into the water first, and we can't do that.'

'We've got to. We gotta relocate.'

Several times she tried to convince him that it was an impossible project, but Coburn wouldn't be deterred. He found a rusty machete in a toolbox on deck and was using it to whack at the fibrous vegetation clinging to the hull. It was backbreaking work.

'Hamilton gave you his word. You don't trust him to keep it?'

'No.'

'But he's your boss. Overseer, supervisor? Whatever you call it in the FBI.'

'He's all of that. But I know how he thinks. As we speak, he's probably already trying to get a location on my cell number.'

'You said disposables were untraceable.'

'Yeah, but I don't know everything,' he muttered.

The harder they worked, the more hopeless it seemed. Honor suggested that they take their chances in the recently stolen pick-up.

'OK, and go where?'

'To my friend. She'd hide us, no questions asked.'

'No. No friends. They'll be watching your friends.'

Eventually she stopped trying to change his mind. She applied herself to helping, and did whatever he asked of her.

Emily woke from her nap. She was chatty and excited by the activity. She got in the way, but Coburn worked around her with surprising patience. She stood on deck and called down encouragement to them as, together, they pushed the unfettered craft off the bank into the water.

Coburn checked for leakage and, finding none, joined Honor at the controls. Her dad had taught her how to start the engine and to steer. Miraculously, she remembered the steps, and the engine belched to life.

Coburn asked about fuel. She checked the gauge. 'We're OK. Dad was preparing for a hurricane.'

He spread a yellowed nautical map over the control panel. 'Do you know where we are?'

She pointed out their location. 'If we head inland, the bayous narrow. There's more tree coverage. Waters are shallower.'

'Since we'll probably have to bail out, I vote for shallow water. Just get us as far as you can.'

They chugged for about five miles before the engine began to cough. The waters were thick with vegetation. Honor steered the boat close to a dense cypress grove, where Coburn dropped anchor.

She cut the engine and looked at him for further instruction.

'Make yourselves comfortable.'

'What?' She exclaimed.

He folded the map and stuffed it into the pocket of his jeans, then set his pistol on the control panel. 'I'll take Hawkins's. You keep this one. It's ready to fire. All you have to do is pull the trigger.'

'What are you doing?'

But he was already out of the wheelhouse, lowering himself into the waist-deep water. 'Can't leave the truck back there.'

Chapter 7

Diego was shopping in a Mexican supermarket when his cellphone vibrated. He stepped outside to answer. 'You ready for me?'

'Yes,' The Bookkeeper said. 'I want you to watch someone.'

'What? What about Coburn?'

'Do as I tell you, Diego. The man's name is Bonnell Wallace.'

Before he could voice his objections, he was given two addresses, one for a bank and one for a residence. With exaggerated boredom, he said, 'Do you want him to know he's being watched?'

'Not yet. Keep me posted on anything he does that's not part of his daily routine.'

Diego clicked off and returned to the store. The Bookkeeper's stupid assignment would keep for an hour or two.

HONOR WAS SITTING on the bunk beside her sleeping daughter, listening to the rain and her own heartbeat, when she heard a bump. She slid the pistol from beneath the mattress and crept up the steps.

'It's me,' Coburn said.

With profound relief, she said, 'I'd almost given up on you.'

'It was a long way back overland. By the time I got there, it was dark. Then I had to find a road. Only waterways were on the map. I finally found a gravel road that runs out about a quarter of a mile from here.'

His clothes were soaked. 'I'll be right back,' she told him. She descended the steps and returned with khakis and a T-shirt. 'They were in a storage compartment. The trousers will be too short.'

'Doesn't matter. They're dry.' He peeled off Eddie's LSU T-shirt and replaced it with her father's, then began unbuttoning the jeans.

She turned her back. 'Are you hungry?'

'Yeah.'

She went back down and flicked on the lantern to locate the food she'd set aside for him. By the time she returned, he'd swapped trousers. Using his fingers, he ate his canned chicken and crackers. She fetched cookies to appease his sweet tooth.

He was sitting on the floor, his back propped against the console. She sat in her dad's captain's chair. The silence was broken only by the pelting rain and the crunch of cookies. 'Will they find us?' she asked.

'Uh-huh. It's only a matter of time.'

'When they find us, will you . . .'

'Go peacefully? No. I'm not quitting till I get The Bookkeeper.'

'How did it work? The business between him and Marset?'

'Well, here's a for instance. Each time a truck passes from one state to another, it has to stop at a weigh station. Those arms extending over the interstate near state lines look like streetlights, but they're X-ray machines that scan trucks and cargo. Agents see a truck that looks suspicious, or that hasn't stopped at the weigh station, it's pulled over and searched.'

'Unless the person monitoring it is on the take and lets it pass.'

'Bingo. The Bookkeeper created a market out of doing just that. Sam Marset, I believe, was one of the first clients.'

'Royale Trucking. Are all the employees crooked?'

'Not at all. Those six who died with Marset, yes. He had a separate set of books that only he and one other guy ever saw.'

Honor pulled her feet up to the edge of the seat, looped her arms around her legs. Quietly she said, 'They'll kill you.'

He bit into another cookie. 'Hamilton's told everybody I'm already dead. Wonder how he'll wiggle out of that one.'

'It doesn't bother you that you could die?'

'Not particularly. I'm surprised that it hasn't happened yet.'

Honor picked at a cuticle that had been torn loose while they were working on the boat. 'You know how to do things.' She glanced at him. 'Survival things. Did you learn those skills in the Marine Corps?'

'Most of them.' He didn't elaborate.

'You were a different kind of Marine to my father-in-law.'

'Yeah, I was different. No marching in formation for the kind of Marine I was. I had a uniform, but didn't wear it but a few times. I didn't salute officers, and nobody saluted me.'

'What *did* you do?'

'Killed people.'

She had suspected that. She'd even deluded herself into thinking she could hear him admit it without flinching. But the words felt like blows to her chest, so she carried the subject no further.

He finished his last cookie. 'We need to go through it again.'

'Through what again?'

'Eddie's life.'

For the next two hours, Coburn hammered her with questions. He wanted to know about every aspect of Eddie's life. When did his mother die? How did she die? Was he close to her family?

'What does any of this have to do with what you're looking for? Coburn, please. I'm tired. Can't we wait until morning and pick this up again then?'

'We may be dead in the morning.'

'Right, I may die of exhaustion. In which case, what's the point?'

He dragged his hand over his face. He stared at her long and hard through the darkness. 'You or his dad. One of you has it.' While he thought, he repeatedly socked his fist into his opposite palm. 'Who ruled Eddie's car wreck an accident?'

'The investigating officer.'

'What's his name? How did he happen on the wreckage?'

Honor stood up and went out onto the deck but stayed near the exterior wall of the wheelhouse so the slender overhang of the roof would protect her from the rain.

Coburn followed her. 'What?'

'The officer who investigated Eddie's car crash was found floating in a bayou a few weeks later. He'd been stabbed.'

'Unsolved homicide?'

'I suppose. I never heard any more about it.'

'Thorough, aren't they?' He stood shoulder to shoulder with her, staring out at the rain. 'What did Eddie like to do? Bowl? Golf?'

'All that. He was a good athlete. He'd hunt and fish.'

'Where's his fishing and hunting gear? Golf bag?'

'At Stan's. And so are his bowling ball and his bow and arrow set.'

'I'm gonna have to pay Stan a visit. Describe Eddie. Was he serious and studious? Moody? Funny?'

'Even-tempered. Conscientious. But he liked to have a good time.'

'Was he faithful?'

She glared at him. 'Yes. He was faithful. We had a good marriage. I didn't keep secrets, and neither did Eddie.'

'He kept one. Everybody keeps secrets, Honor.'

'Oh really? Tell me one of yours.'

A corner of his mouth tilted up. 'Everybody but me.'

'Absurd thing to say. You're wrapped up in secrets.'

He folded his arms over his chest. 'Ask away.'

'Where did you grow up?'

'Idaho, near the state line with Wyoming. In the shadow of the Tetons.'

That surprised her. 'What did your father do?'

'Drank. Mostly. When he worked, he was a car mechanic.'

'He's deceased?'

'For years now.'

She looked at him inquisitively.

Finally he said, 'He had this old horse that he kept in a corral behind our house. He never gave it a name but I did. One day he saddled it and rode off. The horse came back. He didn't. They never found his body. Of course they didn't look very hard.'

Honor wondered if the bitterness lacing his voice was aimed at his alcoholic father or at the searchers who had given up on finding his remains.

'Dad had ridden that horse near to death, so I shot it.' He stared out into the rain. 'No great loss. It wasn't much of a horse.'

She let a full minute pass before she asked about his mother.

'She was French Canadian. Tempestuous. She and I parted ways long before I joined the Marines. My first tour of duty, I got word that she'd died. I flew to Idaho. Buried her. End of story.'

'Brothers or sisters?'

'No.' His facial expression was as devoid of feeling as his life had been devoid of love from any source. 'No cousins, aunts, uncles, nobody. When I die, I'll just be history, and nobody will give a damn. Especially me.'

She was angry, she realised. 'Don't you value your life at all?'

'Not really. Why do you care?'

'You're a fellow human being.'

'Oh. You care about mankind in general, is that it?' He turned the rest of his body towards her. 'So why didn't you beg him to come get you?'

'What?'

'Hamilton. Why didn't you tell him where you were so he could send someone to pick you up?'

She took a shaky breath. 'Because after the past day and a half, I don't know who to trust. I guess I chose the devil I know.'

He inclined an inch towards her. 'Why else?'

'And . . .' Her throat was tight. 'Because of Eddie.'

'To preserve his reputation. That's why you're here with me?'

'Yes.'

'I don't think so.'

And then he pressed into her. First his thighs, then his chest, and finally his mouth. She made a whimpering sound, but she realised that her arms had gone around him instinctively, and that she was clutching his back, his shoulders, her hands greedy for him.

He kissed her open-mouthed, and when she kissed back he cupped her head in his large hand and kissed as if to suck the very breath from her. Boldly his hand covered her breast.

That brought Honor to her senses. 'I can't do this,' she gasped, and shoved him away. He stood there, his chest rising and falling.

'I'm sorry,' she said, meaning it to the bottom of her soul. But was she sorry for him, or sorry for herself?

She rushed through the door of the wheelhouse, down the steps, and into the cabin.

EMILY CAME AWAKE, sat up, and looked around. It was still kinda dark, but she wasn't scared. Mommy was lying beside her on the smelly bed. Coburn was in the other one. They were both asleep.

She hugged Elmo against her and dragged her bankie along as she scooted to the end of the bed and climbed down. She went up the steps to look at the room with all the funny stuff in it.

Mommy had sat her in the crooked chair and told her that it used to be her grandpa's seat, and that he had let her sit in his lap while he steered the boat. But she'd been a baby, so she didn't remember. Her mommy probably wouldn't like it if she went any further, so she tiptoed back down the steps. Then she spied the phone at the foot of Coburn's bed.

Yesterday, while Mommy and Coburn were cutting bushes off the boat, she'd asked if she could play Thomas the Tank Engine on Mommy's phone. Both of them had said 'No!' Mommy had said if she touched the phone, she'd have to go to Time Out. She didn't understand why, because when Mummy wasn't using the phone, she would let her play games on it.

Mommy wasn't using her phone now, so she probably wouldn't mind if she played a game.

When all the pretty pictures came on the screen, she tapped on Thomas the Tank Engine. Concentrating hard, she started with the wheels, then added the engine and the smokestack, and all the other parts. Each time she worked the puzzle, Mommy told her how smart she was. Mommy knew she was smart, but Coburn didn't.

She crept towards the head of his bunk. 'Coburn?' she whispered.

His eyes popped open. He looked at her funny, then looked over to where Mommy was sleeping before looking back at her. 'What?'

'I worked the puzzle. The Thomas puzzle, on Mommy's phone.'

She held it up for him to see, but she didn't think he really looked at it, because he jumped off the bed so fast he banged his head on the ceiling. Then he said a really bad word.

DEPUTY SHERIFF CRAWFORD was surprised to discover that their destination was a derelict shrimp boat. As hiding places went, it was a sorry choice. Maybe Coburn was becoming desperate.

Using only hand signals, they approached the craft. The team consisted of himself, two other sheriff's deputies, three Tambour policemen and two FBI agents. After their techie got the signal from Honor Gillette's cellphone, and the triangulation was successful, it had taken an hour to determine how to get to the isolated location and forty minutes to drive there. They'd hunkered down among the trees, watching for signs of life aboard the boat as the sun rose.

Crawford had motioned the men forward. They stepped lightly onto the deck. Crawford was the first inside the wheelhouse, the first to hear movement coming from below, the first to aim at the man coming up the steps.

Stan Gillette stepped out of the passageway into the wheelhouse with his hands raised. In one of them, he was holding a cellphone. 'Deputy Crawford. You're late.'

HE'D MADE THE KID CRY.

When he'd wrenched the cellphone from her hand, she'd let out a howl that could've raised the dead. It got her mother up, all right.

He'd practically slung Emily over his shoulder, shoved Elmo and bankie into her chubby arms, then grabbed Honor's hand, and dragged her— protesting—up the steps, through the wheelhouse and onto the deck. Honor had baulked at stepping into the water, but he'd pushed her, and she'd managed to splash her way out of the shallows, stumbling twice during their dash to the pick-up. The kid had kept a stranglehold on his neck, wailing in his ear over and over, 'I didn't mean to.'

They were well away from the boat now, but he didn't know what time the kid had turned on the phone. At best, they couldn't have much of a head start.

Honor shushed Emily as she hugged her. The kid stopped crying, but when he glanced over, he was met with four reproachful eyes.

He finally pulled into the parking lot of a busy truck stop, where the pick-up wouldn't be noticed among so many similar vehicles. For thirty seconds after he cut the engine, no one said anything. Finally the kid said in a trembling voice, 'I'm sorry, Coburn.'

He blinked several times. He looked at Honor, and when she didn't say anything, he looked back at the kid, whose damp cheek was still lying against Honor's chest. He mumbled, 'Sorry I made you cry.'

'That's OK. Can we have breakfast now?'

He considered, then said, 'Why not? What do you want?'

'Would you rather I go?' Honor asked.

'I don't think so . . .' His gaze moved over her tousled hair and snug T-shirt. 'You'd attract attention.'

Her cheeks turned pink. She had ended last night's kiss, but that didn't mean she hadn't liked it. Face averted, she said, 'Anything you get will do.'

He put on the cap and sunglasses he'd found in the truck, and, as he'd expected, he blended with the other customers. He brought sandwiches to the cash register and paid. As soon as he'd handed the food to Honor, he started the truck and drove away.

While driving, he ate the sandwich and sipped the coffee, but his mind was on his next course of action. There wasn't much time for decision-making. 'You mentioned a friend yesterday,' he said.

Honor looked over at him. 'Tori. I trust her implicitly.'

He pulled off the road and dug his cellphone from his pocket. Then he laid it on the line. 'I gotta dump the two of you.'

'But—'

'No buts. Only thing I need to know, when you're free of me, are you going to call in the cavalry? Doral, the police, the FBI?'

'I won't call in the cavalry.'

'All right. Do you think your friend would hide you?'

'If I ask her to.'

'She wouldn't betray your trust?'

She gave an emphatic shake of her head.

It went against his nature, as well as his training and experience, to trust anyone. But he had no choice. 'OK. What's her number?'

'It won't work if you call. I'll have to.'

'If you do, you could be implicated.'

'Implicated? In what?'

He glanced at Emily, who was singing along with Elmo. Coming back to Honor, he spoke softly. 'Implicated in anything that may come down when my deadline expires. If I do nothing else, I'm going to take care of Doral.'

'You can't just kill him,' she whispered.

'Yeah, I can. I will. I am.'

Visibly distressed, she said, 'I'm so far out of my element here. I know you're doubtful about Stan. But he would—'

'Not an option.'

'He's my father-in-law, Coburn. He loves us.'

He lowered his voice even more. 'Do you want Emily to witness the confrontation between us? He's not going to let me just walk into his house and go through Eddie's things. Whether he's partnering with The Bookkeeper or an honest citizen safeguarding his dead son's name, he's going to resist my intrusion. Not only that, he'll be pissed with me for dragging you into this.'

Her expression was a giveaway. She knew he was right.

'What's Tori's number?'

EVEN BEFORE TORI CHECKED the light beyond her shutters, she knew it was an ungodly hour for her phone to be ringing. She groaned and buried her head into her pillow. Then, remembering the events of yesterday, she grabbed her phone. 'Hello?'

'Tori, did I wake you up? It's Amber.'

Tori flopped back on her pillow. 'What? It had better be good.'

'Well, just like you instructed me, the first thing I do each morning after turning off the alarm is to turn on the sauna in the locker rooms. Then I check voicemail. This morning, somebody left a weird message at five fifty.'

'Well, what was it?'

'"What does Barbie see in Ken?"'

Tori sat bolt upright in bed. 'That's all she said?'

'Actually it was a man.'

Tori thought on that, then said, 'Obviously it was a crank call.'

'Are you coming in today?'

'Don't count on it. Cover for me.'

Tori ended the call and bounded out of bed. She skipped doing her hair and make-up, which she *never* skipped, and dressed rapidly. Grabbing her keys and handbag, she left through the front door.

But halfway to her car in the driveway, she noticed a beat-up truck parked across the street. She couldn't tell whether anyone was behind the wheel, but Doral's threat came back to her.

Maybe she'd been watching too many crime shows on TV, but she'd never seen the truck on her street before. She'd rather be paranoid than stupid. Rather than continuing on, she bent and picked up the morning newspaper lying in the grass. Pretending to read the front page, she retraced her steps back into the house. Then she slipped out of her back door and walked to the house behind hers. She knocked on the door.

It was answered by a buff young man, a client who never missed a workout. He pushed open the screened door and motioned her in. 'This is a surprise! Coffee?'

'Thanks, no. Listen, can I borrow a car? I gotta go . . . somewhere . . . in sort of a hurry.'

'Something wrong with your Vette?'

'It's making a funny noise.'

She hated telling such a transparent lie. He'd become a loyal friend.

Finally he asked, 'The Lexus or the Mini Cooper?'

UPON SEEING STAN, Crawford exclaimed, 'What the *hell*?'

'My daughter-in-law's cellphone,' Stan said, extending it to Crawford.

He snatched it from Stan. 'I know what it is. How the hell did you get it, and what are you doing here with it?'

'Well, one thing I'm *not* doing with it is playing Thomas the Tank Engine,' Stan retorted. 'It's Emily's favourite game.'

Crawford activated the phone. From the screen, the cartoon steam engine smiled up at him. 'So they have been here.'

'Yes, they were definitely here, but they're gone.'

To Crawford's further consternation, Doral joined them from the cabin below. Crawford holstered his gun. 'Mrs Gillette must have called and told you both where she was. Why didn't you notify me?'

'Honor didn't call anybody,' Stan said.

The deputy's eyes landed on Doral with an accusatorial glare. 'If she didn't call you, then one of your late brother's friends in the police department must have tipped you that we'd got the signal. If I find out who it is, I'll nail his ass to a fence post.'

He was right, of course. A police officer friend had called Doral with news of this latest development. Out of loyalty, Doral had in turn called Stan. While Crawford was still pulling together a team, the two of them had been speeding here.

Doral smirked. 'I'd pay to see that,' he said, and left the trawler.

Crawford ordered two officers to search the boat for clues. He sent the rest out to search for footprints, tyre tracks, anything. When he and Stan were alone, he said, 'Couple of things, Stan. Mrs Gillette obviously had access to her cellphone. Why didn't she call 911? If she wanted to be found, wouldn't she have done that instead of letting her little girl play games on her phone?'

Stan schooled his expression not to change. *If she wanted to.* 'You said a couple of things.'

'You might want to reconsider who you ally yourself with.'

'Why?'

'I received a ballistics report. The bullet that killed Fred Hawkins didn't match any fired during the warehouse murders.'

Stan offered an explanation. 'Coburn would have dumped the guns he used at the warehouse. He used another to shoot Fred.'

'Or,' the deputy said, 'he wasn't the warehouse shooter.'

Chapter 8

'She's a babe.'

It was the first time Honor had spoken in five minutes. Even Emily sat still and untalkative in her lap.

Coburn looked at Honor. 'Come again?'

'Tori will knock your eyes out. She's a babe.'

'What Tori is,' he said tightly, 'is not here. We've been waiting an hour.'

'She'll come. Just be patient.'

But he looked like a man whose patience had run out an hour ago when they had arrived at the designated place. He looked around. 'We're like sitting ducks. Right out in the open.'

'It's safe. No one knows about it except Tori and me.'

'Maybe she forgot that silly code. What's it mean, anyway?'

'It means Ken's a dork.' When she and Tori had first sworn an oath on it, they'd been giggling girls. Then they'd continued to use it into their teens to communicate whenever one needed to see the other immediately. It meant, 'Come now, this is an emergency.'

Of course when they were in high school an emergency had amounted to an adolescent trauma. Today's emergency was for real.

'Why here?' he asked.

'Here' was an ancient oak tree. Imposing and magnificent, it almost appeared artificial, like something from a Hollywood set.

'Meeting out here in the countryside added to the thrill of sneaking out, I suppose. We came across the tree out here in the middle of nowhere and claimed it as our own.'

Coburn sat up, alert. 'What kind of car does she drive?'

'A Corvette.'

'Then that's not her.' He reached for the pistol at his waistband.

'Wait! That's not her car, but that's Tori. And she's alone.'

The small, unfamiliar car bumped across the creaky wood bridge and followed the rutted path to the tree, stopping twenty yards short of it. Honor opened the passenger door so Tori could see her. Emily scrambled out and ran to her, shouting, 'Aunt Tori!'

Tori alighted from the Mini Cooper and swung Emily up into her arms. 'You're so big! I won't be able to do this much longer.'

'Guess what,' Emily said, wiggling free of Tori's hug.

'What?'

'Coburn said if I would just be quiet and let him think, he would get me an ice cream. Only not now. Later. And guess what else. We slept on a boat and the beds didn't smell nice, but it was OK 'cause we're on a 'venture. I woke Coburn up and he said a bad word but he isn't mad at me.'

'My goodness, we've got a lot to catch up on,' Tori said.

Over Emily's shoulder, she was looking at Honor and telegraphing unspoken questions. She kissed Emily's cheek, then set her down and extended her arms to Honor. For several moments they just held each other tightly.

Finally, Tori released her. 'I've been worried sick.'

'I knew you would be, but there was no help for it.'

'The news stories led me to fear . . . Well, I'm just awfully glad to see you and Emily in one piece. Did he . . .? Are you . . .? God, I'm so *relieved*. You look like something the cat dragged in, but you seem fine.'

'We are. Basically. I'm sorry you were so afraid for us. He wouldn't let me call you until this morning. And even then he wouldn't let me call you directly. I wasn't sure you'd get the message. But he—'

'"He" being *him*?' Tori watched Coburn as he came towards them. In an undertone she said, 'Kidnapper? I should be so lucky.'

Honor made the introductions. 'Tori Shirah. Lee Coburn.'

Coburn didn't acknowledge the greeting. He was looking towards the bridge that Tori had crossed. 'Is your cellphone on?'

She was taken aback by the question, but answered. 'Yes.'

'Turn it off.'

Tori looked at Honor and, when Honor nodded, she retrieved her phone from her handbag in the car and turned it off.

Coburn asked, 'Were you followed?'

'No. I made sure.' She told them about borrowing the Mini Cooper after seeing the truck parked on her street that morning.

'What made you suspicious of the truck?' Coburn asked.

'Doral Hawkins came to see me and said if I heard from Honor, I'd better notify him, or else.'

'He threatened you?' Honor asked.

Tori shrugged. 'Stan came by, too. I must admit that he was less obnoxious than usual. I guess fear's taken the shine off his brass.'

'What's he afraid of?' Coburn asked.

'You left a trail of dead bodies, then took Honor and Emily. Stan has a right to be more than a little concerned, don't you think?' Tori said.

'Coburn didn't murder those men in the warehouse,' Honor said. 'And he didn't take Emily and me by force.'

Tori looked from one to the other. 'I sorta gathered that. So, what gives?'

'The fact is that he's—'

'No.' He put his hand on Honor's arm to stop her from revealing his identity. 'The only thing she needs to know is that you and Emily must stay underground until all this shakes out.'

'She deserves an explanation,' Honor argued.

'Excuse me.' Tori raised her hand and addressed Coburn. 'Keep your secrets. I've already volunteered my services.' Then she said to Honor, 'Emily isn't afraid of him, and kids are good gauges of character. In any case, you summoned me, and I'm here. Tell me what you want me to do.'

'Get them away from Tambour,' Coburn said before Honor could speak. 'Right now. Don't tell anybody. Can you do that?'

'I own a house on Lake Pontchartrain. Would that do?'

'Who knows about it?' Coburn asked.

'I got it in my divorce settlement. I don't go there much.'

Honor was listening to them, but she was watching Emily. Her hair was unbrushed. There was a tear in her top. Meals had been irregular. Yet she seemed perfectly content. She'd found a stick and was happily etching patterns in the mud.

'She'll need some things,' Honor remarked.

Tori gave Honor's arm a pat. 'I'll take care of everything.'

'You can't use credit cards. Do you have cash?' said Coburn.

'I can get what I need,' Tori said. 'All I have to do is ask.'

'Ask who?' Coburn wanted to know.

'My current beau.'

'No. Nobody can know where you are.'

'He wouldn't tell.'

'Yeah, he would. If the right people got to him.'

He said it with such conviction, that even Tori was daunted by what he implied. 'We'll pool our resources and make do.'

He appeared satisfied with that, but stressed that Honor and Emily must get into hiding before being spotted.

'I'm not going with Tori,' said Honor.

Honor's declaration startled Tori speechless. Coburn was more outspoken. 'The fuck you're not.'

She had come to the conclusion that she couldn't just dust her hands of this. Since Eddie's death, she'd allowed others to oversee her decisions. Widowhood had made her insecure and cautious. She didn't like the woman she was now. She said to Coburn, 'I'm not going to let you brush me off.'

'Not going to *let me*? Watch, lady.'

'You're the one who dragged me into this.'

'I didn't have a choice then. Now I do.'

'So do I. I'm going to see this through, Coburn.'

'You could get killed.' He pointed to Emily, playing with her stick. 'You want to leave her an orphan?'

'You know better than to ask that,' she shot back angrily. 'But this time I won't be coerced. *I* want answers about Eddie.'

'I'll get them for you.'

'That's just it. I need to get them. Because I didn't do it before. I should have insisted on a thorough investigation of his car wreck. I never posed a single question, not even after the officer who found Eddie was murdered. I let everyone take over my decision-making. *I'm* making this decision. I'm staying on until I know what really happened to my husband.'

Softly, Tori said, 'That's honourable and all, honey, but—'

'I'm not doing it just for me. He needs me.' She nodded at Coburn. 'You can't find what you're looking for without my help.'

He stewed for a few moments, but she knew she'd won the argument even before he turned to Tori and repeated his instructions.

Tori gave him the general location of her house on the lake shore. 'It's about a two-hour drive. Shall I call you when we get there?'

'Is there a land line at the house?'

She recited the number, which Honor memorised, as she knew Coburn did. He said, 'Let us call you. Don't answer the phone unless it rings once, and then again two minutes later. And leave your cellphone off.'

Finally, all the details had been discussed, and it came time to part with Emily. Struggling to keep her tears in check, Honor hugged her close. Emily was too excited over the prospect of having time with her aunt Tori to

376 | SANDRA BROWN

notice Honor's emotion. 'Are you and Coburn coming to the lake, too?'

'Maybe later. Right now, you're going with Aunt Tori all by yourself.' Honor tried to keep a brave face. 'Give Mommy a kiss.'

Emily kissed Honor's cheek enthusiastically, then held her arms up to Coburn. 'Coburn. Kiss.'

He'd been acting as though on sentry, obviously impatient with the protracted farewell. Now his gaze dropped to Emily.

'Kiss,' she repeated.

After a long, expectant moment, he bent down. Emily looped her arms around his neck and kissed his cheek. 'Bye, Coburn.'

'Bye.' He stood up, pivoted quickly, and started walking back towards the truck. 'Hurry up,' he told Honor over his shoulder.

Emily scrambled into the back of the Mini Cooper. Tori promised to drive with special care until she could stop and buy a car seat. She eyed Honor warily. 'Sure you're doing the right thing?'

'I'm not at all sure. But I've got to do it anyway.'

Tori smiled ruefully. 'You always were the Girl Scout.' She hugged Honor tightly. 'I can't even pretend to understand it all, but I'm smart enough to realise that you're trusting me with Emily's life. I'd die before letting something bad happen to her.'

'I know you would. Thanks for this.'

'You don't have to thank me.'

CLINT HAMILTON was on the telephone with Tom VanAllen, who was giving him an account of the morning's events. VanAllen sounded apologetic, which didn't surprise Hamilton, because Coburn had outfoxed the authorities again.

When VanAllen concluded, Hamilton thanked him absently, then remained silent for nearly a minute while he absorbed and analysed the new information. Finally he asked, 'Any sign of a struggle aboard the boat?'

'I'm emailing you some pictures. It's a shambles, but if you're asking if they found fresh blood or anything like that, then no.'

'The footprints. Did they indicate that Mrs Gillette was being dragged? Heel skid marks, anything like that?'

'No, sir. In fact, Crawford has come right out and suggested that she's not a hostage as originally believed.'

Everything that Tom was saying lent credibility to what Hamilton had heard from the widow herself during their phone conversation yesterday. Forsaking law and order, trusted lifelong friends, and even her father-in-law, she had allied herself with Lee Coburn.

'What about the tyre tracks?'

'The tyres came as standard issue on several makes of Ford pick-ups, model 2006 and 2007.'

'That narrows it down to several thousand trucks in Louisiana alone.'

'It's a daunting number, yes. State agencies have ordered that every Ford truck of those model years be stopped and checked. Meanwhile, Mr Gillette is very concerned about his daughter-in-law and granddaughter. He came straight here from the shrimp boat and—'

'Explain to me what he was doing there when the authorities arrived.'

VanAllen shared Deputy Crawford's suspicion that Doral Hawkins and Stan Gillette had a direct pipeline into the Tambour PD. 'Crawford thinks they've got moles inside the sheriff's office, too,' Tom said. 'And Gillette went ballistic over Crawford's insinuation that his daughter-in-law was "in cahoots" with Coburn. Said that if his family wound up dead, their blood would be on my hands.'

Hamilton considered his decision for several seconds, then said, 'Tom, Mrs Gillette and her little girl are in danger, but not from Coburn. He's one of ours. He's an agent.'

After a momentary pause, VanAllen said, 'Crawford asked me point-blank if he was. I said no.'

'Where did he get the notion?'

'Rumour mill, he said.'

That was troubling. The rumour had to have originated in Tom VanAllen's own office, based on the fishing Hamilton had done yesterday. Shelving that issue for the moment, he gave Tom background on Coburn.

'I recruited Coburn straight out of the Marines and trained him personally. He's one of our best undercover agents. He took Mrs Gillette and the little girl from their home for their own protection. On that score, you can ease your mind. What you should be concerned about is the seepage of information out of your office.'

VanAllen's voice vibrated with anger. 'Why did you deliberately mislead me about Coburn?'

'Because his mission was sensitive. There's some bad stuff going on down there, and everyone is susceptible to corruption.'

'If you didn't trust me, why did you appoint me to this job?'

'I appointed you because you're the best man for the position.'

VanAllen gave a bitter laugh. 'Well, in light of my position, can you tell me why Coburn was planted inside Sam Marset's company?'

Hamilton talked him through the secret op. 'Essentially he went in to unmask the players. Discovered more than he bargained for.'

'The Bookkeeper.'

'The Bookkeeper. Coburn was on the verge of making an ID.'

'So why haven't you made arrangements for him to come in, share what he knows?'

'I tried,' Hamilton said. 'He wants to finish what he started.'

'How noble,' VanAllen said snidely. 'The truth is, he doesn't trust this office and his fellow FBI agents. Where does Mrs Gillette fit into this?'

'Coburn thinks her late husband died with secrets to reveal about The Bookkeeper. The target on Coburn's back gets bigger every minute he's out there.' Having reached the heart of the matter, Hamilton said, 'That's why I need you to bring them in. We need to finish this thing.'

COBURN CLIMBED BACK INTO the pick-up truck, trying to ignore the damp spot on his cheek where Emily had planted a kiss. He wanted to wipe it away, but doing so would be an acknowledgment that he felt it. Better to attach no significance to it. But as he watched the Mini Cooper disappear, he realised that he was going to miss the kid's chatter.

When Honor joined him in the pick-up, he gave her a dirty look for having lagged behind, but he didn't say anything because she was holding back tears, and the last thing he needed was a crying jag.

As he started the truck, he mentioned the tyre tracks they would have left near the boat. 'No way they could have missed them. If these tyres were put on at the factory, they'll be on the lookout for this make and model. We need another set of wheels.'

'You plan to steal another car?'

'I do. From the family that supplied the truck.'

They drove for twenty minutes along back roads. Coburn had a flawless sense of direction and was able to relocate the house from which he'd taken the pick-up. It was a mile from its nearest neighbour, and the mailbox was still bulging with uncollected mail.

He guided the pick-up up the drive, pulled into its original spot, and cut the engine. The garage was twenty yards from the house. Exterior stairs led to quarters above it, but Coburn was interested only in the car he'd seen inside the garage yesterday. There was an old padlock securing it, but he used a crowbar from the toolbox in the pick-up and, within seconds, was raising the garage door.

The sedan was old, but in good shape. The keys were dangling from the ignition. It took a couple of tries, but it started. He drove the car out of the garage, then put it in park and got out. He looked at Honor, and hitched his chin towards the passenger side door. 'Get in.'

'HAS HE GOT AN alarm system?'

'Yes.'

'Do you know the code?'

'Yes.'

'Can we get in without being seen?'

'Possibly. At the back corner of the house, there's an exterior door going into the garage. It has a keypad, but I know the code. There's access to the kitchen through the garage.'

They'd already driven past Stan Gillette's house twice, but Coburn wanted to be certain he wasn't walking into an ambush. Befitting Gillette's character, his was the neatest house on the street.

Coburn drove past it and circled the block again.

'He's not there,' Honor said. 'He doesn't put his car in the garage except at night. If he were in the house, his car would be in the driveway.'

'Maybe this is a special occasion.'

Two blocks away from Gillette's street was an empty playground. Coburn pulled the car into the lot and they got out. 'We're in no particular hurry,' he said. 'Just out for a leisurely stroll. OK? Wouldn't hurt for you to smile.'

'This coming from the man who doesn't own one.'

They fell into step and walked along the perimeter. They reached Stan's house without mishap. Honor raised the cover on the keypad and pecked in the code. They slipped into the garage, and he pulled the door shut behind them. Daylight coming through high windows enabled them to see their way to the kitchen door. Honor stepped inside and disarmed the alarm.

Coburn listened for sixty long seconds. 'I think we're OK.'

Most operating rooms weren't as sterile as Stan Gillette's kitchen. Coburn figured the sterility was a reflection of the man himself. Cold, impersonal, unyielding, no emotional clutter. Which, he realised, was also an accurate description of himself.

Honor led him into what had been Eddie's bedroom. He pointed her towards a bureau. 'Empty the drawers. I'll start on the closet.'

It seemed that Gillette hadn't disposed of anything belonging to his son. Resisting the temptation to rush, Coburn tried not to overlook anything. Thinking that Eddie's police uniforms would be a logical hiding place, he examined each lining and pocket. An hour passed.

Another hour went by. Coburn was on borrowed time and it was getting away from him. He glanced at Honor to ask again about her father-in-law's routine, but the question died before he asked it.

She was sitting on the bed, going through a box of medals Eddie had won for sporting contests. She was crying silently.

'What's the matter?'

Her head came up. 'What's the *matter*? This is the matter, Coburn. This!' She shoved the box away from her. 'I feel like a grave robber.'

What did she want him to say? *I'm sorry, let's leave.* A moment passed while they just looked at one another.

'Never mind,' she said. 'I don't expect you to understand.'

She was right. He didn't understand why this was upsetting her. He'd done worse things. But Honor didn't need to know about it.

'Where's Stan's room?'

TWO HOURS LATER, the house was in a state similar to Honor's when Coburn had finished with it. The only place that hadn't been searched was the garage. In the extra bay, a spick-and-span fishing boat sat on its trailer. Hunting and fishing gear was so nicely arranged it looked like a store display. Along the back of a worktable, paint cans had been perfectly lined up. Tools were neatly arrayed on a pegboard wall.

'Damn,' Coburn said. 'It would take days to go through all this.' He nodded towards the small loft that was mounted just under the ceiling in one corner. 'What's up there?'

'Mostly Eddie's sporting gear.'

A ladder had been built into the wall. Coburn climbed it and stepped onto the loft. 'Hand me a knife.' Honor got one from the worktable and passed it to him. He used it to slice through the packing tape on a large box. Inside, he found an archery target, baseball, basketball, soccer ball and football.

One by one, he tossed them down to her. In a second box were uniforms. He searched them all. Found nothing.

When he came down, Honor was holding the football. Smiling, she said, 'Eddie was quarterback of the high-school team. His senior year, they went to district. He was too small to play college ball, but he'd go out and throw passes whenever he could get somebody to catch them.'

Coburn held out his hand. Honor gave him the football. He plunged the blade of the knife into it. She cried out and reflexively reached to take it back, but he worked the knife to increase the size of the hole, then shook it. Nothing. He tossed the deflated ball onto the worktable.

When he came back around, she slapped him. Hard. 'You're a horrible person,' she said. 'The coldest, most heartless, cruellest creature I can imagine.' She stopped on a sob. 'I hate you. I really do.'

At that moment, he pretty much hated himself. He was angry and didn't know why. He was acting like a complete jerk and didn't know why. But he seemed incapable of stopping himself.

He took a step towards her. 'You don't like me?'

'I *despise* you.'

'Is that why you kissed me last night?'

She spun away, but he reached out and brought her back around. 'That's what you're really pissed about, isn't it? Because we kissed.' Lowering his face closer to hers, he whispered, 'And you liked it.'

'I hated it.'

He released her arm. 'Don't beat yourself up over it. Humans are animals, and animals mate. That's as much as that kiss meant. You didn't cheat on your dead husband.'

Before she could respond, he pulled out his cellphone. By now Hamilton would know about this morning's close call on the shrimp boat. Coburn wanted to know what the fallout had been.

He placed the call. Hamilton answered immediately. 'Coburn?'

'Good guess.'

'You pulled a fast one this morning. Where are you?'

'Try again.'

'I've set it up with Tom VanAllen for you and Mrs Gillette to come in. He's as solid as Gibraltar. It'll be safe. I give you my word.'

Coburn held Honor's stare. His cheek still stung where she'd slapped him, where hours ago her daughter had left the wet imprint of a goodbye kiss. He wasn't used to dealing with people who wore their emotions on their sleeves. No wonder he was cranky.

'Coburn?' Hamilton said.

'I'll call you back,' he said, and clicked off the phone.

Chapter 9

'He lied to you.'

Tom VanAllen made a shrugging motion. 'Not outrightly.'

'He deliberately misled you. What would you call it?' Janice said.

He would call it lying. But to admit how gullible he'd been would make him look even more ridiculous to his wife.

He'd come home to help her with Lanny, who'd kept them up most of the night moaning. In the end, he'd fallen asleep, but it had been a rough night. That, coupled with Tom's professional crisis, was making both of them feel particularly whipped today.

After tending to Lanny, he'd declined her offer of lunch but instead had gone to the den to tell her about Hamilton's trickery. He'd noticed the computer was on, and she admitted to having spent time investigating the websites of some of the better perpetual care homes within a reasonable distance.

Tom regarded that as a step forward. Of sorts. Paradoxically it was a forward step that led to an end. He was almost relieved to have another crisis diverting his attention from that one.

'How do you know he's telling the truth now?' Janice asked. 'That man Coburn seems no more like an FBI agent than—'

'Than I do.'

Her stricken expression was as good as an admission that he'd taken the words out of her mouth. 'What I meant was that Coburn sounds like someone who's cracked. He killed eight people, counting Fred Hawkins.'

'Hamilton claims Coburn didn't shoot those men in the warehouse.'

'Then who did?'

'He didn't say.'

'Does he know?'

Tom shrugged.

She exhaled a gust of breath. 'So he's still playing head games with you.'

'He's paranoid about leaks. With reason.'

'Why didn't Coburn call you for help?'

'He wanted to maintain his cover. Besides, Hamilton is his exclusive go-to guy.'

'Until now.' Janice didn't try to disguise her bitterness. 'Now that his boy wonder has his back against a wall, Hamilton dumps it on you to bring him in. If it goes wrong, you catch the blame.'

She was right, of course. 'It may not even happen. Coburn doesn't trust the agency, and, frankly, he'd be crazy not to be cautious. If Marset was as dirty as alleged, God knows what kind of evidence Coburn's collected. Anyone who did illicit trade with Marset probably has a contract out on him. It's got Hamilton worried.'

'He wants Coburn alive.'

'He wants the evidence Coburn obtained.' Tom glanced at his wristwatch and then reached for his suit jacket. 'I need to get back.'

As he walked past her towards the door, she reached for his hand. 'Tom, this could be an opportunity for you to prove your mettle. Show Hamilton your stuff. And Coburn. And everyone.'

'I'll do my best.'

He got as far as the front door before realising he'd left his keys.

He retraced his steps to the den, but then drew up short. Janice had returned to the sofa. She had her cellphone in hand, her thumbs tapping the touch screen. In under a minute, he and his problems had been forgotten. She was engrossed in her own world.

'Janice?'

She jumped. 'Tom!' she gasped. 'I thought you'd left.' She came to her feet. 'Did you forget something?' Her pitch was unnaturally high.

He nodded at the phone in her hand. 'What are you doing?'

'Playing my word game.'

'Let me see.' He extended his hand.

'You're interested in my word game? Since when have you—'

He lunged and snatched the phone from her hand.

'Tom!' she cried in shock.

When he held it out of her reach and read the text message, she said his name again, this time with a soft, remorseful groan.

'I'M PUTTING YOU on alert. Be ready to move at a moment's notice.'

Diego gave a sarcastic huff. 'What? And miss all this fun?'

He'd been watching Bonnell Wallace's mansion since before sunrise and had followed the banker as he drove out of the gate. For hours, he'd been watching Wallace's car where it had remained in the employees' lot at the bank. In addition to being bored, Diego disliked being assigned a mindless job that any moron could do.

'I sense some malcontent in your tone, Diego. I have a reason for assigning you to watch Wallace.'

Well, so far the reason had escaped Diego but the prospect of a more exciting job perked him up. 'Today's the day I get Coburn?'

'Coburn is an undercover FBI agent.'

Diego's heart bumped. Taking out a Fed, that was trippy, man.

'You'll have to move with extreme caution. You'll know the details when I'm ready for you to know.'

Then the line went dead.

HONOR AND COBURN made it back to the playground parking lot without incident. They got into their stolen car and drove away.

Only then did Honor ask Coburn about his brief exchange with Hamilton. 'What did he say?'

'He wants us to turn ourselves over to Tom VanAllen. He said VanAllen's solid and that we'll be safe in his custody.'

'Do you believe him?'

'If VanAllen is that solid, why didn't Hamilton let him in on my op? That makes me nervous. I'd have to be eyeball to eyeball with VanAllen before I could gauge his trustworthiness.'

'And the other part? About his ability to protect us.'

'I have even less confidence in that, but I'm running out of options.'

'I would say so. You've resorted to puncturing harmless footballs.'

He ignored that, but she hadn't really expected an apology.

'The thing is, I know I'm right. Eddie did have something.' He looked over at her as though daring her to contradict him.

They'd been keeping to the outskirts of town, where there were clusters of houses now and then, but no organised neighbourhoods. Coburn pulled into the parking lot of a run-down strip centre and cut the motor. For several minutes, he sat deep in thought. Finally, he reached for his cellphone.

'I'm going to make this quick. Whatever I say to Hamilton, you go along. You gotta trust me, OK?' His blue eyes bored into hers.

She nodded.

He placed the call. She heard Hamilton's brusque voice. 'I hope you're calling to tell me you've come to your senses.'

'There's an old train on an abandoned track.'

He gave Hamilton the location on the outskirts of Tambour.

'VanAllen only,' Coburn said. 'I mean it. I feel one tingle down my spine and we're outta there. I send Mrs Gillette to VanAllen. But I'm keeping her kid with me until I'm certain everything's—'

'Coburn, that's—'

'Ten o'clock.' He disconnected and turned off the phone.

WHEN STAN RAISED his garage door using the remote on his car's sun visor, Eddie's basketball rolled out onto the driveway.

That could only mean one thing.

He killed the engine and got out, sliding his knife from the scabbard strapped to his ankle. No one was inside the garage. When he spotted Eddie's deflated football on the worktable, he was seized by a cold fury.

He moved swiftly but silently towards the door that led into his kitchen. He thrust the door open. The warning beep of his alarm didn't engage. The house was perfectly still. Honed instinct told him that there was no one inside. He moved from room to room, surveying the damage. *Coburn.*

And Honor. Searching the rooms this thoroughly would have taken hours. An impossible task for one man working alone. Stan's heart constricted painfully at her betrayal.

Stan had been beating the bushes all day, railing at VanAllen, calling Honor's friends and acquaintances. Doral, who had a man watching Tori Shirah's house, had informed him that Tori hadn't left it all day except to retrieve a newspaper at dawn.

Stan's gut instinct had said otherwise. He remembered a place in the country that Eddie had shown him, a place Honor believed was her secret. Eddie had confided that he'd followed her one night when, following a brief phone call, she'd abruptly left the house with a flimsy and transparently false explanation. But her mysterious errand had amounted to nothing more than a meeting with Tori. Eddie had laughed it off, saying their clandestine meeting was probably a holdover from their high-school days.

It was just possible that the tradition continued. Stan wondered if Honor had sent Tori a distress signal which she had withheld from him and the authorities. Acting on that hunch, he'd driven to the remote spot. He'd seen recent tyre tracks, but more than that, he'd noticed irregular letters etched in the mud: E M I L y.

On his way back to town, he'd called Doral to say Doral's man was wrong. Tori wasn't at home, she was with Honor and Emily.

Now, as Stan retraced his steps through his house, his cellphone rang. It was Doral, and he could almost hear him grinning. 'My guy at the FBI office called. Coburn is sending Honor in.'

TOM VANALLEN ARRIVED at the designated place at two minutes before ten o'clock. He turned off the motor of his car, and the silence was complete except for the sound of his own breathing.

He wasn't cut out for this cloak-and-dagger stuff. He knew it. Hamilton knew it. But Coburn had set the terms.

The rusting train was to Tom's right. Praying he wouldn't screw up, he checked the lighted hands on his wristwatch. He wondered if his heart could withstand the pounding for another minute and a half.

He watched the second hand tick off another few seconds, making an involuntary sound of despair as his mind tracked back to the scene that afternoon, when he'd caught his wife on her cellphone. Caught her in the act, so to speak.

Some of the words on the screen were so blatantly sexual, they seemed to jump out and strike him. But he couldn't associate them with Janice. His wife. With whom he hadn't had sex in . . . He couldn't remember when the last time had been.

The last text someone had sent her was a salacious invitation, and the reply she'd been composing was a graphic acceptance.

'Tom—'

'Who is it?'

'It's no one . . . I don't know . . . he's just a name. Everybody uses code names. Nobody knows—'

'"Everybody"?'

He tapped on the corner of the screen to display the senders from whom she'd received text messages. He tapped on one and several exchanges appeared. He accessed those sent by another sender with a suggestive code name. The names were different, but the content was nauseatingly similar.

He looked at her with horrified wonderment.

She met him eye to eye. 'I refuse to apologise. What I have to live with day in, day out, God knows I need to amuse myself. It's a pastime! Rather pathetic, but harmless. It doesn't mean anything.'

He stared at her. 'It means something to me.' He picked up his car keys and stalked from the room, leaving her calling after him.

The last thing he heard her say was, 'Don't leave me!'

Now, hours later, the sound of her plea echoed inside his head.

He'd been so damned angry. But leave her? Walk out and leave her to cope with Lanny alone? He couldn't do that.

He checked the time. Straight up ten o'clock.

'Make yourself seen,' Hamilton had told him.

He got out and walked forward, stopping several yards beyond the hood of the car, as Hamilton had directed. He could hear his own heartbeat. He didn't hear the man. He had no forewarning that he was there until the barrel of a pistol was jammed into the base of his skull.

WHEN COBURN HAD TOLD Honor what she was to do, she'd protested. 'You never intended to send me to meet VanAllen?'

'Hell no. Somebody in this op is working for The Bookkeeper. Probably lots of somebodies. The Bookkeeper is afraid of what you know, or suspect, and will want you taken out as bad as he does me.'

'He can't just have me shot.'

'Of course he can. You could become an "accidental" casualty.'

He had parked their stolen car in the garage of a defunct paint and body shop, where the gutted chassis of other cars had been left to the mercy of the elements. When she'd asked him how he knew about these places, he'd said, 'I make it my business to know.'

They had waited in the stifling garage for more than a hour before he began giving her instructions. 'Stay here,' he'd said. 'If I don't come back a few minutes after ten, drive away. Collect Emily and get as far away as this car will take you. Then tell Hamilton you won't come in to anybody except him.' He'd given her his cellphone, recited a number, and told her to memorise it.

She had repeated it back. Then he'd gone through it all again, stressing that she couldn't trust anyone, except possibly Tori. 'But they'll try to pick up her trail in the hope of it leading to you.'

She'd tried to assimilate everything he told her. When he'd said all he had to say, he'd got out of the car, rubbed his fingers in the dirt and oil on the floor, and spread the gritty residue over his face and arms. Then he'd passed her Fred's revolver. 'Don't talk yourself out of pulling the trigger, or you'll be dead. OK?'

'OK.'

'Don't let your guard down for a second. Remember, when you feel the safest, you'll be the most vulnerable.'

'I'll remember.'

'Good.' He'd taken a deep breath, then said, 'Time to go.'

'It's not nine o'clock yet.'

'If there are snipers in place, I need to know where they are.' He'd stood and looked at her for several seconds. 'You know, as kids go, yours is OK.'

She'd opened her mouth to speak, but could merely nod.

'And the football? It was a mean thing to do. I'm sorry.'

Then he was gone, and she'd been left alone in the darkness.

Where she had remained for more than an hour now.

She was worried about Emily and Tori. She thought of Stan, and how badly she felt about turning his home inside out. Her thoughts often returned to Coburn and the last things he'd said to her.

It was a mean thing to do. It might not have been the most eloquent of apologies, but Honor didn't question its sincerity. His eyes had conveyed his regret as well as his words. *I'm sorry.* She believed he was.

His harsh childhood had made him cynical. The things he'd seen and done while in service to his country had hardened his heart even more. Whatever he said and did was unfiltered because hesitation could be fatal. He didn't worry about future regret because he didn't expect to live to re-examine the pivotal decisions of his life.

Everything he did, he did as if his life depended on it. The way he ate, apologised . . . kissed . . . was like it was for the last time.

That brought Honor's thoughts to a complete standstill, and she experienced a jarring realisation. 'Oh God,' she whimpered.

Suddenly flying into motion, she pushed open the car door and scrambled out. She struck out in a dead run for the railroad tracks.

Why hadn't she realised it before? Coburn didn't expect to return from this meeting with VanAllen. In his way, he'd been telling her goodbye.

He'd said all along that he didn't expect to survive, and tonight he'd gone in her place, probably sacrificing himself to save her. But his thinking was flawed. No one was going to shoot her. If The Bookkeeper believed she had something that would incriminate him, she wouldn't be killed until he had discovered what it was. That was as good as a bulletproof vest. But Coburn had no such protection. She was his protection.

Chapter 10

'Coburn?'

Coburn pressed the pistol more firmly against VanAllen's neck. 'Pleased to meet you.'

'I was expecting Mrs Gillette.'

'She's couldn't make it. If the sharpshooters who've got me in their night-vision sights kill me, she'll stay perpetually lost.'

VanAllen shook his head slightly. 'There are no sharpshooters.'

'Tell me another one. Wireless mike? Are you talking for the benefit of everybody out there listening in?'

'No. You can search me if you don't believe me.'

Coburn deftly stepped round VanAllen, but kept his pistol aimed at his head. When he came face to face with the man, Coburn sized him up. Desk jockey. Probably with neither the guts nor the cunning to be on the take. Which was why the man truly didn't know about the sniper on the water tower. Or the one in the caboose window.

'Where are Mrs Gillette and the child?' VanAllen asked. 'They're my chief concern.'

'Mine, too. Which is why I'm here and she's not.' Coburn lowered the pistol to his side.

VanAllen wet his lips. 'You can trust me, Mr Coburn. I don't want this fouled up any more than you do. Is Mrs Gillette all right?'

'Yes, and I want to make certain she stays that way. Here's what's going to happen. You're going to order the local PD to call off the manhunt for me. I can't have a bunch of trigger-happy yokels on my ass.'

'Crawford isn't going to shrug off eight murders.'

'Homicide detective?'

'For the sheriff's office. He's investigating Fred Hawkins's murder. He sort of inherited the warehouse murders when Fred—'

'I get the picture,' Coburn said. 'Talk this Crawford into granting me a reprieve until I can bring Mrs Gillette in safely. Then I'll brief him on the warehouse shootings and Fred Hawkins.'

'He won't go for it. Maybe if you gave me information that I—'

'No, thanks. Your office leaks like a sieve and so does his.'

VanAllen sighed, looking worried. 'It all relates to The Bookkeeper, right? And it's big?'

'Right.'

'Can't you tell me anything?'

'If you were supposed to know, Hamilton would have already told you.'

The man winced. 'OK, I'll do my best with Crawford.'

'I'll bring Mrs Gillette in, but I'll choose my time and place. I'm still on the trail of something, and I intend to finish the job that Hamilton assigned me. You can tell him that. Now, let's get in the car. We'll make it look like I'm going peaceably.'

'Look like?' He glanced around. 'Look like to who?'

'To the snipers who've got me in their cross hairs.' Coburn frowned at him. 'Come on, VanAllen. The only reason they haven't taken me out already is because they don't know where Honor Gillette is. You and I will get in the car and drive away.'

'Then what?'

'Somewhere between here and your office in Lafayette, I get out. When you arrive, surprise! I'm no longer in the car with you. You arrest whoever baulks first, because that's who had the snipers in place. Got it?'

VanAllen nodded uncertainly. He turned and walked to the driver's side of the car and opened the door.

Coburn opened the passenger side door and was about to get in when he sensed motion in his peripheral vision. A shadow streaked past the gap between two of the freight cars. Coburn dropped to look beneath the train and saw a pair of legs on the other side sprinting away. He started crawling in that direction and was almost under the train when a cellphone rang.

Coburn swivelled his head, caught VanAllen as he reached for the ringing telephone attached to his belt.

Coburn looked beneath the train and at the man fleeing from it.

Then to VanAllen, he shouted, '*No!*'

HONOR WAS WINDED. She hadn't thought the train tracks were that far from the garage until she began covering the distance. Her steps became slower the farther she ran. Her heart felt on the verge of bursting but she ran on, because Coburn's life could very well depend on her reaching him. Finally she reached the tracks.

She spotted the old train near the water tower, then the automobile parked near the train. She saw the two figures standing in front of the hood. As she watched, Coburn went round to the passenger side. The driver got in and closed his car door.

A heartbeat later a ball of flame bloomed into the night sky, illuminating everything around it in the red glow of Hell.

The repercussion of the explosion knocked her to the ground.

DORAL HAD THE DUBIOUS pleasure of informing The Bookkeeper.

'My guy in the FBI office had just enough time to plant the bomb on the car and programme in the phone number. But it worked exactly like it was supposed to. Bam! They never had a chance.'

The silence on the other end was palpable.

'I witnessed it myself from the water tower. All of us got the hell away immediately. Nobody ever knew we were there.'

Still silence.

Doral cleared his throat. 'There is one thing. It wasn't Honor who showed up. It was Coburn. Which is better when you think about it.'

'But those weren't your instructions. That wasn't my plan for Coburn.'

'We got two FBI guys tonight,' he said. 'That should impress that cartel.'

But The Bookkeeper didn't seem all that impressed. What did he have to do to make up for letting Coburn escape the warehouse? Now that Coburn and VanAllen were dead, the only remaining threat was Honor. She had to be eliminated. Doral accepted that. Just as he'd accepted having to kill Eddie.

He and Fred had tried to persuade The Bookkeeper to rethink that mandate. They'd bargained for his life to be spared. Did Eddie, their boyhood friend, really have to *die*? Maybe just a stern warning or a threat either real or implied would work.

But The Bookkeeper hadn't made an exception even for Eddie. He'd crossed a line. He had to go. Doral and Fred had made it as quick and painless as possible, while still making it look like an accident.

Doral hoped he could devise something that easy for Honor.

Of course before Doral could do anything, he had to find her.

With the mind-reading skills that often gave Doral gooseflesh, The Bookkeeper said, 'Coburn's dead, and he was the only person who knew where Honor is. How do you plan to find her?'

'I'm going to focus on Tori Shirah. Because when we find her, we find Honor and Emily.'

'For your sake, I hope you're right, Doral. For once.'

The Bookkeeper hung up without saying more. Doral closed his phone and realised his hand was shaking.

He drove his pick-up out of the crowded parking lot of the tavern where he'd stopped to toast his success with the car bomb. He joined the stream of vehicles that were homing in on the area near the train tracks where VanAllen's car still smouldered.

The area had been cordoned off. Flashing strobes of emergency vehicles gave the scene a surreal aspect. Doral heard a dozen versions of what had taken place and who was responsible, none of which were right. Playing the role of city manager, Doral pledged that law enforcement officials were doing all they could.

He'd been glad-handing for about an hour when he saw the coroner backing his van away from the burnt-out car. Doral motioned for him to lower his window. 'Any guess who was in the car?'

'The driver?' The coroner shook his head. 'No idea. Wasn't enough to make a positive ID.'

'What about the other one?'

'What other one?'

'The other person. On the passenger side.' He hitched his thumb over his shoulder. 'Somebody said there were two.'

'Then somebody said wrong. There was just the one.'

The earth dropped out from under Doral.

COBURN HAD BEEN PARTIALLY beneath the train when the bomb detonated, which is what had saved him. Triggered when VanAllen answered his cellphone, the explosion had instantly obliterated most of VanAllen and demolished the car.

When Coburn crawled out from under the boxcar, burning debris showered him, scorching skin, hair and clothing. With no time to drop and roll, he batted out the burning patches as he ran like hell the length of the train.

The man in the caboose had saved his life. Had it not been for his running away, Coburn would have been standing in the open passenger door when VanAllen answered his phone. Coburn rounded the caboose and ran in a crouch along the weed-choked tracks, trying to keep a low profile against the glow of the burning car.

He was almost on top of Honor before he saw her, and even then it took him a second to process that the form on the tracks was Honor. With full-blown panic, he thought, *Oh God, she's dead. No!*

He bent over and dug his fingers into her neck for a pulse. She slapped at his hands and screamed bloody murder. He was glad she was alive, but, at the same time, furious with her for endangering herself. He scooped her off the ground and up against him.

'Stop screaming! It's me. Are you hurt?'

He looked her over. She didn't have any wounds that he could see. Her eyes were open and staring at him, but unfocused.

'Honor, we've got to get away from here. Now! Come on!'

He jerked on her hand as he struck out running, trusting her to come along. She did, although she stumbled before gaining her footing.

When they reached the garage, he opened the door, shoved her inside, then rolled the door shut. He didn't even wait for his eyes to adjust to the darkness, but guided her by feel to the car. He secured her in the passenger seat, then got in on the driver's side.

He pulled off his T-shirt and used it to wipe off the grease camouflaging his face and arms. The shirt came away blood-smeared.

He looked over at Honor. Her teeth were chattering, and she was hugging herself tightly. He didn't attempt to snap her out of her daze. For the time being it was just as well that she had shut down.

He got out of the car and opened the garage door. He drove out of the garage, his destination the only place he knew to go.

THIS JOB SUCKED.

By now, Diego should have been washing Coburn's blood off his razor. Instead, he'd wasted all day baby-sitting the fat guy's car until he left at ten past five. The Bookkeeper had said to follow him, so Diego had followed him through rush-hour traffic. He'd gone straight home to his mansion.

That had been hours ago, and no one else had come or gone.

After collecting his pay for this job, Diego would get himself a new phone and disappear off The Bookkeeper's radar. As though he'd conjured up a call, his phone vibrated. He pulled it out and answered.

'Are you ready for some action, Diego?'

'You hafta ask?'

The Bookkeeper issued him new instructions, but they were a far cry from what he'd waited all day to hear. 'You're conning me, right?'

'Change of plans, but this is related. Just do as I tell you.'

'What do you want me to do with him after?'

'That's a stupid question. You know the answer. Get on it.'

Diego disconnected. For several minutes, he remained in his hiding place and analysed the mansion. Then, keeping to the shadows and moving with the stealth of one, he found a place at the back of the property where the wisteria vine on the estate wall was thick and the lighting thin. He went over the wall.

THE PLACE WAS still deserted. The padlock on the door of the detached garage was exactly as Coburn had left it. The black pick-up hadn't been moved from where he'd parked it that morning.

He parked the sedan beside it and they got out. Honor, still functioning in a fog, looked to him for direction. 'Let's see what's up there,' he said, nodding towards the room above the garage.

They climbed the staircase attached to the exterior wall. The door at the top of the stairs was locked, but Coburn found the key above the doorjamb. He opened the door and flipped on the light.

The small room obviously had been occupied by a young male. Sports posters and pennants were tacked to the walls. The bed was covered with a stadium blanket. A nightstand, a chest of drawers and a vinyl beanbag chair were the only other pieces of furniture. Coburn crossed the room and opened a door, revealing a small bathroom with a shower stall.

He tested the taps on the bathroom basin. Water gushed from both faucets. He found a drinking glass in the medicine cabinet, filled it with cold water, and passed it to Honor.

She took it gratefully and drained it. He ducked his head into the basin and drank straight from the faucet. When he came up, he wiped his mouth with the back of his hand. 'Home sweet home.'

'What if the family comes back?'

'I hope they won't. At least not until I've used their shower.'

She tried to smile, but it fell flat. 'Who blew up the car?'

'The Bookkeeper has somebody inside the FBI office. Somebody privy to information.' His lips formed a grim line. 'Somebody who's gonna die as soon as I find out who he is.'

'How are you going to do that?'

'Find your late husband's treasure, and we find that person.'

'Was VanAllen—'

'He was clueless.' Tersely, Coburn recounted their conversation. 'The naive bastard really thought we were all alone out there.'

'Somebody set him up to die.'

'Along with you.'

'Except that you took my place.'

He shrugged with seeming indifference.

She swallowed the emotion that was making her throat ache and focused on something else. She pointed towards his shoulder. 'Does that hurt?'

He looked at the patch of raw skin. 'I think a piece of burning car upholstery fell on me. It stings a little.' His eyes moved over her. 'What about you?'

'No. I guess I'm lucky.'

'Why'd you leave the garage?'

The question took her off guard. 'I don't know. I just did.'

'Were you going to throw yourself on VanAllen's mercy?'

'No!' Before he could say anything further, she motioned towards his head. 'Your hair's singed.'

Absently he raked his hand over his hair as he moved to the chest of drawers. He found a T-shirt and a pair of jeans. The T-shirt would do, but the jeans were too large. 'I'll have to make do with your dad's khakis.'

'We're both a mess.' She was still wearing the clothes she'd had on when they'd fled her house yesterday morning.

'You use the shower first,' he said. 'I'll see if I can find us something to eat in the main house.'

Without another word, he left. Listlessly, Honor forced herself to move. The bar soap in the shower was locker-room variety, but she used it liberally, even washed her hair with it. The towels were thin smelt reassuringly of Tide. She finger-combed the tangles out of her hair, then dressed in her dirty clothes. She carried her damp sneakers out with her.

Coburn had returned, bringing with him various staples he'd set out on top of the chest of drawers.

'No perishables in the fridge, so they must have planned to be gone for a while. And these are for your jeans.' He held out a pair of kitchen scissors.

He'd already hacked off her dad's trousers at the knees. 'Thanks.'

'Dig in.' He motioned towards the food, then went into the bathroom and closed the door.

She hadn't eaten since the breakfast sandwich, but she wasn't hungry. She did, however, take the scissors to her jeans, leaving them with a ragged edge just above her knees. It felt worlds better to be rid of the fabric that was stiff with dried swamp water.

She turned off the ceiling light, switched on a small lamp on the night-stand, then moved to the window and separated the curtains.

It had been an overcast day, but the clouds had thinned out. Wisps drifted across a half-moon. *I see the moon, and the moon sees me.* The song she and Emily sang together caused her heart to clutch with homesickness for her daughter.

Hearing Coburn emerge from the bathroom, Honor hastily wiped the tears off her cheeks and turned back into the room. He had dressed in the cut-off khakis and the oversized T-shirt. He was barefoot. And he must have found a razor because he had shaved.

He looked up at the extinguished ceiling light, then over at the lamp on the bedside-table. 'Why are you crying?'

'I miss Emily.'

He raised his chin in acknowledgment. 'Did you eat anything?'

She shook her head. 'I'm not hungry.'

'Why are you crying?' he asked again.

'I'm not.' Even as she said it, fresh tears slid down her cheeks.

'Why'd you risk your life? Why'd you leave the garage?'

'I just . . . I don't know.' The last three words rode out on a sob.

He started walking towards her. 'Why are you crying, Honor?'

'I don't know. I don't know.' When she reached her, she said once again in a hoarse whisper, 'I don't know.'

For what seemed like the longest time, he did nothing except stare into her tearful eyes. Then he raised his hands to either side of her face, slid his fingers up through her hair, and cupped her head. 'Yeah, you do.'

Angling his head, he kissed her as passionately as he had the night before, but this time she didn't fight the sensations it evoked. She couldn't have even if she had wanted to. His large hands moved to her hips and drew her up against him. And when he growled against her lips, 'Are you gonna stop?' she shook her head and drew him back to continue the kiss.

They kissed recklessly and hungrily, She tried to get a grip on her spinning universe, but she kept slipping . . .

'Honor.'

Gasping, she looked into his face.

'Put your hands on me. Pretend this means something.'

With a whimper, she wrapped her arms around him and drew him in.

Chapter 11

For Clint Hamilton the wait was agonising.

An hour ago, an agent in the Lafayette office had called to inform him that the meeting between Honor Gillette and Tom VanAllen had ended disastrously with a car-bomb explosion.

Since receiving the staggering news, Hamilton had been alternately pacing his Washington office or sitting with his elbows propped on his desk, supporting his head.

He waited. He paced. He wasn't a patient man.

The anticipated call came shortly after 0100 EDT.

Unhappily the update confirmed that Tom VanAllen had died in the explosion. 'My condolences, sir,' the agent in Louisiana said.

'Thank you,' Hamilton replied. 'And Mrs Gillette?'

'VanAllen was the only casualty.'

Hamilton nearly dropped the phone. 'What? Mrs Gillette? Coburn? The child?'

'Whereabouts unknown,' the agent told him.

Mystified, Hamilton processed that even as he was being told that an arson inspector from New Orleans was assisting the investigation. He asked if VanAllen's wife had been notified.

'Two agents have been dispatched to the VanAllen home.'

'Keep me posted on that. I also want to know anything else you hear, official or not. Especially about Coburn and Mrs Gillette.'

He ended the call and slammed his fist on his desk. Why the hell hadn't

Coburn called? Although, he grudgingly admitted, a car bomb wouldn't exactly inspire an agent's confidence in his agency, would it?

Hamilton decided that the situation could no longer be handled long distance. He needed to go there himself. He placed a series of calls and secured clearance from his superiors. He asked for a squad of agents trained for special ops. 'I want them at Langley, geared up and ready to board the jet at oh two thirty.'

Everyone with whom he spoke asked why he was flying men down there when he could use personnel from the district office in New Orleans. His answer to all of them was the same.

'Because I don't want anyone to know I'm coming.'

WHEN HER DOORBELL RANG, Janice VanAllen ran to answer it, not caring that she was wearing only her nightgown. She had a look of concern on her face when she pulled open the front door.

Two strangers stood there. One was male, the other female, but their dark suits and serious expressions were practically identical.

'Mrs VanAllen?' The woman palmed a leather ID wallet. Her partner did the same. 'Special Agent Beth Turner and Special Agent Ward Fitzgerald. We're from Tom's office.'

Janice's chest rose and fell on short breaths. 'Where's Tom?'

'May we come in?' the woman asked kindly.

Janice shook her head. 'Where is Tom?'

They remained silent.

Janice made a keening sound and gripped the door. 'He's dead?'

Special Agent Turner reached for her, but Janice jerked her arm back. 'He's dead?' she repeated, this time on a ragged cry. And then her knees gave way and she crumpled to the floor.

HONOR SMILED SHYLY and burrowed her face into Coburn's chest.

He gathered her close. They had moved to the bed and were lying with their legs entwined. 'What was its name?'

'What?'

'You'd named the horse you had to shoot. What was its name?'

He glanced down at her, then away. 'I forgot.'

'No, you didn't,' she said softly.

He lay still and said nothing for the longest time, then, 'Dusty.'

She propped her fist on his breastbone and rested her chin on her fist, and looked into his face. He held out for several moments, then lowered his gaze to her. 'Every day when I got home from school, he'd amble over to the fence like he was glad to see me. He liked me, probably because I fed him.'

'I doubt that was the only reason he liked you.'

'He was a horse. What did he know? Dumb thing to be talking about.' He tugged on a strand of her hair, then studied it thoughtfully as he rubbed it between his fingers. 'It's pretty.'

'Thank you. It's seen better days.'

'You're pretty.'

'Thanks again.'

He took in all the features of her face, but eventually his eyes rested on hers. 'You hadn't been with anybody since Eddie.'

'No.'

Eddie had been a wonderful and ardent lover, and she would cherish for ever sweet memories of him. But Coburn had a distinct advantage. He was alive, warm, virile, and inclining towards her now.

His kiss was languid and sexy. Their hands explored. She discovered scars on him that she kissed in spite of mild protests. He kissed her rib cage, turning her on her stomach. He pecked kisses down her spine. 'My oh my. Who would have guessed?'

Knowing what he had discovered, she said primly, 'You didn't corner the market on tattoos.'

'What inspired you?'

'Two Hurricanes at Pat O'Brien's. Eddie and I spent a three-day weekend in New Orleans while Stan kept Emily.'

'You got drunk?'

'Tipsy. I was easily persuaded.'

'What is it?'

'A Chinese symbol, maybe. I can't remember,' she said quietly.

He stared into her eyes for several moments, then pulled away and lay on his back, staring at the ceiling.

She turned onto her side towards him. Quietly she said, 'When this is over, I'll never see you again, will I?'

He waited for a beat or two, then gave a shake of his head.

'Right,' she whispered, smiling ruefully. 'I didn't think so.'

'I haven't made a secret of who I am, what I'm like. Yeah, I've wanted you naked from the minute I saw you, and I made no secret of that either. But I'm not a hearts-and-flowers guy. I'm not even an all-night guy. I don't hold hands. I don't cuddle . . .' He paused, swore. 'I don't do any of that stuff.'

'All you've done is risk your life to save mine. More than once.'

He looked at her.

'You asked me why I left the garage,' she said. 'Now I want to ask you something. Why were you coming back to it?'

'Huh?'

'You'd told me that if you didn't return within a few minutes after ten o'clock, I was to drive as far from Tambour as possible. So, for all you knew, that's what I'd done. After nearly dying in that explosion, you could have run in any direction to get away, but you didn't. When you found me, you were racing back to the garage. To me.'

He didn't say anything, but his jaw tensed.

She smiled and moved closer to him, aligning her body along his. 'You don't have to give me flowers, Coburn. You don't even have to hold me.' She laid her head on his chest just below his chin. Her hand curved around his neck. 'Let me hold you.'

DIEGO HELD THE RAZOR'S EDGE to Bonnell Wallace's Adam's apple.

Wallace was proving to be a stubborn son of a bitch.

Getting into the house had been easy. The alarm hadn't been set, so he hadn't had to strike immediately and then run like hell to get away before the cops showed up. Instead, he'd been able to sneak in and get the layout of the house before Wallace knew he was there.

He thought he'd caught every break, until he realised Wallace was in the study, in plain view of anyone who happened by on the street.

The soundtrack of a television show had covered his footsteps as he'd climbed the staircase. The first floor had bedrooms along both sides of a long hallway, but Diego had soon discovered the master suite. He had made himself at home inside the walk-in closet. An hour had elapsed before Wallace came up to the room.

From inside the closet Diego had heard the chirps of the security system as Wallace punched in the code numbers to set it for the night. But he'd decided not to worry about that until he'd figured out how to overpower a man twice his size.

Wallace had obliged him. As soon as he'd entered the bedroom, he'd headed for the adjacent bathroom and unzipped. He used both hands to aim.

Diego had come up behind him and pressed the razor to his throat. Wallace had cried out in shock. Reflexively he'd reached behind him and tried to ward off his attacker. Diego had sliced at his hand.

Wallace had stopped struggling and asked, 'What do you want? Money? Credit cards? Take what you want and get out.'

'I want Tori. Where is she?'

Wallace had been taken aback. 'She's not here.'

'I know that, jerk face. I want to know where she is.'

'I don't know. I haven't seen or heard from her today.'

Diego had cut an inch-long slice in Wallace's cheek. 'It's the ear next time. Where is she?'

'I don't know,' Wallace had said. 'I had one text this morning, saying she had to leave town. She didn't say where she was going.'

'Where's your phone?'

Wallace had sucked in air. 'I tossed my phone on the chair when I came in here. Go look. I swear.'

'You want me to go see if your phone is in the bedroom? Fine. Only thing is, I'll have to kill you first, because I'm not letting go of you until you tell me what I want to know or until you're dead.'

'I think you're going to kill me anyway.'

Now, after five minutes of this song and dance, Diego was ready to be done with Wallace. 'One more time. Where is she?'

'I don't know. But even if I did, I wouldn't tell you.'

Diego moved like a striking snake, but he didn't cut Wallace's throat. Instead, he dashed his head against the toilet. The big man fell to the floor. Diego used a monogrammed towel to wipe his razor clean. The cellphone was exactly where Wallace had said.

Rapidly, he made his way downstairs, avoiding the front windows. He accessed Wallace's text messages. Tori. Eight forty-seven a.m. She was leaving town at short notice, but didn't say where. Next Diego looked at Wallace's call log. No calls from her. The fat man had been telling the truth.

Diego used his phone to call The Bookkeeper. He recited Tori's cellphone number and explained the text message.

'All well and good,' The Bookkeeper said tightly, 'but where is she?'

'Wallace doesn't know.'

'Doesn't? Present tense?'

'What good would it do to kill him? He didn't see me.'

'No loose ends, Diego. What, have you gone soft?'

'I haven't. But once I open a door to this place, all hell's gonna break loose. If I can't outrun the police, I don't want to be caught with a dead man.'

'You're refusing to deliver what I asked for?' There was a long silence. 'You've disappointed me, Diego.' The silkiness of The Bookkeeper's tone sent a tingle down Diego's spine.

Anyone who knew anything about The Bookkeeper knew what happened to people who disappointed or failed. Diego's stomach lurched. He disconnected and, without even considering the consequences, opened the kitchen door. Alarm bells went off. The noise was deafening, but it barely registered with Diego.

He sprinted across the terrace and over the lawn to the estate wall, used the leafy vine to reach the top, and jumped. He heard the whoop-whoop of approaching sirens, but he took the most direct route to his stolen car, even though it was out in the open. He pulled away with a squeal of tyres.

COBURN HAD BEEN TRAINED to sleep as efficiently as he'd been trained to do everything else. He woke up after two hours, feeling revived if not rested.

Honor was still lying as though welded to him. Her right hand was on his chest, and he was shocked to realise that, in sleep, he'd covered it with his left hand, keeping it directly over his heart.

He had to admit: She'd got to him. This demure woman, who'd been faithful to her husband, but who had made love to him with the same fervour with which she'd fought him two days ago, had crawled under his mean ol' hide. And it scared him. Because never in his life had he needed or wanted anybody needing or wanting him. Good thing that this set-up was short term. And if she wanted to hold him, fine. As long as they both understood that the intimacy was temporary.

But there was no denying how good it felt having her against him. Maybe, while they were fitted together like this, he'd kiss her. And if she woke up, smiling and drowsy, and kissed him the way she usually did, he would probably lose it. He'd have no choice. Afterwards, he would tease her about her tattoo above her shapely bottom.

Then he'd tell her what his vocation would be in his next life. He'd be a tattoo artist that specialised in women who went on Hurricane binges and got tattooed—

His lazy train of thought suddenly derailed.

He pushed her off him and leapt from the bed. 'Honor, wake up!'

Startled out of deep sleep, she came up on her elbows and shaded her eyes when he turned on the light. 'Is someone here?'

'No. Turn over on your stomach.'

'What?'

He planted his knee beside her and rolled her over. 'Your tattoo. You said you got tipsy and were persuaded. Persuaded to get tattooed?'

'Yes. I didn't take to the idea at first, but Eddie sort of double-dog dared me. I finally gave in.'

'And he chose the spot.' Coburn squinted down at the swirling pattern. 'What does it say?'

'I told you, it's a Chinese symbol of some kind. Eddie chose it. In fact he designed it.'

They stared at one another for several seconds, then Coburn said, 'We just found the treasure map.'

TORI'S CELLPHONE RANG for the umpteenth time, and for the umpteenth time she was sorely tempted to answer it. Bonnell had called her throughout the day and a dozen times in the past hour.

She longed to talk to him. So what if he wasn't handsome? He wasn't an ogre. She knew his infatuation for her was genuine. He'd be concerned over her sudden departure to parts unknown.

If he'd put two and two together, he'd have figured out that her leaving was connected to her friend who'd been kidnapped. Maybe he had late breaking news on the search for Honor and Emily. She could practically feel the urgency each time her phone rang.

After sending that one short text to Bonnell, she'd heeded Coburn's instructions, even though she'd questioned the necessity of taking such precautions. Half an hour after arriving at the house, she and Emily were making mud pies near the lake shore. She'd been enjoying herself so much that it was easy to forget why the two of them were on this excursion.

But whenever her phone rang and she saw that it was Bonnell, she'd experienced a pang of guilt, until now, lying in bed and missing his company, she'd decided no harm could come from one short conversation.

She sat up and was about to reach for her phone on the nightstand. Instead she screamed.

A man wearing a ski mask was standing at the foot of her bed.

He lunged and clamped his gloved hand over her mouth. She fought him like a swamp panther, shaking off his hand, then baring teeth and nails. Her muscled and toned body wasn't just for show. She tried to yank off his mask, but he got his fingers round her wrist and jerked it so hard she heard bones snap. In spite of herself, she screamed in pain.

Then he knocked her in the temple with his pistol grip. Darkness descended like a velvet blanket as Doral backed away and aimed.

HAMILTON'S JET SET DOWN at Lafayette Aero at 0340. The six men who disembarked with him unloaded their gear and stowed it in the two black Suburbans waiting on the tarmac. Within minutes, the team was speeding away in the darkness.

Hamilton gave his driver the VanAllens' home address. He wanted to pay his respects to Tom's widow. It was presumptive to call at this hour, but hopefully she'd be up, surrounded by friends and kinfolk. What he feared, however, was that he'd find her alone.

Hamilton didn't waste the travel time in the van. He placed a call to the sheriff's office in Tambour to speak to Deputy Crawford.

Hamilton identified himself. 'The bureau lost a man down there tonight. *My* man. Tom VanAllen. Are you investigating the case?'

'I was initially. Once VanAllen was ID'd, your guys took over. Why aren't you talking to them?'

'I have been. But there's something you should know since it relates to your other cases. Tom went to that abandoned train track tonight to pick up Honor Gillette and bring her into protective custody.'

Crawford assimilated that. 'How do you know?'

'Because I brokered the deal with Lee Coburn.'

'I see.' The deputy was quiet for several moments. 'We've only got one body in the morgue. So what happened to Mrs Gillette?'

'Excellent question, Deputy.'

'Did Coburn set up VanAllen?'

Hamilton chuckled. 'If Coburn had wanted VanAllen dead, he wouldn't have troubled himself to use a bomb.'

'Then what are you telling me, Mr Hamilton?'

'Somebody besides Coburn and me knew about that meeting, and whoever it was wanted Mrs Gillette dead. Somebody planted that car bomb expecting to get two birds with one stone, a cop's widow and a local FBI agent. Somebody was made awfully nervous by that pairing so they acted swiftly to prevent it.'

'"Somebody". Any idea who?'

'Whoever is listening in on this conversation.'

'I don't follow.'

'Like hell you don't. Your department's a sieve. So's the PD, and I suspect Tom's office, too.' He paused to see if Crawford would dispute that. 'I'm not telling you how to do your job, Deputy, but unless you want an even higher body count, double your efforts to find Mrs Gillette and Coburn.'

'Is she with him voluntarily?'

'Yes.'

'Thought so. Does Coburn work for you?'

Hamilton said nothing.

'Did he *recruit* her for some reason? That's what it looks like to me. What are they onto that's got people wanting them dead?'

Hamilton didn't answer that one, either.

Crawford sighed. 'They've successfully stayed under the radar for three days, Mr Hamilton. I don't know what else I can do, especially since, as you say, other forces always seem to be several steps ahead of me. But if I manage to flush them out, what then?'

Hamilton said tersely, 'I'm the first person you call.'

Chapter 12

Coburn pulled the car to a stop at the kerb in front of Stan Gillette's house and said, 'You ring the doorbell. I'll take it from there.'

He could tell Honor was conflicted about what they had to do, but she stepped onto the porch and rang the bell. Coburn pressed his back to the wall adjacent to the door and slipped the pistol from his waistband.

'What are you doing with that?' she said nervously.

'He may not welcome our company.'

'Don't hurt him.'

'Not unless he forces me to.'

Footsteps approached, the door was opened, and then several things happened in rapid succession.

The alarm system began chirping. Stan seized Honor's arm and drew her across the threshold. Coburn sprang into the entryway, kicked the front door shut, and ordered Honor to disarm the security system. Then he pushed her out of harm's way when Gillette lunged forward and swiped at him with his knife. The tip of the blade cut through Coburn's oversized T-shirt and found skin.

'Stop it, old man,' Coburn shouted. 'We need to talk to you.'

Honor was practically weeping. 'Stan, please! Stop!'

But Gillette didn't relent. Coburn tried to grab his knife hand and missed, and Gillette drew another vicious arc. When the blade connected with Coburn's forearm, Coburn attacked with everything he had in him until a well-placed blow caused Gillette to stagger backwards. Coburn seized his knife hand and twisted until Gillette cried out and dropped the knife.

Coburn got him face down on the floor, planted a knee in his back, and jerked his hands up between his shoulder blades.

Honor was openly weeping.

Coburn said to her, 'There's a roll of duct tape on the worktable in the garage. Bring it to me.'

'You're a dead man,' Gillette snarled.

'Not yet.' But the cut on Coburn's arm was gushing blood.

Honor returned with the roll of tape. Coburn told her to bind her father-in-law's hands. She tore a strip from the roll and wound it around Gillette's wrists. Coburn bound his arm wound and the two of them got Gillette secured to a kitchen chair.

Honor got the full brunt of Stan's animosity. 'I thought I knew you,' he told her. 'How can you do this?'

'*Me?* You came at Coburn like you would kill him. You gave me—us—no choice. Stan, please—'

'Even if you have no regard for Eddie's memory, how dare you put my granddaughter's life at risk.'

Coburn could tell that Gillette's tone pissed her off, but she replied evenly, 'Actually, I've been protecting Emily and myself.'

'By teaming up with him?'

'He's a government agent.'

'What kind of agent stages a kidnapping?'

'I knew that would make you frantic with worry. I wanted to call and tell you what had really happened, but I couldn't without jeopardising our safety. Mine. Emily's. Coburn's too. He's been working undercover in a highly dangerous position, and—'

'And he's flipped,' he said. 'Whacked out. Happens all the time.'

'He hasn't flipped. I've spoken with his supervisor in Washington, Clint Hamilton. He has absolute trust in Coburn.'

'So you thought you could, too?'

'Coburn saved our lives, Stan. He protected Emily and me from people who would've harmed us. Like the Hawkins twins.'

He barked a laugh. 'That's ridiculous.' He shot Coburn a furious look. 'What kind of nonsense have you been feeding her?' Turning back to Honor, he said, 'Those men wouldn't touch a hair on your head. Doral hasn't stopped searching for you and Emily since you disappeared. His brother lay dead, but he's been—'

'Pumping you for information about them, about where they might be, who might be sheltering them?' Coburn said.

Gillette's chin went up a notch. 'Doral's been a loyal friend. He's gone without meals, sleep. He's turning over every rock—'

'Doral's been desperate to find us before any branch of law enforcement did. Why is that, I wonder?' Coburn let Gillette chew on that. 'Doral and Fred Hawkins shot Marset and the other six.'

The older man stared up at Coburn, then laughed a mirthless laugh. 'You say. You who stands accused of that mass murder.'

'Fred would have killed Honor, and probably Emily, too, if I hadn't shot him first. Ever since last Sunday, Doral's been trying to mop up the mess he and his brother made in that warehouse.'

'I don't believe you. I've known those boys their whole lives.'

'Are you sure you know them? Did Doral tell you he broke into Tori Shirah's house?' Coburn saw surprise in the older man's eyes. 'Threatened her if she failed to contact him when she heard from Honor?'

'How do you know it's true? If you heard it from Tori, I'd say the source is unreliable.' He turned to Honor. 'Is Emily with her?'

'Emily is safe.'

'Coburn, your time is up,' said Gillette.

'Really?' Coburn leaned down. 'How do you know it's up?'

Gillette's eyes narrowed fractionally.

'The Hawkins twins don't strike me as bright enough to run an organisation as sophisticated as The Bookkeeper's.'

Gillette looked to Honor. 'What's he talking about?'

'Hey.' Coburn nudged the man's knee, drawing his attention back to him. 'Somebody with an authoritative personality and a god complex has been giving Fred and Doral their orders. I've got my money riding on you.'

'I have no idea what you're talking about.'

Coburn made a show of checking his wristwatch. 'You're either staying up awfully late or getting up very early. Why are you fully dressed? Even wearing shoes. Why are you all spit-and-polish at this time of morning?'

Gillette only glared.

'You know what it looks like to me?' Coburn continued. 'Like you're on standby for something. For what? For a showdown with me, the federal agent who's put a real crimp in your crime chain?'

Hostility radiated from Gillette, but he remained silent.

Coburn straightened up slowly. 'The only reason I might second-guess myself is because I really can't see you ordering the murder of your own flesh and blood. Your overblown ego wouldn't let you destroy your own DNA.'

Gillette began struggling against the tape in frustration and rage. His gaze shifted to Honor. 'For God's sake, why are you just standing there? Has he brainwashed you into believing this garbage?'

'He's convinced me that Eddie's car wreck wasn't an accident.'

Gillette stopped struggling as suddenly as he'd begun.

Coburn nodded. 'Eddie died because he had incriminating evidence on a lot of people. Not just low-life types, but prominent citizens like Sam Marset and law-enforcement personnel who streamline the trafficking of drugs and weapons.'

Honor said, 'Eddie was killed before he could expose them.'

'Or,' Coburn countered, 'before he could blackmail them.'

'Drugs? Blackmail? My son was a decorated police officer.'

'Then prove it. If you're so sure of Eddie's honour, you should be eager to help us find what Eddie stashed before he was killed.'

Gillette's glare turned even more malevolent, but finally he ground out the question, 'What the hell *are* you looking for?'

'We don't know, but we have a clue.' Coburn motioned to Honor. 'Show him.'

She turned her back to Gillette, raised her shirt, and tipped down her waistband to expose the small of her back. She explained when and how she'd got the tattoo. 'That was Eddie's design, only two weeks before he was killed. He didn't want to place me in danger by giving me the item outright. Coburn figured out that the tattoo says Hawks8.'

It had taken a while to decipher the figures concealed within the intricate swirls and curlicues of the seemingly random pattern. The significance of the time and intimacy required to unravel the puzzle wasn't lost on Gillette.

'You went to bed with this guy.' Gillette bristled with censure.

Honor didn't flinch. 'Frankly, Stan, I didn't need your permission. I won't apologise for it. Now, what does Hawks8 mean?'

Gillette's chin lowered. The ferocity in his eyes faded, and there was weariness in his voice. 'The Hawks was a soccer team up in Baton Rouge. Eddie played one season with them. He was number eight.'

Coburn asked, 'Is there a picture of the team? A uniform?'

'Nothing like that. It was a ragtag league. They mostly got together on Saturday afternoons and drank beer after the games.'

'Keep an eye on him,' Coburn said to Honor. He went into Eddie's bedroom, where he remembered finding a pair of soccer cleats in the closet. He had examined each shoe, but perhaps he'd missed something. He took the cleats from the closet, dug his fingers into the left shoe, then ripped out the inner sole. A minuscule piece of paper dropped into his lap.

He unfolded the note and read the single printed word: BALL.

On his dash from the room, he rounded the corner of the door so fast, he grazed his shoulder, which jarred his injured arm. It hurt so bad, it made his eyes water, but he kept running.

'What it is?' Honor asked as he raced through the living room.

He slapped the small note into her hand. 'His soccer ball.'

'I put it back in the box in the loft,' Gillette called after him.

Coburn made it back from the garage in seconds, cradling the ball. With Honor and Gillette watching expectantly, he pressed it as one would test a melon's ripeness. Noticing that one seam was crudely sewn, he picked up Gillette's knife from the floor and ripped the seam. He pulled back the leather flap he'd created.

A USB key fell into his palm.

He locked eyes with Honor. He walked quickly to the master bedroom and Stan's computer. Activating it, he inserted the key into the port.

Eddie hadn't bothered with a password. There was only one file on the key, and when Coburn clicked on it, it opened immediately. He scanned the contents, and when Honor joined him he couldn't contain his excitement. 'He's got the names of key people and companies all along the Interstate 10 corridor between here and Phoenix where most of the stuff from Mexico is dispersed. But better than that, he's got the names of corrupt officials. And I recognise some of those names. Marset had dealings with them.'

He pointed to a list. 'He's a weigh station guy who's on the take. Here's a used-car dealer in Houston, who supplies vans. Two cops in Biloxi. Oh my God, look at all this.'

'Does it identify The Bookkeeper?'

'Not that I see, but it's a hell of a start.' He pulled his cellphone from his pocket, but the battery was dead. Quickly he took out Fred's phone. When he saw the read-out, he frowned.

'What?' Honor asked.

'Doral has called three times. And all in the last hour.'

'Doesn't make sense. Why would he call Fred?'

'He wouldn't,' Coburn said thoughtfully. 'He's calling me.' Suddenly overcome by foreboding, he depressed the call icon.

Doral answered on the first ring. In a jolly voice, he said, 'Hello, Coburn. Good of you to call back. Someone here wants to say hi.'

Coburn waited, his heart in his throat.

Elmo's song came through loud and clear.

When Honor heard the song, she clapped both hands over her mouth, but started screaming behind them. Fear, a foreign emotion to Coburn, struck him to his core. The Bookkeeper had Emily.

'OK, Doral, you've got my attention,' he said.

'I thought I might. Lies and booze worked like magic with that airhead gym receptionist Amber. Nice place Tori has there on the lake.'

Coburn's hand formed a fist. 'You hurt that little girl and—'

'Her fate is up to you, not me.'

Honor still had her fingers clamped over her lips. Above them, her eyes were wide with anguish. Coburn dispensed with the threats and asked what the terms were for getting Emily back.

'Simple, Coburn. You disappear. She lives.'

'By disappear, you mean die.'

'Those are the terms. Non-negotiable.' Doral gave him instructions. 'Honor drives away with Emily. Then it's you and me, pal.'

'I can hardly wait,' Coburn said. 'But one last thing.'

'What?'

'Since you've botched everything so bad, why are you still breathing? The Bookkeeper must have a reason for keeping you alive. Think about it.'

DORAL DISCONNECTED, muttering a stream of vile language.

Coburn was playing him. He was well aware of that. But Coburn was good at it. He had tapped into Doral's worst fear: he was nothing more than a flunky and, after everything that had gone wrong over the past seventy-two hours, an expendable one.

He looked over his shoulder into the back seat where Emily was sleeping, dosed with Benadryl so she wouldn't put up a fuss when it became clear that Uncle Doral had fibbed about why he'd taken her in the middle of the night from Tori's lake house.

They'd not gone far before the questions started. 'Are you taking me to Mommy? Where's Coburn? He's gonna buy me an ice cream. Can I see them?' They'd become numerous and unnerving, and he was glad his sister had once remarked on how the liquid antihistamine affected kids. He'd stopped at a 7-Eleven, bought a bottle of the medication and a cherry Slurpee, and soon after drinking the laced slush, Emily was sleeping soundly.

That's when he'd called The Bookkeeper, who'd been furious after the screw-up at the tracks. He wasn't praised for a job well done, but he actually thought he heard a sigh of relief. 'See if you can get Coburn to answer your brother's phone. Set it up.'

Now things were in place and all he had to do was wait. He faced forwards, unable to look into Emily's angelic face and acknowledge what a creep he was for exploiting her affection for him. Eddie's kid. He'd killed her father. He'd have to kill her mother, too. Making an orphan of a sweet little girl was a hell of a career.

But before that, he was going to kill Lee Coburn for killing Fred.

IMMEDIATELY AFTER COBURN disconnected from Doral, he punched in the number of Tori's lake house and got voicemail.

'What's Tori's cell number?'

Honor lowered her hands from her mouth. Her lips were white. They barely moved as she dully recited the number.

That call also went straight to voicemail. 'Dammit!'

Tremulously Honor asked, 'Coburn? Is Emily alive?'

'If they had killed her, they wouldn't have anything to bargain with.'

He could tell she wanted to believe it. *He* wanted to believe it.

'Is he holding her hostage at the lake house?'

'Sounded like he was in a car.'

'Do you think Tori is . . .' She couldn't bring herself to finish.

Coburn punched in 911 and when the operator answered, he gave her the address of Tori's lake house. 'A woman there has been assaulted. Send police and an ambulance.'

Honor was trembling. 'Will they kill my baby?'

He refused to lie to her. 'I don't know.'

She made a sound of such abject despair that he put his good arm round her and pulled her hard against him, laying his cheek on the top of her head. 'We've got to call the police, Coburn.'

'We can,' he said quietly. 'She's your kid, Honor. Whatever you decide, I'll go along. But I think if you bring the cops into it, The Bookkeeper will know in a matter of minutes.'

'And Emily will be killed.'

He nodded bleakly. 'Probably. The Bookkeeper wouldn't back down. I know that's not what you want to hear, but I won't lie.'

She gnawed her lower lip. 'The FBI office?'

'Is no better. Case in point, VanAllen.'

'So it's up to us?'

'I'll do whatever it takes to save her life.'

'Whatever it takes.' Both of them knew what that implied. 'That's the deal, isn't it? You for Emily.'

'That's the deal.' But he didn't say it with his customary shrug.

'I don't want you to die,' she said huskily.

'Maybe I won't. I've got another good bargaining chip.' He released her and sat down at the computer.

'We don't have time for this.' Honor stood, wringing her hands. 'Where do they have Emily? Did you hear her crying?'

'No.'

'She has to be afraid. Why wasn't she crying? What does that mean?'

'I'm trying *not* to think about it.' Her near hysteria was justified, but he tried to tune her out long enough to concentrate on what he needed to do hurriedly but without making mistakes.

He opened Gillette's web browser, went into a web-based email service, and accessed his account. He sent the file on the USB key as an attachment to an email, then logged out and closed the browser after clearing the browser history. The address to which he'd sent the file was assigned to only one computer, and it could be opened with a password known only to him and Hamilton.

The job done, he stood up and placed his hands on Honor's shoulders. 'If it wasn't for me, you could have died of old age without ever knowing the significance of that tattoo. None of this would have happened.'

'You're apologising?'

'Not for what I've done. For what I'm about to ask you to do. If you want Emily back alive—'

'Tell me what to do.'

FOLLOWING HIS CONVERSATION with Hamilton, Crawford had stepped outside the building, whose walls had ears, and used his cellphone to call police officers and sheriff's deputies he trusted implicitly. He'd asked for immediate assistance to beef up his search for Mrs Gillette, her daughter and Lee Coburn.

He had a secret meeting with those whom he'd enlisted and asked some to re-patrol areas. He dispatched others to follow up on various leads, everything from the crazy lady who called in at least once a day reporting sightings of Coburn to a rural couple who'd returned from a Mediterranean cruise to discover that their car had been stolen, their kitchen had been rifled, and their garage apartment had been inhabited by at least two people. The towels in the bathroom were still damp.

He hadn't liked having his hand spanked by Hamilton of the big, bad FBI. He decided to interview Mrs Gillette's father-in-law himself.

Stan Gillette, who popped up anywhere the action was, had what seemed to be a direct line into local law enforcement. His association should have ended when his son died. That bothered Crawford.

He didn't want to wait until daylight. He'd wake him up and go at him hard. People dragged from bed were groggy and disorientated and more likely to make mistakes.

But he arrived at Gillette's house to find it lit up like a Christmas tree. Crawford felt a tingle of apprehension. The front door stood ajar. He pulled his service weapon from its holster. 'Mr Gillette?'

Getting no answer, he pushed the door open and stepped into a living room that looked as if a cyclone had gone through it. In the centre, securely taped to a straight chair, was Stan Gillette. His head was bowed low over his chest.

The man let out a moan just as he reached him. 'Is anyone else in the house?' the deputy whispered.

'They left. Coburn and Honor,' Gillette replied hoarsely.

Crawford reached for his cellphone.

'What are you doing?' Gillette asked. 'Hang up. I won't have my daughter-in-law arrested like a common criminal.'

'You need an ambulance.'

'I said forget it. I'm OK. Are you going to get me out of this chair?'

As Crawford sawed through the tape with the sharp point of his pocket-knife, Gillette filled him in on what had taken place.

'They took the USB key?' Crawford asked. 'What was on it?'

'They refused to tell me. Coburn reminded me that when a Marine has a duty to perform, he doesn't let any obstacle stand in the way. He said, "Intentionally or not, you could be an obstacle." Then he slugged me. Next thing I know, you're here.'

'Where's your computer?'

Gillette led him down a hallway and into the master bedroom. Crawford sat down at the desk and activated the computer. He didn't find anything, nor had he expected to. 'I'd like to take your computer. Give it to the department techies, see if they can find what was on that—'

He drew up short as he turned. Stan Gillette was holding a deer rifle in one hand and pointing a six-shot revolver at him with the other.

Chapter 13

'It's Coburn.'

Hamilton yelled at him through the phone. 'About time. Damn you, Coburn! Are you still alive? Mrs Gillette? The child?'

'Honor is with me, but they've got her daughter. I just talked to Doral Hawkins. The Bookkeeper wants to trade. Me for Emily.'

Hamilton exhaled noisily. 'Well, that sums it up.'

'Listen, I found what I've been after. Turned out to be a USB key loaded with incriminating information.'

'On who?'

'Lots of people. Locals. Some not. A load of stuff.'

'You've actually seen it?'

'I'm holding it in my hand.'

'To swap for Emily.'

'If it comes to that. I don't think it will.'

'What's that supposed to mean? No more damn riddles, Coburn. Tell me where you are, I'll get—'

'I emailed you the file a few minutes ago. I didn't send it to your regular email address. You know where to look.'

'So it's good stuff. But it doesn't ID The Bookkeeper?'

'We weren't that lucky. But it probably makes him traceable.'

'Good work, Coburn. Now tell me—'

'No time. I've got to go.'

'Wait! You can't do this without back-up. I spoke with Crawford. I think I can safely vouch for him. Call him and—'

'Not until Emily is back with Honor. Then she'll notify the authorities.'

'You can't confront these people alone.'

'That's the condition of the swap.'

'That's the condition of every swap!' Hamilton shouted. 'Nobody sticks to the conditions. You could get that little girl killed!'

'Maybe. But it's a sure thing she'll die if cops and Feds swarm the scene.'

'Doesn't have to be that way. We can—'

Coburn disconnected, then turned off the phone. 'Bet he had some choice words for me,' he said to Honor as he tossed the phone onto the back seat of the car.

'He thinks you should call in reinforcements.'

'Just like in the movies. Give him his head, he'd have an army of Stallones who'd only mess it up.'

She was rubbing her upper arms, a sign of her anxiety.

'Honor, I can call Hamilton back. Have him send in the cavalry.'

'Two days ago, you wouldn't have given me an option,' she said, her tone throaty and intimate. 'Coburn, I—'

'Don't. Whatever you're about to say, don't.' Her misty expression alarmed him. 'Don't delude yourself into thinking that I'm a different person than I was when I crawled into your yard. I'm still mean. Still me.'

He made himself sound harsh, because in an hour, possibly less, one way or another, he would exit her life as swiftly as he'd entered it. He wanted to make that exit painless for her, even if it meant wounding her now. 'I haven't changed, Honor.'

She gave him a wan smile. 'I have.'

WHEN HAMILTON and his men arrived at the VanAllen home, there were no other vehicles there. The widow was passing the night alone. But she wasn't sleeping. Lights were on inside the house.

Hamilton rang the bell, and waited. When Janice didn't respond, he wondered if maybe she was asleep, after all. The VanAllens' invalid son, he remembered, needed round-the-clock care. Perhaps the lights in the household never went out.

He rang the bell again, then knocked. 'Mrs VanAllen? It's Clint Hamilton,' he called through the door. 'I know this is an extremely difficult time for you, but it's important I speak to you right away.'

Still getting no response, he tried the latch. It was locked. He reached for his cellphone, scrolled through his contacts, and called the house number. He heard the phone ringing inside the house.

After the fifth ring, he hung up and shouted, 'Bring the ram.'

The SWAT team joined him on the porch. 'This isn't an assault. Mrs VanAllen is in a delicate state of mind. There's also a disabled boy. Take care.'

Within seconds they busted through the door. Hamilton barged in, the others fanned out through the rooms behind him.

Hamilton found Lanny's room at the end of the hall. It had the sweetly cloying odour unique to the bedridden. But except for the hospital bed and medical paraphernalia, everything was perfectly normal. The television was on. Lamps provided a soothing ambient light. There were pictures on the walls, a colourful rug on the floor.

However, the tableau of the motionless boy lying on the customised bed was almost gothic. His eyes were open but his stare was blank. Hamilton walked to the side of the bed to assure himself he was breathing.

'Sir?'

Hamilton turned to the officer who had addressed him from the doorway. His aspect conveyed SITUATION as he hitched his helmeted head towards another part of the house.

DORAL SAW THE CAR HEADLIGHTS approaching from the side street. Show time. Seated in his borrowed car, he took one last drag on his cigarette, then called The Bookkeeper. 'He's right on schedule.'

'I'll be there soon.'

Doral's heart hitched. 'What?'

'You heard me. I can't afford for you to screw up again.' Then the phone went dead.

It was a slap in the face. But, he supposed, the collaboration with the Mexican cartel hung in the balance, so The Bookkeeper was taking no chances of something else going wrong.

Coburn had stopped the car about forty yards away, its idling motor an uneven growl in the stillness beneath the football stadium bleachers, where Doral had chosen to do this. This time of year, the place was deserted. It was on the outskirts of town. Ideal location.

Coburn was screwing with his head again. But he also wasn't going to come any closer until he saw that Doral did indeed have Emily.

Doral got out of his car. Crouching lower than the roof, he opened the rear door and lifted Emily out. Her body was limp, her breathing deep as he placed her on his left shoulder.

What kind of man would use thirty-five pounds of sweet little girl to save his own skin?

All he wanted was one crack at Coburn.

He placed his gun hand in the centre of Emily's back so that it could be seen. Then he stood up and walked round the hood of the car, forcing himself to appear perfectly relaxed, although his heart was knocking.

Coburn's car began to roll forward at a snail's pace. Doral's gut tightened. He squinted against the headlights. The car came to within fifteen feet of him and stopped. He called, 'Turn off the headlights.'

The driver got out. Despite the glare, he made out Honor's form.

'What the *hell*? Where's Coburn?'

'He sent me instead. He said you wouldn't shoot me.'

'He said wrong.' *Shit!* He hadn't counted on having to kill Honor face to face. 'Move away from the car and raise your hands.'

'Coburn's nailed you, Doral, thanks to Eddie. Coburn found the evidence he had collected.'

His mouth went dry. 'I don't know what you're talking about.'

'Of course you do. That's why you killed him.'

'Are you wearing a wire?'

'No! Coburn has already got what he came for. He doesn't care what happens to me or Emily now. But I care. I want my daughter.'

Doral gripped his pistol tighter. 'I told you, get away from the car.'

She stepped from the cover of the open door, hands raised. 'I won't do anything, Doral. I'm leaving you to the legal system. Or to Coburn. I don't care. All I care about is Emily.' Her voice cracked. 'She's not moving.'

'You've got only your friend Coburn to blame for this. All this.'

'Why is Emily so still?'

'Where is Coburn?'

'Is she *dead*?' Honor screamed hysterically.

'Where's—'

'You've already killed her, haven't you?'

Emily stirred, then lifted her head and murmured, 'Mommy?'

'Emily!' Honor shouted and extended her arms.

Doral backed away towards his car. 'Sorry. Coburn screwed it all up.'

'*Emily!*'

Emily started squirming against him.

'Emily, be still,' he hissed. 'It's Uncle Doral.'

'I want my mommy!' she wailed and began thumping him with her small fists and kicking at his thighs.

Honor continued shouting her name. Emily screamed in his ear.

He released her. She slid to the ground, then ran directly towards the headlights. Doral aimed his pistol at Honor's chest.

Before he could get off a shot, something smacked him in the back of his head. Simultaneously the car's headlights went out.

He blinked wildly, trying to restore his vision, even as he realised what Coburn's strategy had been. Blind him, rattle him, deafen him, and then attack from behind. He spun round in time to catch the full brunt of Coburn's impetus as he launched himself over the hood of Doral's car, landing on him like a sack of cement and forcing him down onto the ground on his back.

'Federal agent!' he shouted.

Coburn's impact had knocked the wind out of Doral but he had been fighting all his life. Instinct kicked in along with a surge of adrenaline. He whipped his gun hand up.

A gunshot rang out.

COBURN BACKED OFF DORAL.

There wasn't much blood, actually, because Coburn had fired point-blank into the man's chest. In death, he didn't look all that sinister, only bewildered, as though wondering how someone as clever as he could have been done in by a soccer ball.

Coburn patted down his body and pocketed his cellphone before walking to the car where Honor was sitting, clutching Emily.

'Is she OK?'

'Limp as a dishrag and asleep again. He must've given her something. Is he . . .'

'In hell.'

'He refused to surrender?'

'Something like that.' He paused, then said, 'You did good.'

She smiled shakily. 'I was scared.'

'So was I. First time for everything.' They shared a long look. 'You get Emily to a doctor and have her checked out.'

He lifted Emily from her and gently placed her in the back seat.

'What are you going to do?' Honor asked.

'Call this in to Hamilton. He'll want the skinny. He'll want—'

'Lee Coburn?'

The quiet voice, coming from behind him, surprised them both. Honor looked beyond him and registered puzzlement. Coburn turned. The woman was expressionless when she pulled the trigger.

Coburn grabbed his middle and sank to the ground.

Honor screamed.

Coburn struggled to remain conscious, but it was a hell of a fight. He'd been shot twice before. This was different. This was bad. He worked his way into a half sitting position but kept his palm clamped over the pumping hole in his belly. He tried to bring into focus the ordinary-looking woman who had shot him.

She was ordering Honor at gunpoint to stay inside the car. Already she'd disarmed him. He could see his pistol on the ground a short distance away, but it might just as well have been a mile. Fred's .357 was under the driver's seat, but Honor couldn't get to it.

She was sobbing, asking the woman, 'Why, why?'

'Because of Tom,' she replied.

Tom VanAllen's wife. *Widow*. But for a woman who'd just committed a crime of vengeance, she seemed remarkably cold-blooded.

'If Tom hadn't gone to those train tracks to meet Coburn last night,' she said, 'he would still be alive.'

Last night. The eastern sky had taken on the blush of predawn. Coburn wondered if he'd live to see the sun break the horizon.

He hated that he would bleed out with Honor watching. And what if Emily woke up and saw the blood gushing out? He'd dragged Honor and her through enough already. He'd always thought that when his number came up, he would be OK with it. But, oh God, this was bad. Really bad.

These were useless thoughts to be entertaining when he should be trying to figure out something. Something just beyond his grasp. Something winking at him like that last holdout star in the lightening sky above Janice VanAllen. Something he should've caught before now. Something—

'How'd you know?' As he gasped the question, he realised what the something was. 'How'd you know I was at the tracks?'

Janice VanAllen looked down at him. 'Tom told me.'

That was a lie. If Tom had told her anything, he'd have told her that he expected to meet Honor. She'd learned it from somebody else. Who? Tom's agents wouldn't have known.

The only people who could have told her were the ones who'd planted the bomb and been there to make sure it went off.

Honor was sobbing, begging her to call for help. 'He'll die.'

'That's the point,' Janice VanAllen said coldly.

Coburn sagged forward and groaned through clenched teeth.

'Please, let me help him,' Honor implored.

'He's beyond help. He's dying.'

'And then what? Are you going to shoot me, too? Emily?'

'I won't harm the child. What kind of person do you think I am?'

'No better than me.' Coburn cut a vicious swath with Stan Gillette's knife, which he'd slid from his cowboy boot. It connected with Janice VanAllen's ankle and, he thought, probably had sliced through her Achilles' tendon. She screamed. Her leg buckled and, when it did, he found enough strength to topple her with both his feet.

'Honor!' He tried to shout, but it came out barely a rasp.

She practically fell out of the car, seized the pistol that Janice had dropped, and aimed it at her. 'Coburn?' she asked breathlessly.

'Keep the gun on her. Cavalry's here.'

SQUAD CARS WERE SPEEDING towards them from a dozen directions. The first to reach them bore the sheriff's office insignia. The driver and passenger were out in a flash. The uniformed man had his pistol drawn. Stan Gillette was carrying a deer rifle.

'Honor, thank God you're all right,' Stan said as he ran to her.

'Mrs Gillette, I'm Deputy Crawford. What happened?'

'She shot Coburn.'

Crawford and two fellow deputies took over guarding Janice, who was writhing on the ground. Other officers ran over to Doral's corpse.

Stan reached for Honor and hugged her. 'I forced Crawford at gunpoint into bringing me along.'

'I'm glad you're here, Stan. See to Emily, please. She's in the back seat.' Honor pushed herself free of his hold and shouted for the EMTs scrambling out of the ambulance to hurry, then dropped to her knees beside Coburn.

She touched his face. 'Don't die. Don't you dare die.'

'Hamilton,' he said.

'What?'

He nodded and she turned. Two black Suburbans were disgorging officers wearing assault gear, along with a man who looked even more intimidating than they, although dressed in a suit and tie.

He made a beeline for her. 'Mrs Gillette?' he said.

She looked at him. 'Coburn is badly wounded.'

Hamilton nodded grimly.

'Why aren't you in Washington?' Coburn growled up at him.

'Because I have a pain-in-the-ass agent who won't follow orders. We were at her house.' He nodded towards Janice. 'We found evidence that she was going to leave the country. We found notes, texts on cellphones, indicating that she had a vendetta against Coburn over what had happened to Tom. I called Crawford, who'd received word of gunshots in this area. I left one man behind to stay with her son and got here as quickly as I could.'

'Let go.' Coburn snarled at the paramedic who was trying to get an IV into his arm and slipped his hand in his pocket. He took out a cellphone and held it up where Hamilton could see. 'Doral's. Before he got out of his car, he made a call.' He used his bloodstained thumb to work the phone, and depressed a highlighted number. 'He called The Bookkeeper.'

Seconds later, all heads turned towards the sound of a ringing cellphone coming from the pocket of Janice VanAllen's windbreaker.

For Honor the next hour and a half passed in a blur. After making his startling revelation, Coburn lost consciousness, which made it far easier for the EMTs to get him into the CareFlight helicopter.

Honor considered it a miracle that Emily had slept through the entire traumatic event. On the other hand, a sleep that deep was worrisome. She was transported to the ER via ambulance.

Honor rode to the hospital with her, but once there, her insistence on remaining with Emily was overruled. While Emily was being examined, Honor and Stan waited anxiously. There was an awkwardness between them that had not been there before.

Finally Stan said, 'Honor, I owe you an apology.'

'After what I did to your house? After binding you to a chair?'

He gave her a stiff grin. 'You tried to explain your motivations. And my apology goes beyond what's happened over the last couple of days. Ever since Eddie died,' he said uneasily, 'I've held you in strict control. We both know it. I've been afraid that you would meet a man, fall in love, and I'd be ousted from your lives. Yours and Emily's.'

'That would never have happened, Stan,' she said gently. 'You're our family. Emily loves you. So do I.'

'Thanks for that,' he said huskily. 'I made some ugly remarks about your personal life. I'm sorry.'

'I know it offended you to think of Coburn and me together.'

'As you said, it's none of my—'

'No, let me finish. It's occurred to me that Eddie knew my tattoo would be discovered only by a lover. Who else would have seen it? He trusted me to choose that man wisely.' She paused. 'I loved Eddie. You know that. He'll be enshrined in my heart until I draw my last breath.' She reached for his hand. 'But he can't be enshrined in my life. I've got to let go and move on.'

He nodded, his eyes suspiciously moist. Honor was still clasping his hand when Deputy Crawford joined them.

'Your friend, Ms Shirah? NOPD responded to your 911. She was found alone in the house with a gunshot wound to the head.'

'What! Oh my God!'

'She underwent surgery to remove the bullet. I spoke with a friend of hers named Bonnell Wallace, who's with her. She's in a stable condition. The surgeon told Mr Wallace that it appears the bullet did no permanent damage. He predicts a full recovery.'

Weak with relief, Honor leaned her head against Stan's shoulder. 'Thank God. Have you heard anything about Coburn?'

'I'm afraid not. I'm sure Hamilton will be in touch.'

Not long after that, the paediatrician who'd examined Emily arrived and confirmed that she'd ingested an excessive amount of antihistamine. 'I'll let her sleep it off. She'll be closely monitored. But she shouldn't have any lasting effects,' he said.

Honor and Stan were allowed to go along as the staff transferred Emily to a private room. She looked small and helpless lying in the hospital bed, but measured against what could have been, Honor was grateful to have her there.

She was bending over her, stroking her hair, loving the feel of her, when Stan quietly spoke her name. She straightened up and turned.

Hamilton was standing just inside the door. Holding her gaze, he said, 'I thought I should tell you in person.'

'No,' she whimpered. 'No. *No.*'

'I'm sorry,' he said. 'Coburn didn't make it.'

Epilogue

Six weeks later

'You sound surprised, Mr Hamilton. Didn't Tom ever mention to you that I'm brilliant? No? Well, I am. Before Lanny was born, I had a bright future as a business consultant and financial planner. All my career plans had to be abandoned. Then, a few years ago, I decided to apply my know-how to another endeavour.

'And I was in a perfect position to do so. Who would suspect poor Janice VanAllen, mother of a severely disabled child and wife to a man totally lacking in self-confidence and ambition, to initiate and orchestrate an organisation as successful as mine?'

Here she laughed.

'Ironically it was Tom who planted the idea. He talked a lot about illegal trafficking, the profits to be made, the government's futile attempts to stop the tide. Mostly he talked about the middleman, whose risk of capture is

limited because usually he's hidden behind a screen of respectability. That sounded smart and attractive to me.

'*Tom was an unchecked source of information. I asked questions, he gave me answers. He explained to me how criminals got caught. All I had to do was get to the men who caught them, and, through men like Doral and Fred Hawkins, offer them a handsome bonus for slacking.*

'*Suffice to say, Mr Hamilton, my little cottage industry became extremely lucrative. That was important. I had to save up for the day when Lanny would no longer be an impediment. After he died, I wasn't about to stick around. I'd had it with Tom, with my life. I'd earned an easy retirement. Millions of dollars were waiting for me in banks all over the world.*

'*But then Lee Coburn came along, and I had to accelerate my plan to skip the country. Lanny . . .' Her voice turned thick. 'Lanny would never have known the difference. It's not like he would have missed me, is it? In exchange for a guilty plea, you swear to me that he'll be placed in the very best facility in the country? And he'll get Tom's pension?'*

'*You have my personal word on it.'*

'*Tom would want that. He was devoted to Lanny.'*

After a short pause, she said, 'That sexting . . . that isn't me. It was simply a means of coded communication. It was just a way to explain all the telephone activity in case Tom became suspicious.'

'*Didn't you have misgivings about killing Tom?' said Hamilton.*

'*Of course! But there simply was no other way. I grieved for him. Honestly, I did. But this way, Tom died with honour.'*

After another pause, she said, 'I guess that's everything. I suppose you'll want me to sign something.'

Hamilton reached across his desk and punched the button to stop the playback.

Honor and Stan, who'd been invited to the district office in New Orleans to listen to Janice VanAllen's recorded confession, had sat motionless for the duration of it, astonished by the casualness with which she had confessed her crimes to Hamilton several days earlier.

'She had Eddie killed,' Honor said quietly.

'As well as a lot of other people,' Hamilton said. 'Based on the information on that USB key, we're making definite progress. But as she said, it's almost futile. The criminals are multiplying at a rate much faster than we can catch them. But we stay at it.'

'There's nothing that implicates Eddie,' Stan averred. 'And no one was more taken in than I was by the Hawkins twins. Yes, I used Doral to get information, but I never had an inkling of what they were doing. I stand by my record. You can check it.'

'I did,' Hamilton said, giving him a congenial smile. 'You're as clean as a whistle, Mr Gillette. And nothing implicates your son in any wrongdoing. According to the superintendent of the Tambour PD, Eddie offered to do some covert investigative work. Possibly he'd picked up vibes when he was moonlighting at Marset's company. In any case, the superintendent sanctioned it, but when Eddie was killed, he didn't connect the car wreck to Eddie's secret investigation.'

Hamilton stood up, signalling that the meeting was adjourned. He shook hands with Stan. Then he clasped Honor's hand between both of his. 'How's your daughter?'

'Doing well. She doesn't remember anything of that night, thank God. She talks about Coburn constantly and wants to know where he went.' After an awkward silence, she continued. 'And we've been to see Tori twice at Bonnell Wallace's house. She's going to be fine, which is a miracle. For once, Doral didn't hit his target.'

'I'm glad they've recovered,' Hamilton said. 'I commend you for your courage and fortitude, Mrs Gillette. Thanks for coming today.'

'Thank you.'

'We appreciate the invitation,' Stan said. He started for the door.

Honor hung back. 'I'll be right there, Stan. Give us a minute.'

He left the office and when she heard the door close behind him, she said to Hamilton, 'Where is he?'

'I'm sorry?'

'Don't play dumb, Mr Hamilton. Where's Coburn? He didn't die.'

He sighed. 'Mrs Gillette, I know how distressing—'

'Don't talk to me like I'm no older than Emily. Where is he?'

'He told me that if you should ever ask—'

'He *knew* I would ask.'

'He threatened me with bodily harm if I didn't say he was dead. But he also made me swear that if you ever questioned it, I was to give you this.' Opening a drawer, he withdrew a white envelope.

She could barely breathe as she worked her thumb beneath the flap. Inside was a sheet of paper with one line written in a scrawl.

It meant something.

She closed her eyes and pressed the sheet of paper against her chest. When she opened her eyes, they were damp with tears. 'Where is he?'

'Mrs Gillette, you went through a terrible ordeal together. It's only natural that you formed an emotional attachment, but you and he could never work. You'd be letting yourself in for heartbreak.'

She planted her palms flat on his desk, and leaned to within inches of him. 'Where. Is. He?'

HE'D BEEN COMING to the airport every day for the past two weeks, ever since he'd been able to leave his bed for more than a few minutes at a time. The third time he'd been noticed loitering in the baggage claim area, a transport agent had asked him what he was up to.

He'd shown the guy his badge. Although he didn't look much like the photo any more—he was paler and twenty pounds lighter—the guy could tell it was him. He'd made up a story about working a case undercover, and from then on, they'd left him alone.

He still used a cane, but he figured that, with luck, he could toss the damn thing away in another week or so. He'd made it all the way from his bedroom to the kitchen without it this morning. But he didn't trust himself to navigate the busy baggage claim area where people were notorious for grabbing suitcases and making a dash for the rental car counters. After all he'd been through, he didn't want to be mowed down by a civilian.

Even with the cane, he was sweating by the time he reached the bench on which he customarily sat to await the arrival of the plane from Dallas, because, if you were travelling from New Orleans to Jackson Hole, in all likelihood, you took the route through Dallas Forth Worth.

The bench afforded him a view of every passenger exiting the concourse. He cursed himself for being a fool. She probably had bought Hamilton's lie; Lee Coburn was dead. End of story.

One day far into the future, she'd bounce her grandkids by another man on her knee and tell them about the adventure she'd had one time with an FBI agent. Emily might have a vague memory of it, but that was doubtful. How much did a four-year-old retain?

And even if she'd questioned his demise and received his note, maybe she hadn't caught on to the message. Maybe she didn't even remember their love-making. If he ever had it to do over, he'd say more. He'd make it clearer to her that it had meant something. If given another opportunity, he'd tell her . . .

Hell, he wouldn't have to tell her anything. She'd just *know*. She'd look at him in that certain way, and he'd know that she knew how he felt. Just like she had when he'd told her about having to shoot Dusty.

What was its name?

I forgot.

No, you didn't.

Without him having to put it into words, she'd known that the day he'd had to put that horse down was the worst in his memory. All the killing that came after hadn't affected him like that had. And Honor knew it.

Thinking about her caused him to ache. It was a pain that went deeper even than the one in his belly where he'd been stitched up. He took strong medications at night so he could fall asleep, but there was nothing he could do to get past the ache of desiring her, of wanting to feel her against him, sleep with her hand over his heart.

And, even if she had understood what he was trying to tell her in that cryptic note, would she want to be with him? Would she want Emily around him twenty-four/seven? Would she want her little girl influenced by a man like him, who knew how to kill?

She'd have to see something in him that maybe even he didn't know was there. She'd really have to want him. Have to love him.

The PA speakers crackled, announcing the arrival of the 757 from Dallas. He stood up shakily, leaning heavily on his cane.

He called himself a masochist for putting himself through this torture day after day.

He braced himself for the disappointment of having to go home alone.

He braced himself for happiness like he'd never known in his entire life.

He watched the door they would come through.

sandra **brown**

Profile

Born:
March 1948, Waco, Texas.
Raised:
Fort Worth, Texas.
Previous jobs:
Model, TV weather forecaster.
Pen names:
Rachel Ryan, Laura Jordan, Erin St Claire.

Published novels:
70+.
Favourite music:
Classic rock, country, classical.
Favourite movies:
Doctor Zhivago, *The Godfather*.
Website:
SandraBrown.net

Sandra Brown began her long and prolific writing career more than thirty years ago, when she lost her job at a television station. On a dare from her husband, Michael, she decided to try writing a book, something she had always dreamed of doing. To prepare, she bought a pile of romance novels and writing 'how-to' books and ploughed through them. Then she sat down at her typewriter and penned her first novel. 'It was scary then and it's no less scary today. Unfortunately there is no magic formula—none I know of anyway—for putting words on paper that hopefully someone will find compelling enough to read.'

It wasn't exactly success at first try, but it was close. One publisher turned her down, but a second one bought her manuscript. Sandra Brown quickly wrote more romances, publishing them under various pseudonyms.

From those early days, her star has risen steadily. After writing over forty-five genre romances, Sandra Brown longed for a bigger challenge. Thus, she experimented with adding suspense to the mix. 'I think of my books now as suspense novels, usually with a love story incorporated,' she says. 'They're absolutely harder to write than romances. They take more plotting and real character development.'

She has had dozens of *New York Times* best sellers, and has sold multimillions of books worldwide. She's one of a select few authors (the others being Stephen King, Tom Clancy, J.K. Rowling and Danielle Steel) to have had three books on the best-seller list simultaneously. So what does Sandra Brown think are the key ingredients of this success? 'If you study the best-seller lists, you'll notice that the only thing the books have in common is that they're on the lists. Every author on there has found a niche for him or herself. They write their "thing" and they've found an appreciative audience for it. I think success relies a lot on tenacity and just plain hard work. To be a success at anything, you've got to work at it. So far, I haven't found a short cut to writing a book. It can only be done one word at a time.'

So just what is her process of writing a novel, from conception to revision? 'I get the idea and work with it until it lets me know it wants to be a book. (Some ideas don't.) Then I write a ten-to-fifteen-page synopsis for my editor, in which I let her know who the main characters are, what the big problem is, how that problem is going to get worse, and how it will be solved.

'This is a road map, nothing more. I know where I'm going, just not how I'm going to get there. After I begin writing, I rarely consult the synopsis again. I put the characters in place, get them into big trouble, and then let them show me where this scene or that scene will take place. Some of the best plot twists, even I didn't see coming until it was right there. Some of the best characters weren't even in the synopsis.

'I do four drafts: the first is the plotting draft, the second is the crafting draft, the third is for pacing and to make sure all the loose threads are tied up, the fourth is for polishing.'

In *Lethal*, Sandra Brown returns to one of her favourite settings, rural Louisiana. The changes that this state has undergone as a result of Hurricane Katrina, along with increased crime and corruption on Interstate 10, which bisects the state, are what led to the idea for the book.

Plus, Brown uses one of her favourite tricks in *Lethal*. 'Isolating the characters from the world is one of my favourite plot devices,' she says. She likes to throw her characters into life-threatening circumstances, where they really have to trust each other or perish. 'I love writing the mental cat-and-mouse,' Brown says. 'I love testing the characters to see if they'll go with what their common sense tells them, or if they'll trust their gut instinct and go with what they feel. That's a dilemma to which everyone can relate, isn't it?'

Brown also tries to make her suspense realistic, and that can sometimes lead to complications. In *Lethal*, she ran into trouble with cellphones. 'Cellphones have done more to destroy good plots than any other single thing I can think of,' she says. She had to learn about 'burners'—throwaway cellphones that are untraceable—after becoming aware that with new technology, cellphone calls could be easily traced. 'I bought one for research,' she says, 'and felt like a drug dealer.'

Writing a book a year does not leave Sandra Brown with much time to relax, but, when she does have a spare moment, she loves to go to the movies, to travel, and to host get-togethers with family and friends. And, of course, her favourite pastime is reading.

The Haunting
Alan Titchmarsh

How can the mysterious disappearance of Anne Flint in 1816 have any impact on the life of history teacher Harry Flint some two centuries later?

That's the question that Harry is hoping to answer, for with a failed marriage and a teaching career firmly behind him, he's decided to research his ancestors.

As he digs ever deeper, the more he realises that the past is just as unpredictable as the present . . . and much closer than he could ever have imagined.

The Streamside, Hampshire

16 April 1816

It was not a day for death. For a start, the weather was all wrong. It was one of those perfect days: the sort that occurs only a handful of times each year. Air as clear as crystal; a day when the whole world seems to sparkle and glisten—freshly laundered by a shower of rain, buffed up by the gentlest of breezes and then polished to perfection by clear sunlight.

On this April day, at a quarter to nine in the morning, Anne Flint took advantage of her mistress's absence in the hope of changing her life. She lifted the latch on the heavy oak door and slipped from the Manor House without a backward glance. The events that had occurred since she had risen that morning at five o'clock had made her more determined than ever . . .

A bucketful of ashes can be quite heavy. If you are small. And slight. And slender of wrist. Anne had struggled down to the vegetable garden where old Mr Moses, who used to be the groom, now tended a few desultory rows of cabbages, swedes and turnips. She would not see him: he did not rise until half past eight at the earliest, and it was not yet half past six. As usual, Anne emptied the bucket gradually along the path that led to his dilapidated shelter. The bucket emptied, she retraced her steps to the house and stored it in its usual place in the cellar. As she climbed back up the cellar steps, she heard the firm footsteps of Mrs Fitzgerald walking down the passage above her.

Anne took the precaution of picking up a bottle of vinegar and a box of salt from a stone shelf behind the open cellar door. At first, she thought she might escape being seen by hiding behind the door, but that strategy was invalidated by the housekeeper who, thinking that the door had been left open by mistake, went to close it and saw the junior housemaid, salt and vinegar in hand, standing flat against the wall.

'What are you doing there? Idling?'

'Just coming out of the cellar, Mrs Fitzgerald.'

'You are out of the cellar. Why is there any need to stand behind the door?'

'I was—' Anne held up the box and bottle to show the fruits of her mission.

'They are doing no good in your hand. They need to be applied to the brass. Get your bowl and cloth. There's plenty to clean before breakfast.'

'Yes, ma'am.'

Anne had cast her eyes downwards, partly out of shame, and partly from weariness. There seemed no respite from this daily round. Oh, she knew she was lucky to have work at all, and she was not shy of it. It was just that this was not the sort of work she wanted to do. Not now.

Mrs Fitzgerald, of robust constitution, four feet eight inches of rough black linen and a collar of starched white cotton, read the situation. 'And there is no earthly point in you dreaming about being a lady's maid when you cannot even polish the brass or lay a fire.'

'But I can, ma'am. I do!'

'To your own satisfaction, perhaps, but not to mine.'

Anne bowed her head. 'No, ma'am.'

'Now, off you go. Bowl and cloth from the cupboard, the salt and vinegar you have.'

'Mrs Fitzgerald, do you think I might—?' Anne did not have time to complete the question.

'If you are asking to be let out of the house again, the answer is no. I have never objected to you taking a few minutes off from time to time. You know that. But you were gone for two hours yesterday, and such an abuse of privilege is not to be countenanced. You will work through.' And with that the housekeeper turned on her heel and headed off down the passage again.

For two whole hours, Anne rubbed at door handles and fingerplates, and anything that looked as though it should have glinted. She rubbed until her fingers ached, the vinegar merciless at discovering cuts.

The longcase clock in the hall struck the half-hour. She glanced up at the black hands on the dial. Half past eight o'clock. Silently, Anne walked along the passage that led to the linen cupboard and the pantry. There was no sign of Mrs Fitzgerald. She walked back and put her head round the doors of the kitchen and the scullery. The housekeeper was nowhere to be seen.

Swiftly, Anne replaced the salt and the vinegar in the cellar then along the passage she went, listening at the foot of the stairs for voices. They were faint—somewhere upstairs Sir Thomas Carew was talking to Mrs Fitzgerald.

She knew the tone of each voice in the household. Sir Thomas's was deep and rumbling, Lady Carew's gentle and soft; Mrs Fitzgerald's had an Irish lilt and a hard edge to it. The voices of the two sons, when they came home, were hard to distinguish from one another, but neither of them was in residence: Master Edward was away with the militia, and Master Frederick in London at his uncle's chambers.

But she had no time to think of them now. In a few minutes Mrs Fitzgerald would come back downstairs. If Anne was to leave and make her assignation it must be now. She took a woollen shawl from the hook in the kitchen, threw it round her shoulders and slipped out of the door.

Beyond the wrought-iron gate in the high wall to the side of the house lay a narrow path of bare earth that snaked its way under overhanging branches of hazel and quickthorn. Anne followed the path until it forked beneath a sturdy oak, then took the turning that led down to a grassy bank. At the bottom ran a stream, bordered by sweet flag and youthful meadowsweet, that was yet to send up its froth of creamy flowers. The stream was not a river; that distinction it could lay claim to a couple of miles down the valley. Now it was barely six feet across and ankle deep, shimmering as it flowed in whispering eddies over the pebble bed.

Anne flopped down on the bank and squinted as the sun, slanting through the osiers, caught her in the eye. For a few minutes she did nothing more than breathe, then, pulling her feet up close, she undid the long laces of her boots and slipped off first one, then the other, before reaching up under two layers of calico to find the ribbons that secured her stockings. She slid them from her legs, slipped down the bank a little farther and lowered her slender white feet into the clear water.

She gasped at the coldness of the water, then smiled. How wonderful it was to be free of the black boots and thick stockings. To be free of everything. Maybe today she would finally make her escape from the drudgery.

The prospect was too exciting to contemplate; she would take her mind off it. As she dangled her feet in the water, she reached into the pocket of her apron and pulled out a small book. A piece of purple ribbon marked her place. She had not got far with the book, but her reading was improving.

Anne had never had a formal education. She had no family: at least, none that she knew of. She had begun to read at the orphanage, encouraged by a kindly beadle who would sit beside her and take her through her alphabet, and read with her each day from the Book of Common Prayer. She did not mind too much that he sat so close to her; only when he began to touch her did she suspect he was not the kind man she had at first imagined him to be. From then on, she had made sure she was never alone with him. A few months later, she was sent into service.

Now, she had to manage for herself. She might be alone, but she was determined that would not always be her situation. One day she would meet a handsome young man and fall in love. Those were the sort of stories she liked to read. She had found a box full of books while cleaning the attic, took great care to ask if she might borrow one. Mrs Fitzgerald had looked at the faded title. 'Romantic. Well, if you must. But do remember that life is seldom quite so exciting.'

But Anne had liked the story. It had taken her several months to read, and then she was allowed to borrow another and another. The book she carried with her now told of how a highwayman came and swept a young girl off her feet. She was not at all sure that she wanted to be swept away by a highwayman, but it excited her to imagine what it might be like to live a little dangerously. Her heart missed a beat at the prospect.

Reality soon reinstated itself. No one looked like sweeping her off her feet. She was fifteen, not bad-looking, with her red-brown hair and a fair complexion. At least Sam told her that. Said that she was 'very presentable'. But what did he know? Sam was the yard boy in the stables. Sam would never get anybody. Certainly not her. He could read and write, it was true, but it would take someone special to win her hand. Not someone like Sam, with his warts and his big feet. She sighed heavily and made to read on, but it was too fair a day to be engrossed in a book. Carefully, she laid the purple ribbon between the pages and slipped the book back into her pocket.

Anne glanced around. The person she had hoped to meet was nowhere to be seen. She tied the laces of her two boots together, slipped a stocking into each of them and hung them round her neck, then withdrew her tingling feet from the water and rubbed them on the soft grassy bank to dry them.

The sun rose in the sky and slowly her dreams began to fade. It seemed as though the day that had promised so much would not be special after all. She had better return.

As she clambered carefully up the steep bank from the stream, Anne did not see a figure standing not far from her, by an oak tree. It moved, blending into the shadows . . .

St Jude's School, Winchester

16 April 2010

'It's boring, sir.'

Harry Flint looked over the top of his glasses, the better to see the youth who was addressing him. 'What do you mean, "boring"?'

The boy shrugged. He was not one of the brightest in the class, but then neither was he a total no-hoper, nor one of the tiresome troublemakers.

'Just . . . well . . . what has it got to do with us? It's history.'

Harry took off his glasses, slid from the desk on which he had been sitting and walked across to the window. He looked out across the school yard to the fields and meadows beyond. It was one of those perfect days: the sort that occurs only a handful of times each year. Air as clear as crystal; a day when the whole world seems to sparkle and glisten—freshly laundered by a shower of rain, buffed up by the gentlest of breezes and then polished to perfection by clear sunlight.

'What's it got to do with you?' He asked the question softly, rhetorically. But he nevertheless received a reply.

'It all happened ages ago. All this stuff about kings and queens. It doesn't make any difference to us.'

Harry repeated the boy's words slowly. 'It . . . doesn't . . . make . . . any . . . difference . . . to . . . us.'

He turned to face the boy and the rest of the class. A sea of wary faces gazed at him. They could sense his mood was changing.

'Just because something happened a long time ago—in this case about two hundred years ago, Stephens—does not mean that it does not affect you today, or that it is unimportant. The past'—Harry glanced about the room—'Wilson, what does the past do?' he asked of a studious lad, who might hopefully come to his aid.

'It informs the present, sir.'

The rest of the class let out a low moan.

'It informs the present and allows us to place our lives in context.'

Feet shuffled under desks.

Harry sighed heavily. 'The reign of George the third, while from your point of view as far away from your own lives as'—he sought a suitable analogy—'Harry Potter or Spiderman, is part of your history. Not everything that happened all those years ago is dull or unimportant or irrelevant.'

He scanned the room once more, hopeful of a glimmer of interest or a spark of enthusiasm. None came.

'Here was a king who lost America, who is remembered as being mad—which is far from the truth—whose grasp of agriculture and encouragement of architecture and the arts was matchless, who was subjected to the most fiendish treatment at the hands of doctors to cure him of ailments they didn't fully understand, and who died blind and deaf, handing over his kingdom to a self-indulgent son who squandered his talents.'

A hand went up halfway back in the classroom.

'Yes, Palmer?'

'Sir, can we go to Brighton?'

Before Harry could answer, the air was riven by a metallic clanging. The boys began to clear their desks of books.

Harry raised his voice. 'We'll continue this fascinating discussion on the fate of King George on Monday. Thank you, gentlemen.'

'Thank you, sir.' The words emerged through the sound of chairs scraping against the wooden floor and feet clattering out of the classroom.

Harry sank down into the chair behind his desk. The repetition of facts over the years had wearied him. Maybe they had a point. Maybe it wasn't relevant any more. Perhaps he had been doing the job too long. Well, this was his last term. When the summer holidays finally came they could say goodbye to Flinty—and George III, too, for that matter. And what then?

If only he knew. That was the thing about the future: it was all so uncertain. So uncomfortable. Not like the past. You knew where you were with the past. Things slotted into place perfectly. Neatly. He liked neatness. Orderliness. That was his problem. That was why he was on his own now . . .

It was no time to brood. The rest of the afternoon was clear and it was Friday. He would go out. Leave the classroom behind and shake off the grey mood brought on by an ungrateful bunch of twelve year olds.

Harry glanced up at the coat of arms fixed to the wall above his desk. It was of a swan on a blue ground with the school motto beneath it—*Nitor donec supero*:'I strive till I overcome.' *Some hope*, he thought.

He slid his books into a holdall and walked towards the door. Where to go? Down by the river. Being near to it always made him feel better.

As he left the classroom he glanced again at the coat of arms and smiled ruefully. St Jude. How appropriate. The patron saint of hopeless cases.

The Fulling Mill, Hampshire

17 April 1816

The first they knew of it was when the hammers slowed. 'Another branch must have come down,' shouted William Palfrey, the miller, to his wife Agnes. 'Send Jacob along; I'll need help to clear it.'

The life of a fulling miller was not, he reminded himself, an easy one. Prices of raw materials continued to rise, and of the finished product—the thick and rich felted cloth—well, they continued to haggle over it every day. And the bloody hammers thumping . . . Flour: that's what he should be milling. Still, at least he was away from the town, making a living on the banks of a river. No one would prise him away from it.

The miller made his way down the rickety wooden stairs and pushed open the door adjacent to the mill stream. The storm two days before had interrupted their work more than he would have liked. It was fine now, but branches that the earlier spell of weather had dislodged often took a day or two to find their way down to this stretch.

The sturdy wooden framework that William and his son Jacob had erected across the river usually caught these wayward branches before they could find their way into the mechanism, but they would then gather around them more and more debris and slow down the flow of water that powered the hammers. It was a simple matter to pull them free, but it usually took more strength than William possessed—fighting against the flow of flood-water—and he called upon his son for the requisite muscle power.

William walked round to the mill leat to see what was causing the problem. The water seemed to be flowing over the top of the barrier quite evenly; there was no branch sticking up to show where the blockage had begun. He held on to the corner of the archway under which the water flowed in order to look along the barrier. It was then that he saw not a broken branch, but a pale hand protruding from a waterlogged sleeve.

ONCE WILLIAM AND JACOB had fished the body out of the river and hauled it up onto the bank, they stood silently for a few moments. This was not a vagabond or a drunk who had fallen in and drowned. The person on whom they gazed wore the clothes of a housemaid. Her hands were pale and soft. Her auburn hair clung to her pallid cheeks and her green eyes stared vacantly at the sky as she lay like a broken china doll on the soft grass of the river bank.

'What shall we do?' asked Jacob, his face as pale as that of the young girl's on whom he gazed.

William ran a gnarled hand over the snow-white stubble on his chin. 'We'd best tell Sir Thomas. He'll know what to do.' The miller stared again at the lifeless body. He recognised the fabric of her dress. It was of a thick gingham, a small check. Pale blue. She must be one of Sir Thomas's house-maids: this was the uniform of the more lowly members of the squire's domestic staff. But how had she come to be here? It was at least two miles to the big house. Up there the water was shallow, the river nothing more than a gurgling stream. And where were her boots and her stockings? Had she been paddling and lost her footing?

There was little point in wondering: William Palfrey knew that these were questions to which he was unlikely ever to have an answer. Deaths were deaths and were invariably down to old age, disease or misfortune. One of the three. Only the last of these gave him pause for thought. The misfor-tune of slipping was tragic but straightforward. But if the girl had not fallen or slipped . . . He shook his head to clear it of unwelcome thoughts.

'Saddle the horse,' he instructed his son. 'I'll go and find Sir Thomas.'

The River Bank, Hampshire

16 April 2010

He should not really be there. He should be marking. Or preparing. Or . . . well, something constructive, rather than sitting on the banks of a river. Oh, to hell with it. They would assume that he was hard at it in the public library or somewhere suitably dreary: conscientious Harry Flint, no life except for that which he finds in his books.

He could feel one of those Peggy Lee 'Is That All There Is?' moments coming on. They were occurring more frequently. The onset of his forties seemed to coincide with pointless self-analysis, mainly as a result of the unexpected solitude that life had thrown his way.

He breathed deeply, in the hope of dispelling negative thoughts and the fog that seemed to fill his head. Chalk dust might be a thing of the past thanks to interactive whiteboards, but these days there were other things to cloud a teacher's mind. Futility and frustration, for a start. And loneliness.

It was two years now since Serena had left him. Bored, she'd said. Fed up with taking second place to his books, and tired of a lack of fire in their relationship. Her announcement had hit him like a sledgehammer.

They had met through mutual friends: she a high-flying lawyer, he the steady schoolmaster. It was she who kept long hours—coming home from work close to midnight. She who, when she was at home, sat at a desk in their joint study and pored over pink beribboned bundles while he cooked and cleaned, put a glass of wine at her elbow. How could he be the one who had caused it all to fall apart? By being too easy-going? Too tolerant?

He hadn't seen it coming. She'd admired his quiet self-containment at first. And his wit. And his memory for quotations. Well, he liked to think so. She had, after all, intimated as much. Hadn't she? At first, when their love was fresh and exciting? He remembered her telling him that he made her laugh. The difference of their worlds—and of their outlook—was what had brought them together, each fascinated by the other. In the end it was what drove them apart.

Serena's world was light years away from his own. The parties they went to at her friends' were riotous affairs: men with loud voices and women with low-cut dresses and high-pitched laughs. It was not that Harry was a prude—far from it—or that he didn't like laughing. He did. But they were just not his sort of people. When he answered their questions about teaching and history, he was aware of their gradually diminishing attention. Of their eyes drifting over his shoulder to see if there was anybody more interesting in the room.

Six months after they married, Serena moved out, and he had neither heard nor seen anything of her since. He had tried contacting her, but texts and phone messages went unanswered. And so, eventually, he gave up trying.

The reason he had waited until he was nearly forty before he got married was because he had wanted to be sure. Didn't want to make the same mistake as his parents. They had seemed to be so happy when he was a boy. It later became apparent that they had stuck together solely for his sake: their only child. Only when he went off to university did they tell him they were going their separate ways. Now they were both dead.

It had made him wary, determined not to commit himself until he was absolutely sure that 'this was the one'. It had been Serena who'd convinced him that they were made for each other. Told him not to be such a stick-in-the-mud. They'd spent a weekend away in Paris just a month after they had met, walking along the banks of the Seine, looking at the bookstalls and the flower kiosks, lunching in small cafés, dining in cosy restaurants and lying in until almost noon, to be woken by the bells chiming out over the silvery rooftops. What a dream it all was . . .

He reached down and picked up a pebble. It was round and smooth in his grasp, a comforting sort of thing to hold. He raised his arm and tossed it into the swiftly flowing water, where it landed with a deep-toned 'plop'. A few seconds and the ripple that it had set up had disappeared.

Handing in his notice had taken courage. That's what he liked to think. His capacity for stupidity might have been borne out by an unwise marriage, but this decision was, in a way, a rebellion. Proof that he was not boring. Or predictable. Or unadventurous.

He had no idea what he would do, but he was not without funds. The only kind thing that Serena had done was to say she would not ask him for any money. She earned more than he did, she had conceded, and, being a lawyer, had no appetite for litigation on her own part: 'A waste of time. The only people who win are the lawyers. And I don't want to hurt you.'

As if she hadn't already. But he was grateful for that crumb of generosity of spirit. So what now? Leaving the flat they had shared was the first step. Within the month the new owners would take over. Time he got a move on. Literally. But where to? He liked it in this part of Hampshire.

He would begin looking today. On this bright April afternoon. Spring: a good time to start a new life. A good time to move on. He got up from the grassy bank and walked towards the car. He would go into town and look in the estate agents' windows.

It was time that he found out who he really was. What his destiny might be. He almost laughed out loud at the ludicrousness of such a thought. But he would make a start. He would grab a fistful of particulars from every estate agent down Winchester High Street and then go home to sift through them. With any luck there would be something suitable and then he could get down to work. Not school work, but the tracing of the ancestry that had occupied him since a few weeks after Serena had left.

That, and studying the lives of the saints, filled most of his otherwise idle hours. The interest in saints had been a spin-off. He was curious to discover how ordinary people had managed to lead such extraordinary, even fantastical lives. But as interests went, martyrdom and genealogy were not likely to set the world—or another woman—on fire.

The Manor House, Withercombe

17 April 1816

Sir Thomas Carew, baronet and the local magistrate, had met the miller in the hall of the Manor House at Withercombe. His face had been grave and his voice raised to little more than a whisper. The body, he had instructed, should be brought there immediately. He would inspect it, and only then could it be transferred to the back room of the Bluebell, the local inn, where the coroner's court could convene and give its verdict. He had also given his opinion that the miller's cart would be the most suitable form of transport. That would create a minimum of fuss. William Palfrey had returned to the mill, and the same grey cob that he had ridden to the Manor House had been hitched up to his cart.

Jacob now sat up-front with his father, glancing back every now and then to check the security of the sad load as they rattled along the lane towards the Manor House. The girl was covered in a sheet of coarse grey felt—a poor, uneven bolt that his father had rejected as unfit to be sold on. Jacob noticed that the cloth had slipped a little and revealed one of the her pale feet.

'Pa, stop!' he called, still looking backwards. The miller pulled on the reins and halted the cob. Jacob jumped down from the box and adjusted the cloth, tucking it under the girl. Then he climbed up beside his father again. William Palfrey flicked the reins and bade the horse walk on.

Jacob was fifteen and, like most boys of that time, was no stranger to death. He knew that babies died, hours or days or weeks after being born, quite often in these parts. And old folk in their fifties and sixties. He had seen their bodies laid out when he called with his father to pay their last respects. There were epidemics, too, when no one was safe, not even the strongest youth. But on a warm spring day, when there was nothing evil going around and no reason for a young maid to fall foul of miscreants and footpads by his stream, in his valley, it all seemed so wrong. He had never seen such a beautiful corpse.

His father noticed Jacob's expression. 'No reason to upset yourself,' he murmured.

'Beautiful,' whispered Jacob. 'So beautiful.'

'Aye. 'Tis a sad day when girls of her age are taken from us.'

'How did it happen, do you think?'

'Lost her footing, I shouldn't wonder. The river stones are slippery at this time of year—the weed has begun to grow on them.'

'So her boots and stockings would be by the river? Where she fell in?'

'Like as not.'

'I will go and look for them when we get back.'

William nodded his assent.

THEY ARRIVED, after twenty minutes or so, at the Manor House, and the miller drove the cart to the stables. The cob's hoofs clattered loudly in the courtyard and the wheels of the cart emitted a metallic, rasping sound. On hearing them, the groom came out to meet them. Timothy Jencks was a small, fine-featured man whose grave expression suited the task that lay ahead of the miller and him—that of carrying the body into the stables' grain store—where Sir Thomas would inspect it.

William and Jacob got down from the cart and Jacob took the horse's reins. The miller and the groom greeted each other with a nod. The two men then eased the felt-covered body from the back of the cart and bore it across to the stables, where they laid it on a long, rough table that was usually used for the mixing of grain and mash for the horses.

No sooner had they done so than Sam, the yard boy, put his head round the corner of the grain store and asked, 'What's goin' on, guv'nor?'

'Never you mind,' retorted Jencks. 'You get about your business.'

The youth was not to be deterred. 'That there a body?' he enquired.

The miller nodded.

'I've told you, be off,' Jencks reiterated. 'Nothing to do with you. Sir Thomas will be here presently and will not want you around.'

It was not that Sam did not hear the words, rather that what he saw over-whelmed him so much that he was drawn towards the body. The grey felt covering had left part of the girl's dress on view, and a corner of coarse blue gingham hung down over the edge of the table. The boy walked forward and took it reverently in his hand. 'One of ours,' he murmured.

'Just you go and . . .' Timothy Jencks's words of warning went unheeded as Sam lifted the edge of the damp grey felt, the better to see the face of the body that lay in front of him. What his eyes beheld caused the colour to drain from his face.

Before he could say anything, however, a commotion in the stable yard caused the three men to turn round.

'Take these dogs away! I distinctly asked Stuart to shut them in.' Sir Thomas, endeavouring to make his way across the cobbles, was being impeded by two springer spaniels and a pointer that had, not unreasonably, assumed they were in for some sport on this fine spring morning. He was irritated, and his flushed cheeks contrasted even more than usual with the white mutton-chop whiskers that framed his face. The three dogs had caused their master to lose his footing—and now his temper—on the uneven cobbles of the yard. It was Jacob who caught him before he toppled over, and Sir Thomas gave the youth a nod of gratitude.

'Reaper, Stalwart, Oscar—AWAY!' At the sound of the thundered admonishment, the dogs hastened off in the direction of a footman, who was now running across the stable yard to make good his earlier omission.

Regaining his dignity, the magistrate, local squire and lord of the manor now nodded at William and looked enquiringly at his groom, who motioned him towards the table on which the body lay.

Sam was still standing alongside it, causing Sir Thomas to glance at his groom as though to admonish him.

'I'm sorry, Sir Thomas, he just . . . well . . .'

Annoyed that yet another member of his household was demonstrating how little dominion he had over his charges, Sir Thomas interrupted, 'Sam, come away! This has nothing to do with you. Go about your business.'

Sam looked round, his face still white, and said, quite simply, ' 'Tis not her. 'Tis her dress, but not her.'

Confused as well as annoyed, Sir Thomas asked, 'Not whom?'

'Not Anne. Anne Flint. 'Tis not her . . .'

Sir Thomas stepped up to the table and looked down at the fair, pale face that looked upwards but past him with vacant eyes.

'Good God!' he muttered, softly. 'No. Indeed, it is not.'

He remained silent, looking down at the body, as though unable to believe his eyes. Then he became aware of the miller standing at his shoulder.

'I thought,' said William, 'that she must be one of your maids. Her dress is of your household, I think, sir.'

'It is. It most certainly is, but . . .' Sir Thomas spoke musingly, looking unseeingly at the miller as he did so. 'One of my housemaids went missing yesterday. She left the house in the morning. Mrs Fitzgerald had just scolded her. I was upstairs instructing Mrs Fitzgerald and it was she who saw her go. On occasions, I was told, the girl would slip down to the stream and Mrs Fitzgerald usually turned a blind eye. She was a good girl. These . . . dalliances with nature seemed . . . well . . . important to her.'

'But this is not her?'

'No.'

'And the girl has not returned?'

'No. She has not.'

Sam looked agitated. 'Something must have happened to Anne. 'Tis her dress, sir.'

'We do not know that, Sam,' snapped Timothy Jencks. 'It is one of our housemaids' dresses, but that does not mean it is Anne's.'

Sam shook his head defiantly. 'Look . . .' He stepped closer to the body and pointed to a short length of purple ribbon that protruded from the apron pocket. 'This is Anne's. She used it to mark her place. In books.' Tentatively, he slid his hand into the pocket of the dead girl's apron and withdrew the purple ribbon. He turned to Sir Thomas with a look of desperation on his face. 'No book,' he murmured. 'Only the ribbon.'

Under other circumstances, Sir Thomas would have uttered an exclamation of the 'Bless my soul' or 'Good heavens' variety, but on this occasion he said nothing, just carried on staring at the face of the girl.

'So,' said the miller softly, 'we do not know who she is.'

'Oh, yes,' said Sir Thomas. 'We know who she is.' He remained gazing at the girl's face as though transfixed. 'Are you acquainted with the Earl of Stockbridge?' he asked.

'I know of him, sir. From the big house at the foot of the downs.'

'Hatherley.'

'Yes, sir. Hatherley.'

'The earl has three daughters. This is the youngest of them. Lady Eleanor. Or rather, it was . . .' Sir Thomas broke out of his reverie and carefully replaced the coarse cloth over the face of the dead girl.

'I should have known,' muttered William. 'Her hands—they were soft. Not at all like those of a housemaid.'

'No,' said Sir Thomas. 'Not at all.'

William shook his head. 'So what was she doing wearing a dress that belonged to your maid?'

'I have absolutely no idea, Mr Palfrey. No idea at all.'

Sam turned away from the group and stumbled out into the yard. If this was Anne's dress, then where was Anne?

St Cross Apartments, Winchester

17 April 2010

Harry did not sleep well. Perhaps it was due to worrying. Well, there was no perhaps about it, really. Worrying was a way of life to Harry Flint. But he had, he considered, just cause on this bright Saturday morning. In the space of the next few weeks, he would need to find himself a new place to live and a new job. With the sale of the flat going through, and by drawing on what his parents had left him, he would be able to afford a small place without having to commit himself to a mortgage. He should count himself lucky. He *did* count himself lucky. Sort of . . . He showered and made himself a pot of coffee before sitting down at the kitchen table.

He reached across it and pulled towards him the two piles of estate agents' particulars that his trawl of the high street the previous day had yielded. He had done a preliminary sifting the night before, taking out all those properties that did not fulfil his requirements. The larger pile he now picked up and dropped in the wastepaper bin, the smaller he spread out on the table. There was nothing that set his heart on fire.

He sat up and looked around him at the flat. Three of the four walls that surrounded the large sitting room were clad, floor to ceiling, in books. Books on history, books on art, books on Georgian architecture and furniture. How could he face putting all these into store and going into rented accommodation? He would apply himself. It was spring; the house market traditionally moved faster in spring. Surely there was something out there?

He was torn, however. He really wanted to get on with the project that eased his mind, that of researching his roots. Finding out what had gone before seemed to offer more in the way of stability than what lay ahead. So far, he had been moderately successful, having traced back five generations. Now it had started to become tricky.

Where had his great-great-great-grandfather—the delightfully named Merrily Flint—come from? The Internet drew a blank. Perhaps parish records in dusty ledgers were the only gateway to his past. That would mean foot-slogging. But not today.

He looked back at the table and the four properties that had made his short list. A semidetached cottage—1920s—in Alresford. Out of town, but still accessible. He could not say that it really excited him.

A bungalow in St Cross. He looked again at the details. He really was not ready for a bungalow: he could still climb stairs. Why on earth had he kept that in? He lobbed it, along with the Alresford semi, into the bin.

A town house with views of the cathedral. On four floors. Georgian. With a manageable walled garden. Perfect. Until he looked at the price. It was way beyond his means. He threw it into the bin after the semi and the bungalow.

There was one property left. Two sheets, paperclipped together. He eyed the particulars. It was detached, true, so that fitted the bill. It had a small garden. It was Victorian, not Georgian, but . . . well, it was reasonably priced and the rooms would accommodate both him and his books. He checked the address. Unfortunately, it sat right alongside the A31.

Harry flopped back in his chair. So that was that. Nothing. Not a single affordable property that he could feel comfortable living in. He picked up the details to throw them after the others, removing, as was his habit, the paperclip. The second sheet, he assumed, would be directions to the house on the A31.

As he removed the clip, the second sheet was revealed and his heart skipped a beat. The front page showed a small, detached, thatched cottage. Something about it spoke to him. The garden in front of it was overgrown, the cottage itself barely visible through a haze of apple trees and brambles. The thatch was in reasonable condition but the dwelling had clearly been unoccupied for some time. It was likely to be damp. He totted up the number of rooms: a small hallway, two reception rooms, kitchen, cloakroom, two bedrooms and a bathroom upstairs. Not really enough to make the place a viable proposition.

He turned over the sheet of paper and checked the price and the level of council tax. Well, it was affordable. Then he saw an additional paragraph and a small map: 'In addition to the cottage, there is a small stone-built outhouse, which was once a miller's storeroom, on two floors. It has potential to be converted into a granny annexe, subject to planning permission.' *Or a library*, thought Harry.

The map was the final coup de grâce. It showed the location of the cottage and indicated quite clearly its curtilage. The garden that surrounded it, overgrown though it might be, ran down to the banks of the River Itchen. He looked at the name of the property: Mill Cottage, Itchen Parva.

The feeling of possession was overwhelming. Then he checked himself. A romantic-sounding name was insufficient reason to take on a liability.

But then the name was not the reason. The river was the reason. The name just . . . well . . . added to its emotional pull.

He glanced at his watch. A quarter to nine. The estate agent would not open until at least nine thirty. What was the likelihood of them being able to arrange a viewing that day? Well, the property was empty. Perhaps it would not be a problem.

For the next forty-five minutes he tried to occupy himself, then, as the bracket clock on the chest of drawers struck the three-quarter hour, he set off for the estate agent's office.

The Manor House, Withercombe

17 April 1816

Sam stumbled across the stable yard without knowing where he was going. His head swam, his stomach churned and a deep sense of bewilderment swept over him as he walked past the open doorways where Leger and Botolph, Thistle and Alderney pushed out their heads and munched the hay from the wooden racks that Sam had filled that morning. He rounded the corner, out of sight of the three men, and sat down on the edge of the stone water trough. His head in his hands, he tried to get some kind of purchase on the events that had unfolded. Where was Anne? Why was someone else wearing her clothes? And why was this someone else a lady, and a dead lady at that?

The whole scenario was beyond the compass of his comprehension. The clock above the stable struck nine. The horses were fed and mucked out. Timothy Jencks was fully occupied dealing with his master, the miller . . . and a dead body. Sam stood up and walked, then ran along the edge of the yard and out through the ornate iron archway at the end of the stables into the parkland beyond.

After a few minutes he was at the edge of the stream—Anne's favourite spot, he knew—and he flopped down, panting. He flung off his leather jerkin and drank from the cool water of the stream, before remembering what had happened there and regretting his action. Tears came unbidden to his eyes. He liked Anne. He liked her a lot, even though she had spurned him and told him that she could never be his. They were too young, she had said, and not suited.

Too young? And now where was she? Who was she with? He hoped and prayed that she was safe. Impatiently, he wiped the tears from his eyes, got up and walked along the edge of the stream, looking for something that might show where she had been. But there was nothing—nothing but the flash of a kingfisher and the plop of a young trout darting for cover.

For fully half an hour, he sat on a smooth boulder above the stream, his thick brown hair falling over his eyes, before getting up to go. He put on his leather jerkin and, as he did so, he saw something dark among the sword-like leaves of flag iris at the streamside. He bent down and picked it up. It was a small leather book, rather battered and faded on the spine. He opened it and read the title: *The Highwayman's Bride*. It was Anne's book. It must be. She'd had an obsession with highwaymen over the past few days. Said that one day she would be swept off her feet. Surely she could not simply have been taken? Kidnapped? And what of the earl's daughter wearing her dress? What was Anne wearing? So many questions and not one answer. But he had Anne's book, he was sure. After looking over the area to see if he could find anything else, he decided he would go back to show the book to Timothy Jencks and Sir Thomas. They would know what to do.

THE BODY WAS CARRIED by servants to a small anteroom in the Manor House. The Bluebell Inn was no place for a lady of rank, Sir Thomas had decided. The body was laid on an oak table and covered with a white linen shroud—more suitable than the poor-quality grey felt the miller had supplied.

Sir Thomas would go in his chaise to inform Lord Stockbridge. They would harness the horses immediately and hope that on their arrival he would be there. He thanked William and Jacob for their trouble and sent them on their way. They made the journey home in silence, both of them thinking on the likely outcome of this mystery.

THE YARD WAS SILENT when Sam returned, the book tucked safely into the pocket of his jerkin. He could not find Timothy Jencks, and both Alderney and Leger were absent from their stalls. The doors of the coach house were also open and the chaise was gone. Sam deduced what had been going on in his absence and hoped he would escape a scolding on Mr Jencks's return, for leaving him to harness the two greys on his own.

Sitting on the rim of the old stone horse trough once more, he took out the book and fingered the rough leather binding, then opened it and flicked through the pages, vainly hoping that it would offer some kind of clue to the whereabouts of a girl without whose presence he felt bereft.

AS THE CHAISE RATTLED its way to Hatherley, Sir Thomas Carew mused on how he could best approach the matter. There was no tactful way in which you could tell a man that his daughter had been found drowned. He looked out across the Hampshire countryside and wondered how such a tragic accident could occur on such a glorious spring day.

Eventually, they turned into a long drive lined by lime trees, shimmering in their lush April finery. Sheep grazed in the parkland to either side, looking up in a vaguely interested way as the chaise went past. The house itself was a model of elegance, built during the brief reign of Queen Anne, with tall, white-framed windows and a pleasingly porticoed front door.

Timothy Jencks was relieved to find a servant in front of the house: without Sam beside him, he did not want to leave the horses unattended while he went to the front door. Timothy gave the man a wave of acknowledgment and instructed, 'Sir Thomas Carew of Withercombe to see the earl.'

The servant nodded and mounted the stairs to the front door, opening it and disappearing inside. Within a few moments the horses had come to a standstill and the servant had returned from the house wearing a dark green footman's coat. He opened the door of the chaise and Sir Thomas alighted.

'Lord Stockbridge is in the library, sir, if you will follow me.'

Sir Thomas nodded and did as he was bid. In the hall, he briefly composed himself before crossing to enter a large room lined with oak bookcases.

The earl was as small and slight as Sir Thomas was large and round. Among the tables, books, folio cabinets and globes, he was not at first visible. But then Sir Thomas saw him standing by the fireplace with his back to the flames, his face wearing a look of foreboding.

'Your lordship.' Sir Thomas bowed respectfully from the neck.

'Sir Thomas.' A less demonstrative bow from the earl.

'I come, I am afraid, with grave news.'

The earl's expression did not alter and he remained still, both hands thrust under the tails of his dark blue coat, his eyes fixed on Sir Thomas.

'It is your daughter, Eleanor. She is at the Manor House at Withercombe. I am afraid that she was discovered this morning by the miller from Itchen Parva.' Sir Thomas fought for the right words. 'She is, I am afraid—'

'Dead?'

The earl's candour momentarily caught the baronet off guard. He nodded. 'I am afraid so. She was found early this morning in the river alongside the mill. There was nothing the miller and his son could do. We brought her . . . that is, her body . . . to the Manor House.'

A silence sat uncomfortably on them. Then the earl asked, quite slowly and with little trace of emotion, 'Do you have a daughter, Sir Thomas?'

'No, sir. Only sons. Of daughters I have no experience.'

The earl nodded. 'They are not easy. When they are very young they are rash and rebellious, and when they are older they are intransigent. They do not listen to reason. They have minds of their own.'

Sir Thomas half smiled sympathetically. He would have loved a daughter. To spoil. To make a fuss of him. To tease him as daughters did.

'They are a drain on one's finances, a cause of grey hairs, a thorn in one's side, and yet . . .' The earl paused, unable, for a moment, to continue. 'They are any father's delight. Her uncle is due to come and see her today. Back from Italy. She was the apple of his eye, too.'

Sir Thomas knew that he could not escape the next obstacle. 'Milord, there was one strange circumstance. Lady Eleanor was wearing . . . the clothing of my housemaid, Anne, who has, I am sorry to say, gone missing.'

The earl did not respond, but upon his face was a look of incredulity.

Mill Cottage, Itchen Parva

17 April 2010

'What do you mean, sold?' asked Harry in disbelief. 'You gave me the particulars only yesterday afternoon.'

'Sellers' market, sir. Things are moving fast at the moment. Spring, you know.' The young estate agent looked as though he had been born just a few weeks ago, though his attitude was more akin to that expected of a long-standing member of the House of Lords who owned half of Cirencester.

'I am well acquainted with the seasons and know that April is in spring. What I don't understand is why—barely fifteen hours ago—you would give me the details of a property that you now tell me is sold.'

'Well, it is not exactly sold, sir, but it is under offer.'

'But they haven't bought it yet?'

A slight flush appeared in the young man's cheeks. 'They have not yet exchanged contracts. That will occur once they are happy with the survey and their solicitor's searches. We expect completion within the month.'

Harry was lost for words. Eventually he asked, 'Is there any chance I can have a look at it?'

'As I say, sir, it is under offer.'

'And if the offer falls through?'

'Very unlikely, sir. This is, after all, a highly desirable property—'

'A highly desirable property that needs a master builder to make it habitable and a JCB in the garden, which at the moment is as impenetrable as the Forest of Arden.' Harry held up the particulars and pointed to the photograph of the picturesque ruin.

The bell on the door of the estate agent's office broke into their conversation with a resounding 'ping', and a middle-aged couple entered. The young man looked relieved and seized the opportunity for respite that they offered. 'Excuse me a moment. Sir? Madam?'

'Could we arrange a viewing of the bungalow in Oliver's Battery?'

'Of course.'

'Might I have the keys then?' Harry broke in. 'So that if your current sale falls through, you have something in the way of back-up?' He spoke in a voice that brooked no contradiction: the better part of twenty years of teaching small boys had offered ample opportunity to refine an intimidating tone.

It did the trick. With Pavlovian predictability, the young man said, 'Of course, sir,' and handed over the keys.

IT WAS, UNDOUBTEDLY, a rash thing to do: to see the cottage now would simply pile on the agony. And agonising it most certainly was. Perhaps if he had viewed it in filthy weather, in wind and rain, on an autumn day, he would have seen it for what it was—a tumbledown pile of stones topped by a battered straw hat. But it was another perfect spring day. Bees and brimstone butterflies beset him as he fought his way through the brambles in the wake of prospective buyers who had gone before. Dog roses feathered his path, pushing their paper twists of buds heavenwards. Ancient and tortured apple trees towered over him, their stooping boughs encrusted with pale green lichen, their branches festooned with blossom as pink and white as coconut ice. How could something so neglected and ignored be so beautiful?

Reaching the peeling front door, he pushed in the key and turned it. For a door so battered it opened with ease and in silence, and he peered into the two rooms to right and left. Both had fireplaces, and small windows that let in a surprising amount of light. He explored upstairs—a primitive bathroom and two small bedrooms with dormer windows. In spite of the age of the cottage it did not smell of damp and decay. It was just . . . well . . . empty. Waiting. Expectant.

He let himself out of the back door and battled his way through the undergrowth to the outhouse, a large stone-built and gable-roofed structure that sat to the west of the cottage. Inside, a plain wooden staircase led to what must once have been a hay loft. Harry felt the walls: bone dry. Try as he might, he could not stop himself from imagining what life would be like there. And then he remembered the river.

He locked the door of the outhouse behind him and set off in search of the bottom of the garden. At first, all he could hear was birdsong: a robin, and then a yellowhammer, then house sparrows chattering in a bay tree, and blue tits and chaffinches . . . and then, through the birdsong, he heard the sound of the river. Finally, he reached the grassy bank that sloped to the water's edge and gazed on the clear stream as it waltzed gently by. The Itchen was perhaps twenty feet wide there, and three feet deep. A proper river.

HARRY DROPPED OFF the keys, asking to be called if the current buyer had a change of heart, and went home disconsolate. Five hours later he took the call that he had told himself would never come: the previous buyer had got cold feet and Mill Cottage was his if he wanted it.

So it was that Harry Flint became saddled with a crumbling thatched cottage in an overgrown wilderness on the banks of the River Itchen. The funny thing was, it already felt like home.

Rakemaker's Close, Old Alresford

17 April 2010

Harry could see from the look on their faces that they thought he was quite mad. What they said confirmed his suspicions.

'It's falling down, dear!' was Pattie Chieveley's verdict on the particulars.

Her husband, Ted, was more comprehensive in his condemnation, 'It's a complete heap. You'll be a slave to it, Harry! It will drain your bank account. And thatch? I mean, do you know what the fire risk is like?'

Harry smiled. 'I know. Daft, isn't it? But the place just spoke to me.'

The Chieveleys had become, in a way, surrogate parents to Harry. When he had joined St Jude's five years previously, Ted had been the headmaster. The two had got on, sharing a fondness for Georgian England and the literature of the time.

Harry had known that they would not approve, encouraging and helpful though they had been to him over those past rocky months. They were anxious for his wellbeing, and worried that he had completely lost the plot and was about to commit his life savings to a lost cause.

'Have a Scotch,' muttered Ted. 'Might restore your addled brain and make you see things more clearly.' He moved to the sideboard and poured his wife a Martini, and himself and Harry a generous measure of whisky.

Pattie picked up the conversation. 'If you're sure it's what you want . . .'

'I am,' said Harry. 'I know it's in a bit of a state.'

'Ha!' Ted almost choked on his whisky.

Pattie gave him a withering look and he refrained from further criticism. She was a touch more astute than her husband. Sharp-eyed and sensitive to mood, she knew just when to let her husband ramble on, and just when to stop him in his tracks.

The only other close friend Harry had was a very different kettle of fish to these two. Rick Palfrey taught maths at St Jude's. Where Harry was introverted and introspective, Rick was best described by words beginning with 'out'. Outgoing, outspoken and, on occasion, in Harry's opinion, outrageous. Like the Chieveleys, he had helped Harry come through the tough times.

'What does Rick think?' had been Pattie's next question.

'Haven't told him yet.' Harry took a slug of Scotch. 'I'm seeing him tonight. For a curry.'

'Cobra then,' offered Ted.

'What, dear?' Pattie Chieveley looked puzzled.

'Cobra beer. Good with a curry.' Ted rose from his chair and walked to the sideboard. He glanced at Harry. 'Another one? To give you courage?'

'No. I'd best be off.' He looked at his watch. 'Meeting Rick in an hour.'

Ted looked blank for a moment, then asked, 'What was I doing? Oh, yes.' He refilled his own glass. 'Well, I hope he succeeds where we've failed.'

'What do you mean?' asked Harry.

'In putting you off.'

Bluebell Inn, Withercombe

19 April 1816

They had no idea Sam was there. Inside the Bluebell Inn, the coroner was addressing a jury of twelve men drawn from the local hundred—the division of the county of Hampshire over which he presided. They were ranged around the figure that lay on the scrubbed pine table; Sam could just make out its shape between their warm-coated bodies. He sat on a wooden bench at the side of the inn, where the cool spring breeze whipped at his neck and chilled his calves through the coarse weave of his stockings. The clear, bright weather of the past few days had been replaced by more typical April fare—blustery, with showers.

It was three days now since Anne had disappeared, and there was still no sign of her, nor any word as to her whereabouts. He had asked the local coachman for news on his daily return from London but, in spite of calling at towns and villages along the lanes that led from Winchester to the capital, the coachman had seen or heard nothing of her.

Sam sneaked round the side of the inn and leaned on the frame of the open door, the better to hear the conversation that emanated from the taproom and to shelter from a sudden shower that threatened to soak him to the skin. At first the low growl of voices was indistinct above the patter of the rain on roof and road but, little by little, some phrases drifted more clearly from the inner gloom and through the open door: 'A sad affair' was one. Then, 'His lordship should have kept a closer eye. Not done for young women of good birth to be abroad on their own.' And a phrase that he would never forget as long as he lived: 'Death by misadventure.'

Mill Cottage, Itchen Parva

29 May 2010

When the last packing case had been brought into the cottage, Harry told himself that it did not look too bad. Rick told him what it really looked like: 'A heap of shit.'

'Do you mind? If that's the best you can come up with, you can push off.'

Rick dumped the box he was carrying on the floor of the kitchen. 'Hey!

If that's all the thanks I get for giving up my Saturday, then I will push off.'

'Well, this place has seen a lot over the past three hundred years. So just you give it a bit of respect. Anyway, where did you put the beers?'

'Where they were meant to be put three hundred years ago—in the larder.' Rick nodded towards the door in one corner of the kitchen. 'Where's your fridge?'

'Left it at the flat—the new owner bought all the white goods and the new one hasn't arrived yet.'

Rick made a sound something between a harrumph and a grunt and leaned on the draining board of the butler's sink, while Harry went into the larder and came out with two bottles of beer. 'Opener?' he enquired.

Rick fished in the pocket of his jeans. 'Here you are.' For a few moments the two were silent, all but draining their bottles of beer, then Rick said, 'So, where's this river, then?'

Harry nodded in the direction of the garden. 'Down there. Want a look?' He pushed open the back door and led the way through the thicket of brambles and bindweed, on through the emerging thistles and dog roses, which had now decorated their leafy stems with single flowers of palest pink.

'Where are we going?' asked Rick. 'Up the Amazon?'

'Not quite,' retorted Harry. 'Down the Itchen.'

Holding his hands and beer bottle over his head, Harry wove through the undergrowth in the direction of the bottom of the long garden. After much jostling and slashing at the tangle of stems with a well-placed boot, the two men arrived on the river bank. For the first time, Harry heard Rick in complimentary mode: 'This is lovely,' he said. 'Is it all yours?'

'Twenty yards of it.'

'Well, I can see why you wanted it now. I'd be down here every day.'

Harry laughed. 'It'd be wasted on you. The peace and quiet would drive you mad. Good for picnics, though, when I've cleared the garden. You can bring Rachel and Tilly down, if you want.'

'Oh, it's a *garden*. I hadn't realised. I thought it was a nature reserve.'

Harry looked about him. 'Yes,' he mused. 'It'd be a shame to spoil it. Perhaps I'll just make paths through it and let the wild flowers grow.'

Rick turned to look back up the garden. Between the dense canopy of hawthorn and goat willow, he could see the mellow brick of an adjacent house. 'Who lives there?'

'Don't know yet. Haven't called on the neighbours.'

'Smart house. What I can see of it.'

'It's the old mill,' said Harry. 'Bigger than this.'

'Oh, the big house?' asked Rick, with mock reverence.

'Just a mill—nothing grand. A fulling mill, where they used to make felt. The water powered the hammers, which beat the fibres into thick cloth.'

'I see. Bet they're stuck up,' remarked Rick. 'Having the bigger house.'

'They might not be. It doesn't always follow—'

Their musings were interrupted by a woman's voice.

'Hello?'

Neither of them could see where the voice was coming from, and they craned their necks in the direction of the sound.

'Over here.'

Between the dog roses and the hawthorn they could pick out the movement of some form of life. They made their way towards the sound until they had a clearer view. The voice belonged to a woman. She was dark haired, quite pretty, thirty-something, Harry judged. But it was Rick who was first to greet her. 'Hello! Are you the neighbour?'

'Yes. Are you?'

'No. That's him.' He muttered under his breath, 'Worse luck.'

Harry butted in, 'Just moved in—yesterday and this morning.'

'We saw. I thought you might like . . .' There was a pause, during which the woman spotted the beer bottles. 'Oh, I was going to offer you a coffee.'

'That's very kind,' replied Harry. 'Only . . .' He held up his beer bottle.

'Yes, I see. Too late.' The woman laughed: a light, rippling laugh. It came as a pleasant surprise. Harry hadn't heard that kind of laugh for a while.

'So you live in the big house?' asked Rick.

'Oh, not that big, actually.' She smiled. It was a lovely smile, Harry thought. So did Rick.

'I'm Harry. Harry Flint. This is—'

'Rick Palfrey. Just helping him move in.' They were about ten feet away from her now, but the brambles prevented any closer contact.

'Alexandra Overton. My friends call me Alex.'

Harry nodded.

She saw the slight confusion on his face. 'I mean, you can call me Alex.'

'Yes.'

Rick stepped in to ease the conversation along. 'Been here long?'

'About two years. Just about got the place sorted out. Your turn now.'

Harry smiled ruefully. 'Yes.'

'Look, this is silly. Why don't you come round? I'm making a spot of lunch; we might as well say "hello" properly.'

'Oh, I . . .' Harry hesitated.

'Brilliant,' said Rick. 'But have you got any soap? It's one thing Harry seems to have lost on the journey, and my hands are black.'

She grinned. 'I think I might find some.'

They made their way back through the wilderness to the back door of the cottage. Once they were in the kitchen, Rick said, 'You're in there!'

'What? Don't be ridiculous.'

'She's lovely. What a bit of luck!'

'It is a bit of luck, yes, having a nice neighbour but—'

'Well, you never know.'

'Rick, I am not on the lookout, in the market, or anything like that.'

'All the same, it's nice to know that it's close at hand when you need it.'

'Look, I've already told you to push off for being rude about the house. If you're going to start fixing me up with my next-door neighbour, you really can go and take a running jump.'

'All right, all right. I just think Ted and Pattie are all very well, but a guy needs to mix with his own age group as well.'

'I do mix with my own age group. I mix with you.'

'Yes, but in case you haven't noticed, I'm married, so there's no point in you raising your hopes there.'

Harry picked up a tea towel and threw it at him. 'Silly sod. Anyway, the next-door neighbour's husband wouldn't be very pleased.'

'Not sure there is one.'

'What do you mean?'

'No wedding ring.'

'Good God, you don't miss much, do you?'

'Old habits . . .'

'Don't let Rachel hear you.'

'Oh, she knows.'

They left the cottage and closed the gate behind them before walking across the patch of freshly cut grass that led to the Old Mill. As they approached the front door, it opened, and Alex Overton stood in front of them smiling and welcoming them. At her side was a small girl of about six or seven. She smiled at them. 'Hello,' she said, 'I'm Anne.'

The Streamside, Hampshire

16 April 1816

Anne Flint reached the top of the bank and looked about her. There was still no sign of anybody. Today was not to be the day after all then, despite the promise she had been made yesterday.

The sun was rising now and the blue sky growing paler. A breath of wind began to ruffle the narrow leaves of the osiers. She realised that she had better return home. To a short break Mrs Fitzgerald might turn a blind eye, but a longer absence would be frowned upon—unless she did not go back at all. She decided it was better not to think about it. Mrs Fitzgerald had warned her about what was expected of young housemaids: did Anne know that most housemaids stayed in their jobs much less than a year? That they then thought they would better themselves and go off to London. Did Anne really want to end up at a hiring fair? Standing in a line with all the other maids up from the country and hoping for a position in a busy town household? Had she not seen the engravings in Sir Thomas's library? Those by Mr Hogarth of *The Harlot's Progress*? Did she really want to end up like Moll Hackabout? Did she know what life was like in a bawdy house? Anne had wondered how Mrs Fitzgerald was so well informed, but the thought of it now made her shiver and she sat down and began to put on her stockings and boots.

It was at this point that a figure caught her eye. Someone was standing under an oak tree not far from her. Her heart leaped. Was it a vagabond, come to rob her? Or a highwayman? But there was no horse. Just the solitary figure in a long black cloak. As the figure approached, she could feel her heart thumping in her chest. She wanted to back away, but there was only the stream behind her and her boots were not yet laced up. She remained fixed to the spot, unable to move.

'I startled you. I'm sorry.'

The words surprised her. Not only for their apologetic tone—nobody apologised to a housemaid—but also because they were spoken by someone she had thought would not be coming to the streamside after all, despite the plans she had made. The figure removed the hood that covered its head.

'I was watching you. You seem very happy this morning.'

Anne bobbed out of courtesy. 'Yes, ma'am.'

'What do I keep telling you, Anne? You are not to call me ma'am! It makes me feel so old.'

The girl in the cloak was of her own age. Her hair was a similar colouring to Anne's, and her complexion equally pale.

'Sorry . . . er . . . miss.'

The girl laughed. 'It is becoming warm.' She undid the ribbon that fastened her cloak and let it fall, catching it over her arm as it did so and revealing a plain dress of soft pink.

Anne gasped a little.

The girl looked at her questioningly.

'I'm sorry . . . only . . . it is such a pretty dress,' apologised Anne.

Eleanor shrugged. 'It is nothing special. Just a day dress.'

'Better than mine.' Anne looked down at her own tired gingham.

'But yours is practical. Better for running away in.'

Anne smiled shyly and her cheeks began to colour. 'Do you mean . . .?' She hesitated. '*Today?*'

The girl looked Anne in the eye. 'Only if you are sure.'

Anne's heart beat faster. 'Oh, yes. I am sure. Is he . . . is Mr La—?' She took a deep breath and said slowly, 'Is Mr Lavallier . . .?'

'Yes. He is coming. He will bring a spare horse from Winchester. Then we shall all three return there to board the Portsmouth coach at noon.'

Anne could not speak.

'Would you like to walk a while?' The girl indicated the narrow pathway that ran beside the stream.

Anne nodded. As they began to walk she said, 'I have not ridden before.'

'I suspected so. That is why we have but two horses. You shall ride with Mr Lavallier and I shall take the other horse. We will keep you safe, Anne; you need not fear.' The girl looked about her. 'What a perfect day! Are you nervous, Anne? I have to confess that I am very nervous. It is just as well that I have you for company or I suspect I should take fright and go home.'

'I am not very good company,' Anne confessed.

'Compared with what I have left behind, I think that you are. My elder sisters think that I am far too young to have any life at all; it is all very well for *them* to be engaged in searching for a husband, but every day they tell me that I am still too young. My father is of the same mind. Do you think fifteen is too young to become engaged?'

Anne could not recall ever being asked for her opinion. She had thoughts and feelings, right enough; but they had never been sought by anyone.

'I think that *I* am not quite ready to be engaged to be married.' She thought of Sam, and her opinion was confirmed beyond contradiction.

'That is just how I felt.'

'But not any more?'

'No.' Eleanor looked about her. 'He cannot be far away now.'

IN THE WEEKS that had gone before, Anne had come to look forward to meeting Eleanor Stockbridge on the river bank. At first she had thought that her ladyship would be all lofty and above herself, but she discovered that for one brought up an earl's daughter, Eleanor had little of what Mrs Fitzgerald would have called 'side'.

'Where do you live?' Anne had asked at their first, chance meeting.

'Hatherley. Underneath the downs.'

'But that is several miles away.'

'I know. And I should not have walked so far in these shoes.' Eleanor had lifted the hem of her dress and revealed a pair of silk shoes with short heels. 'Not really made for walking in, but I left in something of a hurry today.'

'Were you in trouble?'

'Not exactly. My father was being tiresome and I needed some fresh air. I did not mean to walk so far but my thoughts were carried away and before I knew where I was . . . here I was.'

Eleanor had laid her cloak across the rough bark of a trunk of a fallen willow, and had motioned to Anne to sit beside her. 'You must tell me where you come from, and I shall tell you all about me, and then we really will get to know one another.'

Over the weeks they had met by the stream several times and talked of their lives and aspirations. Eleanor had listened attentively to the story of the orphanage, and the unpleasantness with the beadle, and Anne's desire to be a lady's maid; then she had related the events of her own brief life at Hatherley, until Anne felt that they had known one another for a long, long time.

As the weeks progressed, Eleanor had hatched a plan to elope with her intended—Mr Lavallier—a man she had met at the Basingstoke Assembly Rooms and whose father had plantations in far-off lands.

Anne recalled the moment when the intended scheme was first described to her. Eleanor had spoken softly, as though fearful of her secret being overheard, even though they were alone by the stream. 'He is a very handsome man,' Eleanor assured her. 'And a gallant one. We do so love one another, but he dare not ask my father for my hand lest he be refused. We plan to run away together.' She saw Anne's eyes widen and quickly asked, 'You do understand, don't you? There is no chance of my father agreeing to the match. My age and the distance from England of Mr Lavallier's interests would make my marrying him out of the question.'

'What will you do? Where will you go?'

'To Portsmouth first; then we shall set sail for the West Indies. Do you not see, Anne? This is my chance to escape and live a *real* life.' Eleanor saw Anne's eyes light up. 'And you. Would not you like to experience things?'

'Oh, yes, ma'am . . . I mean to be a lady's maid.'

Eleanor laughed with delight. 'You could be *my* lady's maid! But I would rather be your friend, Anne.'

A look of concern crossed Anne's face. 'Our housekeeper, Mrs Fitzgerald, says the likes of you and me can never be friends. She says the most we can hope for is friendliness, but not friendship.'

Eleanor sighed. 'Perhaps.'

'Don't you have a lady's maid?' Anne asked.

Eleanor looked downcast. 'Yes. Weaner. She is very old. Almost forty.' Then she brightened. 'But you *could* become my lady's maid, Anne. As we are the same age it would be much more congenial. I could call you "Flint" if that made you feel better. We would have such fun together, you and I.'

All that was several weeks ago, and yesterday Eleanor had come with news that on the morrow Mr Lavallier would bring horses to the streamside and that Anne must travel with her as her maid.

They had spoken for a long time about it until Anne, judging where the sun was in the sky, saw that she must have been gone from the Manor House for two hours. Two hours! Mrs Fitzgerald would be . . . she must return at once.

'But you will come back? Tomorrow?' Eleanor had asked.

'Tomorrow? I . . . I'm not sure . . .'

'Oh, Anne, you must. I cannot run away with Mr Lavallier on my own.'

And now here was Eleanor with her cloak over her arm, waiting for her lover to gallop to her rescue and spirit her away to foreign lands. But they would not be travelling alone, as she would be going with them. Anne pulled her shawl closer about her and waited . . .

The Old Mill, Itchen Parva

29 May 2010

They sat at either side of a scrubbed oak kitchen table eating cheeses, salami and warm granary bread. The coffee did not materialise, but a bottle of wine did—the better, said Alex, to celebrate a new arrival.

'Where are you from?' asked Anne. She was a bright child with intelligent eyes, and she looked closely at them as she leaned on the table with both elbows.

'Hey! Don't be nosy,' admonished Alex. 'And take your elbows off the table when you're eating.'

'But I'm not eating. I'm talking.'

Alex raised her eyes heavenwards and shot an apologetic look at Harry.

He smiled across at the girl. She was engaging in an unaffected way. He answered her as best he could. 'I've come from St Cross—the other side of Winchester. I teach at a school in town. But not for much longer.'

'Have you been sacked?' asked Anne.

Rick and Harry both laughed.

'No. I've decided to leave,' Harry replied. He noticed how the sunlight streaming in through the window glinted on Anne's auburn hair. 'What about you? Where do you come from?'

'Here. The Old Mill in Itchen Parva.'

'And before that?'

'Southampton.'

'And which do you prefer?'

Anne looked quite serious as she stood up from the bench on which she had been sitting. 'Here. I like the country. Much nicer than the town. I like the river, too.' And then she asked, 'Please may I leave the table?'

'Of course,' said Alex. 'Off you pop—but stay away from—'

'I know, I know . . .' The girl picked up a large stuffed dog and tucked it under her arm before going out of the door and into the garden.

The two men looked after her. 'Quite grown-up,' murmured Harry.

'More grown up than the thirteen year olds I have to teach,' agreed Rick.

'A teacher too, then?' asked Alex.

'Yup. Both of us. For our sins . . .'

'Subject?'

'Maths,' said Rick.

Alex glanced at Harry.

'History.'

'Oh, much more my bag,' confessed Alex.

Rick suppressed a smile, and Harry kicked him gently under the table. 'How about you?'

'I help out at the local day centre. No time for anything permanent: single parent and all that.'

'Oh?'

'Widowed. Two years ago. That's when Anne and I moved. Not a happy time, but I tried to protect her from the worst.' She paused. 'Anyway, enough of that. Makes me sound either desperate or despairing, and I'm neither.'

Reacting to the uncomfortable turn in the conversation, Harry made to change the subject. 'Know much about this place?' he asked.

'The mill? I know that it's very old, and that it was a fulling mill. And that it is a full-time job looking after it, but that there is nowhere else that I'd—or should I say, we'd—rather be.'

'Isn't it a bit big for you?' asked Rick.

'You'd think so. But we don't rattle. And I do have rather a lot of books.'

Harry sat up.

'Not you as well,' said Rick with a groan.

'I'm sorry?'

'This guy here is Hampshire's answer to the British Library.'

Alex's eyes lit up. 'Really?'

Harry replied defensively, 'He exaggerates. I just have rather a lot.'

'What sort of books?' said Alex.

'Oh, all sorts.' Harry felt embarrassed. He wasn't ashamed of his books, but he would rather have kept the conversation anodyne, bland. He pushed back his chair. 'We'd better get out of your hair.'

He got up from the table, Rick following reluctantly. 'Thanks for lunch,' said Harry, trying as best he could to sound bright. 'I'll get you round for a drink. Both of you. As soon as I can find a clear surface to put a glass down and somewhere to sit.'

'That would be lovely. You know where we are if you need anything.'

Harry nodded. 'Thanks.' He shook hands with her rather formally and looked out of the window to where the child was lecturing the stuffed dog. 'Good to meet you. And Anne.'

Winchester Cathedral Library

3 June 2010

Harry had been to the cathedral in Winchester often before, but until now he had not discovered the library. Its entrance was far from impressive, and those not looking for it would easily pass by the doorway, little knowing what treasures lay above their heads. Once through the door, a simple sign indicated that the staircase led to the 'Library and Triforium'.

Harry climbed the stairs and turned right at the top, into a small, narrow room that had an oak-framed glass case running down its centre. The four volumes of the Winchester Bible lay open in the glass case in front of him. Avidly Harry read its history. Commissioned in 1160 by Bishop Henry of Blois, and taking some fifteen years to complete, the handwritten Bible had been copied out by a single scribe and had utilised the craftsmanship of six different illuminators for its exquisitely painted initial letters. When he had drunk in enough of its riches, he turned and entered the room opposite.

Harry had wondered if the cathedral library might be the sort of place where he could do more research into his ancestry, or which might offer him an insight into the place where he now lived. That sort of information, he was told by the curator, could be found upstairs in the Triforium Library. Did he have an appointment? He regretted that he did not, but the kindly woman led him upstairs anyway, opening the glass cases of the less impressive upper library and allowing him to take down the volumes she thought might be of use.

Harry knew his father and grandfather had moved away from the area but, before them, three generations of Flints had all resided and worked in this part of Hampshire. His grandfather, Henry Richard, had been a printer in London's East End and, along with his wife, Mary, had been killed in the Blitz; in fact, the Flint family had not fared well in either of the two world wars. Prior to the wars, all the members of Harry's family that he had been able to trace had worked on the land. But the trail dried up when it reached his great-great-grandfather Henry's parents: Merrily, born in 1816, and Elizabeth Henry, whose surname had clearly been handed down to first-born sons from generation to generation.

Merrily had been described in the birth certificates of his children as a 'shepherd' and his wife as a 'domestic servant'. But who were Merrily's parents? Finding Merrily's own birth certificate was the key, and it would mean scrutinising parish registers and perhaps the National Archive.

This was the task ahead of Harry. But right now it was Mill Cottage that interested him. Who had lived there and what had they done? For over an hour, he pored over two volumes, their pages allowing him to build up a picture of the goings-on around his humble Mill Cottage at Itchen Parva.

There had been another village back then; well, more of a hamlet really: a scattering of cottages. Withercombe, it had been called. There had been a manor house and a fulling mill. Many of the buildings had disappeared over the years, fallen victim to fire or flood, pestilence and general neglect, while the manor house had succumbed to fire in the 1950s. The buildings that remained had been absorbed into a newer village.

Gradually, Harry linked together the disparate pieces of this geographical jigsaw, discovering as he did so that the Old Mill next door to him, and his own cottage, had once been leased by a family called Palfrey. He smiled to himself. He had done all this work to trace his own ancestry and had ended up finding out more about Rick's family. He would take great delight in telling Rick that the house in which Alex Overton now lived had once been occupied by Rick's ancestors. With that pleasing little nugget jotted down in his notebook, he left the cathedral library and headed for home.

The Fulling Mill, Hampshire

20 April 1816

'What does that mean, then?' asked Jacob Palfrey of Sam the yard boy. '"Misadventure"?'

'Means what it says. She 'ad an adventure and it went wrong.'

'What sort of adventure?'

'I know not. They took her back to Hatherley after the inquest. They will bury her there, I expect, with the rest of her family. The ones that's dead.'

Three days after finding the body, Jacob was still feeling out of sorts. 'S'all wrong,' he kept murmuring to himself. 'It ain't right.'

The events of that bright spring morning had brought the two friends even closer together, and they took what little comfort they could from chewing over the matter almost every day. Sam, like Anne before him, had to choose his moments to escape with great care, lest Timothy Jencks took exception to his absenting himself for too long and exacted retribution.

'No sign of your Anne, then?' asked Jacob.

'She weren't my Anne.'

'Not for want of tryin' though, eh?' A rare smile broke out on Jacob's lips.

'I did find one thing,' confessed Sam, reaching into the pocket of his jerkin. He pulled out a small book. 'She were readin' this.'

'Where d'you find it?'

'In the sweet flags by the stream. She must have dropped it. Or it fell out of her pocket.' He turned the book over in his hands.

Jacob held out his hand and Sam passed him the small volume. Slowly he read the title out loud, '*The Highwayman's Bride.*'

'She liked to dream about things,' said Sam defensively. 'Doesn't mean she was ever going to run away.'

'You don't think that's what she's done then? Just upped and left?'

Sam shook his head.

'Why not? You say she didn't like her job—what's to stop her running off?'

Sam paused for a moment and looked at his feet. 'She would've told me.'

Jacob smiled again, half mocking, half indulgent. 'So there was something between you?'

'No. There was not. But I am sure she wouldn't have gone without saying something. Or leaving me a note. She could write as well as read.'

'So what else could've happened?'

'She could have been taken.' Sam put his hand out and Jacob returned the book. He put it back in his pocket.

'Do you think she knew someone?'

'Not sure. She did say she had a friend.'

'A man friend?'

'She wouldn't say. Liked having her secrets. But she never said she would leave. She wanted to be a lady's maid.'

'She would have had to have left to do that, wouldn't she?'

'Maybe.'

'You know something else?' asked Jacob.

Sam hesitated. 'By the stream . . . there were hoofprints in the mud . . .'

The clock over the stable struck the hour.

'I'd best be away.' Sam picked up his pitchfork.

'Think you she is dead?' asked Jacob bluntly.

Sam shook his head vigorously. 'I knows she ain't dead. I just knows.'

BACK AT THE FULLING MILL, Jacob Palfrey asked his father what he thought.

'Maids like that is forever running away. Most goes to London. They has hirin' fairs there. They likes girls up from the country.'

'You do not think she may be dead, then?'

William Palfrey looked up from his work. 'No body yet,' he said.

In his room that evening, Jacob sat down at the oak table tucked underneath the eaves and, by the light of a single candle, filled in his diary. He and Sam had been the only ones of his contemporaries to leap at the chance to learn to read and write when the governess from the Manor House had offered to teach anyone, who cared to master it, the art of penmanship.

> *Apr. 20 Still no sign of Anne. Sam do say she might have been taken by who he know not. He seen hoofprints in mud by the stream and found her book in the sweet flags. Father think she has run away and we will see her no more. Father to Winchester with three bolts of cloth. Fine bright day.*

His daily life thus recorded, he blew out the candle, got into bed and pulled a rough woollen blanket over his head, the better to keep out the wind that was now whistling between the roof tiles.

Mill Cottage, Itchen Parva

4 June 2010

Harry could have left it longer than a week, but Alex had been so hospitable on the day of his moving in that it had seemed churlish to postpone returning the compliment. He had knocked on her door after returning from school and asked if she would like to come round for lunch with Anne the next day, Saturday. Lunch, Alex had said, however, was not possible: she had promised Anne a trip to Winchester.

'Perhaps another time,' Harry said, happy to let the appointment slide, his initial obligation having been fulfilled.

'I could do supper tonight,' she had replied. 'Anne's going to a sleep-over and I'll be on my own.' Then she had realised the potential imposition and did not want him to feel that he was being cornered. 'Or we could both do lunch next Saturday . . . oh, no, sorry: school spring fair. Oh, dear—'

'Supper tonight, then.' Harry had said. 'That's fine. About seven thirty?'

'Perfect! I'll have had a chance to get back and smarten myself up.'

And now it was a quarter past seven. Harry went through a mental check-list: white wine in the fridge (he'd plumped for a Chablis—champagne might appear to be too celebratory and load the evening with excessive significance) and a bottle of Merlot open by the log fire.

He looked about him and smiled to himself at the modest transformation of the previously bare sitting room. He had found a home for a few dozen of his books on pine shelves he had constructed in the narrow alcoves at either side of the fireplace, while three small table lamps dotted about the place gave it a warm glow without showing up too many of the flaws in his barley-white emulsion. He had found secondhand curtains in Winchester and arranged the furniture that had come with him from St Cross in a way that meant he did not have to fall over it when he crossed the room. A couple of watercolours decorated the two unadorned walls, and a scrubbed pine table under the end window had turned that into a dining area. The old sofa, placed to one side of the fire, could do with a couple of bright throws to hide its threadbare arms, but they could come later.

The fire crackled in the grate and broke in on his thoughts. It was followed by the bouncing ring of the little bell that hung by the front door. Harry ran his hand through his hair in the hope that it would be enough to make him presentable; the clean navy-blue shirt and chinos would have to do the rest. He opened the door.

Alex's first words were unexpected: 'How sweet!' Thinking that he might assume she was talking about his appearance, she added, 'The bell, I mean.'

'Oh . . . it was here when I came. I think it's probably pretty old.'

Alex held up a bottle of champagne. 'I thought we ought to celebrate.' She saw the look of slight embarrassment on Harry's face. 'A new house. You can't really toast that with plonk, can you?'

'Er . . . no. Lovely. That's very kind.'

'It is chilled. I've had it in the fridge all day. Goodness, this is nice.'

Alex had entered his house, and his life, it seemed, like a whirlwind, as she remarked on this picture and that pair of curtains, the fact that the walls had been painted and the floor covered with an old Persian carpet. 'It's as if you've always been here. How very clever. Most men can't do that. They move their furniture in and it looks like a secondhand shop.'

Harry found himself grinning.

'What is it? asked Alex. 'Oh, I'm sorry. Listen to me, going on like a steam train. I've hardly drawn breath.'

'No. Not at all. I'm glad you like it.' Harry had found two wineglasses. 'Sorry about these; the champagne flutes were in a box that one of the removal men dropped on the kitchen floor.' He handed Alex a glass of fizz.

'Here's to you and your new house . . . cottage . . . palace!'

'I'll settle for cottage. And here's to you—my first guest, if you don't count Rick. And not many people do.'

'Is he a pain?' asked Alex, with a look of genuine concern.

'No, not really. He's a good mate. Thick and thin and all that. And mainly thin. Anyway, no time to talk about him. Thank you for coming.'

'Thank you for asking me.'

They sipped their wine in an awkward momentary silence; then both spoke at once, and laughed at their mutual nervousness.

Harry motioned her to sit down on the sofa, while he sat in the armchair opposite her. For the first time, he had a chance to look properly at Alex. Her hair was thick, shiny and dark, lightly brushing her shoulders. Her deep brown eyes shone in the firelight and the honey-coloured sweater she wore over cream trousers showed off her figure not in an obvious way, but flatteringly nevertheless. He did not remember her being quite so good-looking, but then reminded himself that he had seen her only in her garden and then over her kitchen table on a Saturday morning.

He made polite small talk for a few minutes and then excused himself while he got up to bring the smoked salmon starter to the pine table.

Gradually, from being an effort, the conversation became more relaxed. They talked easily together about Harry's plans for doing up the cottage, the state of the garden, where he would put his books and what he would do when he had finished teaching—about which, he had precious little to offer.

He had bought a chicken pie for the main course. 'Sorry,' he said. 'It's not homemade.'

'Who cares?' Alex said. 'It's very nice to be sharing it.'

Harry felt an unfamiliar kind of warmth coming over him. As they ate it, he said, 'We've done nothing but talk about me. What about you?'

Alex thought for a moment. 'We lived in Southampton. I was married to a barrister. We'd been married for eight years and then . . .' She paused momentarily. 'He died. It was all very messy and traumatic. Anne was five at the time so it was upsetting for her, but she didn't understand fully and I knew she'd get over it.'

Harry looked at her quizzically but said nothing.

'I was a barrister, too,' she continued. 'We were in the same chambers. That's why I have so many books. Not as interesting as yours. Torts and litigation, not Titian and Lautrec.'

'Very good,' said Harry appreciatively. 'And after he died, you came here?'

'Yes. I needed a fresh start. I felt Anne and I both did.'

'And what do you . . . how do you . . .?'

'Fill my days? Well, as I mentioned, I do a bit of work down at the local day centre, but really I concentrate on Anne.' She paused again, then said, 'I'm very aware of being a single mother and all the things people think.'

'What do you mean?'

'Oh, you know. That I must be on the lookout for someone. That no one's husband is safe—that sort of thing.'

'Seriously?'

'Oh, you wouldn't believe. I spoke to a very nice man outside the school gates a few months ago. Just a pleasant chat about children and things while we waited for ours to come out. The next thing I know, he doesn't come any more; his wife does and gives me a lecture on staying out of her life.'

Harry's expression made Alex laugh. 'It's true, unbelievable as it sounds!'

'So you're not—'

'On the market? One day, maybe. I've had a gentle dabble on the Internet but . . . oh, now I am beginning to sound desperate. And this is not the conversation I wanted to have. Not at all appropriate. I'm so sorry.'

'No. I'm sorry. I shouldn't have asked. It's just that—'

'It came up. I know. Look, I'd better be going.' Alex got up from the table.

Harry got up, too, and rather surprised himself by saying, 'I'd rather you didn't. I really don't mind what anybody thinks. And I certainly don't think . . . well . . . anything. Except that there's a pudding in the fridge and it would be a shame not to eat it.'

He was surprised to see a tear roll down Alex's cheek. She sat down softly on the sofa and said, 'Oh, dear. I'm so sorry. Too intense. Too sensitive. Too everything . . .' and she smiled at him as another tear sprang unbidden from her eye.

Harry sat down alongside her and put his arm round her shoulders.

'I'm afraid I'm not very good at this,' she said. 'Not very good at anything much.'

'You're a bloody good next-door neighbour,' he said. 'Shall we settle for that for a while?'

The Streamside, Hampshire

16 April 1816

The sound of horses' hoofs filled Anne's heart with a mixture of hope and fear. She pulled her shawl tight about her and turned, with Eleanor, to see a horseman galloping down the meadow beneath the oaks. Within seconds she felt the hot breath of the black stallion on her naked arms, thrilled to the whinnying of the grey mare reined in at its side, and saw the sparkle in her friend's eye as he leaned down from his horse and cupped the back of Eleanor's head in his hand.

'You came!' she said.

'Of course I came. Did you doubt me?'

'Not for a minute. And yet . . .'

The horseman slipped from the saddle, took Eleanor in his arms and kissed her on the lips. Anne could but look on embarrassedly, wishing that she were somewhere else while the two completed their intimate greeting.

Eleanor eased away from the youth in the dark green coat. 'Roderick, this is Anne. I told you of her.'

Roderick Lavallier bowed smartly from the neck and said with a glint in his eye, 'Of course. Are you ready for adventure, Anne?'

Anne nodded. She was incapable, at the sight of the kind of man she had dreamed of, had read about in her books, of anything more than a weak smile.

'Then we must go.'

Anne looked at him as he turned again to Eleanor. He was tall and angular, with high cheekbones and bright blue eyes, his thick brown hair tied back with a glistening black ribbon. *Sir Thomas's sons*, thought Anne, *are handsome enough, but Roderick Lavallier makes them seem plain by comparison.* And, oh, the way he dressed! His dark green coat was caped at the shoulders and his riding boots and breeches were spattered with mud from the ford he had crossed at the bottom of the field. In the white silk stock at his neck, a single pearl glistened.

'You must change,' he instructed the two women.

They looked at him questioningly.

'If Anne is to ride with me, as you suggested, Eleanor, then she must wear your clothes. It would not do for a gentleman to be seen riding with a maid. In such a case we might well be stopped.'

The two women looked at each other and then Eleanor laughed. 'Over here, Anne. We must exchange our dresses behind the trees. No one shall see us. We need change nothing more, and Richard has brought another cloak for you, have you not?'

The man nodded. 'But hurry. We must catch the coach to Portsmouth within the hour.'

The next few minutes passed in a haze for Anne. Eleanor helped her remove her dress as Roderick Lavallier obligingly attended to the horses, and looked in the other direction to avoid any embarrassment.

The two women were of almost exactly the same build and, for the first time in her short life, Anne found herself wearing a rich pink day dress and gloves, topped with a riding cape. Such was the excitement that she could hardly bring herself to speak.

The two, however, were unable to exchange shoes—Eleanor's feet were a little bigger than Anne's. Laughing, Eleanor slipped her delicate shoes back on, giggling at the sight of Anne's sturdy boots: they peeped out incongruously from beneath the pink dress and the all-enveloping cloak.

Anne then buttoned Eleanor into her old gingham dress and tied on the apron. Eleanor finished the look by wrapping a short cape around herself and then said brightly, 'Look, Anne, we have become each other. Is this not a little strange?'

It was indeed strange, and suddenly Anne began to wonder what she had become a part of. Now that her dream had become reality, the seriousness of her situation began to dawn on her. But there was no time to change her mind: Roderick Lavallier lifted Eleanor onto the side-saddled grey and handed her the reins. Then he turned to Anne. 'Hold my shoulders,' he instructed. Anne did as she was bid, and felt Lavallier's arms round her small waist. She could not recall when her heart had beaten faster.

The gleaming stallion threw its head to one side. 'Steady, Jupiter!' murmured Lavallier, as Anne was lifted up into the saddle. She instinctively held on to the stallion's neck, and Jupiter pawed at the ground and gave an impatient snort. For the first time Anne felt real fear, but then Lavallier was up astride the horse behind her. 'Hold very tightly to the pommel,' he instructed, and then turned to Eleanor. 'Are you ready?'

'I am ready, my love,' she cried, excitement in her every word.

He flashed her a wicked grin, dug his heels into the black stallion, and the three of them galloped off up the river valley towards Winchester.

St Jude's School, Winchester

7 June 2010

'Walk, don't run, Palmer!' The boy disappeared into the distance of the school corridor with no perceptible reduction in horsepower, and Harry turned into the staff room and flopped down into a chair.

'Had enough?' enquired a bright voice. It was Rick. 'You should try maths with twenty-two seventeen year olds whose testosterone levels are off the Richter scale.'

'At least you can give them problems to solve that will occupy them for a few minutes. It's more difficult when Palmer and his cohorts are trying to persuade you to let them act out massacres and battles.'

'Strong coffee then?'

'Very. Thanks.'

Harry wondered how long it would be before Rick probed him about the 'weekend assignation', as he called it. His question was answered almost immediately: 'Well? How did it go?'

Harry glanced at his watch. 'Twenty-three seconds. A personal best. It went very well, thank you.'

'That it? No blow-by-blow account?'

'No blows exchanged. She was just . . . well . . . very nice.'

'Oh, I was expecting a bit more than "very nice", to be honest.'

Harry glanced around. The staff room was large, with small groups of teachers scattered in different areas. The arrangement made it easier to have relatively intimate conversations without being overheard, provided you took the precaution of keeping your distance from those of a curious disposition. 'I think she was a bit scared, if you must know. A bit nervous.'

Rick looked surprised. 'What, with you? Mr Unthreatening?'

Harry ignored the jibe. 'I think she's been hurt a lot. Since . . . you know, since she lost her husband.'

'Did she say how he died?'

'No. And I didn't ask. It didn't seem right.'

'And did you tell her all about your ex?'

'No. We didn't get round to that.'

'Ah, one of those who likes to talk about herself—'

Harry jumped in. 'No. I don't think so. Just a bit lost. A bit like me.'

Rick put two brimming coffee cups on the table. 'God, you two must be fun when you get together.'

'Well, it was fun. It just got a bit sort of . . . introspective. Anyway, the object of our meeting was just to be sociable.'

'You make it sound like a Women's Institute AGM.'

Harry took a sip of his coffee. 'When I've anything to report, you'll be the first to know.' And then he remembered something. 'Oh, and I've some news for you on a different topic.'

'What's that?'

'Your ancestry.'

Rick sighed. 'You do lead a heady life, don't you?'

'No, listen. This'll surprise you. The old fulling mill next door to me— well, the family who were the tenants, back in the early 1880s, their name was Palfrey.'

'Bugger me!'

'So if you are as native to these parts as you claim to be, then it looks as though Alex Overton is living in your old family home. Unless, of course, it's a different branch of Palfreys.'

'How did you find this out? Did she tell you?'

'No. I did some research at the cathedral library. There's not much there in the way of local history but, as luck would have it, there were a couple of books that made reference to Itchen Parva, and the mill and the Palfreys.'

Rick brightened. 'Could I claim it back, do you think? Or at least claim rights over the people who now live in it?'

'Doubtful.'

'Well, well, well . . .' Rick fell silent for a few moments and the two of them continued to sip their coffee. Then he said, 'Perhaps I should get that old trunk down from the attic.'

'Which trunk?'

'Oh, there's an old trunk my granddad gave me. Never really bothered to look at it. Probably just old notebooks and stuff.'

'What? You've had it all this time and you never thought to tell me?'

'It doesn't interest me, Harry. I live in the present and it's the future that concerns me. There's no point in living in the past. Look where it's got you.'

Harry took all manner of light-hearted insults from Rick, but this one stung more than most. 'Not very kind.'

'No. I'm sorry; I didn't mean to—well . . . I just think you should start putting all this historic stuff behind you. That's where it belongs. Make a new life based on where and what you are now. Stop living in the past.'

'I can't. It haunts me. There's something to it, something that is of the present.' Harry paused and sighed. 'Oh, I don't know. It's all so confusing. Maybe you're right. It hasn't actually got me anywhere, has it?'

The bell signalling the end of the break resounded through the school, and the members of staff stood up as one to take their crockery to the communal sink. Rick and Harry drained their mugs.

'Have you thought of'—Rick looked round to make sure no one could hear—'Internet dating?'

Harry nodded. 'Tried it a couple of times.' He shuddered. 'Strange who turns up when you say your interests are history, genealogy and the lives of the saints.'

Rick shook his head. 'I'm not surprised.'

The Streamside, Hampshire

16 April 1816

Having gone for what seemed like minutes without drawing a single breath, Anne now found herself panting as the horses galloped side by side along the bank above the stream. The pounding of the beast beneath her, the sound of its roaring breath and the shine on its rippling ebony coat, coupled with the closeness of a man—as close as she had ever been held in her entire life—mingled exhilaration with raw fear. She occasionally glanced to her left where Eleanor, her cape flying, was riding the grey mare; the eyes of horse and rider were as bright as each other.

'How long do you think?' asked Eleanor, shouting to Roderick above the sound of the pounding hoofs. The mare, not as strong as the stallion, was struggling to keep up.

'Around four miles—it will not take us long and then we shall be aboard the coach and you can rest.'

As the track beside the stream widened, the mare came alongside the stallion. Aware of her close proximity and of her tantalising scent, Jupiter suddenly turned his head to the left and bit the mare on the neck. With an ear-splitting whinny, the mare careered sideways then stopped in her tracks and reared up. Eleanor, whose horsemanship was by no means slight,

fought to control her mount and, at first, it looked as though she would succeed. But, when Lavallier reined in the stallion and turned sharply to go to
Eleanor's rescue, as the black horse approached the grey reared up again,
and this time Eleanor was thrown. She let out a sharp cry as she tumbled
from the saddle, her leg becoming entangled with the stirrup leather. Again,
the stallion lunged towards the mare, but this time the mare took avoiding
action. Her head thrown to one side, she galloped down the bank towards
the stream, trailing Eleanor behind her like a rag doll, stopping only when
she had reached the water.

'Eleanor!' Lavallier's voice cut through the air as he spurred his horse
towards her. Anne could do nothing but cling on for dear life. Reaching the
stream, Lavallier leaped from the saddle and dashed to Eleanor's side as she
lay, half in and half out of the water, her head resting on a boulder.

Lavallier looked up in desperation. 'Help me!' he cried to Anne.

With difficulty, Anne slid down from the stallion and ran to Lavallier's
side. She said nothing, but gazed in horror at the lifeless form of Eleanor on
the bank of the stream. It had all happened so quickly. Perhaps if she shook
her head she could go back some minutes and stop it from happening. But
no, she was there, looking down on her friend whose eyes were wide open
and focused on nothing. The smile had vanished from her lips and her
cheeks were drained of all colour.

Lavallier looked at Anne, his face a mixture of horror and disbelief.
'How could it have happened?' he asked.

Anne could do nothing more than stare. And then she began to shake,
and tears trickle down her cheeks.

'Anne, you saw, did you not? It was nobody's fault. The horses . . .' His
voice faded and he turned again to look at Eleanor. Her face was expressionless, her cape and her shoes had been lost in the chase, and she lay in
her servant's clothes among the sweet flags and the rushes.

'Oh, my love,' murmured Lavallier softly. 'Oh, my love, my love! We
were to have been married . . .'

By now Anne's body was racked with sobs. 'What shall we . . . do . . .?'
she asked, through staccato breaths.

Tenderly, Lavallier stroked Eleanor's cheek and then, with the finger and
thumb of his right hand, he gently closed her eyes. 'Goodbye, my love.'

He stood up, looking down at the body and, in that moment, a change
came over him. Anne saw it quite clearly: the face that had borne so much

love and tenderness now hardened; the jaw was set, the eyes cold as ice. Roderick Lavallier drew his cloak around him. 'We must go. There is nothing we can do here.'

'But where?' asked Anne.

'To the coach, and then to Portsmouth. You must come with me.'

'But I cannot,' Anne exclaimed through the sobs.

'You must. You cannot stay here. What would people think—when they found you?'

'I . . . I do not know, but—'

'They would accuse you of murder. You are wearing Eleanor's clothes. They would think you had robbed and killed her, and then taken her clothes and dressed her in your own to confuse.'

The rising fear Anne felt was evident in her voice. 'But I did not—'

'It will make no difference. You are a servant; Eleanor was a lady. The law takes little heed of servants.'

A sea of confusion surged through Anne's brain. What could she do? What Roderick Lavallier said was true, even though the reality was completely different.

'We should go to Sir Thomas. He will know what to do,' she offered.

'And how will we explain our circumstances? Shall we admit that we were to run away to Portsmouth and then sail to the West Indies? Shall we explain why you are wearing Eleanor's clothes and she yours? What do you think will be the squire's response to such a revelation? And how will Eleanor's father, Lord Stockbridge, treat me? And you? For abducting his daughter you will be hanged, Anne, and I shall be transported. Our only recourse is to continue with our journey, and for you and I to travel as husband and wife.'

The conversation was interrupted by an ear-piercing shriek. The stallion had made one more attempt to attack the mare, which had aimed a well-placed kick at its hocks. With a loud whinny, the grey took off across the meadow at a gallop.

'We have no choice now, Anne. We have only one horse. We must travel together or you must return and face the consequences.'

'But what about Eleanor?'

'We can do nothing for Eleanor now, God rest her soul. She has gone. She is not Eleanor any more. She is a body, and bodies are found every day in town and country.'

His coldness horrified her. To think that just a few moments ago she had been swept off her feet by this handsome buccaneer of a man—the kind she had so often read about in her books. *Her book! Where was her book?* But there was no time to think of it now. The man she had thought to be a dashing hero now frightened and revolted her in equal measure.

Lavallier lifted her into the saddle and she felt his arms round her waist once more. Only this time a different kind of thrill ran through her body: a thrill born of terror.

The Old Mill, Itchen Parva

7 June 2010

'I just wanted to apologise,' said Alex.

'There really is no reason why you should,' replied Harry.

'Oh, I think there is. I was far too intense and you probably wanted to run a mile.'

'It's very considerate of you to say so,' said Harry, 'but you are really quite wrong. I'm very flattered that you bothered to tell me anything.'

'And we never really talked about you.'

'Just as well, really. Rick thinks I've nothing interesting to say.'

'This Rick seems to be quite a large part of your life. You're not joined at the hip, are you?'

'Sometimes I wonder,' muttered Harry, then he smiled. 'No, not really. He can be a real pain in the arse but he's got me through quite a lot.'

After school, Harry had popped in to see Alex. They were now sitting in her kitchen early in the evening, on the same day that Rick had lectured Harry.

'Anyway, I was able to tell him something for a change. I went to the cathedral a couple of days ago. Do you ever go?'

'Once a month or so. I like going to evensong. I find it . . . helpful.'

'I stand at the back myself sometimes,' said Harry. 'Just to listen. To let it wash over me. It's, well, comforting.'

Alex did not add any more, fearing that any conversation about religion would be a turn-off.

Harry continued, 'I went into the library and found a couple of books that talk about this place—the Old Mill.'

'Really?' Alex's eyes brightened. 'What did they say?'

'That the people who lived here at the beginning of the nineteenth century were called Palfrey—Rick's family name.'

'Good heavens! And is he local?'

'Yes, and never lets me forget it.'

'So this place was probably lived in by his ancestors?'

'Could have been. He's promised to look in an old trunk his grandfather gave him. I ask you: he knows I'm interested in history—especially family history—and he's never mentioned it. Typical.'

'Let me know what you find. I'd love to know more about this place.'

'You don't find it boring, then? History, genealogy—that sort of thing?'

'Not at all. I love knowing what's gone before, who's gone before.'

Then, before Harry had time to respond, a small face appeared round the doorway. 'Can I come and say good night?'

Anne Overton was wearing pyjamas with a pattern of small horses prancing all over them, and clutching the stuffed dog he had seen before, which was possessed of even less fur than he had remembered.

'Of course.'

'Good night, Harry,' she said.

'Good night, Anne.'

She walked over to him and looked up into his eyes. 'Can I give you a good-night kiss?'

Harry was momentarily thrown off guard and then recovered himself enough to say, 'Yes, of course you can.'

He bent down and felt a small pair of lips kiss him softly on the cheek. For a moment he felt quite overcome with emotion. *How silly*, he thought. *A small girl kisses you on the cheek and you become all sentimental.*

Her mission accomplished, Anne said, 'Good night then,' and turned and disappeared through the doorway.

Harry looked at the empty doorway, unsure of what to say, then he glanced at Alex and saw that her eyes were glistening.

'She doesn't often do that. You're very honoured.'

He wanted to ask whether she meant, 'She doesn't often do that to the men I have around,' or just, 'She doesn't often do that to anybody,' but he resisted the temptation, smiling gratefully when Alex poured him a glass of red wine.

'So,' she said. 'Are you going to tell me how you come to be living on your own?'

IT WAS MIDNIGHT by the time he left, and there was an awkward moment at the door when the form of parting had to be decided upon. The discomfort was minimised by Alex, who bent forward and kissed him on the cheek. 'Thank you for coming. For your company.'

'Thank you for listening,' he said. 'I'm sorry if it all sounded pathetic.'

'Not pathetic,' she replied. 'Just sad.'

Harry shrugged. 'That's me. Sad old man . . .'

'That's something you need to work on,' said Alex with a glint in her eye.

'What?'

'The self-esteem. There's no reason for it to be quite so low. You're quite good-looking and, if you don't mind me saying so, quite bright as well.'

'Well, thank you. It's a while since I had such a compliment.'

'I can keep them coming if you like.'

He smiled. 'That's probably enough for me to be going on with. I don't want to get above myself.'

'Somehow I don't think you could.' She hesitated. 'Shall we do it again?'

'That'd be nice. Only . . .' Harry hesitated. 'I'm very conscious of . . .' He gestured upstairs to where Anne would be sleeping.

'Well, she's going away next weekend. To stay with a schoolfriend in Bournemouth—they've got a holiday apartment overlooking the sea.'

'Oh. And are you busy? I mean, say, on Saturday night?'

'Not at all.'

'We could go out if you like. Dinner? Theatre? Movie?'

'Dinner sounds good. We can talk more then. I rather like talking to you, Mr Flint. And listening, of course.'

For the first time in as many months as he could remember, Harry Flint went to sleep with a smile on his lips.

The Portsmouth Road

16 April 1816

Anne sat silently on the seat opposite Roderick Lavallier in the coach as it bounced along for the twenty-nine and a quarter miles to Portsmouth.

For most of the journey, she had tried to avoid his eyes, and gazed out of the window. Lavallier had twice warned her not to speak once they had dismounted at Winchester, lest it become obvious by her long Hampshire vowels to all about her that this was no 'lady', but a girl of lowly birth.

The only sounds that filled Anne's ears were the jangling of the harness, the clatter of the wheels and the rhythmic sound of horses' hoofs over cobbles and tracks, through mud and mire.

And now the hardness of the ground beneath the hoofs told her they were not far from their destination. Through the window of the coach, Anne could see the towering form of Portsdown Hill as they went past Cosham—at least, she imagined that was what it must be, having heard its lofty eminence spoken of by Mrs Fitzgerald. And then came the realisation that she would not see them again: Mrs Fitzgerald and Sir Thomas, Sam and Mr Jencks, Mr Moses and his vegetables; they were now all a part of her past. She felt tears forming in her eyes and rubbed them away impatiently. This was no time to be feeble.

She was sure now that Lavallier was a dishonourable man, and she was conscious that she knew nothing of him or his background, save that Eleanor had said his father had plantations. But how could she believe even that, having observed the way he had behaved when he had discovered that Eleanor was dead? Dead! That word—so filled with anguish and finality—she never could have imagined it being applied to Eleanor, who had been so brimful of life in the all-too-brief spell that they had known one another.

The horses slowed now to a steady walk, and the noise from the streets grew louder as they entered Portsmouth. To have arrived there by coach on any other occasion would have thrilled her, and Anne felt, beneath the wave of fear that enveloped her, an anger that she had been robbed of what under other circumstances would have been an exciting adventure. She had never even travelled in a coach before, let alone as far away as Portsmouth, and now here she was, overwhelmed by the sight of masts, towering hulls and flapping sails.

The coach turned into the yard of an inn and much commotion now surrounded them. With little delay, the four horses that had brought them from Winchester were unhitched by the ostlers and another fresh team made ready, while almost before the door of the coach had been opened, the passengers' luggage was being handed down from the roof.

Lavallier motioned to Anne to remain in her seat until the other passengers had vacated theirs. Only when the interior of the coach was empty, and they heard the voice of the coachman shouting, 'All change!', did Lavallier rise from his seat and step out through the door, offering Anne his hand. As she alighted into the salt-laden air, the whole of Portsmouth seemed to envelop her. Seagulls screeched above their heads, adding their plaintive wails to a cacophony of sound composed of rolling casks and cartwheels, hawkers crying their wares, hauliers and carters exhorting everyone to move aside and sailors, drunk and sober, uniformed and roughly clad, swarming like bees up and down the gangplanks and docksides. It was as if the whole of the city were out on the streets.

Reeling as though she had been dealt a blow about the head, and with a sickly feeling in the pit of her stomach, Anne found herself being steered along the dockside by Lavallier, his arm clamped securely about her waist. At the end of the dock they turned up a side street that seethed with even more humanity: it spilled from the doorways of ships' chandlers and coffee houses, from shops selling exotic objects and richly coloured carpets, from butchers' and bakers', greengrocers' and fruiterers', with their produce piled high in colourful pyramids. Before she had time to take it all in, Lavallier motioned her through a small archway and into some kind of office.

'Sit there,' instructed Lavallier, pushing Anne down onto a hard wooden chair in one corner. Above the polished counter she read the heading on the large blackboard to which the men behind the counter kept referring: 'SAIL-INGS', it said, in large gold letters, while underneath it were chalked the names of ships: '*Leviathan*' and '*Osprey*', '*Venus*' and '*Mermaid*', '*Dolphin*' and '*Blue Moon*', their times and dates of departure indicated alongside them.

Lavallier untied the cord at the neck of his cloak, unbuttoned the coat beneath it and sought in his coat pocket for a slender bundle of papers, which he took out and examined. As he did so, he took his place behind a gentleman whose transaction was clearly nearing completion, all the while glancing regularly in Anne's direction, checking that she was still with him.

The man in front of Lavallier raised his hat to thank the official behind the counter and, as he departed, Lavallier took his place and began to engage the official in conversation. Anne seized her brief opportunity. Without a backward glance she got up from the chair and slipped silently out of the doorway. Pulling her cloak tightly about her, she wove her way swiftly up the alley, past the vendors and the passers-by, under canvas awnings and between carts and crates and barrows until she emerged, eventually, in a small square. It was quieter there, but she did not linger. She crossed the square and zigzagged her way through more alleyways and narrow passages until, at last, she had left the seething mass of humanity and, more importantly, Roderick Lavallier, behind her. She had shaken him off; she had escaped. She stopped for a moment to catch her breath, leaning on a wall to one side of a house, in yet another square.

The moment of triumph was brief. She had, indeed, rid herself of her captor, but now the only thing of which she was entirely certain was that she was alone in a strange and frightening city, and that she was totally lost.

Hotel du Vin, Winchester

12 June 2010

Harry picked Alex up in his old Volvo estate at half past seven.

Alex's first question surprised him and made him laugh: 'How long did it take you to get ready?'

'About three times as long as normal,' he admitted.

'Me, too. Actually, more like four.'

Her openness was refreshing, but it did nothing to ease his state of mind. Were things moving too fast? What did he expect of this relationship, which, as yet, hardly qualified for the term. Did he want it to be a relationship?

Banishing these thoughts from his mind, he asked, 'Did Anne get off to Bournemouth all right?'

'Just about. She's a born country child—never happier than when she's picking wild flowers, netting minnows in the river, or just out in the garden with Mr Moses.'

'"Mr Moses"?'

'Her dog. That threadbare animal that she carries under her arm.'

'Funny name for a dog.'

'She found him down by the river—someone had dropped him in the rushes. We left him on the garden fence for days to see if anyone would come by and pick him up, but they never did, so Anne said she'd give him a home until his rightful owner turned up.'

'How long ago was that?'

'A couple of months.'

'So Mr Moses is now a part of the family?'

'The most important part. She talks to him. Tells him things.'

'What sort of things?'

Alex looked thoughtful for a moment. 'She doesn't say, usually. But at least it means she's articulating her thoughts, rather than bottling them up.'

'You're not a bottler, then?'

'I thought we were going to talk about you tonight, not me.'

Harry took the comment kindly and swung the Volvo into the car park behind the Hotel du Vin. Once inside, they were ushered to a corner table, and inconsequential conversation followed over the menu and the wine list.

Orders taken care of, they chinked their glasses as Alex said, 'Now it's my turn to find out about you.'

Harry told the rest of the story of his frenetic courtship with Serena, of their brief marriage and hasty divorce, and did his best to sound neither maudlin nor self-pitying.

'She sounds dreadful,' offered Alex, as he wound up his story.

'No, not dreadful. We were blissfully happy at first. But the differences rose to the surface and before we knew where we were, it had all crumbled.'

'But did you feel uncomfortable about some things from the beginning?'

'I never really got on with her friends. But it was Serena I'd fallen in love with. You can't dislike someone because you don't like their friends.'

'No, but you can judge them a bit by the company they keep.' She said it gently but firmly.

'Yes, I suppose you can . . . on reflection.'

Alex asked, 'Is she with anyone now?'

'No idea. It's almost as if she never existed. As if our marriage never happened. I wonder sometimes if it was all a dream. But then that's Serena. Once she's made up her mind about something, there's no going back.'

'Or looking back?'

'No.' He thought they had talked enough about his misfortunes. 'How about you? Do you ever look back and think "What if . . ."?'

Alex leaned back in her chair. 'Oh, yes. About so many things.'

Harry thought it would probably be a mistake to probe further. This was meant to be a happy evening out. He had already dragged the conversation down with his own tale of woe—better to be upbeat.

'Goat's cheese tart?' It was the waiter's voice. 'And the lobster bisque?'

They fell upon the food as though they had not eaten in days.

'You probably think I'm a real no-hoper,' confessed Harry. 'Bringing a girl out to dinner and talking about my ex-wife, and then ordering "surf and turf"—I mean, how unimaginative.'

'Are you?' asked Alex.

'I hope not. If I am, I'm determined to change. That's why I'm making a new start. In a new house and with a new career. If I can find one,' he added.

'Well, I don't think you're a no-hoper at all. Just a bit bruised. That sort of thing saps confidence. I've seen it happen enough times to know.'

'Do you have lots of friends?' he asked.

'Not any more . . . I mean, not since we've moved.'

'Choice or circumstance?'

Alex looked uneasy, and then said softly, 'A bit of both.'

IT WAS HALF PAST TEN by the time Harry pulled into the gravel drive of the Old Mill. The rest of the evening with Alex had been devoted to lighter fare—the kind of music they each liked, whether Venice was better than Florence, whether the coffee in Florence was better than in Rome.

The last topic gave Harry the excuse to ask Alex back to his, rather than having coffee in the hotel. She accepted happily, but on their arrival back at the Old Mill she said, 'Look, why don't you come and have coffee with me; my place is probably warmer for a start. I've got an Aga.'

'Show-off,' countered Harry.

'Oh, you'll get one, I guarantee. Once you've been through your first winter here by the river, you'll realise how nice it is to be warm.'

Alex opened the door into the kitchen, lit by a single lamp on the windowsill, and then walked through a low archway into the sitting room, where the dying embers of a log fire glowed softly behind a tall wire guard. She took two small logs from a wicker basket and dropped them on the grate. There was a brief shower of sparks before the fire flickered into life and small flames began to lick at the dry birchwood.

Harry had not been in this room before, and he looked about him, smiling at the warmth and friendliness of it. There were two soft sofas facing each other in front of the fire—he took a seat in one of them—their loose covers partially hidden by throws of heather-coloured tweed. Stripped-pine book shelves flanked the fireplace and a grandfather clock ticked sonorously in one corner, while a furnished doll's house sat in the other. Odd chairs held piles of books, and a bunch of old-fashioned roses stood on the low table between the sofas, the soft pink, purple and crimson petals of the flowers now cascading onto the magazines beneath the bowl that held them. It was naturally stylish and comfortable.

'Very nice,' he murmured—to himself, so he thought.

'You like it?'

He was startled to realise that he had spoken out loud. 'Very much.'

Alex made the coffee and brought it to the sofa where Harry was sitting. 'Music?' she asked.

'It should be me doing this,' countered Harry.

'Well, make the most of it.' Alex went to an iPod that rested between two speakers and, within moments, Ella Fitzgerald was singing.

Alex flopped down beside him. 'What are you doing tomorrow?'

'I don't know, I haven't really thought. I did have plans to crack on with tracing . . .' And then he realised he was not remotely interested in his ancestry. Not right now. He turned to her and asked, 'What about you?'

'Free day. I can do what I want.' Alex looked at him and smiled, and before he knew what was happening, he had his arms round her and they were lying back on the sofa, kissing.

Portsmouth

16 April 1816

'Lost your way, dear?'

Anne was shaken out of her trancelike state by the voice in her ear. She turned to discover the smiling face of a woman who looked rather elderly, but whose mode of dress was that of a much younger woman. Her petticoats were full and voluminous, while her dress was of a satin once fashionable but now passé and, judging by the stains, infrequently laundered. Around her shoulders lay an elaborate wrap that had seemingly once belonged to a member of the fox family, and upon her head sat a collection of feathers. The woman's cheeks were the colour of a Quarrenden apple and her lips as red as blood. Several soot-black beauty spots decorated the skin around her mouth and eyes: the whole vision rendered Anne lost for words.

'What's a nice girl like you doing on her own in Portsmouth?' The individual arrangement of teeth added sibilance to the question.

'Lost,' blurted out Anne, without thinking.

'Oh, we're lost, are we? And do we have any money?'

Anne shook her head.

'Well, it's a good job you bumped into Old Phoebe then, ain't it? What's your name, dear?'

Warning bells rang in Anne's head as she told her. She had heard about the likes of 'Old Phoebe' and knew what they were about: Mrs Fitzgerald had made sure of that. 'I don't . . . I mean—' Anne suddenly burst into tears.

'Well, does you need help or doesn't you?'

It seemed futile to claim to the contrary, when it was patently obvious to anyone, including Old Phoebe, that she did.

'What sort of help?' Anne heard herself ask.

'Shelter, a room for the night. A position.'

'A lady's maid,' countered Anne defensively. 'That's my position. I'm going to be a lady's maid.'

'Of course you are, dear. Eventually. But, in the meantime, you'll need a roof over your head, some food, and the wherewithal to find yourself that position, won't you?'

Anne could not bring herself even to nod. She kept glancing over her shoulder in the direction of the shipping office—or at least, the direction in which she assumed the shipping office was.

'Someone looking for you, dear? Someone who worries you?'

Anne nodded and Old Phoebe saw the terror in her eyes. 'There's dreadful men abroad. Men the likes of which I will have no truck with. My men are nice men. Every last one.' She reached into her battered velour reticule and pulled out a square of fine linen, edged with lace. It did not glow with the whiteness of her mistress's handkerchiefs at the Manor House, but it was kindly proffered and Anne managed a very weak smile.

'Wipe your eyes, dear, and come along with Old Phoebe. You need only stay as long as you want. I will not hold you there.'

Anne shook her head violently. 'I need to get back to the Manor House.'

Old Phoebe looked sympathetic. 'Which Manor House is that then?'

'At Withercombe.'

'Withercombe . . . mmm . . . is that a long way away?'

'It is in Hampshire.'

'So is Portsmouth, dear, but this is a large county, and you'll need the coach fare to get back there.'

'But I have no money,' protested Anne. 'Not even a farthing.'

' 'Tis of no account, ducky. 'Tis of no account. Them as comes with me seldom has. Not at first. But they soon becomes more comfortable.'

Anne dabbed at the tears that still rolled down her cheeks. What was the alternative? At least if she went with Old Phoebe she would be in her own county and able—if the old woman was to be trusted—to earn enough money to be able to afford her fare home.

'What would I have to do? To earn some money?'

'Just be nice. To my gentlemen.'

'But I've never—'

'No, dear, of course you haven't. And Old Phoebe ain't the sort to make you do things against your will.' The old woman looked about her; she seemed keen to be on her way. 'Make your mind up, dear, I've things to do.'

For a brief moment, Anne considered declining the old woman's offer and continuing her journey through the busy streets of Portsmouth but, just then, a gaggle of passing sailors, clearly the worse for rum, tumbled by. One of them grabbed at Anne's skirt and asked, 'Ready for a good time, lady? Better than the usual, ain't ya?'

Old Phoebe put a protective arm around her new charge and swung at the tar with her stout parasol. The handle caught him smartly about the left ear and his companions fell about laughing at his misfortune.

'No need for that, you old bizzom,' retaliated the sailor.

Anne looked at the woman. 'All right. But just until I get enough money.'

At this Old Phoebe smiled and put her arm through Anne's. 'You just stick close and we'll be there in two shakes of a sailor's leg, if you sees what I mean.' She looked Anne up and down as she bustled her across the square and down another alleyway. 'Nice dress, dear. We'll have to find you one or two more like that.'

Anne shot her a worried glance.

'Oh, don't you worry. You won't have to pay for them; we'll find one or two nice gentlemen who'll be happy to provide you with pretty clothes.'

'For being a lady's maid?' asked Anne hopefully.

'Of a sort, dear. Of a sort.'

Mill Cottage, Itchen Parva

13 June 2010

Ordinarily, Harry did not mind when Rick turned up unannounced, but when he arrived on the doorstep at 9 a.m. on Sunday, he was less than welcoming. 'Do you know what time it is? What day it is?'

'Yes to both.' Rick looked strangely uncomfortable.

Noticing his friend's demeanour, Harry made to sound more welcoming. 'Come in, then. Coffee?'

Rick nodded. He was clearly preoccupied, his manner distant.

'Are you all right?' asked Harry.

'Yes. I'm fine.' Rick tried to sound more relaxed, but his body language contradicted his efforts. 'What about you?'

'Couldn't be better,' responded Harry, as he held the kettle under the tap. 'But you look as though you're about to deliver bad news . . .'

Rick shrugged. 'Sort of. Not exactly bad. There's probably nothing in it.'

Harry looked concerned. 'Let me be the judge of that.'

Rick sat down at the kitchen table and reached into the inside pocket of his leather jacket. He pulled out a sheet of folded newsprint. 'You know my granddad's trunk I was telling you about? Well, I thought I'd get it down and have a look at it. Granddad clearly put things in it when they cropped up, so the newer stuff is on the top. I found this.' He unfolded the sheet and handed it to Harry.

At the top of the left-hand page was a picture of the Old Mill and below it were a few brief lines on its history, remarking that it had been in the Palfrey family for several generations until it had been sold to another family in the 1960s, and that it was on the market again for the first time in a generation. Harry checked the date of the clipping—2008: two years ago. As well as showing a picture, it also listed the full particulars of the house.

'So when did your grandfather die?'

'Last year. I've had the trunk only a few months. It was you mentioning it all that made me go up to the attic to get it down.'

Harry made to hand the clipping back. 'There you are, then—you're on the trail of your family history. Your granddad clearly knew all about it.'

'Yes. I suppose that's why he kept the clipping.' Rick did not take it from Harry's grasp. Instead he said, 'There's something else. On the other side.'

Harry turned over the page and, as he did so, felt his heart thump. There, in the centre, was a picture of Alex Overton on the steps of the Crown Court in Winchester, accompanied by two men in suits. The headline caused him to sit down: SOUTHAMPTON WOMAN CLEARED OF ASSISTING HUSBAND'S DEATH. The colour drained from his cheeks.

'I thought you ought to see it,' said Rick. 'I thought you ought to know.'

'Yes,' said Harry softly. 'Yes, of course.'

The dense silence was interrupted by the whistling of the kettle. Rick got up from the table and poured the boiling water into the cafetière. 'The important thing is that she was cleared.'

Harry looked up and held out the newspaper clipping. 'Would you read it to me? I don't think I can bring myself to . . .'

Rick took the clipping and read as levelly as he could: '"At Winchester Crown Court, the Hampshire barrister Alexandra Templeton—"' He looked up. 'She must have changed her name after the case—"was today cleared of assisting in her husband James's suicide. Templeton, thirty-six, himself a barrister, had been suffering from premature-onset Alzheimer's disease for two years. His death, from an overdose of sedatives, had been the subject of a police investigation in which his wife Alexandra, thirty-five, was accused of having aided his suicide. The Judge, Mr Justice Westmacott, in his summing up, said, 'This was a sad case of a bright and intelligent man suffering from the cruellest of diseases and being cared for throughout by a wife for whom he had the highest regard and whose selfless attention to his needs was never less than admirable. From the evidence we have heard, I am confident that Mr Templeton decided to take his own life and that he was in no way assisted by the woman who had loved and cared for him. He clearly felt that he could no longer be a burden upon his wife and family or upon society. His note to that effect would appear to be his own work and that of himself alone. There is no evidence to suggest that Mrs Templeton was in any way a party to her husband's taking of his own life. She leaves this court without any stain upon her character and has the deepest sympathy of those here today. This is a sad case that should, in my opinion, never have come to court.'"'

Rick carefully folded up the paper and laid it on the table.

For a few moments neither of them spoke, then Harry said, 'But if she was clearly innocent, why *did* the case come to court?'

'I wondered about that. I asked my mum if she could remember anything about it. She said there was something about a neighbour who told the police that Alex had something to do with it.'

'Why didn't we know about it, or hear about it?' asked Harry. 'We don't live that far from Southampton.'

'Probably school holidays—we could both have been away.'

Harry asked, 'Why do you think your grandfather kept it?'

'It must have been coincidence, I reckon,' said Rick. 'I suppose it just happened to be on the other side of that piece about the family home.

I mean, what else could it be? He wouldn't have known the Templetons.'

Harry looked as though the weight of the world was upon his shoulders.

'I didn't show it to you to worry you, or to make you feel any differently towards her,' Rick said.

Harry ran his hand through his hair. 'It's a bit of a jolt, that's all.'

Rick poured the coffee into mugs. 'She hasn't mentioned it, obviously.'

'Well, no,' said Harry. 'And there's no reason why she should. She was exonerated. Cleared of any involvement.'

Rick stirred lots of milk into his mug and drank off half his coffee with one gulp. 'There were obviously some who weren't convinced, I suppose, which accounts for the move and the change of name.'

'Are you saying—?'

'No. No! Just thinking out loud, really.' Rick took a sip of coffee and then asked, 'Do you think it's her maiden name—Overton—or just one she picked at random?'

'I'm sure she'll tell me when she's good and ready.' Harry's voice was louder now and his manner more assertive. 'Until then . . .' He threw his hands in the air and looked questioningly at Rick.

Rick finished his coffee and got up to go. 'Yes, well, I'm taking Tilly to see *Mary Poppins the Musical* this afternoon. Rachel's off playing tennis.'

Harry looked at him incredulously.

'It's what fathers have to do,' said Rick. 'See you. And . . . I'm sorry.' He closed the door behind him sheepishly, leaving Harry with thoughts as confused and tangled as the garden that ran down to the banks of the river.

72 Godolphin Street, Portsmouth

16 April 1816

The doorway was not, at first, obvious. It opened off a side street some way from where Old Phoebe had encountered her newest prospect.

Anne was confused and frightened. Torn between running off and encountering the menacing Lavallier once more, and committing herself to the charge of a woman of dubious repute, she was still endeavouring to convince herself that she had little choice but to follow the old woman when they were through the doorway, and Old Phoebe was pushing her up the three steps into a gloomy interior.

Anne began to be truly fearful. Old Phoebe read the signs and made to reassure her: 'Worry not, my dear. It may not be as grand as the house you have been accustomed to, but we are very welcoming at number seventy-two.' She cleared her throat extravagantly and then called out, 'Mr Pontifex! Where are you, Mr P? New visitor to meet you.'

Old Phoebe pushed Anne before her into a shadowy passage, along past curtained doorways. As they neared the end of it, a small head peeped out from between two dusty swags of crimson velvet bordered with black velour pompoms. It fringed the face of an elderly man with elfin features and made him look like something from a travelling side show. For a moment Anne wanted to laugh out loud, but fear overcame her once more.

'Mr Pontifex, this is Anne.'

Mr Pontifex brushed aside the curtain and stepped out into the hallway. In the half-light Anne could see that he had an angular and crooked body and was quite unable to stand upright. His head was a shiny pale dome, fringed by wispy white hair, and his nose was pointed. Anne half expected his ears to be pointed, too.

'Ah! Hello!' said the goblin. He looked Anne up and down with curiosity.

Old Phoebe broke in on both their thoughts. 'This is Anne. Lost, I'm afraid, and without any means of getting home. So, Mr Pontifex, I took her in. Offered her shelter and sustenance before she heads off on her way back to . . . where did you say it was, dear?'

'Wither—'

'Somewhere in Hampshire,' cut in Old Phoebe, clearly not in the least concerned as to the precise identity of Anne's domicile. 'Do you think we can look after her, Mr P?'

The little man smiled and Anne saw that he had even fewer teeth than Old Phoebe. 'Of course!' he croaked. 'Nothing easier!' She flinched a little as he reached out and took the fabric of her dress between his fingers. 'Nice, very nice.' Then he looked at Anne questioningly. 'Your own gown?'

'Yes,' replied Anne, hastily.

Pontifex nodded. 'I see. Only you don't sound . . .' He shrugged, deciding not to pursue his line of questioning. Then he brightened. 'Refreshment— that is what you will be requiring. After your long and tiring day. Follow me, Miss Anne . . . this way.' He led the way farther down the passage and ushered Anne through another curtained doorway into a parlour, stepping back smartly to let Old Phoebe pass in front of him.

Old Phoebe slipped the fox fur from her shoulders. 'Yes,' she said, 'we have had a bit of a morning of it, Mr P. Muffins and porter, if you please.'

At this Pontifex raised his eyebrows and muttered, 'Bread and porter, right away, with pleasure,' and scuttled out through another door.

'You just sit down and make yourself at home, dear, while Old Phoebe changes into her house clothes, yes?'

Anne said nothing but perched on the end of a chaise longue as the old woman swept out after Mr Pontifex, leaving her to take in her surroundings.

It was not a large room, but it had tall windows in the end wall. The curtains reduced the amount of light that filtered in, but Anne could still make out the main features of the room, which seemed filled to bursting with furniture and ornaments. The walls were hung with large pictures of young women whose pale bodies were draped with translucent muslin or clad in chemises, like those worn by the fine young ladies who occasionally visited the Manor House with Master Edward and Master Frederick. They were reclining at ease on sofas like the one on which Anne was sitting. Tall stands carried potted palms with browning fronds, and chairs and tables, none of them matching, were dotted in haphazard fashion about the room, which was peppered with candlesticks of brass and mahogany. An abundance of shawls seemed to have been strewn over every stick of furniture.

Anne's first thought was that she would have felt the sharp edge of Mrs Fitzgerald's tongue had she left any of the rooms in the Manor House in this deplorable state: even the ashes had not been cleared from the grate in the black iron fireplace. Perhaps that would be one of her first jobs.

Mr Pontifex and Old Phoebe had been gone for several minutes now. Anne's anxiety continued to build and she took deep breaths of the sour-smelling air to try and clear her head.

A night. She would stay for one night only. Maybe two. Quietly, without meeting anyone but Old Phoebe and Mr Pontifex. She would do some cleaning and washing—clear the grates and shake out the dusty rugs here and in the other rooms of the house. She would stay just long enough to raise the money for her coach fare. Then she would return with haste to the Manor House, hoping that they would forgive her foolhardiness, that Mrs Fitzgerald would consider that the events she had endured were enough to have brought her to her senses, and that there was no need to punish her further. She realised now that it had been a mistake: she was not at all ready to leave her present life and seek adventure.

Then she thought of Eleanor lying by the stream, and her eyes began to fill with tears. They must have found her, surely? Noticed that she was wearing Anne's clothes. What must they have thought? It was only because she wanted to be a lady's maid that these disasters had occurred. Her life had changed for ever in a matter of a few hours.

She remembered Lavallier and shivered. She knew that if she stayed with Old Phoebe for a single night he was certain to have boarded his ship and sailed for wherever he was bound. Tomorrow she could safely walk the streets again, discover the times of coaches to Withercombe . . . no, the coaches did not stop at Withercombe. She would take the coach to Winchester, she remembered now. From there she would have to walk. But in which direction? Again, with a stab of anguish, she realised just how little she knew of the wider world. She knew neither where she was nor how to return from whence she had come.

'Here we are, then!'

Anne started at the interruption to her thoughts. Mr Pontifex had re-entered the room, bearing a wooden tray upon which sat three small pewter tankards and three slabs of bread cut from a loaf. A curled lump of ochre-coloured cheese and a knife accompanied them.

Old Phoebe followed in his wake. The fox fur and layers of shawls had been replaced now by a voluminous amber-coloured cloak of faded silk. It had puff sleeves that made its inhabitant look even more voluminous, and upon her head sat a mobcap of black lace. Her cheeks were freshly rouged and she seemed to float upon a vapour of the smell of stale roses.

'Luncheon!' she exclaimed, greeting the arrival of the bread and cheese and porter with a level of enthusiasm that Sir Thomas would have reserved for his eight-course dinner on Christmas Eve.

Anne looked up at the two of them—the woman appearing in a vision before her like some extravagantly decorated cottage loaf, and the man who seemed to be nothing more than a dried-up spider. As his bony hand reached out towards her, proffering a foaming tankard of porter, she wanted more than anything to leap up from her seat and dash down the passageway and out of the door. Instead, her hunger and thirst overrode all other sensibilities. She took the tankard from the beaming spider and drained its contents in one. A feeling of warmth immediately enveloped her and she managed a weak smile in the direction of the plump old woman.

'Bread and cheese?' said Phoebe. 'Got to get your strength up, haven't we?'

Mill Cottage, Itchen Parva

13 June 2010

Harry had thought seriously about calling Alex and coming up with some excuse to avoid them spending the day together. The thought of an entire day with her—a prospect that, the night before, had seemed so full of promise—left him feeling ill at ease. Should he bring the subject up? Would she be aware that he knew? Had she assumed all along that he had known about it but had just been too polite to say anything?

He had the phone in his hand at one point, but put it down again, cursing himself for his lack of faith in her. But it wasn't that. Or was it? How could he go into this relationship unsure of whether or not the object of his affections had helped her husband to kill himself? The judge seemed pretty sure she had not. And even if she had, she would have done so on compassionate grounds. Wasn't it more cruel to watch someone you loved, who wanted to die, suffering day after day?

No. He could not go there. He would have to trust his instincts: Alex was the one person he had met since his separation from Serena with whom he felt totally at ease. He chastised himself for allowing himself to fall for her so completely in the space of a couple of weeks: he knew he had, in those moments when he dared to be honest with himself. Whatever else he felt about Alex, there was a deep and underlying respect. But why? He tried to analyse what was at the root of his . . . admiration for her. For that was what it was. He admired her determination, her generosity of spirit, her relationship with her daughter. Her taste. They seemed to like the same things: she hadn't even blenched when he had mentioned his interest in tracing his ancestry or the lives of the saints and that, surely, was the supreme test.

He should stop brooding. Call her and ask her what she wanted to do, when she wanted to meet. To ring her now and call it off would not only be distrustful, it would be cowardly.

Anyway, he would not call her on the phone. He would go round.

HARRY FOUND ALEX down at the bottom of her garden, sitting in an old canvas chair on the banks of the chalk stream, gazing at the water. She did not see him, and he looked at her, sitting in a white cotton skirt that she had pulled up to expose her shapely legs to the June sunshine. She wore a simple navy-blue vest that flattered her curves, and he felt a flip in the pit of his stomach.

She seemed to be miles away, cradling a mug between her hands and staring into the clear depths of the gently rippling stream. He hardly wanted to break the spell; instead he wanted to stand watching her. To admire the curve of her neck, the fall of her hair, the deftness of her fingers.

And then a moorhen called—a loud 'chook' that rang through the still morning air—and at the same time a twig snapped under his foot. She turned and saw him and smiled. 'I wondered whether you would be up yet,' she said. And he knew then that whatever had been before did not matter. Somehow, for some reason, it could all be explained. And on this sunny Sunday morning, the best thing was that he was there with her, in a part of the world that he loved and which had somehow welcomed him home.

SHE MADE HIM LUNCH—a simple affair of pâté and crusty bread, fresh strawberries and local cheese. He opened a bottle of muscat brought from his tiny cellar. 'Too sweet,' she said with a glint in her eye, as she saw the label.

'Just right for summer days,' he countered and, when she tasted it, he could see that she knew he was right. He lowered it into the water at the stream's edge to keep it cool, and when they had lunched and finished the bottle, they wandered indoors and up to her bedroom. It seemed the most natural thing in the world. The ease that was so in evidence when they talked was mirrored in their lovemaking—gentle and tender. For some while afterwards, they lay in each other's arms, the dormer window open, letting in the sounds of birdsong and gently whispering willow wands.

72 Godolphin Street, Portsmouth

16 April 1816

The small room that Old Phoebe had shown Anne into was on the fourth floor of the dusky house in Godolphin Street, reached by ever-narrowing stairs, so narrow that the old woman had had a deal of difficulty in forcing herself up them.

'You rest here a while, and wash off the cares of the day,' Old Phoebe had instructed Anne, adding, 'I'll be back in a little while.'

It was still light outside, but the drapes across the casement cast the space into a deep gloom. The room was sparsely furnished: a chest of drawers, over which a fringed shawl was thrown, was topped by a china basin and ewer. This was clearly where Anne was meant to 'wash off the cares of the day', but the water had a brown colour to it and Anne thought the better of any contact with it. Behind it hung a small and clouded looking glass.

A hard, button-backed chair was pushed into a corner and, from where she sat on the brass bedstead, Anne could see that the bottom had come away and that brown horsehair was falling out of it. Two wooden candlesticks, perched on the mantelpiece of the small cast-iron fireplace, added to what little light there was, their flickering flames making frightening shadows on the wall. The room smelt musty: the dust beneath the bed was almost half an inch thick, and the counterpane was stained.

Anne did not like to remove any clothing, but her feet were aching now so she untied and slipped off her boots and rubbed her toes. Simultaneously, she realised how tired she was. She pulled up the hood of the cloak she still wore so that it covered the back of her head, then lay back upon the lumpy palliasse. Soon the room faded from view and she was lost in sleep.

IT WAS, SHE IMAGINED, only several minutes later that she woke. Surely no more. For a few moments she could not recall where she was but then, with a fearful dawning of realisation, she remembered what had happened. Her head seemed to be filled with some kind of fog, and her bones ached, but the sleep, although uneven, had replenished some of her strength.

She sat up on the bed and blinked. The candles still flickered on the mantelpiece but they were slightly taller now than they had been before she had fallen asleep. Then she looked down at her body and started. It was no longer clothed in the pink dress, but in a loose-fitting, translucent chemise, topped with a threadbare silken cloak—a more modestly cut version than that worn by Old Phoebe when she had shown her up to her room.

Quickly she slipped from the bed and crossed to the looking glass. Fuzzy though the reflection was, she could see that her hair had been rearranged and tied in place with a ribbon. Her cheeks looked pink and her lips were a darker shade of red than normal. Her heart beat loudly in her chest now. Who had done this to her, and why? She sat down heavily on the bed, with the growing realisation that it was unlikely that she would be dressed like this if Old Phoebe wanted her to empty the grates and polish the furniture.

Unbidden, a phrase from *The Highwayman's Bride* came into her mind:

'In the bawdy house, he had his wicked way with her.' Her heart was beating rapidly now. While never completely sure what 'his wicked way' would be, Anne felt certain that it was not something that she would enjoy; neither was it something that she was in any way ready to experience. Then the images of Moll Hackabout in Sir Thomas's library came flooding back to her. Was this what she looked like? Was this about to happen to her? She had never really wanted to be a highwayman's bride; she knew it was all a silly dream. And she was certain that she did not want to be a—she hardly dared even think the word—'harlot'.

How could she have been so foolish as to have gone there? What did she imagine that Old Phoebe and Mr Pontifex wanted of her, other than that she would be expected to . . . she fought to avoid the thoughts that swam around in her head.

But she was aware of sounds now. The house that had been so quiet seemed to echo with distant murmurings. They were not the voices of the old man and woman. They were younger voices, voices with more energy and vigour, both male and female. And the house smelled differently: a sickly, smoky vapour seemed to envelop everything and made her feel light-headed. And then there were footsteps upon the wooden stairs leading to her room. A single pair of footsteps. Anne breathed heavily, wondering what could possibly happen next. After a few moments, she saw the tarnished brass knob turn, and the door of her room began to open.

As it swung wide she had a clear view of her visitor. The figure who stood before her, a glass in his hand, caused her heart to leap. 'Well, well,' he said softly. 'If it is not Anne Flint.'

Mill Cottage, Itchen Parva

19 June 2010

It was a decision taken by both of them the previous Sunday evening, that to live too much in each other's pockets at first would not be a good thing. Not so much for them as for Anne, whose world had been troubled enough by her father's death two years ago. At that point, Harry had been on the verge of clearing up the one area of unease in his mind and raising the subject of James Templeton's death, but he had let the moment pass.

The end of term was just a month away now and he began to feel quite excited about the prospect of his new life. On this rather cloudy Saturday morning, he set about the one bit of house reorganisation that he had decided was necessary. The upstairs bathroom was at the end of the landing and should he ever have guests, the inevitable meeting on the landing with sponge bag and towel could be avoided only if he made a doorway into the bathroom from his own bedroom, and fitted a bolt to both that and the outer door. That way he would have what amounted to an en suite arrangement, but on leaving he could slip back the bolt of the door to the landing to show that the bathroom was vacant.

It seemed a simple-enough job; the wall was not load-bearing. All he would need to do was knock out a portion of the lath-and-plaster wall, insert a new doorway, plaster round it and fit a new door. Simple. But filthy.

He had sheeted up the passageway and all the other doorways so that he was cocooned in the bathroom itself. Having pinned up a sheet on the opposite side of the wall to prevent the bedroom being filled with dust, he opened the bathroom window to let in much-needed fresh air, and then hacked away at the old wall, its brittle plasterwork tumbling onto the dust sheets below. Having taken the trouble to invest in a face mask and goggles, the resulting discomfort was not as bad as he had feared, but the combination of lime and horsehair filled the air with a fine dust.

Through the gloom he heard a voice calling, 'Bye, Harry!' It would be Alex and Anne on their way to the village fête but, when he finally made it to the window—looking like Toad of Toad Hall in his goggles—there was no sign of them. Ah well, they would be back that afternoon to regale him with stories. With a light heart he continued to chip away at the plaster.

Slowly the opening grew in size and, once he had reached the lines that he had drawn on the wall to mark its outline, he stopped and laid down his hammer and chisel. There it was: a new doorway. Strange how different it made the two rooms look; his bedroom appeared larger now, and so did the bathroom. He stepped from one to the other and then back again.

He went downstairs to get a breath of fresh air and to make a cup of coffee. As he crossed the kitchen he saw them coming down the garden path: Alex and Anne. The girl waved and Alex shouted, 'We won't disturb you; we're just off. See you this afternoon.'

By lunch time he had managed to fit the new jamb in place and to plaster around it. He congratulated himself on both his speed and the efficiency of the job, running his hand up and down the new timber with pride. He would not hang the door today; that he would do when the plaster had gone off properly and the whole thing had settled. Now he would clean up, though he knew that for days, and maybe weeks, there would still be dust settling on every surface.

As he folded up the last dust sheet, from out of the corner of his eye he caught sight of a figure walking up the stairs. Alex and Anne must have come back early. But when he turned there was no sign of anyone. He shook his head. It must have been a speck of plaster in his eye.

DOWN BY THE CHALK STREAM, the fresh air was especially welcoming. He opened a bottle of beer and sat down on the grassy bank. He would lunch alone today, down here; but his reverie was broken by a voice he had not heard for some weeks.

'Can I come down? Are you at home to visitors?' Harry swung round and saw the figure of Pattie Chieveley as she gamely picked her way between the dog roses that threatened at any moment to remove her clothing.

'Hello!' Harry was genuinely pleased to see her.

'You haven't been round for a while, so I thought that if the mountain couldn't come to Muhammad . . .'

Harry rose to his feet and went to greet her. 'I'm sorry, I've been so tied up with . . . this place and—'

'I know, dear, and don't you worry. I quite understand.'

Harry put his arms round her and gave her a big hug.

'Oh, careful, dear. I'm not as strong as I was.'

Harry grinned. 'You? You're as strong as—'

'Now don't say "as strong as an ox", dear, or I'll begin to think that Ted's home cooking is taking its toll.'

'Ted? Cooking? Are you serious?'

Pattie smiled, and then Harry noticed that her eyes had filled with tears.

'Hey! What's the matter?' Without waiting for an answer he put his arm round Pattie's shoulders and led her back through the garden to the house, sitting her down in a comfortable chair by the kitchen table.

'There you are. Would you like coffee?' he asked. 'Or something stronger?'

'Coffee would be fine, dear, thank you.'

Harry went about the coffee-making quietly, casting a glance at Pattie now and then, but he was unwilling to press her.

After a few moments she said, 'Well, you've made it very cosy, Harry.

Most men can do "macho"—is that what they call it? But not cosy.'

Harry grinned as he put a mug in front of her. 'I take that as a compliment.'

'And what a lot you've accomplished in the time.'

'Yes,' murmured Harry. 'What a lot . . .'

Pattie noticed the preoccupied look. 'I won't keep you,' she said, sipping her coffee.

Harry came back down to earth. 'No. I mean, don't worry. It's lovely to see you and I'm not doing anything in particular—not now. I've just finished knocking through a doorway from the bedroom to the bathroom upstairs. So that if I have guests, we don't have that—'

'That polite "after you" on the landing?' finished Pattie.

'Exactly.'

'Just like you,' she said. 'Very thoughtful.'

'I try,' said Harry. 'But enough about me and my house. How are you . . . and Ted? Is everything all right?'

'Not really.'

'Is it Ted?' asked Harry.

Pattie nodded. 'When you last saw him, what, a couple of months ago, he was all right, most of the time. Just occasional lapses of memory. A bit forgetful. He'd go to the fridge and stand with the door open wondering whether he was there to put something in or take something out.'

'Well, I do that,' said Harry.

'It's got worse. Sometimes he's clearly . . . well, somewhere else.'

'Do you think it's anything to worry about? I mean, anything serious?'

'I'm afraid so.' Pattie took another sip of coffee. 'He's been for tests. He doesn't know what for—just that they were routine: a checkup. The doctor called me in on my own the following day. Ted's suffering from dementia. He's got Alzheimer's disease.'

Harry sat down beside her. 'What's the prognosis?'

'Not good. They've told me to keep a close eye on him.'

'But you can still leave him at home on his own?'

'Sometimes. He can be fine for a while—often for a few days at a time—and then he'll just be . . . well . . . sort of absent. He'll sit in his chair and not really be with me. He mutters, too. Things I can't make out.'

'Do you think you can carry on looking after him?'

'For now. While he's like this. But they've warned me that he might change quite quickly. That he might become violent, and if he does that . . .

I won't be able to manage him.' Pattie finally dissolved into tears. 'Oh dear, Harry; forty-seven years we've been married and it has to end like this . . .'

Harry put his arm round her shoulders and gently rocked her as she sobbed. 'Oh, Pattie. If there's anything I can do . . .'

Pattie lifted her head. 'I don't think there's anything anyone can do. It's just one of those things. But the saddest thing of all is that the Ted I know is gradually disappearing, and one day he'll be gone altogether.' She managed a brave smile. 'You've no idea how dreadful that is, Harry. No idea at all.'

The Old Mill, Itchen Parva

19 June 2010

'You know, he really was a prick!'

Harry was surprised at Alex's outburst, especially since Anne was within earshot.

'Who was?'

'That Carew bloke. The one who goes around in his Range Rover as though he owns the place.'

'It's not a Range Rover, it's a Porsche Cayenne.'

'Well, there you are—even worse, then.'

'And he does own the place—well, a few cottages. And the bit of land the fête was on.'

'Just because some distant ancestor used to live in the Manor House here—when we had one—it doesn't mean that he can stomp around the place like . . . like . . . Lord Muck.'

Harry handed Alex a glass of red wine and tried to suppress a smile. 'Why so angry though?'

'Because he backed into me and then told me it was my fault for being so close. And now I shall need a new headlight and all he got was a scratch on his Range Rover's—'

'Porsche's—'

'Porsche's bumper! Stupid little—'

Harry cleared his throat and nodded at Anne, who was having an in-depth conversation about the afternoon's events with Mr Moses.

Alex stopped mid-tirade. 'Oh, I'm sorry.' She grinned, guiltily. 'I'm just cross about my headlight, that's all. Stupid man—no wonder he's divorced.'

'So tell me about this, er . . .' He lowered his voice and mouthed the word 'prick'. 'I don't know much about him.'

'He's some distant relative of the old lord of the manor when there used to be one—at Withercombe. There's nothing much there now except a few old cottages.'

'That's right,' replied Harry. 'I read about it in the cathedral library. There was a big fire at the manor in the fifties. That was the time when nobody wanted rambling old houses, and they pulled it down in the belief that it had little lasting value. Tragedy.'

'Oh, I know,' said Alex. 'But they used the stone to build a lot of local walls. The one outside my front garden was built from it.'

'I wonder if there's any in my garden?'

'Oh, I shouldn't think so. Your house isn't smart enough.'

Harry shot her a look, then saw the smile stretching across Alex's face.

'Cheeky blighter,' he countered. 'Anyway, tell me about this . . . er . . . "merchant banker".'

Alex flopped onto the sofa and Harry perched on the arm of the one opposite. 'Sir Marcus Carew?'

'Sir Marcus, eh? Very "lord of the manor".'

'Funnily enough, I think he *is* a merchant banker. Has one of those new houses outside Alresford—you know, on the Cheriton Road.'

'Smart.'

'Showy,' retorted Alex. 'The rumour is that he claimed the title through some legal wrangle. Anyway, that's just gossip, and I really don't care for that.' She looked thoughtful for a moment, as though she were admonishing herself for saying such a thing, then she continued, 'But he's not very nice to people. And he never looks you in the eye: always talks to your breasts.'

Harry spluttered on his wine. 'If there's a red wine stain on your sofa now, it was your fault,' he said. 'Anyway, did Anne have a good time?' He looked across at the child, still deep in conversation with her stuffed dog.

'Yes,' said Alex, and her voice sounded more relaxed. 'She just loves animals, and there were lots there—chickens and quail, even alpacas and sheep. Oh, and the local beagle pack. All she wants now is a real Mr Moses.'

'Maybe you should get her one.'

'With her at school all day and me out at the day centre? The dog would be here on its own a lot, and that wouldn't be fair.'

'I could look after it.'

Anne looked up. 'I said that Harry wouldn't mind.'

Alex looked across at the girl and frowned. 'I thought you were playing with Mr Moses.'

'I am. But I can still hear.'

Alex looked at Harry with a long-suffering expression, 'What am I to do?'

Anne cut in. 'Let me have a dog.'

'One day, sweetheart, but not just yet. Let's get a bit more settled.'

'But if Harry can help . . .'

'Harry has only just moved in and it wouldn't be very fair if we asked him to look after our dog straight away, would it?'

The child sighed and went back to playing with Mr Moses.

'Anyway, how did your day go? Do you have an en suite bathroom now?'

'Well, I have a hole in a wall. A very neat hole, but just a hole. En suite sounds a bit grand for a cottage.'

'Can we come and look?'

'Of course.'

Alex turned to Anne. 'Do you want to see Harry's en suite bathroom?'

'What's on sweet? Anything to do with pudding?'

Harry laughed. 'Not exactly. It's a bit boring really. Just a doorway between the bedroom and the bathroom.'

Anne turned to the stuffed dog. 'What do you think, Mr Moses? Shall we go and have a look?' She turned back to Harry. 'Mr Moses says that would be very nice.'

'I SEE WHAT YOU MEAN,' said Alex. 'It's just a hole. But a very nice hole. And it does make a difference.'

Harry walked through from the bathroom to the bedroom and then back again. 'See? Luxury!' He looked around. 'Where's Anne?'

'Anne?' Alex called her daughter. There was no reply. 'Anne? Where are you, poppet?'

Harry went into the spare bedroom. Anne was standing against the far wall, her face as pale as chalk, clutching Mr Moses tightly to her chest.

Alex was at his shoulder. 'What's the matter, sweetheart?'

The child did not answer, but continued to gaze straight ahead of her.

'Aren't you feeling well?' asked Alex. 'Come on, let me take you home.' She walked across the room and put her arm round her daughter. 'Goodness, you're cold.' She rubbed Anne's upper arms, looking at her with concern.

Anne shook her head. 'The lady,' was all she said.

Alex took her hand and led her downstairs and out into the garden. Harry followed. Once they were in the garden, the colour began to return to Anne's cheeks and the sun came out from behind a cloud.

'That'll warm you up,' said Alex. 'It's been a bit of a chilly day, that's all.'

Anne shook her head. 'It was the lady.'

'Which lady?' asked Alex.

Anne pointed towards the cottage. 'The white lady. In there.'

72 Godolphin Street, Portsmouth

16 April 1816

Anne Flint gazed upon the form of Frederick Carew with wide-eyed incredulity, eventually managing to blurt out, 'Master Frederick!'

'You remember me?' He smiled at her.

'Why, yes, sir. Of course!'

'And what on earth are you doing here, Anne? So far away from home.'

The words came flooding out. 'Oh, sir, please don't be angry with me. I thought I was to be a lady's maid and so agreed to go with Lady Eleanor and Mr Lavallier but there was the most dreadful accident and Mr Lavallier took me with him on his horse and brought me to Portsmouth and tried to get me to sail with him to the West Indies but I escaped and—'

'Stop, stop!' Frederick Carew raised his hand—the one that did not contain the bumper of red wine—and bade Anne slow down and repeat the entire story. Carefully, he lifted the tails of his green velvet coat and lowered himself onto the chair in the corner of the room. Perched on the edge of her bed and tugging nervously at the sleeve of her chemise, Anne related the events of the day—a day that seemed to have started at least a week ago, so eventful had been her past few hours.

Frederick listened closely, occasionally sipping his wine. His attention did not waver. 'And now you are here,' was all he said at last.

'Yes, sir.'

'And have you a plan? What do you propose to do?'

'To return to Withercombe as soon as I have the money to pay for my carriage fare.'

'I see.' Frederick smiled.

She had forgotten just how winning was the smile of Sir Thomas Carew's younger son. He was as handsome as ever, with that rich hank of fair hair that would keep falling over his pale blue eyes. How the housemaids gossiped about him. Even Mrs Fitzgerald would sometimes colour up as he addressed her and flashed her that amazing smile.

'It is good fortune that you bumped into me, is it not?' he said.

'Oh, yes, sir! Such good fortune.'

'But the story you tell me is not one that will cause you to be favourably received upon your return to Withercombe, is it?' The smile faded now, and Master Frederick looked more serious.

Anne's hopes, having been raised momentarily, were dashed again by his accurate summary of her circumstances.

'No, sir.' She hesitated, then asked, 'Do you think you could explain it for me, sir? To Sir Thomas, and Mrs Fitzgerald? So that they would not scold me but would understand that I had learned my lesson?'

'I could try, Anne. But there is the question of the death of Lady Eleanor. That simply cannot lightly be explained away. There is likely to be a lot of ill feeling. Grief. Tragedy.' He sighed. 'People are very often swayed in such circumstances.'

'Sir?'

'They will find it very hard to take you back, Anne. Your actions, though not responsible directly, were in some way entwined with the loss of Lady Eleanor Stockbridge. Her father is very important in the county.'

'Oh, but, Master Frederick, it were none of my doing! I only did what I were bid.'

Frederick smiled indulgently. 'That may be so, Anne, but you can see how others might view the situation differently, in the light of those disastrous and tragic consequences.'

The relief that Anne had felt on encountering a man who had seemed to promise salvation was rapidly evaporating and she felt tears spring unbidden to her eyes. 'What am I to do then, sir?'

Frederick Carew thought for a moment, then he rose. 'Would you grant me a moment's leave, Anne?'

Anne nodded and sniffed back her tears. As her master's son left the room, she lay back on the bed, her head reeling. It was only then that it occurred to her to wonder what on earth he was doing in the house of Old Phoebe and Mr Pontifex.

EVENTUALLY, ANNE SAT UP on the edge of the bed and wrapped her arms around herself, as if to protect her virtue. As she did so, the door opened once more and Old Phoebe entered. She was carrying a tray. 'Here we are, dear. Look what I've brought you. A nice bumper of wine!'

Anne shook her head. 'No. No, thank you.'

Old Phoebe sighed, then she rested the tray on the corner of the chest of drawers, gathered her skirts and deposited her not inconsiderable weight on the edge of the bed, next to Anne.

Phoebe took her hand and patted it. 'I know what you are thinking, my dear. But there are some things in life that we must needs do if we are to get on. I recall when I was your age that I, too, was to be a lady's maid in a grand house.'

Anne shot her a brief glance.

'Yes, dear. Just like you. But I realised that we cannot always have what we want, just when we want it. Sometimes we have to use our feminine wiles to get what we want. Do you know what "wiles" are, Anne?'

Anne looked straight ahead, and shook her head.

'They are what we ladies have to use if we are to get the better of men. Master Frederick says he will help you to get back to Wither . . . wherever it is you are from, but I do think he will need a little encouragement to do so. What has happened is very serious, and it would be unreasonable, would it not, to expect Mr Frederick to put his own reputation at risk just to save yours?' She patted Anne's hand again, almost absent-mindedly. 'And so, what I suggest you do is, when Mr Frederick returns, you show him just how grateful you are for his help.'

Anne looked at her pleadingly. 'But how can I do that? I have no money.'

'Bless you! Mr Frederick has no need of your money. He has plenty of that himself. No, what Mr Frederick needs is for you to be kind to him. Nice to him.' The old woman looked at the young girl sitting next to her. 'You do understand what I mean, Anne, do you not? When Mr Frederick returns, he will ask you to sleep with him.'

A look of incredulity spread across Anne's face.

'And before you sleep, he may ask you for certain signs of affection.'

Anne did her best to understand. 'Like . . . kissing?'

'Yes. Like kissing. And holding you.'

'But Mr Frederick is the master's son. If I were to be found doing that, I should be dismissed. Mrs Fitzgerald would not approve of such—'

The old woman cut in. 'Mrs Fitzgerald is not here now. This is a different household. And Master Frederick is very handsome, is he not?'

'Oh, yes, but—'

'And you are a very beautiful girl, Anne.' Old Phoebe rose from the bed. 'I shall go now. Take a sip of your wine; it will make you feel better. You will be nice to Master Frederick, Anne, will you not?'

Anne nodded gently but, as the old woman closed the door behind her, she fought back tears. Quickly she got up from the bed and walked to the chest of drawers. She lifted the bumper of wine and took two large gulps. Its fiery taste burned the back of her throat. From somewhere deep inside her, she knew she must find reserves of strength that she had, until this moment, never had need to call upon.

The gentle tap at the door startled her. She took another sip of the wine, dabbed at her lips with the sleeve of her chemise, put down the glass and said in as clear and steady a voice as she could, 'Come in.'

The Old Mill, Itchen Parva

19 June 2010

After Alex had put Anne to bed, she sat with Harry under the old Bramley apple tree down by the stream. His thoughts turned to Pattie Chieveley and Ted, but he did not like to bring up the subject. Instead he asked, 'Will Anne be all right?'

'Oh, I should think so,' said Alex, topping up his glass from the bottle sunk into the long grass at her feet. 'She saw such a lot of things at the fête today and she probably just had a bit of an overload. You know what she's like with things that crawl, fly or scamper.'

'A proper country child,' offered Harry. 'You could get her some chickens. They don't take much looking after. A small coop and a run, that's all. She can feed them before she goes to school and again in the evening. It would give her something to look after.' He paused, then continued enthusiastically, 'Marans. Cuckoo Marans. Now they're sturdy blighters. Or Welsummers—lovely brown eggs.'

Alex grinned at him. 'How come you know so much about chickens?'

'Oh, we had a neighbour who used to have them when I was a kid. I got some pocket money for collecting the eggs.'

'Well, well, well. I never thought of you as a poultry farmer.'

'Oh, there are lots of things about me that you don't know.'

Alex looked a little uneasy.

Harry immediately realised the implication of his remark and made to put her at ease. 'Like the fact that I can recite the entire list of the kings and queens of England from 1066 to the present day.'

Alex threw her head back and laughed. 'You are silly.'

'Silly but brimful of fascinating information.'

She leaned forward and squeezed his hand. 'And the best company since I don't remember when.' She looked up at the sky. 'Sunday tomorrow. The weather's improving. Why don't we go for a picnic? I'll show you where the old Manor House was. Withercombe. There're only a few cottages there now, but the views across the water meadow are good.'

72 Godolphin Street, Portsmouth

16 April 1816

Frederick Carew stood just inside the door of Anne Flint's room, a half-drained bumper of red wine in his hand. His coat and waistcoat were unbuttoned, and the stock at his neck hung loose. Anne thought she detected, for a moment, a look of nervousness upon his face. But the moment quickly passed, and he smiled that disarming smile of his. Realising, instinctively, that she must somehow survive this encounter, Anne stood up, smiled back at him and asked, 'What do you require of me, sir?'

Frederick cleared his throat. 'I gather Old Phoebe has explained the situation to you?'

'She has, sir.'

'And that it will be extremely difficult for me to argue your case, but that, nevertheless, I am prepared to make some endeavours on your account?'

'Yes, sir.'

'You are very beautiful, Anne.'

It was not at all what she had expected, and her colour heightened.

'Perhaps you do not realise how beautiful.'

Anne stood frozen, unable to move. No one had told her before that she was beautiful. Sam had told her she was 'presentable', but that had seemed a grudging comment, and one that was probably offered only to persuade her to go and kiss him behind the stables or down by the chalk stream.

Frederick Carew took the few steps necessary to approach her. She could feel her heart beating in her chest again. He put down his glass upon the chest of drawers and raised his right hand to her face, gently stroking her cheek with the backs of his fingers. He did not speak now, but with his left hand pulled at the ribbon that held the silken cloak about her shoulders. Loosened of its ties, the cloak slid silently to the floor, and Anne stood before him in nothing but the translucent chemise. Drawing on strengths she hardly knew existed, she managed to smile a gentle smile and to avoid wrapping her arms around herself to hide her near-nakedness.

Frederick took off his coat and his waistcoat, and lay them on the chair, gazing at Anne all the while. Then he stepped up to her again and took her in his arms, pressing his lips to hers. Before she had a chance to think further, he had taken hold of the chemise in both hands and lifted it above her head.

'Oh, Anne,' he murmured, 'you really are quite, quite beautiful.' Delicately he traced the outline of her curves with his right forefinger and leaned forward again, feathering her shoulders with soft and gentle kisses.

Anne arched her neck away from him, but then felt a novel sensation of freedom infusing her entire body. It came over her in a great wave that took her completely off guard. She began to breathe more heavily, as did Frederick, his hands exploring her soft young body's graceful curves.

Suddenly, she pulled away from him, gasping for breath. Then, without taking her eyes off him, she slid quickly between the covers of the bed. She thought for a moment that he might be angry, but then he smiled. It was not a wicked smile, but one of excitement and desire. For the first time in her young life, she felt the merest sensation of power.

Frederick took off his breeches and then his shirt. His body was, as the ladies of the household had suspected, a paragon of muscle and sinew. Without pausing he slid in beside her.

The events of the next few hours were to transform the rest of Anne's life.

IT WAS DAYLIGHT when she woke. There was no clock in the room and so she had no idea of the time, save that there was little noise coming from the street below. Silently she eased out from under the sleeping Frederick's arm and slid from the bed. He stirred slightly, but when she had satisfied herself that he was still fast asleep, she hurried across to the window and lifted the curtains a little. It was a clear spring morning and Portsmouth had been freshly rinsed by a shower of rain. She could see the gilded hands glinting on a church tower several streets away: it was half past five o'clock.

Without making a sound, she slipped on the chemise. But where were her clothes—the ones in which she had arrived? Carefully she slid open the drawers of the chest. *Be there, please be there!* she thought. The two upper drawers were empty, save for some faded hanks of cloth. She closed them gently. Master Frederick stirred a little and murmured something inaudible. Anne froze. Then his breathing fell back into a steady rhythm. She opened the larger of the two drawers at the bottom of the chest and— joy!—there was her cloak. The other revealed her dress and undergarments. But where were her boots? She could hardly travel barefoot. Anxious now, she dressed as quickly and as silently as she could. Then she caught sight of Frederick's coat upon the chair, the corner of his pocket book just visible in the inside pocket. Should she do it? Would he still speak up for her to Sir Thomas and Lord Stockbridge? There was no guarantee that he would do so, regardless of her actions. Perhaps it had all been just a ruse to get her to . . . well, she had done that now and would have to take her chance.

She eased the pocket book from its resting place and opened it. Three five-pound notes nestled inside it. She could not take those. A country girl carrying such a large amount of money would arouse much suspicion. Coins. Where were his coins? She felt in the pockets of the coat. Success! A purse! She would not take it; but just a modest amount of the contents—a single gold sovereign, four shillings and eight pence three-farthings. That should be enough to get her on her way. Perhaps he would not even miss them. As she returned the purse to the pocket of the coat, she noticed something underneath the chair. Her boots! She picked them up and tiptoed to the door. As she turned the handle Frederick stirred again, and this time she heard him murmur, 'Anne . . .'

Not pausing to see if he had woken, she slipped through the door, closed it behind her and padded quickly downstairs in her bare feet. Reaching the front door, she then saw the next obstacle in her way: three large bolts. She put down her boots and set to work. She grasped the bottom two and slid them silently to one side, but the uppermost bolt was beyond her reach. She looked about her in the dark hallway; in the shadows stood a mahogany hall chair. She lifted it up and stood it against the door, then reached up and grappled with the bolt. It was stiff, but applying all her strength she managed to pull it free. It shot back against the metal stay with a sharp crack.

Swiftly now she replaced the chair and reached for the doorknob to effect her escape. As her hand began to turn it, so another hand lay upon her own. A spare and bony claw it was. Anne turned to see the form of Mr Pontifex beside her. He was grinning and chuckling to himself. 'Are you going somewhere, Anne?' he asked. 'So early in the morning?'

Mill Cottage, Itchen Parva

20 June 2010

There was plenty to keep Harry awake that Saturday night: his developing relationship with Alex being uppermost in his mind. It was both ironic and sad that what was potentially the most enjoyable prospect in his life for a long time was clouded by the knowledge that Ted Chieveley would soon cease to be the father figure that he had become. And then Harry felt ashamed of dwelling on how the loss of such a man would affect himself rather than Pattie Chieveley. What must it be like for her—watching the man she had loved for four decades gradually disappearing before her eyes?

He turned over and tried to sleep, but there was a coldness about the room that chilled him to the bone. It was June, for heaven's sake, and it had not been a bad day. Why, then, did he feel frozen?

The doorway. It must be the new opening from the bedroom to the bathroom. He had clearly created a draught. And yet he could not feel any air movement, as such. Old houses: that's what it was. They always said that the thick walls in old houses kept them warm in winter and cool in summer.

His mind was whirling, full of thoughts of Alex and Anne, Pattie and Ted. Anne: he would see her today—along with her inseparable companion, Mr Moses. Perhaps today he would get to know her a little better.

THE REMAINS of the Manor House were, as Alex had suggested, just that. There were a few low walls, but they disappeared into the hummocky banks above the river. A hundred yards away three or four cottages—once simple dwellings for artisans and ostlers—sat tidily inside their white picket fences, done up now with window boxes and pretty front gardens replete with hollyhocks and marigolds, snapdragons and tobacco plants.

'Is this it?' asked Harry.

'Yes,' replied Alex. 'I told you there wasn't much.'

'Was it very grand?'

'Apparently. There was a stable block and parkland around it. The river ran through it—there are the water meadows.' Alex pointed to the chalk stream snaking away into the distance.

'How old was it?'

'Well, I think it must have been Elizabethan—with additions, probably.'

Harry shook his head. 'How on earth could they have knocked it down?' He sat down on a grassy knoll just across from the cottages. It was an idyllic spot: rolling Hampshire countryside dotted with clumps of oak and ash trees. The distant sounds of sheep and traffic did little to disturb the peace and calm that pervaded a scene which, but for the absence of the big house, had probably not changed for a century or more.

Alex nodded. 'Nobody wanted to be lumbered with big, old houses that cost a fortune to keep warm and watertight. Did you know that between 1920 and 1955 we lost an average of thirteen country houses a year?'

Harry looked surprised. 'And I thought I was the one with a mind for useless facts.'

Alex shook her head. 'They're not useless. They keep us informed.' She looked at the faint tracery of ruins. 'They teach us a lesson—not to let it happen again.'

Harry sought to lighten her mood. 'It could have been worse, of course. Sir Marcus Carew could have been living here. Just how impossible would he have been then?'

Alex grimaced. 'Yes, there is that, I suppose. We should be grateful for small mercies; but he probably wouldn't have been living in it, anyway. He's only a distant relative of the old squire's. He's a pale shadow, really.'

'Talking of shadows,' said Harry, 'do you believe in ghosts?'

'What on earth brought that on?' asked Alex.

'Just yesterday, when Anne said she saw something at Mill Cottage.'

'Oh, I wouldn't worry about that.'

'Only last night . . . well, it's probably nothing, but I can only describe it as . . . a coldness in my bedroom.'

'You haven't got central heating and it was a clear night,' said Alex matter-of-factly.

'No, it was more than that. There was a real chill about the place. An icy chill. Not a draught; the air was quite still, but really cold.'

Alex looked thoughtful. 'It would make sense, I suppose, wouldn't it?

With what Anne said yesterday. About seeing a woman in white.'

Harry laughed. 'I didn't see a woman in white.'

'No, but Anne thought she did. And why would she say that if she hadn't?'

Harry looked down towards the streamside where Anne was showing wild flowers to Mr Moses. 'Well, she has got a vivid imagination.'

'Imagination, yes. But she doesn't make things up—not in a deceitful way. I thought it was just tiredness, but she really did seem to think she'd seen something in your cottage. She was as white as a sheet.'

'Oh, and there was the voice,' added Harry.

Alex looked confused. 'What voice?'

'Well, when I was knocking out the doorway, I was sure I heard you shout my name, calling goodbye. But you weren't there when I looked out of the window, and then you really did say "goodbye" later. Odd. I didn't gave it a second thought at the time but . . .'

'There is a theory that spirit manifestations occur when the dwelling they inhabit is disturbed in some way.'

'Like me knocking a hole in a wall?'

Alex nodded. 'Exactly like you knocking a hole in a wall.'

'So I've disturbed the spirit of the place?'

'Probably someone who lived there once. Or who died there. It could just be confused. Making its presence felt.'

'I'd never have thought of you as believing in ghosts,' Harry said.

'I'm open-minded. It wouldn't do to say that I don't believe in something just because I've never experienced it, would it?'

'No, I suppose not.'

'So, do *you* believe in them?' asked Alex.

Harry sighed. 'I'm rapidly thinking I'm going to have to.'

72 Godolphin Street, Portsmouth

17 April 1816

Edwin Pontifex could see the terror in Anne Flint's eyes as he grasped her hand on the knob of the door. 'Are you leaving us so soon?' he asked.

Anne looked into his eyes, hoping to see some kind of compassion there. There was none in evidence. Her mind raced. She could not be stopped now. 'I must go,' was all she could stammer. 'I must—'

'But Mistress Phoebe will be expecting to see you when she rises, which will be'—he pulled a small pocket watch from his waistcoat—'within the hour.' He looked pensive, then slipped the watch back into its pocket. 'And what of Master Frederick? Will he not be disappointed that you have left? Is he not about to make amends for your earlier misdeeds?'

'They were not misdeeds! Not mine!' exclaimed Anne.

'But may be perceived as such, as I understand?'

'Yes, but—'

'Then that is the way it shall be. You will find it very difficult to regain your old position. Things change, Anne. The world does not stand still. We can never go backwards.' Pontifex tilted his head so that he appeared even more lopsided than usual. 'I would rather you stayed with us, Anne. You see, Mistress Phoebe will be very cross with me when she discovers that I let you go without saying goodbye to her. She gets very angry with me when things do not go according to plan. I really would rather you stayed.'

Pontifex stretched out a scrawny arm towards the hallway, urging Anne to walk that way rather than through the door and out into the street. He was not a strong man: she could simply have pushed him aside and run away, but something made her hesitate. There he stood, half crouching in the shadows, his expression a mixture of fawning obsequiousness and veiled threats. She saw him now for what he was—an acolyte at the court of Old Phoebe. A dogsbody like herself.

'Why should I stay?' she said at last. 'So that I can be like you?'

Pontifex looked bewildered for a moment, then wounded by her candour.

She continued, 'I am young. I have a life ahead of me. I won't be held back, that I won't, not by the likes of you and Old Phoebe. I may have been bad, I may have done wrong things, but it is not that I am bad, just that . . .' She was lost for words now, unable to articulate her feelings.

'Circumstances got the better of you?' offered the crooked man.

Anne nodded. 'Yes, circumstances . . . that's all.'

Pontifex nodded thoughtfully. 'And you think that running away from here will let you escape a terrible future in a disreputable house, and that when you get to wherever you are going then life will be fine once more and that you will meet the man of your dreams and live happily ever after?'

'I know I cannot hope for that. But I *must* hope for better than this.'

The old man looked crestfallen. 'What about old Pontifex? What's to become of him?'

'Do not try to turn me from my will. You have had your life and chosen what to do with it. Mine is just beginning and I will not be'—she sought for the word and finally it came—'diverted. No. I will not be diverted.'

The words echoed around the empty hallway, causing Pontifex to raise his crooked finger to his lips, encouraging her to speak more softly. 'And what will you do for money,' he asked, 'to escape from this—' he looked about him '—this den of iniquity?'

'I have sufficient for my needs.'

Pontifex regarded her quizzically. 'But when you came here yesterday you had nothing. No coach fare. Not a farthing for a piece of bread.'

Anne looked nervous. 'I found some.'

Pontifex nodded. 'In the pocket book of Master Frederick?'

Anne could feel the coins in the pocket of her coat. Now she withdrew them and held them out in her hand. 'One sovereign, four shillings and eightpence three-farthings. I done my sums.'

'A good night's work,' confirmed Pontifex.

At this, Anne threw the coins at him and they clattered from his cowering form onto the bare floorboards at his feet. 'I ain't for buying. I took them for my coach fare, that was all. Master Frederick had his way with me; I only wanted to go home.' There were tears of anger and frustration in her eyes now. In a world where she had done her best to please those whom she had served—last night making the ultimate sacrifice—it seemed that no one would take her for what she was: an honest, simple girl who wanted a better life than the one dealt to her by the unfeeling hand of fate.

Fighting to hold back tears, Anne now elbowed Pontifex aside and made for the door again. At that moment a voice boomed from upstairs, 'Mr Pontifex? Is that you? What is the commotion?' Old Phoebe had been woken by the disturbance and had come to discover its origins.

Anne's hand was on the doorknob now, and again she felt a bony claw grasp it. In desperation she turned to push Pontifex away again, but saw that he was holding out his other hand towards her.

'You are right not to steal, Anne. It can only lead to trouble. I will replace the money. Take these instead.' He lifted up Anne's hand and dropped into it four silver crowns. 'They should help you to get home.' He gave her a flicker of a smile and added, 'And without causing too much suspicion.'

Anne did not speak but her wide-eyed expression showed both her aston-ishment and her gratitude.

'Mr Pontifex!' The strident voice echoed again down the stairway and across the hall.

'Now go,' he said, opening the door onto the street.

The morning light flooded in so strongly that the old man had to shield his eyes. Anne, too, was dazzled by its brilliance, and the heady aroma of morning air, horse dung, sea salt and reawakening life. She turned on the top step. 'Thank you,' she murmured. 'Thank you so very much. I shall . . .' She paused for the briefest of moments. 'I shall never forget you.'

Pontifex smiled and shook his head. 'Best that you do, my dear.'

And then she heard footsteps coming down the stairs and the rustle of petticoats. Without a backward glance, she ran down the steps and away through the carts and the carters, the sailors and the street urchins, in the direction of what she hoped was the coach to Winchester.

The Streamside, Hampshire

20 June 2010

'Do you remember when you were like that?' asked Alex.

'Oh, yes. Sometimes I think I still am like that,' confirmed Harry.

'Me, too.'

They were watching Anne, lost in her own little world with Mr Moses, down by the banks of the stream. At that moment she was oblivious to them and everything around her, except for that which was a part of her present, intimate world. A look of intense concentration was upon her face as she picked first one wild flower, then another, and showed them to her canine companion, identifying them one after another in her clear little voice, 'This is water figwort. Can you see its tiny pockets? And this one is water mint. Here you are, Mr Moses: smell it. Isn't it lovely? Mummy says it's good with roast lamb. I'm not sure about that.'

'Do you worry about her?' asked Harry.

'Doesn't every parent? I worry about her crossing the road, about getting on at school, about . . . well . . . just about everything, I suppose. I worry more than anything over whether she'll grow up a balanced child. With a sense of proportion. Fairness. With a sense of values.'

'Like yours?'

'I suppose.'

They were leaning back against the trunk of an old oak tree, each at an angle, so that they spoke without looking at one another.

'Do you want her to have what you had as a child?' asked Harry.

'Some of the things I had. Loving parents. A happy home. I'd quite like her to have siblings. One day . . .' She quickly changed the subject. 'What about you? What would you wish for a child?'

'Security. Knowing that when you came home everything would be the same as it was when you left. That life would not change too soon, too suddenly. That your parents would be happy with each other—and with you.'

'For ever?'

'For ever.'

'That's a bit of a tall order nowadays, isn't it?'

'I guess.'

'So was your childhood secure?' asked Alex.

'It was in that I knew we wouldn't starve. My parents stuck together for as long as they could—for my sake, I suppose—but they weren't happy. I'm not sure that it was a good thing that they clung on for so long. But then, when is a good time to break up?'

'Did it scar you—emotionally?'

Harry thought for a moment. 'I'd like to say "no", but that wouldn't really be true. It made me wonder if I could have done anything to stop it.'

'But how could you? It was their relationship, not yours.'

'But I was a part of it. It knocked my confidence.'

Alex looked at him sympathetically.

'It's a funny thing, confidence,' Harry continued. 'You see people who have it in spades—like Marcus Carew—and you wonder where they get it from. Then there's Muggins here who has to grope for every ounce of the stuff. Pathetic, really. Lack of confidence is something I wouldn't wish on anybody. At best it's debilitating, and at worst a crashing bore. People tire of it, assume it's some kind of affectation, but in reality it's a pain in the arse.'

'Nature or nurture?' asked Alex.

'Nurture, I think. It's like an incurable disease contracted early in life.' He thought for a moment, then said, 'Oh, I don't know; perhaps you are born with it. One thing I do know is that it never goes away.'

'Does it affect your . . . relationships?'

Harry grinned, ruefully. 'When everything's going well it seems to fade away. But when things start to go wrong and you're powerless to do anything, it comes roaring in at you and you realise it has just been waiting to pounce.'

'Is that what happened when Serena left?'

Harry nodded. 'Like a raging tide. Like I said—pathetic.'

'Not really. It just shows that you're a sensitive soul.' She smiled at him. 'I rather like sensitive souls.'

Harry laughed. 'That's a relief. You seem to have found one here. Sensitive to mood, sensitive to changes in atmosphere, sensitive to . . . ghosts?'

'Of the past?'

'I hope not. Time to move on.' He turned to Alex. 'At the right pace.'

Alex leaned round the tree and kissed him on the cheek. 'Go and talk to Anne while I get the picnic ready.'

Harry got up and ambled down to the stream. Anne looked up as he approached. 'Mr Moses likes the smell of mint.'

'Good,' said Harry, dropping down on the grass beside her. 'So do I.'

He put out his hand and stroked Mr Moses on the nose. 'I'm sure you'll have a real dog one day.'

'Oh, Mr Moses is real; it's just that he's different real.'

'So what sort of dog would you like—when you get one? Large or small?'

Anne thought for a moment. 'Small. Then he wouldn't get in Mummy's way or knock me over. I like Mrs Armstrong's dog but he's a labrador and a bit excitable. Sometimes he can barge into you and it really hurts.'

'Who's Mrs Armstrong?'

'My teacher. She's very nice. She knows about wild flowers, too.'

Harry watched as Anne gathered buttercups and clover, plantains and water mint into a bunch. She was a pretty child, her red hair glinting in the sunshine. Then she surprised him by asking quite clearly and levelly, 'Do you like Mummy?'

He hesitated for a moment, then said, 'Yes. I like her very much.'

'Enough to marry her?'

'Well . . . who knows what might happen? But I like her very much.'

Anne was looking him straight in the eye now. 'But you'd need to love her to marry her?'

'Yes. Of course.'

'Do you? Do you love her?'

Harry looked thoughtful. 'What would you like me to say to that?'

'I'd like you to say that of course you love her.'

'You wouldn't mind?'

Anne shook her head.

He found it hard to suppress a smile. 'Well, then, you won't be disappointed when I tell you that I do.'

'Good.' She turned back to Mr Moses. Then, having considered her next question, she looked at Harry again and added, 'Are you *in* love with her? Because that's different, isn't it?'

Harry said nothing for a few moments and then confirmed, 'Yes, I am.'

Content, the girl returned to her flowers, but Harry made to attract her attention once more. 'There is one thing,' he said.

Anne looked up.

'I want to keep it a secret just a little bit longer.'

Anne nodded. 'OK,' she said. 'I can keep a secret.' Then she picked up Mr Moses and walked up the grassy bank towards her mother.

Portsmouth

17 April 1816

In spite of the early hour, the streets of Portsmouth were already astir, for sailing ships begin their voyages according to tides, not clocks. Tars with shiny broad-brimmed hats swarmed over the streets, weaving their way, bags on shoulders, between horses and carts, costermongers and carriages, towards the vessels packed along the quayside, each straining at their thick ropes and hawsers, anxious to be away. As anxious as Anne herself. Each ship bound for heaven knows where, just like herself. Everywhere there seemed to be parallels with her own situation—the unpredictability that lay in front of her was overwhelming.

Anne pushed on through the melee as the street cries fell upon her ringing ears: 'Hot pies!', 'Carry your bags, milady?', 'Lemons! Oranges! Fresh from Spain!' Realising how hungry she was, Anne slipped her hand into the pocket of her cloak to check on the safety of the four crowns. They were still there. She would break into one of them to eat, for already she was feeling light-headed. But an orange would not suffice. She bought, instead, from a sturdy youth with a tray of hot pies and felt herself salivating at the prospect.

Anne found a corner against a warehouse wall, where a stone bollard provided a welcome seat. Putting the crisp pastry to her lips, she tilted back her head and savoured the warm and nourishing gravy as it ran over her tongue. Eagerly she devoured both pastry and meat, feeling the strength returning to her body.

She needed a plan. What would she do? She could not go straight back to the Manor House—assuming that she would be able to work out how to get there—as there was little likelihood of her being accepted with open arms. And there would be questions. All kinds of questions: about Eleanor, and Mr Lavallier—if they knew of him.

A coaching inn. That was what she needed to find. If she could locate a coach, journeying through the streets of Portsmouth, she could follow it to its destination and board a carriage there. Yes, that was what she would do. The crowds were becoming so thick that the carriages were compelled to travel slowly—if she walked briskly, she could just about keep up with one, provided she did not trip over her skirts.

She saw coaches now, but they were travelling in different directions. Which were coming into town and which departing? She looked around for inspiration. Standing a short way off, outside the Fountain Inn, was a man reading a paper.

'Excuse me, sir . . .'

The man lowered his paper and peered at her over his spectacles.

'Please could you tell me which coaches is coming into town and which is going out?'

The man—perhaps in his late sixties, portly and clearly well-to-do, since his coat was well cut and his top hat brushed—pondered for a moment, endeavouring to reconcile the courtliness of the young woman's dress with her apparent lack of the finer points of grammar. But, sensing a maiden in distress, he smiled at her regardless and enquired where was it she wished to go.

'Winchester, sir.'

'Now there is a coincidence; for I myself am bound for Winchester and will be happy to escort you to the coach. Do you have a ticket?'

'No, sir. But I do not want to be any trouble. I am happy travelling alone.'

The man shook his head. 'I think that inadvisable. Portsmouth is full of blackguards and drunken sailors, even at this early hour. Better that you are in company.' And then, seeing Anne's discomfort, he added, 'I can assure you that I will make no demands upon you, for I have my paper and do not wish to impose. But you have no ticket, you say?'

'No, I do not. Not yet.'

'Why then, come inside the Fountain Inn. Coaches for Winchester depart from here.'

Anne thanked the gentleman and gave a little bob before entering the Fountain Inn and purchasing a ticket from the clerk behind the coaching desk. He hardly looked at her, which came as a great relief, and said nothing as she handed over an entire crown to pay for her journey.

'The Regulator leaves at eight o'clock, miss,' he said. 'You can wait in there'—he indicated a small room to the side of the taproom—'or else take the air and come back at half past seven o'clock when we starts loading luggage.' He looked up from his ledger and took in the fact that Anne would not be needing to load any luggage. 'Five minutes to eight o'clock, then,' he muttered, and went back to his ledger.

That was it; she had done it. She had booked her passage as far as Winchester. During the course of her journey back, she would have to work out what to do on her arrival. Where to go and who to see. For the life of her she had absolutely no idea.

Anne spent the better part of two hours outdoors rather than confine herself to the taproom. The old gentleman was true to his word: apart from ensuring that she was not bothered by sailors or tradesmen, he kept a discreet silence, engrossed in his paper, while Anne sat upon a wooden bench.

Soon the coach arrived, and once the passengers had been disgorged and their luggage had been handed down to porters eager at the prospect of a tip, the coach was swept out and made ready for the return journey. When the horses had been changed, the postboy doffed his hat to indicate that all was ready, and the old man held out his arm to escort Anne across the cobbles, helping her up the two steps into the coach. Having confirmed that she was perfectly happy, he took off his hat and placed it on the seat beside him, before resuming the scrutiny of his paper.

The two of them were quite alone inside the carriage on the first leg of their journey—to the Red Lion in Fareham—and, soon enough, to the sound of a yelping horn, they drew to a halt outside the inn. Her companion turned to Anne and said, 'We shall have company now, I suspect.' The old man took out his pocket watch and checked the time. 'Not too long now. My brother will send his chaise to meet the coach at Winchester. Perhaps I might be able to offer you passage should you be travelling in the same direction?'

'Oh, no. I am not sure—'

'It really will be no trouble, should you care to tell me in which direction you are to travel onwards.' Then the old man paused and smote his knee. 'But, forgive me, I omitted to introduce myself. My name is Nicholas Stockbridge. Brother of the earl. Perhaps you have heard of him?'

The Old Mill, Itchen Parva

20 June 2010

'Can I get her some chickens then?' Harry asked Alex, once Anne had gone to bed and the two of them were alone in the kitchen.

Alex gave him an old-fashioned look. 'Oh, go on then. But not too many.'

'Great! I'll have a scout round and see what I can find.'

'But what about a hen house? Don't we need a coop or something?'

'Just leave it all to me.'

'But it will cost quite a lot—'

'Hey! Did you hear me?' admonished Harry. 'I said, leave it all to me. A present for Anne. It's time she had something alive to look after.'

Alex frowned. 'Mr Moses is alive to her.'

'Yes, but looking after a stuffed dog is not the same as looking after—'

'Unstuffed chickens?'

'Quite. They'll be good for her, show her what real animals need—regular care and attention.' He saw the look of concern on Alex's face. 'Not too much, though; that's why chickens will be perfect, and at least they produce something—unlike a rabbit or a guinea pig. Oh, and chickens don't bite.'

'No,' agreed Alex, 'but they peck.'

'Dirt and grass, not humans . . . Well,' reflected Harry, 'not very often.'

'They could have your eye out,' countered Alex.

Harry looked at her and saw that she was laughing. 'Do you remember when your mother used to say that? When you were playing with anything remotely pointed: "Don't do that, you'll have your eye out"?' Then he noticed she had gone quiet. 'Oh, sorry. Did I . . .?'

'No. I lost my mum quite early, that's all. Brought up by Dad. She never had the chance to offer me any advice—about sharp objects, puberty or . . . men.' Then she saw Harry's discomfort. 'Oh, don't worry! I got over it years ago. The wounds have mended. I've had others to occupy me since.'

'Like losing your husband?' It came out unbidden. For so long it had been the elephant in the room and now he had let it loose, thoughtlessly.

'Yes.'

It was too late now to retract. 'You never mention him.'

'Don't I?'

Harry shook his head. 'I don't want to pry or anything.'

'No. You ought to know. Come on, let's take a bottle down to the stream. It's warm enough outside and I can hear Anne from there if she needs me.'

They strolled down the garden in silence. Harry was nervous as to what he was about to hear, wishing that he had not brought up the subject; and Alex was wondering how best to explain things.

An old wooden table and two chairs sat underneath one of the willow trees. Alex poured them each a glass of cool white wine and leaned back in her chair. 'You didn't read about it in the paper then?' she asked.

'No. Well, not originally. But Rick found an old one the other day and showed it to me.'

'Oh. I see.'

Harry made to explain, a hint of anxiety in his voice. 'He just came across it. What he really found—in his grandfather's chest—was an advertisement for the sale of this place. His family used to own it, years back, and his grandfather had cut out the page and kept it. The story of your . . . court case . . . was on the back. It was just an odd coincidence.'

Alex nodded. 'I saw the advert when I read the paper. I took it as a sign, I suppose. A happy coincidence, a pointer as to where I should go and what I should do. You know: when God closes a door he opens a window, that sort of thing. I—that is, we—wanted a fresh start.' She took a sip of her wine. 'Here seemed as good a place as any and, when I saw it, everything just fell into place; well, as much as anything could back then.'

Harry waited for a moment and then asked, 'So who suggested that . . . well, that you had a hand in James's suicide?'

'Some old biddy who used to dote on him. He used to help her with her legal affairs after her husband died. She didn't like me at all. Used to call James up at every hour of the day and night. Got very shirty when I answered the phone and suggested to her that it would be kinder to call him in business hours between Monday and Friday.'

'Were she and James—well, you know . . .?'

'Oh, heavens, no! She was far too old, not at all his type.'

'So when did . . .?'

'James's illness start? About four years after Anne was born. It was little things at first—lapses of memory. Disorientation. He'd be there but his mind would suddenly be elsewhere. The progression was fairly rapid in the early stages. And then came the worst bit of all—the personality change.' Alex took a large gulp of wine and put down her glass on the table. 'He started to get violent. Lashing out for no apparent reason. I can tell you that a thirteen-stone man can't half pack a punch. I used to lay witch hazel in by the crate. But then I really started to worry that he might hurt Anne. I thought it would be best if he went into a home, but I just couldn't bring myself to do it. Before I could work out what to do, he took his own life.'

'At home?'

'Yes. That's when I realised that he must have known what was happening. That he didn't feel he could go on.'

'And Anne?'

'She went into herself. Became very self-reliant. She still is, I suppose. But I worried. Bottling things up is not a good thing—especially for a child.'

'How could anyone think that you were involved with James's death? I mean, for it to come to court?'

'Oh, James's client was very persuasive, and once the police become involved they have to satisfy themselves that there are no real grounds for prosecution.'

'So why did they prosecute?'

Alex shrugged. 'Who knows? I can tell you that it was the most dreadful thing that's ever happened to me. It's only now that I'm beginning to get myself together again.' She smiled ruefully. 'You're taking on a basket case.'

Harry reached across the table and squeezed her hand. 'Oh, I don't think so.' Then he asked 'How did he . . . I mean, what did he use . . .?'

'Sleeping tablets. I came home with Anne and found him sitting in a chair with the pill bottles beside him.'

'So you had an alibi anyway?'

'Not exactly. I came home at lunch time on my own to check that he was OK. That was enough to make them think that it was possible that I'd helped him.'

Harry got up from his chair, walking over to the stream. 'Do you think it's ever acceptable to help somebody to end their life?'

Alex stood up and walked over to him. 'No, I don't.'

He turned to look at her. 'Not even when you love them more than anyone else in the world and you're watching them suffer, knowing that it will end in a painful death?'

'No, not even then. It is agonising, more painful than I can begin to tell you, and the most heartbreaking experience in the world next to losing a child. But I don't think we can play God under any circumstances.'

Winchester

17 April 1816

The sky was darkening as they reached Winchester and, as the coach pulled into the yard of the Royal Hotel, there was much commotion. Luggage was unloaded, ostlers came and unhitched the steaming team, and passengers disembarked from up on the box and inside the coach, assisted by the postboy.

The old man turned to instruct Anne to follow him, but she was not to be seen. He shrugged and went into the hotel to enquire as to the whereabouts of his transport. The landlord explained that the earl's chaise had been delayed. A horseman had come to apologise; some family problem had meant that the household had been thrown into disarray. The old man frowned. This was odd: his brother was a man who prided himself on his efficiency. He went into the hall of the hotel and ordered a pint of ale.

ANNE USED THE CONFUSION of the coach's unloading to slip into the shadows, and from there edged her way out of the yard and onto the street. But which way to go? Some way from the hotel, seeing a man walking towards her, she lifted her arm to attract his attention and asked, 'Excuse me, sir. Could you point me in the direction of Withercombe?'

The man smiled and lifted his hat. 'Of course. When you come to the end of the street here, you will find that the road forks. Take the right fork, and then after a mile take the left fork. Keep straight along that road and it will lead you, eventually, to Withercombe.'

Anne made a small bob and said, 'Thank you.'

The man raised his hat once more, then a look of concern crossed his face. 'But it is seven miles. Surely you are not to walk all that way?' He looked up at the sky. 'It will likely rain before too long.'

Anne smiled, her relief palpable. 'Thank you, sir. I shall not mind the rain now that I know I am on the right road.' And with that she turned and walked off in the direction that had been pointed out to her. The man watched her go and shook his head. The distant rumble of thunder confirmed his suspicions that the young woman was in for a soaking.

Anne had gone a little over a mile before the rain started. The high road had become a track, wide enough for only a single coach—not that many came this way—and there were occasional passing places for farm carts and teams of horses. The gently rolling Hampshire downland to right and left, emerald in its spring livery, seemed to be nudging her on, and then she saw the river. Her river. The chalk stream, the River Itchen, snaking its way across the meadows, teasing the long wands of willows that trailed across its shimmering surface and singing now with the sound of rain. The acrid tang of freshly moistened earth came to her nostrils. This was the smell of the countryside she was used to: of crushed grass and bruised leaves, of river water and morning rain.

She did not mind the rain at first. It refreshed her and seemed to be washing away the shocking events of the previous day. For they were indeed shocking. She had felt brave at the time, determined to survive the ordeal. But now, in the cold and rain-soaked light of day, came the terrible dawning of reality. That only yesterday she had witnessed the death of her one true friend. That she had been run away with, escaped from the evil Lavallier, fallen into the clutches of Old Phoebe and, as for the night and Master Frederick . . . It was at this point in her recalling of events that her emotions overcame her and she collapsed sobbing on a fallen tree trunk by the banks of the river, as the rain beat down upon her. What was to become of her? Where did she think she was going? And what would happen when she got there? Did she really think that they would welcome her at the Manor House? Eleanor's death would surely be known now, and her own disappearance in some way linked with it. They must have found her body down by the river. And her own book. It would be lying near the river bank, for that was where she had rested it when they were changing clothes. In the rush to mount the horses and be away, she had not picked it up and transferred it into the pocket of her new garment. *My book and Eleanor's body* . . . the words kept turning over and over in her mind.

Perhaps Mrs Fitzgerald would understand. Would help her. But Mrs Fitzgerald had clearly been exasperated by her recent actions. Why else would she have lectured her the previous morning and forbidden her from going out? And yet she had defied her and taken off without asking.

Oh, why had she done it? Why could she not have realised that her life at the Manor House was a fortunate one? That Sam was her sort of boy and not some dreamed-of highwayman who would whisk her away? She had indeed been whisked away, and look where it had led.

On she trod, with faltering steps, getting colder and colder. She could feel the rain—growing heavier by the minute—penetrating her clothes now. Soon she would be soaked through, and already the weight of the saturated garments was beginning to tire her.

Ahead of her there was a wooden finger post, pointing the way to somewhere. Eventually, she reached it and, shielding her eyes, read the two names—'Martyr Worthy' to the left and 'Alresford' to the right. There was no mention of Withercombe.

Which fork to take? Which was nearest to Withercombe? Martyr Worthy or Alresford? Think! She must try to remember the man's instructions. Had she turned to the right or to the left at the last fork? Right! She had turned right—she could remember that quite clearly. She must now turn to the left.

Her head bowed against the rain, she pushed forward in the direction of Alresford. She had walked just a few hundred yards before her head began to spin and the ground to rise upwards.

Within moments the rain had ceased but, by that time, Anne was no longer aware of the vagaries of the weather.

The Manor House, Withercombe

21 April 1816

Jacob Palfrey had been every bit as troubled by Anne's disappearance as Sam the stable lad, though he did not give much away to his friend. He found Sam this April morning, mucking out the stables. Sam looked up from his task and enquired, 'You be not working this morning then?'

'Father is gone to Winchester with cloth. I cannot work the mill alone.'

Sam scraped at the dung that clung to the floor of the stable. 'Well, I have no time to stop. The master is to go by carriage to see Lord Stockbridge at noon and I must ready the horses.'

Jacob looked about him. 'I see no horses.'

Sam stood up and stretched his aching back. 'They be tethered by the coach house.' He nodded in the direction of the end of the stable yard.

'Ready for harnessing.' He put down the long-handled shovel and picked up the wicker basket of dung, walking out of the stable and round to the back of the building where he added it to the heap of straw and equine ordure.

Jacob followed him. 'No more news?'

'Not until the master returns.'

'You think then we shall know more?'

'Only if he cares to tell Mr Jencks of any developments.' Having emptied the basket, Sam walked back to the stable and hung it from a hook on the wall, before crossing to the coach house to harness Leger and Alderney. Jacob followed him like a spaniel.

'You can help me pull this out if you have nothing else to do,' instructed Sam, indicating the chaise that nestled, gleaming, in the end coach house, alongside a larger, monogrammed carriage.

The two horses tossed their heads as Sam fastened bits and bridles, collar harnesses and traces. Looking on at this strange and confusing arrangement of leather and brass that Sam handled with a deftness born of habit, the miller's son could not help but be impressed, though nothing on earth would have caused him to acknowledge the fact. His own understanding of horsemanship stretched no further than harnessing his father's cob between the shafts of the simple cart that took their cloth to market.

At the sound of footsteps and general commotion at the archway that led from the Manor House to the stables, Jacob melted into the shadows and left his companion to hold the horses' bridles while Mr Jencks and Sir Thomas crossed to the chaise. Sir Thomas had on his best tailcoat and Timothy Jencks his day livery: this was an outing of some note, clearly.

'Sam,' acknowledged Sir Thomas. 'All ready?'

'Yes, sir,' confirmed the boy.

The baronet mounted the chaise, cane in hand, heaving himself around until he was comfortable. The horses shifted their weight and blew heavily.

Timothy Jencks stepped up to the box and took the reins. 'Just hold for a moment, Sam,' he instructed. 'We have another passenger.'

Sam looked questioningly at the groom.

'Master Frederick is home and he is to accompany the master.'

At that moment, across the yard, strode a fair-haired young man, dressed in a long green coat and carrying in his hand a tall hat and a pair of yellow leather gloves. He nodded at Sam. 'All right, Sam?'

Sam felt surprised that the baronet's son should have remembered his name. Master Frederick had been up in London at his uncle's chambers for almost a year now. What could have brought him back to Withercombe? His love of the town and all it had to offer was well known. This was a courtesy visit, obviously. Either that or he had come to ask his father for money. That was what all sons of rich gentlemen did; it was well known.

Sir Thomas coughed loudly and Master Frederick was dissuaded from any further conversation with the stable lad. Instead, he nodded resignedly at Sam and sat down opposite his father, who took his cane and tapped smartly upon the polished woodwork, at which signal Timothy Jencks urged the horses out of the yard and away down the drive.

BY THE END of the day, Sam had news for his friend. At the Bluebell Inn, over a half-pint of ale, he told Jacob all that he knew. The crumbs of gossip that Timothy Jencks had let drop were few in number and they did not concern Anne. The story was that Lady Eleanor had been going to elope with a man called Lavallier. A man who had, since that day, completely vanished. Just like Anne.

St Jude's School, Winchester

21 June 2010

'Just over three weeks to go, thank God.' Rick dumped a heap of exercise books on the table in the staff room and took from Harry's proffered hand the mug of coffee that was waiting for him. 'Christ, you look knackered!' was his secondary remark, as he sat down in a chair.

'No. You mean "Thank you for the coffee", I think.'

'That as well. But you do look knackered. Not sleeping?'

'Not much, no.'

Rick grinned. 'All loved up?'

'No! Haunted.' Harry slumped into the chair next to Rick's. 'There's something going on in that house of mine and I don't know what it is. Cold winds. Draughts. I've never really thought much about ghosts—or poltergeists—but I am beginning to . . .'

'Is it menacing?' Rick leaned forward.

'No. At least, I don't think so. It's just . . . well, a presence I suppose. I did think I saw something out of the corner of my eye when I was knocking a hole from the bedroom to the bathroom to make a new doorway. And I thought I heard a voice, too, calling my name. But nothing since then.'

Rick looked sceptical. 'Are you sure you're not being a bit fanciful? I mean, you have got a lot going on in your life at the moment—new house, new relationship. It could just be cold feet.'

'At the moment it's cold everything,' replied Harry, frowning. 'And I'm not fanciful. There's a real chill about the cottage—upstairs, anyway—and it wasn't there before. And Alex's little girl, Anne, was convinced that she saw something. A lady, she said: a lady in white.'

'Sounds like a ghost to me. Perhaps you'd better have it exorcised.'

'Oh, for goodness' sake. This isn't a movie!'

'No! I'm serious,' Rick said. 'You can have things like this sorted out. There was a piece in our parish magazine—'

Harry looked incredulous. 'You read your parish magazine?'

'Not me. Rachel. Tilly goes to Sunday school . . . Anyway, apparently every diocese actually does have somebody whose job it is to go to houses or . . . buildings . . . or whatever, and deal with, you know, visitations.'

'Well, that's a relief.'

'So you'll do it then?'

'I mean it's a relief to know that it's just not my imagination.'

Rick took a large gulp of the coffee. 'It's something the Church does and they do it more often than you'd think. I'd seriously consider it if I were you. That way you might get some sleep at night. Or at least, if you didn't sleep, it would be due to doing more exciting things.'

'Cheeky bugger,' said Harry.

'So, what's the latest?' asked Rick.

'If you're going to ask for a progress report every time we meet, I'm going to stop talking to you,' said Harry.

'Just interested, that's all. Just keen for you to be happy.'

'Well, we spoke about the newspaper clipping. Eventually.'

'And you're convinced that she's innocent?'

Harry lowered his voice to a whisper. 'Well, of course she was innocent. It was some jealous old biddy who had a crush on James—her late husband—apparently. Just muck-raking. She really put Alex through it.'

'And the Old Mill? Did she know it was in the same paper?' Rick asked.

'Yes. She saw the advert too, apparently, when she was reading the piece about the case. Thought it was divine intervention.'

'There's rather a lot of divine intervention in your life at the moment, isn't there?'

'Rather too much if you ask me,' confirmed Harry. 'You've heard about Ted Chieveley?'

'Yes. What a bugger.' Rick threw Harry a sympathetic glance. 'Bit of a coincidence, that happening to Alex's husband and now to Ted. History repeating itself.' He drained his mug and got up to go. 'Oh, I almost forgot. I've been delving around a bit more in my grandfather's trunk. Just a tick . . .' He walked over to the row of lockers arranged along one wall, pulled open the door of the one marked 'R. Palfrey, Mathematics', and withdrew from the top shelf a small and battered book, which he tossed casually in Harry's direction. 'Here you are,' he said. 'Some kind of notebook. Kept by one of my ancestors—Jacob Palfrey, I think his name was. I haven't really had much of a chance to read it. The writing's a bit hard to fathom, but you never know, there might be something interesting in there.'

Mill Cottage, Itchen Parva

24 April 1816

'I still think we should tell the squire,' said William Palfrey. ' 'Twill not be long before he finds out and then we shall be in trouble.'

With a note of impatience in her voice, Agnes Palfrey addressed her husband, 'And what do you suppose would have happened? What could the squire have done that we have not?'

The miller shook his head. 'There is trouble here. They has been looking for yon maiden for a week now. Vanished, she has, they thinks. Into thin—'

'Oh, do stop, William. 'Twas you who found her, I admit, but 'twas both of us who gave her shelter. And we cannot know for certain who she is . . .'

'That we do, woman. 'Tis the maid from the Manor House as sure as sure. Clothing of a lady and hands of a housemaid. 'Tis plain to see.'

'And a human being for all that. When you found her, she had hardly a breath left in her body. Of course you did right by bringing her here. There will be plenty of time to tell the squire once we know she is well enough. The fever is passing now. We must build up her strength, and then she can answer the questions she will surely be asked.'

'And if we are discovered?'

'If we are discovered, we will explain that we have done what anyone with plain decency would have done—brought a stranger back to life from the brink of death. And that is no crime. Besides, we are far enough away from the Manor House to keep the matter from those who live and work there.'

'They will find out, mark my words.'

'Not if we keep our peace. They has no reason to come this way.'

'And what of Jacob? And the stable boy at the Manor—Sam?'

'Jacob has been told that should he breathe a word of what has occurred to anyone at the Manor House, then he can consider that there is no longer a roof over his head here.'

At this the miller shrugged and left the room, muttering. He was not happy, but he was wise enough to know that should he cross his wife, his life would be even more uncomfortable than if he were to cross the squire. He went back to the mill and his hammers, but even the sound of their rhythmic thumping could not erase from his mind the worry of his discovery.

He had been journeying back from Winchester with an empty cart, alone. The rain had been so heavy that his head was bowed low under the oilskin that kept out the worst of the weather. At the Martyr Worthy junction, he had noticed what he thought was a grey-black bundle of discarded clothing upon the verge. Irritably, he had pulled on the reins and stopped the horse, who did not even try to pull at the grass as the rain pelted down.

Alighting from the cart, he had walked over to the bundle and pulled at the cloth, starting when his actions revealed a pale and rain-washed face. Swiftly he had lifted up the crumpled body, weighing no more than the clothes themselves it seemed, and carried it across to the cart. He was far from certain that the young girl—for it was a girl, he could see that now—was alive.

He had laid her gently in the cart, immediately behind the box where he sat and where she would be sheltered from the rain, pulling the tarpaulin he kept to protect his cloth from foul weather over her. Whipping the reins across the horse's back, he had travelled now at a brisk trot in the direction of the mill.

Agnes Palfrey had been quite clear what they should do. While most would have sent for the doctor, it was her opinion that such an action would, in all probability, lead to problems, not to say expense. If this young girl was who they thought she was, then taking her up to the Manor House and exposing her to the squire would, like as not, result in serious consequences.

The girl had a fever. But Agnes Palfrey had sat with enough of her relations to know what to do in the case of a fever. She would minister. William could complain all he liked, but the girl was young and healthy—if a little frail—and would, with God's help, come through.

SEVEN DAYS after they had found her, Anne opened her eyes and took in her surroundings. Agnes Palfrey was by her side at the time. At first came the disorientation, then the fear, and finally the insistence on rising, dressing and going on her way. This sequence of events was rapidly quashed by Agnes who, sensing the likelihood of such a reaction, had taken care to remove all traces of Anne's clothing, so that all she had to protect her modesty was the cotton nightdress in which she had slept.

'But how long . . .?' asked Anne feebly.

'A week. Seven long days you have been here.'

'But where . . .?'

'The cottage. At the mill. The fulling mill. I am Mrs Palfrey. My husband William it was who found you. Lying by the Winchester road.'

Anne sat up and her eyes began to fill with tears as the realisation of her plight flooded over her.

'Now, now. There is no need for that.'

'Oh, but, Mrs Fitzgerald—'

'Mrs Fitzgerald will be told when the time is right.'

'Does anyone know I am here?'

'No one except William and myself, and our son Jacob, who has been sworn to secrecy.'

'But he knows Sam, the stable boy and—'

'And should he breathe a word to anyone, he knows that the wrath of his mother is akin to the wrath of God. He will tell no one.'

Anne flopped back onto the pillow and murmured, 'I fear I have been very wicked. I do not know as I shall be forgiven.' Her face was white, and her auburn hair framed it so that it seemed to have been carved from alabaster.

'It is the way of the world,' said Agnes softly, 'that pretty young girls is taken advantage of.' She was speaking to herself as much as to Anne, and she wondered what might have befallen this young maid, so innocent and unworldly. She would keep her peace, for the time being, and help the young girl to mend.

AT THE MANOR HOUSE, Sam listened daily for news of Anne. He could not understand why none was forthcoming. Mr Jencks mentioned the subject not at all, not since the day that he had taken Sir Thomas and Master Frederick over to see Lord Stockbridge. They had all returned with faces as long as a week, and nothing more had been said.

Jacob had stopped coming round to see him now, too. He had no idea why. Normally he enjoyed the sport of baiting Sam, knowing that he was fond of Anne. He would tease him about her, suggest that she had not been the pure young girl that Sam had taken her for. Now he must have grown tired of the pastime. But for him, Sam, nothing would erase Anne from his mind, and her little book would stay safely in the box beneath his truckle bed.

Mill Cottage, Itchen Parva

21 June 2010

Was it, wondered Harry, that because he now had more fulfilling things to occupy him than tracing his ancestry and researching the lives of the saints, they had assumed less importance in his life? The very phrasing of the question in his mind seemed to highlight the truth and it brought him up short. Almost made him laugh out loud at the absurdity of the comparison. How could the past possibly be as important as the present? Or the future? And then he heard his own voice resonating across the classroom of his mind: 'The past informs the present and allows us to put our lives in context.'

Well, maybe. But with the end of term rapidly approaching, the future loomed large in his mind and context seemed irrelevant. What sort of future? With Alex? Doing what? Sighing heavily, he flopped into a chair by the kitchen window and looked out over the botanical garden that passed for a lawn. Time he got down to sorting out the garden as well, except that he rather liked it the way it was. Enjoyed the overgrown loucheness of it all.

Tired after a busy day, he leaned back in the chair and closed his eyes. 'God, grant me a better sleep tonight,' he muttered. 'Free of nature's icy grip.' It must be nature really, mustn't it, rather than supernature? Only people with overly vivid imaginations were in touch with that side of . . . whatever it was. He opened his eyes and glanced up the stairs, then he started. A glimpse of something white. Leaping from the chair he ran to the stairs and bounded up them two at a time to the landing. Nothing. There was absolutely no sign of any lady—in red, white or blue. Lack of sleep had started him hallucinating. Well, if not hallucinating, then making his imagination more vivid.

He showered and changed, then went to the phone to call Alex. But there was no reply. He felt slightly deflated. He'd been unaware that she was going out . . . he checked himself. She did not have to tell him every time she wanted to leave the house.

His mind went back to their last conversation. She had believed that he had accepted her version of events, hadn't she? But had there been a note of distress in her voice? Disappointment that he had questioned her too deeply about where she was when James took his own life, and on her feelings about assisted suicide? He'd only been curious, had only wanted to understand her more. But supposing she had misread that and had thought that he was questioning her honesty? What then?

She would have been hurt. She would have felt a sense of betrayal, that the man she was in a relationship with had needed to make sure that she was not capable of helping her husband to die. And what if she had been? Was it the work of a wicked and evil person to ease the burden of a loved one, knowing that their subsequent departure from this world and absence from your life would leave you feeling so wretched as to be unable to carry on? Surely that was not selfish? Quite the opposite.

His thoughts turned to Pattie and Ted Chieveley, now going through the same situation themselves. He would go round and see them at the weekend. Though what he could say, or in what way he could help, he had no idea. He thought of Pattie and Alex being in the same position. What would Pattie do, compared with what Alex had done?

He flopped into the chair again. Such introspection was getting him nowhere. Alex would be back soon—Anne would have to be put to bed—and then he would slip round to see her. He would reassure her that he was there for her, come what may. The past was the past and they both needed to move on. Could they move on together?

He drummed his fingers on the chair arm, and then remembered the little book that Rick had handed to him in the staff room earlier that day. He went and pulled it from his school bag.

The notebook was covered in a kind of rough felt. On the inside front cover he read: *Jacob Palfrey—His Book. 1815. The Mill on the Itchen, Hantshire.*

The writing was not exactly spidery, but difficult to read, nonetheless.

The spelling was, in some cases, highly original (the schoolmaster in him would take some erasing) and the first entry was typical of such notebooks:

Christemas day—Cold and bitter. River frozen at hedges. With father and mother to church. Mother say fine sermen. To me dull. Home for goose and pudding then out. Hard walking in snow and ice. Geese on field. Watercress beds frozen. Gorse in bloom.

He read on:

Boxing day—To Manor House for meet. Snow and ice still on groun but non so cold. Houns giving much tong. Walked four hour after houns. One fox to ground. One catched. Sam say he kissed house maid under misseltoe yesterday. She clout him round ear. Serve him right. He say I be jelous. Pushed him over in snow and telled him that house maid looking for better than he. Know the girl. Pretty and good spirit. Name of Anne.

27 December—Thaw setting in. Dripping trees. Father starts milling again as river thoring. Do not care to work today. Too much ale on Boxing eve. Father not pleased with me. Says must shape mysel. Mother say nothing. Only four days of year left to see out.

The diary made Harry smile, though so far there was nothing of significance within its covers. What was he hoping for? Revelations? Unlikely. But he would carry on over the next few evenings—dipping into it and deciphering the scrawl. He was not so rooted in the past as he had been before he met Alex and yet the quest for knowledge of his forebears was still there. Perhaps it was the fact that having got as far back as Merrily Flint in 1816, he did not want to leave it at that. The mysterious Merrily Flint. It was the name as much as anything that drove him on.

It was a quarter to eight now. He called Alex again but there was still no reply. He climbed the stairs to his bedroom. He needed to fit an architrave to the new doorway and had still to measure up and order the door itself.

He pulled out his tape measure and jotted down the measurements on the back of an envelope. But, as he turned to go back downstairs, the air that suddenly surrounded him was so cold it was almost palpable, and he gave an involuntary shudder.

'What is it?' he found himself asking out loud. 'What do you want? Who are you and why are you here?'

He did not expect an answer and was not disappointed when none came. Having checked every room on the first floor for open windows, and finding none, he went downstairs again and poured himself a large Scotch. The fire that burned its way down his throat and into the core of his body had the desired effect of settling him.

Standing at the bottom of the stairs, Harry looked up towards the landing and declaimed in a loud voice, 'White lady, pink lady, lady in red, lady of the bloody lake, fast lady, foxy lady . . . will-o'-the-wisp . . . whoever you are—you are perfectly welcome to stay here. I mean you no harm and I am very happy to live with you. Just stop making the place so bloody cold.'

BY NINE O'CLOCK there was still no sign of Alex, and Harry was beginning to tell himself that she was clearly engaged in something that she had omitted to tell him about. It did not matter. He was not her keeper.

Having brought in some timber from the outhouse, he set to and began to construct the architrave round the doorway. By eleven o'clock it was in place, and he had managed to fill in around it with plaster. The dust filled his nostrils and he went out into the garden to inhale a lungful of clear air.

He would wander round to the Old Mill, just to see if she was back. He could see a light in her window. So she must be in. Was her car in the drive? Yes, it was. But parked alongside it was a Porsche Cayenne.

Hatherley

21 April 1816

'Good morning, Sir Thomas.' A nod. 'Sir.' Another nod—one for each of the visitors. It was the second time in a week that the squire had had reason to call on his distant neighbour, and he had scant hopes that on this occasion the atmosphere would be more congenial than on the last, for he feared that the information that Frederick, his younger son, had to impart would be little better received than the tragic news he himself had delivered just a few days earlier. The house steward ushered Sir Thomas Carew and his son into the spacious, black-and-white-tiled hallway. 'If you will just wait here, sir.'

'Of course.' Sir Thomas nodded and the steward retreated into the library, closing the heavy mahogany door behind him. The two men stood in silence. The air was filled with the scent of lily of the valley—Sir Thomas noticed a large bunch on the marble-topped hall table, where a sturdy bracket clock ticked sonorously. By way of avoiding any dialogue with his son, the squire stepped forward to examine the timepiece and to check against it the accuracy of his own pocket watch. Satisfyingly, there was barely half a minute between them, and the squire slipped his half-hunter back into his pocket and patted it securely in place.

At that moment, the door of the library opened and the steward declared, 'His lordship will see you now, sir . . . sir.' With a modest bow he held open the library door and ushered in the two uneasy gentlemen, having taken from them their walking canes and headwear.

Both men were relieved when the earl bade them sit opposite him on a gilt sofa, while he himself perched elegantly on the front edge of a matching fauteuil. Lord Stockbridge came straight to the point: 'I gather that you have some information concerning Lady Eleanor?'

'We do,' confirmed Sir Thomas. And then, 'Or rather my son Frederick has information. He had the good fortune to encounter someone who witnessed the events and could offer a first-hand account of the tragedy.'

'Really?' The earl leaned forward, eager for reliable information.

'Yes, sir.' Frederick hesitated. 'It seems that Lady Eleanor was to . . . er, well . . . that she was to . . . elope with a certain gentleman.'

The earl held Frederick's gaze. 'I suspected as much,' he said. 'Headstrong girl. Would not be told. Would not wait. Do you know the identity of the gentleman in question?'

'I do, sir. His name was Roderick Lavallier.'

'Damn the man!' Lord Stockbridge half rose from his seat and then sat down again. 'Absolute rogue, a blackguard if ever there was one; though I am happy to say he is not of my acquaintance. Do you know of his whereabouts?'

'His plan was to travel to the West Indies. He was endeavouring to spirit Lady Eleanor away with him when she unfortunately fell from her horse and dashed her head upon the stones of the river bank.'

'But she was a fine horsewoman.' The earl was speaking almost to himself now. 'Rode to hounds from an early age . . . But tell me, young man, how came you by this information? You say that you encountered someone who had seen the occurrence at first hand?'

Frederick replied very calmly. 'I did, sir. I was playing cards in Portsmouth—at Lady Rattenbury's. Seated at the table was a gentleman who had been riding by when the tragedy happened. He witnessed the entire scene and saw exactly what transpired. The horseman and -woman were riding at some speed along the river bank. The two horses were, it seems, a stallion and a mare, and the stallion was taking a considerable interest in the mare.'

'Foolhardy combination,' murmured Sir Thomas.

'On a particularly treacherous stretch of ground—quite close to the river bank—Lady Eleanor's mare was bitten on the neck by Lavallier's stallion and she reared up in fright. Lady Eleanor did her best to rein in the mare, and she had, it was thought, succeeded, but then the stallion lunged at his quarry yet again and the resulting action was too much for her ladyship, who was thrown to the ground and—'

'Yes, yes, I understand,' Lord Stockbridge interrupted. 'But why did this fellow you met at cards not dismount and go to Eleanor's assistance?'

'By all accounts he saw Lavallier galloping off, once the tragedy had occurred, and, thinking to apprehend the man, rode in pursuit. Alas, Lavallier's stallion outpaced the gentleman's mare after less than a mile.'

'And did he not then return to Lady Eleanor, as any gentleman should have done, to offer her assistance?'

Frederick cleared his throat. 'He did, sir. But by that time Lady Eleanor's body . . . Lady Eleanor was no longer there, and neither was her horse. The gentleman assumed that Lady Eleanor must have recovered from her fall—however severe—and journeyed home.'

Looking at his father for approval, and receiving a curt nod of assurance, Frederick leaned back on the sofa and concluded, 'That is all I know, sir.'

Lord Stockbridge let out a heavy sigh. 'Well, at least we know the story now. And what a tragedy it is. Oh, foolish girl . . . And this damned fellow Lavallier, where is he now? On the high seas, free to press his attentions on some other unsuspecting heiress.'

'I fear he will not be doing so,' said Sir Thomas.

'And how can you be sure?' enquired the earl.

'The ship upon which Lavallier would have sailed for the West Indies would have been the *Leviathan*—'

'But he will be too far away to be arrested now,' complained the earl. 'Even knowing the name of his vessel. And I am quite sure that once he sets foot in that colony, he will be beyond the reach of the law and the constabulary.'

'It looks as though we shall not be in need of the law or the constabulary, Lord Stockbridge, for the Almighty himself has taken care of matters.' Sir

Thomas reached into the long pocket of his tailcoat. 'I have here a copy of today's *Examiner*,' he said, a portentous note in his voice. 'There is a report of a ship capsizing at sea in a terrible storm off Cape St Vincent. All hands were lost. The ship was the *Leviathan*.' He proffered the newspaper.

'Bless my soul,' said the earl. 'If ever there was a case of divine intervention . . .' He scrutinised the paper most carefully and then asked, 'May I?'

'Please do retain it, sir.' Sir Thomas coughed and adjusted his wig.

'Well, gentlemen, I thank you for the information you have vouchsafed to me, though I cannot pretend to have more than a strange satisfaction as a result of these revelations.' Lord Stockbridge slipped the paper onto the table beside him and thought for a moment. 'We have accounted then for this Lavallier, but what of your maid—the one who exchanged costume with my daughter? Is there any news of her?'

It was Frederick who answered, smoothly, 'It seems that he took the maid with him to Portsmouth, but it is unclear whether or not she boarded the ship with him.'

'How so?' asked the earl.

'The gentleman who witnessed the accident thinks that he may have caught sight of her there.'

'But is there nothing more definite than that? Nothing that can prove with certainty that this girl is alive and still on these shores?'

'Alas, no, sir.'

'But was the girl a party to the whole sorry business, or simply swept away by Lavallier against her will?'

'We cannot be certain—' said Frederick.

Sir Thomas interrupted. 'It seems I may have been mistaken as to the girl's nature, milord. If the situation is as my son reports it, then I fear she may well have had a hand in all this. I fear, also, that we shall never see her again.' He shook his head repeatedly. 'A sorry, sorry affair. All I can do, milord, is offer my deepest sympathy and regrets. Frederick told me of the news just yesterday, and I decided that we must journey to you without delay and apprise you of the situation.' Sir Thomas rose to leave.

The earl got up from his chair. 'Well, Sir Thomas, I thank you.'

Frederick, following the earl's lead, rose also.

As they collected their hats and canes from the steward in the hall, Lord Stockbridge addressed Frederick. 'Should you encounter again the gentleman who witnessed the events of last week, perhaps you would be good enough to ask him to come and see me here at Hatherley, for I would very much like to hear the unfolding of events from his own lips.'

Frederick smiled his most winning smile. 'I will indeed, sir. Though I fear it unlikely, for I believe he, too, was sailing for foreign parts.'

St Jude's School, Winchester

22 June 2010

Harry did not really feel like talking to anybody at break time on Tuesday morning. He was sitting quietly in a corner, catching up on his marking, when Rick walked in and said brightly, 'Morning, Harry!'

Harry said, 'Morning,' without looking up.

Rick made a coffee and slid into the seat next to Harry. 'What's up?'

Harry answered, again without looking up, 'Just getting on with work.'

'Oh,' said Rick. 'That sort of morning. Sorry I asked.' He took a sip of his coffee.

Harry closed the topmost exercise book and said, 'No, I'm sorry. Just a bit weary, I suppose. Up late last night doing DIY.'

'Mmm,' said Rick. 'I've heard it called some things in my time, but that's a new one.'

Harry let slip a rueful smile. 'I wish,' he said.

'Oh, dear. Lovers' tiff?'

'Keep your voice down,' said Harry. 'I don't want the entire staff room to know about my private life.'

'I should think they're fascinated. Harry Flint, the man who keeps himself to himself, revealing the intimate secrets of his nights of lust—'

'Do you mind? Anyway, I am not having nights of lust.'

Rick looked sympathetic. 'So, what's happened to love's sweet idyll, then?'

'I'm not sure.'

'I feel a "but" coming on.'

'We don't live in each other's pockets, and I know I shouldn't be feeling like this, but . . . well . . . Alex didn't get in till late last night. I didn't know where she'd been, and she didn't call, but when I went out at eleven o'clock for a stroll, guess whose car was in the drive next to hers?'

'Can't think.'

'Marcus Carew's.'

'Sir Marcus Carew? The gay divorcé? That old lecher?'

'The same. She was absolutely incandescent about him a few days ago. Said he was an arrogant prick.'

'Oh, well, I should think she's bound to be having an affair with him then. You know what women are like. The ones they hate, they come round to loving in the end. It was just the same with me and Rachel. She couldn't stand me at first. Couldn't bear to be in the same room.'

'I know how she feels,' murmured Harry.

'No—seriously. But I won her round in the end. Maybe that's what Marcus Carew's up to. I mean, Alex is an attractive woman. If you want to be in there, boy, you'd better pull your finger out. Never mind all this "Let's take it easy, let's not rush things" sort of stuff.'

'But that's ridiculous,' protested Harry. 'She really can't stand him.'

'Come on! Lovely as Alex is, she's a woman, and women like to be noticed. I'm not saying she's leading you on, but you can't expect her to be totally frank with you, can you? Not yet. I mean, what sort of commitment have you made to her? Nothing. You've just admitted to her that you like her a lot . . .'

Harry raised his eyebrows.

'Well, all right,' Rick conceded, 'I don't know the precise details of your conversations, but from what you tell me there's an agreement not to rush things, to see what develops. All I'm saying is, you've no hope of anything developing unless you do something positive to progress things. Hell, I'm not for rushing in, but if you're as keen on Alex as you seem to be, then offer her something more definite than "Let's see how it goes". I don't know any woman who'd find that much of a commitment. And with old Carew showing an interest, she might just think that she'd be better off there.'

'That's absurd! There is no way she'd—'

'Don't you be so sure. Alex is a single woman with a young child to bring up—education and all that sort of thing. Her child is the most important thing in the world to her. The one constant. When she starts weighing things up, who's the better bet for the future of her child: a baronet who works in the City, or a soon-to-be-out-of-work teacher with no job prospects?'

'When you put it like that—' said Harry weakly.

'There's a danger of complacency here, Harry. You need to assert yourself a bit more and show her that at the very least you see a future ahead of you. At the moment, you're just the sweet guy next door who's very nice to her. But it's not going to be long before she wants more than that. If Marcus Carew is sniffing around there, then your warning bells should be ringing.'

As if to emphasise the point, a loud bell did at that point ring, and the various members of staff in the room got up from their chairs. Before any of them could leave the staff room, however, the door opened and a familiar figure walked in, wearing a suit and tie and carrying a briefcase under his arm. Ted Chieveley smiled brightly and asked, 'Where's my first lesson?'

At first there was a stunned silence. No one really knew what to make of it. Perhaps it was a joke: the old headmaster had come back to say hello and this was just a light-hearted jest. But something in his eyes told them that this was not the case. Those who knew of Ted's condition (and they were relatively few, Pattie having been circumspect in her spreading of the sad news) had expressions of foreboding; those who did not were simply thrown by the unexpected sight.

It was Deirdre Tattersall, the RE teacher, who broke the silence. 'Headmaster,' she said softly. 'How lovely to see you again. Won't you come in and sit down?' From her slightly theatrical and gently patronising tone, it was clear that she was one of the few who understood the situation. 'Can I get you a cup of coffee?'

'That would be nice,' replied Ted, as he sat in the chair indicated by Deirdre. He had a faraway look in his eyes, and now clutched his briefcase to his chest as if to protect the contents. Looking up at Deirdre, he said, 'The results. I have the results. Here in my briefcase.'

'Splendid,' responded Deirdre. 'You just sit there and I'll make you a nice cup of coffee.' She shot Harry a look that said 'Get help'. Harry made to leave the room to call Pattie; he did not need to, though, for as he reached the door, Pattie came into the staff room.

Harry could see the concern etched into her face, but she attempted to make light of the situation. 'Ted! There you are. I've been looking for you. I was getting worried. You went off without saying where you were going.'

Ted looked up from the chair, still clutching his briefcase to his chest. 'Did I? It's very important that I take care of the results. I've just come to put them in the safe.'

Pattie walked over to him. 'Well, you're here now. You can hand them over and then we'll go home, shall we?' She bent down and made to take the briefcase from him, and it was then that a change came over Ted.

'No!' he said loudly, snatching the briefcase away from her. 'No, you can't!' And then, swiftly and with no warning, he brought the case down so heavily on Pattie's head that the old woman reeled for a moment, then keeled over sideways and crumpled to the floor. Rick leaped forward, attempting to save her from the full impact of a heavy fall, but his progress was impeded by the coffee table and Pattie's head hit the linoleum-covered concrete floor of the staff room with an ominous thud.

A collective gasp from the room was followed minutes later by the hasty arrival of two paramedics, who moved swiftly to Ted's side and took an arm apiece. Harry instantly relieved one of them, indicating that he would be better employed attending to Pattie, who was lying quite still on the floor.

Under instructions from the other paramedic, Harry firmly but carefully eased Ted out of the chair and across the room. Ted was weeping silently, the crisis having passed and an awareness of his actions having dawned.

Harry spoke softly and encouragingly. 'It's all right, Ted. Pattie will be fine. We'll just get you both to hospital and then you'll be all right.'

'Yes. Yes. I didn't mean to,' sobbed Ted. 'I didn't mean to . . .'

Rick was standing over Pattie, watching as the senior paramedic attempted to resuscitate her. It was Deirdre Tattersall who took the lead and marshalled the rest of the staff. 'I think we'd better return to our classrooms, ladies and gentlemen. The bell has gone.'

The staff did as they were bid. Only Deirdre and Rick remained, watching with concern as the paramedic continued in his endeavours. Repeatedly he applied pressure to Pattie's chest and repeatedly he listened for signs of breathing. Then, after several minutes, he stopped and sat back.

'She's breathing,' he said. 'But only just. She's had one heck of a blow to her head. We'll get her in and have her X-rayed. I can't think she'll be going anywhere for a few days. But then neither will her husband.'

Mill Cottage, Itchen Parva

27 April 1816

Slowly Anne Flint mended. She would sit for much of the day on an old fallen tree down by the river, gazing at the gently rippling water. Agnes wondered for how long a fifteen-year-old girl could sit without saying anything, without a need to share her troubles, but she concluded that Anne's introspection was a part of her recovery, a way of learning to deal with what had happened. Whatever had befallen her on her brief adventure, it was clearly of such gravity that the girl had been deeply disturbed.

William Palfrey went about his business with similar circumspection. He had made his feelings clear about the girl's presence at Mill Cottage and now remained silent on the subject.

It was Jacob who had the greatest difficulty in keeping his counsel, for much as he teased Sam about his liking for the girl, he knew in his heart that the youth cared for her and was troubled by her disappearance. It was this, rather than any willingness to spread gossip or share confidences, that led him early one morning to accost his friend on the banks of the chalk stream.

Sam had already mucked out the stable and had been allowed half an hour's idleness with a crust of bread and an apple—a late-stored pippin that was more wizened than he would have liked, but of reasonable flavour. He was biting into it absent-mindedly when Jacob sat down heavily beside him.

Sam started and almost choked. 'You made me jump!' he said accusingly.

Jacob smiled. 'Should have been listenin' out then. What you doin'?'

'Nothin' to speak of. Finished my chores and eatin' my apple. Mr Jencks says I can 'ave a set by the river.' Then he looked thoughtful. 'What you doin'? What brings you up here?'

Jacob hesitated. He knew that what he was about to tell Sam might result in all manner of consequences, and he could not predict Sam's reaction to what he was about to say.

'What be the matter? Why d'you look so sheepish?' asked Sam.

'That business with Lord Stockbridge's daughter . . .'

Sam stopped chewing, his face frozen at the prospect of news that he somehow dreaded but which he was nevertheless eager to hear.

Jacob continued, 'I've more news. You heard nothing from Mr Jencks?'

Sam shook his head.

'Well, it seems that that Lavallier feller and her ladyship meets up all right to elope, but then it all goes wrong. She falls off her horse and hits her head. Stone dead. He gallops off with Anne. Takes her with him.'

Sam turned to face Jacob square-on. 'Takes her where?'

'No one knows. 'Cept that he's been lost at sea in a ship. Foundered off Cape St Vincent. Dead he is. Dead and gone.'

'And Anne? What about Anne?'

Jacob realised the cruelty of keeping Sam in the dark any longer. 'You are not to tell a living soul, promise me that?'

'Cross my heart, I promise,' said Sam, gesturing to his chest, with a look on his face that was a mixture of eagerness and fear.

Jacob looked about him to make sure that they were quite alone and then said, 'She is with my mother at Mill Cottage.'

Sam leaped to his feet, a look on his face of such relief and joy that it quite took Jacob by surprise. 'Then I must go and see her! Is she well? What does she say? How did she escape?'

Jacob shook his head. 'You must not go and see her. You must not tell a living soul what I 'ave telled you.'

'But the master . . . does he know?'

'Nobody knows except my mother, my father and me. My mother swore me to secrecy and if she do find out that I telled thee, I shall be banished. I only tells you so that your mind is at rest. I knows you was worried. I could see, like. But until my mother says, we cannot tell a soul.'

Sam flopped down on the bank. He sat for a few moments, staring at the water and then asked, 'How do you know all this?'

'Father talked to Mr Jencks.'

'But Mr Jencks ain't said nothin' to me.'

''Tis not general knowledge. But Mr Jencks hears things in the chaise on the way to Lord Stockbridge and he tells my father.'

'Who did know then? Who did find out this information?'

''Tis from Sir Thomas's son—Master Frederick. He did meet a man who seen it all 'appen. The man tells Master Frederick and Master Frederick and Sir Thomas goes to Lord Stockbridge and tells him.'

'And they knows about Anne?'

'They knows she was there, and that the Laval man rides off with her, but they know not where she is now or even if she be alive.'

'But how can you keep it secret from them? They will find out. The mill is only a few miles from here.'

'No one comes to the cottage. No one from the Manor. You is the only one outside the family who knows where Anne is.' Jacob reiterated his warning, 'You must promise me that you will not tell a soul.'

Sam nodded eagerly. 'I promise.'

Jacob nodded, satisfied, and got up to go.

Then Sam asked, 'When can I see her?'

Jacob shook his head. 'You cannot. I have gave my word to my mother. If she do find out I broke it, then . . .'

Sam looked crestfallen. To know that Anne was alive was the best thing he could have hoped for, but to be unable to see her was the cruellest of blows. She was but a few miles away, but for all that she might as well be at the other side of the world. As Jacob went off towards his horse and cart, Sam tried to convince himself that he must abide by his word. He would have no difficulty in keeping the knowledge to himself, but somehow he must try to catch a glimpse of Anne. Somehow.

IT WAS A LONG WAY to walk, especially on uneven ground. But that evening, when his duties were done, Sam excused himself from the stables and wandered off in the direction of the river.

Checking that he was out of sight of the Manor House and the stables, and staying as close to the hedge for as long as he could, he walked downstream in the direction of the fulling mill. For an hour and a half he walked, more confidently now that he was clear of his home, past twists and turns in the river where the water ran swift and deep and then chatteringly over pebbled shallows, until eventually the distant rooftop of the mill hove into view, sheltered, as it was, by alders and willows.

The sound of the mill race grew louder as he approached, and his heart beat faster. He stuck close to the trees now, trying to remain in the long evening shadows as much as was practically possible, though from time to time great cushions of brambles forced him out into the open. But his shirt was a dull green and his leather jerkin brown; he would not stand out and, if he were careful, he would be able to approach closely without being seen. If he could just get a glimpse of her, that would be enough! To see for himself that she was well and had survived her ordeal. He could not hope to speak to her—that would be too much to ask; but he would endeavour to get close to the mill and peer through a window, perhaps see her in the candlelight: dusk was beginning to fall now and soon it would be dark.

Slowly he edged towards the mill. He stood still for a moment to catch his breath and to plan a route across the rough grass of the copse to the side of the mill. He could see a window there, the interior of the mill illuminated by the gentle glow of candles.

There were hazel bushes scattered about the edge of the copse, and hawthorn and elder. They were dense enough to give him cover, and the sweet smell of their blossom—just beginning to open—lay thickly on the air.

For a few moments he stood silently in the evening shadows, confident that he had not been seen. And then, at the moment when he least expected it, a voice in his ear almost made him jump clear of the ground.

'Sam! What you be doing here?'

It was Anne! She stood there in front of him as clear as day. Anne! Looking just like she always had. But there was something different about her too. She had been gone only eleven days, but she had about her face a kind of weariness. It was not the sharp and vital expression he was used to. There was nothing of the teasing look that he had come to take for granted. He found it impossible to speak, and she could see his look of disbelief.

She sought to reassure him, 'It is me,' she said. 'Anne. I am here but you must not tell anyone.'

Sam shook his head, still speechless.

'Why did you come?' she asked. 'How did you know?'

'J-J-Jacob,' he stammered. 'Jacob told me.'

'He will be in such trouble,' said Anne.

Sam quickly made to defend his informant, 'He made me promise not to tell. I shall not. I shall not tell a soul.'

Anne nodded. 'I know you will not.' She smiled at him kindly, with a look that melted his heart.

'Oh, Anne,' he said. And then his words came flooding out in a torrent: 'I were that worried. I knew not what had happened to you. Where you had gone. And then we found the body—with your clothes on it. At first I thought it were you. Then I saw it were not. Then you had disappeared and nobody did know where you were. Where has you been, Anne? Where has you been?'

Anne shook her head. 'I cannot say. Not yet awhile.'

'Will you come back to the Manor?' asked Sam eagerly.

'I cannot. Not yet. Maybe not ever. I know not what the future holds for me, Sam. I have been ill used. I am not the Anne you knew ten days ago.'

'Eleven,' corrected Sam. 'I been counting.'

Anne smiled again. She had spurned this callow youth but a fortnight ago, had spurned him for the past two years. How she regretted that now. For he was indeed young—as young as she, and every bit as innocent as she once had been—but he meant well, and it was clear that he thought much of her. How she had teased and taunted him, and yet he still had feelings for her! But she knew that if he were ever to learn the bitter truth, then he would be on his way without a backward glance: how could he still care for her after what had happened? She bowed her head, as the feeling of shame that she had become so used to enveloped her once more.

Sam spoke again. 'It do not matter, Anne. It do not matter what happened on the road. I will still look after you.'

'Do not say that, Sam. Not until you knows. And I cannot tell you yet.'

There was the sound of a latch being lifted on a wooden door. Anne glanced at the mill and a worried look crossed her face. 'You must go, Sam, before you is discovered.'

Sam stood, rooted to the spot.

'Promise me you will say nothing?' asked Anne.

'I promise.'

'Now be gone.' And with that Anne walked swiftly across the rough grass to the door of the mill. She looked back at him only briefly before she closed the door behind her, but it was enough to let Sam know that she had been glad to see him. He would never let her down. Not ever.

Mill Cottage, Itchen Parva

22 June 2010

The sadness that Harry felt when he went home on the evening of Pattie and Ted's disastrous encounter was of a depth he had not experienced since Serena's departure. He had, to all intents and purposes, lost the two people who for the past five years had been his adopted parents. Pattie would warn against his excesses, often with no more than a 'Do you really think so, dear?' And Ted. Dear Ted, who offered guidance when it was asked for—and when it wasn't, but always with Harry's best interests at heart. A kindly man. A gentle man, with a gentle wife who now . . .

Harry dropped his bag onto the kitchen table and went in search of a stiff drink. Why hadn't he been to see them more frequently of late? That way maybe he could have seen the direction things were going and done something to help. Pattie had said there was a danger that Ted might become violent, but Harry had not expected it to happen so quickly. It was barely two months since his condition had been diagnosed. Maybe it was something to do with the drugs they had given him? But such conjecture was fruitless. What had happened had happened, and there was little point in recriminations, even those aimed at himself.

As he poured himself a generous Scotch, he realised that for the first time he could completely understand how Alex must have felt when James had gone through the same sort of character change. Nothing had prepared him for the alteration he had observed in Ted's behaviour. It had come like a bolt from the blue: the transformation of a dear and cherished friend into . . . what? And Alex had lived through this nightmare with the man she loved most. The father of her daughter. The agony must have been unbearable.

He flopped down on a chair at the kitchen table and gazed at the amber fluid in his glass. He took a fortifying gulp and felt the liquid burn down his throat. It would be good to talk things over with someone. Well, one particular person. But he would not go round. He hadn't the energy and, anyway, what was the point? If, as Rick suggested, Marcus Carew was making a play for her, then let him. If that was her kind of guy, so be it.

A tap on the door broke in on his introspection.

'Can I come in?'

In truth he had half expected her to come round. She was probably going to make some excuse about being busy for the next few days. Well, he would cope. He had managed without a woman for the past two years and there was no reason why he could not carry on doing so.

Alex saw his expression and the glass that he cradled in his hands. 'What on earth's the matter?'

Harry explained the events of the afternoon as Alex sat opposite him, listening intently as history began repeating itself. He looked up as he got to the end of the story. 'So there you are. So many things change in such a short space of time.'

'Yes. Yes, they do.' She thought for a moment. 'What will you do?'

'Nothing I can do. Ted will be taken into care. Pattie will be in hospital for a while—I don't know how long. All I can do is go and see them. I don't suppose it will be long before Ted doesn't recognise me, but I'll still visit him. As often as I can. I should have been to see them more than I have—'

She interrupted and laid her hand on his. 'It wouldn't have made any difference, you know. There's no way you can stop it.'

'I know. I just feel—'

'Guilty.'

'Yes. For not doing more for them, and for not realising just how tough it must have been for you.'

'Oh, don't go there. There really is absolutely no point in feeling guilty. It achieves nothing. I can tell you that from experience.'

Harry nodded and took another gulp of the whisky. Then he said, 'I'm sorry; I didn't ask you if you wanted a drink.'

'No, thanks. Not at the moment.'

'No,' he said. 'No, of course not. Other things to do . . .'

She looked surprised. 'No. I just don't fancy a drink, that's all.'

'Oh. I thought maybe you were going out. With him, you know . . .'

Alex looked puzzled. 'With who?'

'Carew. The man whose Porsche Cayenne was parked outside your house at eleven o'clock last night.'

Alex half laughed. 'What?'

'Well, it was, wasn't it? And there's me thinking that you thought he was a prick. How wrong can you be?'

Alex was taken aback by Harry's unexpected attitude. 'Well, very wrong as it happens.'

'Mmm?' Harry drained his glass and stared at her. Self-pity was beginning to take over.

'Yes, his car was parked outside my house last night and, yes, he was inside with me. But only for about ten minutes.'

'At eleven o'clock?'

'Yes, at eleven o'clock. Because I'd taken Anne to another sleep-over before I went to the school to help them with a fund-raising evening at which Marcus Carew was present and at which I told him in no uncertain terms that he owed me some money for the repair to my car headlight that he had smashed. He went home to get his chequebook and then came round and handed a cheque to me in person. All of which would have been quite laudable had he not tried to grope me in my own house—stupid me for letting him over the threshold, but as you weren't around I had to manage for myself. Which I've been quite used to doing for a couple of years now.'

There was a rising note of anguish in her voice, and Harry could see tears in her eyes. He sprang up from the table. 'I'm so sorry,' he said, wildly. 'It's just that Rick was going on today about how I'm so slow and how Carew would be getting in there and—'

'What is it with you and Rick? When are you going to stand on your own two feet and make your own decisions? What does Rick know about me?'

Harry made to put his arm round her, but she pulled away and turned from him.

'I thought we understood each other better than this,' she said.

'So did I,' said Harry contritely. 'It's my fault. It's just been such a bloody day and things build up and . . . this house and . . .'

She turned to face him. 'You can't go on blaming things on this house. You haven't given it a chance. You need to get to know the place better, then you'll get the feel of it. It's just the same as with people. There's an initial attraction, but if that isn't built on then the whole thing falls apart.'

Harry looked into her eyes, 'Is that what you think has happened to us?'

Alex met his gaze. 'Not as far as I'm concerned, no. But I could do with a bit of proof.' She turned her head away and he walked towards her, cradling her in his arms from behind.

'I'll give you the proof whenever you want,' he said. 'And I'm sorry for getting hold of the wrong end of the stick, for listening too much to a mate, for not being patient enough with my house and for not—'

'Enough,' said Alex gently. 'Enough.'

He turned her round to face him, lifted up her chin with his hand and kissed her gently on the lips. 'I'll try not to cock things up again.'

Alex smiled. 'Let's just keep going, shall we?' she said softly. 'We've a summer ahead of us and it would be nice to enjoy it.'

Harry kissed the top of her head. 'Yes,' he said. 'It would.'

Hatherley

30 April 1816

Lord Stockbridge was at supper in the dining room at Hatherley. There were but two of them at the table, and while it might have been more sensible to have taken their repast at a smaller board in the library, it seemed to the earl that any vestige of normal life that could be clung to was a comfort. In the old days, when the house was full of voices and children and a wife, this was where they had dined. Since his brother Nicholas had returned from Italy, he had reverted to this arrangement, the one concession being that they dined at one end of the long, polished board of mahogany rather than having to shout at each other along its entire length.

The earl's brother had had the great misfortune to arrive on the day that Eleanor's body was discovered, and so had been bound up with the tragedy from the start. Lord Stockbridge had taken pains to keep Nicholas informed of every development, and as the cheese and port arrived on this particular evening, they fell once more to talking about the events surrounding that day, as indeed they had for the better part of two weeks.

Their conversation surrounded the revelations of Frederick Carew.

'I find it a curious coincidence,' said Nicholas, 'that young Carew encountered the very man who saw the tragedy unfolding.'

'A coincidence, but a fortunate one,' said the earl, 'for without his information, we should have remained in the dark as to the precise nature of Eleanor's death.' He took a sip of port. 'Though I cannot, in truth, claim to gain much in the way of solace from such revelations.'

Nicholas cut himself a large piece of Stilton and proceeded to peel back the skin of one of the figs that he had brought with him from Italy. 'Are you well acquainted with the Carew family?' he asked.

'I am acquainted with the father,' confirmed the earl. 'I have little knowledge of the sons. One I believe is in the militia, and the other is a barrister. They return home but rarely. The boy Frederick—the one who came here with his father—he is the barrister, as I understand it.'

'You have no personal knowledge of either son, then?' asked Nicholas.

'None,' confirmed the earl.

'I see.' Nicholas considered for a moment and took a bite of the fig. Then he said, 'While I have no knowledge of the elder son, I do have some knowledge of his younger brother. I would like very much to have listened to his story. And perhaps to have questioned him further.'

The earl looked surprised. 'I was not aware—'

'I had resisted saying so. I hardly wanted to add to your discomfort. But it seems the boy has something of a reputation with the ladies: he is a little too free with his attentions.'

'And how came you by this information?'

'I was delayed a little in Portsmouth—some problem with my trunks and valises—and chanced to spend one or two evenings in the company of what passes for Portsmouth society. It seems that Master Frederick Carew has not endeared himself to Portsmouth hostesses, on account of his reckless gambling and dalliances with the ladies.'

'But, sir, every young man has "dalliances with the ladies".'

'Brother, the ladies with whom Master Frederick has dalliances are not the sort one would want to boast about. Neither is he discreet. His conduct has resulted in his being declared unwelcome at more than a handful of households in that city.'

'Indeed. Well, that is as maybe, but he is certainly an habitué of Lady Rattenbury's, for that is where he learned of the events concerning Eleanor. From the gentleman who witnessed them at first hand.'

'That cannot be,' contradicted his brother. 'There must be some mistake.'

'No. No mistake. I remember quite clearly that he informed me—while he was here, in the presence of his father—that he had encountered the gentleman who had witnessed Eleanor's accident at Lady Rattenbury's.'

'Then, brother, you have been most grievously ill-informed.'

The earl sat back in his chair. 'I do not understand.'

'The very house where I was apprised of Master Frederick's lack of popularity with Portsmouth society was that of Lady Rattenbury. It was she herself who told me. She will not have him in her house.'

Winchester

26 June 2010

This particular Saturday morning, Harry found Anne surrounded by felt-tip pens, colouring in the shapes of a book of animals at the kitchen table of the Old Mill. 'Do you like colouring?' he asked.

'Yes. Very much.'

Their brief conversation was interrupted by Alex, who was in a hurry: 'I have to go to the optician's in Winchester.' She turned to Anne. 'You'll have to sit and wait while Mummy has her eyes tested.'

'But I'm colouring,' responded Anne, without looking up.

'I'll tell you what,' said Harry, 'why don't I come too, and while your mum is choosing the most wonderful pair of specs that will make me appear more handsome than ever, I'll take you to see the best bit of colouring that's ever been done.'

Anne looked up. 'Where? In Winchester?'

'Yup.'

Anne thought for a moment, then put down her felt tip and said, 'OK.'

THEY SPLIT UP by the Butter Cross, Alex going off in the direction of her express optician's, and Harry walking with Anne through Great Minster Street into the Cathedral Close.

'But this is the cathedral,' Anne said as they walked towards the west front. 'They don't have colouring books in the cathedral. I mean, I know they have some in the cathedral shop, because Mummy bought me one, but they're not exactly special. Nice. But not special.'

'Well, the colouring book I am going to show you is far better than those.'

'Can I have a go with it?'

'Er, no. But you can have a very close look at it.'

'Oh.'

'You won't be disappointed.' They were in the cathedral now and Harry guided Anne towards the narrow staircase that led up to the library. At the top of the stairs, Harry pointed to the doorway that led into the small room.

'In there?' asked Anne.

Harry nodded. Anne walked through the door and saw the four volumes of the Winchester Bible, lying under the glass cover, their illuminated letters glowing from the ancient pages. She gazed at the work before her, then slowly walked along the length of the cabinet, peering at each of the four books. When she reached the final volume she looked up and said softly, 'It's beautiful. When was it coloured in?'

'You guess.'

'It must be a long time ago. A hundred years?'

'Nope.'

'Two hundred years?'

'Nope.'

'Five hundred?'

'Nope, nope, nope.'

'How many then?'

'Eight hundred and forty years ago.'

Anne's eyes widened, 'No!'

'S'true. It took one man fifteen years to write it and six men all that time to paint the letters.'

'How do you know they were men?' she asked.

'Well, because in those days it was the men who did this sort of work, not the women.'

'Did the women stay at home and do the washing and the cooking?'

'I suppose so.'

'Not very fair, that.'

'No,' agreed Harry. 'Not fair at all. But today, if they were making another one, perhaps they'd let you have a go.'

'No. I don't think so. I'm not as good as all that,' admitted Anne. She walked down the length of the glass case again, and this time Harry could hear her gently humming to herself. He had to bite his lip to avoid telling her that this was why he had become a teacher: because of those rare and fleeting magic moments when you could open a child's eyes to something unexpected. Especially when it involved history. This particular feeling— the one he had at this very moment—was what gave him the greatest lift. Maybe he should stop teaching ungrateful adolescents and turn his attention to primary school teaching? The prospect of such a challenge lifted his spirits and that was something that had not happened in a long while. He would give it further thought. Yes, he would seriously think about it.

With unusual brightness he asked, 'Shall we go now?'

Anne nodded.

'But you did enjoy it?'

Another nod.

'And it is a good colouring book, isn't it?'

'Mmm.'

They were walking through the retrochoir behind the altar, when suddenly Anne grasped Harry's hand. He could feel her body trembling.

'What's the matter?' he asked.

The child simply stared at the wall ahead. Harry looked in the direction of her gaze and saw a stone carving let into a niche in the wall. It was palest grey, almost white, and of a robed woman, except that it lacked a head.

'The lady,' murmured Anne.

'She seems to have lost her head,' said Harry lightly.

'The white lady,' continued Anne.

'Oh. You mean at the cottage?'

Anne nodded.

'And she didn't have a head?' asked Harry.

'Yes,' said Anne softly. 'She did have a head, but her dress was like that.'

Harry regarded the monument. 'Ecclesia,' he said. 'She was a lady who represented the Church and all it stood for. The long dress would be her robes.'

'Robes . . .' murmured Anne.

'Yes. They wore long dresses from ancient times right up until—oh, about a hundred years ago.'

'Like the white lady.'

'If you say so.'

Anne turned to him. 'Is she still there?'

'Well, I don't know; I haven't seen her.'

Anne looked disappointed, and Harry didn't want her to think that he did not believe her. 'But I have—well—felt her presence,' he said.

Anne continued to gaze at the statue. 'She was carrying something.'

'What sort of something?'

The child didn't answer, but gazed again, almost mesmerised, at the figure.

'Would you like to go and have a drink and wait for Mum?' asked Harry.

Anne took a moment to answer. Then she said, absently, 'If you like.'

They had left the cathedral and were making their way back to the Butter Cross when suddenly Anne said, 'Why don't you ask me what I would *really* like.'

Harry smiled and asked, indulgently, 'So what would you really like?'

'I'd like you and Mummy to get your act together.'

For the first time in a long while, Harry was lost for words.

The Manor House, Withercombe

1 May 1816

Sir Thomas Carew understood that the matter was serious when Lord Stockbridge sent word that he would call upon his neighbour at eleven o'clock that morning, and that he would expect to find both the baronet and his son in residence. Upon receiving the message, Sir Thomas immediately summoned a servant and told him to fetch Master Frederick.

Some twenty minutes later, his younger son stood in front of him.

'Lord Stockbridge has sent word that he will be here at eleven. It is now'—he took his half-hunter from his waistcoat pocket and squinted at the dial—'a quarter past ten o'clock. You will be properly dressed and waiting upon me within thirty minutes, Frederick.'

'Father?'

'His lordship has asked specifically to see us both.'

'But why is that? I had understood that our interview last week had been conclusive. I have no more information that I can pass on.'

'That may well be the case, but his lordship was quite insistent upon the matter, and is to bring his brother Nicholas with him.'

'His brother?'

'Yes. He has newly returned from Italy and I gather he spent a few days in Portsmouth. Perhaps you encountered him at Lady Rattenbury's during your recent stay?'

At this Frederick looked uneasy, and shifted his weight from one foot to the other. 'I cannot say that I recall.' He pushed his blond fringe from his eyes and turned to avoid his father's gaze.

'No matter. I am sure we will discover the true nature of his lordship's enquiries within the hour.'

BEHIND THE STABLES, at the other end of the social spectrum, Sam was attempting to bring a pile of equine ordure under control.

He had, as Anne had entreated him, stayed away from the mill cottage, but it had been four days now, and four days is a long time when the heart of a young man yearns for the company of his girl. Not that she was his girl. But maybe, if he persisted, she might just come round to his way of thinking. He was sure that she was not to blame for Lady Eleanor's death; that was something he could believe without an ounce of doubt. Nor was he particularly eager to find out precisely what had happened. It was enough for him that she was safe, though he did worry as to how long she could remain at the mill cottage without being discovered.

Tossing aside the long-handled shovel, he checked that Mr Jencks had gone about his duties. He had been summoned by the master to wait in the house through luncheon. It was a task the groom loathed and Sam knew that he would be in a foul temper on his return, but that would not be until half past two o'clock. If Sam were sharp about it, and ran most of the way, he could get to the mill cottage and back again before he was missed.

He checked his jerkin pocket. Safe in the knowledge that he had what he needed, he retraced his steps of four nights before and made his way along the river. In little less than an hour he saw the roof of the mill and his heart began to beat faster. It was a fine May Day morning, and Anne loved to be outdoors. Surely she would not be cooped up inside on such a day as this?

His thoughts were vindicated by the sight of a slender figure sitting on a fallen tree trunk by the river. Silently he snaked his way through the bushes and came into her vision only when he had reached the end of the fallen tree.

'Sam! You startled me!' she said. And then, 'You promised not to come.'

'That I did not,' said Sam, defiantly. 'I promised to tell no one that you was here. And that I have not—will never—do.'

Anne smiled at him and then a worried look crossed her face. 'But Mrs Palfrey is in the house baking bread. She may well come out at any minute for a breath of fresh air.'

'If she do, she do. I ain't afeared.'

Anne was flattered by his bravery. Somehow he looked more grown-up to her than he used to. She could no longer see any sign of warts, just a sturdy youth of reasonable looks who seemed to want to look after her. She should be grateful, really. But now it was too late for that—

Sam interrupted her thoughts. 'I cannot stay, for I will be missed, but I brought you something.' He slid his hand into the pocket of his jerkin and pulled out a small leather book.

Anne caught her breath. 'Where did you find that?'

'By the stream. The day after you left. I went looking for you and found it on the bank.' He passed it to her and she took it from him, running her hand over the spine and reading once again the words: *The Highwayman's Bride*. And then she bowed her head and began to cry.

'Don't,' said Sam, anxiously. 'Don't cry, Anne. I thought you would be happy to have it back.'

Anne nodded her head. 'Oh, I am, but then I am not. It was the start of all my troubles. Dreaming of something different. Something I thought I could find, but that I now know all too well I cannot.'

Sam sat down beside her on the fallen trunk and nervously ran his hands over the surface of the bark-free timber. Then he tentatively lifted up his arm and drew her head to his shoulder. She made no move to resist, but sobbed gently until he could see her tears running down the front of his jerkin.

'It will all come out all right,' he said. 'I am sure of that.'

Anne shook her head and dried her tears on the sleeve of her cotton dress—a dress worn by Agnes Palfrey in her younger days. 'No, Sam. Life will not be the same again. But I must make the best of what is left.'

'Where will you go? What will you do?' asked Sam.

'Mrs Palfrey has a sister. In Devon. I shall go there for a while.'

'But Devon? That be miles and miles away.' He looked wounded, and she took pity on his evident pain at her planned departure.

'Only for a time. Until this has calmed down. Until I has been forgiven.'

'But forgiven for what? It were not your fault, were it?'

'No. It were not. But I were there and I must pay for that. And for other things. Things I cannot—will not—tell you, Sam. Forgive me.' She stood up from the fallen trunk. 'Thank you for my book. It was kind of you. I am sorry that it made me cry. It was just that—'

'I know. It upsets you to have it back.'

'No. Not just that. It upsets me that I did not know what I had until I turned my back on it.'

Sam looked confused. He was anxious now. Anxious to get back before he was missed, and anxious to discover when he could see Anne again.

'Can I come back?' he blurted out.

Anne shook her head. 'I must go from here. I am deeply sorry.' She leaned forward and kissed him gently on the cheek and, by the time that he was aware of what was happening, she had disappeared from view.

SAM ONLY JUST MANAGED to get back to the Manor House in time for Mr Jencks's return to the stable block. Far from being in his usual foul temper after such duties, however, today he had a glint in his eye. As if he had been party to some news that he could not wait to share. But it would not be shared with Sam: Mr Jencks's news would have to keep until that evening in the Bluebell Inn. Then, within a few hours, it would be round the village. He should have felt pangs of guilt at being disloyal to his employer's son, but Master Frederick had always been a little brat: driving his horses too hard, and expecting Timothy Jencks to clean up after him. The groom had seen it coming. It was about time Frederick had his comeuppance.

INSIDE THE MANOR HOUSE, Sir Thomas was directing a final sermon at his younger son: 'And when you have packed, you can summon Mr Jencks, who will take you and your trunk to Winchester. You will not darken these doors again. I shall explain to your mother that you have been called away and that I am uncertain as to when you will return. Should you manage to find employment in foreign parts, in a land where the morals are more in tune with your own, then you will receive a small allowance to keep you there. I shall expect a letter from you when you are settled.'

For the first time, Frederick Carew's face bore a look of some contrition. 'Father, there is one thing that I did not reveal to Lord Stockbridge about the servant girl, Anne, who gave me the information in Portsmouth. I have reason to believe that she may be being given shelter nearby.'

Sir Thomas sat down heavily on a sturdy oak chair. 'And how do you come by that information?'

'I listen, Father.'

'Yes, that I have come to realise. And in the most unfortunate places.'

'Do not be hard on her, Father. I am quite convinced that she had no part in the affair, but was just an innocent pawn.'

'So you have told us. It would have been kinder, would it not, if you had spoken up and spoken truthfully at the outset.'

Frederick shrugged. 'Ah, well, Papa. Water under the bridge now.'

'Get out!' said Sir Thomas softly.

'When I have—'

'GET OUT OF MY SIGHT!'

Frederick did not argue. His father was a large man and he was not above striking his son. Frederick bowed curtly from the waist and left the room.

Sir Thomas thumped his fist on the table. 'Mrs Fitzgerald! Mrs Fitzgerald! Damn her, where is the woman?'

A shuffling sound from outside the door betrayed the presence of the housekeeper, who entered rather too quickly to have convincingly made the journey from her quarters. 'Yes, sir?'

'You heard all that, I presume?'

'I'm sure I don't know what you mean, sir.'

'Come, Mrs Fitzgerald; you have worked for me for long enough to be aware of the fact that I understand your modus operandi. Make your enquiries, and discover the whereabouts of this girl, Anne, will you?'

'Of course, sir. I think I know where to begin.'

'She will need help, I dare say. And shelter. When you find her, tell her that she will not find me lacking in compassion. I have a son whose treatment of her has fallen far short of the standards that I would like to think should be upheld in this family. It is time that at least one member of this family showed her some kindness.'

Sir Thomas was speaking as a gentleman; it was a description that, to his considerable chagrin, was unlikely ever to be applied to his younger son.

FREDERICK SAT in the back of the chaise as Timothy Jencks drove him to Winchester, cracking the whip with more than a little relish.

The matters of which Frederick had apprised his father, Lord Stockbridge and his brother Nicholas were only partially complete. While he had given detailed information of the events of the fateful morning when Eleanor had come to grief, as related to him by Anne, leaving out not a single fact, he had been somewhat vague concerning the precise location of their meeting and the means by which it had come about. It seemed sufficient for the three gentlemen's needs that he should explain that he had bumped into her in Portsmouth, recognised her as being one of his father's household staff and, having observed her apparent distress, had listened while she poured out her story. That the encounter had occurred purely by chance the three senior parties had accepted. Why should they not? That much was perfectly true: when he had opened the bedroom door at Godolphin Street and found her sitting on the bed in front of him, he was taken quite by surprise. That the girl had taken flight and given Frederick the slip was true also. And it had seemed quite unnecessary to relate any details concerning the portion of the story that took place after dark. Such information could lead only to embarrassment for all parties.

He was quite certain that the servant girl would not mention it herself. He had been sure of that at the time, too, for he had learned long ago how to differentiate between a reluctantly compliant servant and one with manipulative and malicious intentions. After all, she had left his funds intact, in both his purse and his pocket book. Were she to be the sort of girl who would capitalise on such an encounter, she would have already done so. No. It was clear that the girl was to be trusted. He could be on his way with no pricking of conscience. While he might not have behaved exactly as his father would have wished, he could now rest assured that all loose ends had been tied up.

Frederick's arrogance and self-assurance blinded him to one particular consequence of his actions. It was an obvious one. And one that was to have more lasting repercussions than any of the others.

Mill Cottage, Itchen Parva

Christmas Day 1816

Anne Flint gave birth to her son on Christmas Day. The baby was a month early coming and, despite the diligent ministrations of Agnes Palfrey and Mrs Fitzgerald, the child's mother gently slipped away from them. For the two women, who had seen many comings and goings in their lives, it was the most serene of deaths, and also one of the most heart-rending.

Ice held fast the wheel of the mill that winter, while snow and biting wind had tightened their grip on the river and the water meadows for two whole months. The ice seemed to creep into the heart of Sam, too, as he sat outside the mill cottage on that fateful day, knowing that he should not be there, but certain that he could be nowhere else.

Mrs Fitzgerald had gone to the miller's wife for information almost immediately the squire had sent word to find Anne, in early May, for the miller's travels to and from Winchester resulted in his picking up crumbs of information on all manner of movements and events. Somehow, it had come as no surprise to discover the girl in the care of Agnes herself.

There had been discussion of Anne's return to the Manor House, but when it had become clear that she was with child, such thoughts were banished. Agnes would care for her at Mill Cottage, and Mrs Fitzgerald would share the load as much as her household responsibilities would allow.

It astonished Anne that not once did either woman admonish her and, as time passed, Anne became deeply grateful to the two women who shared their mothering duties. In this role she saw quite a different side to the Mrs Fitzgerald she had known of old.

As to the identity of the child's father, neither Agnes Palfrey nor Mrs Fitzgerald made any reference to it. Anne wondered if they suspected the truth. Master Frederick had, after all, been banished from the household at the very moment of her own return to Withercombe, but she herself would give nothing away. The baby was to be hers and no one else's.

Sam did not know what to think. At first he was angry, angry at Anne for giving of herself so freely. But it was Jacob who reasoned with him that such might not have been the case. The revulsion that had crept over him was soon followed by sympathy, and then an overwhelming feeling of sadness at his loss. Anne had made it clear to him on that day when he had returned her book that she would see him no more. But he would never give up thinking of her, never give up believing that one day she would be his. She would come round and learn to like him—maybe love him—if he were patient, if he were always there.

Sam sat on the fallen tree trunk until his body was as cold as the dead and icy timber beneath him. And then he heard the small and agonising cry of a baby. His heart leaped. He ran as fast as he could to the door of the cottage and beat on it with his fists; already the tears were running down his face. He would care for them both—Anne and the baby. He could help; then she would see how much she meant to him.

He had known at once when he saw Mrs Fitzgerald's face. Knew what had happened. That she had gone from him: gone from them all. The housekeeper had put her arms round him and rocked him as he howled, failing to staunch her own tears, which coursed down her cheeks and disappeared into the rough weave of her linen smock.

''Twas quiet,' she murmured. 'She slipped away. There was no pain . . .'

Sam looked up at her. How could there have been no pain? Anne had died giving birth. Seeing the disbelieving look, the housekeeper made to console him. 'Peaceful at the end. She held the baby in her arms. Gave him a name.'

Between the heaving sobs that racked his body, Sam asked haltingly, 'What is he called? What did she call him?'

Mrs Fitzgerald smiled. 'Merrily. She called him Merrily.'

The youth held her so tightly that she felt she would almost stop breathing. And then she said to him, 'Anne said that I was to tell you she was sorry. She was sorry that she let you down.'

Again, Sam gazed at her disbelievingly. Mrs Fitzgerald nodded. 'I think she realised in the end, Sam. Realised just a little too late.'

Mill Cottage, Itchen Parva

17 July 2010

The combination of a lifted burden and the fear of the unknown left Harry slightly light-headed at the end of term. There was the expected presentation on the final day in the school hall, where he had been surprised at the level of enthusiasm shown by the boys when he had received a smart laptop. It quite took him aback. He had made a brief speech, doing his best not to sound like Mr Chips, and went to pack his bag.

Rick put his head round the door of Harry's classroom. 'That it, then? Galloping off into the sunset?'

'Sort of.'

'So when will I see you?'

Harry shrugged. 'Around.'

'Well, don't leave it too long. We're off camping in the Dordogne. I'd rather be in a nice little hotel on the Riviera, but that's teachers' pay for you.'

Harry smiled. 'Your choice,' he said, softly.

'What about *your* choice? Made any decisions?' asked Rick.

'Yes. I'll keep you posted.' Harry picked up his bag, slapped Rick on the shoulder and walked out of St Jude's for the last time.

He had hoped that Alex and Anne would be around on his first weekend of real freedom. But the two of them had gone to Bournemouth for a week. It was rather an anticlimax. Without Alex—and Anne—he somehow felt deflated. They had become, he realised, a part of his family.

He would busy himself until their return. Potter about in the garden a bit—bring some order to the chaos—and start sorting out his books in the outhouse, where they had lain in their boxes since the day he had moved in.

And the diary. In the evening, he would delve more deeply into its pages. It had lived on his bedside table for the past couple of weeks and he had dipped into it from time to time, but it seemed to contain little of import.

ON THE SATURDAY NIGHT, having spent the day in the garden, mowing paths through the long grass, cutting back brambles and pruning wayward apple trees, Harry poured a glass of wine and opened the felt-backed book yet again. The diary had begun on Christmas Day 1815 and had now reached April of the following year. It was around this time that the entries became more interesting. Harry smiled at history repeating itself. Though Harry's Anne was younger than the girl Jacob wrote about, there were similarities—both had auburn hair and freckles, and both were clearly capable of winding men around their little finger.

Harry suddenly realised that the book in his hand was, of course, a history of Alex's Old Mill and his own place. As well as being Rick's history—that of the Palfrey family—the diary contained something of his own history now: that of the house in which he had come to live.

As he read on, the story began to unfold. Of Jacob's friend, Sam—a stable boy at the Manor House—there were asides: *Beat Sam with the horse shoes* and *Caught a trout today. Sam catched naught.*

Reading from the beginning of the diary again, Harry began to build up a picture of the two lads and their youthful rivalry. As the months passed and winter turned into spring upon the faded pages, and the story became much more compelling, the entries became longer and more detailed. Harry sat entranced, reading of the death of Eleanor Stockbridge and the fact that she had been clad in Anne's clothing. The story of Anne's disappearance began to unfold. Between the lines, Harry could detect Jacob's anxiety—and also Sam's—at her absence. Although Jacob wrote of Sam only briefly, and most often in scathing terms, it was clear that Sam had felt Anne's absence even more acutely than his friend.

After a few days, Anne had clearly come back and, in spite of the fact that she seemed to have worked as a maid in the Manor House, on her return she had stayed here, in the Mill Cottage, with Jacob's mother and father. There was no further explanation of the death of Eleanor Stockbridge, apart from the suggestion that she was eloping with a man called Lavallier and had fallen from her horse. Anne's part in the story remained a mystery.

There was mention of the squire—Sir Thomas Carew—and references to his son. Jacob was clearly not enamoured of the man, for he described him variously as 'that blagard Master Frederick' and 'yon Frederick'.

Harry wondered now if the maid Anne and the miller's son Jacob were destined to become man and wife, with Anne being accommodated in Mill Cottage rather than the Manor House. What other explanation could there be for her relocation? Throughout all of this, Anne's surname remained frustratingly absent from the pages.

Then there were further comings and goings with Frederick Carew and his father, the former clearly leaving the household under a cloud. But the entries became erratic at this point. *Like all youths who begin a diary*, thought Harry, *the initial good intentions wear thin*. He flipped forward and noticed that the final entry was more comprehensive:

Christmas day 1816. Anne Flint has her baby. Mother and Mrs F in cottage helping her. Sam say he not go away but set by river on log crying. When father and I comes to see, mother tells us of Anne's death. She were only fifteen and I feels dreadful. Jencks comes for Mrs F and takes news back to squire. Hope Master Frederick do rot in hell. Think he father though Anne never say. Anne do lie in upstairs bedroom of cottage at front. Baby in room next door. She to stay there until she be buried in three days time. Mother say she will care for baby. I know not what to think. Sam Overton do not speak. Father say he will get over it and that time heels. Baby do not cry much. Anne gave it name before she die. Say it to be called Merrily. May God protect us in the coming year. Amen.

Harry gently closed the book and put it down. Such a small and insignificant volume, but one that had answered questions that he had been asking for years. The answers had lain, undiscovered, in Rick's grandfather's trunk for goodness knows how long. For the first time Sam's surname had been mentioned: Overton. It would be too much of a coincidence for Sam to be related to Anne, wouldn't it? There was, after all, the village of Overton nearby. He had to pinch himself to believe that it was true. He had found the mother of Merrily Flint, and her name was Anne. And Anne had been loved by Sam Overton. The family connection continued. He sat back in the chair and closed his eyes, and gradually the fog began to clear. The ghost in the room upstairs. It had been carrying something, the seven-year-old Anne had said. Yes, of course it was. It was carrying the baby from whom it had been separated by death. The baby was Merrily. The knocking of the doorway from one room to the other had reunited them.

Harry opened his eyes. Why was he being so fanciful? How could any of this be proved? But, somehow, deep down, he knew it all made complete sense. He had been searching for months for his roots. Now he had not only uncovered them, but found that by some strange serendipity he had bought the very cottage in which they had been put down, and maybe even fallen in love with someone whose ancestor had been in love with his own. How weird was that? No, not weird. Comforting, that was what it was. Ordained. Meant to be. He had been guided there by a force or forces unknown. Why should that be so odd? Why, in a world of microchips and messages being sent by satellites through the airwaves, should something as old and established as intuition and fate be thought absurd? It made perfect sense. That, he told himself, was why history was so satisfying. Why it 'informs the present and allows us to put our lives in context'. He would never have to tell it to a classroom of boys again, but it heartened him to prove it true for himself.

So that was that. He knew his roots and he had come back to them. And in the house next door, having returned unknowingly to her own roots, was someone he would be happy to spend the rest of his life with. It was not given to Harry to feel confident on anything like a regular basis, but on this particular topic there was not a shred of doubt. He just hoped that she would feel the same way.

But something niggled him about the revelations he had just uncovered: there was one fly in the ointment in the ancestry thing. He went to his new laptop and connected to the Internet. Half an hour later he had the information he needed. Alex would return and, when she did, he would 'get his act together', as Anne had requested.

The Old Mill, Itchen Parva

18 July 2010

Alex and Anne returned earlier than expected, on the Sunday. The child had quite enjoyed her day in Bournemouth, she said, but had informed the assembled company that she would not be able to stay any longer because they had to go home to see Harry, who would have some news for them. It was quite important, she said.

Alex had done her best to persuade her that she was being silly, and that many arrangements had been put in place so that she could spend a week by the sea, not just a day, but in the end she had given in. Alex and Anne returned—the mother baffled, the daughter content.

When, that evening, Harry proposed to Alex in the sitting room at the Old Mill, Anne was listening upstairs with Mr Moses. She took in the situation and then whispered to him, 'There, I told you so.' Neither of the parties downstairs heard her, though both knew that their love for one another was in some way enhanced by a small girl who seemed sensitive to the kind of feelings and atmospheres that more experienced and supposedly sophisticated adult minds are inclined to overlook.

'I know it seems sudden,' confessed Harry. 'I mean, I know we've only known each other a couple of months . . . but the thing is . . .'

'It feels like longer,' said Alex. 'Almost as if we've known each other all our lives.'

Harry could hardly believe what she said. He told Alex all that he had gleaned from the diary—of Sam Overton and Jacob Palfrey, of the other Anne and all the things that had befallen her. Well, almost all. He did leave out one name, for fear of spoiling the story. Alex listened silently and, at the end, said, 'How astonishing. Sam Overton and Anne Flint. Now we know two Annes. And both of them auburn. Such a coincidence. It's almost as if you've come back to where you were meant to be, that we've all come back to where we were meant to be. The ghosts have been laid to rest.'

'Not quite,' said Harry. 'There is still the question of Merrily's father.'

'Who do you think it was? Will you ever know?'

'Not for certain. It was only a rumour . . .'

'A rumour?'

'Yes. Nothing was ever proved, but I've also been doing a bit of digging on the Internet. It seems that the most likely candidate was one Frederick Carew—younger son of Sir Thomas Carew, baronet: the local squire who lived in the Manor House.'

'Oh, heavens!'

'Now the thing is, both Frederick Carew and his elder brother died without male issue.'

Alex's face took on a look of dawning horror. 'You don't mean . . .?'

'Well, as you said some time ago, Sir Marcus Carew has dubious claims to the title, since he was a very distant relative. However, thanks to the Internet, and various fascinating web sites, I have been able to trace my direct line of ascent from Sir Thomas, which, no doubt, a DNA test would prove beyond doubt.'

'So you are the rightful heir to the Carew baronetcy?' Alex murmured.

'With one flaw.'

Alex brightened. 'Of course! You're illegitimate!'

'I most certainly am not! But Merrily was.' Harry adopted a heavy judicial tone and clutched at an imaginary pair of lapels to make his legal point: 'And so, regrettably, my dear Alex, I have no legal claim on the title and therefore I shall not be able to make you Lady Carew.'

'Thank the lord for that!' Alex laughed, a laugh of relief and of contentment. 'I don't think we need anything else,' she said.

'Neither do I. I've found out all I need to know. I think my family can rest in peace now—every last one of them. And we won't inform Sir Marcus for fear of undermining his confidence, though you can keep it at the back of your mind the next time he makes a pass at you.'

'So it's our secret?' asked Alex.

'Ours alone. Mind you, I can't wait to tell Rick when he comes back from France. He doesn't know that our family association goes back two hundred years.'

'Do you think he cares?' asked Alex.

'I think deep down he's a sensitive soul. He just doesn't like to show it.'

'Not like you.' She said the words softly, putting her head on his shoulder.

'No. Too sensitive for my own good, me.'

'Like someone else I know,' said Alex, casting a glance upstairs.

'Well, as you say, we have everything we want now,' said Harry, stroking the back of her head.

And then a little voice cut through the stillness.

'Not quite,' it said. 'We still haven't got a dog.'

Both Alex and Harry laughed as Anne walked down the stairs, trailing Mr Moses behind her. She came over to the sofa and squeezed her small, pyjama-clad body between them.

'Do you believe in happy endings?' Harry asked her.

Anne looked thoughtful. 'Not always,' she said. Then she brightened and looked into her mother's eyes. 'But I do believe in happy beginnings.'

PERHAPS GHOSTS BELIEVE in happy endings, for there were no further disturbances at the Mill Cottage, and the atmosphere in the upper rooms became increasingly warmer. But then, after almost 200 years of being alone, I suppose Anne and Sam had finally been reunited. In a funny sort of way.

alan **titchmarsh**

Profile

Born:
Alan Fred on May 2, 1949, near Ilkley Moor, Yorkshire.
Family:
Wife, Alison; daughters Polly and Camilla.
Further education:
Oaklands Horticultural College, Herts; Royal Botanical Gardens, Kew.

First TV appearance:
BBC *Nationwide* 1979.
Homes:
House in Hampshire; flat on the Isle of Wight.
Interests:
Vintage cars, steam trains, bell-ringing, singing, acting.
Website:
alantitchmarsh.com.

When you first thought of writing *The Haunting*, was it the idea of the back story, set in 1816, or the modern-day love story that made you reach for your pen?

It was the mixture of the two—and a love of that particular period of history, which I wanted to explore to see how it related to our own.

When you write, do you, in fact, use pen and paper or a computer?

I'm a computer man—so much easier to do edits and juggle around—and easier to send to the publisher, too, by clicking a button. When I first started to write I used an old black and chrome typewriter, which I still have. Well, you never know . . .

Do you write your novels in your house in Hampshire or at your flat in the Isle of Wight? Is there a special, tucked-away place where you settle down to it?

I sometimes write on the Isle of Wight, but mostly in the barn alongside our house, where I have a loft/study and a library of books.

Did you enjoy the challenge of planning and crafting a story that moves between two different time zones? Would you do it again?

Each period is a great 'palate-cleanser' for the other. As a writer, it's refreshing to be able to switch from one to another.

History teacher Harry Flint has a love of everything from the Georgian era. Is this a period in history that you especially like, too?

Oh, yes. It was an age of elegance, both in terms of architecture and fashion, and also a fascinating period in history, too, with George III on the throne, and the loss of America . . .

'Not quite,' it said. 'We still haven't got a dog.'

Both Alex and Harry laughed as Anne walked down the stairs, trailing Mr Moses behind her. She came over to the sofa and squeezed her small, pyjama-clad body between them.

'Do you believe in happy endings?' Harry asked her.

Anne looked thoughtful. 'Not always,' she said. Then she brightened and looked into her mother's eyes. 'But I do believe in happy beginnings.'

PERHAPS GHOSTS BELIEVE in happy endings, for there were no further disturbances at the Mill Cottage, and the atmosphere in the upper rooms became increasingly warmer. But then, after almost 200 years of being alone, I suppose Anne and Sam had finally been reunited. In a funny sort of way.

alan **titchmarsh**

Profile

Born:
Alan Fred on May 2, 1949,
near Ilkley Moor, Yorkshire.
Family:
Wife, Alison; daughters
Polly and Camilla.
Further education:
Oaklands Horticultural
College, Herts; Royal
Botanical Gardens, Kew.

First TV appearance:
BBC *Nationwide* 1979.
Homes:
House in Hampshire; flat
on the Isle of Wight.
Interests:
Vintage cars, steam trains,
bell-ringing, singing, acting.
Website:
alantitchmarsh.com.

When you first thought of writing *The Haunting*, was it the idea of the back story, set in 1816, or the modern-day love story that made you reach for your pen?
It was the mixture of the two—and a love of that particular period of history, which I wanted to explore to see how it related to our own.

When you write, do you, in fact, use pen and paper or a computer?
I'm a computer man—so much easier to do edits and juggle around—and easier to send to the publisher, too, by clicking a button. When I first started to write I used an old black and chrome typewriter, which I still have. Well, you never know . . .

Do you write your novels in your house in Hampshire or at your flat in the Isle of Wight? Is there a special, tucked-away place where you settle down to it?
I sometimes write on the Isle of Wight, but mostly in the barn alongside our house, where I have a loft/study and a library of books.

Did you enjoy the challenge of planning and crafting a story that moves between two different time zones? Would you do it again?
Each period is a great 'palate-cleanser' for the other. As a writer, it's refreshing to be able to switch from one to another.

History teacher Harry Flint has a love of everything from the Georgian era. Is this a period in history that you especially like, too?
Oh, yes. It was an age of elegance, both in terms of architecture and fashion, and also a fascinating period in history, too, with George III on the throne, and the loss of America . . .

Is there a little piece of you in Harry and perhaps in the stable lad, Sam, too?

More than a little. Harry shares my own sensibilities in many ways, though I've been luckier in marriage! And Sam is, perhaps, me as a lad. Not terribly successful with the girls!

Have you done research into your own ancestors? If so, did you find a link to your love of gardening?

A fan once traced back for me as far as the late eighteenth century. Nothing very remarkable—mainly folk who lived off the land, which is comforting. But I'm not a future King of England!

Harry is comfortable chatting with his neighbour's perceptive and sensitive little daughter, Anne. Were those convincing, touching scenes easy to write?

As I write them the scenes are quite real to me. They have to be or they don't ring true. When a novel is going well it's like taking down dictation from the characters—simply listening to their conversations and transcribing them. But I do occasionally throw spanners in the works—it's the way that fiction, and the story, comes alive.

You have many interests, including music, history and art, and in the novel you write vividly about the Winchester Bible in the library at Winchester Cathedral. Is the cathedral a place of inspiration for you?

I think it's the most wonderful building. I compere a carol concert there every Christmas to raise funding for the choristers and it's a very special evening for me.

To date you've written three memoirs, numerous gardening books, newspaper and magazine columns, as well as eight novels. What has brought you the greatest satisfaction and enjoyment?

I enjoy the solitude of writing and the one-to-one communication with the reader. Writing fiction is, perhaps, the greatest 'escape', in that I can lean back on my imagination.

Is there one thing you would love to do in your life that you haven't yet had a chance to do?

I hardly dare ask to do anything else. But a small part in a good stage comedy . . .

It seems 2012 is going to be busier than ever for you with your new three-hour Saturday-morning radio show on Classic FM. Are you excited about that?

I listen to Classic FM all the time so it was a great treat to be asked to be a part of the team. I'm delighted to be sharing my love of music with listeners every Saturday morning. My own taste is for Baroque, Viennese and English music—quite a mixture!

What do you do to relax?

I potter in my garden, delve into books and drive an old car round the lanes near our house. I love messing about in boats, too, when I get the chance. Oh, and listening to music!

What three words do you think best describe you?

Tenacious, loyal and lucky.

COPYRIGHT AND ACKNOWLEDGMENTS

THE FEAR INDEX: Copyright © Robert Harris 2011.
Published at £18.99 by Hutchinson, an imprint of The Random House Group Limited.
Condensed version © The Reader's Digest Association, Inc., 2012.

THE HOUSE OF SILK: Copyright © Anthony Horowitz 2011.
Published at £18.99 by Orion Books, an imprint of The Orion Publishing Group Ltd.
Condensed version © The Reader's Digest Association, Inc., 2012.

LETHAL: Copyright © Sandra Brown Management Limited 2011.
Published at £12.99 by Hodder & Stoughton, An Hachette UK company.
Condensed version © The Reader's Digest Association, Inc., 2012.

THE HAUNTING: Copyright © Alan Titchmarsh 2011.
Published at £18.99 by Hodder & Stoughton, An Hachette UK company.
Condensed version © The Reader's Digest Association, Inc., 2012.

The right to be identified as authors has been asserted by the following in accordance with
sections 77 and 78 of the Copyright, Designs and Patents Act, 1988: Robert Harris, Anthony
Horowitz, Sandra Brown, Alan Titchmarsh.

Spine: Shutterstock. Front cover (from left): Erik Isakson/Tetra/Corbis (Design by
GlennO'Neill; (centre left): www.designedbydavid.co.uk; (centre right): © Landov; (right): Lisa
Spindles Photography Inc./Getty Images (woman), plain picture/Etsa (background). 6–7:
images: Shutterstock; illustration: Rick Lecoat@Shark Attack; 154 © The Times/NI
Syndication. 156–157: images: Shutterstock; illustration: Rick Lecoat@Shark Attack; 294 ©
Adam Scourfield. 296–297 images: Harvey Schwartz/Photolibrary; Daryl L. Hunter – The Hole
Picture; Sami Sarkis/Photographer's Choice RF; illustration: Narrinder Singh@velvet tamarind;
428 © Ron Rinaldi/NY. 430–431 illustration: Jim Mitchell@The Organisation. 574 © Niall
McDiarmid.

Printed and bound by GGP Media GmbH, Pössneck, Germany

020-276 UP0000-1